THE ROUND TOWER

COLOUR BLIND

THE ROUND TOWER

COLOUR BLIND

Catherine Cookson

LONDON NEW YORK SYDNEY TORONTO

This edition published 1997
By BCA
By arrangement with Transworld Publishers Ltd

First Reprint 1998

CN 2033

Printed and bound in Great Britain by
Mackays of Chatham PLC, Chatham, Kent

CONTENTS

THE ROUND TOWER

To John Foster White
My publisher for many years
and always my friend

Contents

I have you fast in my fortress,
And will not let you depart,
But put you down into the dungeon,
In the round tower of my heart.

And there will I keep you for ever,
Yes, for ever and a day,
Till the walls shall crumble to ruin,
And moulder in dust away!

HENRY W. LONGFELLOW.

BOWER PLACE

Bower Place

The four heads were almost wedged together as they looked out of the small open window of the fitting shop and leered at the uniformed schoolgirls walking down the public pathway that ran between the railings cutting off Affleck and Tate's Engineering Works, on one side, and the firm's playing fields on the other.

'There's a new one there the day; I haven't seen her afore.'

'Coo! haven't you? Why, that's God-Almighty's daughter.'

'No kiddin'.'

'Aye, it is. They usually send the Bentley to the Convent for her.'

'They're not gona let on the day.'

'Let them get by and when they think we're not gona say nowt I bet yer life they'll squint round.'

'There! What did I tell you.'

As one of the four girls slanted her glance backwards towards the men, the tallest of them shouted, 'What yer gona be when yer grow up? . . . Oh! a tart, are you?' He shook his head, 'Eeh! that's nice. Let me know when you're done an' I'll come an' have a nibble at yer.' When the girl's head jerked upwards,

17

the man's voice, louder now, called, 'How about a bit of homework first?'

'Never mind bloody homework, see to the dayshift!' The voice brought the heads from the window, and three of the men returned sheepishly to their benches, but the fourth one who had been doing most of the talking rubbed his greasy hands through his hair and remarked nonchalantly, 'Oh, aye.'

'None of your lip, Taggart; don't come the smart Aleck with me. Now get back to your bench, and bloody quick.'

As the man moved away he said as if to himself, 'All right, Gussie?' then, 'Oh, pardon –' he looked sideways – 'or should I say Mr Cotton?'

Angus Cotton let out a string of oaths, then went to close the window. The girls, farther along the path now, were looking back, and he stared at them for a second before banging the window closed. He now glanced round at the bowed heads of the ten men of whom he was in charge, then walked to the end of the shop where, on a bench, lay a large sheet of paper on which was a square and a compass, and his teeth began grating together as he continued to work out measurements on the paper.

About five minutes later he took a rough sketch to a bench to the right of him, where stood an oldish man. 'Can you follow that, Danny?' he asked. 'Or will I take it along to the drawing-office and have it polished up?'

Danny Fuller surveyed the drawing, then said, 'I'll have a shot.' His casual reply meant that his hand would make the work as accurate as any machine could. He was studying the drawing when he said, 'There'll be trouble if you don't do something with that big head. Every day they're at those lasses. One of these times they'll go home and tell their folks what's been said in passin', and then there'll be sparks flying. Taggart comes out with some red rivets I'm tellin' you. An' if I was you I'd make it me business to be in the shop around this time when they're leaving school, 'cos I'm tellin' you, lad, they come out with things. The day was nothin'.'

'I don't suppose they say anythin' that those daisies haven't heard afore.'

'They're at the Convent, lad.'

Angus Cotton turned a humorous glance on the old man. 'And you think that's any protection the day? Their real education can start when they turn the telly on.'

'Oh, I don't suppose those lassies are allowed to look at the telly much.'

Angus now thrust out his hand and pushed Danny, saying, 'You're fifty years behind it, Danny. I bet you if you heard them talkin' among themselves your last three hairs would rise.' He flicked the thin fringe of white hair hanging over the collar of the old man's coat, then returned to his bench.

But as he worked he thought, 'He's right about Taggart. I'll bloody well have to sew his mouth up if it's the last thing I do; it's stretching too wide for peace.' Yet he knew he'd have to get Taggart for something else other than chatting up the lasses. The fellows in this shop had always chatted the lasses. Any lass that came along that path expected it, and some could give as much as they got, but, as Danny said, those were Convent school kids.

It was thirty minutes later when Mr Wilton caused an uneasy stir by marching through the shop, calling, 'Cotton! Cotton!'

'Aye. You want me?' Angus came from under a machine, straightened his back and stood wiping his hands on a rag as he looked into the infuriated face of a man who had to be reckoned with in Affleck and Tate. Mr Jonathan Ratcliffe might be the manager but it was his second in command whom the employees had to answer to usually. But Angus never let Wilton, or anybody else for that matter, think he could intimidate him. As he waited for the assistant manager to speak he said again, 'You want me?'

Mr Wilton now seemed to find difficulty in getting out his words. 'What's been going on here?' He flung his head from one side to the other, swallowed deeply, then added, 'Can't you control these louts?'

'Control these . . .?' Angus didn't repeat the word. There was only one lout in this shop, and even he wouldn't thank anybody for putting a name to him. He said stiffly, 'I don't know what you're gettin' at.'

'You'll know soon enough when the boss is finished with you. He's at white heat; he's had two parents phone him within the last ten minutes because their daughters cannot pass down the Cut without filth being strewn over them.'

'Oh . . . Oh!' Angus nodded his head.

'You know then?'

'I know nowt about filth; I know the lads have a crack now and again.'

'A crack? What are you talking about, man? These are schoolgirls from the Convent, and one, for your information, happens to be Mr Ratcliffe's daughter.'

Angus felt his body stiffen. He hadn't noticed Van there; she never came this way.

'You'd better get along, and sharp; he wants to see you. And there'll be some sweeping out of this shop if I have anything to do with it.'

Angus turned a cool eye on Mr Wilton. He liked Wilton as much as he did God-Almighty Ratcliffe.

20

Perhaps he liked Wilton less because he had more to do with him. He walked past him now and took off his overall and hung it on a nail; then, looking into the narrow, pale face of the assistant manager, he said, 'There are lots of places looking out for sweepings these days, Mr Wilton. One should bear that in mind.'

He heard a sound that could have been a chuckle coming from the direction of Danny Fuller's bench; then he went out of the shop, through the sheds, across the car park and into the building that housed the offices.

He took the lift to the third floor and stepped out into the panelled hall, looked about him for a second, then crossed to a door which bore the name 'Jonathan Ratcliffe' on a gilt-lettered board. He didn't bother to knock on the door because he knew he would have to pass the secretary before he could get into the holy of holies.

Miss Morley raised her eyes and looked at the burly shock-haired workman. She didn't ask what his business was, she knew. 'Wait a minute,' she said stiffly.

As she went towards a far door Mr Wilton came panting into the room, and he checked her, saying, 'I'll see to this,' and went swiftly through the door, closing it after him, and Miss Morley turned and favoured this Angus Cotton with a glance that told him plainly what she thought about him and all his kin: Dirty-mouthed individuals.

It was on the point of his tongue to say, 'Now look here you, get this straight,' when the door opened and Mr Wilton said crisply, 'This way, Cotton.'

Angus was a second before moving, and then his step was slow, and as he passed Mr Wilton he looked him straight in the face before turning his attention to the man sitting behind the big black desk at the end of the long room.

Although this was only the second time that Angus had been in the boss's office, he guessed he knew more about this man than did any of the thousand employees in the firm.

He had been eight years old when his mother first went to work at the Ratcliffes' house, as a daily. That was all they could afford in those days, because although Jonathan Ratcliffe was a draughtsman and earning good money, both he and his missus thought big, and spent big. As his mother said, they knew what they were doing right from the start, for the guests they wined and dined were always people of influence. And it had paid off. Oh aye, it had paid off for Mr Ratcliffe, for he was the big noise of the town now. All you needed was a little bit of brain, a good bit of influence and a cart load of luck, not to mention the art of sucking up. It was the sucking up that had pushed him over Mr Brett's head. If anybody should be sitting in that chair now it was Mr Brett, and everybody in the place knew it, but Mr Brett was still in the drawing office.

'Remember the last time you were in this office, Cotton?'

Neither the tone nor the words startled him as they were meant to.

'I remember, sir.'

'You were then doing rough work in number one shop, and out of regard for your mother's long service with my family I wanted to help her, so I didn't only have you transferred to number three, I put you in charge of number three.'

Angus drew in a deep breath that pushed out his waistcoat, and he let it out again before he said, 'You

22

put me in number three, sir, on the recommendation of Mr Brett, who had seen some of my drawings and thought I should be given a chance to develop.'

Jonathan Ratcliffe brought his fist firmly down on the blotting pad, and he thrust his face forward slightly as he said below his breath, 'Mr Brett's recommendations would have counted as nothing unless I gave the word; surely you have the sense to understand that. And let me tell you, I was criticised from a number of quarters for going over other recommendations and pushing you up. Such chances don't often come the way of men from the floor in number one, not at your age anyway, and with your slight experience . . .'

'Did you have me here, sir, just to tell me this? Because if you did then I've got me answers ready for you. The first is, I'm doing a good job along there, a damn fine one, Mr Brett says . . .'

'Be quiet! How dare you! You're forgetting yourself, Cotton. You take advantage because of your mother. But since you ask, no, I didn't bring you here to remind you why you were promoted but to tell you that in my opinion – no matter what Mr Brett might say – you are not making a damn fine job of running number three because you cannot control the men under you. It is coming to something when parents demand to speak to me on the phone because their daughters are insulted every time they pass the works: schoolgirls having filth hurled at them, bar-room chatter, obscenities, and you allow it to happen.'

'I allow nothing of the sort.'

'You were present.'

'I was WHAT!'

'One of the girls said so, she even described you. Big, fair hair . . .'

'Well, she's a bloody liar, that's all I can say.'

'Will you moderate your language, Cotton. I think you forget who you are, and where you are.'

'I don't forget either, sir; an' I say, if she says I was there she's a bloody liar. I heard the lads at the window and I went and stopped them and shut the window . . . But anyway –' he lifted his hand airily – 'what's all the fuss about? You know yourself, sir, that all along the east side of the building where the Cut is the men have always chipped the lasses.'

'These are not lasses, these are Convent school girls, young ladies.'

'Huh!' Angus's head jerked backwards, and the sound infuriated Jonathan Ratcliffe further. The one desire he had at the moment was to get rid of this fellow for good and all, to say, 'Get out! You're finished.' But there were two simple reasons why he couldn't put his desire into action. The Union was one, and the second had even much more bearing, his wife. If he were to sack young Cotton they would lose Emily's services. Now, when they had the money to employ four servants, even with the wages they demanded today, they were quite impossible to come by. Helps came and went by the week in the house; only Emily was constant. Even if her blunt manner was as big a trial to his wife as was her son's I'm-as-good-as-you attitude, nothing must happen to cause Emily to give in her notice. That would be disastrous; especially at the present time with Susan's wedding in the offing and the Braintrees likely to drop in at any time.

He made a great effort to mollify his tone, but he could not look at the fellow as he said, 'Well, I'll overlook it this time – not that the parents concerned will, I can assure you – but should it occur again,' he now raised his eyes without lifting his head, 'I will be forced to

24

take very strong measures. By the way, who are the men concerned?'

'Does it matter?'

'Of course it matters.' He was barking again.

'Roland, Weekes, Naylor . . . and Taggart.'

'I'll get Mr Wilton to deal with them, but,' his finger wagged now accompanying each word, 'I'm holding you responsible, Cotton. Remember that. That's what you're paid for, responsibility. That's all.'

He watched the big figure turn slowly about, and when the door closed on him he drew his lips tightly in between his teeth and muttered to himself, 'Insolent swine! . . . Trash.'

Jonathan Ratcliffe left his office at six o'clock. Miss Morley was still working, as was Mr Wilton, but the rest of the works seemed entirely deserted. There were only three cars standing in the car park and it was with a sense of deep irritation that he noticed a man with his head under the bonnet of a Volkswagen. As he unlocked his car door he asked, 'Something wrong, Arthur?'

Arthur Brett straightened himself and smiled grimly, saying, 'Third time in a week it's packed up on me. I'll have to get the garage to come and fetch it.'

There was nothing for Jonathan Ratcliffe but to say, 'Well, hop in.'

As he drove his Bentley through the gates that the watchman held open for him, he remarked casually, 'You want to change it.'

'Yes . . . yes, I know that.'

'Well, can't you?' He cast a swift glance towards the man whom he had lived next door to for the past eighteen years, the man who made him feel uneasy when in his presence, the man whose head he had jumped over, which jump had enabled him to take another two jumps into dead men's shoes, men who had died apparently long before their time. Well, as he had told himself often before, some were destined to move upwards and some to remain stationary. Arthur Brett had remained stationary because he had no push, no initiative; he was a plodder. What was more, he'd never had to strive for anything in his young days, he'd had it on a plate from when he was born. It wasn't good to have things too easy when you were young, not if you wanted to go places.

When he stopped at the traffic lights he stared ahead as he said, 'I've been having trouble with Cotton.'

'You mean Angus?'

'Who else? There's only one Cotton on the books as far as I know.'

'What's he done?'

'Spewing filth from the shop window at the Convent school girls.'

'Angus! I can't believe it. He's a rough customer, but his roughness doesn't take that form, I'd lay my life.'

'He's your golden-headed boy, isn't he Arthur?'

'No, he's no golden-headed boy of mine, but he's got ideas. Given the chance, he'll do things. Pity he hadn't had more schooling though. But he's no fool . . . No, he's no fool.' His voice had sunk on the last words and there was a silence as they drove along the embankment, round the park and up Brampton Hill, until Jonathan Ratcliffe said, 'The trouble is he can't control the fellows under him. Apparently, they are at this every day.'

'You can't hold him responsible for that.'

'Oh, can't I?' Jonathan cast a glance sideways. 'That I can. If his men are hanging out of the windows, they're not working. I'm going to put a stop to it.'

26

Halfway up the hill the car turned right down a wooded lane and came to a stop at the end of a line of larches, and as Arthur Brett went to get out of the car he said, 'Thanks, Jonathan.' Then standing on the kerb he bent down and, looking through the window, said slyly, 'Whatever you do to Angus will react on Emily; I don't think Jane would be pleased if Emily went, do you?'

For answer Jonathan slammed in the gears and drove past the remaining larches, past the blue sitka trees that marked his boundary, through the imposing iron gate and up the dull pink composition drive that led to his equally imposing-looking house.

Bower Place, as he had named his house, was both a source of pleasure and irritation to him. Pleasure, because he had designed it himself. Its situation was one of the best in the town and its value had risen phenomenally in the last five years. He had paid old Brett five hundred pounds for the two acres in 1949, and it had cost him four thousand to build the house. Now he wouldn't take a penny less than twenty thousand for the place, not with the money he had spent on it lately, and if only his ground had access to the river that would put another five thousand on it.

This was the irritation, the fact that Arthur Brett, with all that river frontage, wouldn't sell him a yard of it. He was as stubborn as his old man had been. There he was, without a penny to bless himself with – it took all his salary to keep his place going – yet he wouldn't part with one of his six acres. It was sheer spite, that's what it was; Arthur was jealous of him because he had got the post he thought should have been his by rights.

At times he became so angry that he thought he'd sell his place to a speculator and let him run up a twenty-storey block of flats. That would fix Brett. And it could be done.

Oh yes, it could be done. At other times he could see the council confiscating some of Brett's six acres, and running up council houses. What did he want with six acres anyway? He never touched his land, it was like an African jungle.

He entered the house and marched through the hall, throwing his hat on to the marble and gilt hallstand, then went into the lounge where his wife and two daughters were seated. They all looked at him, and his wife spoke first. She said briefly, 'Well, what have you done about it?'

'I spoke to him.'

'Who?'

'Cotton, of course.'

She rose to her feet. 'It was him then?'

'Well, not by what he makes out. He said it was some other fellows in the shop. But he's in charge. What did happen?' He turned now towards his younger daughter, where she was sitting on the couch, one leg curled under her.

'Nothing as far as I'm concerned.'

'Nothing as far as you're concerned!' His thick greying eyebrows were beetling. 'Well, well! this is news. The other three were concerned; their parents were concerned. I suppose what shocked their girls didn't shock you.'

'I didn't hear anything, Father.'

'You were with them, weren't you?'

'Yes, of course.'

'And you didn't hear anything?'

'I was thinking. I didn't even know the boys were at the window.'

'Boys! Boys! They were men, and they were throwing filth down on you and you tell me you didn't hear them?'

The girl turned her head on to her shoulder and closed her eyes, and her mother said sharply, 'Vanessa! Now don't take that attitude, your father is talking to you.'

Vanessa Ratcliffe unwound herself from the couch and stood up straight and looked at her father. She was almost as tall as he, and a good three inches taller than her mother. Her hair was a dark chestnut and fell straight on to her shoulders at the front, but tapered to a point in the middle of her back. Her eyes were brown and round, and the skin over her cheekbones spread to her lower lids without making the slightest hollow. Overall, her face was long and thin, but her lips were full, and when she smiled the corners of her mouth looked square. Her body was unformed and flat. In appearance, she took after neither her mother nor father, nor did she hold any resemblance to her elder sister, Susan, because Susan was a replica of their mother; with Ray, her ten-year-old brother, who had been sent out of the room a few minutes earlier, she had one thing in common, the colour of her hair.

Vanessa was sixteen years old and she was at the turbulent, unrestful stage of adolescence. For weeks now she had been irritated by her family, her girl friends, and everyone about her; what was more, she was experiencing a feeling that both frightened and intrigued her. She knew what it was all about but she could do nothing about it. They talked about it at school, but that didn't help, only tended to make it worse.

'I asked you a question.'

'I've told you, Father. I don't remember hearing anything, only the boys . . . men shouting. Anyway,' she shrugged her shoulders, 'they always shout down at the girls, and that's why they go along that path. They needn't, you know.'

'Do you mean to tell me that they go along there . . .?'

'Yes, Father, I do. Lucy Fulton goes that way every day just to egg them on.'

Jonathan Ratcliffe swallowed deeply, then said, 'Well, the Fultons didn't phone me, but Mrs Herring did, and Kathy Young's mother. Was this the first time they'd been that way?'

'I don't know because I don't usually go home with them. But anyway, why should those two make such a fuss? You should hear how they talk.'

'Be quiet!' Jonathan Ratcliffe looked as if he were about to burst. 'What are things coming to? Been attending the Convent school since they could walk and you telling me they . . .' His indignation wouldn't allow him to go on.

'Well they do. And after all,' she gave a little laugh, 'we're not infants you know, Father; I'm sixteen and a half and Kathy Young is seventeen . . .'

'Be quiet, girl! I don't care if you're twenty-six and a half, I wouldn't expect you to listen unmoved to the spewing of the fitting-shop louts. The trouble with you, girl, is you've no sense of dignity. The Convent has failed lamentably there. Don't you realise that you're the daughter of one of the leading families of this town.' He almost said 'THE leading family'. 'And what are people going to think if you take such talk casually, while other girls are squirming . . . Where are you going?'

'Upstairs to do my prep.'

'Well, get that defiant look off your face; and bang that door after you if you dare.'

When the door was not closed at all Jane Ratcliffe hurried down the room and shut it; then returning to the fireplace and looking at her husband, she said in her prim, thin voice, 'Now you'll understand when I tell you what I've got to put up with; she's getting more difficult

30

every day. I never had this with Susan.' She looked at her elder daughter. 'She's getting worse.'

'It's a phase; it'll pass.' Susan smiled at her mother knowingly. She had no great love for her sister – they had always been at loggerheads – but since her engagement she had felt much more kindly disposed towards her. She knew what was wrong with Vanessa; she was suffering from the same complaint herself, but soon that feeling would be alleviated; only four months and she would be married. She wished it was four weeks . . . four days . . . four minutes. Yes, four minutes. Oh, she knew what was the matter with Vanessa all right. And if her mother had any sense she'd understand too. But sex was a taboo subject in this household. Her mother would have you believe that babies came by kissing. 'Mind, Susan; if a boy should try to kiss you keep your lips closed. Mind, now; keep your lips closed.' That was the sex instruction she'd had. When she had children she'd tell them the whole caboodle at ten. Yes, ten. Ten wasn't too young; just look at Ray. He didn't need any sex training that little devil; you could see the knowledge in his eyes. Give him another five or six years and her father would really know what trouble meant, she was sure of that. But she was getting out of it, and oh, Lord! wasn't she thankful. No more church twice on Sundays. Brian's connections might be county and titled, but she felt sure of one thing, they were as godless as they came.

When her mother said to her father, 'I told Emily,' Susan rose to her feet; she just couldn't sit and listen to another debate on Emily.

'Do you think that was wise?' Jonathan Ratcliffe looked at his wife under gathered brows.

'Yes, I do. You see, she took the call from Mavis Herring, and as usual she had her ears cocked, and when

Mavis said point blank that her Rona had stated that Angus Cotton was one of the men, well, I inadvertently repeated the name Angus Cotton. I said, just like that, Angus Cotton? Are you sure? And there was Emily standing at the kitchen door all eyes and ears, so I just had to tell her. But, as I said, I think it was best; she has heard our side of it now, and when she gets home and hears Angus ranting off because he was hauled over the coals she'll understand why. Oh!' She pursed her lips and her left eye twitched in a nervous fashion. 'It's all so annoying. Why do we have to be bothered with such things at a time like this when I've so much on my mind and Brian's people coming at the week-end? By the way, you didn't really go for Angus, did you?'

Jonathan Ratcliffe now bent his head forward and hunched his shoulders up, and the action told her that he was deeply irritated, and this came over clearly in his voice as he snapped, 'Yes, I went for him. But not as much as I would have liked to. It maddens me to think that I have to put up with that ignorant upstart's attitude simply because we cannot do without his mother . . . Look, Jane.' He now stabbed his finger towards her. 'I'm sure if you put yourself out and went around the agencies you'd come across someone.'

'Don't talk nonsense, Jonathan.' Jane Ratcliffe drew herself up to the limit of her five feet four inches. 'You know for a fact that I need another two in the house and can't get them.'

'Well, you should do what Irene is doing.' He jerked his head backwards in the direction of the Brett house. 'Take an au pair girl.'

Jane Ratcliffe turned her head towards the french windows and focused her eyes on a white-painted, wrought-iron chair standing on the terrace, and she surveyed it for almost a minute before she said, 'We've had all that out before. I'm not having any more foreigners in the house; I'm not going through that again and I think it very tactless of you, to say the least, to re-open the subject.'

Oh, my God! Jonathan Ratcliffe almost said the words aloud but his Chapel training prevented it. He could blaspheme and swear in his mind, but not even his wife's finickiness, nor her narrow outlook with regard to pretty Swedish girls would permit him to take the Lord's name openly in vain. He turned and left her without further words, and as he reached the top of the broad shallow stairs he saw his younger daughter coming out of her bedroom. She turned her head in his direction for a moment, then turned it away again. There was something defiant in the action; there was something defiant in the way she walked to the bathroom; her whole body was expressing defiance. He wasn't startled when the desire came to him that he wished it were possible to take a horse whip to her. Fifty years ago he could have done it. He remembered his mother saying that her father had horse-whipped her because she had committed the deadly sin of entering a theatre. It didn't matter if the play was Uncle Tom's Cabin, she had disobeyed his wishes, and she carried one of the marks of his anger visible on her neck for the rest of her life. He had never felt sorry that his mother should be so treated; he had been in entire agreement with his grandfather's attitude. A man had to stand by his principles, he had to be master in his own house. It might be considered an old-fashioned adage, but he thanked God that it still held true in some families.

As the bathroom door closed and he opened his bedroom door he thought, 'Yes, one of these days

I will chastise you, madam.' But as he took off his coat he remembered her saying she was sixteen and a half years old. Soon she'd be beyond the age of open chastisement. Well, he would see, he would see.

24 RYDER'S ROW

24 Ryder's Row

Looking down on Ryder's Row from the embankment you could well imagine you were viewing the efforts of a model railway enthusiast who had stuck a short row of houses next to the goods yard at the foot of the embankment to give a natural touch to his lay-out.

The cottages were surrounded on three sides by the accoutrements of the railway company, the embankment, the goods yard, and the cleaning sheds; the end of the row fronted the main road that ran between Fellburn and Newcastle.

Over the years the occupants of the Row had become immune to the clanking and clashing of wagons, to the hissing of steam, and now the thunder of diesel engines. Some of them had been born amid the noise, and Emily Cotton was one of these.

The Cottons had always considered themselves fortunate that they lived in the last house because their back yard was twice the size of any other in the Row, and they had only one wall through which could permeate their neighbours' conversation and their own loud interchange.

Saturday morning was usually the time when their interchange was at its loudest and most penetrating, for on a Saturday morning neither Angus Cotton nor his sister, Rose, nor Emily was at work. But on this particular Saturday morning the intermittent exchange between Angus and Rosie had been comparatively quiet. Although neither of them would admit it openly, they thought the house dead when their mother wasn't in it. Without her, there was no incentive to have a bust-up, or a cracking laugh. They sometimes said, 'Coo! in't it peaceful without her'; then they would look at the clock and wish the hours away until she burst in on them.

'She's late, isn't she?' Angus put his head into the narrow scullery and looked at Rosie where she was emptying two tins of soup at once into a pan.

'I bet she's gone to the jumble on the way back; trust her not to miss that.'

'Workin' Saturday mornin'! They'll have her there on Sunday after this. Why the hell doesn't she give it up! There's no need for her to stay on there; she's done enough, she's past it.'

'Don't you tell her that.' Rosie jerked her black hair out of her eyes. 'She'd scalp you.'

'Well, let's face it. She can't do it all. Just look at this place. It's like a pig-sty; she's had enough by the time she gets in, and she doesn't need the money now. I'm goin' to have it out with her.'

'Don't be so bloomin' daft, our Angus, and use your loaf. You know old Ratcliffe would wangle you out of the shop if mam left there . . . You know it.'

'I bloody well know nowt of the sort.' Angus thrust his square chin aggressively towards her. 'That's what I'm wantin' to put to the test. What do you think I feel like, being carried on her shoulders . . . at least that's what they think. But let me tell you, I got into that shop through my ability. Mark you that, through my ability.'

38

'All right; don't bawl your head off, I can hear you.'

The clank, clank, clank of shunting wagons filled the silence between them, until Rosie said, 'Here she is.'

As the back gate opened there came the sound of a train whistle and it seemed to pipe Emily Cotton into the house. She came in backwards, thrusting her thick, firm buttocks against the door and from her arms she dropped on to the table an assortment of garments, exclaiming, 'There! What do you think of that lot?'

'Oh, Mam! Look at the bread.' Rosie retrieved the loaf from underneath the clothes, then swiftly began picking up one article after another. Holding a jumper up in front of her, she said, 'Oh, this is all right. What did you give for it?'

'Threepence.'

'Here, I got you a couple of shirts; they'll do for work for you.' Emily threw two garments towards her son and he caught them, and without looking at them he threw them on to a chair, saying, 'I've told you, Mam. I don't like wearin' other blokes' gear.'

'You were bloody glad to wear other blokes' gear, let me tell you, once on a time.'

'Well, I'm not any more, Mam; so don't get them for me.'

'God!' Emily Cotton lowered herself into a straight-backed chair and lifting one foot slowly up on to her knee she stroked her swollen ankle vigorously, and it was to it she addressed her remarks as she said, 'Talk about out of the frying-pan into the fire, I've spent most of my bloody life with upstarts. That lot along there; their noses in the bloody air so much they have to have their necks massaged. And now I come to me own house and me son tells me that he's got too damned big to wear another bloke's shirts. Let me tell you,' she

39

lifted her head to him, 'you'll never be able to buy shirts of that quality in your lifetime. Let me tell you that.'

Angus stared at his mother for a moment. Then, the corner of his mouth moving upwards, he went towards her and, leaning forward, put his big hands on her shoulders and brought his face down within an inch of hers and said, 'Emily Cotton, that's where you're wrong. One of these days I'm goin' out and I'm goin' to buy six of the best bloodiest silk shirts in all this bloody town, and I'm goin' to wear them for work just to let them see.'

As Rosie's laugh burst forth Emily put her hands up and grabbed handfuls of her son's hair and, shaking his head none too gently, she grinned widely back into his face, saying, 'Aye. An' you will an' all.' Then giving him a push, she ended, 'But in the meantime, you'll bloody well wear these shirts for work else I'll know the reason why.'

The three of them were laughing unrestrainedly now, Angus with his hand covering his face, Rosie leaning over the table, her forearms buried in the pile of old clothes, while Emily, her head back, her mouth open, thumped her broad knees with her clenched fists; then, wiping the back of her hand across her nose and mouth, she exclaimed, 'Well, this won't do. We don't get paid for laughin'. Get that clobber off the table and let's get somethin' to eat. What you got ready?'

Rosie lifted up the assortment of clothes and threw them into an old armchair, saying, 'Soup, and fish and chips. They'll be soggy by now; I got them nearly an hour ago. An' some Ambrosia rice. By the way, what did you pay for that lot?'

'Four and six.'

'Go on! There's three dresses and two skirts there.'

'I paid four and six, I tell you, I didn't pinch them.'

'That's because you didn't get a chance. Who was on the counter?' Angus cast his eyes sideways at his mother, and she said, 'Old fat arse Flanagan. Nobody's going to pinch much when she's around; although I saw Alice Brownlow stuff somethin' in her bag. Eeh! she's barefaced, that one. Did you hear that Millie Taylor was caught again yesterday in the supermarket? She'll go along the line as sure as life this time. This must be her tenth nap. Well, it serves her right; you can be too greedy.'

'Oh, aye. Well, you remember that, Mrs Cotton, when your fingers start to itch . . . now remember.' As Angus turned to go out of the kitchen Emily threw an old woollen tea cosy at his head, saying, 'Snotty young bugger!'

A few minutes later, when they sat down to their meal at the small square table in the middle of the kitchen, Rosie remarked, on a laugh, 'You know, Mam, I've often wondered how you manage not to come out with something up there.'

'Oh, you have, have you? Well, I'll tell you, Rosie.' Emily's voice took on a pseudo-refined note. 'It's because I know how to pass meself. I always suit me language to the company I'm in – when in Rome they say – an' I'm tellin' you there's nobody can act more refined than meself when I like.'

As Angus drew his hand slowly down his face her voice suddenly changed and she bellowed at him, 'You take the bloody micky, me lad, and I'll skite you out of that door.'

'Who's taking the micky?' His brown eyes were dancing as he looked at her. 'Of course you can pass yourself. You wouldn't have survived so long up there if you hadn't been able to. But, you know, there's somethin' I've often

41

wondered an' all, Mam; I've wondered what effect a real good mouthful of yours would have on them.'

Once more they were laughing, spluttering over their soup. When the laughter subsided Angus asked, 'Did you hear anything more about yesterday's business?'

'Not much,' said Emily. 'Only she informed me that the master was very vexed at the whole affair.' She inclined her head deeply towards Angus, and he inclined his back and said, 'Oh, aye.'

'She was at her most buttery this mornin'. She impressed on me that the master didn't hold you responsible; it was them awful common fellows that you work with.'

'What did you say to that?'

'Nothin', I kept me silence. I find it pays with her. Say nowt and speed the work up and she gets into a tizzy. Oh, don't you worry, I can manage her all right. You don't live with somebody five days a week for eighteen years and not know them inside out. I've been along of her more than I've been with either of you.' She nodded from one to the other. 'That's strange to say, isn't it?'

'And you don't like her?'

Emily looked at her son and said slowly, 'I don't dislike her. I sort of understand her. She's a damned upstart, but she's got it from him, because he's a sanctimonious, hymn-singing, big-headed nowt. An' that's only half of it, because he's deep and calculating into the bargain. An' that Susan takes after him. An' I'm another one that'll be delighted when the wedding comes off, for then she'll be away from under me feet.'

'Have you seen much of her fellow?' asked Rosie.

'Oh, he's been in twice this week. He's not a bad sort . . . I'll tell you somethin'. He's not got one quarter of the side they have. Although he has one uncle a lord

42

and one an admiral, he acts just like any other fellow. "Hello, Emily", he says. "How goes it?"'

'He doesn't; you're kiddin'.' Rosie flapped her hand at her mother.

'I'm not kiddin'. An' don't you start mickying either. That's what he said. He came into the kitchen when I was gettin' lunch, and that's what he said. "Hello, Emily. How goes it? What you hashin' up?"'

'He did?'

'Aye, he did. An' I'll tell you something else. He said I was a fine cook. An' that's more than me family's ever said to me.'

'But your family never tastes your cookin', so how are we to judge? I ask you. How are we to judge?' Angus spread his hand out, palm upwards, giving emphasis to the question, and he expected her to laugh or come out with a mouthful at him. But when she dropped her fork, which was halfway to her mouth, back on to her plate and, looking at it, said dully, 'I'm sorry I've neglected you,' his face showed utter dismay.

'In the name of God, woman!' He scraped his chair back. 'Don't be so bloody soft. You know I was only pulling your leg. If you don't cook at the week-end it's our fault because we won't let you. Isn't it, Rosie?'

'Aye, Mam. Look.' Rosie put her hand gently on her mother's thick arm. 'You're tired, that's what it is. He was only pullin' your leg. You neglect us! As Angus says, don't talk so dippy; where do you think we'd have been if it hadn't been for you goin' out to work. We've never wanted for anything in our lives, an' it's thanks to you.'

Emily bowed her head and closed her eyelids tightly, and as the tears welled up they came one to each side of her. Their concern making them tender, they put their hands about her shoulders.

43

'Look,' said Angus; 'you're in need of a holiday, a break . . . a long one.'

'I'm in need of no holiday.' Emily's voice was quiet.

'Well, you want a change, Mam.' Rosie stroked the blatantly dyed black hair. 'What about going to the club the night; you haven't been for weeks. That's an idea, isn't it?' She looked up at Angus. 'I'll get Stan to come along. We were going to the pictures, but he doesn't mind where he goes as long as he can have his slap and tickle.' She pressed her lips together and giggled, then said, 'What about it, eh Angus, the club?'

'I'm game. It should be a good night. We'll have a knees-up, eh?' He brought his face down to his mother's, and she blinked rapidly and sniffed, then smiled and said, 'Aye, that'll do me good, a knees-up, even if I can't get me feet off the floor.' She looked at her swollen legs. 'Anyway, I think I'll go and put them up for an hour now.' She rose stiffly to her feet, and Rosie went with her along the narrow passage and watched her mount the stairs before returning to the kitchen. There she looked at Angus and said, 'Funny. I've not seen her like that afore.'

'She's tired.' Angus's voice was low. 'I'm tellin' you, she's tired, she's worn out.'

'But she's not old,' said Rosie sadly; 'she's just fifty odd.'

'Well she's had enough in the last twenty years to make her feel eighty. I wonder she hasn't cracked up afore now.'

'But I've always thought she was as strong as a horse.'

'Horses get old. Don't you know that? Even horses get old and tired . . . Go on up and see how she is.'

When Rosie entered her mother's room Emily was lying

on the bed, her stockinged feet showing the prominent
hump of bunions. Her stomach was pressing up a hillock
under her skirt band and her square, heavy face looked
pallid in contrast to the colour of her hair.

'You all right, Mam?'

'Oh aye, lass; just a bit tired.'

Rosie sat on the edge of the bed. 'Anything worryin'
you?'

'Aye.' Emily stared at her daughter for a full minute
before saying, 'Yes, there's somethin' worryin' me.'

'What then?'

'Angus.'

'Angus? Why you worrying about him? He's all right.
He's fine and fixed.'

'Aye, he's fine, but he's not really fixed, not securely
fixed. Do you know something?' Emily pulled herself
up on the pillows and, supporting herself on her elbow,
she leant towards her daughter and whispered, 'If I was
to leave up there the morrow he would have Angus out
of that shop afore you could blink.'

'Mr Ratcliffe! He couldn't do that, Mam. He'd have
to have a reason. If he sacked him for nothing he'd have
the whole shop out, the whole place out. You remember
last year when they came out because of John Petrick.
They were out three weeks but they got him reinstated
in the end. They couldn't do anything to Angus.'

'There's ways and means, lass. An' I bet you what you
like he'd have put the whole blame for yesterday's business
on him if they weren't frightened of losin' me.'

'Well, I can understand them not wanting to lose
you, Mam, because they won't get anybody like you
in a hurry.' Rosie patted her mother's hand, and Emily
said firmly, but without bumptiousness, 'I know that,
an' they know that, and the missus knows if it wasn't

for Angus I'd have left there two or three years back.'
Her voice suddenly dropped and she said, 'I'm tired,
Rosie.' Then she put in quickly, 'I'm not bad, I'm just
tired. Tired, lass, tired of working for other folks. I want
to stay in me own house and get it shipshape an' have
the meals ready for you both when you come in . . .
Aw, I know you won't be here much longer, you'll be
gettin' married. And Angus an' all, he'll find somebody
to his likin' afore long, if he doesn't take May, and then
likely I'll be wishin' I had a job. But I can always get a
job. Aw, that doesn't worry me, but in the meantime I
want a space, not just a week off, or even a fortnight –
she's promised me a fortnight – I want a month, two,
three, a year.'

'Oh, Mam!' Rosie dropped sideways and laid her head
against her mother's shoulder and her voice had a broken
sound as she said again, 'Aw, Mam.'

'There, there, don't upset yourself. And mind,' she
pushed her daughter's head away from her, 'now don't
you bloody well go downstairs and tell him. Now
mind you.'

'I'm not daft, Mam. But I can tell you this. He could
get a job anywhere. There's dozens of places he could
start the morrow, on Monday at any rate.' She gave a
little laugh now.

'Yes, I know that, but not with the prospects there are
at Affleck's. Mr Brett recommended him to chargehand
and he can recommend him further. I want to see him
be something, lass, not just a workman like his dad and
my dad and their dads afore them. I want to see our
Angus rise, and he can, given half a chance. You know
it was only because of the set-up in this house that he
left school when he did to help look after your dad, an'
him being bad so long. You see,' she swung her legs

46

over the edge of the bed until she was sitting side by side with Rosie, and she started to pull the knuckle of each finger in turn as she went on, 'you need education to rise, not so much brains. Ratcliffe hasn't any more brains than a louse to my mind but he had education. An' look where it got him. A grammar school education and a few kicks in the backside and he's at the top of the tree now. Aye, you need education and our Angus hasn't it, not the kind he needs to push him on, so he's got to get there in some other way.'

'But where do you expect him to get, Mam? He's in charge of his shop; he'll not get much higher than that in Affleck's.'

Emily turned her face towards her daughter and the words came under her breath, but they were weighty as she said, 'He could get himself into the drawin' office where the draughtsmen are. That's why he's been goin' to evening classes on the quiet. He doesn't know that I know he's been goin'. Did you know owt about it?'

'No, Mam. Evening classes! Our Angus?'

'Aye, our Angus.'

'He's twenty-four!'

'Twenty-four or not, he's goin'. But mind you –' she poked her finger into Rosie's chest – 'don't you let on for God's sake, else he'll stop. You know what his temper's like. If he wants us to know he'll tell us in his own good time. Now go on downstairs afore he comes up an' tell him I'm all right.'

When Rosie entered the kitchen again Angus asked, 'How is she?' and Rosie replied, 'She's all right. She's goin' to have a nap.'

'All right. All right. She's not all right. An' I know why she won't leave up there, she thinks it'll affect me. I know, and she's a bloody old fool. He can do nothing

47

to me and he knows it. You know something?' He turned round and looked at Rosie across the table. 'That man Ratcliffe has hated my guts since I was a nipper.'

'But why?'

'I think I know; in a sort of way I know.' He went and looked out of the window and down the narrow back yard. Then he said musingly, 'It was him that stopped me playing with Van. I remember the day. It was just after Dad died. Me Aunt Mary had you, an' me mam told me to go up there after school and she'd slip me a bite to eat. She was workin' late because they were havin' a dinner or somethin' – they gave dinners when they couldn't meet their grocery bills. Anyway, this day I was keeping out of the way round the back when Van comes on me. She was about five at the time. Well, there happened to be a garden barrier on the back path, you know one of those wooden ones, an' I put her in it and started to wheel her up and down. An' she laughed so much I thought she would burst. It must have been her laughin' that brought his lordship round, and he bellowed so loudly that he startled me and I nearly upset the barrer and her an' all. After he had ordered her in he stood looking at me with a look on his face that he sometimes has now, as if he considers me so much slime that should be washed down the drain. Yet even on that day he didn't go for Mam and tear her off a strip. But I never got the chance to play with Van again. Anyway, I've worked out this theory about Ratcliffe's attitude to me. It's just this. He can show his dislike for me and nothin' comes of it, but if he did it to Mam she would leave, and knowing this he not only hates me guts but hers an' all.'

'Go on. You're just imagining things. They think the world of her.'

48

'Think the world of her! Why? They think the world of her because she's necessary to them. They won't get a woman like Mam the day. Who they goin' to get to work from eight till five for five quid a week, turning her hand to anything from cooking to waiting on the "At Home" do's and their blasted dinners? Think the world of her! If she died the morrow they wouldn't come to her funeral.'

'Oh, you're too bitter against them, our Angus.'

'Not me, I've just got them taped, him most of all. He'd like to kick her backside out of the door. You see she doesn't kowtow to him, she answers him straight – without the bloodies of course.'

They both laughed softly now, and Rosie said, 'Eeh! I wonder what they'd think if they heard her going on sometimes?'

'Do them good. God! wouldn't I like to hear her let rip at them.' He boxed the air and Rosie said, 'Well, that reminds me. When you're gettin' it out of your system why aren't you at the match the day? Is your back still hurting?'

'I've left.' He was still punching the air, dancing round the table now, boxer-fashion, on his toes.

'You've left?' Her exclamation was high.

'Aye.'

'Are you barmy altogether? You broke your neck to get in, and it was an honour.'

He stopped abruptly and repeated, 'An honour? From who?'

'Well.' Rosie tossed her head. 'With Callow, the solicitor, playin', and that young Brownlow in the accountant's office.'

'To hell! Who's Callow, the solicitor, and Brownlow? Don't forget Ted Robson's the star player, and he's a

49

bricklayer. And Andy Thompson, what does he do? He carts ballast. If they had to depend on the white collar bods they wouldn't have a team at all. Honour!'

'Well it was,' Rosie persisted. 'It isn't everybody who is asked to join the Rugby team in this town. You must be barmy leaving it.'

'Well, I have left.'

'Does me mam know?'

'No, she doesn't.'

'When did this happen?'

'Two weeks ago, if you want to know.'

'When you hurt your back?'

'Yes, when I hurt me back; when somebody hurt me back, jumping on it with both feet. For the last year I've been asking meself what it's all about. Why get half-killed every week? I've had me ribs nearly kicked in, me shins torn. There was one time last year I nearly had me neck broke. And so I asked meself why I was doing it? And then when you're playin' away, the drink. Swimming in it. I don't mind a drink, you know I like a drink, but oh, God! the stupid things they get up to, the way they carry on. I used to an' all, I did me share, but I happened to be solid and sober one night when I went along to the Bull late. They had been at it a couple of hours, and aw, it turned me stomach over. They had put a nappie on Bill Webster. That's all he had on, a nappie, an' there he was sittin' in the middle of the floor sucking his thumb and slobberin', and Alec Turner was playin' the mother. I tell you, Rosie, I nearly spewed.'

'Well, it's only a bit of fun.'

'Well, it's not my kind of fun.' He nodded his head at her.

'You know what, our Angus?' She pursed her lips and grinned. 'I think you're goin' through a bad time. It can't be adolescence, so it must be an early change. I should warn May.'

The old tea cosy flew through the air again and she ran into the scullery laughing, and he was laughing as he went into the front room, which was his room.

The front room was twelve feet by nine. In it was a single divan bed, a new acquisition, an old chest of drawers, a hanging wardrobe, a small table in the corner near the window, and a gas fire in front of an open grate. The floor was covered with blue-and-white check linoleum and there were blue cotton curtains at the windows. The room was tidy and, if not bright, it was clean. No matter what condition the rest of the house got into Emily saw to this room.

Early change. He grinned to himself and jerked his head, then pulled a straight-backed chair up to the table on which were a number of books and some drawing paper, but he didn't start to work. He rested his elbow on the table and supported his chin on his hand, and he gazed through the narrow aperture of the curtains, across the street to the high, faceless wall of the railway sheds. An early change. Well, he might not be going through an early change but there was something wrong with him. He didn't know what, except, as he put it, he was at sixes and sevens with himself. He knew this much though. If it wasn't for his mam he would pack up the morrow and clear out, he would that. Ratcliffe, Afflecks, the lot would go to hell . . . What about May? Oh, May an' all for that matter.

THE LARCHES

The Larches

As they went out of the door it began to rain and Rosie said, 'Oh lord! me hair'll be flat. Why the devil can't we have a car, our Angus? Nearly everybody else in the street's got one 'cept us.'

'Aye; and look at them.' He thumbed a derelict looking specimen they were passing. 'I'll get a car when I can afford one, not one from the scrap.'

'You'll get no car at all,' said Emily, 'if you want to stay alive. Remember Sammy Cullen afore Christmas. I bet where he is the night he wishes he had never seen a car.'

'His was an old wreck, Mam,' said Rosie. 'You can get a nearly new one for a couple of hundred from Hallows.'

'Listen her!' exclaimed Angus. 'A couple of hundred! Why don't you get Stan to fork out and buy you a car?'

'He will an' all. That's what he's goin' to do if he wins the talent spot next week, goin' to put it down on one.'

Angus gave a ha-ha of a laugh; then nudging his mother, he said, 'Why don't we go in for the talent spot, Mam, eh? You could do your bit poetry, you know.

"Between the dark and the daylight,
When the night is beginning to lower,
Comes a pause in the day's occupations
That is known as the children's hour.
I hear in the chamber above me
The patter of little feet . . .'"

He was pushed into the gutter. 'You'll hear the crack of me hand across your lug, me lad, if you don't stop takin' the micky. I'll tell you one thing, they learnt you poetry in my day. Aye, at a council school at that.'

'Eeh! The Children's Hour.' Rosie shook her head. 'It used to petrify me, that, Mam, when you used to say it to me.

"I have you fast in my fortress
And will not let you depart
But put you down in the dungeon
In the round tower of my heart."

You used to say it to me to send me to sleep but it always sent me into nightmares; I was always cryin' to get out of dungeons.'

They were laughing hilariously as they boarded the bus. They were still laughing and talking, and all at once, when they alighted in the main street, and they were a few yards from the club entrance and passing a tobacconist's, when Angus said, 'You go on in, I'm goin' to get some baccy.'

'Baccy? You?' Rosie had hold of his arm.

'Aye, baccy, me. I've decided to smoke a pipe. Better for your lungs, they tell you.'

Their laughter vied with the noise of the traffic, and

as they parted he tried to control his face before entering the shop.

Carsons was a big shop, the best in the town. A number of people were inside, and he did not notice the young girl until she moved a step to allow a man to pass her, and then he said, 'Why, hello, Van.' He had almost said Miss Van. It was just a habit, the Miss. Sometimes he added it to her name and sometimes he didn't.

'Oh, hello, Angus.' Her face, which had been solemn in repose, brightened.

He bent his head down to her. 'You takin' to smokin'?'

'No.' She smiled widely at him. 'It's father's birthday on Monday.'

He looked her up and down, then whispered, 'I didn't recognise you without your school rig; you know, it's the first time I've seen you out of school uniform in years.' He jerked his head. 'You look different.'

She stretched her face slightly up to his and whispered back, 'And you know something, Angus? I feel different.'

They both chuckled, then moved a step forward as another customer left the counter. They were silent for a moment, he staring ahead towards the cigarette-laden shelves; then turning to her again, he whispered under his breath, 'Don't often see you down this way,' and she answered as softly, 'I don't often get down this way; I've been let out.' And they exchanged an understanding smile.

When her turn came to be served she asked for a box of cigars and paid over thirty shillings for them. As she turned from the counter he said, 'Be seeing you, Van.' And she nodded at him and answered, 'Yes. Be seeing you, Angus.'

A minute or so later, when he left the shop, she was standing in the shelter of the doorway and she turned to him and said, 'What a night! I'm going to wait here until the bus comes across the road and then make a dive for it.'

He peered at her in the dim light, saying, 'This is one time when I wish I had a car. We were just talking about a car when we left the house, me mother and Rosie. They said I should have a car.'

'Are they here?' She nodded towards the street.

'They're in the club; we're goin' to make a night of it.' The corner of his mouth moved characteristically upwards.

She looked into his face, hers unsmiling now, and she said, 'You do enjoy yourselves, don't you? I mean Emily and Rosie and you, you do enjoy yourselves.'

'Oh, I don't know, not more than anybody else. Life's very dull at times.' In his mind he was talking to a very young girl, a girl who had everything, yet whom he was sorry for in a way, whom he had always been sorry for in a way. He said now, 'It's about time you splashed out at dances, isn't it? Country balls an' that?'

'The school dance is as far as I've got so far, Angus; but I'll likely start in the autumn.'

'Well, that's something to look forward to.' He paused and stretched his thick neck upwards out of his collar before saying, 'By the way, Van, there's something I'd like you to get clear.' He now rubbed the side of his forefinger across his chin. 'It's about yesterday's business. You know I wouldn't have let that happen if I could have helped it, but the lads –'

Her gloved fingers lightly flicked his sleeve. 'Look, Angus, forget it. All that fuss. They ask for what they get, I know that.'

'Yes, but nevertheless, the fellows should mind their tongues . . . I didn't know you came along that way?'

'I don't as a rule, but I was going to my friend's house and apparently she uses it as a short cut,' her lips pressed together for a moment, 'because she likes to egg them on.'

He stood looking down at her. She was wise in a way was Van. He'd always felt that. Different from the rest, inside as well as in appearance. She was turning into a lovely looking lass, and she would get lovelier. With startling suddenness there came into his chest, just below the ribs, a strange feeling, and for a moment he felt he had been cut off from life; he felt empty, sort of lost. The feeling so enveloped him that he didn't notice a car drawing up to the kerb. When a man got out and came into the shop doorway, Vanessa said, 'Oh, hello, Brett,' and the man answered on a surprised note, 'Why! Vanessa.' Then he looked at Angus and added, 'Hello there, Angus.' He didn't show any surprise that Angus Cotton, one of the floor men, should be standing in a doorway talking to the manager's daughter. But, on the other hand, Angus showed a great deal of embarrassment.

'Hello, Mr Brett,' he said; then added quickly, 'Van . . . Miss Van here got caught in the rain. She's waitin' for a bus.'

'Waiting for a bus? Well, it's a good job I came along. I won't be a minute, Vanessa. Go on in the car; Irene's there.'

'Oh thanks. That's fine. Good-bye, Angus.' She smiled at him.

'Good-bye, Van.' They were alone again for a moment. 'Be seeing you.'

'Yes; be seeing you, Angus.'

As she got into the back of the car she said, 'Hello

59

Irene,' and Irene Brett turned round in her seat and said, 'Hello, Vanessa. A beastly night, isn't it?' Then after a slight pause she added, 'Wasn't that Emily's son you were talking to?'

'Yes, Irene. I just met him in the shop a minute ago.'

Vanessa always thought of the woman she had known from a small child as Irene Brett, not Auntie Irene. Susan called her Auntie, but she herself had stubbornly refused to call their neighbour Auntie, or her husband Uncle. She had even amazed her parents by going so far as to address Arthur Brett by his surname. When she was asked why, she said she didn't like the name Arthur, she liked Brett, and so he had been Brett to her ever since.

This familiarity had always incensed Irene Brett. She now sat looking at the rain-smeared windscreen, and she was again feeling annoyed that she could find nothing to say to this girl. She had always considered Vanessa a deep, withdrawn type of girl, and she felt now that she was indeed right about her being deep. She didn't believe for a moment that she had met Angus Cotton by accident. This wasn't the first time she had seen them together; a fortnight ago she had seen them both standing talking outside the Technical School. Now what would she want outside the Technical School? It was miles away from the Convent, and from Brampton Hill. She had felt for a long time that Jonathan and Jane were going to have trouble with this one. They weren't going to be able to plan her life as they had done Susan's. Anyway, perhaps they'd be satisfied in wangling one daughter into the fringes of the titled set. They'd never let up, those two, get there or die.

Her thoughts, touching on the second main grievance of her life, gathered momentum and she became lost in her hate, and she started as the door opened and her husband took his seat, saying over his shoulder, 'Don't often see you in the town, Vanessa.'

'No, I don't often come down. But it's Father's birthday. I was getting him a present.'

'It's his birthday is it?'

'Yes, he'll be fifty on Monday.'

'Fifty! Well, well. Yes . . . yes, he will be fifty.' He was talking as if to himself. When he got the car going he added, 'Time doesn't stand still; no, time doesn't stand still.'

There wasn't another word spoken until they turned from Brampton Hill into the side road; then Vanessa said, 'Just drop me at your gate, Brett, that'll be all right.'

'No, I'll take you along.'

'No, please. It's eased off.'

'All right, just as you say.'

When she got out of the car she said, 'Thanks for the lift, Brett. Good-night, Irene.'

They both said together, 'Good-night, Vanessa.'

A few minutes later they went up the steps, through the glass-covered lobby and into the dark, panelled hall, and there, as Irene Brett took off her hat and coat, she remarked casually, 'Well, what do you think of that?'

'What?'

'Her standing talking to that Angus Cotton.'

He hadn't looked at her before, but now he turned round and faced her. Then after staring at her for a moment, he said, 'Angus Cotton and Vanessa? Well, why shouldn't she talk to him? They've known each other all their lives. I remember them playing together.'

She threw up her head, closed her eyes and turned from him, and as she went into the high-ceilinged, old-fashioned looking drawing-room, she said, 'Your

61

simplicity makes me want to scream. It must be all of ten years or more since Jonathan put a stop to that. But of course you wouldn't remember anything so mundane.'

She turned round now and watched him coming slowly into the room, and when he came near her she said, 'I saw them together outside the Technical School only a few days ago. And that's not the only time.'

Arthur Brett surveyed his wife. There were times when he had to screw his eyes up to get her into focus, when he had to remind himself that he had lived with this woman for twenty-five years, that she wasn't a stranger whom he didn't know. He said quietly to her, 'What are you trying to make of it?'

'What am I trying to make of it?' She stressed the I. 'I'm only making a statement. What do you think would be Jonathan's reaction if he knew that she was talking to that fellow in the main street?'

'I don't know, Irene; and I don't care very much what Jonathan would think. But I would think it strange if those two met in the street and passed each other. And whether Jonathan stopped them playing together years ago or not, I can recall when Angus was a big lump of a lad and Vanessa was seven or eight or more seeing them together in the garden.'

'Well, you've seen something that nobody else saw, because if either Jonathan or Jane had known there'd have been an abrupt stop put to it. And I think a stop should be put to this if they don't want consequences . . . That fellow! He's like a great big Irish navvy. I think at least Jane should know about it.'

'And I think,' there was a hardness in Arthur Brett's usually soft, lazy-sounding voice now, 'I think you should mind your own business and not take it out of Jane through Vanessa.'

'Take it out of . . .! What are you talking about? What are you insinuating?'

'Just that you're not too pleased, are you, that Jane is getting Susan married into the Braintrees. But you can't do much about that so you intend to make her uneasy through Vanessa. That's it, isn't it?'

'How dare you! How dare you suggest such a thing. You're making me out to be a vile, mischief-making . . .'

'I'm not making you out to be anything but what you are, Irene.' As he turned from her she hissed at him under her breath, 'Don't leave me like that, Arthur. Listen. Listen to me. Do you hear?'

Not until he was at the room door did he turn, and then he said quietly, 'I'm not going to listen to you, Irene; I don't happen to be a member of one of your committees, nor a fellow councillor whom you are rating, nor yet a delinquent up before you on the bench. There are a number of things you can't make me do, Irene, and that's one of them; listen to you.'

When he closed the door behind him and she was alone she stood with her two hands pressed tightly over her thin lips. She could understand why women committed murder. He hadn't the gumption he was born with, yet he was inflexible about what he considered his ideals, his principles. Oh, God, how had she of all people got stuck with someone like him! She knew the answer to this, but she had long refused to think about it.

She now walked to the couch, and with her hands still in the same position she sat herself down. She did not lean back against the couch for support, her thin body remained erect. She had a good figure and she looked after it, as she did her complexion and her hair. She was looked upon as a smart woman, but no one had ever said she was good-looking or pretty . . . or charming, but she was often referred to as clever and business-like. She was a committee woman and could get things done, at least outside her own house and family.

After a moment she lowered her hands to her lap and her eyes moved slowly around the room. She almost hated this room, this whole house, as much as she did its owner. The place had never been redecorated inside or out for years, yet he had only to sell two or three acres of land and the whole place could be renovated. Even if he could have been persuaded to sell some of the furniture, some of these ugly monstrosities, this would have gone a long way towards lightening and refurnishing the house.

There was a Queen Anne secretaire on the landing for which he had been offered three hundred pounds, and in a corner, over there, in the recess that hardly saw the light of day, was a William and Mary side-table. There was a very old mahogany commode in Colin's bedroom that would be worth a small fortune at Sotheby's. There were French chairs dotted all over the house, the tapestry so threadbare the wadding was sticking through, and there was no hope of having them re-covered; he wouldn't even allow her to put loose-covers on them. There wasn't one of the twelve rooms in the house that didn't hold a piece of furniture that would bring in hundreds, but because his grandfather had furnished this house for his bride in 1892 he thought that was sufficient reason why it should remain as it was for his life. She knew that he had even made a will to the effect that all the furniture couldn't be sold on his death; certain pieces he had willed to the three boys with a request that they would think twice before parting with them. He had dared to tell her that he was going to do this. Spite. Spite, that's what it was, and all because she wouldn't supply him with his needs. His needs indeed! If he came into her room again she would tear his face off. Only last week he had dared to try to get into bed with her. Why? Why? When he cared as little for her as she did for him. She had warded him off for years with the excuse that she didn't want any more children, and nothing was safe . . . And nothing was safe. Michael, her youngest son, was only six years old. Fancy, on the verge of forty having become pregnant again! The shame of it almost killed her. She had hardly been able to face the boys . . . Boys? Colin had been almost a man then: eighteen, and Paul thirteen.

And last night he had dared to try it on again, even knowing how she felt about him. Again she had to ask herself, Why?

Upstairs in his room, Arthur Brett was asking himself the same question. Why? Why, when their love was dead, so dead you forgot when it had died, did you re-visit the corpse? Why did you want to put your arms around it, put your mouth on its mouth, press your body into it, work over it, struggle with it, even knowing it wouldn't move? It never had moved during all the years of their married life. The act had been an act of sufferance on her side and had brought him humiliation; yet he suffered humiliation a thousandfold in going to her and begging for his body's easement. Why? Why didn't he go down to Bog's End? He could find ease in Bog's End. He could reel off the names of at least eight men he knew on his floor who visited Bog's End regularly. He had just to say one word to Will Hobson and he'd be fixed up. The times he had made up his mind to say that word to Will. He would be determined when he had left the house in the morning that the first thing he'd do would be to see Will and put an end to this torment. He always got as far as seeing Will but he never mentioned Bog's End. Again why?

Perhaps it was because at these moments he would remember that but for his grandfather's taste for high living, and his father's easy goingness and lack of business sense, he might today be Will Hodson's employer, because the firm of Affleck and Tate had once belonged to the Bretts. His grandmother's name was Affleck. She had brought the business – much smaller than it was now admittedly, but nevertheless a thriving concern – she had brought it to one Arthur Brett, a handsome, loving, carefree individual, who had a taste for good furniture, good wine, entertaining, and horses, which tastes he indulged right up to the middle of the thirties. He died at the table drinking wine; he actually died in toasting his white-haired and still beautiful wife. It was all very romantic.

He could remember the night his grandfather died as if it was yesterday. It was a beautiful summer evening, and he was home from boarding-school. He was sitting at his grandmother's right hand and he was looking at her profile as she gazed down the table towards her big, corpulent, but still handsome husband. When he fell forward over the table she gave a thin high scream and then became quite still. Three days later she herself died. His father said that was as it should be; they both had enjoyed life and one couldn't exist without the other.

His own father had almost repeated the pattern in his approach to life and way of living. It wasn't until Arthur himself was seventeen that he realised that Affleck and Tate was no longer their firm, that the shares had been sold gradually until their holdings were now non-existent, and that all that remained of the once-affluent Afflecks was the house and land; and, of course, the furniture, the furniture which his father wouldn't part with even to keep up some kind of appearance in the town.

He was nineteen when he met Irene Bailey, and she was a year older than him, and he hadn't thought he was deceiving her by not explaining the financial position in which his parents stood. After all, thinking socially, she was of little consequence in town. Her father was a schoolteacher, elementary. She was attractive and vivacious, and he had fallen deeply in love with her, besides which he was full of admiration for her. She hadn't got to the high school, but she had supplemented her elementary education by going to night school. She could talk intelligently; she only had to have a smattering of any subject and she could give the impression of knowledge.

He knew she was flattered by his attention; also that she was impressed by the big house, and the fact that he was the only son of the Bretts, and that they were Affleck and Tate.

He had told her casually before they were married that they were no longer Affleck and Tate, and he imagined at the time that it had meant nothing to her, but he knew now that she married him because she thought she could do something with him, restore him to the lost eminence of his grandfather, if not in the works, then along other lines.

But he was not cut out for other lines; except perhaps he could have been manager of Affleck and Tate. Oh yes, yes, he could have been manager, and he should have been manager because, after all, Affleck and Tate was in his blood so to speak. Yet all this had been forgotten when a certain Jonathan Ratcliffe, whom incidentally he had befriended when he first came into the drawing-office, inveigled himself into the good books of the board, by what method he had never been able to find out, and he had been too proud to enquire. Of course there had been the usual tittle-tattle about sucking up; but any move upwards brought this reaction. Anyway, Jonathan had gone from the drawing-office to the building across the yard, and there had become assistant to the under-manager, Rowland. Yet he must be fair. That was likely as far as he would have got if both Bowden, who was manager at the time, and Rowland, who took his place, hadn't died within the next five years.

Life was odd. He went to the window and looked out through the leafless trees. There, in the distance, he could see Jonathan's house. It was lit up. They were entertaining again, likely Susan's fiancé's people. He liked entertaining did Jonathan; it was a mark of his power. They were rarely asked next door, because he embarrassed Jonathan. He also knew he angered him. He had still things Jonathan wanted, the river frontage, for instance, and the land, all of it. The land. Oh, yes, all of the land.

He turned from the window and went out of the room and was crossing the landing when his eldest son, Colin, came up the stairs. They blinked at each other over the distance and Colin's look said, 'You two been at it again?'

Arthur knew that his eldest son saw him through the eyes of his mother. This didn't boost one's morale. Still he had the consolation of Paul. Paul was different. Paul was the replica of himself, quiet, easy going; clever in a way. But what was the use of being clever in a way, you had to be clever in all ways. He doubted somehow if Paul would be any different from himself in this way either. He had no push. He wanted to meander through life like they both used to meander at night through the wood, then sit in the old summerhouse looking at the river and talk, or be silent, and sometimes laugh. Paul was the only real companion he'd had in his life. Irene had made certain of Colin and was making certain of Michael, but she could do nothing with Paul. Paul had stuck to him as if he was his own sweat.

Irene had made no fuss about Paul going to college. He knew that she had welcomed the fact that the other part of her husband would be out of the house. She was at her worst during the holidays, but the holidays were the only thing he lived for. And this year they would be short, at least for him, because Paul was going abroad on a walking tour. He had wanted him to go along, and if there had only been the two of them he would have jumped at the chance, but he couldn't see himself being one of a party of four exuberant youths.

After his bath he went straight to bed. This wouldn't interfere with the routine of the house; he rarely had anything to eat after teatime. Later on, when they had all retired, he might go down to the kitchen and make himself a hot drink and sit by the stove. He liked sitting by the stove. He had sat a lot in the kitchen when he was a boy; it had been a different stove then. The old one had exploded one day and the cook had fainted. She had been a big old Irish woman, and when she came round the first thing she said was, 'Oh God, have I been blown into heaven?' And they had all laughed and laughed. They had laughed a lot in this house at one time. Everybody in it had been compatible; there had been no in-law trouble when he was young. His mother and father had lived all their married life with his grandfather and grandmother, and he himself had brought his bride to live with his mother and father. It was from then that the laughter had eased off.

It was around ten o'clock when he heard Irene come upstairs and go to her room. She did not look in on him. That, too, had ceased a long time ago. He lay for a time, his book lying on top of the quilt, his two hands flat on the open pages, and he staring down at them as he asked himself questions to which there were no answers. When eleven o'clock struck he switched the light off and got up and opened the curtains. He was surprised to see the moon shining brightly. The rain had stopped and the tangled garden below him and the long stretch of wood beyond looked like an enchanted forest. He pulled his dressing-gown about him and sat on the broad windowsill, with his knees up under his chin. He could still do that for he wasn't pot-bellied. There was no movement outside, no wind; March was in but she was with-holding her signs. It could have been a June evening except that it would be cold out. He had always wanted to write poetry; there seemed such a lot of poetry locked up inside of him. He envied people who could write. There must be great easement in writing, pouring out your feelings and being able to read them back to yourself. Not only must it be alleviative, but also satisfactory. That's why he missed Paul so much. Paul, in a way, had been his form of release, his outlet.

As he stared at the treetops his eyes were caught by a movement down below to the left of him. There was a shadow crossing the open space, which was the north side of the Ratcliffes' garden. There were no open spaces in his garden. It took gardeners to create open spaces, and he himself was no gardener for the simple reason he hated to cut anything down, even weeds. Killing in any way was abhorrent to him, but he didn't give this reason for the neglect of his garden. He just said that he was no gardener, also that he was innately lazy.

The shadow disappeared, then reappeared again in a patch of moonlight. It was making for the gate in his boundary fence, the gate which allowed the Ratcliffes' access to the river bank, his river bank. He had had the gate made when Jonathan first built the house. A second before the figure disappeared again into the shadows he recognised Vanessa. Now what would Vanessa be doing out at this time of night? He turned and glanced at the clock. Ten minutes to twelve. He now turned his gaze towards the Ratcliffes' house. The lights were all out.

Once more he focused his gaze in the direction of the gate. It was impossible to see if she had come into the wood. But she had been making for the gate. When, five minutes later, he had not seen her return up the garden, the reason for her midnight stroll came to him as he remembered what Irene had said earlier in the evening, and he muttered aloud, 'Oh no! No!'

It was one thing Angus Cotton speaking to her in the street, but it was entirely another thing meeting her secretly, and at this time of night. The wire fencing at the bottom of the wood was broken in several places where it bordered the side road. The children were always coming in for cob nuts or bluebells. Angus could easily come in that way and walk along by the river bank to the summerhouse.

God! No! He liked Angus. He was a good, honest fellow, and he had brains of a sort, but to start anything with Vanessa! He began swiftly to pull his trousers on. One thing was certain. If there was anything in this, Jonathan would blame him for giving the fellow ideas above his station. He had already used that very term.

He got into his coat, took his shoes in his hand, then

71

opened the door softly, and, crossing the landing, he went down the back stairs that led directly into the kitchen, then let himself out at the side door.

The night air made him shiver. As he took the side path around what had once been the rose garden he asked himself what he would say to them. Well, he could just be taking a stroll. That was it. He couldn't sleep and had come out for some air. Then he would get Angus on one side and let him have it. Oh yes, he'd let him have it. This kind of thing couldn't go on. It wasn't only because Jonathan would blame him, it was because a girl like Vanessa mustn't get herself mixed up with a fellow like Angus. No matter how decent he was, it just wouldn't work out. He liked reading mythology and tales of princesses and plough boys, but these were only to entertain that section of the mind that remained for ever in youth. The fate of the princess and the plough boy in real life could only spell disaster. In a sort of way his own romance had been like the prince and the beggar maid. Not that Irene would thank him for placing her in that category.

The path was well worn, and last year's leaves had been trodden into mush by his own feet. He entered the wood, and although he was in deep shadow he found his way unerringly between the great oak tree which dominated the top of the wood and the forked group of three birch trunks that stood to the right of it; then through a thicket of spidery hazel trees, and on to a pathway again. He was careful to keep to the path so as not to tread on to the carpet of wood anemones and the sprouting daffodils and narcissus. In another week or so the wood would be a picture of white and gold with a sprinkling of blue, and when the blue took over he would think again the sky had fallen. He now turned sharp right and to the gate that gave access to the wood. It was open, pushed back on its rusty hinge. He left it like that, then walked quickly in the direction of the river and the summerhouse.

He paused by the landing stage and looked along the bank and up the rise to where the summerhouse stood. The moon was lighting up the scene as if it was daylight. He strained his ears but could hear no sound of voices. God, but this was going to be awkward. Yet she might not be there at all, she might have gone back. No, she would have closed the gate after her if she had gone back. They always closed the gate so that Michael's puppy wouldn't again get through into Jonathan's garden and play havoc among the formal beds. No, somehow he had no doubt but that she was still here, and in the summer-house. Well – he squared his shoulders – he couldn't stay out all night, he'd better get it over with. His feet made no sound on the grass bank as he approached the wooden structure that had a disintegrating veranda and a thatched roof in a similar state. Three steps along the veranda took him to the door. To his surprise it was open and, further to his surprise, there was Vanessa, her hand held tightly against her cheek, sitting on the slatted form staring at him.

'Vanessa!'

'Oh, Brett. Oh!' She put her other hand up to her face and closed her eyes. 'Oh, you did give me a start.' She swallowed deeply now as she gazed up at him. 'I . . . I nearly had a fit.'

He was blacking out the moonlight, and in the shadow of himself he could only see the dark gleam of her eyes, their brown now appearing like pieces of jet. 'What on earth are you doing here, on your own?'

'Oh, well.' She rose to her feet, then dropped her head and said again, 'Oh, you did give me a fright, Brett.'

'You're shaking.' He had hold of her arm. 'Sit down. I . . . I didn't mean to frighten you. But why are you out here at this time of night?'

'Oh, I often come down. I hope you don't mind, Brett.'

'Mind? Of course not. But why?'

'Well, I suppose it's because I'm restless, I can't sleep. This is only the second time I've been here this year; it's a bit cold yet.' She shrugged her shoulders upwards around her chin. 'I started to come down last summer. I could have sat in our garden but it wasn't the same, I wanted to look at the river. You really don't mind?'

'Don't be silly.' He turned his head away from her. Then looking at her quickly again, he asked, 'You're . . . you're not in trouble of any sort?'

'No. No, of course not, Brett. Trouble? What trouble could I be in?' This was followed by an embarrassed silence. She was sixteen and a half, as she had informed her father, and she knew what trouble she could be in, but she didn't think Brett was referring to that kind of trouble. Cecilia Tomache had had to leave school last year because of a similar trouble, but she was well over seventeen. She said airily now, 'Well, it's now my turn to ask why you are out at this hour?'

'That's easy to answer. I saw you coming down, and I may as well tell you I wondered what you were up to.'

'Oh, Brett, you didn't!'

'I did, young woman, I did.'

They were laughing softly together. 'Who did you expect to find me with?'

'Well now.' It would never do to tell her the truth, so he stroked his chin and pretended to think deeply before he said, 'Seeing that Susan might well one day be Lady Braintrees I thought you would at least be hobnobbing

74

with a count.' He looked at her. 'Yes, a count, Italian. But on second thought, no. Italian counts are two-a-penny, and it would have to be someone exclusive for you, a prince. Yes . . . Now who are the eligible princes? There's not many left. Now let's see . . .'

'Oh, Brett, you are funny.' She pushed him. 'I'll settle for something less than a prince.'

'Well, don't do too low. Now mind, I'm telling you.' He wagged his finger at her. 'Aim high. Aim high, young woman.'

The moonlight was falling across their faces, just below their eyes, but he could see the expression in hers as she said, 'Who are you thinking about, Brett, when you say I should aim high? Me, or mother and father?'

It was a sobering question, and the bantering went out of his voice as he answered, 'I wasn't thinking of them, I was merely being funny. When the time comes, high or low, you'll know.'

He had said to her, high or low, yet a few minutes ago he had been worried stiff in case she had given her young freshness to someone like Angus Cotton. People never said what they meant. He was no exception.

She was looking out of the door now down the slope on to the moonlight water and she said, 'I want to get married some time, Brett, but I . . . I don't want it manoeuvred, like Susan's. Brian's young, but if he had been as old as father I think she would have been manoeuvred into it, and she herself would have wanted to be manoeuvred into it, she's got a thing about titles. She's as bad as mother.' She turned her head sharply towards him. 'People make me sick, Brett.'

'People make me sick too, Vanessa.' He laughed tolerantly.

75

'Yes, I should imagine they do, Brett, because you've had what is known as a dirty deal, haven't you?'

His eyes widened as he stared at her. Then he said, 'How did you come by that impression?'

'Oh!' She shook her head quickly. 'Father, Mother, the things they say. Father's guilt complex. He feels awfully guilty about you. I know he does; that's why he blusters.'

'Nonsense, nonsense, Vanessa. Good gracious, child, you do have queer ideas about some things.'

'I haven't, Brett. You know I haven't. And I'm not a child, I'm going on seventeen and I'm very, very worldly.' She bowed her head in a deep obeisance towards him, and he threw back his head and laughed aloud, only to check it quickly as he whispered, 'I could be heard from the road, and if the night patrol was passing he'd be in here like a shot. And what would he think, finding us here at this time of night, eh?'

'He'd think the worst, Brett.'

'Vanessa!' There was astonishment in his voice, yet he was still laughing.

'I told you I'm very worldly.'

He looked at her with his head on one side. 'You're very sweet, Van. I used to call you that when you were young but your father didn't like it. Vanessa is her name, Vanessa she must be called . . . Come on, I think we'd both better be making for indoors.' He rose to his feet and put out his hand and pulled her upwards, and as they went out on to the veranda she said, 'Paul will soon be home; you'll be happy then, Brett, won't you?'

He stopped dead and stared at her. 'What makes you think I'm unhappy without Paul, Vanessa?'

'Oh, I don't know, just the way you look, sad like,

76

lost. Yet you never look like that when you're with Paul. You know when you were together at Christmas, you remember at the party, I thought to myself you were like twins.'

'Oh, my dear, that's the best compliment I've had in my life. Thank you, Vanessa, thank you.' He bowed deeply from the waist.

'I mean it.' She turned from him and went down the steps on to the grassy slope, saying over her shoulder, 'I like Paul, I like Paul better than anybody I know, except you.' She was laughing widely as she turned her glance back towards him.

He laughed back at her, then said, 'I am deeply honoured, ma'am, deeply honoured.' And he added, 'Seriously, I am.'

'I am looking forward to Paul coming. He's good fun.'

'You like Paul, really like him?'

'Yes, yes, I do. Would you like me to marry Paul, Brett?'

'Vanessa, what's got into you tonight? It must be the moon.'

'Yes, I think it is the moon because I'm being very forward, aren't I? I'm not usually like this, am I? They say I don't talk enough. They think I'm reserved. Sulky, Father calls it. But I've always talked with you, and I can feel forward with you and know you'll not tick me off.'

Again they were laughing, smothered laughter.

'But would you, would you like me to marry Paul, Brett?'

'Since you ask, Vanessa, I would. It would make me very happy if you married Paul. But that's up to you and Paul.'

'Yes, that's up to me and Paul, and Paul doesn't even know I exist.'

'Nonsense, Paul's very fond of you. I know that.'

'Yes, as the kid next door.'

'Well, you know,' he said thoughtfully, 'up till last summer, even up till Christmas, even up to yesterday, you did appear like the kid next door, but not any longer.' He held up his hand warningly against her attack, and they were laughing softly again as they entered the shadows of the trees. He whispered to her now, 'Keep your voice down,' and they said nothing further until they reached the gate, and there, looking up at him, she murmured below her breath, 'I feel better, better than I've done for weeks. There was a dinner tonight, and, oh, it was boring.'

'You were down for dinner?'

'Yes, of course. Don't you know that I'm a young lady and must be initiated into society?' The bantering tone left her voice and she said, 'You know, sometimes, Brett, I think I'm in one of Jane Austen's novels; the pattern in our house is just like that. Mother talks about "getting one ready". In this day and age, "getting one ready"! I ask you. When they are already talking of school children getting married and going back to school. It's true, it was on the telly. She's still living in her youth, even in her own mother's youth. There's no fun, Brett. You know, down on the main street where I was tonight, you know when I was talking to Angus, there's a club. They were going, his sister and Emily, and they would be laughing and singing and enjoying themselves up till midnight. It made me feel sad, forgotten somehow. Not that I want to go to clubs, but some of the girls from school, younger than me, they go out on a Saturday night to dances. The Golf Club have a wonderful dance once a month. But what happens to me? I'm allowed down to dinner to be "got ready". Got ready for what, Brett? Not to get married, not really, you don't really need to be got ready to get married, do you? I should imagine that comes naturally, doesn't it?'

'Well.' He was stumped, he was stumped by the whole train of her conversation.

'I know what I'm being got ready for, Brett. I'm being got ready to hook someone in the Braintree set. Oh, I know all about it, and it makes me furious inside.'

'Take it slowly, dear,' he said gently. 'I know how you feel, I really do, and when Paul comes home you'll go off to a dance together. It'll be arranged in some way.'

She sighed deeply. 'It won't be arranged, it can't. Father will see to that, and in any case I wouldn't want to go to a dance with Paul because it would be on sufferance.'

'Don't talk nonsense, he'd be delighted to take you, because, you know, you're a very, very attractive young lady. In fact, I could say truthfully you're a very beautiful young lady when you're not scowling, and if I'm not mistaken you're going to cause some havoc in the male world before you're much older.'

'Do you think so, Brett?' Her voice was eager. 'Really? You're not just being soothing?'

'No, I'm not just being soothing. It's a prophesy, and all my prophesies come true.' He raised his hand, and again they were laughing gently. Now he pushed her through the gateway, saying, 'How do you get in?'

'Up the fire escape, on to the second landing, and once I'm there and anyone should open their door I'm just coming from the bathroom.'

'You're a minx.'

'How did you get out?'

'Down the back stairway.' Again he pushed her. 'Go on, sleep well. See you tomorrow.'

She moved a step from him, then turned swiftly towards him and, reaching up, she kissed him on the chin, saying, 'You are the nicest man I know, the very nicest.'

He stood perfectly still until he imagined she had reached the side of the house where the fire escape was, then he moved slowly up through the wood, his head bent on his chest, and when he re-entered his room again he switched on the light and looked at himself closely in the mirror. Then he held his hand a few inches from his face as if he was cupping the face that had kissed his.

As he went to sleep he thought, 'And I went out to tear a strip off Angus Cotton!'

PART ONE

1

Vanessa just managed to board the train with the assistance of a lift and an, 'In you go!' from a porter. She stumbled over the feet of the second-class passengers and excused herself; then she went out into the corridor and down the train towards the few first-class compartments. She was passing the last compartment in the corridor when the sight of the sole occupant of it brought her to a halt and she said, 'Why! hello, Angus.'

'Oh, hello.' Angus got hastily to his feet, dropping the paper to the floor as he did so. He retrieved it and threw it on to the seat before saying, 'Fancy meeting you here.'

'Yes.' She nodded and smiled at him.

'Lookin' for a seat?' He looked down at her.

She hesitated just a moment, and his chin jerked up as he said, 'Oh, you're going down to the first. I'm sorry.'

'Don't be silly.' She moved into the compartment and sat down; immediately he sat opposite to her, saying, 'You're not at school the day? That's a daft question, but I mean . . .'

'I've been to the dentist.'

'In Newcastle?' His thick, sandy, well-defined eyebrows moved upwards. 'I thought we had an overflow of them in Fellburn.'

'I had to see a specialist. I'm getting an extra ration.'
She pressed the corner of her mouth back and upwards
to reveal a small tooth jutting out between the roots of
two others.

'Good lord! Cutting your milk teeth again? Aw,'
his smile widened, 'in your case it would be a wisdom tooth.'

She laughed. 'Wisdom, huh! Wisdom. By the way,
while we're explaining why we aren't at our particular
jobs, why aren't you at work?'

'Oh.' He leant back. 'I've been to a funeral.'

'A funeral?'

'Yes; me uncle's. We haven't seen him for years, ten
or more, but me mother thought somebody should go.
It wasn't decent like,' he mimicked Emily's words, 'to let
him be put away and not one of the family near him.'

'But why didn't she . . .?' Her voice trailed off and
she ended lamely, 'Oh yes. Oh yes, the company.'

He nodded at her slowly and repeated, 'Yes, the
company.'

'But if she had asked mother, I'm sure it could have
been arranged.'

He stared at her. He didn't say she did ask mother,
but that mother said it would be very inconvenient, and
wouldn't it be simpler for Rosie to attend the funeral? No,
Rosie was just a lass and, what was more, she couldn't
abide funerals. Then it must be arranged that Angus
should have the day off; she would see the master. And
she had seen the master, and here he was.

His silence and his intent look implied the facts of
the case to Vanessa and she thought, 'Oh, Mother!'
Then merely for something to say she said naïvely,
'But how are they managing in your shop without
you?'

His bellow of a laugh could have been heard above the noise of the train and he wiped his eyes and said, 'You know, it's funny but I've never been able to make out how the firm managed to carry on afore I got into the shop. An' you know something else?' He now leant forward and rested his elbows on his knees and brought his face level with hers. 'I bet there's twice as much work done in that shop that day, because, you see, I've got a friend, oh a very dear friend.' He stretched his upper lip well over his teeth and pulled a face before he continued, 'One, Jim Taggart. He likes me so much that he'll get his blokes to work twice as hard when I'm out of the way and he'll say to me the morrow, "What do you think of that, Angus? We didn't slack, eh?" but what he's really sayin' is, "I can get twice as much work out of the . . . out of them than you, boy."'

'He sounds a horrible individual.'

'He's not really, he's just ambitious; it's funny what ambition can do to you. It made me hate his guts; it's also made me take up evening classes just to show him that I'm goin' places.'

'You're going to evening classes, Angus?'

'Yes, the Tech. You know; I met you outside.'

'Oh, I thought you were just passing, I didn't realise.'

The eyes looking into his were full of interest; her smile was sweet. She was slim and long and beautiful. He gazed at her. Who would have thought she would have grown into this? And there was more to come. She would be a stunner in a few years' time. She could get anybody . . . anybody. Bye, she looked lovely. And she was lovely, because besides everything else she had a nice nature. As his mother always said, she'd been nice right from a bairn. And to think that he once used to put his arms around her and hump her up on to his bike or lift her into the barrow. She would have forgotten all that but he never would. If he had been brought up differently perhaps he would have had a girl like her, beautiful and untouched. Aye, she looked untouched, not like the paw-patterned misses that got in the club and thereabouts. Not like May . . . funny about May. He had thought he loved her until the other night she had told him she had been with two other blokes. She felt she had to tell him, she said, because she loved him. He had been with her himself more times than he could remember, but he had intended to marry her, so it was different. But from then he just couldn't. He had scudded away like a frightened rabbit; or a better description in his case, with his bulk, would be like a shying buffalo. He knew his attitude was unreasonable, oh aye, he knew that, but it was different for a man. A fellow had to have it; it was as necessary as a morning cuppa, or the evening pint; but with a lass . . . well, it was different. Oh yes, he had worked that out an' all. If they all preserved their virginity it would be pretty hard on the males in general. But there would always be lasses who wanted it and no responsibility, no marriage ties, they wanted it for the cash they could get out of it . . . Yet May hadn't wanted cash. Give May her due, the only thing May had wanted was him. He felt bad about May, but there it was. He had this kink in him, and he couldn't do anything about it. If and when he married he'd like to make sure he was the first buyer at that particular stall, but as things went the day she'd have to be pretty young or so bloody ugly that nobody would have wanted to try their luck. He laughed inwardly, and it brought a quirk to his lips, and Vanessa asked, 'What's tickling you, Angus?'

'Oh!' he straightened up. 'I was just thinking about

something.' He leant back against the seat. 'What are you going to do when you leave school?'

She, too, leant her head back against the seat then she turned it towards the window and looked out on to a stretch of green countryside that lay between the towns as she said musingly, 'I don't know. Sometimes I think one thing, and then another, I just don't know.'

'What do your people want you to be?'

'Oh.' She was looking at him again, her face stretched, her brown eyes wide, the thick lashes on her lower lids forming dark circles on her high cheekbones. 'A duchess. A countess. Queen of the Outer Isles.'

They were laughing together and he brought his head forward as he said, 'You've got them weighed up, Vanessa.'

Her face suddenly became straight. Yes, she had her people weighed up, but she knew it wasn't right to discuss them with Angus Cotton, nor have him laugh at them. With Brett, yes, but not Angus for, after all, his mother was their daily.

Oh lord! lord, stop it! It was as if she was being reprimanded by an elder self. You're talking like Susan. He's right, I've got them weighed up; he's got them weighed up; and Emily's got them weighed up. They know as much about us as we do ourselves, more, in fact, being lookers-on. She was fond of Emily, very fond of her, and not in the way her mother was either. Her mother kept saying, 'What would I do without Emily?' but she wasn't thinking of Emily, she was thinking of herself and the difficulty in getting staff. Emily was a common woman; she talked common and she acted common, yet there was something lovable about her. She was the only one who had cuddled her. She used to do it on the quiet in the kitchen. She could never

87

remember her mother cuddling her. Angus was like his mother. He, too, was what you would call common; but he was nice for all that. There was something about Angus that she liked. It was odd when she came to think about it but there were only two men with whom she could really talk without stopping to think of every word she said. Angus was one, and Brett the other. They seemed alike in some way. Yet they were as far apart as the poles; Brett with his soft, cultured way of speaking, against Angus with his hard, thick, North-country intonation and his appalling lack of grammar.

She said seriously now, 'Emily's feet are badly swollen.'

'Aye, yes; I've noticed that.' His tone matched his cynical look.

'She should rest more. I mean when she gets home.'

He stared at her for a full minute before saying quickly, 'She's got a house to look after besides yours, you know. She's got me coming in at night, tearing hungry, and Rosie. She needs to eat an' all.'

'Oh, I'm sorry, I really am, Angus. I didn't think.'

'It's all right, oh, it's all right. But I know you're right, she should rest. I might as well tell you, I've been at her to leave your place for a long time now.'

Her hand went instinctively to her lips and her face showed dismay. 'No, Angus! Oh, the house wouldn't be the same without her. As for mother, well, she'd go round the bend. The people we've had over the last three years, part-time dailies, au-pairs, gentlewomen,' she poked her face towards him on the last title, 'the lot. But whoever came or went, Emily was there. I think Mother would really go potty if Emily left. And she knows it's hard on her, Angus; and she does try to get help for her. She's even offered them factory wages, but they just won't do housework.'

'Can you blame them?' The question was soft.

'What? Oh! Well, I suppose not.'

'Have you ever done housework?'

'I do my own room at times.'

He stared at her again without speaking, then laughed gently as he said, 'And why should you do housework or do your own room when you're going to be a duchess, or a countess, or Queen of the Outer Isles?'

'Oh, Angus, you're making fun of me.'

'No, I'm not. No, honest, 'cos I could see you carryin' any of those positions off right to the tee.'

'I couldn't, Angus. Susan could, but not me. And I would get bored.'

'Bored? Not you. Wait till you get going and you'll enjoy yourself, you'll be belle of the ball, top of the pops, the lot.'

Her face was bright with laughter again. 'You're very comforting, Angus. You know, you always were. I'm so glad I ran into you. I was feeling down in the dumps, and this,' she pointed to the offending tooth, 'this has been giving me gyp for days. Look, we're running in. Hasn't the time flown?'

He stood up. 'Yes, that's the quickest half-hour I've known for a long while. I wish the time went like that at work.'

They went into the corridor and walked to the end of the coach, and when the train stopped he got out and gallantly helped her down the high step on to the platform. As they went through the barrier together a young man standing among a group waiting to get on to the platform said, 'Hello there, Vanessa.'

89

She turned her head and answered on a high note, 'Oh, hello there, Colin. You going into town?'

'Yes.'

'I've just been.'

He nodded at her, then looked to the side where stood Angus Cotton; then he nodded again. 'Good-bye,' he said.

'Good-bye, Colin. Be seeing you.'

'That was Colin Brett.' She looked at Angus as they went out into the station yard and he said, 'Aye, I know.'

'Oh!' Her voice was hesitant now. 'I thought perhaps you mightn't know him; he doesn't work in the yard, he's an accountant in Forrester's.'

Oh, aye, an accountant in Forrester's, was he? By the look he had given him you'd think he was God Almighty in paradise. He knew Colin Brett all right; they were both of the same age. He had played with him once or twice when he had gone up to the house, but Colin Brett wasn't the kind who would remember that. Oh no, he was an accountant in Forrester's. He'd likely be a member of the Conservative Club and the Golf Club. Had he been a member of the Rugby Club he would have spoken to him in the dressing-room, he would have drunk with him in the pub afterwards, but he would hardly have recognised him in the street, particularly if he was with any of his women folk. Oh, aye, they were living in an age of social equality. Social equality, his backside!

'I'm gettin' the bus here,' he said abruptly. 'Been nice seein' you.'

'It was nice seeing you, Angus. I'll tell Emily I came down with you.'

'Do.' He nodded at her, then turned on his heel and

crossed the road to the bus station; and she walked some distance behind him wondering at his sudden change of manner. She had to get the bus, too, not the same one as he was getting but the one next to it; he could have walked across the road with her, he had walked out of the station with her. But all of a sudden he had looked grim and bad-tempered, like Emily did when something upset her. Had she upset him? Had she said anything? Oh, bust and botheration. That was people. Everybody seemed at sixes and sevens lately.

When she boarded her bus she saw him standing on the pavement opposite his; he was talking to a girl. She was of medium height and a blonde. Her skirt was well above her knees; she was wearing a short, hairy coat like imitation fur. She looked common.

As she took her seat in the bus she did not retract her use of the word this time for the girl did look common, cheap. Well, she supposed that was the kind of girl Angus would go for. Men usually went for blondes, they said, some time or other.

As the bus turned out of the square it came to her with a kind of shock that Angus was a man. He was no longer a youth or a young fellow, he was a man. A big, virile, rough, coarse man, yet she had chatted to him in the train as if there was no difference between them with regard to age. Somehow she didn't think she'd ever chat to him again like that.

The house was quiet when she entered, it seemed empty. She looked into the lounge but no one was there. In the dining-room the table was set for dinner. There were eight places. This was the second time the Braintrees had been here within the last three weeks. The table looked nice, all gold and silver, the gold being the daffodil heads her mother had arranged in a flowing line down the centre of the table. She used to cringe when, as a child, she saw her mother wiring the heads for a flower display. Her mother was very clever at arranging flowers.

When she went into the kitchen Emily was at the stove. 'Oh, hello there. You back? Did it hurt?' she said.

'No, not at all. Well, he didn't do much. I've got to go again next week. By the way, guess who I came home with on the train?'

'The Lord Mayor.' Emily closed the oven door and added, 'Would you like a cup of tea?'

'Oh, yes, Emily, if there's any going ... Where's Mother?' Her voice had dropped on the question and Emily answered as quietly, 'Upstairs, having a nap afore the fray. She's jiggered.'

As Emily took down two cups and saucers from the cupboard Vanessa looked at the back of her legs. There was no shape in them; her ankles were the same width as her broad calves.

'What are you looking at? Oh, me feet? Oh, they're giving me gyp the day; I feel they're going to bust any minute.' She put the cups and saucers on the table. 'I'm gonna put them in some epsom salts as soon as I get home.'

'After you've made the dinner for Angus and Rosie?'

'What's that you say?' Emily held her head to one side and screwed up her eyes.

'I came back in the train with Angus.'

'Aw, you did, did you?' Emily now took the kettle from the Aga plate and mashed the tea. 'And he told you that I'm a poor soul who has to go home and cook for the family, eh?'

'No, no, he didn't, not like that, but he said he'd been trying to get you to leave us.'

'Oh, that! You don't want to listen to him. And look, Miss Van.' She turned quickly. 'Don't you go scaring your ma. Well, what I mean is the missus has got enough on her plate without worrying about being left high and dry. By the way.' She leant against the rail of the stove and a smile spread over her broad, flat face. 'That one that came for interview this mornin', she took one look at the place and skited out of the gate as if we had turned a hose on her.'

'She wouldn't even give it a try.'

'Give it a try? You should have heard what she said. An' what she wanted. Double time for waiting on dinner at night. I said to the missus she should have asked her if she thought this was a factory. I tell you, they don't want work, Miss Van; they won't work the day.'

As Emily again turned to the stove and lifted the teapot Vanessa once more let her gaze drop to the feet encased in a pair of old leather slippers that had once belonged to her father. Her father had big feet, he took size ten, yet the slippers, stretched as they were, were still too small for Emily's feet.

'You should put your feet up in the afternoon, Emily. You know, Mother told you to.'

'Well, I've had them up. I've just got off me . . . I just got out of the chair a minute or so afore you got in. I haven't done a hand's turn since half-past two.'

'What's happening tonight?'

Emily handed Vanessa a cup of tea, then said, 'Oh, I'm slipping home for an hour, then coming back.'

'It wouldn't surprise me if Angus doesn't let you.'

Emily now turned fully about and surveyed the only member of this household for whom she had any liking, and she said tersely, 'Since when did Angus Cotton tell me what and what not to do? It's all arranged. Miss Susan's dropping me off in the car at half-past five and picking me up an hour later, and let Angus have anything to say on the matter and he'll get a mouth . . . I'll tell him somethin' that he won't forget in a hurry. Because he can boss the men under him at the works it doesn't say he can do the same at home. An' I've told him.' She jerked her head. The statement carried pride that her son was in the position to boss men, and this fact was not lost on Vanessa.

'Have a piece of cake?' Emily asked the question with a conspiratorial air. 'Walnut cream sponge.'

'Oh, yes, Emily, please.'

Emily went to the pantry and returned with a large shive of cake and, placing it before Vanessa, said, 'Get it down you in case we should have visitors.'

It was a rule that 'the children' weren't to eat in the kitchen, and Emily had always seen that Susan complied with it and also Master Ray. Oh yes, she kept firmly to the order where that young demon was concerned. She spoke of Ray now, saying, 'Oh, by the way, we had some high jinks here just afore lunch. His nibs climbed the spout and got stuck on the roof near the garret. How, in the name of God, he got up there nobody knows. He got up but he couldn't come down.' Her body began to shake with laughter now.

'What happened?' Vanessa, too, was laughing quietly.

'They had to phone the works for extra ladders.'

'No! Never.'

'It's the truth I'm tellin' you. They brought a lorry and two blokes, and one of them went up and got him. Oh, you should have heard the master.'

'Where's Ray now?'

'In his room . . . It'll be nice when the holidays

are over, peaceful like. Thank God for schools, I say.'

Vanessa was laughing openly with her hand over her mouth to still the sound; then rising and taking the plate to the sink, she said, 'Thanks, Emily; that was lovely.'

'Leave those, I'll see to them.'

'No, no, I'll rinse them.'

'Leave them and go on your way. Go on.'

Vanessa rinsed the plate and cup and saucer under the hot tap; then turning and bowing her head stiffly towards Emily, she said, 'There.' It was as if she had assisted her with some major household task, and the look on Emily's face seemed to bear this out as she said, 'You always were stubborn, Miss Van. But get along with you; you don't want your mother to come down and find you here. Go on now.'

As Vanessa ran lightly up the stairs she thought again of Emily's feet, and the thought took her into the bathroom that she shared with Susan, and there, from her own particular cupboard, she took a plastic bag and filled it almost to the top with a proprietary brand of bath salts that promised to relieve all the aches and pains the body harboured.

Downstairs again, she went hurriedly into the kitchen where Emily was sitting down now and, putting the bag in her lap, said under her breath, 'These are very special salts. Bathe your feet with them, they're bound to do them good.'

'Aw, lass, aw, that's real thoughtful of you, Miss Van. Ah, that is. Thanks.'

Vanessa stood for a moment looking down into the smiling face; then she ran out of the kitchen and up the stairs again with a strange feeling of happiness inside her. There was something in what you learned at church, she supposed. Kindness had its own reward. She felt very good.

The dinner was over. Emily, her feet encased in black shoes, had brought the coffee into the drawing-room and now Susan and Brian were going to run her home. They had just gone out of the room together. They looked happy and self-satisfied. Vanessa thought perhaps Susan, too, was feeling the rewards of charity. The conversation over the last fifteen minutes had been between her mother, Mrs Braintree and Susan, and it concerned Emily. Their mother said, as always, she didn't know how she would exist without Emily. She spoke of Emily as if she was a very old family retainer. She said as much without actually using the term. Mrs Braintree said how lucky she was to have such a faithful servant, yet such service could only have been maintained through kindness. Susan put in with deceptive casualness that she was in the habit of running Emily to and from her home. Her mother said it was all a matter of consideration.

The Braintrees had brought their younger son with them. He was eighteen years old and pimply. His name was Alan and he talked big about cars. He was standing now, talking to her father. She watched her mother rise from her chair and come towards her. She was smiling. She still smiled as she bent over her and said under her breath, 'What is the matter with you, Vanessa? Have you gone dumb all of a sudden? Why can't you talk to Alan?'

'Because he wants to talk, you can't get a word in.' Vanessa's face looked sulky.

'Don't be difficult, child. Your father's noticed it. You're being difficult. You don't want to make him angry, do you? Now you get up and go and talk to Alan.'

96

As she looked back into her mother's face Vanessa almost said, 'He's no good wasting time on, he'll never come into the title, not unless Brian dies,' but what she said was, 'I'd like to go upstairs.'

'You'll do nothing of the kind. You'll stay here until they go.'

As she turned away she was smiling again.

After a while Vanessa rose to her feet and gradually made her way towards Alan Braintree, but he took no notice of her; he continued to talk cars to her father. Cars were his only interest, the only thing he could talk about. What was more he did not want to be left alone with Vanessa Ratcliffe. She made him uneasy. She was one of those clever sticks of girls, and he had no time for clever sticks.

Half an hour later, when Susan and Brian returned, they all sat down to a game of bridge. It was a comparatively short game and the guests left at half-past eleven. At twelve o'clock all the lights in the house were out, and at five past twelve Vanessa went down the fire escape and into the garden. It was moonlight again, but tonight the clouds were scudding across the sky and the wind was high.

It was nearly four weeks since Brett had found her in the summerhouse, and she had been down there at least half-a-dozen times since. Twice when it was black dark. She had been a bit scared those times, yet excited. The first time she had gone into the woods after that particular night she had half expected Brett to appear again, and on each occasion since she had hoped she might see him. He was nice, was Brett. But tonight she didn't expect to see him. It was too late; the whole world was asleep.

She could have fallen asleep at any time during the

97

dinner or after, particularly during the bridge, but now she felt wide awake. She had never felt so wide awake and so filled with unrest. She felt unhappy. Was it because Susan was so happy? Was she jealous of Susan? Yes, she supposed she was. She wasn't jealous of her having Brian, or marrying into the Braintrees, but she was jealous of her getting married. She was nodding at herself as she went through the gate and into the deep shadow. One had to be honest with oneself.

Perhaps if she had a boy she would feel different. But boys didn't make for her. Look at Alan tonight. Not that she'd wanted anyone like him, the spotty oaf. But still, he hadn't been attracted to her at all. Boys didn't seem to be attracted to her; what was wrong with her? Rona and Kathy, they'd had boys since they were fourteen. Of course, their mothers hadn't known, but Rona's mother knew now, and Kathy took Harold Blackett home. And neither Rona nor Kathy were good-looking. She considered she was better looking than either of them; she wasn't being conceited. No, because she knew she wasn't as good-looking as Lucy Fulton, because Lucy was beautiful. But she wasn't bad-looking; she had nice hair and eyes. So, what was wrong with her? It was the same when she went to a party. Look at the parties last Christmas. All the necking that went on, but the boy that was with her just sat and played with her fingers. There must be something wrong with her somewhere. It must be something inside that boys sensed.

Further on, the wind lashed a branch against her face and she covered her cheek and bent her head against the pain of it. When she looked up again she saw the figure crossing a dappled moonlit space. First of all her heart seemed to stop still in fright because it didn't look like Brett, not as tall; then she realised he was walking with his head down. Before he was aware of her she called softly, 'Brett! Is that you, Brett?' She watched him stand motionless, looking in her direction, and when she reached him she said, 'You gave me a start again, I didn't think it was you. What would have happened if it hadn't been you?'

He didn't speak, he just stared into her face, which was illuminated in moving patterns of moonlight.

'What's the matter, Brett? Are you sick?'

'No, no. I had the beast of a headache, I had to come out. But . . . but why are you out at this time? It's well past midnight.'

'I couldn't sleep.' She turned away from him, walking in the direction of the river. 'I felt all het up inside. Oh, I don't know.' She turned again, expecting to find him by her side, but when she looked back he was still standing in the same place, and she retraced a few steps and said anxiously, 'There's something wrong, Brett. What is it? What's the matter? You . . . There's nothing happened to Paul?'

'Oh, no, no; he's all right.'

'You've heard from him?'

'Yes, we had a letter yesterday.'

'Is he having a good time?'

'By all accounts, the time of his life.'

'You're missing him, aren't you? Going off like that the second day of his holiday. You . . . You didn't expect it.'

'Oh, yes. Yes, I did.'

'No, not until the summer, and remember,' she gave a little laugh, 'he was going to take me to dances. You promised.' She took hold of his arm and shook it. She was endeavouring in her own way to lighten whatever depression had fallen on him, because even in this light she could see that his face was almost the colour of chalk. He never had much colour but she had never seen him looking so pale.

'Come on,' she coaxed. 'Come on down to the summer-house and let's talk.'

'No, not at this hour. You'd best get back indoors. What if they should miss you?' His voice was stiff.

'They won't miss me.'

'I'm going up, Vanessa; it's late.'

'All right then.' She made her voice sound a little huffy. 'You go on up and I'll go and sit in the summerhouse and muse.'

She had gone half-a-dozen steps towards the river again when he joined her. He had his head bent once more, and he muttered something that she couldn't hear above the wind, but she didn't question what he had said. She suddenly felt gay and excited. It must be the wind and the moonlight and the fact that she – and Brett – must be the only people in Fellburn to be walking in a wood at this time of night.

When she slipped her hand into his arm she brought him to a stop again and he turned his face to hers, pleading with her now. 'Van, be a good girl, come on back.'

'Look, we're there.' She pointed across the clearing to the summerhouse, then tugged him forward.

They sat on the step and she pulled the rush mat from the middle of the floor to make the seat more comfortable, and then, joining her hands round her knees, she said, 'There.' She had the same feeling now as when she had taken Emily the bath salts, she felt good. What she was doing she felt was good for Brett. He was lonely. She knew that he didn't get on with Irene. She had gauged that much from snatches of conversation she had overheard between her mother and father, and latterly between her mother and Susan.

'What is it, Brett?' she said now. 'You're worried. You can tell me. Is it about the yard?'

He was about to say no, but he said, 'Yes.' He'd have to tell her something. 'Your father gave me the chance to go to Holland, Germany and round and about. You know Mr Cribber is in hospital and likely to be there for the next two or three months. He's the representative. Your father wanted me to take his place. Temporary, that is . . .'

'And you're going to?'

'No. No, I turned it down.'

'But why? Why, Brett? It would be a kind of holiday for you.'

'Oh, for a number of reasons. But the main one, I think, was I'd have to be away from here for weeks on end. You know I've never been away from this place for longer than three weeks in my life, and even after a week I long to be back.'

'You are funny, Brett.'

'Yes, I suppose so.'

Their faces were turned to each other, and she nodded slowly at him as she said, 'But I can understand. I can understand how you feel. It's the trees and the river and the house, and it's yours. Yes, I can understand. I often wish we had a bit of woodland. Oh. Oh,' she put her hand on his arm again, 'I don't mean that you should sell it to father. I would say don't sell it to father, hang on to it. I would if it were mine. But I would like a garden with trees in it. Ours is so formal, you feel you're in the park. I wouldn't be surprised any day to see some women coming through the gate pushing prams.' She laughed, but he didn't laugh with her.

She said now, 'Are you worried because you refused? I mean, did it upset Father? He hates doing anything without getting loud applause.'

'Oh, Vanessa!' Now he was laughing a little.

'Oh, I know I shouldn't talk like that, but you see I know him. I've said that before to you, haven't I, that I know him?' She joined her hands once more round her knees and began to sway a little back and forwards as she asked, 'Why isn't love a sort of natural thing like growing hair or cutting your second teeth, I mean loving your parents. You're theirs and they've brought you up, and you should just love them out of gratitude if for nothing else. It worries me.' She stopped swaying and turned her face towards him again and repeated, 'It worries me. Can you understand that, Brett? I don't love them and it worries me.'

He nodded, then said thickly, 'You can't love to order, even your parents.'

'I think about it a lot, Brett, I mean loving people. I . . . I can't even like them. There are so few people I really like. I thought I used to like Rona and Kathy and Lucy, but I don't any more. I used to have a thing about Kathy when I was fourteen and now I think she's silly and I was stupid for having a pash on her. And, I . . . I don't like Susan, Brett. Fancy me saying that about my own sister, but I don't like her. And Ray. At times I loathe Ray. You know the only person I like in our house is Emily. She's fat and at times doesn't look over-clean, and she's common. I mean . . . Well, Mother says she's common, they all say she's common. They need her services but behind her back they say she's common. And she is, but I like her. Why should I like her better than Susan or Mother or Father?'

'I can't answer you that one, Vanessa; perhaps because she's more natural, hasn't got so many skins.'

'Do you dislike people, Brett?'

'No, not really. I find it hard to dislike people.'

'Even Father?'

'Yes. Yes, even Jonathan.'

'As you get older will it become easier to love people?'

'In your case perhaps.' He smiled tenderly at her. 'You'll find somebody that stirs you, makes you feel warm, somebody that you can't bear to live without seeing every minute of the day and night; you'll love like that one day, then everything will be ironed out. You're going through a difficult period; it happens to us all.'

She said now, 'You know I was thinking today there were only two men I could talk to, Angus and . . . and you. I could love you, Brett.'

She didn't know why she had said it, perhaps because he needed comfort. When she leant her head on his shoulder and put her hand through his arm, the result of her action surprised and frightened her for a moment; she felt his whole body quivering, and then to her dismay she saw his head droop over his knees, and she watched him cover his face and his hands.

'Brett! Brett! What is it? Oh, Brett, don't. Don't. What have I done? What have I said?' She put her arms round his shoulders, and when her hand covered his it became wet with his tears. 'Oh, Brett, Brett. Dear Brett.' She pulled him round to her. His head drooped on to her shoulder; his wet face was buried in her neck. When she heard him murmur, 'Oh God! Oh God' as if he was in pain, she held him more tightly to her, stroking his hair, patting him, soothing him. When, a few minutes later, she held his tear-stained face between her hands

103

and looked into his eyes she became consumed with pity and love, a first love, a love that expected no future, a love that consumed itself in its very creation, a love that was made up of curiosity and desire.

When, locked together, they dropped sideways on to the wooden floor, he hoisted her farther into the summerhouse, and when his hands moved over her she could not have stopped him if she had wanted to for the gentle Brett had vanished and a strange man was tearing her apart, choking her with his tongue and rending her in two with his body.

Her curiosity was being satisfied.

2

'It's the beer talking,' said Emily.

'Now, Mam, it isn't the beer. I haven't passed me quota; I've had me six and that's all.'

'You can't kid me.'

'No, I can't kid you, Mam.' Angus bent over the back of the chair where Emily was sitting with her feet up on a cracket, and he nipped one of her sagging chins as he repeated dramatically, 'No, I can't kid you. I'll have to confess, I've had a drop of hard.'

'I knew it, else you wouldn't be talkin' so damn soft. You know you can't carry it. As for this hair-brained scheme of joining up with Fred Singleton, you can forget it. You're not leaving the yard. Head of a shop at your age and wantin' to give it up. And for what? To start a one-man . . . all right, a two-men, haulage business, when the neighbourhood is infested with haulage businesses.'

'I know that, Mam, the big bods. But . . . but the big bods can't carry all the work they've got in. That's what I've been tellin' you. They sub-contract, you know, let it out.'

'I know all about it.' Emily now brought her feet from the cracket. 'And I'm tellin' you this, you're not puttin' your bit of money into any bloody racket Fred Singleton can think up.'

'Fred's a good lad.'

'Then why hasn't he made his fortune afore now?'

'For the simple reason he didn't have enough to start with; he's just got one lorry and he's on his own. Now if he had two or three . . .'

'Bought with your money like.'

'Aye, bought with my money like, then we would be in clover.'

'Do you know where the most clover grows, Angus Cotton? In the Bankruptcy Court. You big gowk, I'll talk to you in the mornin' when you're sober.'

Angus was standing with his hand to his brow and his eyes closed when the door opened and Rosie came in, accompanied by Stan, and before they had time to close the door Emily cried at them, 'You want to hear what this 'n is on about now; he's talkin' of puttin' his bit in with Fred Singleton and startin' a haulage business. Haulage, I ask you. Bloody silly bugger.'

Rosie looked from Angus where he was sitting at the end of the table now, his head resting on one hand, an oily smile covering his face and his lips moving back and forward over each other, and she laughed outright. Their Angus always looked funny when he was carrying a drop; he was never bad-tempered, like some. Wanting to rouse her mother still further and wanting a laugh, she said, 'Well I don't think it's a bad idea, not really. I mean if you put five thousand down and pay the rest in instalments.'

Angus let out a roar of a laugh and cried, 'Aw, Rosie! Aw, Rosie! That's good. Trust you.'

'I don't see anythin' to laugh at.' Emily was glaring at Rosie now. 'He's serious, it isn't a joke. He started

106

this afore he went out an' he was solid and sober then.'
She turned to Stan now and demanded, 'What do you
think, Stan? You're on the factory side of cement, you
should have your ear to the ground about this kind of
thing, haulage.'

'Well.' Stan walked to the table and took a seat opposite Angus. Then looking at Emily, he said, 'If you had
a few hundred about you, and the strength of a bull an'
plenty of nerve you could get through.'

'There you are. There you are.' Angus's arm was
extended high above his head. 'Nerve, he said. And the
strength of a bull; and a few hundred. Is anybody more
qualified than me?' He got to his feet and banged his
chest with his clenched fists. 'Oo! Oo! . . . Oo! Oo!'

The Tarzan call was too much for Emily. She joined
in the laughter and she laughed till the tears ran down
her face . . .

But Emily didn't laugh the following morning when
Angus informed her he was going to have a run out with
Fred Singleton. But she did not go for him either, she
pleaded with him.

'Look, lad,' she said. 'It's only three hundred and
seventy five but it's taken a bit of gettin'. Don't be a
bloody fool, lad.'

'Listen, Mam.' He was speaking as quietly as she was.
'I'm not bein' any kind of a bloody fool, I'm not committing meself, I'm just goin' out to see this lorry.'

'If Fred Singleton thinks he's on a good thing why
can't he buy another lorry?'

Angus sighed. 'Aw, Mum, he's got a wife and six
kids and his widowed mother living with him. It
takes every penny. But he tells me at times he can
turn forty a week, not all the time, but pretty often.
But with a couple of lorries running and the prospect

of more there's no reason why it shouldn't be forty every week.'

'As long as it lasts, lad; these buildings won't be goin' up for ever.'

'You heard Stan last night, Mam. They've got plans out for along the river that'll take another ten years.'

'Listen. Listen to me. I don't want you to leave the yard. There's a sort of, well, call it status, or prestige or whatever you like, but you're chargehand of your shop an' you've got it.'

'God, Mam.' His tone was scathing. 'Chargehands an' foremen, they're two a penny. As for prestige, that went down the sink years ago. You're living in the past, Mam. Men don't look up to them a step above them these days, they spit in their eye. You should hear Jim Taggart at me.'

'What's Jim Taggart? Scum. Scum, that's all he is.'

'Well, there's a lot of scum about and you find that out once you've been put over them. Anyway, Mam, I've got a fancy for being me own boss.'

'Well, what about all this evening-class business you've been goin' at?'

'Oh that'll come in handy, nothin's ever lost.'

'And what if you want to get married and your money goes down the drain?'

'If I want to get married, Mam! Who's talking of gettin' married?'

She turned from him and went into the scullery, and from there she shouted, 'May was round here last night. She had been to the club lookin' for you.'

'Oh, aye.'

'You're not playin' fair by May, Angus.'

'That's my business, Mam.'

'It can be your business but I still say you're not

playing fair by her. Three years you've known her; you should be married now, with a bairn.'

'Oh, for God's sake! Look, Mam, you can stick your finger in any pie that I'm eatin', but with regard to May, or any other piece, that's my business. Now, I'm tellin' you.' He walked towards the scullery door and addressed her back. 'I'll marry when I think fit, May or anybody else I want to, but it'll be when I want to. Now understand that.'

He went out without saying good-bye, but the frame of his mind was conveyed to her as he banged the door, and she hurried into the front-room and watched him go down the street. He was a fine figure of a man, and he was as well put on as any gentleman in the town. He knew how to dress did her Angus. The cut of his overcoat suited his broad shoulders. He was wearing one of those new velour sporty hats. She shook her head. It was a motion of pride, but as she turned from the window she exclaimed aloud, 'The stubborn bugger.'

Angus went with Fred Singleton in his old car to Morpeth. He saw the lorry that was for sale, but thought they were asking about twice what it was worth, and so they returned the way they had gone, nothing settled.

On the return journey they stopped just before closing time and had a drink and discussed the situation for the twentieth time. 'I'm not going to jump into anything, Fred; I've got a good job as you know, an' what's more I've got me mam to consider. As I say there's plenty of time.'

'There's not, you know, Angus; there's not. There's other fellows borrowing money to start up.'

'Well, why don't you borrow to get another lorry?'

'Well, as I've told you, I'd have to take on another

bloke. What I want is a partner, somebody who'll carry his weight, like you. Tough, with a level head on him. And, I don't mind admitting this to you Angus, somebody who'll be able to do the correspondence like, the writin' and bargainin'. I'm not much good at it. If I did things in writin' I would get farther, but everythin' is by word of mouth, you know.'

Angus nodded, then said, 'I'm sorry, Fred, but I'm gonna leave it for the time being. Not too long; no, not too long, but just for a week or so. I've got to consider, you see.'

It started to rain as they left the pub and when they were about two miles outside of Fellburn and taking a side road that was bordered by the open fell, Angus suddenly said, 'Hold your hand a minute, Fred, stop her!'

'What!'

'Stop the car. Stop her a minute.'

When the car had stopped Angus swung round in his seat and looked out of the rear window. Then, leaning across Fred, he said, 'Pull the window down a minute, I want to see over there.'

Over there was a young girl walking by herself. She had a raincoat on with a collar turned up and a scarf round her head. She was walking with her hands in her pockets and her shoulders hunched.

'Who is it? Somebody you know?'

'Aye.' Angus nodded his head. 'I wonder what she's doin' out up here on her own, in the rain. Hang on a minute, will you?'

Fred grinned and said, 'Oh aye; I've all the time in the world.'

Angus got out of the car and went up the bank on to the fell. The girl had her back to him now, but there was no mistaking Vanessa. He would have picked out her walk and her style from a hundred; but he didn't call her name until he came abreast of her, about six yards distant, and then she turned and looked at him and he said, 'I thought it was you. What you doin' up here in the wet? You lost?'

She stared at him, her mouth slightly open; then she said, 'Oh, hello, Angus.'

'You lost? I mean it's pourin'. Do you like being out in the wet?'

'I don't mind. I wanted to have a long walk.'

'Do you want a lift back?' He nodded over towards the car. 'There's another two miles to go, three to your place.'

She followed his gaze, then said, 'No. No, thanks.'

He was now standing in front of her and he peered at her through the driving rain for a moment before saying, 'You all right?'

'Yes, yes.'

'You look peaked.'

'Oh, I'm all right.'

'Look.' He came close to her. 'You're not tellin' the truth, are you? You're not all right. What's up?'

'Nothing nothing.'

'Mam said you'd been off colour and had a cold, tummy upset; you'd been off school for a week or two.'

'Yes, I have. I've had a cold but it's better now.'

'Well, you don't look better. And you won't stay better long in this. Come on, get into the car.' He put out his hand towards her but she shrank back, saying, 'No, no; I want to walk.'

He continued to look at her for some minutes before he said, 'All right,' then turned abruptly away and went towards the car. And there, bending down to Fred, who was sitting smoking, he said, 'Do you mind finishin' on your own? I feel I'd better see her home.'

'Oh, aye. But you're not goin' to enjoy yourself very much, it beltin' like this.'

'Oh, it's nothing like that, man.' Angus put his fist against Fred's shoulder. 'She's the daughter, you know, where Mam works. She's been ill and I think she still is. She looks odd to me; I think I'd better see to her.'

'Please yourself. But . . . but you'll think about the other, won't you?'

'Aye. Yes, I promise, Fred, I'll think about it. And I'll let you know one way or the other in a week or two. All right?'

'All right.' Fred's face looked crestfallen as he moved off, and Angus, turning, went on to the fell again. Vanessa was some distance further away now and he had to hurry to catch up with her. When he came to her side he said, 'Well now, which is the shortest way home?'

She stopped and again she looked at him with her mouth open. Then lowering her head and moving it from side to side, she said, 'Look, Angus, I'm all right, really I am.'

'Well, if you're all right, it's a poor look-out for the bad 'uns. It strikes me you should be in bed. You look as white as lint and you're shiverin'.' He put his hand on her arm. 'Come on. An' I'm standing no nonsense; if we're going to walk we're going to do it briskly. And you want to get home and get into bed. You shouldn't pick days like this to take a tramp; although,' he remarked as if to himself, 'it wasn't so bad earlier on. But this is our summer, flaming June. Look, we'll cross over the top,' he pointed into the distance, 'an' go down by the river and over the stepping stones. That'll cut almost a mile off and bring us to the end of Mr Brett's wood.'

When her body jerked he thought she had stumbled, and he put out his other hand to steady her.

They walked some distance in silence, until it became embarrassing to him and he said, 'Mam tells me you're leaving school at the end of this term.'

'Yes.'

'I thought you were staying on until you were seventeen next year?'

'I'm seventeen in August.' For the first time she turned and looked at him. 'In exactly six weeks and two days I'll be seventeen.'

He was slightly nonplussed by both her voice and her manner but he said airily, 'Well, it's plain to be seen you've got it worked out to the hour.'

'Yes, to the hour.'

What was wrong with her? There was something amiss. He hadn't seen her for some time, not since that day they had travelled up from Newcastle and he had got himself narked by the way young Brett had looked at him, and he had left her abruptly. Surely, she in her turn hadn't been narked about his manner . . . Could be, could be. What did she expect him to do? Bow and scrape. He said, 'Haven't seen you for some time, not since that day when we came up on the train together. I . . . I had to leave you rather sharp, there was somebody I wanted to see.'

She was looking at him again. She didn't for the moment know what he was talking about; and then she remembered him walking away and talking to a cheap-looking girl.

CHEAP LOOKING. CHEAP LOOKING. CHEAP LOOKING.

113

The words were re-echoing in her mind, as words were doing a lot lately. Significant words such as cheap, consequences, retribution, sin, scandal, death, suicide, water. Yes, water. But she would never drown, she was too good a swimmer; and they hadn't gas in the house, only electricity and the Aga. This only left the aspirins, there were all kinds of aspirins in the bathroom cupboard. If only Brett would come back. If he knew he would do something about it. He would take her away. She hadn't a doubt but that he would take her away.

For days after it happened she hadn't been able to think of him without wanting to be sick. For days and days after, she could feel his body on hers; she could see his part naked flesh as he rolled off her exhausted, finished. When she had finally come to herself she had for the first time experienced loathing, loathing of herself and him. But it was too late, the thing was done, the beastly horrible slimy thing was accomplished.

Some parts of the episode had faded from her mind and there was only a feeling left about them, but she still remembered the sound and sight of his crying. He had started to cry again, he had cried as he had kissed her all over; he had cried until she had kicked herself free from him and run through the wood in panic. And the panic was still with her, and only his presence could ease it.

If she could only hide her panic until he came back then it would be all right, they would go away. He would get a divorce and they would marry. That's how things were done.

'What? I'm sorry I wasn't paying attention.'

'I said, had you decided on anything, a job or anything?'

'No. That is Mother and Father want me to go to France to stay with a family; my French is weak.' She tried to put a smile to her words but it wouldn't come.

He helped her across the stepping stones; then they went up the bank and along the towpath that ran by the side of the river, and fifteen minutes later they came out into the lane where the wire fence that bordered the Brett ground ran down into the river. She had her head down as she walked up the narrow lane towards the road. They were about half-way along the lane, and silent once more, when her name being called brought them both to a startled halt. There were two voices calling, 'Hi, Vanessa! Hi, Vanessa!' and the voices appeared to be coming out of the air.

She looked up into the trees, and Angus's gaze followed hers and he said, 'There's somebody up there in the trees.'

She was walking on again. 'It's Ray,' she said, 'and Michael Brett. They've built a platform in the oak.'

'Good for them. But it gave me a bit of a gliff hearin' your name being called out of the sky.' He was looking at her profile, waiting for her to say something, but she didn't, and when they came to the end of the lane he stopped and said, 'Well, here's the parting of the ways. Now you take my advice and go to bed; you look as if you're sickenin' for something. Have you had the doctor?'

'No; I'm all right really and . . . Thanks.' Her voice trailed off, and he added with a smile, 'For forcing meself on you? But me mam would never have forgiven me if I'd left you up there in the rain all by yourself. You looked lost.' He leant his head slightly to the side. 'If you go on this way you'll be losin' your looks, you know, an' you don't want that to happen, do you? What's the duke or the count goin' to say?'

When she swung away from him without a word of goodbye he stood gazing after her until she disappeared into her own gateway; then he turned towards home . . .

Emily was having her Sunday afternoon rest when he arrived, and he went straight upstairs and into her room. She was sitting up in bed with a cup of tea in her hand and she said, 'Oh, so you're back. Well, what's happened?'

'Enough of that after.' He sat down heavily on the foot of the bed and began: 'Look, Mam, when we were comin' down the fell lane about two miles out, Fred and me in the car, I saw Van meandering across the fells in the rain and I got out and asked if she would like a lift, but she wouldn't come, and she was in such a state that I let Fred go on and I brought her back.'

'Here?' Emily straightened herself up.

'No, no. Don't get yourself agitated. I mean home; we came the river way. She was in a state, Mam. She looks bad.'

Emily lay back and closed her eyes for a moment before saying, 'Oh, she's been like that for a week or two. The missus hasn't known what to do with her, nor me for that matter. We used to have a crack at one time but I've not been able to get a word out of her, not for days. It's exam nerves, that's what the missus says.'

'Exam nerves? Good God, is that what it is?'

'Yes, they all get it when they're sitting for "O" levels; sick, tummy upsets, the lot.'

'Christ!' He banged his forehead with his double fist. 'Me thinking she was going into the old-fashioned decline or somethin'. Well, I'll be jiggered. You know, she hardly opened her mouth all the way, and when she did she was so bloomin' dramatic you'd think she was rehearsing for a play. Once or twice I could have laughed, but then she looked so bad.'

'Oh, they take it seriously.' Emily nodded. 'I remember Miss Susan and her "O" levels. She was sick, an' in the night an' all, and the lazy little beggar wouldn't get up. I remember that bed I had to tackle the next mornin'. Well now, tell me what happened about Singleton.'

'Oh, they were asking too much, far too much. I told them when they came down to practically half I'd think about it.'

'What did Fred say?'

'I told him that I'd give him me answer one way or the other in a few weeks' time.'

'Well, it'll be the other if I've got anything to do with it.'

He stood up, then poked his head down to her and said, 'Yes, Mam. Yes, Mam.'

'Go on with you.'

'Where's Rosie?'

'She's in her room. There should be some tea in the pot.'

'I'm not havin' your leavings, I'm goin' to make fresh.'

'You don't need to make fresh, it's just been made.'

As he went out of the room he said to her over his shoulder, 'Don't be so stingy; you'd think you bought it. I like making fresh pots of God Almighty Ratcliffe's tea. Anyway, I brought his daughter home out of the wet.' He pushed his head back round the door towards

her. 'That's a good 'un. It's the title of a story: Out of
the Wet.'

'You're not just wet, lad, you're drippin'.' Emily lay
back and gurgled at her own joke; then she emptied her
cup, saying to herself, 'Thank God. But he's got sense,
our Angus. I needn't have worried.'

3

'You're mad. You must be mad.'

'Yes, we're all slightly mad, Mrs Ratcliffe.'

'But you are.' She checked herself from adding, 'or drunk.' It was a well-known fact that he was a tippler; hadn't Mrs Carey objected to his breath when he visited her? She would change; she had been thinking about it for a long time.

The doctor seemed to read her thoughts, and he buttoned up his coat briskly as he said, 'Mad, drunk, or daft, Mrs Ratcliffe, your daughter is pregnant.'

There was the word again; it hadn't really registered the first time. Pregnant. PREGNANT. Oh, no, no! This couldn't happen to them. Not only was he mad, she was going mad. The wedding in six weeks' time. Their position. Oh, Jonathan! He would go insane. This would drive him insane. Jonathan couldn't stand things like this. When they happened to other people's daughters he condemned them out of hand; but to his daughter! Where? How? What had they done to deserve this? WHAT? The question was spiralling in her head. She heard the doctor say, 'Come along now, sit down. It isn't the end of the world; these things are happening every day.'

Every day. Every day. Every day. The words carried her into a dead faint.

Doctor Carr went to the drawing-room door and in no small voice yelled, 'Emily! Emily!'

'Aye, doctor. What is it?' Emily came scurrying across the hall. It was one of the quirks of the social set-up that Doctor Carr should also be her doctor.

'Your mistress has fainted.'

'Good God! What caused it?' She was hurrying past him to the couch.

'She's had a bit of a shock.'

'About . . . about Miss Van?' She was loosening the front of Jane Ratcliffe's dress as she spoke, and she turned her shrewd glance up at the doctor.

'Yes, about Miss Van.'

'Has she caught something? Infectious or something? She'll go mad,' she nodded down towards the prostrate figure, 'if anything happens to put a spoke in the weddin'.'

'This will put the spoke in a number of things, Emily, if I'm not mistaken. Look, go and make a cup of tea. And be quick about it.'

Emily straightened up and was in the act of hurrying away when she turned and looked at him and said, 'God Almighty! You don't mean . . .?'

'Yes, I do mean.' He nodded at her. 'And go on and get that tea made.'

Oh no! No! What's the world comin' to? NO! Not Miss Van. God in Heaven! She went into the kitchen and stood gripping the edge of the table. That's what had been wrong with her all these weeks. But who would have suspected Miss Van! Examination nerves, everybody said. Aw, no! No! She just wouldn't believe it. She rammed the kettle on to the top of the hot plate.

120

But the doctor . . . the doctor had just examined her. The missus had insisted on him coming because Van wouldn't get up out of bed to go to school. She kept saying she wasn't feeling well, and begod, she wouldn't be feeling well . . . But who? . . . Who did the child know? Child? She was a child no longer, she was nearly seventeen. She herself had been married a week after her seventeenth birthday. But in this class, this house, it was different; they were still children at that age. Aw, she answered herself, there were no children these days. But, in any case, God strike them down dead the one who had brought it about. It would be Van this would happen to, the nicest of the bunch; it always happened to the nice ones. 'Hurry up you!' She scraped the kettle backwards and forwards on the hot plate.

The master? Oh, God Almighty! There'd be high jinks the night. When he got wind of this they'd have to tie him down, because he was a sanctimonious prig, was Jonathan Ratcliffe. He went to the most fashionable church in town and subscribed handsomely to the fashionable charities, but let a fellow come to the door and ask for a bit, as they used to years ago – not now; they didn't need to now – and he showed them what charity was. Oh, there'd be hell to pay the night in this house.

When she took the tray of tea into the room Jane Ratcliffe was sitting up, her head supported in the wing of the couch, and as Emily held the cup to her lips Doctor Carr said, 'I think your husband should be here. May I use your phone?'

For answer Jane Ratcliffe just raised her eyes.

It took some minutes to convince Jonathan Ratcliffe's secretary that the doctor had no intention of leaving a message and that he intended to speak to Mr Ratcliffe.

'Yes?' Jonathan's voice was abrupt, and Doctor Carr's matched it as he said, 'This is Carr speaking. I think it would be wise if you came home for a while.'

'Home? What on earth for? What's the matter? Something happened?'

'Yes, something's happened, Mr Ratcliffe.'

Doctor Carr's words were clipped. 'Your wife has collapsed.'

'My wife! But . . . but I thought you were calling to see Vanessa.'

'I have seen Vanessa.'

'What's the matter with her?'

'I don't think we can go into this on the phone; you'd better come home. I can't stay; I have another call to make, I'm late already.' On this he banged down the phone, returned to the drawing-room and said quietly, 'He'll be here shortly. Now just take it calmly. I'm leaving you some tablets. If you need me give me a ring.'

Jane Ratcliffe didn't speak, she didn't even move her head; she was in a state of shock.

At the door Doctor Carr motioned Emily towards him, and as he picked his bag up from the hall table he said under his breath, 'The one upstairs could do with a drink too, Emily.'

'Aye, Doctor, aye. I'll see to it.'

But Emily didn't get the chance to take a tray upstairs until fifteen minutes later, because her missus kept hanging on to her hand, staring up into her face while not uttering a word. That was, until the master walked into the room, and then she released Emily and whimpered, 'Oh, Jonathan.'

Emily hurried out of the room with the tea tray in her hand and, standing in the hall for a minute, she

122

wondered whether she could get a cup upstairs in time to fortify the lass before he started on her.

A few seconds later she knocked gently on Vanessa's door, then went in.

Vanessa was sitting on the side of the bed in her dressing gown. To Emily she looked all eyes, teeth and hair. She said softly, 'You could do with a cup, lass?'

'Emily.'

Emily looked at the quivering face, and she said, 'Aye. What is it, hinny?' She was no longer talking to Miss Vanessa, only to a lass, who, like many another, and better, before her, had been laid down.

'Oh, Emily!'

'Now, now, now, don't take on. Drink this up. You'll be havin' visitors in a minute; your father's downstairs.'

The cup rattled on the saucer and Emily had to steady it. 'Come on now, drink it up.'

Before Vanessa had drunk half the cup of tea there came the sound of quick muted footsteps across the landing; then the door was thrust open.

Jonathan Ratcliffe stood aside to allow Emily to leave the room, and he allowed his wife to pass in; then he closed the door quietly, which spoke of the control he had put himself under. But when he looked at his daughter sitting with bowed head on the side of the bed his control vanished, and he almost sprang towards her.

'Look at me!'

Her head remained bowed until his hand shot out and jerked her chin up. He did not say, 'Is this true?' but, 'You dirty, dirty little slut! You filthy little slut!' There were dobbles of saliva spurting from between his clenched teeth. 'Who was it?'

Petrified, she stared up into his face. This is what she had been afraid of, this moment, in case her fear of him would cause her to betray Brett. She knew she must do nothing until Brett came and he would do the telling. He would stand up to her father. This once he would stand up to her father.

'Answer me, girl.'

When the only answer he got was the wide stare from her eyes it was too much. He struck her once, twice, three times before she fell backwards over the bed.

Jane Ratcliffe was clinging to him now crying, 'Jonathan! Jonathan, no! Not that.' She forced him back. Afraid herself now of the wild stare in his eyes which he kept fixed on his daughter. Using all her strength, she led him out of the room.

On the landing, he stood, his eyes unblinking as he fought the desire to return to the room and tear every stitch off her and flay her until she cried out for mercy. He should have done it. He glared at his wife for a full minute; then, taking a handkerchief, he rubbed the sweat and saliva from around his mouth.

'What's to be done? What's to be done?' Jane was whimpering now.

He moved down the landing, still wiping his mouth; then ground out through his handkerchief, 'She'll have it taken away.'

'Taken away? But Jonathan, that's illegal.'

'Don't be stupid, woman!' He turned on her. 'Nothing's illegal if you can pay well enough for it. But one thing is certain; there's going to be no baby born on the side in this house. And think, just think what this will mean if the Braintrees get wind of it; it could ruin everything. Their outlook might be modern but they're narrow underneath. Remember the other night? Remember when he was on about cleaning up certain quarters of the town?' He put his hand to his head, then turned and looked towards

Vanessa's room again and asked, 'Who? Who? That's what I want to know.' When he brought his infuriated gaze round to her he demanded, 'Have you no idea?'

She shook her head in bewilderment. 'I can't think I don't know . . . anyone.'

'Well, you should know, woman. It's your duty to know. There's a man somewhere, boy or man; she can't be having a baby through auto-suggestion.'

As they went down the stairs Ray came from the narrow passage that led to the second bathroom and he watched his parents' heads disappear before turning and looking towards Vanessa's door. Vanessa was going to have a baby. He knew how people had babies; Clive at school, had told him. He had shown him how it was done in the lavatories . . . He bit on his lip. Vanessa was going to have a baby. He was grinning as he went out down the back staircase to Michael's tree house. He would whistle to Michael, he should be back from school now. He would tell him Vanessa was going to have a baby.

Emily stood at the table and looked at Angus where he was standing with his coat in his hand. He had taken it off but he hadn't hung it up. She said, 'I wanted to tell you afore Rosie got in. I promised him faithfully I wouldn't utter a word. He got me in the study and made me swear I wouldn't let on. They're goin' to have it taken away as far as I can gather . . . Don't look like that, lad, but I know how you feel. I've never got such a gliff in me life. Honest to God, I was floored.'

'Can't be true.' Angus's voice was rumbling in his throat. 'Van? No, not her. She's only a kid and – '

'Look, lad, you know as well as me, they're hardly out of the cradle afore they're fallin' with bairns these days.

You haven't to go any further than three doors down. Fourteen years old.'

'Oh, I know, I know.' His voice was suddenly high and harsh. 'But you don't judge the world on Betty Halliday, do you? We're talking about Vanessa Ratcliffe . . . How did it happen? Was she raped?'

'Oh, lad!' Emily put her hand to her head, swinging it from side to side. 'You're askin' me, and they're askin' her, and they can't get one word out of her. And they don't know any fellow she's been with. She doesn't go round with fellows; she hasn't even got a boy friend. There were three lasses, Lucy Fulton, Kathy Young, and that Rona girl. They come to the house for tea. Those are all she ever sees. At least, that's what everybody thought . . . And then they nearly had another casualty on their hands. I thought Susan was going to go clean up the pole. She went up the stairs and I heard her screaming from down in the kitchen. The missus had to go up an' stop her. You know, it could put a spoke in that one's wheel, a scandal like this.' Emily sighed now and ended, 'Well, there's nowt we can do about it, so go and have a wash, and by that time your tea'll be ready.'

He went towards the scullery, saying, 'I've got no appetite the night, I'll just have a cup of tea for now.'

'You'll eat your tea. I've cooked it.' She was barking at him.

In the scullery he stripped off his shirt and went to the sink and began to wash himself, pausing every now and again to stare at the wall. He felt sick, actually sick, like he did sometimes on a Sunday morning when he had gone over his quota on a Saturday night, and he knew this was only the beginning. Later on tonight, when he was in bed and could think quietly, it would be worse.

As he dried himself he stood looking out of the window

126

on to the back yard, and he did not think, 'Poor kid. What luck!' but aggressively, 'Why had she to do it? Her!' She had been a kind of symbol to him, the queen who smiled at the shoe-maker, the princess who touched the hand of the swine herd. He had likened her to the characters in the books that had once been Susan's and hers and had been passed on to Rosie. She had been in his mind something so aloof that even when he thought of her he had to look upwards. She was, he realised at this moment with a mixture of astonishment and scorn at himself for being such a fool, the reason why he had cooled off May when she let on about having the other fellows. He had indeed been a bloody fool. He didn't like feeling a bloody fool. He turned to the kitchen door and said, 'She could have been attacked or somethin'.'

'I don't think so, lad,' said Emily flatly. 'If that had happened she would have come home in a state at the time. Lasses don't keep things like that to themselves. No, it was no rape to my way of thinkin'. But whoever it is, she's keepin' mum about him. But, oh, the look on her face as she sat on the side of that bed when I took a cup of tea up to her. That is afore he saw her. She looked like all the lost souls in the Bible; all eyes she was and them full of fear. Oh, I can't explain how she looked. And them gettin' the doctor for exam nerves. That's the only funny part about it.'

He turned back into the scullery. Funny part . . . exam nerves. By aye. She had exam nerves all right. That is why she had been wandering around the fells in the rain and he had taken her home as if she was a little bairn who had lost her way. Oh, she must have been laughing up her sleeve at him. God, but wasn't he the bloodiest of bloody fools. He recalled how he felt as he walked by her side, proud, sort of humble and grateful, all mixed up together. He had always felt grateful to her because she spoke to him. But all the while they had walked over the fells she was pregnant. She had been with a fellow. She knew all about it.

He wondered how many times she had done it, and who with. Likely some pimply groping grammar-school twirp, some sixth former; a boy at school, but a man when he got out of the gates and stuffed his school cap in his pocket.

'Come an' get your tea.'

He went into the kitchen and, looking down at the two chops bordered by fried potatoes and tomatoes, he said, 'I couldn't stomach it.'

Emily glared at him for a moment; then, wagging her head, she said flatly, 'All right, we'll say nothin' more about it. I'll warm it up after for you. Go and get yourself changed and have a pint; you'll feel better.'

Yes, he'd get himself changed and have a pint. But he wouldn't feel better; he'd only feel more of a so and so fool because the beer would unlock the secret places in himself, that only it and dreams had the power to do; places in which he would wander as he had done on the fells the other day and hold conversations with her. He didn't just talk at these times, he conversed, speaking correctly. He always spoke correctly in the secret places; there was nothing about himself to be ashamed of in the secret places. He had no need to be aggressive in the secret places for there he had an ease of mind and a demeanour that could only elicit admiration – and from the one person he wanted, had always wanted, admiration . . .

He returned at eleven o'clock. He had been on the hard, and Emily had to put him to bed and she was dismayed. She had always known he was fond of Miss

Vanessa, right from she was a bairn, but not all that fond. You see, you thought you knew everything, but there were things you didn't know, even about your own.

In the kitchen Rosie asked, 'What's brought this on in the middle of the week?' and Emily replied, 'Miss Van; he's cut up.'

'Huh!' said Rosie. 'What the hell for! That's rich, that is. He wants to tell that to May.'

'Now, now,' said Emily. 'You can be sorry for her.'

'Sorry for her, me backside. She had everything, an' she wanted that an' all; she couldn't wait. She's asked for it, an' boy, she's got it. Sorry for her! You're askin' something, aren't you? She always got on my wick.'

What Rosie was saying was that she had sense enough to be jealous of the advantages that had fallen to the lot of Vanessa Ratcliffe and she was now feeling a little compensation for the gaucheness that she experienced whenever she was in Vanessa's company. That Vanessa was nearly three years younger than herself made no difference, it was her manner that created the disadvantage.

4

Irene Brett hadn't been so happy for years. She couldn't wait to go next door to offer her condolences.

She had made her son repeat again and again what Ray had said to him, and she linked this with having seen Doctor Carr driving in next door when she was coming home not more than two hours ago. She wished her patience would allow her to wait until the day after tomorrow when Arthur would be home. Not that he would feel as she did because in a way he had been fond of Vanessa, always taking her part; but he would be bound to feel some satisfaction over this calamity falling on Jonathan. As great as the difference was between her and Arthur, she could, she told herself, joy with him in this. How are the mighty fallen. Ah, yes, that saying was applicable to their neighbour. It was another Jonathan in the Bible it was said of. She would have to look it up so that she could quote it pat to Arthur when she told him; and she would also point out to him that she had been justified in her suspicions. She could almost say she had been expecting this outcome; she had always known that, beneath that reserve, Vanessa was a cheap little piece. Her choice of a partner had proved that; she couldn't have picked much lower. Really, really, when you came to think about it.

She looked at the clock; it was turned seven. She would go next door now . . .

Susan opened the door to her and her manner indicated the state of her mind for she stammered and said, 'Oh, hel-lo, Auntie;' then added, 'Mother's resting.'

'Yes, I expect she is, Susan, but I just want to see her for a minute.' She slipped into the hall and turned and faced Susan, who was slowly closing the door. Then bending towards her, she whispered, 'I . . . I don't know whether to believe it or not, children carry such tales, but if it isn't true, your mother should do something with Ray.'

'Ray!' Susan moved her head in small jerks. 'What's . . . what's Ray done?'

'It's not what Ray's done, it's what he's said. Look, Susan; is your mother in the lounge?' She turned and walked across the hall, and Susan, after a moment's hesitation followed her almost at a run and pushed open the door, saying, 'It's Aunt Irene, Mother.'

Jane Ratcliffe turned sharply round. Her face was pale and her eyes red, and on the sight of Irene Brett she turned as sharply away again, saying, 'Oh, Irene, I've got a headache.'

'Yes, dear, I expect you have. I . . . I was just saying to Susan. I thought I had better come over. It's about Vanessa.'

Jane Ratcliffe looked as if she had been frozen into stillness. Her body slightly twisted, she stood gaping at Irene Brett, then she almost whimpered, 'Vanessa?'

'Yes.' Irene's voice was low and sympathetic. 'Ray has told Michael something utterly fantastic and I think you should speak to him.' She looked now from Jane to Susan, and unmercifully she went on, 'He said that . . .

Well, I really don't know how to put it, but he said that . . . well, the fact is he said that she is going to have a baby.' Her voice faded away as if in shock, and for the second time that day Jane Ratcliffe almost fainted. She groped backwards at a chair and sat down; then looked up at her daughter, and Susan turned away and walked towards the fireplace.

'Oh, I am sorry, Jane. Oh, I am. It's appalling. What can I say? What a terrible thing to happen. I . . . I didn't believe it, but, well, if it's true he should be horse-whipped, or put in jail. If I had him up before me, oh I would give him enough time to cool him down I can assure you. It's a pity the birch has gone. I say that again and again.'

Both Susan and her mother were staring at Irene now.

'You know who . . . who it is?' It was Susan asking the question, and Irene looked at her and her eyebrows moved slowly upward as she asked on a high, surprised note that sounded genuine, 'Don't you?'

Susan turned her gaze on her mother, and Jane Ratcliffe, calling to her aid all the dignity of which she was capable, straightened her back and said, 'Who do you imagine has done this thing to Vanessa, Irene?' She asked the question as if she herself already knew the name of the perpetrator.

'Well,' Irene shook her head as if in perplexity. 'I mean . . . Well, I thought. Well, it's no use beating about the bush. I've told Arthur about the number of times I've seen them together, and Michael saw them last Sunday from up in the tree house. He saw them coming across the river. He was with Ray; they shouted to them.'

'They shouted to them! Who? Who was with her?'

'Why Angus, Emily's Angus. Didn't you know?'

Jane's hand went slowly to her throat. She told herself that she mustn't faint, not again. She had thought that nothing worse could happen, but it had, and the consequences were terrifying. Angus Cotton . . . Emily's Angus. NO. She could never have degraded herself with Angus Cotton; he must have taken advantage of her. That was the only thing; he had taken advantage of her. Yes! Yes! That was it, and she was frightened to say anything, knowing how they all valued Emily's services . . . Emily's services? Oh, no! Oh, no! This would mean she would lose Emily. It was too awful. What would Jonathan say? What was more to the point, what would he do? In anger Jonathan could be terrible. Oh, why had this come upon them? Why? And Irene Brett standing there gloating. She got to her feet, saying, 'If you'll excuse me, Irene. I'm sure you understand . . .'

'Yes, yes, of course, Jane; I understand. And if there's anything I can do, anything at all, I'll only be too – '

'Thank you. Show Irene out, Susan.' She didn't say Aunt Irene, and the tone she used and the words themselves were in the form of an insult, as she meant them to be; and of this Irene Brett was aware, but she continued to smile her sympathetic smile, and she touched Susan's hand at the door as she said, 'Good-bye, Susan dear. And I wouldn't let it upset any of your plans.'

'Cat! Mean, narrow-faced cat!' Susan was speaking aloud as she re-entered the lounge, and going straight to her mother she stood before her and cried, 'Angus Cotton. No wonder she wouldn't say anything. Angus Cotton. Dear Lord! Can you believe it, Mother? Angus Cotton!'

Jane Ratcliffe could believe it; yes, she could believe it. Vanessa had always been fond of Emily's Angus. But she knew she must never voice this. She looked up at Susan and said, 'He must have forced her.'

Susan was scornful. 'She's not a child.'

'She'd be a child in his hands; he's a great big bulky individual.'

Susan turned away, her face screwed up in distaste, saying, 'Bulky. Horrible. The big oaf!' Then swinging round again, she demanded, 'What am I going to do? It's out now; it'll be all over the town tomorrow. I could murder that boy.' She clenched her fists, then ended, 'Why did you have to talk in front of him?'

'Don't be silly,' said Jane Ratcliffe wearily. 'As if we would have said anything if we had known he was about. He must have been outside the door or somewhere when we were upstairs.' She put her hands to her head as she added, 'And when your father comes in I just daren't think what will happen. I just daren't think.'

'I can see something even worse than that. Just think what will happen when you confront Emily with this tomorrow morning. Have you thought of that?'

Yes, in a way she had thought of it. Not what Emily's reactions would be, but that Emily would now leave her. The thing she feared had come upon her.

Emily stood for a full minute without speaking; then she startled her mistress by yelling, 'You're a bloody liar! And she is an' all if she says it's him.'

'Emily! You're forgetting yourself.' Jane Ratcliffe's pale, pained countenance flushed.

'Forgettin' meself? You stand there and accuse my Angus of puttin' her in the family way. Miss Van who he thinks about as a child still, an' you tell me I'm forgettin' meself.'

'Well, there's no need for language.'

'No need you say, no need? Begod! you'll hear somethin' more than this afore you're finished. Wait till he gets wind of it. Just wait till Angus gets wind of this. Anyway, who said this? Did she say it was him?'

'No, but . . . but deducing from what we know it can only be him. She's been seen a number of times with him lately.'

'Where, might I ask?'

'Well, they were seen coming across the river last Sunday. And they've been seen in the town together . . . She doesn't know anyone else, Emily – she hasn't any boyfriends – he can be the only one . . .'

'Listen to her.' Emily banged her head with her fist. 'You're talkin' through the fat of your neck, woman.' Gone was the cultivated servile manner of years. Her mistress was now just a woman who was accusing her son of taking down a girl. She could have been May's mother, or that of any lass in Ryder's Row. 'There must be thirty thousand blokes in this town altogether,' she flung one arm wide, 'and you're pickin' on him because they were seen talkin' together. He's always talked to her. Or I could say, she's talked to him. She's never passed him in the street like the rest of you.' She turned her glare on Susan, who was standing gripping the back of a chair. 'Let me tell you, I know my Angus, and he would as soon have broken into the Convent and raped one of the nuns as he would have done that lass up there.' She thumbed the ceiling. 'Well now. Well now.' She was tearing off her apron. 'This is the end. I've stood you, the lot of you, for years, but this has put paid to it. But afore I go I'm havin' a word with your daughter.'

'You're not to go upstairs.'

'I'm goin' to see her and you're not goin' to stop me.' Emily glared into Jane Ratcliffe's face.

'She'll only say to you what she said to us, that it wasn't him. She's maintaining that because she doesn't want to cause further trouble.'

'Further trouble!' Emily brought her chin into her neck. 'You don't know anythin' about it yet. Wait till my Angus hears of it, then you'll know what trouble means.'

As she marched out of the room and across the hall Jonathan Ratcliffe came down the stairs, and he stood in an advantageous position on the bottom step and looked down at her with open loathing on his face; and she glared back at him as she said, 'I want to see your daughter.'

His teeth moved tightly across each other and he ground through them, 'After I have seen your son. And if you know what's good for both of you, you won't go yelling your head off about this.'

'Huh!' She gave a mirthless laugh. 'I've just told her.' She nodded back towards the drawing-room door where Jane Ratcliffe was standing. 'I've just told her you don't know what you're in for when he gets wind of it . . . Yelling me head off. Huh!'

'I know what I'm in for.' His voice was deadly calm now. 'But as yet your son doesn't. He's the one you should worry about. Now I presume you're going; well do, and as quickly as possible.'

She was nonplussed for a moment by his manner. She looked up into his thin, bony face, then she turned her gaze on the woman for whom she had worked for years, and her lip curled upwards from her teeth and, squaring her shoulders, she walked from them with exaggerated dignity.

In the kitchen she grabbed her hat and coat from behind the scullery door, screwed her feet into her outdoor shoes, tore her aprons out of a drawer, then went to a cupboard to find a piece of paper with which to wrap them, and as she pulled it out she saw a tarnished silver milk jug and sugar basin. They were among other oddments that her mistress had pushed away in this cupboard from time to time to save cleaning. With a swift movement she grabbed them up and put them in the middle of her aprons. She had worked for these, and much more, they were only Elkington A1 silver, not solid, but they would fetch something. Aye, by God she had worked for them; she wasn't going out empty-handed. And if she had only thought of it at the time she would have asked for a week's money in lieu of notice, but she had been paid last night.

Without a backward glance she walked out of the kitchen, banging the door behind her, but when she left the drive and entered the road she had to stop and lean against the railings for a moment because her whole body was shaking. What should she do now? His lordship there would go to the office within the next half-hour and send for Angus, and if he threw it at him the same way as the missus had thrown it at herself then only the Lord knew what would happen. She had better go to the works and warn him. But how she was going to put it she didn't know . . .

It was a bus ride and twenty minutes later when she came to the gates of Affleck and Tate and told the gate man she wanted to see her son.

'Oh!' he said. 'Angus Cotton? Oh well, look. Just follow the road straight on, take the first turning right across the open space, and anybody there will tell you where his shop is.'

Another seven minutes and she saw him coming towards her and her throat swelled and her body began to shake again.

'What is it?' He was holding her arm. 'Something happened to Rosie?'

She shook her head. 'Is there any place I can sit down for a minute?'

He looked about him. There was a wooden cask lying on its side, and with a heave he righted it and pushed it against the wall, then led her to it. 'What is it?' he said again anxiously.

She looked up into his big, rugged face, tender at the moment with his concern for her. She wetted her lips, but she couldn't speak because she was realizing that he would now lose his job. In some way or another Ratcliffe would get rid of him; if not altogether, because of the Union, he'd knock him to the bottom again.

'Look. Look, what's happened? Why aren't you at work?'

She grabbed hold of his hands. 'Listen to what I'm gona tell you, an' don't go mad, don't shout.' She looked about her at the different men moving about the yard. 'I . . . I went in this mornin' like . . . like ordinary, you know, an' . . . an' she sent for me. Susan come and said – I'd just got me hat and coat off and me shoes changed – and she said her mother wanted to speak to me. I went in never thinkin', and then – ' She tightened the pressure on his hands, swallowed again and shook her head before muttering, 'Now, Angus, please, please, for God's sake don't go mad, but,' she had to close her eyes as she whispered it, 'they're blamin' you for Vanessa.'

When there was no movement of his hands within hers, when there was no yell or volley of oaths, she opened her eyes and looked up into his face, and then she realised he hadn't taken it in; or, if he had, thought it was funny. He was actually smiling. And then he took his hands from hers and, going to the wall, put his forearm on it and dropped his head against his wrist, and his shoulders began to shake. But he made no sound. Then turning, he looked at her and said, 'They're blaming me for dropping Van?'

She nodded at him.

'You mean,' his voice was louder now, 'you mean they're blaming me?' He dug his fingers hard into his chest, making a metallic sound. 'Christ! You're joking, aren't you?'

'No, son, I'm not jokin'. I came straightaway 'cos when he gets in,' she jerked her head upwards, 'he'll likely be sendin' for you.'

'Huh!' His sandy brows knit together and again he said, 'Huh!' It was the beginning of a deep laugh that never materialised. He looked up at the high façade of the shops; then looking down at her again he said, 'Well, they must be bloody well hard up to pin it on somebody when they've picked on me. But why me?'

'Because you're the only one who she's been seen with. That's what they said.'

'What did she say?'

'I didn't see her; they wouldn't let me. But the missus said they had faced her with it but she kept denying it because she – she didn't want to cause trouble.'

'Cause trouble did you say?' He was bending over her, his look full of mock enquiry. Then straightening himself, he said, 'God Almighty! Mam, it's bloody well fantastic, isn't it? Me an' her!'

'You've said it, lad, fantastic. What'll you say when he sends for you?' She was breathing more evenly; she was relieved beyond measure that he had so far taken it sort of calm like.

'What'll I say?' he said. 'Now, you leave it to me. Oh, just leave it to me. But you're wrong, Mam, about one thing. He won't send for me here, not about that he won't. He won't want the whole place to know about that, not if I know Mr Ratcliffe. He'll want it hushed and he'll hush me up an' all one way or another. You'll see I'll either be pushed out, or,' he bent his head towards her again, 'I'll be pushed up.'

'Pushed up?'

'Aye, Mam, pushed up, to keep me quiet.' He jerked his head slightly.

She now stood up, and they looked at each other. Then she said grimly, 'Knowin' you, an' your kind of reaction, it'll be the out not the up you'll get.'

'True, true, Mam, but just you wait. He'll try it on, you'll see. That's if the lady concerned doesn't name the right man and straighten things out, and herself into the bargain.' His voice now ended on a bitter note. He put out his hand and said grimly, 'Come on; I'll take you to the bus, an' you get home and put your feet up. There's one thing.' His voice lightened just the slightest. 'You'll be able to have your house clean again and the meal on the table when we come in. It's odd how things happen . . . I've had to become a dad-dy,' he drew the word out, 'before I could get you to leave your job, Mrs Cotton.'

He put her on the bus outside the works gates, and he left her with a smile. But it disappeared immediately he re-entered the gates. His reactions now were becoming normal to him. His temper was beginning to boil. His thoughts, bitter and cynical, made his face hard and ugly, yet there was among them a feeling he couldn't pin down. It would be later in the day when he would realise that he was flattered that the Ratcliffes should even think he had given their daughter a baby . . .

It was an uneasy morning in the shop, uneasy for all

140

the workers; even old Danny Fuller enquired what had got into him. 'Don't bark me head off, lad,' he said. 'If you want me to do anythin' just ask me, but don't bark me head off.'

It was round half-past eleven when the call came.

'You're wanted up top,' said the messenger boy. 'Boss's office.'

But when he got up top, his body stiff with tension, he was confronted by Mr Wilton.

Mr Ratcliffe, Mr Wilton said, was indisposed. He wanted these papers immediately and he wanted him, Angus Cotton, to deliver them. Why this should be, Mr Wilton didn't know. But, it wasn't altogether unexpected. Brett had been trying for a long time to give Cotton another push up. But he was no favourite of the boss, nor of himself. He didn't like the fellow, or the idea of him getting any status.

He handed Angus the envelope, and Angus looked at it and all he said was 'Thanks'; then turned on his heel and walked out.

Jane Ratcliffe herself opened the door to him as Susan had refused to do this office. After barely glancing at him she inclined her head to indicate that he should enter the house, then she led the way to her husband's study where she opened the door and again indicated by a movement of her head that Angus should enter the room.

Jonathan Ratcliffe was in a place of authority behind his desk, which was set in a corner of the room with a window to the side of it so that the light fell fully on anyone who was sitting on the chair in front of him.

But Jonathan Ratcliffe did not ask Angus to be seated. He himself sat, his hands gripping the arms of the revolving chair, and stared at the figure confronting

141

him. He had disliked many people in his life, he had hated a few, but the combined hate he had ever experienced was nothing compared to the feeling he had for the man opposite to him. He had sat here for the last half-an-hour thinking about this man, his thoughts taking him right back, back to the day he had first seen him, when he had disliked him on sight. Even as a boy there had been something about Emily Cotton's son that caused him to grit his teeth, and as the years mounted so did his dislike. He saw Angus Cotton as a brash, utterly common individual; added to this he was powerfully built, making his own thin frame appear like a reed, which did not improve matters.

He glared up at him now. This was the man who had dared to handle his daughter. Her loud screams and protests had only convinced him more firmly that it was nobody else but this obnoxious individual who had brought her low.

He was preparing himself to speak, to say one word, 'WELL?' but before he could utter it Angus threw the envelope on to the blotting pad, remarking caustically, 'You wanted that. Or did you?'

It was with something akin to a feeling of triumph that he saw Ratcliffe's jaws tighten until the cheekbones shone white through his skin. He could get this man on the raw; he had always known it. He, too, had his memories from a boy. Perhaps his determination not to knuckle under to him right from the start was the reaction to hearing his mother saying, 'Yes, ma'am,' and 'Yes, sir.' His mother wasn't made for knuckling under either, but she'd had to do it. They'd had to eat.

Ratcliffe picked up the envelope and slapped it on the table as if it were a cane, saying as he did so, 'You know the real reason why I sent for you.'

'Aye!' The words sounded casual. 'I understand I'm giving your daughter a baby.'

'You dirty . . .!'

'Hold it. Hold it.' The careless attitude was gone. Angus was leaning over the desk, his hands flat on it. 'I'm warning you. Don't use any of those terms on me.'

Jonathan Ratcliffe had to swing his chair round before he could rise. Then when he was on his feet he said, 'You've taken advantage of a young girl of good family; you've taken advantage of the fact that your mother . . .'

'I'll take advantage of the fact that we're alone here without witnesses and bust your mouth open for you, MR. RATCLIFFE, and then I'll bloody well take you to Court. How would you like that? Justice is impartial. That's what they say. Well, I would see that it was impartial in this case.'

For a second Jonathan Ratcliffe knew a moment's fear. It was two-pronged. It was a fear of being physically handled, also the fear that he had made a mistake. But this reasoning was quick to reassure him on the latter point. Last night they had gone over everybody she knew; there was not one boy they could name that she had seen more than once in the last six months. They had gone over her movements for weeks past. She had been in the house most evenings doing her homework. When she went to the pictures it was with Kathy, or Rona, and, he, himself, had picked them up in the car, having insisted on this because the High Street was usually full of hooligans at night. The only person she had been seen with was this man here. He had made it his business this morning to go next door and have a word with Irene Brett. She said she had seen them together at least four times during the past few weeks.

She told him of the night she had seen them standing in the shop doorway together, and Arthur had insisted on bringing her home. She also remembered to tell him of the time Colin had seen them coming off the train together.

Added to this was the tale his son had gone over for him yet again, of how he had seen his sister being helped over the stepping stones in the river by Angus. They had come from over the fells and they had come up the road and stood talking near the railings. He had shouted to them and then Angus had gone away.

He said grimly, 'Threatening won't help you any, Cotton. We may be in Court together yet, but I'll give you a guess as to who will be on trial, and what is more I haven't to guess why you have done this.' He leaned forward again. 'You wanted to inveigle yourself in, didn't you? You were determined to get up into the drawing-office by whatever means in your power. You couldn't get there owing to your lack of education and limited brains so you used . . .'

Angus's arm flashed upwards, his fist doubled and looking like a huge hammer head, but whether it was the width of the table between them and the fact that Jonathan Ratcliffe stumbled back against the wall, or that in the nick of time he realised what he was about to do, his fist dropped with a crash on to the oak desk, the force lifting up a cut-glass inkwell from its brass stand, and as it shuddered back into place again he bent his head deeply over his chest and drew the air into his lungs. After a moment he lifted his eyes to where Jonathan Ratcliffe was still standing against the wall, his face looking like a piece of new lint, and he muttered thickly, 'You and your bloody job! You can stick it. Right from this minute, you can stick it. Do you hear? I'm finished. As for brains I've got more in me little finger than you've got in your whole body. The whole works, the whole town knows how you got into the top office, by leap-frogging poor Mr Brett . . . Sucking up. Do you know what your nickname is in the yard, and around? Do you know it?' He was yelling now. 'It's Tit Ratcliffe. That doesn't need much working out, does it? Tit Ratcliffe, the biggest sucker-up in the game an' the biggest upstart into the bargain, because your father was no better than any of ours. A little huckster grocer's shop, that's what he had. But he scraped and saved and sent you to college, and what did you learn there? To suck up, Mr Ratcliffe!' He gave an imitation of spitting. Then straightening himself, he ended, 'There's one thing I want afore I go, an' you'll not get me out of this house unless you do it. You'll bring her in here, and she'll face me, and she'll tell you if it was me or not.' There was a long pause before he said, 'Well, get going an' ring your bell.'

And Jonathan Ratcliffe did just that. He rang the bell. He was shivering with rage and humiliation; the only thing he wanted now was to get this man out of his sight. There was part of him wishing that the position was reversed, at least physically, that he was broad and tough and had fists like hammers because with them he would batter Angus Cotton to a pulp. Tit Ratcliffe! How dare he! . . . How dare THEY!

When the door opened he did not look at his wife but muttered in a voice that she did not recognise, 'Bring her down.'

During the time they waited Ratcliffe sat down before his desk again and Angus stood facing the door, and when she came in he hardly recognised her. Not only were her eyes swollen but her whole face was swollen,

145

and there was a dark patch on her cheekbone as if she'd had a blow. She looked even younger than when he had last seen her walking on the fells in the rain, and . . . she looked frightened.

After a moment's hesitation she came straight to him and, standing in front of him, she looked up into his face and said, 'I . . . I'm sorry, Angus. I told them. I've told them but they still won't believe me. I'm sorry. Oh, I am sorry.'

Her words, instead of convincing her father and mother, only proved to them still further that this was the man and that because of her fear she was frightened to name him; fear of what might happen to him at the works, and through that how Emily would be affected, because they knew she had always been very fond of Emily too.

Angus, now looking down at her, asked quietly but stiffly, 'Have I ever touched you?'

For answer she lowered her head and shook it slowly.

'Have I ever made any improper suggestion to you, or said anything out of place?'

Again there was a shake of her head.

'They say you're goin' to have a baby and I'm the father.'

Her head went further down and still kept shaking.

'If they're right then I should marry you, shouldn't I?'

He had never intended to say any such thing and his words came as a shock to her and brought her head up with a jerk. 'But . . . but you won't. I mean, you're not . . .' The look on her face made him sick; the prospect had terrified her.

She turned frantically now and looked from her mother

146

to her father, and she said again, 'He's not! He's not!' She cupped her face with her hands and began to rock herself and Jonathan Ratcliffe cried sternly, 'That's enough!' then nodded to his wife, and she came forward and took hold of Vanessa's arm and led her from the room.

But before she passed through the door Vanessa turned and looked over her shoulder at Angus and whimpered again, 'I'm sorry, Angus. I'm sorry.'

Now Angus moved towards the door, but he, too, turned before he reached it and he asked tersely but rather flatly now, 'Well, does that convince you?'

Jonathan Ratcliffe wanted to bawl a loud 'No!' but what he wanted above all things at the moment was to be rid of this man, and so he remained silent.

A few minutes after the front door banged Jane Ratcliffe came into the study and, moving slowly towards her husband, she said, 'He wouldn't admit it?'

'No; but it's him all right. I'm more convinced than ever now. Did you see how she went? "I'm sorry Angus. I'm sorry Angus. I'm sorry." She'll be sorrier before she finishes.' He gulped in his throat. Then nervously moving papers about on his desk, he said, 'I'm going into Newcastle to see Muxlington again. I'm sure he could do it, but he won't. But he'll arrange about London. You can say she's going to visit relatives, anything. When she comes back and there's no sign of it, it'll give the lie to Irene's tongue.'

'People will still think . . .'

'Yes, they'll think,' he said bitterly. 'And they'll always think. And they'll know, but she won't have any baby.' He turned on her. 'Understand Jane. She's not going to have any baby.'

'Doctor Carr?'

'I'll settle with Doctor Carr. He can't do anything.

She'll have a miscarriage. Anybody can have a miscarriage. And if he knows what's good for him he'll keep his tongue quiet, else he'll find himself and his bottle out of practice. He's not fit to be on the books anyway. Now go up and tell her what's arranged. And stand no nonsense. Tell her from me, if she knows what's good for her she'll comply . . . and quietly.'

But Vanessa didn't comply, and quietly. She wasn't going to London, she said; she wasn't going to have the baby taken away.

Then what, asked her mother, did she intend to do?

Vanessa could give no answer to this question until tomorrow. Brett would be here tomorrow, and when he knew what had happened everything would be smoothed out. There would be trouble. Oh yes, there would be more trouble. But they would be away from it all. Tomorrow night she would go down to the summerhouse as soon as it was dark, and he would be there because Irene would certainly put him in the picture the minute he got indoors. She would have her cases packed ready and then they would go off. They would go through the wood, out into the main road that way. She could see it all plainly.

'You're not to think of seeing him again. Do you hear me, Vanessa?'

'What . . . You mean, Augus?'

Jane Ratcliffe bit on her lip. Her daughter wasn't stupid, far from it, she was much brighter than Susan, yet her responses were those of some dim child. 'Who do you think I mean, girl? And don't take that attitude with me. There's only one person responsible for your condition . . . at least I hope so.' The implication startled even herself, together with the fact that she had voiced it. 'Now I've told you. Your father is arranging for you to go to London. You'll go into a nursing home, and when it's all over you'll go to Great-Aunt Jean's and stay there until your father considers it fit for you to come home again.'

'Oh no, I won't. I won't go to Great-Aunt Jean's.' Vanessa was startled into protest. 'You're not going to shut me away with Great-Aunt Jean, out in the wilds in Scotland, so don't think you are.'

She was about to protest further when she reminded herself there was no need. Great-Aunt Jean who lived in a cottage on a hill six miles from a town, surrounded by her hens, dogs and goats, with her Bible-reading and hymn-singing – the only form of entertainment she allowed – Great-Aunt Jean wouldn't see her, whatever happened, she would die first. But there would be no need for that. She must be quiet and just let them think she was going to go along with them. She turned from her mother and sat down and looked out of the window, and Jane Ratcliffe, taking her change of attitude for acceptance of the situation, said firmly, 'There now, let's hear no more protests. The time is past for that attitude. It's all settled.' Then she went downstairs to tell her husband.

Vanessa spent the following day cleaning her room, and Susan's. Since, her mother said, she had been the means of depriving them of Emily's services she would have to learn to do things for herself in future. She also delegated to her the cleaning of the two bathrooms, and she ordered her to have her meals in the kitchen because her father couldn't bear to sit at table with her . . .

By six o'clock she knew that Brett was home. Ray brought the information into the house. She heard him call, 'Did you know Uncle Brett was home, Mammy?

He's brought Michael a cowboy outfit with a gun. Not a real one but pretty like it. It shoots pellets. It's in a holster.'

That evening was the longest she had spent in her life. She sat looking out of the window in the direction of the larches. She could see part of the side of the house through the trees, but she wouldn't be able to see him until he came right to the fence that divided the grounds. And he didn't come. He wouldn't come out until it was dark and they were all in bed.

She herself was in bed pretending to be asleep when her mother looked in before going to her room. She felt her standing staring towards the bed, then the door clicked shut. She waited a full half hour before she went down the fire escape. She didn't take her cases with her; he mightn't be able to get away immediately, he would have to go to the bank for money tomorrow. She had thought about all this. But she'd take them and hide them in the wood when the arrangements were made.

There was a moon due but it wasn't up yet, but she had a torch with her. She was trembling from head to foot as she neared the river. She wondered what he would look like. Remembering him over the past weeks he had seemed to get younger and younger until she imagined he was almost her own age.

She knew he was in the summerhouse before she reached it. She stood below the steps and played the light through the open doorway, and there he stood. His face was brown, for he had been in the sun for the last three weeks, yet it was an odd kind of brown, and he didn't look young, not even youngish; he looked old, very old . . . and different.

She whispered softly, 'Brett!' but he didn't answer her, he just stared into the light.

She couldn't bear the look on his face; it looked all twisted and misshapen. She switched off the light and said, 'Say something. Say something to me, Brett.'

For answer he reached out and pulled her to him and pressed his lips to her forehead, and she clung to him for a moment before bursting into tears. He still held her as he led her the few steps to the wooden seat and they sat down together. He did not say, 'There, there, don't cry'; he uttered no word of comfort, and after a while his silence told on her and she pulled herself from his arms and peered at him in the darkness. 'It's been awful, Brett,' she said. She heard him gulping in his throat before he spoke. Then his words sounded ordinary and not suited to the occasion. 'Yes,' he said, 'it must have been.'

'I haven't told them, or anyone. No one knows, Brett.'

'Thank you, my dear.' He could have been giving thanks for someone offering him bread and butter, and his peculiar attitude eventually got through to her and she exclaimed on a high note, 'Brett, I'm going to have a baby!'

She thought he said, 'Oh, Christ!' Then he was holding her hand and talking. 'I'm sorry. I'm sorry Vanessa. You'll never live long enough to know how sorry I am. I didn't stay away because of this. You understand? I stayed away because I couldn't bear to see you. I didn't know this had happened. I thought it might, but again I dismissed the idea. Most . . . most women don't at their . . .' She felt the movement of his body as he swung his head widely on his shoulders. 'It was just that I wanted to pull myself together. When . . . when I finished the firm's business I got in touch with your father and asked him if I could stay on for my holiday. I wanted time, time, and . . .' he almost added, 'enough satisfaction for my body's needs to keep me away from you.' And he had certainly done his best in that direction during the past three weeks. No man could have done more.

She put in breathlessly now, 'What are we going to do, Brett?' She felt she must give him a lead because she wanted to be reassured quickly that he was going to take her away, but when after a moment he asked flatly, 'What can we do, child?' she was stunned into silence. And now he was asking her, 'What did they say? What do they intend to do?'

'They . . . they want to send me to London to have it taken away.'

'Well . . . well, that's the best thing, dear.'

'But Brett! Brett!' Her voice sounded full of terror. 'I can't. I won't. I won't have one of those operations. It showed about them on television. People die.'

'Hush, dear. Hush. It won't be that kind of operation. They'll send you to a clinic, to a good man. Those girls who die, they go to old women in back streets, ignorant people. You'll be all right. And when you come back . . .'

She withdrew her hands slowly from his. She was no longer peering at him. Her eyes were wide, staring out of her head into the blackness, and her voice sounded like that of a child's who had been told that they weren't going on holiday after all. 'But . . . but I thought you would take me away, Brett. I thought we would go away. You don't love Irene. You said you didn't. You said that night you had never loved her for years; she was cold and hard. You said she was. You said if only you could take me away' – 'Fly away with you, my princess,' were the words he had used – 'you could get a divorce and . . . and we could be married. I . . . I want to have the baby, I really do, Brett, I do. I feel I would like a baby, but . . .

152

but not unless I'm married. I want to be married, Brett.'
Her voice, filled with pleading and fear, was like a thin
whistle coming up from her bowels.

When he groped over her knees for her hands she felt
herself shrinking inwardly, yet she allowed him to bring
them to his chest and press them there as he said, 'Oh,
my darling, Vanessa, if only we could. If only we could.
But it's impossible, child. There's so many things against
it. You see, it would be difficult, almost impossible, for
me to get started again at my time of life. And I haven't
any money by me, and we'd have to live some place.
What is more, Irene would never divorce me, never. I
know that. And there's . . .' He stopped abruptly. It
was impossible to say to her, 'And there's this house
and the wood. I couldn't live long away from either.'
What was more he couldn't bear the thought of starting
a family again. He had no real love for children, which
was likely why his own sons, with the exception of Paul,
had never responded to him. You only got back what you
gave out. He was well aware of that. When he heard her
catch her breath on a sob he wondered if he would have
been kinder to lie and tell her they were going away,
say tomorrow or the day after – but in the long run that
would only make things harder for her.

From five minutes after he had entered the house this
afternoon he knew exactly what he was going to do. As he
listened to Irene pouring out her spleen, openly gloating
over what had befallen Vanessa, he knew then what he
must do, and now, holding the child's hands, his decision
was firmer than ever. If only he had the courage to take
her away. But he hadn't. He hadn't the courage to start
all over again, to face up to the responsibilities that would
attend such an action. Yet at the same time he hadn't the
courage to live without her. He was a weak man and he

knew it. Life had been pretty bleak before the night he had come down into the wood to send Angus Cotton packing; but since then it had been sheer hell.

When she withdrew her hands from his he said, 'It's going to be all right, Vanessa. Everything is going to be all right. It wouldn't work with you and me. In a year's time, even in a few weeks' time, you would regret having tied yourself to me. You're young; you haven't started to live yet. I've done you a great injustice, a great harm, but . . . but do what they advise and it will be all right. You can start again, and tomorrow morning,' he coughed here, 'you can tell your mother and father just how it happened and they'll understand.'

'You mean . . . you mean I'm to tell them, not you?'

'Yes, my dear. They must have kept at you to know.'

'Yes, yes, they have.' Her voice sounded far away. 'But they think it's Angus, Angus Cotton.'

'What!' He was on his feet. He seemed to have come alive for the first time since their meeting. 'You mean . . .? Have they tackled him with it?'

'Yes. Father . . . Father brought him to the house yesterday. Emily . . . Emily's left. She was in a state.'

'And you let them think this.'

'No, no! I told them flatly that it wasn't him but they wouldn't believe me. You see, Irene came over and told Mother that she had seen us together a number of times . . . and then Ray and Michael had seen us too.'

'Irene came and . . .' His voice trailed away.

'Yes, and from what I understand she seemed very pleased about it all.' There was a sound of bitterness in Vanessa's voice now. 'She's never liked me and she's jealous of Susan marrying well. I think she hopes that this will, in some way, put a stop to it. Mother and Father are afraid of the same thing. I've to be got out of the way, hushed up. They're going to send me to Great-Aunt Jean's, up in the wilds of Scotland, after I come back from London.' She was talking dully now as if she was accepting what had been arranged for her.

He asked quietly, 'Have you seen Angus?'

'Only yesterday morning in the study. He was very angry.'

Brett made no comment on this but, putting his hand out blindly until he found her arm, he drew her to her feet, saying, 'Come along, dear. Come along. And believe me, it's going to be all right. Tomorrow you can explain everything. It'll be all right.'

'What . . . what about you? What will happen to you?'

'Don't worry about me, dear, everything will work out tomorrow. You'll see.' He led her up the bank and through the wood, and at the gate they stopped and he drew her into his arms and, putting his lips against her brow, he held them there tightly for a moment, then said thickly, 'I just want you to remember one thing. No matter what happens remember this. I love you. I've loved you for a long time, but I've only been aware of it in the past few months. Thank you, dear.' When he pressed her away from him she muttered, 'Will I see you tomorrow?' She was crying bitterly now.

'Yes, you'll see me tomorrow.'

He stood on the same spot for almost ten minutes after she was gone, then he walked slowly up through the trees. He let himself in by the side door and went upstairs; but he didn't go to his own room, he went to his wife's.

After he had switched on the light he stood with his

back to the door. Irene, blinking, pulled herself up in the bed and said, 'Yes, yes. What is it? . . . Oh!' She focussed him through narrowed lids, then asked, 'Is it Michael? Is he sick?'

'No, it's not Michael.' He moved slowly towards the bed, and by the time he had reached the foot she had pulled the coverlet up under her chin. The action was a defensive one that a timid woman might take, but there was no timidity about her voice when she said, 'We've had all this out. No, do you hear, no.'

He stood staring at her, not speaking. He watched her thin mouth form into a button that aged her.

She was hissing at him now. 'You're not back five minutes and this starts again. I thought you would have learned more sense.'

'Do you know something?' His voice was quiet, even gentle. 'I wouldn't want to take you, Irene, if you were stark naked doing a fandango. I saw a naked woman doing that dance when I was abroad. She was fat and ugly and her skin was greasy. Moreover, she smelt. But you know something? Given the choice, I'd take her any day in the week rather than touch you with my little finger . . . Does that surprise you, Irene?'

Her mouth had slackened. It was slightly agape. 'You've been drinking,' she said under her breath. 'You could never carry your drink.'

'No, I haven't been drinking, and you know it. I'm solid and sober and I'm going to talk to you. We've never talked for years, and this will be the last time I'll talk to you, and for that I'm grateful.' He paused, and they stared unblinkingly at each other, until he said, 'Do you know what you are, Irene? Fundamentally, you're a mean, narrow-minded bitch. You're a woman who has fought her way into positions in this town on my name, on my

156

father's name, and his father's name. You're uneducated, unintelligent and without the slightest scrap of breeding. You've had a shot at imitating these various qualities, and you've hoodwinked a few into believing they are your own, but they're only a few. Besides which, Irene, you're cruel. It's a hobby with you, cruelty.'

Her lips trembled before she put in, 'Are . . . are you quite finished?'

'No, not by a long chalk. I'm coming to our neighbours now. Jonathan did me a dirty turn some years ago, but what happened was my own fault. Jonathan got the post over my head because he was ambitious. I'm not. And you've never forgiven him or his, not, let me stress, because of me but because of how it affected you. You saw yourself as the wife of the manager of Affleck and Tate's. You would have carried it off with a high hand, but not half as successfully as Jane has done. She's a snob of the first water, she's a social climber, but, unlike you, she came from a decent family.'

'Get out!'

'I'm not going out until I'm ready, Irene. As I said, we're going to talk. I'm going to talk. Now you, in a way, are on a par with Jonathan. You both came originally from the gutters of Fellburn. Your father was an elementary schoolteacher; his father had been a little grocer and his grandfather . . . You didn't know I knew this, but his grandfather, together with your great-grandfather were well known taggereen men in Bog's End. They both had donkeys and flat carts and they gathered scrap. A couple of Steptoes, but not quite so famous I should say.'

Her hair was pulled tight back in curlers held in place by an invisible net, and the skin at her temples now showed the veins standing up like pieces of thick blue string.

As he paused again they held each other's glance, hers

157

wide, bitter, full of hatred, his scornful, sad, and bitter too. He moved from one foot to the other before going on. 'Your chagrin gave you sleepless nights when Susan burst into the titled set, didn't it? So you looked around for something to spoil, something to smash, and you found it, didn't you? You found it when you saw Vanessa talking to Angus Cotton. Your mean little mind put two and two together and made a dozen. They couldn't be talking unless they were up to something, and so what did you do? You flew next door and named the man, the father of Vanessa's child, didn't you? . . . DIDN'T YOU?' His voice had suddenly exploded in a shout and she leant towards him, gritting out between her teeth, 'Stop it! Stop it! Do you want to raise the house?'

'Yes. Yes, I would like to raise the house. I have something very interesting to say.' There was a considerable silence now and his voice had dropped when he spoke again. 'First, I want to ask you. Do you really, in your heart of hearts, think Vanessa was having an affair with Angus Cotton?'

'There was no need to think,' her voice was thin, low and bitter, 'there's enough proof. And I've seen them together again and again. And the children – '

'Yes, I know all about that. The children saw them together. But . . . but he's not the father of her child.'

'How do you know? What do you know about it? You've been away for weeks, and you took your time in coming – '

'Yes, I took my time in coming back, because I was afraid to face up to my responsibilities. I still am.'

'What are you talking about?'

'If you weren't so dull, woman, you'd realise without me having to put it into words . . . I'm the father of Vanessa's child.'

Slowly she leant back against the bed head. She thought for a moment she was going to have a seizure of some sort. She had to wait seconds, minutes, before her heart stopped racing. Then she muttered, 'You're mad. You're sex mad. It's because you wanted her. I don't doubt but that you wanted her. You've thought of nothing but sex for years. But you, you, wouldn't have dared . . . You . . .'

'Well, I did dare. I had one short amazingly glorious moment of living down in the summerhouse.'

Her eyes were like pieces of flint piercing him. 'I – I don't believe you; you're just making it up. Wishful thinking, that's what it is, wishful thinking. I deal with people like you every week in the courts, people who say they've done things because they want to do them but are afraid to. I don't doubt but you wanted one glorious moment, but you would never have dared, never.'

'Well, I tell you I did dare, Irene. And Vanessa has been waiting for me coming back before she's spoke. She's been very, very brave. She wanted me to take her away. And oh, I would have dearly loved to have done just that. And I would if I'd been younger, and with more nerve and some money behind me. Yet if I could have done this she wouldn't have been happy. She's made for someone young, and she'll get someone young. A girl like her must be made happy, because you know why? She's kind, and kind people, even if they're the biggest rogues or scamps in the world, they're happy, they're made happy in some way. I've seen it again and again . . . Of course there are exceptions. I was kind to you, Irene. And my people were kind to you. But my mother's last years were made miserable through you, and all my married years have been made miserable through you . . . Well, it's finished. Or nearly so. By the

159

way, I'd better tell you I made another will some time ago. Funny, but I must have known this was coming. I've made a stipulation in it that the land and house, when it is sold, mustn't be divided, and it must be sold as one and the money that it brings is to go into trust until Michael is twenty-one. Then it is to be divided between the three boys. I've also left special pieces of furniture to Paul alone. You, my dear, will have the interest on the money until Michael comes of age. After that you are at the mercy of your three sons.'

She was unable to speak. Her whole body was shaking as if with an ague. When he said, 'Good-bye, Irene,' and turned slowly from her she knew what he was going to do. The only thing she didn't know was how he was going to do it. But she didn't get out of bed or say one word to stop him.

5

Vanessa had sat by her bedroom window until almost two o'clock in the morning, and when she eventually did go to bed she didn't sleep, at least for a long time. When she heard her mother's voice saying stiffly, 'Vanessa! Vanessa! It's almost eight o'clock. Come along,' she imagined she had been asleep only a few minutes.

At half-past eight she went downstairs and into the morning room. She had stopped being sick these last two or three mornings and had felt hungry, yet at the same time she thought it wasn't right somehow that she should eat at all.

She had the morning room to herself; her father had already had his breakfast and would now be in his study where he would stay until after nine. There was some bacon under cover on an electrically heated plate, and as she served herself she thought, 'I can't eat, I can't'; yet she ate the bacon and had two cups of coffee and some toast and marmalade.

The sun was shining full into the room and she looked about it, seeming to see it for the first time. It was a beautiful room. Pale grey walls, thick pink satin curtains, two large mushroom-coloured rugs on the polished parquet floor. The sideboard with its gleaming silver, most of which was now going to be put away, and the period dining chairs with their seats and backs upholstered in rose. This had always been her favourite room, and perhaps after today, or tomorrow, or the next day she wouldn't see it any more. After she had told them about Brett – and how she was going to deliver this bombshell she didn't really know – she was going to tell them something else. She was going to tell them she meant to get a job of some kind, any kind, and, what was more, she was going to have the baby because the prospect of having the baby in six months' time was less frightening to her than having it taken away now. She knew that when she told them what she intended to do her father would bring his authority to bear, and if he couldn't force her to go to London he would send her somewhere. It wouldn't matter much to him where she went during the next few weeks as long as she was out of his sight, and not an embarrassment to them all until the wedding was over.

But she was fully aware that she couldn't stand up to her father on her own regarding the baby, particularly when he knew it was Brett's. He would be madder than ever at this disclosure. He would see it as a personal affront, and she daren't think of his reaction. She would need a higher authority to fall back on and she knew she would find that authority in Doctor Carr. She would go to Doctor Carr and say, 'I want to have this baby, I don't want it to be taken away.' And she could hear him now exclaiming loudly, 'If you want to have it, you have it; you're strong and healthy. Don't let me hear any talk of you having it taken away.' After that, let her father try and send her to London. Abortions were illegal and people could go to prison for doing them, or aiding them.

One minute her chin was jerking upwards in support

of her thoughts, the next she had her face buried in her hands biting on the pad of her thumb to stop herself crying. She wished she had someone she could talk to. She felt dreadful inside, lonely, lost, all mixed up and confused.

She sat now, telling herself that she didn't know her own mind from one day to the next, because this time yesterday she was just longing to see Brett, knowing that he would take her away, and last night when she knew that he was going to do no such thing she had been sick. Even when she saw him as a timid, vacillating old man, she had still been sick with disappointment, and fear of what was going to happen to her. Yet this morning, when her mother had wakened her, she was filled with relief that they hadn't gone away together, that she wasn't going to marry him.

It was as she sat wishing that the day was over and shuddering inwardly at the repercussion her news would have on the two households that she heard the screaming. It was quite near, it seemed to be in the garden.

When she hastily pulled open the french windows and stood on the paved terrace the screaming filled the air. She saw her mother come to the drawing-room window, then her father come round by the side of the house. He looked along towards her, then her mother came through the morning room and on to the terrace beside her and she asked, 'What is it? Who is it?'

'Next door.' Jonathan Ratcliffe moved down the garden, saying over his shoulder, 'It sounds like Michael.'

The screaming now seemed to come from the top of the trees, and when her mother followed her father she followed them both, and then they were all standing by the gate looking into the wood, looking at Irene and Colin Brett. Irene was standing with one clenched fist pressed against her cheek, she was looking upwards into the tree house. Colin, too, was looking upwards. He was calling, 'Michael! Michael! Do you hear. Come down. I'll only have to come and fetch you. Come down.'

'What is it? What's the matter?' They all went through the gate and into the wood, Vanessa still walking a few yards behind her parents. As another series of screams came from the tree, Colin mounted the rickety ladder.

'What is it, Irene? What is it? What's upset him?'

Irene Brett turned and looked at Jonathan Ratcliffe, then she looked at Jane, and she gulped and moved her head twice before she said in a strangely controlled voice, 'He . . . he found his father in the cellar. Arthur . . . Arthur's hanged himself.'

No one moved for a moment. Then Jonathan said, 'Oh no! No!' And Jane put her two hands up and covered her cheeks, a characteristic gesture when she was without words. Then they both went to Irene's side, and they murmured over her. But she did not look at them, she looked straight between them and to their daughter, and she said again, 'Arthur hanged himself in the cellar. Do you hear?'

Both Jonathan and Jane Ratcliffe imagined she was repeating herself in this way because she was distraught, but Vanessa was aware that she was telling her she knew why her husband had hanged himself. It was in the hate in her eyes, and she was sending it like an arrow into her. Turning, she flew back through the wood and up the garden, and her parents made no comment on her actions because they knew their daughter had been very fond of Arthur Brett.

Back in her room, Arthur's death was having a strange effect on Vanessa; she was experiencing both anger and resentment against him. Her reasoning told her that resentment towards Brett should have taken effect weeks ago when she knew he had given her a baby. Yet her condition had evoked no such feeling. But his deliberate death had.

She saw him in this moment as Irene had seen him, and she hated him. She told herself that she should have known when he cried that he had no guts, gumption, nothing. He had used his tears to gain her sympathy, to get her to touch him, to hold him. She was glad he was dead, she was, she was. She stood in front of the long mirror and nodded at herself, nodded at her long white face, at her long, thin, leggy body, nodded at her stomach which was showing a slight fullness beneath her dress.

When she lay on top of the bed and buried her face in the pillow she asked herself what she was going to do now. Would she tell them, or would she leave it to Irene? He had told Irene. The thought brought her upwards. He must have told Irene last night after he had left her. She knew what would happen now. When her parents took Irene back to the house she would tell them why her husband had committed suicide, it was all because of their daughter. Oh dear Lord, dear Lord. Like her mother, she was holding her face in her hands.

It was nearly an hour later when her parents returned to the house. She was glad she was alone to meet them. Susan was staying with Brian's people for a week. She didn't think she could have borne to see Susan's face when she knew who it was who had given her the child. Her scorn and distaste would have been too much, even worse than when she had thought it was Angus, for after all Angus was young.

She was standing waiting for them when they came

into the lounge. She watched her father go and sit down in the big chair to the side of the fireplace. She watched her mother sit down on the couch. And she looked at them and waited, but neither of them looked at her. Then her mother said to her father, 'What on earth could have made him do it? The trip was successful wasn't it? Nothing went wrong there?'

'No, nothing went wrong there. Nothing could go wrong there, the stuff sells itself. He got the orders. He was only going to be out there six weeks, which was more than ample, but when I knew Cribber wouldn't be able to start again for at least another six months I phoned and asked him if he would like to go on to Germany and Italy. He seemed quite pleased about it. Then just before he was due to come back he phoned me and said he was going to take his holiday out there, was it all right?'

'Do you think something could have happened on his holiday?'

'How should I know?' He got to his feet. 'She says she doesn't know anything, yet I feel she knows something, that look on her face. She's a bitter pill, is Irene. They've never hit it off for years. I could have understood him doing it if he had been at home for weeks and they'd been having one of their periodical rows, but he just came back yesterday . . . Ah well, I'll have to get to the office. You'd better keep looking in,' he nodded at his wife, 'she's going to need all the help she can get. As for that boy, this'll leave a mark on him for life.'

He went out into the hall, and after a moment Jane Ratcliffe followed him, at least as far as the lounge door, and there she seemed to become aware for the first time that Vanessa was in the room and she turned to her and said, 'You can dust the drawing-room and dining-room.

166

I've got a woman coming for interview at half-past eleven, put her in the morning-room, and should I happen to be next door ring me.'

She wasn't going to tell. Irene Brett wasn't going to tell. She stood gaping towards the closed door. What should she do? If she didn't tell the truth they would still blame Angus, but if she told the truth now they would blame her for Brett committing suicide. She couldn't stand that on top of everything else. And it looked as if Irene didn't want it known. Yes, it looked like that because she'd had plenty of time to tell them. What must she do? She'd have to think.

Five days later Arthur Brett was buried. At the inquest they had brought in a verdict of death while the balance of his mind was disturbed. On the day of the funeral, at which all the professional people in the town were at least represented, the local evening newspaper gave the event full-page coverage. It said that Arthur Brett was a descendant of one of the oldest families in the county. There had been Bretts in Fellburn for the last two hundred and fifty years and that the early Bretts had once occupied the Moat House and owned considerable stretches of land on the outskirts of the town. It went on to say that the late Mr Brett's grandfather had married one Alice Affleck whose family had started the engineering firm of Affleck and Tate.

After reading the report Jonathan Ratcliffe handed it to his wife, and after she had read it she laid the paper down before saying, 'It sounds all very fine, but she is left practically penniless. Fancy him making a will like that; he must have hated her.'

'Well, you haven't had to wait all this time to realise that, have you?' he said tartly. 'But, you know he wasn't only hitting at her when he made that will.' His lips were in a tight thin line now and his voice was bitter. 'He was hitting at me. By what I gather from Colin the land is tied up tighter than ever. It cannot be sold without the house.'

'Would you buy it if it was up?'

'Of course I'd buy it. That's a silly question to ask. But I don't want the house. I'd pull the place down, it's dropping to bits anyway.'

'Did Colin say there was anything against their selling?'

'No; but he'll have Paul to deal with there because he's as daft about the place as Arthur was.'

'Are you going to give her a pension?'

'Yes, she'll get the usual, what he had paid in for.'

'Nothing more?'

'I have little say in that. Any suggestion like that would have to go before the board. And anyway,' he turned his face fully towards her, 'the more she has the longer she's likely to stay there. She likes prestige, does Irene, as you know. But,' he rose to his feet, 'we'll talk about that later. There's plenty of time to deal with that. At present we've enough difficulties of our own. Have you told her?'

'Yes.'

'And she's ready?'

'She didn't say anything.'

'You've got her packed?'

'Yes . . . Jonathan.'

'Yes, what is it?'

'I'm worried about this. At least I'm worried about what Doctor Carr might do. You know she said . . .'

'It doesn't for one single moment matter what she said. And I don't believe she went to Carr. Why didn't he get in touch with me, eh?'

168

'Well, he hasn't had much time, it was only yesterday.'

'If she had been to him at all he'd have been on that phone before now. And I was ready for him. I know a thing or two about Carr that will check his tongue ... By the way, have you written to your Aunt Jean?'

'Yes ... I've asked her to answer by return.'

'Well, that'll be settled. She'll go there straight from the clinic.'

'She says she won't.'

'Oh, does she?' His mouth formed a straight line again. 'Well, it's your business to see that she does. You'll be up there, and you'll take her yourself. And you can tell her that if she knows what's good for her she'll do what she's told.' He paused; then looking upwards, he added, 'It might make a deeper impression if I tell her myself. Go and fetch her down.'

As his wife moved towards the door he said, 'By the way, you didn't leave her in alone? This afternoon, I mean.'

She turned towards him. 'No, of course not,' she said; 'Susan was here.'

He nodded; then said under his breath, 'I wouldn't put it past her to try and sneak out to meet that oaf. If she got what she deserves I'd make him marry her. That would be an object lesson all right ... Go on, bring her.'

He had taken up his stand with his back to the fire, his arms crossed, and he looked towards the door as his wife re-entered the room again. She had one hand cupping her face, in the other she had a letter. She held it out to him without a word, and he met her halfway across the room and snatched it from her and read:

'Dear Mother and Father,

I am not going to London, I am going to have the baby. Doctor Carr said I should. I told you last night but you didn't believe me. What I didn't tell you was he said if you force me to go to a clinic he'll take the matter up. I'm going to get work as I told you. I have taken my bank book. I don't want you to worry about me so I'll write you every week. I'll be all right, I've arranged to stay with a friend. I am sorry I've caused you all this trouble. Tell Susan I am sorry and I hope the wedding goes off all right and she's very happy. Please believe I am very, very sorry that I have upset you.

Vanessa.'

It was too much, he actually took the Lord's name in vain. 'God!' He held his head. 'Where? How long? Ask Susan!' He was yelling now.

'How can I, she's out with Brian?'

'God!' he repeated again as he walked up and down; then smoothing out the letter that he had crumpled in his fist he said aloud, 'I am staying with a friend'; rounding on his wife now he cried, 'A friend! Which friend has she that'll take her? Which friend knows about her condition? One friend, Cotton.'

'No, no, Jonathan, she would never go to Emily . . . I mean to him.'

'Then tell me which friend she has gone to?' He nearly knocked her on to her back as he turned and marched out of the room, and she ran after him, crying, 'Where are you going, Jonathan?'

He was at the door which led into the garage from the kitchen when he barked, 'Where do you think? I'll break her neck . . . and his . . . We'll be the laughing-stock of the town one daughter marrying into the county, the other into Bog's End, and her pregnant!'

'Jonathan!' Her voice was loud now and stern. 'Don't publicise us, not in that quarter. Keep your temper.'

He got into the car and from there he looked at her. Drawing in a deep breath, he bowed his head. 'Yes,' his voice was low now, 'yes, you're right. Keep my temper. But wait till I get her back here, just wait. I'll flay her. God! See if I don't.'

Three times he had blasphemed aloud, which proved to his wife the extent of the depth to which he was moved.

Ryder's Row wasn't new to Jonathan Ratcliffe. He had once or twice, in the early days, brought Emily home after a late session of washing-up from a dinner party, but now, when he drove up the narrow street and he had to edge the Bentley into the space between the railway wall and a dilapidated Rover the rage within him increased. People owning cars in this street!

He knocked twice on the door, the second time banging with his fist. He heard someone shouting, 'Turn that down will you! There's somebody at the front door.' The music of either the wireless or television was lowered as the door opened and in the light of the dim passage bulb he saw the towering bulk of Angus Cotton in his shirt sleeves, neck open showing a dark growth of hair on his chest, and his rage was inflamed still further. This was the man who had dared to touch something that belonged to him, something that was part of him. Again the wish came that he could change places with him physically, just for one minute.

'I've come for my daughter.' He had to thrust the words out of his mouth.

'You've what? What the hell are you on about now! Look, what d'you want here?'

'Don't ask the road; you know. Where is she?'

'God Almighty! You must be bonkers, man.'

'Who is it? Who is it, Angus?' Emily came into the dim light. Then seeing the visitor she exclaimed, 'Why sir!' only to have her words cut off by Angus crying, 'Sir, be damned! Do you know what he's here for? He's here to take his daughter home.'

'Van?'

'Aye, Van. He thinks she's here. I ask you! They won't be told, will they?' Angus turned from his mother and, glaring at Ratcliffe, shouted, 'You won't be told. You won't believe the truth.'

'Keep your voice down.' Emily's own voice was low and harsh. 'You don't want the street to know.'

'It doesn't matter a bloody damn to me who knows. I'm not afraid of anythin', or ashamed either. Has she run away then?'

When no answer came from Ratcliffe, Angus cried, 'Good for her. Good for her.'

For a moment Jonathan Ratcliffe stood bewildered. He hadn't the smallest doubt in his mind but that he would find her here. He didn't believe that Cotton had nothing to do with Vanessa's condition, but he did believe him when he said she wasn't here. So when Emily said, 'Come in and see for yourself, if that will satisfy you,' he turned on his heel and walked to his car. And Angus moved on to the step and watched him, his whole body quivering the while. He stood there until the lights of the car disappeared from the street. Then returning to the kitchen, where Emily stood waiting for him, he asked her grimly, 'Well, what do you say to that?'

Emily sighed and shook her head. Sitting down heavily, she said, 'All I can say, lad, is they're dead sure it's you.'

'You know somethin', Mam?' He leant towards her. 'If I knew as much a few months ago as I do now, it would have been.'

'Don't say that, Angus.'

'I'm sayin' it, Mam, and you can believe me. God! I stuck that girl on a pedestal from when she was that high.' He pointed down to the level of his knee. 'You know I did. As hard bitten as I am I was still under the impression – because I wanted to be under the impression. Oh aye, because I wanted to be under the impression – that there were some virgins left, and she was top of the list . . . top of the pops. Aye, top of the pops. An' all the time she was messing about with some pimply schoolboy.'

'How do you know that it was a schoolboy?'

'I don't know, but ask yourself. She was at the Convent school, wasn't she? If she had been goin' out with a fellow regular, I mean like one of the Braintree set, they would have named him surely, but she was seen with nobody but me. She's likely met the bloke on her way from school; there's plenty of lanes between the Convent and Brampton Hill. There's also the golf course and Poulter's Wood.'

'Oh, Angus, don't say that.'

'Well, it wasn't another bloody immaculate conception, was it?'

'Oh!' Emily rested her face on her hands and muttered, 'I don't want to laugh, it's no laughin' matter.'

'No begod, it's no laughin' matter.' He, too, sat down, and after a moment he spoke as if to himself, saying, 'I wonder where she's gone.'

173

'They'll find her. They'll put the polis on her.'

'I wonder.'

'Of course they will.' Emily's voice was high. 'She's only sixteen, well seventeen in a day or so. But she's nothin' but a bairn.'

Nothing but a bairn. Huh! Angus got to his feet now and walked out of the kitchen and into his room and sat down in the wooden chair opposite the little table. His forearms resting on the table, taking the weight of his slumped shoulders, he stared down at the drawing paper and pencils, and his aggressiveness seeped from him. After a while his eyes lifted to the hanging shelf attached to the wall. His hand went up and he pulled one of the books down and looked at the title. It read 'The King's English, by H. W. Fowler and S. G. Fowler.' It was her who had made him buy that book, her and the fact of being put in charge of the fitting shop. Not that he needed grammar in the fitting shop, he had all the language necessary for the fitting shop, but he knew he wasn't going to stay in the fitting shop. Yet that wasn't the real reason why he bought the book; it was because of how she talked. It had happened he had met her on her way to school one afternoon last year. She was carrying a great armful of flowers, white and pink, and he had admired them and asked their name, and she had said they were called Esther Reads. They were quite a common flower really, she said, at least the white ones were, and she had pointed through the park railings and said, 'Look! There they are, those are they.' It had been that last bit, 'those are they.' It sounded all wrong. Surely it should have been 'those are them'. He knew his grammar was bad, but he felt he was right about that bit, for whoever said those are they. It was like saying 'was you?' So, he had gone and bought this book. But far from helping him it had only confused him further; he hadn't been able to find out from it if 'those are they' was right or not. One thing the book did bring home to him was the fact that he'd never be able to understand grammar. He had never heard of gerunds. What were gerunds anyway? And compound possessives? One thing only came out of buying the book, and that was begrudging admiration for those who did speak correctly. He thought that they must have had their work cut out to learn, and understand, all these two fellows said was necessary to speak English properly.

He recalled feeling a bit down and browned off for a few days after buying the book but it had soon passed. He had a home-spun philosophy of his own: If you couldn't do one thing then try something else.

He could draw, he was a good drawer. But now the chance to draw had been whipped away from him. The drawing office, any drawing office, was now as far from his reach as the moon, that was unless he did the thing properly and went every evening to a technical school, and it was too late for that. Anyway, he had burnt his boats. He was committed now for good or ill to cartage; he had gone in with Fred Singleton. Tomorrow he was to collect his lorry and start. And all this had come about through Van Ratcliffe.

Where was she? Where had she gone? Certainly not to any of the family friends else he wouldn't have come tearing around here. The bloody nerve of the man. He was sure, wasn't he? He was so sure. He picked up the book and rammed it back on to the hanging shelf. Je-hov-ah he would like to get even with that bloke. Wouldn't he just. He'd give half his life, or sell his soul, to get even with him. But what chance had he of that, apart from going and shooting him? And he could understand now why blokes got shot. Yes, he could that!

The door opened and Rosie put her head into the room. 'I hear you've had a visitor,' she said.

He got to his feet and smiled wryly, saying, 'Aye. You missed it; you shouldn't have gone to the pictures.'

'Mam's brewed up. Come on, have a cupper.' She moved towards him, smiling now and adding, 'Because, you know, this is the last night of Angus Cotton, Fitter; from the-morrow mornin', boy, you'll be Angus Cotton of Cotton and Singleton, Haulage Contractors. Just think of that, lad.' She pushed him hard in the chest, and he, punching her back playfully on the jaw, said, 'Aye, just think of that.'

'Come on.' She pulled him towards the door. 'I bet you what you like you'll remember this night. Won't he, Ma?' she called to Emily who was sitting with her feet on a modern oxidised kerb fronting the old-fashioned grate. 'When he's got his big house and his Rolls won't he look back to the night and say, "Remember?" you know, like they do on the telly where the poor lad makes good and buys out the lord of the manor, together with his mama and his papa.' She was giggling. 'That sounded funny, Mama and Papa.'

'Funny or not,' Emily's voice was flat and there was no smile on her face as she said, 'there's many a true word spoken in joke, and I know this much, he'll see his day yet with that bugger.'

On this prophecy Angus jerked his head, whether hopefully or hopelessly it was hard to tell.

A few minutes later, when Rosie had poured out the tea and they were sitting at the table amid an unusual silence, she remarked, 'I wonder where she's got to? She's going to find it chilly out there in the big, big world is Miss Vanessa. It'll be like being thrown in from the deep end.'

Aye, thought Angus, just like that, being thrown in from the deep end.

6

Susan's wedding was over. It had been a big affair; half the county had been there. Vanessa's absence had not been remarked upon. One thing education did, it enabled one to be tactful, at least before the parties concerned.

Jane Ratcliffe explained her daughter's absence by saying that she was on the Continent touring with friends. It was rather an inopportune time for her to be away from home, but one of the party had dropped out and Vanessa had been so anxious to go. She was very adventurous was Vanessa. And she wrote every week, such interesting letters.

The recipients of this information smiled and nodded and said how nice for Vanessa, it was what every young girl should do, travel and have experience.

Jane Ratcliffe wondered if there was double meaning behind these smiling replies. She also wondered where her daughter was. The postmarks had said London, another Brighton, another Eastbourne, one as far away as Torquay. She had been forced to show Vanessa's note and her first letter to Doctor Carr because he had become difficult. He had acted as if they had done away with her. She had become very frightened about his attitude, but Jonathan had taken care of him and they had changed their doctor.

Jonathan said he had washed his hands of Vanessa once and for all, he never wanted to see her again. She herself wasn't so adamant; after all, she was her daughter and she was so young. She still felt the matter should be placed in the hands of the police, but Jonathan went almost mad if she brought up the subject. Perhaps it was because Rowland, the Chief Constable, was a member of his club, and Jonathan thought a lot about his status in his club, yet it would reflect badly on them if Vanessa had the baby in some charity home and the fact was discovered. But she couldn't make Jonathan see this. She was at the other end of the country, he said, and let her stay there. Far better that than under their noses and consorting with that lout; at least she'd had the sense to break away from him.

The house seemed very empty now without Susan, and when Ray started boarding-school – another decision of Jonathan's – she wouldn't know what to do with herself. She would have to take up some charity work to fill in her time. The house was no great concern now, for she had been fortunate enough to get a woman equally as good as Emily, if not better. She had thought for years that the world would come to an end if ever she lost Emily, but, you see, everybody could be done without. This had proved it.

PART TWO

1

It was Rosie who first found out where Vanessa was. It happened while she and Stan were in Newcastle. They had arrived at three o'clock with the intention of looking round before going to the cinema, but they were back in Fellburn by five o'clock.

Angus was in the house but he hadn't yet changed. He had finished work at twelve and spent the hours since going over his lorry in the shed that Singleton rented as a garage. He had bought it cheap and it was acting cheap. In the last three months he had learned a great deal about the mechanics of an engine. He'd had to or go bust, for during the first week the lorry had broken down four times. He knew he had been done over his purchase, and he put it down to experience; it would all add up to knowledge when next he went lorry hunting, but by the look of things at present, he was telling himself, that would be some time ahead. Forty quid a week they could make each, Fred had said. The highest he had touched was thirty. Last week he was down to twenty-four. They both worked all the hours that God sent, but their lorries were not big enough or good enough. The business that had passed them by in the last four weeks made him literally sick, yet he knew that even with new lorries two men on their own weren't going to get very far. He wanted half-a-dozen lorries at least, and the same number of men to go with them. He also told himself he wanted the moon. At the rate he was saving now it would take him a year to buy one lorry and that second-hand. He could have got one on the never-never but he didn't want to start that. He was against hire purchase because he had seen too many of the swabs coming claiming the stuff back around the doors; no, he wanted to pay on the nail. It might be frustrating waiting, but that was what he'd have to put up with. There was another thing. Once he started the never-never business Fred would keep him at it. He was finding he had to be firm with Fred; he was too slap-dash, too easy going.

He was looking dolefully down at the exercise book in which he did his accounts when the door opened and Rosie came in, still in her out-door things. 'What do you think,' she said, excitedly. 'I've seen her.'

'You've seen who?' She could have been meaning anyone at the moment.

'Miss Van, of course.'

His face was straight as he asked, 'Where?'

'In Newcastle. Come on, come into the kitchen, I'm not going to tell it twice.' She turned about and left him, and he followed, but slowly.

'Well, go on,' said Emily. 'Where . . . where did you see her? Stop muckin' about an' tell us.'

'You'll never guess, not in a thousand years. Not her. Would they, Stan?' She looked from Stan to Angus, but Angus didn't speak, he just waited. And then she looked at her mother again and said almost gleefully, 'Servin' in a greengrocer's. A potty, dirty little greengrocer's. Wasn't she, Stan?'

184

'Not Miss Van, no!'

'Aye, Mam, MISS VAN. It was her, Stan, wasn't it?'
She looked at Stan for confirmation, and Stan nodded.
'You said it was.'

'It was.' She looked from one to the other. 'We had
just got out of the bus station and gone round by the
pig market. Stan wanted to have a look at the river and
I wanted to go and have a look at the flats, you know
where Kyle Street used to be. We were wandering about
there, and then we came to some of the streets that hadn't
been pulled down yet, old mucky places you know, worse
than anything round here.'

'Go on, get on with it,' said Emily impatiently.

'I am, Mam, I am. I'm just tellin' you, I'm givin' you
the settin'. Well, we saw this little greengrocer's, you
know, that sells everything; candles, firewood, the lot,
a real huckster shop. There was some pomegranates in
a box outside and Stan here says he wants one and I said
I'd like one an' all. It would be like being a kid again
eatin' pomegranates in the street. Well, Stan went to
the door where there was an old woman servin', and
there was a lass inside serving somebody else, an' it was
as I stood by the window that I recognised her. It was
Miss Van.'

'Couldn't be. She could get a job anywhere. She
wouldn't want to go into a huckster shop; she would
go into one of the big stores . . .'

'Mam,' said Rosie slowly and patiently, 'she couldn't
go into one of the big stores an' she wouldn't get a job
any place, not lookin' like she does . . . she's big.'

'God in heaven! Did you speak to her?'

'No, course not, I kept out of the way, she didn't know
Stan. You know I've never cottoned to her but I felt sorry
for her for a minute servin' in that bruised apple dump.'

She looked at Angus as he said, 'You could have made a mistake.'

'I'm not daft, our Angus; I know her as well as you do.'

'Where did you say the shop was?'

'I told you, where they haven't started pullin' down yet. I don't know what the name of the street was. Do you, Stan?'

Stan shook his head, then said, 'No; but I remember that it was near Murphy Street and it was the end one. There was a big open space filled with rubble behind it.' He added, 'I've heard a lot about her but I'd never seen her afore. She's a good-lookin' piece, even if she's – '

'Watch it! Watch it!' Rosie dug him hard in the ribs and they both laughed; but Emily and Angus didn't join in.

'You goin' to the club, our Angus?' Rosie now asked, and he answered, 'Aye, I might as well. But I'm goin' down to the baths first.'

'You were there last night.' Rosie's voice was high.

'Aye, well. And I'm goin' the night again.' His tone said, 'What you trying to make of it?' He stared at her for a minute before he turned away and went into his room, and Emily, now bending towards Rosie, whispered thickly, 'You shouldn't have let on.'

'Let on?' She screwed up her face at her mother. 'What do you mean?'

Her voice lower still, Emily said, 'Don't be a stupid bugger; about Miss Van.'

'Why not for?' Rosie was whispering back.

'Because it's ten to one if she's in a plight he'll do somethin'.'

'Don't be so daft, Mam.' Rosie pulled her chin to her neck. 'And him being accused of droppin' her. He's not barmy altogether.'

'You don't know him like I do, and he is barmy about some things. If he wasn't barmy he would have married May years ago.'

Rosie now turned her head slowly and looked towards the front-room door and she asked under her breath, 'You mean . . . you mean he's been struck with her?' Her tone was incredulous, and her mother whispered sharply, 'I mean no such thing, he knows his place, but, as I said, if she was in a fix he could be sorry for her an' want to do somethin'. He's not barmy you say, an' I say he's bloody well barmy in some ways.'

During the next week Angus came home every night about the usual time. He would have a wash in the sink or take his soap and towel and go down to the public baths three streets away. It all depended on what he had been loading during the day. Monday night he stayed indoors; Tuesday night he went to the club – Stan gave Rosie this information the following day – Wednesday night he stayed at home again; Thursday night he went to the pictures, and on Friday night he was going to the dogs. But on Friday afternoon he took his lorry into Newcastle.

He found Murphy Street and parked the lorry near a mound of rubble. Dusting down his coat and adjusting his cap he went up the first street and found the huckster shop. There were pomegranates in a box outside, and onions and soft tomatoes. He looked through the window but could see only an oldish woman. He bit tight on his lip before he entered the shop and the oldish woman said, 'What can I get you?'

'I'll have a pound of apples, please.'

As she went to weigh the apples he looked towards the

little back shop but could see or hear no one. 'You've got a young lady helping you?' he asked.

Her eyes narrowed and she peered up at him without speaking, and he said, 'Haven't you?'

'What business is it of yours?'

'It happens that I know her. Can I have a word with her?' He looked towards the back shop again, and she said, 'She's not here, she's off bad.'

'Bad?'

'Aye, that's what I said, bad.'

'You . . . you mean the baby, it's . . .'

'No, I don't mean the baby, it's not due yet. You know about that, but I don't suppose . . .' She looked him up and down and didn't finish, but he finished for her. 'That it could be me. That's what you mean, isn't it?'

'I didn't say nowt of the sort.'

'You didn't need to. Where's she livin'?'

'Why should I tell you that?'

He stared at her and decided to tell her the truth, for her sort could keep mum and he'd have had his journey for nothing, and another night of thinking ahead of him. 'Well you see the truth is me mother used to work for her family and she's been worried since she ran away.'

'And so you want to go back and tell her where she's living so she can carry it to the lass's folks?'

'Nothin' of the sort. Me mother doesn't work for them any more and she's no intention of letting on about her. I just want to see her and have a word with her.'

The woman stared at him again, then said, 'It's funny you findin' her; her people haven't done much searchin'. I don't know what kind of folks they are to let her be on her own, an' her in her state. She's nowt more than a

188

bairn herself and no more fit to be left on her own than a new bride in a barracks.'

He hadn't heard that one before. He must remember that one – A new bride in a barracks.

'It's a good job she stumbled on Nell Crawford's house when looking for a room; if she had got in some places I could speak of, even in her condition, she'd have been eaten alive. But Nell's is all right, an' clean.'

'Where's this Nell Crawford's?' he said.

The woman moved her head impatiently. He had only to go out into the street, she said, and ask to be directed to Nell Crawford's and anybody in this district would show him the way. 'It's 132 Batterby Bay Road,' she said.

Batterby Bay Road! God! Of all the places she could have landed in she had to land in Batterby Bay Road. Nell Crawford, whoever she was, might run a clean house but, if she was in Batterby Bay Road, he'd like to bet his life it was the only one there. He said 'Thanks' and turned on his heel, and when she said, 'You haven't paid for the apples,' he said, 'Oh, I'm sorry. How much?'

'One and fourpence.'

He gave her the money and went out of the shop and he sat in the cab of his lorry for a few minutes biting on his lip. Batterby Bay Road! Good God! They made them in Batterby Bay Road; it was a training school for them. He'd first walked down Batterby Bay Road when he was fifteen. It was on a Saturday night, and he and three mates had come into Newcastle and had dared each other to go down the road.

They had gone down it, but they had come out the other end quicker than they had entered it. They had thought they were great guys to go down Batterby Bay Road and had bragged about it for weeks afterwards, but each one of them had been scared stiff by the tarts.

Tarts of all types, tall and short, young, middle-aged and old 'uns. Not one of them had started yet. Talked about it never-ending, but never got down to it, and, all the opportunity in the world offered them, they didn't that night either.

He took the lorry right to the door of number 132. It was a tall, double-fronted terraced house. It had undoubtedly at one time been the home of a middle-class family. Now its ten rooms had ten separate occupants. Their names were on dirty pieces of paper pinned on a board inside the dim hallway; even the paper bearing the name V. Ratcliffe was thumb-marked. There was a glass door leading out of the lobby, but he found it locked. Looking to the side he saw a bell. He did not hear it ring, but after a few minutes there came the sound of footsteps on the other side of the door, and as it was opened a voice said, 'Haven't you got your key?'

The woman stared up at Angus and added, 'Oh, what do you want? I'm full up.'

'I've come to see a Miss Ratcliffe.'

She was now looking at him in the same way as the woman in the greengrocer's shop. Then she said, 'Ee'. You have, have ya. And what would you be wantin' with her?'

'That's my business.' He stepped towards the door with the intention of entering, but her thin arms checked him with a force that was surprising.

'Don't rush it, lad. Don't rush it. And let me tell you somethin'. If you're after anythin' you've come to the wrong shop.'

He closed his eyes for a second and turned his head to the side, then said, 'Look Missus, what I want is to have a word with Miss Ratcliffe. I happen to know her. Will you tell her that Angus Cotton is here?'

She wagged her head in small movements and her lids blinked over her round black eyes; then she said, 'I'm not deaf. Stay where you are.'

As she mounted the stairs he watched her, and when she was half up them she turned and looked down at him, scrutinising him from head to foot as if she couldn't make him out. Then she continued on her way.

It was a full five minutes before she returned and her manner was unchanged. She said briefly, 'It's the top floor, number eight. And you'd better mind your head on the ceiling on the top flight.'

He was glad she had warned him about the ceiling. The third flight of stairs was dark and he had almost to grope his way up them. The top landing was lit by a fanlight in the roof and the door to the left of him was marked number eight.

He was again nipping his lip as he knocked on the door. After a moment it was opened and she was standing looking at him. She was wearing a loose kind of dressing-gown and he reckoned she must have just got out of bed. Her face, as his mother had once described it, looked all eyes and teeth. He had always thought he had never seen hair the colour of hers, a real chestnut with a gleam of dark red in it. There was no gleam in it today, it was dull and lank. When her lips began to tremble he said, 'Hello, Van.'

'He-llo, Angus.' She gulped on his name. Then standing aside, she said, 'Wo . . . n't you come in?'

He walked into the attic room and tried not to notice how it looked, but his immediate impression made him compare it with the home she had left, and he thought, it's unbelievable! His own home left a lot to be desired, but it was Buckingham Palace compared to this. There was a narrow iron bed under the sloping roof, there was one chair and a small square deal table; there was a hanging wardrobe attached to the ceiling at its highest point near the little four-paned window, and beside a much-battered chest of drawers there stood on the floor a tin tray, on which was a gas-ring and a kettle. When he turned and looked at her she dropped her head and said below her breath, 'Don't say it, Angus. Don't say it.' Then her head still bowed, she said, 'Won't you sit down?' She motioned towards the chair; at the same time she sat down on the foot of the bed.

When he was seated he dropped his hands between his knees and tried to think of something to say, but found it impossible. Of the two, she seemed more in control of the situation. 'How is Emily?' she asked.

Even now he couldn't answer her right away; then after a moment he said, 'Oh, she's fine.'

'Has . . . has she got a new job?'

'No, no. I don't want her to go out any more; she's done enough.'

'Yes, of course.'

There was silence between them again, and in the silence the smell of the place filled his nostrils. The air was dank, dirty, thick. He imagined that the walls were impregnated with muck. He longed to turn round and throw the window open, but the room was chilly. His eyes moved about, looking for a means of heating, and then he saw a tiny gas-fire by the wall at the head of the bed.

When they both broke the silence together he smiled and nodded at her, giving her place, and she said, 'I was going to ask where you are working now.'

'Oh.' He straightened his back against the chair, 'I'm on me own, I'm me own boss. I'm in partnership with a fellow called Singleton. Haulage, you know, contracting.

It's working out fine.' He wanted to assure her about that at least.

'Oh, I'm glad, Angus.' Her head drooped for a moment before she raised her eyes to his again and said, 'I'm . . . I'm sorry, Angus, about the trouble I brought on you and the others.'

'Oh, you've got no need to worry about that. If that's all you're worried about you can put your mind at rest. It did us both a good turn. I mean me mam and me. It set me up on me own, and mam's a new woman now she's had a rest.'

'I'm glad,' she said again.

Now his face became straight and he stared at her blankly for a moment before asking, 'And what about you?'

When she made no reply he leant slightly forward and said under his breath, 'This is no place for you, Van. Why don't you go home?'

'No! I'll never do that, Angus.'

'But why? They're your people.'

She looked at him for a time before saying, 'Yes, they're my people. And if I'd gone on the streets they couldn't have treated me worse. They were terrified, really terrified, about me having the baby. Not because of what it might do to me, but because of the effect it would have on their prestige. You see . . . Father was determined that I got rid of it, and, and I didn't want to.' There was a firmness in her voice that hadn't been there before.

'Well, you know I think he was right. I do. I don't hold with a damn thing he's ever done or said, in fact I might as well tell you I hate his guts, but on that score I think he was right. You could have started again.' She was looking downwards, and he stumbled on, 'You know what I mean. You're young, you would have forgotten all about this, and they would have stood by you and seen you all right.'

She was gazing into his face now and there was a deep bitterness in her voice as she said, 'They would have stood by me, but how? They intended that after I came out of the clinic in London I should stay indefinitely with a great-aunt in Scotland. She lives miles and miles off the beaten track. She has an old couple who look after her. They are over seventy. There's nobody young within miles. The minister visits them on Sunday and they have prayers. He's made a special journey out to her for years hoping that when she dies he'll be taken care of. They haven't a car. There's one taxi down in the village, and that's miles away. I was there last year for a week . . . Mother, too, wants to be remembered in her will.' Her tone was cynical now. 'So I was packed off there as a sort of insurance premium to be raked off later. After two days I thought I would go mad.'

As Angus listened to her talking in a way that surprised him he realised that, although she still looked very young, the girl he had known was gone. But then that was to be expected; the girl would have ceased to be when she started the bairn. It was as his mother said, he was barmy in some ways. Into the silence that had fallen on them he said, 'You've been bad, I mean ill?' and she answered, 'I caught a chill. The shop is rather draughty where I work.'

'Yes, I know.' He nodded at her.

'How . . . how did you find out?' she asked.

'I didn't, it was Rosie. They passed the place last Saturday and saw you.'

'Will . . . will she talk? What I mean is, Angus, I . . . I don't want anyone to know I'm here. You see, I write home every week and my letters go from as far away as London, Devon, and places like that. I give them to Mr Noakes. He's ... he's in number nine.' She nodded towards the door. 'He's a long-distance lorry driver. He, he posts them in London for me, and gets one of his work mates to post them some other place.'

A long-distance lorry driver, Mr Noakes. And what did Mr Noakes expect for his kind service? Long-distance lorry drivers who picked up any slimy piece that thumbed them from the gutter. She didn't know what she was askin' for. Doubtless Mr Noakes would one day inform her. After the bairn was born likely, if not afore; it all depended on how desperate was his need.

She seemed to sense his reaction to what she had just told him and she said, 'He's a very nice man, kind, oldish.' When she shuddered he said, 'You're cold, I'm keepin' you out of bed. Can't ... can't you light the fire?'

'Oh, yes. I have it on most of the time but it got a little too hot and I put it out.'

He didn't believe her, but he didn't go and light it. Instead, he said, 'Where do you eat?'

'I usually have my lunch in a café in the town and bring something in for an evening meal. I manage all right.'

'Van.' He got to his feet. 'I've got to be going now, I've got a load waiting for me,' he nodded towards the window, 'but I'd like to come and see you again. Can I?'

She shook her head slowly, then said, 'No, Angus. I don't think it would be right. If they ever found out you know what they'd say; they would put – '

'Aye, I know what they'd say, and what they would put together. Well, they would be bloody well wrong, wouldn't they?' He lowered his head and said, 'I'm sorry.' When he looked at her she was smiling slightly, the first time the muscles of her face had moved upwards since he saw her, and she said quietly, 'Don't apologise; I've enlarged my vocabulary quite a bit in the last few months. It, it isn't that I don't want to see you, Angus, it's been wonderful seeing you but, but I don't want to cause any more trouble, and you know it would only lead to – '

'Well,' he said briskly, 'let me deal with the trouble and whatever it leads to. Now look. You get back into bed and I'll call later on and bring something back for you to eat. And in the meantime you tell that one downstairs that my intentions are honourable.' He felt he had said the wrong thing, and he blustered, 'Well, I've got to go. There'll be so much ballast waitin' at yon end they'll have me scalped. I'll be seein' you. Now get back into bed. I can't say what time, after six though. Aye, it'll be well after six.'

She was standing at the foot of the bed holding the iron rail with both hands, and she said softly, 'Good-bye, Angus.'

He forgot about the ceiling as he went down the stairs and cursed as he hit his head; then he took the other flights two at a time.

He had already lost two loads but he finished early, parked the lorry in the garage, then went straight to the baths, where he hired a towel and soap. He reached home at five-thirty, and sat down immediately to his tea.

'Aren't you going to have a wash?' said Emily.

'Don't I look clean?' He turned his head towards her. 'I had a bath afore I came in.'

Ten minutes later when the room door closed on him, Rosie said, 'Him and his baths, he'll wash himself away! In the end it would be cheaper to put one in the washhouse. He said that years ago, didn't he?'

'Where's he off to in this rush?' asked Emily under her breath. 'The dogs don't start afore eight.'

'Why don't you ask him?'

Ten minutes later, when he came out of the room, Emily did ask him. Casually she said, 'Where you off to, lad?' and he answered without blinking, 'I'm goin' along to see a fellow about a lorry. This one's drivin' me up the wall; it only goes when it's pushed.'

'A lorry?' Emily's brows gathered suspiciously. 'You never mentioned it afore.'

'I couldn't, I only heard of it this afternoon. A fellow on the site told me I might pick up one cheap.'

'The other one was cheap, and look what it's brought you.'

'Well, I've got me eyes open this time. Be seein' you.' As he went out of the front door he knew that they would both be looking at each other and wondering. Well, he would let them wonder for a little while until he knew what he was going to do. He'd have to do something, but what he wasn't sure. Well, not really.

2

This was his sixth visit to number 132 Batterby Bay Road, and he brought with him, on this occasion, two bags of fish and chips, two half-pint bottles of pale ale, a sliced loaf, a half-pound of Danish butter, and half a pound of cheese. It was Monday and she had started work today.

He knocked on the door and entered when she said, 'Come in.' He hadn't seen her since Friday night and he had worked late on Saturday to make up for lost time, and then to allay his mother's suspicions he had gone to the club as usual; and yesterday he had made himself lie in, after which he had followed the usual Sunday routine. He had gone along to the pub for a couple of pints with Stan, and they had come back, had their dinner and, when his mother had gone upstairs to put her feet up, he had left the kitchen to Rosie and Stan and gone and lain down on his bed; and in the evening they had all gone to the club again, for as his mother had said it was often better on a Sunday night than it was on a Saturday. But here he was, here he was where his thoughts had been every minute during this last week and all the week-end.

He stared at her. She was looking different. She was no longer wearing the slack dressing-gown thing but had on a brown woollen dress that hadn't been cut for maternity.

It was evident that she hadn't expected him so soon, because when he entered the room she was going towards the wardrobe, and he watched her take the dressing-gown from it. When she was about to put it on he said quietly, 'Leave that off.' She turned a surprised look towards him, and as he dropped his purchases upon the table he added, 'You don't have to hide yourself.'

When he turned towards her she was standing in much the same attitude as her mother was wont to do, she was cupping her cheeks with her hands. 'Oh, Angus!' she said, and to this he replied brusquely, 'Never mind "oh Angus"! Get those plates out and let's have this while it's hot. I got skate. I don't know whether you like skate or not, I like it.'

She had never tasted skate; she couldn't remember having it at home, but she said, 'Yes, I like skate.' So deep was her gratitude to him that if he had brought in fried dog she would have eaten it. She brought a dinner-plate and a tea-plate to the table; the smaller one she set before herself, and he said, 'You'll have to sport another meal-size plate, eh?'

'Yes, I must get another plate. She doesn't provide for visitors.'

'She doesn't provide for boarders, if you ask me.' He looked disdainfully round the room.

'It's better than some, Angus.'

He paused with a chip to his mouth, saying, 'You're kiddin'.'

'No, I'm not. There was a place farther down the street. It was terrible, dreadful. And at least the people in this house work.'

'Well, didn't the people in that house?' He was quizzing her.

'Yes.' She had her eyes cast downwards. 'Yes, I suppose so, work of a kind.'

'Aye, of a kind,' he repeated. Then turning the conversation abruptly, he added, 'We're goin' out.'

'What!'

'You heard what I said.' He poked his big face towards her. 'We're goin' out.'

'No, Angus, no. What if we were seen together?'

'You frightened?' He placed his knife and fork down on the table, and she was quick to assure him, 'Oh, not that way, Angus. Not what you mean, no, but I'm frightened that someone might see us and tell Father, and if he saw us together then nothing on earth would convince him but that – '

'Look, Van. Get it into your head he's convinced already. God Almighty steppin' out of Heaven wouldn't convince him otherwise. I told you he came to the house when you ran off, and although he believed you weren't there at that minute he believed that I knew where you were. I'm sure of it.'

'Well, I don't want to prove him right, Angus.'

'Now let's get this straight, Van. You can't stay in this place for ever, you can't come from that stinkin' little shop and bury yourself under this roof seven nights a week until the bairn's born. And that's another point. We've got to talk about this . . . It's no use sticking your head in the sand.' He looked at her downcast face. 'What's going to happen when it's born? You goin' to have it adopted?' He waited, and after a while she said, 'I . . . I suppose I should, yet I don't know. I keep thinking first one way then another. It seems stupid having gone through all this then letting it be adopted. If that's what

200

I'm going to do I think it would have been simpler to have done what they wanted in the first place . . .'

'Aye, it would,' he put in. 'As I said, that's one thing him and me agree on, it would. It would have saved you a lot of trouble and worry, because as it is, you know yourself, you can't keep it. Now where could you keep a bairn here? You could hump him along to the shop and put him in a basket out at the back. That's easy fixed, it's been done afore. I spent me early years in a clothes basket in people's wash-houses when me mother went out doin' a day's washin'; under the table in different kitchens when she went out cleanin'; and once, she tells me, I spent three weeks in a hen cree. The old dear she worked for couldn't stand bairns, and there was an empty hen cree at the bottom of the garden, and there me mother used to dump me.' He was smiling now. 'So you see you could manage that part, that would be easy. But this here house is the problem. You'd have to hump up water from the next landing, and take it down again and empty it. And, you must remember, a bairn needs a lot of water.' He almost added, 'And makes a lot an' all,' but refrained. 'You've got some thinkin' to do about this, Van.'

She kept her head lowered as she said, 'I do nothing else but think.'

'Is there nobody you could go to? I mean, none of your relations or friends?'

'Not one of them who wouldn't be embarrassed to see me and who wouldn't immediately get in touch with Father.' Now she raised her eyes to his and said quietly, 'But I'll manage. I've got this far and I'll manage.'

'Manage be damned!' He jerked his head – he had ceased to apologise to her for swearing. 'You're only at the beginning of it, an' what's more you know nothin' about bairns. By the way, have you made arrangements about having it?'

'Yes, yes, I've done that.'

'Do you go to a clinic, or one of them places?'

'No, I went once, but there were so many people there I . . . was afraid someone might see me.'

'But you can't hide away for ever.'

'I . . . I'm not going to. It's just till it's born, and then the thing will be done and he can't do anything about it.'

'Only press you to get it adopted. That's the tack he'll take then.'

'No, I don't think he would do that. I don't think he ever wants to see me again. I think he'd show me the door if I did go home.'

'How did your mother react to it?'

'She is guided by Father, she always has been.'

He rose from the chair and walked down the middle of the attic. He had to keep in the middle to prevent bumping his head. And he walked the length of the room twice before he spoke again, and then he had his back to her as he asked, 'The fellow. Couldn't he marry you?'

He waited for her to answer, and when none was forthcoming he turned and looked at her. She was sitting staring down at her hands resting on the mound of her stomach, and he went to her now and, dropping on his hunkers before her, he put his hand under her chin and pushed it upwards and asked again, 'Couldn't he?'

'No.' She shook her head.

'Why?'

'It's . . . it's impossible.'

'Nothing's impossible.'

'That is.'

They stared at each other for a moment. Then he rose to his feet and, drawing in a deep breath, said flatly, 'Well, you can't go on like this, you just can't.'

'Other girls do. They survive.'

'Aye, but other girls aren't like you.'

'You'd be surprised. I've seen girls at the clinic. The look in their eyes. You can tell us. Oh, you'd be surprised.'

'Nothin' surprises me, Van. And anyway, I'm not concerned what happens to other girls, I'm just concerned at the moment at what's gonna happen to you.'

She was staring up at him, and slowly her face crumpled; then her body bent forward and she was sobbing into her hands.

When his arms went about her and his hands felt her shoulder blades under her dress his own body stiffened against the touch of her. But only for a moment; then he was clasping her tightly and saying, 'There now, there now. It's all right.' But the more he soothed her the more she cried. 'Look.' He brought her damp hair from her brow and face. 'Don't carry on like that, it'll only upset you. An' the bairn as well. Come on, come on, stop it. Give over. Look, give over.'

But she couldn't stop, she couldn't give over. She had cried before, she had cried night after night when she had first come to this room, but it wasn't this kind of crying. This was a deluge of weeping; the force of it was a hurricane shaking her body. He became worried, not only for her, but that at any moment one of them across the landing would come to the door. That bloke Noakes, whom he had met once and whose age and manner had allayed any suspicions he had had of him, but who in his turn might be thinking her visitor was up to something. He implored her now, 'Van! Van! Don't. Aw, don't.'

203

He led her to the edge of the bed and, pressing her backwards, he said, 'There, there, lie down.'

She was lying on her side now, her face covered with her hands, and he knelt by the bed and held her wrists, and he wished his mother was here – his mother would have known what to do. If she went on like this she'd really be ill. She wasn't only crying, it was more like hysteria. The cure for hysteria, he had read, was a good slap along the lug; well, he couldn't administer that kind of shock treatment, but he could give her a shock. Aye, it was one way to do it.

He had wondered all the week-end how he would put it over and what her reaction would be. Well, now was the opportune time to try it out. He pulled her hands roughly from her face and putting his own down close to hers he said firmly, 'Listen, Van. Listen to what I'm going to say to you. Now listen . . . Will you marry me?'

It worked. After a few minutes her sobs turned to intermittent shudders, and then she was staring at him. Her breath still coming in gasps, her eyes puckered, she was staring into his face. Then stammering, she asked, 'W . . . what did you s . . . say?'

'You heard what I said all right, but I'll say it again. Will you marry me? Under ordinary circumstances this could never have happened, you know it, and I know it, but you're not livin' under ordinary circumstances, are you? That's not sayin' what I've got to offer you is a piece of cake, God knows it's far from it, but . . . but it would get you out of this. And I'll have you off me mind sort of, not worryin' every hour of the day what's happening to you in this warren of pimps and whores. Our house is not a palace, you might think it's a slum, but God, it's better than this, and you'll have me mum to see to you. What about it?'

'Oh, Angus, Angus.' Her face crumpled again, and he shook her hands roughly, saying harshly under his breath, 'Now don't start that again, you'll make yourself bad.'

She was biting down on her lip as he said, 'Think about it. I don't want yes or no now, just think about it. But as I see it, when you're drowning in the deep sea you don't turn your nose up at a floating plank.'

She tugged her hands from his and again her face was covered, and again she was crying, but quietly, and he stood up now and walked to the table, and from there, with his back to her, he said, 'I know it'll be a big comedown for you. I might be looked on as a bit of a catch round our quarter, but from the place where you're standin' I'm less than the dust beneath thy chariot wheels, sort of, an' if you did decide to come to our place,' he didn't say 'to marry me,' now, 'you'd have to stand the racket. And it would hit you from a good many sides. You'd be livin' atween the devil and the deep sea. Your own folks wouldn't own you ever again, so you've got to think on that, and my kind would be suspicious. So I'm warnin' you, do a bit of thinkin' about it. I'll be back the morrow night. But mind, don't think I'm blackmailing you or anything like that, for if you do say no you haven't seen the last of me.'

When he turned to her, she was sitting up, leaning wearily against the iron rails of the bed. He came and looked down at her and he put out his hand and lightly took the hair from behind one ear, and as he touched her the tears welled in her eyes again, and he said brusquely, 'Now, now, stop it. I'm off. Well, you have it. Chew on it. I'll see you the morrow night.' As he reached the door he turned to her and said, 'Think hard; it's usually for life.'

When he reached the bottom of the stairs he stood in

the darkness and wiped the sweat from his face. God! Where in hell's name had he got the nerve from. And if she said no, what then? Aye, what then? He knew what then. His self-esteem would never rise to the surface again. He would shout louder, bluster more and belly laugh at every opportunity, but under his skin he'd be grovelling in the deep, deep chasm that held his self-disdain.

He didn't go straight home but called in a pub and had a double whisky. When he reached the house there was only his mother in and he was glad of this.

She greeted him rather tersely as he threw off his hat and coat, and when he took his seat opposite her at the side of the fireplace she looked at him and waited. In a way she knew what was coming, but still wouldn't believe it.

'I've been to see Van, Mum,' he said.

'Tell me somethin' I don't know,' she answered; then went on looking at a magazine she had been reading.

'Now, look!' He pointed his index finger at her as if it was a gun. 'Don't you start.'

'You're a bloody fool.' She was on her feet, and he cried back at her, 'Aye, I know I'm a bloody fool. But I'm not the first, an' I won't be the last. Are you going to listen to me or not?'

She walked over to the dresser and snatched up a cup and saucer from the rack; then coming to the fire and lifting up a brown teapot that had been standing on the hob for the past hour she returned to the table and poured herself out a cup of tea that looked like tar.

'I'm askin' you.' He, too, was standing now, leaning on the table looking down at her, 'Are you goin' to listen me out?'

'I haven't much choice, have I? I have to listen you out apparently whether I like it or not.'

He bowed his head and fought to control his temper. Then, his voice deep in his throat, he said, 'She's in a frightful state, Mam. Rosie saw where she's workin'. That's bad enough. But if you saw the house where she's livin', you wouldn't believe it; you just wouldn't, Mam.'

'Whose fault is that?'

'We're not talkin' about faults or blame or anythin' else. By the way, I thought you liked her; I thought you liked her the best of the bunch.'

'Aye, I liked her, but I don't like the idea of you gettin' yourself mixed up with her. You got blamed for somethin' you didn't do, and now you're walkin' right into their hands. Do you think anybody would believe that you're not the father now?'

'Do you know somethin'?' His voice was deceptively low. 'I don't care a monkey's cuss what anybody believes. They'll believe what they like in any case, no matter what you say, or I say, or God Almighty says, but I would have thought that you might have had a different attitude, especially under the circumstances.'

'What did you expect? The old family retainer with the heart of gold? . . . Well,' she leant towards him and thumbed her chest, 'that isn't a picture of me. Charity begins at home. What charity I have is needed here. As for her, she should be in her own home, an' gettin' charity there.'

'Well, she thinks different, Mam. And so do I.'

'You do, do you?'

'Aye, I do.'

'And what can you do about it, do you think, except make a bloody fool of yourself?'

'It isn't what I can do about it, Mam, it's what I'm goin' to do. Bloody fool or not.'

She stared fixedly at him before she asked, 'You're goin' to live with her then?'

'Live with her!' He sounded slightly shocked. 'No I'm not going to live with her, I'm going to marry her.' He didn't add now, 'If she'll have me.'

'Christ Almighty!' Slowly she subsided back into her chair. After all, she hadn't expected this. She had expected him to say he was going to look after her or some such damn silly thing. She had even expected him to ask if she could come here to be looked after. Aye, that's what she had expected. But, marry her! Her son, Angus Cotton, marry the daughter of Affleck and Tate's manager! Jonathan Ratcliffe's daughter. He was stark, staring, bloody mad, and she said that to him. 'You're stark, staring, bloody mad. You don't know what you're talkin' about. You! You goin' to marry Miss Vanessa Ratcliffe? Aw, lad!' she shook her head slowly at him while she smiled mirthlessly.

'Not so much of the aw lad. What's wrong with me, anyway? Oh, I know I haven't had an education to match hers, but who's fault is that? It isn't mine. But it's not too late. An' what the hell does education matter after all? It's money that counts, money that sets you up. When you have money you get things, an' they change you. I've seen it.'

'Shut up.' Her voice was quiet.

'Look!' He almost pounced on her. 'Don't tell me to shut up, Mam. An' listen to me. I'm goin' to make money, I'm goin' to change – '

'So can a leopard.' She was scornful.

'My God!' He was standing straight now, taut. 'That's what you think of me, worse than them, and you me own, with the scorn drippin' from your lips.'

She looked at him pityingly now. 'Aye, that's what I

think of you, lad, when you're aimin' at her. I wanted you to rise, I wanted you to rise in Affleck's. I stayed on up there for years just so that it would give you the chance. But I knew how far you could go. You see, I'm of two worlds meself. I've lived up there the best part of eighteen year. You could say it hasn't brushed off on me, an' you'd be right, yet inside I know what's what; I know that oil an' water don't mix. And you and she are oil an' water. And I'm goin' to tell you frankly to your face, lad, that if she's marryin' you she must be pretty desperate.'

He swallowed the truth hard. He gulped on it. His lips worked one over the other until there was no saliva left on them. And then he said quietly, 'That's it, Mam; she's pretty desperate. You've said it. You've said a mouthful, haven't you? But look you here.' His voice was almost gentle now and his movements, when he bent towards her, had no aggressiveness about them, he was just making a plain statement. 'I'll surprise you one day. I'll let you see. I'll let you see as well as the rest. From you up to Ratcliffe, I'll let you see. That's a promise, and whatever else I do, or don't do, you know once given I keep me word.'

She reached out and picked up the cup of black tea again and as she stirred it she said, her voice as quiet as his now, 'There'll be nobody more pleased than me, lad, if you bring it off.'

'If I bring it off! But I haven't got a chance in hell. That's what you're thinkin', isn't it?'

She looked at him and her voice still quiet, she asked, 'Where do you intend to live?'

'Here. Where else? Here.'

'Aw no! No!' Her voice was a roar. 'You couldn't. Where do you think she's goin' to live in here?'

209

'There's my room; it's big enough for two.'

'But, lad . . . Aw,' she was pleading with him now, 'what do you think my life is goin' to be like? If you and her are oil and water don't forget I'm on the same side as you. You'll leave her in the mornin' and I'll have her all day. No, no.' She shook her head slowly, slowly and widely as she gazed at him standing silent now. And she waited for him to speak; and when he did he said, 'And where else could I take her? I can't run two houses, and I'm not leavin' you. As bloody bitchy as you've been, I'm not leavin' you, Mam. You know I wouldn't.'

'Look.' She waved her hand at him. 'You can leave me any day you like, lad. I can fend for meself; I've still got a pair of hands.'

'Aye, and a pair of feet that won't carry you much longer.' He looked down at her still swollen legs. 'Anyway, I'm not taking her anywhere else, I'm bringin' her here.' His voice was gritty again. 'An' she's stayin' here until I can make other arrangements, arrangements that's goin' to suit both you and her, and me.' He thumbed his chest on the 'me'. 'Then we'll talk about it.' As he turned from her she said helplessly, 'Have you thought about our Rosie? She'll go mad. She never cared for her.'

He stood in the kitchen doorway and, looking back at her, said, 'That's a pity for Rosie. Anyway, she's got Stan. It's about time she was married.'

As he turned to go into his room she flung one last missile at him. 'What about May?' she cried. 'What about May?'

He turned again to her and said deeply and bitterly, 'To hell with May. To hell with her and everybody else.'

When his door banged she cried at it, 'You've played her dirty. She served your purpose for years and you've played her dirty. You'll pay for it, lad, you'll pay for it; you can't get away with those things.' Then, turning to the fire, she raised her hands and gripped the high mantelpiece and stood staring down on to the flickering coals. Her world had been shattered into smithereens. She wished she was dead.

3

It was three days later that Angus went to see Doctor Carr. He was the only person he knew who was in sympathy with Vanessa and who might be able to advise him on how to go about getting married legally without her parents' consent.

He had been to the reference library and looked up books on Common Law, but had found nothing to enlighten him about a matter of this kind, and he didn't want to go to a minister until he knew where he stood. He would, he told himself, feel embarrassed as it was, going to a parson, as he'd never put his foot inside a church since he was christened.

Doctor Carr's eyes were whisky hazed as he looked across his desk at Angus, but nevertheless he listened intently to him. His interest had been caught from the moment the young fellow had mentioned the Ratcliffe girl, and he was both astonished and absolutely tickled pink when he heard what he intended to do. Lord, but wouldn't this hit Jonathan Ratcliffe where it hurt most. The situation gave him a feeling of glee never engendered by the whisky, without which he was finding, more and more, he was unable to get through a day's work. But before he advised the young fellow what to do he would ask him a question. He asked it bluntly. 'You the father of her child?' he said.

'No, I'm not.' The answer was equally blunt.

'Oh, well, you know you'll get the blame for it when you marry her?'

'That doesn't matter to me.'

Doctor Carr surveyed Emily Cotton's son. He was a good-looking fellow in a way, well made, tough looking, but working class written all over him. It was a pity he wasn't her type. He said, 'I think it's like this. You'd have to have their consent to a register office marriage, but if your banns are called three times at your parish church and nobody raises any objection the marriage can go ahead, and it's legal. I think that's one set-up. It's a bit tricky but it's been done. Anyway there's always the court. You present him with that alternative and if I know Ratcliffe he'll soon sign because in her condition the verdict would be a foregone conclusion. Which parish are you in?' He asked the question of himself. 'Oh, you must be in St. Edward's. You frequent any church?'

'No.'

'Have you ever?'

'No.'

'Where were you christened?'

'I think it was St. Edward's. I don't know but my mother will.'

'Well now, if I know anything about St. Edward's, it's dying on its feet, and but for a few old dears that go there the place is almost empty. I don't think the name Ratcliffe will have any significance for them. It's worth trying. I advise you to go and see the minister. He's like his church, very old, and he mumbles, which is another good thing in your favour. Take her along with you. You'll both look like an ordinary couple doing the usual thing.' He got to his feet and came round the desk, and when he was confronting Angus, he said, 'And good luck to you.' He didn't add 'You'll need it'; that went without saying.

The following evening Angus brought Vanessa in the lorry to the vicarage, and in a musty, dim lit room he asked that the banns for their marriage should be put up. The old man repeated her name twice. 'Ratcliffe. Ratcliffe,' then he peered at her and said, 'Hm! Hm! You will want your birth certificate and your parents' consent.' They couldn't be sure if he recognised her or not. Angus had the idea that he might not be as old and doddery as he looked.

When they came out Vanessa had her head buried deep in her coat collar. She seemed afraid to look up; or, he wondered, was she ashamed to. He hoisted her up into the cab and then he drove her home to Ryder's Row.

Again there was only Emily in the house. Rosie had refused point-blank to meet her future sister-in-law; there was nobody going to look down her nose at her, not if she could help it. Although Emily had said far better stay and get it over, she had replied, 'Not me. You might have to, but not me.' And now Emily stood self-consciously in her own kitchen looking at the girl she had practically brought up, and she saw her as a stranger. Physically she was changed. Her body naturally had filled out, not only her stomach but her face, and also naturally she looked older. Emily also saw that the girl had entirely gone. Here was a lass, a lass in a jam, and the jam had made her calculating. That was how she saw Vanessa now, and in consequence the feeling she gave out was one of resentment.

'Well, Mam; here we are.' Angus looked at Emily, then turned to Vanessa and said, 'Sit down, sit yourself down.' But Vanessa did not sit down, she stared back at Emily and said softly, 'Hello, Emily.'

'Hello.' There was no Miss Van now, not even Van.

Angus sensed that the situation was going to be more awkward than he had bargained for, and the best thing he could do was to leave them alone for a while, so loudly he exclaimed, 'Look. I'm as hungry as a hunter; I'll slip along and get some fish. All right?' He cast his glance down at Vanessa, and she nodded at him and tried to smile, for he was, she knew, doing his best to help matters along.

They sat silent for a long time after the door had banged, before Vanessa said softly, 'I'm sorry, Emily.'

'Aye. An' you've reason to be; you've brought a lot of trouble on a lot of people.' She moved about the kitchen before she went on, 'And if he isn't the father why are you marryin' him?'

'Be . . . because I like Angus and because he wanted me to marry him.'

'You like him!' Emily stopped and, turning, faced Vanessa. 'Lots of people like him. Likin' him isn't enough, it'll be for life. You know likin' isn't enough if he's goin' to look after your bairn and give you some of his own. You don't get by just on likin'. But you've got a thousand and one obstacles in your way; I suppose you know that?'

'Yes, Emily; I know that.'

'Look round you. Look round you, lass.' She was bending towards her. 'This is where we live. This is where he lives. Come here.' She pulled Vanessa towards the front room and, thrusting open the door and switching on the light, she said, 'This is his room. That will be your room. Look at it.'

Vanessa looked. Compared to the one she had just left it could be termed a palace.

215

'We're cramped for space as it is, but just imagine, with you and the bairn here . . . And there's another thing I'll tell you.' She turned her about and, pulling her almost roughly into the middle of the kitchen again and pointing to another door, said, 'That's the scullery in there. Talk about swinging a cat. Two of us can only just get in together. And beyond that is the door leading into the yard, and at the bottom is the lav. Not the loo here, the lav. Sick or well, wet or fine, you go down the yard to the lav, or do it in your room and have it under the bed. This is the way some folks still have to live.'

Vanessa closed her eyes and Emily, letting go of her arm, thrust herself around and said, 'I'm puttin' it plainly to you; I'm lettin' you see what you're in for. You were brought up with carpets in the lavatories, carpets in the bathrooms, powders and scents and creams, bath sprays, the lot. You're goin' to find this very different.'

Vanessa could say nothing in her own defence; there was nothing really to say; she only knew that she wanted to placate Emily. 'I've been living without all these things for some months now, Emily,' she said. 'I'll . . . I'll be quite pleased to live here if . . . if you'll have me.'

'If I'll have you?' Emily's voice was flat now and her face held a dead expression as she turned and looked at Vanessa again, 'I haven't much choice, lass, have I? I know it's my house; my name appears on the rent book, but Angus has always been the head of it since his dad died, even before, because my man was sick for years. And although I keep sayin' I can look after meself I've been on me feet too long.' She slapped her legs. 'They're lettin' me down an' they're not going to get any better. I know that. It's water. They'll get worse. All the doctor's medicine won't cure what I've got. I stood in your mother's kitchen for years just for one

216

thing, so that your father would push my lad on. And now see where it's got me. Do you know something?' Again she bent towards Vanessa. 'I just can't believe this is happenin'; I think I'm in a sort of a dream, or at the pictures. Daughter of influential man marries fitter . . . Daughter of influential man marries cook's son . . . Daughter of influential man lives in slum. An' that's what the papers 'll say when they get hold of it. At least the local one will, unless your father plonks down on them, 'cos he's got shares in that company, hasn't he?'

Vanessa said nothing. She was trying her hardest not to cry, because she knew that if she cried Angus would blame Emily. She sat down abruptly on a wooden chair near the table and, supporting her face with her hands, she muttered brokenly, 'Emily, I said I'm sorry and I am, but . . . but I'm very tired, I'm sort of lost. When . . . when Angus came that day to my room the first time, I was . . . I was thinking about finishing it all. I'd lain in that awful place for three days and the only person I'd seen was my landlady, and then only once. I wanted to die. If I'd had enough aspirins or tablets, I would have taken them. Angus was the first person who had spoken a kind word to me in weeks, except the woman whom I worked for in the greengrocer's shop; and then she was a very brusque kind of person.' She lifted her eyes and looked at Emily. She could have added, 'Just like you.'

There was silence between them again, and Emily turned to the fire and stared into it. Then after a moment she gave a deep sigh and said flatly, 'Well, what's done's done, I suppose. But it's no use sayin', lass, that I'm goin' to welcome you with open arms because I can't. And then there's our Rosie. You're goin' to put Rosie at a disadvantage.'

'Oh, no. No, I won't, Emily; I – I've always got on with Rosie.'

'You've spoken to her kindly, but she's always been tongue-tied in your presence. Think back. Has Rosie ever chatted with you like Angus has? No. There's as big a difference between Rosie and you as between him and you. Only he's got sex on his side. Oh! Oh!' She raised her hand. 'He's a man. That breaks down barriers of a sort, but not atween women, not atween lasses. You've got every advantage over my Rosie; and Rosie's no fool, she knows it.' She came now to the table and, bending down quite close to Vanessa, she asked quietly, 'It isn't his, is it?'

'No, Emily, no.'

'Well, why didn't you say who it was and get him to marry you?'

They were staring at each other, and then Vanessa said, 'I couldn't do that, Emily.'

'Does he know who it is?'

'No.'

'Do you think that's fair to him?'

Vanessa turned her gaze away, then said, 'Fair or not, I can't ever tell him.'

Emily straightened up, then walked away, saying, 'Well, you're not out of the wood yet. You know what'll happen if your father gets wind of this? He'll come storming along here again . . .'

'I don't think so, Emily. He'll close his eyes to it. I'm quite dead to them, at least him. I'm sure of that. I've just realised lately that he's always disliked me.'

At this point the door was thrust open and Angus came in carrying three paper bags, and the kitchen reeked with the smell of fish and chips.

'Haven't you got the plates warmed?' He looked at

his mother. 'What you been up to?' His voice was loud, covering the embarrassment that pervaded the three of them.

'Put them in the oven a minute,' said Emily; 'the plates won't take a tick.'

A few minutes later they were sitting at the table eating the fish and chips. At least Emily made an attempt to, but all of a sudden she got to her feet and, taking her plate and thrusting it back in the oven, she said, 'It's not ten minutes ago I had me tea, I'll have them after. I'll make a drink.' And on this she went into the scullery.

Angus looked up at Vanessa under his eyelids. She had stopped eating. He put his hand out and pressed hers; then silently he mouthed the words, 'It'll be all right.'

Fifteen minutes later they left the house, and on the journey back to Newcastle they hardly exchanged a word, and not until they were standing in her room did he ask, 'How did she take it?'

'Not very well, Angus.'

'She'll get over it; she'll come round; I know me mam.'

'It isn't fair to her. I . . . we could get a room somewhere . . .'

'We're getting no rooms anywhere, Vanessa. If you're marrying me, as I said you're comin' home; I'm not leaving her to God and good neighbours. There's too many does that the day. Round our place it's littered with old folks livin' alone. Well, she's had it hard enough. And I'm not being easy on her now; I know that, but I'm not making it worse by walking out on her. I explained it all to you . . .'

'Oh, I know, Angus, I know. I'm sorry, but I've been thinking. Is it wise to . . .?' She stared into his eyes, and after a moment he said, 'You're going to marry me. It's

219

settled, so just take things as they come, one at a time. The next hurdle you've got to get over is our Rosie. She won't be as easy as me mam, so prepare yourself . . . Well now, I'd better be gettin' back; I've got to get up early in the mornin'. I'll see you the morrow night, same time.'

He made no move towards her; all he said was, 'Tarah!' and he smiled at her and went out. And she went and sat on the side of the bed, and slowly her head drooped in her hands and as the tears fell through her fingers she muttered, 'Oh, God! Oh, God! What am I doing? It isn't fair to him, it isn't. Oh Brett . . . You! You!' Her thoughts ground to a standstill on her clenched teeth, and she rocked herself back and forward, much the same as Emily would have done.

4

Jonathan Ratcliffe heard of the banns being called in St. Edward's through Mr Wilton. Mr Wilton was standing at the other side of the desk, his face showing deep concern as he explained how he had come by the knowledge. One of the men in the fitting shop had a mother who attended St. Edward's. She had heard the names being called and had put two and two together. Mr Wilton thought Mr Ratcliffe should know.

Jonathan Ratcliffe looked at his subordinate and was unable to speak; then after a moment he thanked him and nodded his dismissal. As Mr Wilton went out of the door he was about to call him back and tell him to keep this knowledge to himself when he realised that Wilton would be the last but one in the whole works who had remained in ignorance of the situation between his daughter and Cotton.

He picked up a steel ruler and endeavoured to break it between his clenched fists. The slut! The low, low slut! The scheming little hussy. It was only three or four days ago that she had written to her mother thanking her for sending her birth certificate, the birth certificate that was supposed to be required by an employer. It had never dawned on them for a moment why she wanted her birth certificate. My God! And she was in the town. But that last letter had been postmarked Islington . . . Islington. She could never have been in Islington; you had to reside at least three weeks in the parish where you were to be married. The scheming . . .! The treacherous . . .! Words failed him. He rang his secretary and told her to get his wife on the phone.

All Jane Ratcliffe could say to her husband's information was, 'Oh, no! Oh, no! But how?' and again, 'Oh, no! Oh, no!' Then she asked, 'What are you going to do?'

'I'll tell you when I get in,' he answered and rammed the phone down . . .

And he told her immediately he entered the house, even before he had taken his coat off. After asking, 'Is anyone in?' and getting her answer, 'No,' he said, 'Can you believe it?'

She shook her head. 'No, I can't make it out,' she said. 'How did she send the letters from those various places?'

'He likely manoeuvred that for her.' And he hit on part of the truth by saying, 'Lorry driver. Long-distance lorry drivers. That could be it. Taking her letters down there . . . And to think you sent that birth certificate and it was picked up and returned to this very town.'

'How was I to know? What are we going to do?'

'I'm going to put a stop to it. Anyway he can't do it without our consent, but by God he's likely forged that. I know what he's up to. Once he's married her he thinks I'll come round, and there'll be a place for him well up the ladder at Affleck's. He was never more mistaken in his life.'

'Do you really think that's his intention?' Her question was tentative and conveyed her doubts and brought him barking, 'Of course, woman! I know him and all his type. He thinks I won't be able to bear them being in this town together, not her living in that quarter and us up here. And he's right. But his plans are going a little awry.' He now beat his fist into the palm of his hand as he cried, 'That girl! She must have a defective streak in her. That's it.' He nodded at his wife as if he had discovered the root of the trouble, then went on, 'I'll straighten that out when I get her home. I'll have her put in care. I will. I will.'

'You're going to fetch her home?'

'Just that. And then we're taking her to your Aunt Jean's, and we're taking her ourselves, every step of the road. And then you're staying with her for as long as is necessary.'

'Oh, Jonathan! I . . . I can't do that. How are you going to . . .?'

'Look, woman. Put first things first. I'll manage and see to Ray.'

It was as if by speaking his son's name he had conjured the boy up, for he turned his eyes slightly to the side towards the passage leading to the kitchen, and there he saw his son standing. This was a thing that annoyed him about the boy; he was always standing in dark corners listening. He yelled at him, 'Come out of that!'

When Ray walked slowly into the hall he said angrily, 'You've been listening again.'

'Not really. Not really, Father; I was just coming out of the kitchen.'

'I've told you about it, haven't I?'

'Yes, Father.'

'What did you hear?'

The boy glanced at his mother, then back to his father again and said, 'About Vanessa going to marry Angus Cotton.'

223

As Jonathan Ratcliffe ground his teeth his wife said, 'It can't do any harm now, no matter what he hears.'

As her husband stalked into the drawing-room she took hold of the boy and drew him into the kitchen, and there she said to him, 'Now mind, Ray, I'm warning you, don't discuss this with Michael. Remember, Michael is only a little boy; you shouldn't talk to him about things that happen in the house. I've told you, haven't I?'

'Yes, Mother.' He stared fixedly at her. He wasn't afraid of his mother; he wasn't really afraid of his father; well, just a little bit. He knew something he would like to tell his father just to see him go red in the face and nearly choke, like he did when he was in a temper. He had forgotten about it for a long time now, but hearing his father talking about Vanessa going to marry Angus had brought it back to his mind. He liked to be able to surprise people. He knew he would have spoken about it before if Uncle Arthur hadn't killed himself, yet he knew that his knowledge was somehow connected with Uncle Arthur killing himself.

The next best thing to surprising his father was to surprise his mother. He said to her now under his breath, 'I didn't think Vanessa would marry Angus, I thought she would marry Uncle Arthur.'

'What did you say?'

'I said I thought Vanessa would marry Uncle Arthur, that he'd give up Aunt Irene and marry her, Vanessa, like they do after a divorce. There were three boys in our form whose parents were divorced.'

Jane Ratcliffe was sitting down now. She had hold of her son's shoulders and was staring into his face. Her lips were moving, but no words issued from them for some time. And then she whispered, 'Ray, what are you saying? Come along, tell me what you know. What makes you think Vanessa should have married Uncle Arthur?'

'Well,' he shrugged his thin shoulders and moved his dark, satanic eyebrows upwards, 'they used to kiss and slop.'

She was doing now what she had never done before, she was shaking her son as if he was a rat, and for the first time in his short life he himself was really frightened. When her hands were still again but still gripping his shoulders, she muttered thickly, 'Tell me, boy, tell me everything. Everything mind.'

His head seemed to be still wobbling and he jerked it once before he said, 'Well, I saw them kissing.'

'You saw them . . .?' She swallowed deeply. 'Yes, go on.'

'I used to go out at night down the drainpipe, and one night I saw her go down the wood and when she came back Uncle Arthur was with her, and they stood by the gate talking, and he kissed her. I was up in the tree house.'

'Go on.'

'And another time I followed her and she and Uncle Brett were in the summerhouse.'

His mother was gripping his shoulders so hard that he hunched them up against his head, and when she relaxed her hold and again said, 'Go on,' he continued, 'Well I saw them sitting on the steps. Uncle Arthur was talking and then they were kissing and things.'

He was surprised the way his mother started calling on God. He had never heard anybody say things like that, except Emily.

There was a long silence now before she said, 'Why didn't you tell me this before?'

'Well – well, I didn't want to give Vanessa away; I – I

knew she would get wrong. And then Uncle went away and I forgot about it until he came back.'

'What happened when he came back?'

He bowed his head, then said, 'She went into the wood, but – but I didn't follow her; I was waiting for Michael. He had promised to sneak out and I thought he would be frightened if I wasn't there and go indoors again. We were going to sleep there all night.'

'Yes, yes, go on.'

'Well I saw Uncle and Vanessa at the gate, the wood gate, and she was crying and he kissed her.'

He was now looking down right on to the crown of his mother's head. He looked at it for a long time before she straightened herself up and said to him in a funny voice, 'Come on.'

When they entered the dining-room she checked what her husband was about to say in a voice that caught his attention. 'Ray's got something to tell you,' she said.

He looked at her face for a moment longer, then turned to his son and said, 'Yes, what is it?'

'I think you'd better sit down.'

He stared at her hard again, but sat down, and she pushed Ray towards him, saying, 'Tell your father what you've just told me . . . all of it.'

Jonathan Ratcliffe said not one word as his son talked haltingly, but when the boy was finished speaking he rose from the chair, pushed his son to one side and walked out of the room, across the hall and into his study. A moment later Jane Ratcliffe joined him, and at the first sight of him she was afraid of what might happen. He looked as if he was on the point of a seizure. His complexion was both red and grey, and the greyness around his mouth had paled to a sickly white. She dared not speak in case she said the wrong thing and incited him more.

When he spoke he surprised her because he didn't speak immediately of his daughter but of Arthur Brett, and not about what Arthur had done to Vanessa but what Arthur had done to him. 'You see,' he said; 'you see why he did it? To spite me. He planned it; he planned it every step of the road; he did it to get his own back. I always knew he'd do something one day. He took it too quietly years ago, too smoothly. He must have been boiling against me all this time; behind that quiet smile of his he was hatching this. He wanted some way to bring me low, and he knew exactly how to do it. And he timed it, he timed it that the balloon would go up before the wedding. Don't you see? DON'T YOU SEE?'

No, she didn't see, not quite the way he was seeing it. For once she saw a situation in its true light, an older man, an unhappy man, playing on the sensitive nerves of a young girl at her most impressionable age. She dared to say now, 'No, don't look at it like that, Jonathan; I'm sure he – '

'You're sure of nothing, woman. I know, I know. Everything fits. He had refused my offer to send him abroad in the first place. Then he got cold feet and thought he'd better get out of the way. The swine. The dirty swine. He expected the balloon to burst while he was away, when she found out she was pregnant . . . and he hoped she would be. You mark my words.' He was stabbing his finger towards her. 'That's what he was aiming at, her pregnancy. Then he would come back and gloat.'

'But,' she felt she had to reason with him, 'but he took his life, Jonathan. He didn't gloat, he took his life.'

'Yes, to spite me, so that people who didn't know the real facts would say he had done it out of frustration. He had done it because I had walked over his head; that's what they would say. He had been brooding over the injustices for years; that's what they did say.'

She knew it wasn't any good trying to combat at the moment his irrational way of thinking, nor in fact in the future; Jonathan was a law unto himself; he would think what he wanted to think; but she voiced now what had been in her mind from the moment Ray had spoken. 'And we accused Angus,' she said.

He stared at her, trying to collect his whirling thoughts, Angus, Angus Cotton. And he was going to marry her. Well, this only confirmed what he had known all along – that slob was determined to rise. Ten minutes ago he was determined to put his spoke in his wheel, but now, no, no, he'd let him get on with it, because one thing was utterly vital: not a breath of this latest development must come to light.

It was evident that she hadn't told Cotton who the father was and he was taking her on trust, on trust that he thought was going to pay off a good dividend later on. Oh yes, Cotton's type did nothing for nothing; he was ambitious, he was a climber. Being one himself, he thought he recognised the same traits when he met them in another man.

She said now, 'What are you going to do about them? I mean about them marrying?'

He hadn't enough cool nerve to go on looking at her as he said, 'Let them get on with it.'

'You mean, you're not going to do anything?' she was addressing his back.

'Just that.' He turned to her again. 'I'd even give them consent, for this thing mustn't leak out. Do you hear? Fetch that boy in. He's got to understand that he must never mention this to a soul. If she's kept quiet we can keep quiet. We've got to. I –

228

we'd be the laughing stock of the town if it leaked out. The past scandal would be nothing compared to what it would be if it was known that Brett,' he ground his teeth, 'the dirty, dirty swine had given her the child.'

'You don't think they know, they guessed? I mean next door? Irene and Colin and Paul?'

'Don't be stupid, woman.' His voice was filled with scorn. 'Do you think that Irene would have kept that to herself? And did we guess?'

'No. But knowing Irene. Yes, I think she would have kept it to herself if she had known.'

'Nonsense! Nonsense! That kind of a woman couldn't keep anything to herself. Go on and bring the boy in. And one more thing. Don't breathe a word to Susan about this, mind. Do you hear me?'

'I hear you; you've got no need to stress the point,' she said.

She did not go immediately into the lounge but stood in the hall trying to collect herself. For weeks now her feelings had been softening towards her errant daughter. She imagined her travelling from one job to another, from one place to another, and the baby's birth getting nearer and nearer, but now her duplicity had wiped away any lingering tenderness. Granted she had been taken advantage of by an older man, but that was no reason why she should now resort to marrying a person like Angus Cotton, someone who was the antithesis of all she had been brought up to expect in a man and a gentleman. She could see herself now accepting the child knowing it was Arthur's, because after all Arthur had been a gentleman; but Emily's Angus! Well, he was nothing more than an uncouth, gauche, ignorant individual, and in marrying

229

him her daughter was indeed sinking to the depths. And there, as Jonathan had implied, she must be allowed to wallow.

It was, after all, a comfort to her that she saw eye to eye with her husband over this unhappy affair.

5

They were married at ten o'clock on a Saturday morning. Emily wasn't present, nor was Rosie, but Stan acted as Angus's best man and the verger made the other witnesses. When the short service was over Vanessa couldn't believe that she was now married, and to Angus Cotton.

As she stood in the vestry she had an overpowering desire to turn and fly out of the church, fly out of the town, to put as much space between herself and him as possible. But she liked Angus, for he was the only one who had been kind to her, the only one who had stood by her; the only one who had accepted her condition and hadn't asked questions, at least after the night he asked her to marry him. And now she was married to him and the enormity of the step she had taken loomed over her like a dark canopy.

Yet she felt she could live with Angus and know a modicum of happiness if it was possible for them to be alone. But she was going back to that tiny little house which was filled with Emily . . . and Rosie, and she was frightened, frightened of them both.

She had lodged with Stan's mother for the past three weeks, so fulfilling the requirements of living in the parish during the calling of the banns. Stan's mother was a quiet woman who asked no questions and talked mostly about the weather, and her Stan. She wished they were going back there, or that, things being as they were, they were returning straight home – she thought of it now as home – so that she would get the meeting with her new mother-in-law and sister-in-law over. But Angus had arranged that they would spend the day in Newcastle. She didn't wonder why this was; she knew it had to do with Emily and Rosie.

And it had, it definitely had. Angus thanked Stan and said rather sheepishly they would have a drink later – which term gave no indication of time. Then he bade him good-bye, and Stan, after awkwardly shaking hands with Vanessa, wished her, ironically, the best of luck, following which he took his departure with unconcealed haste.

At this moment, more than at any time in his life, Angus wanted company, lots of company. If someone had told him years ago that one day he could have Aladdin's lamp and three wishes, he would have used all three to wish that he could some day marry a lass like Vanessa Ratcliffe; and now Aladdin's lamp had been rubbed and he had married, not an imitation of Vanessa Ratcliffe, but Vanessa Ratcliffe herself, and the fact had stilled his tongue, made him self-conscious, yet elated, and at the same time sad, sad because his mother had refused to come to the church.

Last night there had been hell to pay. 'You still goin' through with it?' she had said. 'God Almighty, Mam!' he had bawled back at her. 'Haven't you got it into your head yet? I'm marryin' her the morrow. Come hell-fire or high water, I'm marrying her the morrow.' And to this she had said quietly, which made it all the worse, 'Aye, well, I hope you don't live to regret it.'

Then May had come in. One or other of them had used May as a last straw. Neither of them had liked May; May was common. Aye, there were grades below 24 Ryder's Row.

May was standing at the kitchen table when he came out of the room ready to go and meet Vanessa, and she had said, 'Hello there, Angus.' And he grinned sheepishly and replied, 'Oh hello, there, May. How you keepin'?' To which she had replied, 'How do you think?' She would never have made this answer, not within those four walls, if she hadn't had his mother and Rosie behind her.

Rosie and his mam had gone upstairs and left them alone and May said to him, 'Is it right that you're gettin' married the morrow?' and he had answered quietly, 'Yes, May. I'm sorry an' all that, but it's right.' And to this, and with her voice as quiet as his, she had said, 'You know what you are, Angus Cotton; you're a lousy, rotten twister, you're nothin' but a stinking bugger. I've been good enough for you on an' off for years; I've served your purpose, haven't I? Every time I made a break from you an' got a decent fellow, up you'd pop again and wag your little finger and expect me to come runnin'. And being the bloody fool that I am, I came runnin'. And now this. But don't think you'll get off with it; you'll get paid out one way or the other.'

At this point he had asked her had she quite finished, and she had replied, 'Not by a long chalk. You'd have been married already, and to me, wouldn't you, if I hadn't been such a bloody fool as to tell you the truth?' Her voice was weighed now with bitterness. 'You can do it every night in the week and with as many as you like, can't you? But because I was honest and told you of the other two you cooled off. Like a parson at a strip-tease, you melted away.'

233

When he hadn't answered her she moved towards the door and from there she said, 'Well, I wish you joy of her, and from what I hear you'll need it. She'll make you feel like a worm, that's after she gets rid of the bairn. Once she's had the bairn she won't be scared out of her wits any more. She won't want a life-belt then. It makes a difference having a bairn. I should know, shouldn't I? And when she wakes up and sees the big galoot that she's married she'll ask herself if she was clean barmy, because she will wake up. Oh aye, she will, an' then you can look out, Mr Bloody Big-Head.'

What had upset him more than anything she had said was when she looked around the room and put her head back and laughed mirthlessly, saying, 'And you're bringing her back to this? God Almighty! Even I wouldn't have stood for that. I'm goin' to wish you luck, big boy, because you're goin' to need it. And how! . . . Who put the overalls in Mrs Murphy's chowder.' She ended on a saying that she usually fitted to situations that puzzled or were beyond her. It had always made him want to belly laugh. May had had the knack of making him belly laugh. Vanessa would never have that kind of knack.

They were sitting in the bus now and he turned to her and asked, 'All right?' She smiled faintly at him as she answered, 'Yes, Angus.' After a moment he said, 'We're going to have a spot of lunch, then have a look round.' He paused. 'Is there anything you would like?'

'Like? What do you mean?'

'Something for yourself.' He was smiling into her eyes now. 'Wedding present, sort of.'

'No, Angus, thank you very much.'

'Nothing?' The smile had gone from his face.

'Well,' she lowered her head and shook it slightly, 'I haven't thought; perhaps later.'

'Yes, aye.' He looked ahead again.

They had lunch, then they went to the cinema. They sat side by side and he didn't take her hand. He hadn't touched her in any way except to put the ring on her finger. He hadn't even kissed her at the service, and the minister had made no comment on it. What he would do later on the night, he didn't know. The separate beds would help.

That had been another hell-raising moment when the other single bed had been delivered at the house. On this occasion his mother had bawled at him, 'Well you are marryin' her, aren't you? Look . . . if you want my advice you'll start the way you mean to go on. There's a sayin': You've made your bed and you must lie on it, but there's another sayin': If you don't make your bed the first night, whether it's through being sozzled or not havin' it in you, then there's little chance you'll do any better the second, or the third.'

She was a coarse old bitch when all was said and done, and he had told her so. But she had replied that he was already trying to jump the fence to Van's side where nothing was looked at squarely because it wasn't the thing to do, but he wasn't cut out for politeness, and he would soon find that it was choking him. Her words stirred a tiny fear that she might be right.

It was around seven when they came out of the pictures, and there was a cold drizzle falling, and as they stood under a lamp he said, 'What about a bit to eat, eh?'

She pulled her coat collar up under her chin, and she looked up at him for a moment before she answered, 'I'd rather go home, Angus.'

He smiled broadly. 'Good idea. Good idea.'

He had wanted to put the going home off to the very last minute when he hoped both Emily and Rosie would be in bed. Tomorrow morning everything would look different; everybody would take a different slant at each other; but now she had said she would rather go home, and in a way he knew she was right. Far better get it over with. Anyway, they would likely be out at the club. One thing was certain, Rosie wouldn't be in; Stan would see to that. Stan was a good fellow at bottom.

It took much longer to get from Newcastle to Fellburn by train than it did by lorry, and then they caught a bus from the station to the end of the street. It was pouring with rain when they alighted and he took her by the arm and ran her across the road, and he kept her in the shelter of the railway wall until they were almost opposite the door. But as he made to cross over to the pavement he stopped. He had heard the singing farther up the street but he hadn't thought it was coming from their house. The Conways usually had their wireless blazing away at all hours, but this wasn't the wireless or telly, it was singing, voices singing. There was a difference.

When he pushed open the front door the sound hit them like the backwash of a huge wave. The voices were all raised on the last line of a dated song: 'Now is the Hour.' His hold tightened on Vanessa's arm as he stared along the dimly lit passage. God! She had gone and got company in, which told him one thing even before he saw her, she was bottled. She wasn't the one for having neighbours in. Only twice before in his life had he known her do this, and on both occasions she had been burnt up inside with anger.

He stood in the kitchen doorway almost in front of Vanessa looking at the company. He was surprised to see Stan there, but the look that Stan gave him said, 'I couldn't do anything with them,' and he could see that for himself, because Rosie had had a skinful too.

There was Alf Piggott and his missus from down the street, and Bill Wilson and his missus from next door. Bill had his old concertina on his knee; they weren't relying on the television or the wireless the night. His mother always said she hated the sound of Bill's concertina, but she was singing to it now. As the song ended on different notes, the visitors all turned and greeted him, saying in different ways, 'Congratulations, lad.' They didn't say anything to the bride; they just looked at her, and not at her face but at her distended shape, and grinned.

What Emily said was, 'Well, it's a weddin', isn't it?' She stared across the room at her son, but even her glance did not take in Vanessa. 'Come on.' She got to her feet. 'Some of the old 'uns, Bill. Cock-o-doodle. Play Cock-o-doodle. If you don't I'll bloody well do me poetry piece again:

'I hear in the chamber above me the patter of little feet. Da-da, de-da, de-da.

"Do you think, O blue-eyed banditti,
Because you have scaled the wall,
Such an old moustache as I am
Is not a match for you all?"'

'Cock-o-doodle, for God's sake!' cried Rosie, and after a moment's hesitation Bill was playing 'Cock-o-doodle' and Emily and the others were singing. But Emily's voice was louder than the rest.

'Cock-o-doodle, cock-o-doodle,
I'm the cock of the North.
Cock-o-doodle, cock-o-doodle,
I'm the cock of the North.
Me faather went out on a Saturda' night
After giving me ma a bairn;
He filled up with rum
And came doddering back
And tried to give her mairn.'

With the quickness of a freak wave, anger rose in
him. Grabbing hold of Vanessa, he pushed her past Alf
Taggart's chair, then in front of Stan, and to his room
door, and, thrusting it open, he went inside with her,
saying grimly under his breath, 'It'll be all right. Stay
there.' When he returned to the kitchen his mother was
singing,

'He killed five thousand Irishmen
In the battle of the boiling water.'

Over and over again he had told her that it wasn't the
boiling water, it was the Boyne Water, but now he was
boiling. He yelled at her, 'Stop it! Do you hear me? Stop it!'

'What! It's a weddin', isn't it? It's a weddin'. Everybody's merry at a weddin'. What do you say, Bill? What
do you say, Rosie? We know it's a weddin', don't we?'
She punched her daughter on the shoulder, and Rosie
punched her back, crying,

'You wouldn't take your mother's device,
You wouldn't take your faather's device,
But you took Barney Rooney's device,
And now you've got your belly full of Barney
Rooney.'

238

As the company, with the exception of Stan, howled their appreciation of this quip, Angus's hand drew back above his sister's head. It was only Stan catching at his arm and crying, 'Steady on! Steady on, Angus,' that checked the blow.

'Get out! Do you hear me?' Angus now swept the Piggotts and Wilsons with a look that brought them swiftly to their feet, and when he added, 'Quick, the bloody lot of you!' the male in Mr Piggott rose and he turned on Angus, and shouted, 'Now look here, lad, don't try any of your big – '

'OUT!'

'Whose house do you think this is, eh?' Emily grabbed at the back of Angus's coat, and he swung swiftly round, almost sending her to the floor as he said, 'Shut your mouth, you!' Then he turned his attention to his sister who was standing by the table blinking at him. 'Get up the stairs. Go on now.'

'By damn, you won't tell me what to – '

Stan, now pulling Rosie to the door, said, 'Give over. Give over. Look, go on up. Do as he says. I'll see you the morrow.'

'You're as bad as him. Why, you bugger, you're as bad as him!'

'Go on.' Stan pushed her into the passage and towards the stairs. 'Go on now.'

There was only Angus and Emily left in the kitchen, but the walls seemed to be pressing outwards with the bitterness between them. Emily was sitting by the table, her forearms on it; she was staring at her hands and her head was moving in small, pathetic jerks. He stared down at her, love, compassion and understanding all fighting for a place in his thoughts, fighting against the words of recrimination he wanted to pour on her, fighting against

239

his hate of her. Bending his big head down to hers, he gritted out below his breath, 'That was a bloody dirty trick to play.'

Slowly she lifted her eyes to his and her fuddled gaze swept over his face before she brought out thickly, 'I take after me son, playin' bloody dirty tricks.' He straightened up and her eyes were still holding his when he said, 'I'll talk to you in the mornin' when you're sober.'

She rose unsteadily to her feet; her eyes had never moved from his face and she took two unsteady steps away from him as she muttered, 'I might be sober in the mornin', lad, an' in me right senses, but not you; things'll happen to you from now on like as if you'd taken to drugs. Mark my words. You think she's taken your name but she hasn't, lad; you've taken hers, and you're going to break your bloody neck tryin' to keep up with her. Well, you can go on breakin' it, I'll leave you to it.'

She shambled past him and he said nothing, but he turned and watched her go out of the passage and up the stairs. He watched her until he saw her grotesquely swollen feet and ankles disappear from view through the stair railings; then turning to the fire he stood staring down into it, until, with a swift movement, he brought his clenched fist hard against his forehead. The action caused him to screw up his eyes tightly and he held his fist motionless for some minutes before he dropped his hand.

The house was quiet now and he looked towards his room door. Then the habit of years taking over, he followed the nightly pattern and went down to the bottom of the yard.

When he returned to the kitchen he stood confounded for a moment as to how he was going to tell her to do the same. How different it would have been with May; there would have been no feeling of delicacy in mentioning a lavatory to May; rather it would have evoked laughter. He went into the room.

Vanessa had not even taken her outdoor things off. She was sitting on his chair near the little table; her bag was on her knee and her cases were standing near the wall, where he had left them last night. He went to her and said softly, 'It's all right; she'd had a drop.' He refrained from saying that it was rarely she did anything like this, it would only have worsened matters. He made his lips move into a smile as he added, 'She'll be herself in the morning'.'

'She won't Angus.'

'What do you mean?'

'You know what I mean . . . We couldn't . . . ?'

'No, we couldn't, Van.' He bent his head down until his face was on a level with hers. 'We've had this out. I've got to look after her; not only with money, you understand. Oh, I dare say she would get along with supplementary and one thing and another, but she needs me here; she's always needed me. I explained it all to you about me father. I've been the man in her life, if you can put it like that. She's had nobody else, and she's just lived for me. Whatever happens now I'm stuck with her, whether I like it or not. Sometimes I like it fine, other times, like the night, I don't like it one bit.'

Vanessa sat looking at him. She was sick and weary, weary in her mind and body. She wondered vaguely why this should be happening to her, why she had ever let herself be talked into marrying him. She was finding things out about him all the time, things that repulsed her secretly; the depths of his crudity, the depths of his ignorance; yet there were other depths, such as his

241

depths of loyalty, the feeling of responsibility he had towards Emily, which feeling she imagined out-weighed all others in his life, even his love for her.

Intuitively, because he had never put it into words, she knew that he was in love with her, that he had always been in love with her, and that although he had found her when she was at rock bottom, he was nevertheless flattered that she should consent to marry him. But he covered this up with his off-hand and casual attitude towards her. She also knew that she was afraid of him, afraid of his body and what it might do to her.

'Come on.' He held out his hand, pulling her up. 'You're tired. It's been a day. Get ready for bed.'

Perhaps it was the small jerk of her fingers within his grasp that made him say brusquely, 'Oh, it's all right, don't worry. There,' he pointed to the opposite corner from where his bed stood, 'That's yours. At least for the time being.' He did not add 'until the bairn comes'. Although why he was considering the bairn he didn't know; they said it thrived on a little action, and women liked it at this time; brought them a sort of comfort. Well maybe. And that was all right if they had been at it from the beginning, but to take her now, no, he couldn't. He looked at her blankly for a moment. She looked neither Vanessa Ratcliffe, Miss Van, nor Vanessa Cotton. She was a girl with a protruding stomach and a weary face, and eyes with a sadness in them that seemed to be drawn from the very pit of her.

When he turned from her and said, 'By the way, if you want it, it's down at the bottom of the yard,' her head drooped and she went towards the door, pulling off her head scarf as she did so. It was this act that brought a deep embarrassment to them both, for as she flicked the scarf downwards it caught at one of the little ornaments on the mantelpiece and she was only just in time to save it. The ornament was of blue Venetian glass; it was six inches high and stood in a base of silver, so tarnished now as hardly to be recognizable as such. From its narrow base the vase mounted outwards to a fluted top, and as her fingers gripped the scalloped edge she remembered that her mother had always considered it a nice little vase for roses; they didn't topple out. The vase's disappearance had been noted after one of the dailies had left. Over the years the household had come to look on dailies as members of a pilfering gang, for always, after their departure, something was missing, and, as Emily had said to her mother, 'It's not a bit of use going after them, they've likely sold it, and you'd have to pin it on them anyway.'

She placed the vase slowly back on the mantelpiece among the bric-a-brac. When she lifted her head Angus was looking at her.

'God blast her!' He had forgotten about all her perks, because she hadn't brought home anything of value for some time as there hadn't been anybody to pin the blame on; not that she would have let them stand the racket if there had been any possibility of them being caught. She was thoughtful that way. But the house was dotted with bits and pieces from up there. Why the hell hadn't he thought about it! If she had thought she had purposely done nothing about it. She hadn't thoroughly cleaned this room for weeks now; all she had done was to lick a duster over it. But he himself should have remembered and got rid of the things. There was that silver teapot and jug in the chiffonier in the kitchen. He'd put that in the dustbin first thing in the morning. God! What more could happen?

He went to the door and watched Vanessa walking

across the kitchen, and when she went out into the yard he followed into the scullery and put the kettle on. A cup of coffee might help. After making it he put the cups on a tray and took it back into the room; then he waited. It was after he had been waiting ten minutes that it suddenly came to him that she had been a long time. The back door! She could have gone out the back door. He almost leaped across the kitchen, and when he opened the scullery door and saw her standing there about to enter he leaned against the stanchion for a moment and closed his eyes. It took him a few seconds to pull himself together, and then he said, 'Are you all right?'

'Yes. Yes, I'm all right.' She smiled faintly at him.

'I've made a drink.' He led the way into the room and closed the door.

As they drank their coffee he made several light remarks in order to cover up the awkwardness that lay between them. It was an awkwardness that had nothing to do with sex; it was the awkwardness of two diverse personalities thrown into close proximity. After a while he rose and hung his coat up on the back of the door, saying, 'It won't look so bad when you titivate it up a bit, new curtains and things. She didn't do anything to it because she thought you'd like to have it your own way.'

She, too, rose to her feet. She felt better, quieter inside. She thought the hot coffee must have done her good. She stared at him as he turned towards her. He looked bigger without his coat. The muscles of his arms bulged through his shirt sleeves, his arms looked long and powerful, as did his hands and shoulders; an Irish navvy, one of them had called him. Well, she supposed he did look like an Irish navvy, but he was being kind and thoughtful and she was grateful for any kindness. When he stood in front of her, saying, 'Don't worry;

244

it'll be different in the morning. I mean,' and jerked his head towards the ceiling, she didn't answer, but on an impulse similar to that which had brought her lips to Brett's cheek with the result that she was now married to Angus Cotton, she leaned forward and placed her lips lightly against the corner of his mouth.

It was the first time their faces had come into contact, and the effect was electrifying. The next minute he had her pressed tightly to him. Her body slightly askew, he held her in a vice as his mouth covered hers. But within a minute they were standing apart again and she was gasping for breath while he wiped the sweat from his face with the back of his hand.

'You shouldn't have done that,' he said. 'It was all right until you did that. Asking for trouble, aren't you? What do you think I am, eh? Well,' he strained his neck up out of his collar, 'when I want you I'll take you, in me own time. Get that. In me own time.'

She was unable to speak; all she could do was stare at him. She had only meant it to be a sort of thank you for all he had done. She had never really thanked him; he made it so hard. She watched him go to the switch and put the light out. Then his voice came out of the darkness, saying, 'Get to bed.' And she got to bed. Like a child who had been whipped and was afraid of the lesson being repeated, she scrambled out of her clothes, and because she hadn't unpacked anything she got into her petticoat again, and, groping at the bedclothes, she slid down between the sheets and lay stiff and taut, listening to her heart as its beat thumped in her ears. It was so loud that it shut out the sound of Angus's breathing.

But six feet away Angus listened to her breathing as he lay on his back staring upwards. His mother had been right; he had been a blasted fool, he should have got a

245

double bed. He needn't have touched her; she could have just lain by his side and he could have held her hand. Aw, God, he was kiddin' himself, wasn't he? Lying by her side and holding her hand, when that peck she gave him set him off like a starter gun! But, nevertheless, his mother had something.

Into the silence now there permeated a sound that didn't come from the bed to the left of him but from the ceiling at which his eyes were directed. It was a sound that he hadn't heard for many years, not since the night his dad had died; it was the sound of his mother crying. With a heave he turned on his side and pulled the clothes over his head. Had there ever been a wedding night like this, ever? No! He bet his damned life there never had.

6

Why no one liked the month of November had always, up to now, puzzled Vanessa. She had said once to Susan that it was just a different kind of weather, and all weather was nice. She liked walking in the rain, she liked wind, she liked to lie in bed and hear it whine and moan through the tall chimneys. She particularly liked November, December and January because she associated them with roaring open fires both in the drawing-room and dining-room. She had always had more time to read in the winter. After she had done her homework she would curl up before the fire, preferably in a room which she had to herself, and munch crisps and chew caramels – she didn't care for chocolates.

Now, again, it was November, and she was seeing it as most people saw it; a month of rain, fog, cold, sleet, snow flurries and half light that bore you down.

At ten o'clock on this particular Wednesday morning she stood in the middle of the kitchen and thought, not for the first time by any means, 'I'll go mad, I'll go insane and they'll put me away.' She had been married just over three weeks and, mentally, she had gone through more torment during this period than during all the weeks since the night in the summer-house with Brett. She was learning that there were different kinds of torment. There was the torment of this tiny house, where every word you said above your breath could be heard upstairs, and vice versa, where five steps one way and four the other were all you could do in the privacy of your room.

She knew every square inch of the ground floor of this house, but she didn't know anything about upstairs. Even when she was alone in the house, and that was pretty often, she didn't venture upstairs; upstairs was Emily's and Rosie's rooms, and she didn't want to get any nearer to them than she must. Their resentment of her filled the air when they were indoors, and it stayed with her long after they left the house in the morning, because now Emily was again going to work.

For the first week after Angus had brought her here she was, most of the time, alone with Emily, and Emily would speak to her only when it was necessary. 'Well, aren't you goin' to get him his tea ready?' she had said to her on the first Monday.

'I – I don't know what he likes; I'll leave it to you, Emily.'

'Oh no, begod, you won't, lass. You're his wife; you've got to cook for him.'

She had felt an anger rising in her against Emily, but she had tried to control it. Yet in spite of her effort her voice took on a slight hauteur as she said, 'You know for a fact I can't cook, Emily.'

'You should have thought of that afore. And don't use that tone to me; I'm not up at the house now.'

'I'm not using any tone to you, Emily.' Vanessa was beseeching now. 'I just want you to help me, show me how to cook.'

'I'm sorry; I'll have no time for that, I'm going after a job the morrow,' said Emily flatly.

Vanessa had groaned inwardly. That's what Angus feared she would do, go after another job.

But this was only the beginning. There were the evenings when Angus came in and she put before him what she had cooked, and he rarely ate it; but he soon went through the things she hadn't cooked, such as fish and chips, or peas and pies. She said to him, 'I'll go to cookery classes once it's over,' and he had nodded and smiled at her but hadn't said, 'You'll have other things to do besides cookery classes once it's over.'

As much in an effort to make conversation as to find out his tastes, she had said to him, 'What is your favourite dish?' and when he replied, 'Steak and kidney pudding,' she had said, 'Oh!' There was as much chance of her making a steak and kidney pudding as there was of her making crêpes Suzette, in fact she might have had more success with the latter as she had tried her hand at pancakes.

On Monday of this week she had bought a cookery book only to find that there wasn't an ingredient in the house that was stated in any of the recipes. So yesterday she had ventured into the centre of the town to buy what was necessary, for she didn't like going into the little shops near the house, because the looks she received said plainly, 'So this is who all the trouble's about.'

It was while she was waiting for a bus in the main street that she became aware of two women in a car, held up in a line of traffic, almost at the same time as they became aware of her. They were Mrs Herring and Mrs Young, the mothers of Kathie and Rona. She had been entertained in their homes countless times, and they had always been charming to her, but now they were surveying her with hard, blank stares. Their eyes, in a way, looked sightless, as if they weren't really seeing her.

249

She looked away, and it was all she could do not to run away from the bus queue. She had never felt a 'bad girl' before, but she did now. She wanted to sink down through the earth.

It was unfortunate that this incident should have followed so closely on a row between Angus and Emily the night before.

'Where you goin'?' Angus had asked his mother.

'Out,' Emily had replied.

'You've taken to goin' out a lot of late, haven't you?'

'It's my life, lad. You do what you like with yours, I do what I like with mine. Is there any reason why I shouldn't go out?'

'Aye,' he had yelled at her; 'every bloody reason under the sun, you awkward old bitch you.'

'Don't you call me an awkward old bitch else I'll brain you. As sure as God's me judge, I'll brain you.'

'Try it on then. Try it on.'

Vanessa had stood in their room, her face held between her two hands, and like a child she had prayed: Dear Lord, make them stop. She was dazed by the yelling and shouting that went on in the house. What should be ordinary conversation was conducted in a tone that would have been used only for deep anger in her own home, and she had rarely heard it until she herself had evoked it. At one point when the swearing was filling the house she thrust her fingers into her ears, and when she extracted them it was to hear Angus yelling, 'You've no bloody need to go out workin'. You know you haven't.' And Emily's reply, 'You're goin' to break stones with a bloody great stick, aren't you? Sixteen pounds! You'd get more sweepin' roads. Your own boss, me backside.'

'It was a bad week. I told you . . . in between contracts.

Anyway, what the hell has it got to do with you what I make and what I don't make? I pay the rent and every other bloody commitment in the house, so what are you talking about?'

As the door banged before he had finished speaking, Rosie's voice took over from her mother's. 'You should be bloody well ashamed of yourself, our Angus, speakin' to her like that.'

'Now you, YOU keep your trap shut. I'm standin' none of it from you, because you've turned out to be nothin' more than a damned little upstart. That's what you are. And you've got nothing to be uppish about.'

'There you're wrong; I have got something to be uppish about. And I'm going to remain uppish. I'm not like some people I know gettin' me belly filled at the first opportun – '

When the sound of the blow came to her, Vanessa threw herself on the bed and buried her face in the pillow. A few minutes later when she raised her head she expected to hear Rosie crying, but Rosie's voice, as strident as ever, was yelling, 'You great, big, soft nowt. Don't think you'll frighten me. And you lift your hand again and, begod, I'll do what me mam threatened, I'll brain you. Now mind, I'm warnin' you.'

She had sat on the edge of the bed gripping her hands on the dome of her stomach. She felt dazed by it all. She knew she'd never, never get used to it, at the same time she was amazed by the fact that this was how people lived, had gone on living for years and years. Emily and Rosie and Angus hadn't just started shouting at each other since she had come into the house. Everybody in this neighbourhood seemed to shout. They shouted greetings across the narrow streets as if they were miles away; even the tenants in the new block of flats round the

251

corner in the main street, they shouted from their upper windows down to the children in the play yards. Life here was one big shout, when it should have been a whisper, because there was hardly space to breathe. Perhaps it was because they lived in such close proximity to each other that made them want to shout, to break out.

It had been nearly fifteen minutes later when Angus came into the room, and after looking at her face he said, 'Don't look so worried; there's nobody been murdered.'

'You surprise me.'

He had turned swiftly on her. This was a tone, she knew, she must never use to him. It was the tone she had used to Emily, the tone of her class, slightly haughty, supercilious, condescending, and he reacted to it as such. 'Look, this is our way.' He was yelling at her now. 'It means nothing, well, not all that. It'll work out. I keep telling you it'll work out. I know her.' His voice dropped.

'And Rosie?'

'Aw, Rosie. She's jealous of you, that's what's the matter with Rosie. I always had a soft spot for her. She's jealous of you.'

Following this he had gone to the little table in the corner and sat down with his exercise books, working out figures, and she had taken up her knitting. She was knitting a baby coat; she could knit and sew quite well. They had taught her something in the Convent. It would have been better if they had taught her Domestic Science, but they only taught that to those who wanted to go in for·it. There had been no need for her to study Domestic Science. Somewhere inside she was laughing derisively. She had taken languages, German and French, instead of a meat pudding. She would have given all her

252

knowledge, however limited, to be able to make a meat pudding.

They had been sitting in silence for some time when he turned to her abruptly and said, 'What I want is another couple of lorries, besides two new ones to replace the crates we've got. I missed a job the day because we weren't big enough; a fellow said it would take six lorries but he'd stretch a point if I had four.'

She had no interest in his business or the lorries that he had or hadn't got, but she said, 'Can't you go to the bank and get the money?'

'Oh my God, Van.' He smiled pityingly. 'I'm down to one hundred and twenty-five quid. I don't have a bank account; our dealings are strictly cash. It helps with the tax man an' all. But go to the bank you say. You're talkin' daft.'

She suddenly put down her knitting and straightened her back, and her tone changed again, not to the one that would anger him, but to one filled with protest as she said, 'I'm not a fool altogether, Angus.'

'Look honey, I didn't say you were.' He was leaning over the back of the chair towards her. 'But it's just that you've got a different slant on things.'

'I haven't got a different slant on things, not with reference to the bank. What I meant was, couldn't you go to the bank and raise a loan? I know you've got no money in the bank.'

He pulled a chair round until he was facing her, his knees almost touching hers, and he said, 'Oh, I see. But I ask you; what have I got as security? We don't own this place, not that that would mean very much if we did. I've got nothing as security except a broken-down lorry, the other one is Fred's.'

'Has he no security?'

'Insecurity; a wife and six bairns.'

She said, 'You mentioned an insurance some time ago.'

'Oh, that. It isn't due for another eight years. And then what is it? Three hundred pounds.'

'How long was it for?'

'Fifteen years. I've paid seven.'

'Wouldn't they take that as part security?'

'And me not paid half yet? I don't know about that. But,' he jerked his head, 'I could see. It's an idea. You've given me an idea.' His smile widened and he leant nearer to her and asked now softly, in the voice that he kept for her alone, 'How you feelin'?' These were the only words that his tenderness seemed to supply him with: 'How you feelin'?'

'All right,' she said.

'You always say you're all right. If you were peggin' out you would say you were all right, wouldn't you, because it's the thing to say?'

'But I am feeling all right.'

'No, you're not; you're feeling bloody miserable. There I go.' He wagged his head. 'I told you I was goin' to stop swearing in front of you.'

'It doesn't matter.'

'But it does. If I said I was going to stop swearin' I should stop swearin'; at least in front of you.'

She wanted to say, 'The more you try the more it will emphasise the difference. Don't change yourself; it'll be better that way.'

He looked down at his hands, the nails all broken, the finger tips as hard as pieces of dried leather, and he said, 'You're having it pretty rough, but believe me once it's over everything will be all right, you'll see. And we'll go out; we'll start going places; I'll take you round;

we'll enjoy ourselves . . . Oh,' he wagged his hand at her, 'she'll look after the bairn; she'll be in her seventh heaven havin' a bairn to see to. You'll see. I'm tellin' you. And by that time business will have bucked up, and I'll bet what you like we'll have a car. Not a new one, oh no, not yet, because every spare penny I make I want to push into the business. It's going to be big, I'm tellin' you.' He turned his head almost on to his shoulder and nodded it as if she was contradicting him, and he said again, 'I'm telling you. It's a prophecy if ever there was one, it's going to be big. I mean it to be big. I generally get what I want.' He brought his head slowly towards her again and his hand went out and touched hers.

She always shivered when he touched her. She wasn't repulsed by him, but nevertheless she couldn't stop her limbs shivering when her flesh made contact with his, and each time he was aware of this. She knew it angered him, but he endeavoured not to show it.

He had left the house at seven o'clock this morning, before either Emily or Rosie had come downstairs, and when they did come down she heard them talking. They intended she should.

She felt sick and ill this morning, not only in her body but in her mind. A dark depression had fallen on her. Her thoughts were going round in circles, she couldn't see ahead, yet when she looked back into the past all was brightness. She had had a wonderful home, wonderful parents; she even saw her father as kindly and good, and her mother as sympathetic. She had been going to wear the most gorgeous dress as bridesmaid to Susan. There would have been marvellous people at the wedding. Never before had she thought of Susan's friends or the Braintrees as marvellous, but now, in retrospect, they were all charming and kindly; and none of them raised their voices when speaking. What had segregated her from this wonderful past? It was Brett. He should have known what would happen. But she mustn't blame Brett, at least not all the way. She had liked Brett; she could say she had loved Brett. He was a gentleman, except when . . . Her mind shut out the picture of the moments during which Brett had ceased to be a gentleman.

Emily's voice penetrated the fog of her depression as she called to Rosie, 'Times have changed, lass, times have changed. I was goin' at it scrubbin' for nine hours a day up till twenty-four hours afore you were born, not sittin' on me arse all day. Aye, times have changed.'

When finally the door banged for the second time and she had the house to herself she got up and dressed. She knew what she was going to do, and she knew that she should have done it sooner. She should have done it instead of marrying Angus. She had brought trouble on him and parted him from his family. As Rosie had made it plain a number of times, they had been a happy family once.

She got dressed and went to the little shop around the corner. They hadn't any large packets of aspirins, only strips. She asked for four. At the next shop she bought a box holding twenty-five, and now she was standing in the kitchen and the aspirins were on the table before her.

She knew she must leave some word for Angus, so she went into the room and looked for a piece of drawing paper on which to write, but there was none on the table. There was a piece of paper sticking between two books and she pulled it out, and with it Fowler's 'King's English.' She had been surprised to find that on the bookshelf. Angus and Fowler's 'King's English.' She smiled a pitying smile. He tried, did Angus, he tried. Perhaps she could have helped him here. No, he would never have allowed her to help him with his grammar because that would have meant facing the fact that he needed help in that direction. There was a pride in him that mustn't be hurt. She took the piece of paper and a pencil into the kitchen and she wrote on it: 'I'm sorry, Angus. It was a great mistake; I should never have let you do it. Emily was right. It would never have worked out. Thank you for all the kindness you have shown me. You have nothing to regret, believe me, because you're the only one who has given me a kind word during all these awful months. Thank you, Angus. Vanessa.' She read what she had written and felt that she hadn't expressed herself clearly, hadn't thanked him enough, then she went into the scullery and brought back a glass of water, and, opening the aspirins, she dropped thirty into the water and slowly stirred them. They took a long time to dissolve, and as she waited she thought, I wonder if I'll see Brett. Odd, us both going out the same way; but I could never have hanged myself. When eventually the liquid was a milky mass of whirling particles she raised the glass to her lips. Her hand began to tremble now; then her body; and she knew if she hesitated for one moment longer she wouldn't do it.

When the glass was empty she shuddered and gritted her teeth against the taste; then she put her forearms on the table and sat gazing down at the letter she had written and she wondered how long it would be before the aspirins took effect.

7

They were at break in the canteen. Rosie, Freda Armstrong, her pal and fellow machinist, and two other girls. They were seated at their usual table in the corner and Freda was pouring sympathy over Rosie. The expression of her sympathy was questionable but nevertheless sincere. 'You look awful, Rosie girl,' she was saying. 'Cor! your face is green. I've never seen you as bad as this; it makes you look fifty. You should go home, shouldn't she?'

One of the other girls nodded and said, 'Aye. I would tell the boss, Rosie. Tell her you can't stick it, she's all right. She has it herself.' There was a giggle at this which turned into a laugh when Freda added seriously, 'Now you ain't got no proof of that, now have you? Her sex's been in question afore the day.'

Rosie did not join her laughter to the others but said, 'I wouldn't have come in this mornin' but it meant stayin' at home with that 'un. God, what a life it is now. You've no idea.'

'Does she still put it on?' one of the girls asked, and Rosie replied, 'No, by God, she doesn't put it on with me. I'd swipe her mouth for her if she did. She knows better. She keeps out of me way. Our Angus. Of all the bloody fools, our Angus ... Oh, my God, I do feel sick.'

'If you don't do it for free like you should get married, Rosie, that's what you should do. They say it clears up once you start.'

'It all goes into the first bairn,' said the other girl.

'Aw, shut your traps,' said Rosie, straightening herself up. 'Married, bairns; I'm livin' with it. I don't want to hear any more about marriage, or bairns, so shut up.'

There was silence at the table until the pain in Rosie's stomach brought her bending again, and after a moment she stood up, saying, 'I'm goin' to be sick.'

Ten minutes later Rosie went to the forewoman and told her that she'd have to go home. And fifteen minutes later, when she entered the house, she was still in pain and still feeling sick, but the moment she opened the kitchen door and saw Vanessa sitting at the table with a glazed look on her face and the table strewn with the covers of numerous aspirins she forgot about how she herself was feeling. 'God Almighty!' She put her hand across her mouth; then diving across the room she cried, 'What you done?'

Vanessa's lips moved but no sound came from them, and slowly her head sank on to her arm.

'Oh, God! God Almighty!' The words seemed to issue out of the top of Rosie's head. Then pulling Vanessa upwards, she shook her and cried, 'You bloody young fool you! You bloody young fool. What have you done. Oh, my God!' She let Vanessa's head and shoulders drop to the table again; then she grabbed the letter and scanned the first few lines, before throwing it down and crying, 'Mam! Mam!' She was running between the scullery door and the passage like someone demented. Her mother was at her job. Mrs Wilson next door? No,

259

no, she was a big mouth; there would be trouble. She'd have to get the doctor, and her mother, but if she left her she could die. You made them sick. Yes, that's what you did, you made them sick. What did you make them sick with? Oh, my God! She pulled Vanessa up again and shook her. 'Get up, Van,' she implored as she unconsciously used her name. 'Van! Van! Do you hear me? Come on. Come on.' She was in tears now as she pleaded.

Salt water. Aye, salt water. She dashed to the cupboard and, getting a packet of salt, poured a third of it into a mug and filled it with warm water from the kettle standing on the hob. She was talking and crying and swearing as she worked. 'Bloody fool! I knew something like this would happen. Our Angus, you should be battered. That's what you should be, battered. You should never have brought her here. She can't stand it, she's not made for it. God! if she dies. Come on. Come on.' She grabbed hold of Vanessa's shoulder, but when her head still lolled forward she gripped her hair and pulled her head up and, leaning her back in the chair, she whispered, 'Get this down you. It's going to make you sick. Can you hear me?'

Half the liquid ran over Vanessa's face, but some went down her throat as she gasped and gulped.

Now Rosie tried to get her to her feet but it was impossible, and once more she slumped across the table.

There was nothing for it, Rosie knew, but to get her mother and the doctor. She had her mother's phone number. If she could get a taxi she could be here in ten minutes. She looked once more at the inert figure, then flew out of the house and down to the corner of the street and across the road to where there was a telephone kiosk.

When a strange voice answered her ring she asked if she could speak to Mrs Cotton, it was very important.

When her mother came to the phone, she said quickly, 'Mam, you've got to come. Listen. She's tried to do herself in. Get a taxi, do you hear?'

There was no answer from the other end and she yelled, 'Do you hear me, Mam?' and she thought she heard her mother say, 'Aye, I heard you,' before the click of the phone came to her. She was gasping herself now, and on the point of being actually sick as she phoned Doctor Carr. Fortunately, he was still in his surgery and she began by saying, 'Doctor Carr?' and when he answered, 'Yes,' she said, 'Do – do you remember Vanessa Ratcliffe? She – she married my brother, Angus.'

When again he said, 'Yes, yes, I remember,' she said, 'Well, she's tried to do herself in, in our house.'

'What with?' he asked sharply now.

'With aspirins.'

'What have you done?'

'I've given her salt and water; that's all I could think of.'

'I'll be with you in a minute.'

'Ta, thanks doctor.'

She ran out of the box, across the road again, just missing being run down by a bus, down the street and into the house. It was very quiet and she stood for a moment looking down at the relaxed figure lying across the table, and she put her double fists over her mouth and whispered to her, 'Don't die. For God's sake, don't die.'

She continued to stare at her, not knowing what to do. She couldn't get her to her feet on her own, so perhaps it was better just to leave her there.

Emily was the first to arrive. It couldn't have been

five minutes since she got the phone call. She must have walked straight out of the house, for she was without hat or coat and was wearing a blue print dress with a big white bibbed apron over it. She, like Rosie, stood just within the door and gazed for a moment at the inert figure. Her face looked bleached. Then she whispered in much the same way as Rosie had done, 'Oh, God Almighty! . . . Did you do anything?' Her lips were quivering as she asked the question.

'I – I gave her salt water to make her sick, but it hasn't.'

'Get at the other side of her. Hoist her up. Keep her walking. That's what we must do, keep her walking. Did you get the doctor?'

'Yes, he's comin'. He should be here any minute.'

It was as much as they could do between them to support Vanessa. They pulled her arms around their shoulders and Emily thrust her arm around Vanessa's waist, and they managed to walk her up and down the kitchen twice. And then they could go no further. As they sat her in the chair again her body heaved and out of her mouth frothed the salt water and some of the liquid she had swallowed earlier.

'That's it, get it up, lass. Get it up.' Emily now started to rub her back with a large circling movement, talking in a coaxing, wheedling voice as she did so. 'Come on, come on, have another try. Doesn't matter about the floor.' It was as if Vanessa had pointed out that she was being sick all over the floor. 'If that's all we've got to worry about then we're all right. Come on, lass, get it up.'

'Hoist her again,' she said to Rosie, and as they were about to resume the walk the door opened and the doctor came in.

'Has she got it up?' he asked abruptly.

262

'Just a bit, Doctor,' said Emily.

'How many has she taken?'

'There's the papers.' She pointed to the table. 'Twenty, thirty. I don't know.'

He opened his bag quickly and filled a syringe. Then baring Vanessa's arm, he pressed the needle in gently. 'Get a bowl or something,' he said without turning his head.

It was Rosie who ran to the kitchen for a bowl and placed it at Vanessa's feet.

'Shall we walk her again, Doctor?' asked Emily.

'No, she'll be sick in a minute . . . I hope.' He slanted a bleary glance towards Emily, asking now, 'What's brought this to a head?'

Emily's eyes were cast down and she muttered something, and he repeated scathingly, 'You couldn't say? You couldn't say?'

Emily's head jerked up quickly in the old aggressive manner, only to turn sideways, and, her face averted, she said, 'It's been difficult all round, Doctor; the blame isn't all mine.'

'No, I dare say not, but you could have helped.' He was patting Vanessa's cheeks now, first one and then the other, keeping her head up the while. 'By all accounts, you've been giving her hell.'

Again Emily's head swung upwards; then after a pause she said, 'You've had your ear to the ground, haven't you?'

'I didn't have to put it that far to hear what she's been going through. Angus did a decent thing, if you could use an old phrase, a noble thing, not that it was purely altruistic on his part; nevertheless, he did what many another wouldn't have done, no matter what his feelings. But you've done your best to spoil it, Emily.'

263

'Begod, look here – '

'Don't shout; I should think you've done enough of that.'

'What do you know about it?' Emily turned her back on him, and he said, 'Quite a bit; we've all got crosses to bear. And if I hadn't had my ear to the ground, I would still have known your reaction to the present set-up. You seem to forget I've known you for the last twenty-five years.'

It was in her mind to say, 'And me you, you drunken slob,' but this wasn't the time for retaliation. Perhaps she had retaliated too much. Aye, what he said was true, but who was he to say it, anyway?

The sound of Vanessa retching brought her swiftly round and as she saw the volume of water spurt from the girl's mouth she said deep within her, 'Thank God. Oh, thank God.'

'Oh de-ar, oh de-ar, oh de-ar me,' Vanessa groaned, and Doctor Carr said, 'You're all right.' He was now holding her head against his breast, and as she moaned again he stroked the hair back from her head. 'There now, it's all over. You'll feel better soon.'

She opened her eyes dazedly and muttered, 'I'm sick.'

'Yes. It's all to the good; it's all to the good.' He nodded towards Emily now and said, 'We'll get her to bed.'

Emily and Rosie between them undressed her. Rosie supported her as Emily pulled off her clothes. Neither of them spoke until the doctor, standing at the foot of the bed, said, 'Where's Angus working?'

'He's on haulage. He's with Fred Singleton; they're running a sideline on their own.'

'Can you get him?'

Emily looked at Rosie, and Rosie said, 'They're under contract to Farrer's.'

'Well, I would phone Farrer's and get him here. I think he should see this.'

'Yes, Doctor.' Rosie ran out of the room. She had forgotten entirely about the pain in her stomach and her own sickness.

Emily, now standing close to the doctor at the foot of the bed, asked under her breath, 'Will it harm the bairn?' and he raised his eyebrows and said, 'That's to be seen. It could bring it on . . . Has she been going to the clinic?'

'No, not that I know.'

'Well, you should have seen to it, woman.' He poked his face towards her, and his attitude now brought no feeling of retaliation to her because her conscience was working against her. What she said was, 'Aye, I suppose I should. I should have done many things, but bein' meself I didn't.'

'Being yourself, you're a stubborn, ignorant individual. You know that, don't you?'

'Yes, I know it, Doctor, and I don't need you to rub it in; it takes every man to look to his own house.' They stared at each other; then she added more calmly, 'How was I to know she was working up to this?'

His voice, too, was calmer now as he said, 'You've known her for years. You knew her background, soft, easy, filled with refinements. Your own sense should have told you what this set-up would do to her.' He jerked his chin twice as he looked round the room.

'She seemed to be fallin' in. I thought she was settlin', makin' the best of a bad job. She doesn't show things very much. How was I to know?'

'You, with your experience of people, should know

that there are greater conflicts fought beneath the skin than in any open battle. She couldn't get rid of her inhibitions by yelling and shouting; it isn't done in her quarter. You know that, Emily. Their battles are fought quietly, secretly, not like round here.' Again his chin jerked twice. 'You should know that it's a saving grace to be able to bawl your head off. There's very few suicides in this quarter, whereas in the Brampton Hill area there were four last year, one a close neighbour of hers. If any of them from that quarter had one such row as you have on a Saturday night, say, it would break up the entire family for ever. She's from a different world, Emily. You should have realised that . . . But it's not too late.'

Vanessa moaned now and Doctor Carr went to her side, and when he touched her forehead she muttered, 'Angus. I'm sorry, Angus.'

'Don't worry. Don't talk any more. Go to sleep; you're all right.'

She opened her eyes, then shook her head slightly and whispered, 'Doctor Carr.'

'Go to sleep.'

Rosie came back into the room now. She was panting, and she said, 'They're goin' to tell him when he comes back for his next load.'

The doctor walked into the kitchen and Emily, about to follow him, said to Rosie, 'Stay with her a minute, will you?' Then she pulled the door closed before she asked, 'What are you goin' to do about it? Will you have to report it?'

'I should, yes.'

'But must you?' She was staring hard at him.

And he returned her stare for a full minute before he asked, 'Does anybody else know?'

266

'I'll find out.' She went into the bedroom and came out within a minute, saying, 'No. Rosie's got her head screwed on right. She phoned for me; she didn't even go next door. They'll think it's a miscarriage coming.'

He was nodding at her. 'What did she tell them when she got on the phone to Angus?'

Once more Emily went into the room, and when she came back she said, 'She told them to tell him that Vanessa had been taken bad, that's all.'

Again they were staring hard at each other; then he said, 'There's a possibility she might make a second attempt, and the next time when she's found she'll likely be too far gone to be sick.'

'No such thing, no such thing,' said Emily. 'She won't do it again; I'll see to that. I'm staying here. I'll see to her; I promise you.'

'Well, we'll see.' He sighed; then went to his bag, closed it, picked up his coat from a chair, put it on, and, going towards the door, said, 'I'll be in my surgery around one-thirty. Send Angus along to see me then.'

'Yes, Doctor.' She came close to him again and muttered softly, 'Thanks. I promise you things'll be different. I'll see to her.'

'You've nearly been too late, remember that.'

She closed her eyes and shook her head, as she said, 'Don't worry. It's somethin' I won't forget in a hurry.'

Half-an-hour later the lorry stopped at the door, and Angus burst into the house. 'What is it?' he demanded. 'What's happened to her?'

'She's all right,' said Emily from the other side of the table. 'Don't go in for a minute; Rosie's in there with her. You'd better read this.' She handed him Vanessa's letter. It was no use with-holding it from him because Vanessa would ask him if he had got it when she came round.

His mouth was agape when he stopped reading and he put his hand up and ran it slowly through his rough hair. He did it a second time before he muttered, 'Aw, no. No.'

Emily, her lips compressed to stop them trembling, stared at her son. The dark stubble round his chin was standing out against the dead whiteness of his face. There was a grey dust on his hair and shoulders. He looked all white and grey. She dreaded his onslaught; she dreaded to hear the truth from him that she was to blame for this; and she waited silently. And to her surprise he didn't break the silence, but moved slowly across the room and opened the door.

Rosie was sitting by the head of the bed. She had her hands clasped tightly between her knees; she looked like a very young girl, and she, too, was evidently waiting for the onslaught. She stared at her brother and rose to her feet as he came to the bed. She tried to say something but couldn't. He didn't look at her, and after a moment she went out into the kitchen.

Angus stared down on the long pale face. Her hair was scattered over the pillow. It looked dank and tousy. She looked almost dead. He couldn't take it in that she had tried to die. His mind seemed to have got stuck for he was still repeating to himself, 'Aw, no. No.' Then slowly he began to tell himself things and ask himself questions. He should have realised she was at this pitch. But how could he have told? She had been so quiet; she didn't talk much, and when she did she gave no indication of how she was feeling.

He was a thick-headed numbskull; he had been mad to marry her in the first place; but having done so he should never have brought her back here. Yet what could he have done? AYE, WHAT COULD HE HAVE DONE? Not

268

married her at all; just been friendly to her until she had got on her feet. He had rushed her, taken advantage of the fix she was in.

He knelt down by the bed and, enclosing her thin hands between his two hard dirt-covered ones, he whispered, 'Van! Aw, Van!' He had the desire to lay his head down on her chest and cry.

When she neither moved nor spoke he realised she was asleep, and after a moment he got to his feet and went into the kitchen.

They were waiting for him, standing stiffly within arm's length of each other looking towards the door. He knew they were expecting him to blow them sky high, but he couldn't, he didn't feel that he had a shout or a bawl left in him. He had the sensation of being winded. Moreover, he knew it would achieve nothing to blame his mother now. She couldn't have acted differently if she had tried; she had acted according to her nature, as he himself had, as Rosie had. As he walked towards the table he asked, 'Who found her?'

The moderation of his tongue loosened Rosie's tongue, and she said, 'Me. I – I had to come home, I had the cramp, and when I got in she was sittin' there.' She pointed to the chair. 'I – I nearly went mad meself.' She shook her head. 'I rung me mam – ' she nodded towards Emily, who was staring at her son, and then she ended, 'And I rang the doctor.'

'What did he say?' He was addressing his mother, and Emily moved her tongue over her lips for a moment. She wasn't going to repeat what the doctor said, she wasn't a fool; anyway, he'd likely open his mouth to him when he went along. And that's what she told him. 'He says you've got to go and see him about half-past one.'

'Does – does he think it'll affect the bairn?'

Emily glanced down for a moment. 'It might, he says; we've got to wait and see.'

He dropped suddenly on to a chair and he looked downwards as he asked, 'Have you got anythin' in, a drop of hard anywhere?'

She shook her head. 'No, but Rosie will slip along and get you somethin', won't you, Rosie?'

'Aye; it won't take a minute.'

They were both openly eager in their placating of him.

'It doesn't matter,' he said. 'Coffee will do, black.' He put his elbow on the table and rested his head in his hands. After a time he got to his feet as quickly as he had sat down and, going to the fireplace, stared into the fire as he said quietly, 'There's got to be a change, Mam.'

It was some seconds before she answered, and then briefly. 'Aye,' she said.

'I've got to get her away from here.'

'It would be best,' she said.

'I – I can't do it at once, not straightaway; I'll have to look for something.'

'I understand that.' She was supporting herself against the edge of the table, the nails of one hand digging into the underside of the wood. 'But until you do,' she said, 'I'll see to things. I'll see she's all right.'

He turned and looked at her squarely but didn't speak, and she said, 'I'm gettin' Rosie to phone Mrs McVeigh. I never liked working for her anyway; she's a mean scrub. I'll be glad to be back home.'

He surprised and broke her down at the same time by saying, 'Thanks, Mam.'

'Don't,' she turned from him, her voice harsh, her manner almost back to normal, 'don't heap coals of fire on me head; you know in your heart you're blamin' me for what's happened the day and . . . and, although I don't blame you, I'll remind you that I didn't start this. However,' she turned on him quickly before he had any time to reply, 'it's done and I'm not very proud of me share in it, but as I've said, as long as she's here I'll see to her.'

Rosie came in from the scullery, a cup of coffee in one hand and a sugar basin in the other, and she stood mutely before him while he ladled three spoonfuls of sugar into the cup. She wanted to say, 'I'm sorry,' but you didn't say you were sorry, not openly; you didn't ask for forgiveness, although you might crave it badly to take the fear away from you, the fear that told you that if Vanessa had died you yourself would have been more than a little to blame, for, to use her own words, she had been a bloody stinker.

Her tone when she said quietly, 'I made it strong,' was in itself a plea for forgiveness, and when he answered quietly, 'Ta. Ta, Rosie,' the words were a form of absolution.

They were all sitting quiet now, still somewhat stunned but united, and all three were strangely at peace.

It was as he had been telling Van all the while, things would work out, but when the thought came to him how nearly they hadn't he had to get up quickly and go down the yard.

8

Three weeks later Vanessa lost her baby. Doctor Carr
ordered her into hospital on the Friday night and the
baby was taken away on the Sunday afternoon. It was
eight days later when she returned home. Angus brought
her in a taxi, and as soon as she entered the house she
noticed a difference, particularly in their room. There
were new curtains at the window; the furniture had been
polished and there was a cherry-coloured wall-to-wall
carpet covering the floor. The room had been papered
in a plain grey paper and the old pictures hadn't been
re-hung. The single beds were still there, but they both
had new candlewick spreads. She paused in the doorway,
then looked at Angus and smiled weakly as she said, 'It's
nice, lovely. Thank you.'

He wished she didn't always thank him, not in that
polite way anyhow. He said, 'Rosie picked the colours;
I wasn't any good at it, and me mam not much better.'
He turned and looked at Rosie where she was standing
well back in the kitchen, and Vanessa turned towards her,
too, and across the distance she again spoke her thanks,
in that quiet, polite, courteous way, which would have
befitted an elderly woman but sounded strange coming
from this young girl.

Rosie nodded and smiled self-consciously. She couldn't see herself ever liking her sister-in-law; you never really liked anybody who always seemed to put you at a disadvantage; yet she no longer detested the sight of her. She took a step forward, saying, 'I thought the cherry and grey would go nice together.'

'It does. It looks lovely,' Vanessa moved into the room and to a coffee table on which was now set tea for two people. There were two cups and saucers and a milk jug and sugar basin to match, a plate of bread and butter and another of small cakes. She looked down at it; then turned and looked at Emily, and Emily said, 'I thought you'd like to eat in here.'

'No, Emily, no.' There was a firmness about the shake of her head that silenced the three people looking at her, until Angus said, 'It's all arranged, don't worry; we'll eat here.'

'No, Angus.' She looked straight into his face for a moment, then turned to Emily and said again, 'No, Emily. We eat as before.'

'Oh, then have it your own way.' Angus was tossing his head. It was as if he was giving in reluctantly to some outrageous demand, but what the three women knew in their different ways was, he was pleased and relieved at her decision.

The pattern now was different. The atmosphere in the house was light, even gay, but whereas before Angus had felt that his marriage, for good or ill, was an established fact, he no longer had this feeling of security concerning it, for as each day passed and Vanessa returned to full health, he felt that she could walk out on him any minute; there was nothing to hold her. She wasn't dependent on him to look after her and her child; she could go any place and get a job. She had the looks and figure that models were made out of; she was almost eighteen and she hadn't begun to live; she didn't know yet what it was all about.

Each night when he came back from work he felt sick, until he saw she was still there. He felt that there was one solution to it all; he had to put her in a position similar to the one she had just got out of, and everything would be as it was before.

'Go gently with her,' Doctor Carr had told him. 'She's of a different calibre to you. You've got to realise that. Modern, swingin', or what-have-you, as brash as they are today, early environment counts.' He hadn't minced his words had Doctor Carr. 'Your mother's been an old swine to her,' he said. Then he waved his hand and silenced him by adding, 'I've got three hundred patients in your quarter and four of them are in your street, one next door. You cannot stop people talking.' And then he had ended, 'I'm telling you, go gently with her. It'll pay off in the long run.'

Well he had gone gently for two months, he was burnt up inside. There was no May to go to now to relieve the pressure, and he wasn't picking anybody up. He thought too much of his skin for that; he didn't want to catch anything.

So, like a man who proposed to seduce the girl of his fancy, he planned in his mind how he would take her. They would go out the morrow night, it being Saturday; he would take her to some posh restaurant and they'd have a good dinner and a bottle of wine, and then later . . . well, that was up to him.

As he had been doing every week for the past two months, he called in at the estate agents' office to ask if they had found anything in the way of a flat for him, and

274

today Reg Walker, who incidentally had at one time lived in Ryder's Row, greeted him with, 'No, there's nothing in the way of a flat, Angus, but I wonder you don't go in for a house, or a bungalow.'

'Oh, that's in the far future for me. What I want before a house or a bungalow is a couple of lorries.'

'It's a pity,' said Reg Walker; 'a bungalow came on my books yesterday and it's a snip. It's on the outskirts. Bit out for most people. An old couple had it and they died within a month of each other and their only son is in Australia, and he's given us the O.K. to sell it. Do you remember Arthur Ridley? You know, they had the little hardware shop at the corner of Wolf Lane.'

'Yes,' nodded Angus. 'Yes, I remember them.'

'Well, it's him. I mean his people. He wrote me from Australia and asked me to get rid of the bungalow and furniture; they hadn't any money except a small insurance that paid for the funeral. He's cagey is Arthur Ridley. He once had a huge bill in from a solicitor for something and he's never dealt with them since. That's how I've come to be handling it.'

'Aye.' Angus jerked his head. 'What you askin' for it?'

'Well, it's in need of decoration inside and repair outside, and the gardens overgrown. If it was all done up it would bring anybody's four thousand, and then it would be cheap.'

'Oh, aye.' Again Angus jerked his head, laughing now.

'I'm on the level, Angus.' Reg Walker nodded at him. 'I stated a price of two thousand five hundred and Arthur Ridley agreed, so it'll go for that. And I'm telling you, these days it's an absolute snip. And there's nearly three quarters of an acre of land with it, and you know what land is the day.'

Again Angus said, 'Oh, aye,' but now he neither shook his head nor laughed. He hadn't been doing too badly these last few weeks, in fact he and Fred had split seventy pounds for each of the last five weeks. Of course there was tax off that; but then there were the Saturday runs he did and the three Sunday mornings. They had been for cash and had brought in over eighty pounds. Things were looking up, but he could do nothing big until he got more lorries, and he wanted those more than a house, but he said, 'Have you put it in the paper?'

'Yes; it'll be out the morrow.'

Angus bit on his lip. 'When could I see it?'

'Any time you like. Run you out now if you like.'

'Well, there's no time like the present.'

And so Angus went to see the bungalow, and he immediately agreed with Reg that it was a good buy, an excellent buy. It had six rooms, bathroom and garage, and it overlooked the river and a fine stretch of country. He stood in the road looking back over the tangled garden towards the roof of the bungalow. This was the answer, but it would mean good-bye to the lorries for some time to come because he would still have to help his mother. And taking the bungalow was only the beginning. There would be the repayments, rates, electricity . . . and a phone, not to mention furnishing the whole place. He said to Reg Walker, 'Will you give me until five o'clock?'

'Aye,' said Reg. 'And I won't mention it to anybody in the meantime. But mind, you'll have to make your mind then. I can't hold it, and I dare say after it comes out the morrow it'll be gone by Monday.'

'I'll let you know by five,' said Angus.

*　　*　　*

276

He didn't get into the house until half-past six. Emily had the tea set waiting. 'You're late,' she said; 'I thought you must have run into Van.'

'Run into Van?' He looked towards the room door. 'She's not in?'

'No, she went out early this afternoon; she was going to do a bit of shoppin' or somethin'.'

As he moved slowly towards their room she said, 'Now don't go in there on that carpet with your boots on. I've told you,' and he stopped and looked down at the floor for a moment, then sat down by the side of the fireplace and took off his heavy boots and put on a pair of slippers that were resting on the fender.

'Get your wash . . . You're not goin' to the baths the night?'

'No . . . She's never been out at this time.'

'She could have gone to Newcastle.' Emily was bending down to the oven.

'What would she want in Newcastle, there's plenty of shops here? What was she after, do you know?'

Emily lifted a pie from the oven. Its top was brown and there was a pattern of pastry leaves around the edges. It could have been cooked for the table at Bower Place. She said now, 'Stop your worryin'. Surely she can go out for five minutes . . .'

'It isn't five minutes if she went out this afternoon.'

'Well, anyway, you're not very early yourself; you're nearly an hour past your time. Where've you been?'

He got to his feet and went into the scullery and, stripping to the waist, he started to wash himself before he called out to her, 'I've been after a bungalow.'

She was at the scullery door, looking at him. 'A bungalow?' Her voice was high.

'Aye. Reg Walker had a snip on his books; he offered

it to me. I had to make up me mind for five o'clock; it was as quick as that.'

'How much?'

'Two thousand five hundred.'

'Oh, my God!'

'It's worth four thousand, even as it stands. It wants doing up.'

'That'll take some payin' for. What'll happen to the lorries you were goin' after?'

'They'll have to wait. First things first.'

As he reached for a towel he paused and looked at her and said, 'You'll be all right . . . I'll see to you.'

'Now look.' Her voice was high and held the old aggressive quality. 'Don't you bother about me, lad; I can take care of meself. And there's always supplementary. I don't see why I shouldn't get it; every other bugger in the street's on it. You look after yourself . . . and her. Anyway, if Stan and Rosie marry, an' they're bound to, they'll come in with me, so don't let anythin' at this end put you off.'

He nodded at her.

A few minutes later, back in the kitchen, he said, 'Hold it for another ten minutes or so until I get changed; she'll likely be in by then.'

In the room the fire was burning brightly; it looked comfortable and cheery. Inwardly he was delighted at the change in the room, but it was still small, and to her it must appear like a box.

Where was she? Had she gone? He brought his forefinger to his teeth and bit the end completely off his nail. It would be just like the thing, wouldn't it, him getting the bungalow and her going off all in the same day. What would he do without her? How could he go on without her? How did he go on before he had her?

278

And yet he'd never had her in that sense. He had lived in this room with her for weeks on end and he'd never had her. It was all going to happen tomorrow night. He was barmy, mad. Be nice to her, gentle, Doctor Carr had said. Gentle be damned. He should have taken his rights weeks ago; that would have settled it. She would likely have been well on the way now with another. God it was as his mother had said, he was soft, barmy, a blasted fool. He had worked his guts out these last few weeks to get the money to put down for the lorries and now what had he done with it? Given Reg Walker fifty pounds in advance, and promised him another two hundred and fifty the morrow. That would take every penny of his capital and push him back a year, two years; in fact he might never get on his feet again. Well, it served him right . . . And wouldn't there be some laughter round the doors when they knew she had left him high and dry. They had been waiting for it, betting on it . . . Aw, he knew them.

He went to the narrow mantelpiece and, leaning his forearms along it, he dropped his head on to them and groaned inwardly.

When he heard his mother's voice saying, 'Hello, we thought you had got lost,' he almost sprang to the little table in the corner of the room, and when she opened the door he was emptying his back trouser pocket of notes and silver.

'Hello, there.' He smiled at her. 'You look froze. Where've you been?' He continued to smile at her as he walked towards her.

'I went into Newcastle.'

'Oh. Mam thought you might.' He was nodding at her.

She was taking off her hat and coat. 'It's raw,' she

279

said, 'bitter; it's nice to see a fire.' She bent forward and held her hands down to the blaze and, looking over her shoulder, said, 'You were late, too?'

'Yes. Yes, I've been doing a bit of business . . . What have you been up to? Shoppin'?'

She turned and hunched her shoulders up over her long neck, then smoothed down her mauve woollen dress over her flat stomach before saying, 'I've been after a job.'

When he made no comment on this she said, 'Don't be vexed.'

'Vexed! Me? I'm not vexed. What kind of a job?'

'In one of the stores, Daintrees.'

'Oh. It's a classy shop that.'

'Yes.' She nodded. 'Quite nice. You don't mind?'

If he didn't know what he was going to do tomorrow night, or tonight for that matter, he would have said, 'Mind? You're bloody well right, I do mind. If you can't fill your time in then I'll have to give you something to fill it in with, won't I?' but what he said was, 'I've got a surprise for you an' all.'

'You have?' She waited.

'How would you like a bungalow?'

'Bungalow!' She brought her head forward, her smile widening her large mouth.

'Aye, I've bought one.'

She moved a step towards him. 'You've bought a bungalow? What . . . what kind?' She didn't say, 'You bought a bungalow without me seeing it? I mightn't even like it.'

'Big one. Six rooms. The lot. There was no time to let you know. I had to make up me mind by five o'clock. It's a snip. I'll run you out first thing in the mornin' to see it.'

'Where is it?' Her face was bright and eager.

'Oh, it's a bit outside. Collier Road way, on a rise. You can see the river from the windows.'

The river. Her throat constricted just the slightest; the smile was fading from her face when she brought it back again and said, 'Oh, that sounds lovely. Is it going to cost a lot?'

'No. As I said, it's a snip. Two thousand five hundred. It's worth four, even as it stands. Get it put into shape and you can add another two on to that.'

She glanced towards the door, then said under her breath, 'But, Emily.'

'She knows; she's glad.'

'Are you goin' to let this get spoilt?' Emily's voice, coming from the other room, made them both grimace, then laugh gently, and he pushed her towards the door, saying, 'I'll be there in a tick.'

As Vanessa entered the kitchen Rosie came down the stairs, and she asked immediately, under her breath, 'Did you get it?' and Vanessa nodded and said, 'Yes.'

'What they payin' you?'

'Six pounds ten.'

Rosie shrugged her shoulders. 'That isn't very much; in fact it's nowt. And then you've got your fares to pay.'

'That's only to start with, sort of training period. I'll get commission on sales after two months.'

'What did he say?' Rosie jerked her head backwards.

'Oh, he doesn't mind.'

'Coo!' Rosie again jerked her head; 'that's a surprise.'

'What's a surprise?' Angus came into the room, buttoning his shirt up, and Rosie said, 'It's none of your business.'

'Have you told her?' He looked from his mother

to Vanessa, and when Vanessa shook her head and his mother said, 'No, I've not had time, she's just come down,' he turned to Rosie and said, 'I've got a bungalow.'

'A bungalow? You come into some money or summat? A bungalow? When did this all happen?'

When they sat down to their meal he explained briefly how it had all happened, and then Rosie voiced what was in the back of his mind all the time. 'Well, that's put paid to your gettin' any more lorries, at least for some time,' she said, "cos you'll need furniture and things. Good job you started work.' She nodded at Vanessa, and Vanessa, after a moment, said, 'Yes. Yes, it is.' She herself had forgotten about the lorries for the moment, and yet they hadn't been out of her mind for weeks past; the job she had got today was in a way connected with the lorries.

It was as they finished the meal that Angus, suddenly determining in his mind to push personal matters forward a little, said, 'What about us all goin' to the club to celebrate? Friday night's a good night.'

Neither Emily nor Rosie made any rejoinder, but after a moment's pause Vanessa said, 'Yes. Yes, that's a good idea.'

'Oh, I don't feel like it,' said Emily sitting back in the chair. 'Me feet's killin' me.'

It wouldn't have taxed Emily's feet very much in visiting the club. She would have loved to have gone along tonight and had a bit of a sing-song. It was what she needed, to be in a crowd and yell her head off, but the last time they had gone to the club altogether it hadn't been a success. It was Vanessa's initiation, so to speak, into their kind of entertainment and she had smiled all the while, even laughed at some of the turns, but Emily hadn't seen her almost since she was a bairn not to know that it was a façade covering her real feelings. She knew that even if Vanessa had been challenged she wouldn't have admitted to her opinion of the company, of the drinking, singing, rocketing company, where, although the men were well put on and the women wore dresses that were a good imitation of the Bower Place lot, they acted as they had always done. It would have taken somebody like Miss Susan to say outright, 'Common individuals!'

Rosie wanted Vanessa to accompany them to the club no more than her mother, so she said brightly, 'Why the club? Look, our Angus, why don't you take Van along to some place like Donovan's? Now, that would be a night out, sort of celebration for her getting her job.'

'Donovan's.' Angus cocked his chin in the air and repeated, 'Donovan's. Aye.' He looked at Vanessa. 'Would you like to go to Donovan's?'

'I've never been, I don't know what it's like.' She glanced at Rosie, and Rosie said, 'Oh, it's posh is Donovan's. That's where all the Rugby players get on a Saturday night. Angus used to go, didn't you?'

'Oh, well.' He moved his head from side to side. 'I've been a couple of times, but – ' he turned to Vanessa – 'I wouldn't take you there on a Saturday night.' Then bending towards her he added jocularly, 'But this is Friday. We'll go to Donovan's, eh?'

'Is it . . . is it evening dress or . . .?'

'No, anything,' he answered.

'Your blue one,' Rosie put in, 'that he bought you for Christmas. That would do. It's smart and warm and it's your colour. You look smashing in it.'

Vanessa smiled at Rosie. When Rosie was kind to her, as now, she ceased to think, 'If only you had been like this from the beginning I wouldn't have done it.'

The shame of trying to take her own life was still with her. She felt that her action had been the admission of utter failure. She was like Brett. Brett had given her the child, then had taken his life because he couldn't face up to the consequences. They were a pair, weak; nice, but weak. His weakness had created the child and her weakness had killed it. No matter what Doctor Carr said to the contrary, she would always feel that it was through her attempted suicide that the child had died. It had been shocked into death when on the point of coming alive.

'You're for it, aren't you?' Angus's question brought her mind quickly to the present, and she answered eagerly, 'Yes, yes, of course. I'd love it. That's if we're not too late. I've got to get ready and it's after seven.'

'Oh, places like those don't get going until nine or ten.'

'Well, don't sit there,' said Emily, energetically now. 'An' don't you go on stuffing yourself.' She nodded at Angus. 'Else what's the good you payin' for a meal?'

As he got to his feet he bent towards her, saying, 'I bet you a shilling that no matter what we pay it won't be half as good as this.' He was trying to please her in all ways these days. She was all right was his mam; he had always known it . . .

Half-an-hour later they were both ready, and Emily, looking at them as they stood side by side in the kitchen, thought that whatever differences there was underneath it didn't show much when they were dressed up. She was proud of the way Angus was turned out; nothing flashy about him; he could have come from Brampton Hill itself. He knew how to dress, did Angus, and how to carry himself. He had been to Donovan's before and mixed with them lot. Oh, she had no fear of how he would carry himself in that swell place.

'Bye-bye,' said Vanessa, looking from Emily to Rosie; and they didn't answer as was usual with them, saying, 'Ta-rah,' but said, 'Bye-bye . . . And enjoy yourselves,' they both added.

'Don't wait up mind.' Angus turned from the door and Emily answered robustly, 'Wait up for you? What would I wait up for you for? Go on, get yourself away.'

As they stood waiting at the corner of the street for a bus he looked at Vanessa and said, 'There's one thing missing.'

'What's that?'

'A car. People don't go by bus to Donovan's. You can't get near it for cars.'

'Well, we can get off at the stop before and pretend we've left ours parked at the end of the road.'

He dug her gently in the ribs and jerked his head as he said, 'You've got something.'

He was happy as he had never been happy before. The happiness banked down on that corner of his mind where were piled his worries.

In the bus she asked, with excitement in her voice, 'Is there a place to dance?'

'Aye, a bit of floor, but , . .' He drooped his head to the side to look full into her face. 'Do you dance? Funny, I've never asked you; do you dance?'

'I've had lessons.' Her brows moved upwards.

'But you've never been on a dance floor?' He felt superior. This he could teach her, anyway, because he was a good dancer. Heavily made as he was, he was light on his feet.

'Once,' she said.

'Once!' His look and tone ridiculed her single effort;

then he added, 'If you stand on me toes I'll yell the place down mind.'

When she laughed and looked down at his size ten shoes his happiness moved in all directions through his body; it made him want to grab her to him and hold her tightly, not do anything, just hold her tightly, like his Uncle Dick used to do to his Aunt Ann. They had been married for twenty years but he used to get hold of her and hug her, and she used to laugh up into his face. She was a little woman, round and fat, but there was something between them, a sort of something. He remembered it when he went to his funeral, that day he had met Van in the train. Lord, that seemed ten years ago. Did he ever think then that . . .? Blimey? He would have asked them to cart him away if he had even dreamed of it.

They got off the bus, and when they reached the hotel car park where the cars were spilling over on to the drive it looked as if it was a busy night after all.

'We . . . we mightn't get a table.' His voice was flat. 'I should have had the sense to slip out and phone when I got the idea.'

'I don't suppose it would have made much difference; you likely have to book up a day or so ahead. Anyway, we can always try.' She smiled consolingly at him, and her eyes lingered on his face. She wasn't ashamed to be out with him; that was something she was grateful for. Another thing she was grateful for was, he didn't raise his voice outside. He could bawl and shout in the house; even in their room he shouted to her in ordinary conversation as if she was at the end of the street, but outside his manner was different. He tried, did Angus. Oh yes, he tried very hard. She wished he would let her help him. She had learned a lot over the past weeks about the man she had married. She knew, for instance, that he was in constant fear that she would leave him now that there was nothing to hold her, only a marriage that could be dissolved quite easily, it never having been consummated. She knew that he didn't want her to go to work in case she would meet someone else. She was getting to understand all his little ways, his moods, but this did not alleviate the fear in which she held him, the fear that would be strengthened or erased completely when he began to make demands of her; and the time for that was very near. She knew it; she felt it; it was very near.

Having left their outer things in the cloakroom they walked side by side past the open cocktail bar, past the main bar, across the deeply carpeted lounge that was studded with small tables and groups of people, and towards the dining-room. When they were almost there he stopped and said, 'Would you like a drink first?' He motioned towards one of the tables, and without looking at them she said, 'No. No, I would rather not.' She felt excited; nervous, and strangely more ill at ease than he was.

'Good evening, sir. Good evening, madam. You have a table reserved?'

'No, I'm sorry,' said Angus. 'We just came on speck.' His voice sounded airy.

'Ah!' The head waiter looked straight into Angus's face, and Angus said, 'I'd be obliged if you could find us a table.' The words were a promise and the head waiter said, 'Well, sir, you're lucky, there's been a cancellation . . . and a very nice table. It's in the alcove. Come this way. This way, madam.'

The table was indeed a nice table. It was screened from part of the main room by an ornamental partition, and the head waiter pulled out a chair that backed on to the partition for Vanessa, giving her a view over part of the dining-room towards the space allotted for dancing and to the small platform where four musicians were seated.

When they were alone for a moment Angus drew in a deep breath and adjusted his coat, then said, 'Nice?'

'Lovely.' She nodded across the table at him.

As the band struck up the wine waiter came to the table and handed Angus the wine list.

'Well now.' He looked at it, then across at her and asked, 'What do you fancy?'

'I'll have a sherry,' she said.

'Dry or sweet, madam?' asked the waiter.

'Dry, please.'

Angus, after a pause said, 'Make it two.'

'And for later, sir; you'd like a little wine with the meal?'

'Yes. Oh, yes.' Angus looked at the wine list again. He knew nothing about wines. He could name any make of beer in the country, even the brands that were popular in the South, but of wines he was completely ignorant. He felt the heat of embarrassment creeping up his neck. He saved it getting further by looking over the list and saying to Vanessa, 'Have you any particular fancy?'

Intuitively she knew he needed help and she answered, 'I would like,' she paused as she was about to say, 'a white wine.' Instead she named it. 'A Graves Supérieur or a Liebfraumilch.' She looked at Angus, and the waiter looked at Angus, waiting for the final word. And Angus, taking a deep breath, gave him the final word, and he pronounced it almost as Vanessa had done. 'Graves Supérieur,' he said, nodding once. He couldn't have attempted to pronounce the other tongue-twister.

'Very good, sir. Very good.'

When they were alone again, he stared at her, without speaking now. She knew about wines. The space between them was marked again.

She leaned forward and said to him now, under her breath, and as if she had read his thoughts, 'I only know about them because father used to discuss them with mother when people were coming for a meal.' Her voice trailed away. She knew she had said the wrong thing. As far as she could remember it was the first time she had spoken her father's name to him since they were married. This could spoil everything. She said quickly, 'I'm sorry.'

'What you sorry for? No need to be sorry because you know the name of a wine.' He flapped his hand lightly at her, and ignored the fact that she had mentioned her father.

Then they were ordering dinner. He knew his way about here. This was safer ground; it wasn't the first time he had ordered dinner. That was until he looked at the menu. 'What about a shrimp cocktail to start with?' He was bending towards her.

And she answered, 'Lovely.'

'Two shrimp cocktails.'

'And the main course, sir?'

Again Angus looked at her. She was looking at the menu. It was mostly in French.

He too looked at the menu. He looked at it for quite a while; then he raised his eyes to the waiter and said coolly, 'A steak for me, medium rare.'

'Very good, sir. Very good, and you, madam?'

She did not say Chicken sauté à la Marengo but fried chicken in sauce, please.

When that was over they both relaxed for different reasons.

289

There were couples dancing on the floor now, and when she began to tap her fingers to the tune he said laughingly, 'Now you're not going to get up there and show them until you've had something to eat.'

She laughed softly across at him. They both looked across the room when a roar of laughter came from the direction of the cocktail bar, and as the band struck up a number of couples came through from the lounge and began to dance.

Angus, still looking across the room, said, 'I didn't think that was allowed; I thought the dancing space was only for the diners.' He had the air of a regular patron.

As the noise and the laughter rose above the music, Angus commented, 'They're all high. Looks like a Saturday night after all.'

'You used to come here on a Saturday night?'

'Once or twice after we finished the game.'

'I never knew you played Rugby until tonight.'

There was a twisted smile on his face and he looked at her for a full minute before saying, 'There's lots of things you don't know about me, Van.'

When she lowered her gaze from his he turned it quickly into a joke. 'I've got a medal for life-savin',' he said; 'I once dived into four feet of water and got a bairn up in the baths.' When she gave a little splutter he said, 'It's a fact. There was a gang of lads together and someone shouted that their Willie or some such was drownin' and I ran along and dived in, and it was nearly fifteen minutes later when I came round; I'd hit me head on the bottom.'

'Was anyone drowned?'

'I don't know, I've never found out to this day.' They were laughing openly now. 'And that's not all,' he said.

'You should have seen what I got for doing a good deed.' He lifted the quiff of his sandy hair from his brow. 'Have you noticed that?'

She looked at the scar and said, 'Yes, I had noticed it, and I wondered how you got it.'

'Oh, that was the payment for doing the good deed. I was on top of a bus and a woman was going to go down the stairs. She had a basket of groceries, a huge basket, an' she was hanging on to the top rail. The bus was going round a corner so I said, "Give it here, missis; I'll take it down for you." I was a big brawny fellow of fifteen and she said, "Thanks, lad," and she went down the stairs and me after her. Only I tripped, and it was the iron rail, you know the rail you hang on to, that stopped me falling into the road and, boy, I've never seen a basket of groceries go so far in me life. Talk about the three loaves and the five fishes.'

He had her laughing now, really laughing. Her shoulders were hunched and she had her hand across her mouth, and when she murmured, 'Oh, Angus, don't,' he warmed to his theme. He was entertaining her; she was happy; it was the first time he had seen her really laugh. He said, 'That's nothing. I could fill a book. Every time I've done a good turn in me life I've got it slapped back straight in me face.' Somewhere in the back of his mind he knew this was a tactless remark, and at the same time some part of him was praying that this was one time in his life that he wouldn't have his good deed slapped right back into his face, that life would go on from here and that she would never leave him.

'There was Mrs Halliday's fire,' he said. 'You know Mrs Halliday, five doors down. I was comin' down the street one day and there was smoke comin' out of her window, and she came out yellin' that her gas stove had caught fire, and in dashed brave Angus Cotton. I couldn't get near the stove. "Have you got any salt?" I yelled. Mam was always douching our fire with salt when the chimney caught ablaze, you know, and Mrs Halliday yelled back at me, "What!" and I yelled, "Salt!" She was a very methodical woman was Mrs Halliday and she kept a good supply of stuff in the house – everybody used to go and borrow from her. Anyway, when she pointed I picked up the jar of salt, only it wasn't salt it was sugar, and I threw it on the fire. Believe me we were nearly blown over the railway wall.'

Her head was down, her hands were joined tightly in her lap, her eyes were wet; she looked up at him from under her thick short lashes and asked, 'What was the end to that?'

'The fire brigade. Her whole kitchen was burnt down. Lord, I daren't pass her door for months after that.'

Again she said, 'Oh, Angus.' He was nice. She had always known he was nice. He was trying to make her happy. Oh, if only he could . . .

The steak came medium rare, the chicken and its sauce were delicious. They ate everything on their plates, and then made their choice from a trolley of assorted sweets. Finally there was coffee.

'Will you have it here or in the lounge, sir?'

They decided to have it in the lounge. They walked around the outskirts of the dancing couples, past the head waiter whom Angus thanked for an excellent meal and supplemented his thanks with a piece of folded paper, and they were again escorted to their seats.

Over the coffee Angus looked at her and asked, 'Enjoying it?'

'It's lovely, Angus, wonderful. Do you know,' she twisted round to him, 'this is the first time I've ever been out to dinner. I've never enjoyed myself like this before, never in my life.'

His eyes ranged over her face. All the tenseness had gone from it; she looked soft and warm and beautiful. There was nobody in here who could hold a candle to her; and she had to develop yet. In two or three years' time she'd be a stunner; a little more flesh on her and she'd be something. Did she know that? Was she aware of how she looked to other people? He must keep her. By fair means or foul he must keep her. He knew now that all his life he had wanted her, and he had got her, but when she came awake could he keep her? Because the raw fact was, she wasn't awakened yet, not to anything. She'd had a bairn but it hadn't really touched her.

He got abruptly to his feet now and, buttoning up his coat, said, 'We're going into the fray, it's a quick-step. Have you ever done a quick-step?'

She shook her head. 'I've done the twist. I can do the twist.' She sounded confident.

'Aw, the twist! That went out with the first programme of "Top of the Pops". Quick-step's back, à la ballroom dancin'; it's all back. I even saw a young lad on the telly the other night in "Top of the Pops" put his arm round a girl's waist when they were dancing. Do you know somethin'?' He shook his head at her. 'It looked quite indecent, it did really.'

He had her laughing again when they reached the dance floor. And there he put his arm around her and walked her gently backwards and forwards.

She had a lightness and rhythm all her own, and soon they were moving in motion together and she smiled up at him, pleased that this was so. Two or three times they were bumped into, and occasionally he had to excuse himself for bumping into someone else; the small floor was packed even before the company from the cocktail bar came on to it again.

It was when they were almost knocked off their balance by a stumbling, laughing couple that Angus said somewhat angrily, 'Here, steady on,' and, balancing Vanessa, he glared at the back of the man who had bumped into them, and who was evidently far from sober for he had his head on his partner's neck as he shook with laughter. But Angus's tone piercing his mirth, brought him round and he stared from one to the other. Then, his mouth widening, he said, 'Ah, Good Lord! Cotton . . . And you!' His eyebrows moved upwards as he continued to stare at Vanessa. Then on a hic of a laugh, he said, 'Why; would you believe it? Vanessa Ratcliffe!' He poked his head towards her. 'You know me. You remember at Susan's do? Brian Cornell. Fancy seeing you here.'

'Yes, fancy,' said Angus flatly, putting his arm round Vanessa once more and moving away into the dance.

Within a minute Cornell was at their shoulder again, shouting above the music and the noise, 'We'll have to get together, eh?'

Angus made no reply, and a few minutes later he walked Vanessa back to the lounge.

'You know him?'

She screwed up her face as if trying to remember. 'Yes, yes, I've seen him before. He came to a party of Susan's. And you . . . you know him, too?'

'He was in the Rugby team. Still is for all I know.' He didn't add that Cornell was one of those individuals who would speak to you if he must in the dressing-room, or when he was drunk, as now, but would ignore you flat in the street when he was with his women folk. And they said there was no class distinction these days. God! That was funny. He remembered thinking along the same lines the day he met Colin Brett in the station. 'Have another coffee?' he asked her.

'Yes, I think I will.'

He leaned towards her. 'What about a liqueur? Would you like a liqueur?'

'No.' It was a firm no. 'And stop throwing your money about.' She was smiling gently at him. 'You'll need all you can get from now on.'

'Yes,' he said, 'I know. But this is a night apart.'

They were looking at each other; then her head drooped and she moved the spoon around in her cup as she said, 'I'm glad I've got a job, Angus; it'll help, won't it?'

He didn't answer her for a moment; and then he said, 'I don't want you to go to work, Van. You know that, don't you?'

'But I can't stay at home all day, Angus; there's nothing to do.'

'There will be once you get into the bungalow. There'll be more than you can tackle.'

Once more their gaze held until he exclaimed, 'Aw, don't let's talk about that now. Drink your coffee and then I'll let you stand on me toes again.'

She had just put her cup down when there loomed over them the tall, heavy figure of Brian Cornell. 'Ha-ha!' He put a hand on each of their shoulders. 'I've caught you.'

There was the thing about getting to your feet, Angus knew, when another man came to a table when a woman was present, but he remained seated, his head to one side, staring up into the grinning countenance.

'Spare her a minute?' Cornell's voice was thick and fuddled, and his glance merely touched on Angus as he made his request. But it rested heavily on Vanessa as he said briefly, 'Dance?'

'She's not dancing any more.'

'What!' Cornell straightened himself. 'Now, now. Come on, Cotton; don't play the heavy husband. You should have got over that by now. What is it? Four months? Six months? Anyway, I knew her before you did.' He laughed as he punched Angus not too gently on the back.

'You do remember me, don't you?' He was leaning over Vanessa, his face close to hers. 'Susan's party. You know something? I remember thinking then that you'd beat Susan to a frazzle. Come on, give me this dance?' He caught hold of her arm, but she remained seated.

'Leave go of her!' Angus was now on his feet.

'What! Aw, Cotton, be your age.' Cornell thrust his arm backwards across Angus's chest. 'Don't come the heavy husband, man. You're out of your depths; they don't act like that where she comes from.'

His raised voice had attracted the other occupants of the lounge. There was a man sitting to the right of them who had turned completely round and was listening intently to all that was going on.

'I – I don't want to dance, thank you,' Vanessa said; then looking from Cornell to Angus she added quickly, 'It's about time we were going.'

The look she bent on Angus said plainly, 'Please, please don't make a scene,' and he obeyed it. His jaw stiff, his fists clenched tight, he waited for Cornell to leave them. But Cornell had no intention of leaving them. Sidling down on to the wall seat to the left of Vanessa, he mumbled thickly, 'S'prised to see you; didn't think they would let you up out of the ghetto.'

The next second Brian Cornell was up on his feet

296

again, brought there by Angus's hands gripping the lapels of his coat.

'Come on outside.'

'Go to the devil!' Cornell tugged himself from Angus's hold; then surveyed him with disdain.

'Are you coming outside?'

'You'd better go.' The words came from the man who had taken an interest in the proceedings. He was a youngish forty, dapper looking, small.

'Oh, you, Fowler.' Cornell turned towards the man. 'Well, you keep out of this.'

'Are you coming outside or have I to give it to you here?'

'Have it anyway you like, chum, only don't forget you asked for it.' Cornell's mouth curled upwards.

As they went through the lounge, Cornell shouted, 'Arthur! Tony!' but when Arthur and Tony came from the cocktail bar counter they were stayed by the man Cornell had called Fowler. 'Hold your hand!' he said. 'They'll have it out on their own.'

'What the hell is it all about?'

'You can ask Cornell when it's over.'

It was quickly all over. Out in the open near the car park they squared up to each other.

If Cornell had been sober he would have been a match for Angus, but in his present condition his blows were aimed wildly; not so Angus's. A blow with the right hand to the stomach was immediately followed by a quick left-right to the face. When Cornell stumbled against the wall, his body bent over double, Angus stood back gasping.

There was a small crowd around them now, all men, with the exception of Vanessa, and as she moved to Angus's side he pushed her roughly away muttering, 'Go and get your things on.'

After a moment's pause she turned to obey him, and it was then she saw one of Cornell's friends, with his fist at shoulder level, making for Angus from behind, but he never reached him, for experiencing a feeling of anger that was quite new to her she sprang forward crying, 'Stop it, you drunken beast you.' Whether it was the push she gave the man, or the surprise of being attacked by a girl, he stumbled backwards, and those around sniggered. But the sound died swiftly away as Brian Cornell raised himself up and leant against the wall for support. There was blood running from the corner of his mouth and one eye was already swelling.

Another man, going to Cornell's aid, turned and confronted Angus, crying, 'You should be damned well ashamed of yourself. If there was a policeman about I'd hand you over. They're never here when they're wanted.'

The quiet voice interrupted again, saying, 'You're talking to the wrong fellow; he didn't start it.'

'I saw what he started; I was in the lounge. He attacked him first.'

'Under provocation.'

'Come on.' Angus pushed Vanessa past the men and into the hotel again, where the manager was waiting in the foyer, his face no longer smiling. His voice stiff, he said, 'This is a very unfortunate incident, sir.'

'You should be more particular who you let in then, shouldn't you? And you shouldn't keep on serving drink to drunks.'

'Angus!' There was deep appeal in Vanessa's voice and he turned to her and, biting on his lip, said harshly, 'All right, all right. Get your things.'

She wasn't a minute collecting her coat and hat, and when she returned to the hall Angus was talking to the dapper man; at least, the dapper man was talking to Angus. He turned to Vanessa and said, 'Now don't let this little incident worry you. I was just telling your husband that should anything come of it he can call on me to say my piece.'

'Thank you.' She inclined her head towards him, and, looking intently at her, he smiled and said, 'You don't know me but I know of you. I happen to be Brian Braintree's half-cousin.' Perhaps it was because he felt that both of them stiffened that he added quickly, 'But on the poor side. Brian's father and mine are full cousins but they're not on speaking terms; we weren't invited to the wedding.' He brought his head forward as he pulled a face. 'I recognised you right away. You were at the Taylor's house about three years ago when I was there. You haven't changed much. My name's Fowler, Andrew Fowler.'

All she could say was, 'Oh.' Her face was flushed. She knew he was trying to be nice, smooth things over, but she wished he wouldn't. She felt sure that the very mention of him being connected in any way with her family, or the one into which Susan had married, would make Angus angry. But Angus showed no actual resentment towards the man; in fact, he bade him good-night quite civilly, and when he turned towards the door the man turned with them, saying, 'I'm off too.' And on the steps of the hotel he left them, adding, 'Good-bye. And don't let it worry you. Cornell's been asking for that for a long time.'

They walked across the drive and round by the car park and to the bus stop almost in silence. It was as they were standing there that Andrew Fowler passed them in the car. Drawing up sharply and backing towards them, he asked, 'Can I give you a lift?'

Angus hesitated for a moment, then said, 'Thanks,' and opened the door and helped Vanessa in.

'Where can I drop you?'

'Oh, anywhere near Caxton Bridge,' said Angus in an off-hand manner.

They had gone a little way when Fowler dropped his head backwards as he said, 'You're in the contracting business, aren't you?'

'Yes. How did you know?'

'Oh, I'm an architect. I remember seeing you down at Ralstons, in the office or somewhere, and somebody happened to remark that you had started up.'

Yes, thought Angus to himself; I bet they did. And I bet they added, 'That's him that got old Ratcliffe's daughter into trouble.' Only the term wouldn't have been as polite as that.

'How's business going?'

'Oh, not too bad. Could be better though.'

'How many are you running . . . lorries?'

'Just the two at the moment.' He was talking as if the concern was his own.

'Hmm!' There was a silence after this for a while until Andrew Fowler remarked, 'You really need more than two unless you're always going to be dependent on the big firms.'

As if he didn't know that.

When they reached the bridge, and the car stopped, Andrew Fowler turned to Angus and, handing him his card, said, 'You may want to get in touch with me if they stir anything up about tonight. As I said, I'll vouch for you being provoked. Cornell's a nasty piece of work; I think you'd better know that.'

'I already know it; I've met him afore. We were in the Rugby team together.'

'Oh.'

'But thanks. Thanks all the same. And thanks for the lift. Good-night.'

'Good-night,' said Vanessa. 'And thank you.'

He nodded to them both and said, 'Good-night,' and drove off.

They walked down the main road and over the traffic lights, past the railway bridge and up the street, and just before they reached the door he pulled her to a stop and, peering at her in the dimness, said, 'I'm sorry. It . . . it was such a grand night, but . . . it wasn't really my fault.'

'Oh, I know, Angus, I know. He was a horrible beast, and I'm glad that you hit him.' There was a vehemence in her voice that he hadn't heard before, and he smiled slightly and said with some surprise, 'You are?'

'Yes. I wanted to hit him myself.' She, too, was smiling weakly now. 'I pushed that other man.' She put her hand up to her face as she added, 'I've never done that before in my life; but . . . but I wished I'd had a stick or something.'

He put his hand out swiftly and grasped her round the shoulders and pressed her to him for a moment; then they went into the house.

Emily was in; so too were Rosie and Stan; and Emily turned and looked at them in surprise, saying, 'Well! you're back early.'

'No good?' asked Rosie.

'Very good,' said Vanessa. 'Very good indeed.' She looked from one to the other; then slowly she started to laugh. Leaning against the table she laughed and laughed.

They had never heard her laugh like this; they had never seen her mouth stretch in real laughter. They watched her put her arm around her waist as her laughter grew. It was almost touching on hysteria and they became infected by it. Angus sat heavily down on a chair, and threw his head back. Emily was laughing, as was Rosie and Stan, although they didn't know what they were laughing about.

'What is it? Tell us the joke,' Rosie spluttered, and when Vanessa, gasping and holding her chin tightly, said, 'He . . . Angus had a fight,' Emily's laughter suddenly ceased and she cried, 'MY God! You didn't. Not at the Donovan?'

Vanessa was nodding her head when Rosie, who had also stopped laughing, said, 'Oh, our Angus. You had a fight in the Donovan? Trust you to show yourself up.'

Vanessa was still gasping, and the tears were running down her face, and she tried to check her mirth as she said to Rosie, 'But he didn't, he didn't. There was a man and he was bothering me and he wouldn't stop and,' she glanced at Angus, and the laughter bubbled in her again, 'he – he made him go outside and blacked his eyes.' Her long thin body drooped and she collapsed into a chair.

'Oh, my God!' Emily was no longer amused. Staring at Angus now, she asked, 'Who was he? Anybody important?'

'Oh, Mam!' He too had stopped laughing. 'Important? Who's important? Yes, I suppose you could say he was important. It was Brian Cornell.'

'Cornell? You mean the shop Cornell; him who's got the chain stores?'

'Yes, him who's got the chain stores.'

'Well mind, you picked on somebody to hit, didn't you?'

'Aye, I picked on somebody to hit, Mam; and I'll hit him again if I meet up with him.'

'Good for you,' said Stan. 'I know a bit about Cornell. Beer and bawd Cornell, they call him, and it isn't spelt b,o,a,r,d. He's no good.'

'We agree on that, Stan,' said Angus, nodding across the table.

'Aw dear, dear me,' said Emily, getting to her feet. 'Trust you to get into trouble. I don't know when you have gone out of this house that something hasn't happened to you.'

'We had a lovely dinner,' said Vanessa now.

'Aye, what did you have?' asked Stan, aiming to change the subject.

And Vanessa told them, and in detail, and she ended, 'We had Liebfraumilch with it.' They hadn't, but it sounded better than Graves Supérieur.

'Lieb – what? What in the name of goodness is that when you're out?' asked Rosie.

'It's a wine. Angus chose it.'

Both Rosie and Emily were looking at Angus as if they had never seen him before. They didn't ask what he knew about this lieb-frau or whatever it was, they just looked at him, and he laughed openly at them. He was suddenly happy again, very happy. She was with him; she had said he had picked that wine. He bent forward now and, pointing his finger at his mother, said, 'And there's something more you won't believe. She hit a fellow.' He thumbed in the direction of Vanessa; and now they were all looking at Vanessa, and Emily said in a shocked tone, 'You didn't, did you?'

'Yes.' She nodded her head in small jerks, smiling widely.

'You must be spiffy,' said Rosie.

'No, no; I only had a sherry and two glasses of –' she paused – 'Liebfraumilch.' She brought her head

303

into deep obeisance as she said it again, and Emily said, 'Well, I've heard everything. Was it this fellow, this Cornell fellow?'

'No. I don't know who it was, but after Angus had finished with Brian Cornell this man was going to hit him on the back of the head. I could see it coming, and so I pushed him as hard as I could.'

After a few seconds of silence the kitchen was suddenly filled with gales and gales of laughter. It mounted and mounted. Rosie leant her head helplessly against her mother's flabby breast and they rocked together. Stan shook, and Angus shook, and Vanessa laid her head on her arms, so helpless had she become with laughing.

Never before in her life had Vanessa experienced this exhilarating feeling of laughter. They had never laughed at home, not really. Smiled; oh yes, all the time. But they had never really laughed. She couldn't remember hearing her father laugh out loud. She had seen him chuckle. Even Susan never laughed outright. It wouldn't be the done thing for Susan. And Ray? Ray made noises of glee but he didn't laugh. Nobody laughed like these people, the people to whom she had linked herself, and in this moment she loved them. And it was in this moment that her love for Angus was born.

It was almost an hour later when they went into their room and there, doubling his fist, he said, 'I didn't realise it before but my knuckles are hurting.'

'I bet his face is hurting more.'

They were standing looking at each other on the hearth rug in front of the dead fire, and after a moment he put out his hand and touched her cheek and said under his breath, 'You've been grand the night, grand.'

She looked down; then turned away, saying, 'You'd think I'd been in the fight, I feel so tired.'

It had been his practice to put the light out when they were about to get undressed. He knew this was a daft idea right from the beginning, but once he had started it, it became a habit. But tonight he didn't put it out. He took off his coat and loosened his tie, then reached for his pyjamas that were underneath the pillow.

Vanessa had her back to him. She had taken off her dress and was standing in her slip. Then he was surprised to see her pull her night-dress over her head and do some wriggling motions under it. When her slip and panties dropped to the floor he thought, 'Well! Well!'

He had no tent under which to undress, nor did he need one. As he stripped off his clothes and got into his pyjamas she was getting into bed and she didn't look at him until he came and sat by her side. His weight brought the edge of the divan right down, and she rolled a little towards him. As they stared at each other the sound of Emily's and Rosie's laughter came to them from the rooms above, and, without taking his eyes from hers, he said, 'They're happy.'

She nodded at him.

'They think you're the tops.'

She could say nothing to this. They hadn't always thought her the tops; perhaps it was because they thought she had come down to their level that they had changed their opinion of her.

He said, 'It's been a strange night; a lot has happened.'

She nodded again; she was unable to speak.

'We could have some good times together, Van.' His hand came out and stroked her cheek, then moved down her neck on to the top of her breasts. Her flesh was trembling but she didn't shrink openly from him. Yet she couldn't look at him. He said softly, 'Van! Van!'

When she didn't answer or look at him, he was about to say, 'All right, we'll leave it,' but he asked himself was he daft altogether. Lie there half the night awake, his innards churning as if they were filled with boiling oil? The time had passed for words. They were no longer necessary. Get on with it. That's what he had to do, get on with it. He had made up his mind, hadn't he, that it was the night or the morrow night. If this stillness of hers put him off now it would put him off the morrow, and all the morrows.

As he rose quickly from the bed her eyes sprung wide and she was staring at him as he crossed the room and put the light out; then he was throwing back her bedclothes and the next minute she was in his arms and his mouth was on hers and his hands were over her; and it was quite different from what it had been with Brett.

9

'You're not taken with it?'

She turned from him and looked about her once more. 'Yes, yes; it's very nice.' What she wanted to say was, 'It's wonderful,' and it would be wonderful, she thought, decorating it. She was sure she could do it herself, at least inside. And then there was the garden. Angus could dig it and she would plant it with roses and shrubs and perennials. . . . Yes, she could have said, 'It's wonderful,' but instead she said coolly, 'It's very nice.'

'What's the matter with it? I know it's all brown paint; I don't think it's been painted inside since it was built; but that'll come off. And I'm telling you, if it was done up we wouldn't be getting it for this price.'

'That's the point.' She turned towards him again. 'We can't afford it.'

'Now look!' He spread his fingers wide, almost in front of her face. 'You leave that to me. I'll manage. Things aren't going to stay as they are; I'm going on and up. You'll see.' He jerked his head at her in his characteristic fashion.

She was staring at him in a way she wouldn't have done this time yesterday. There was a confidence about her, an assurance that hadn't been there then. Had it come about because she had defended him last night? Because she had pushed his assailant? Or because she had taken the strain out of her body in loud hilarious laughter? Or had the difference been created because he had made love to her for the first time and she hadn't shrunk from him. Not that she had enjoyed the process. And when afterwards she had lain in his arms and he had fallen asleep, his flesh still pressed against hers, she had asked herself what all the fuss was about, why people craved for this thing, and she remembered her curiosity concerning it that had kept her awake at nights, made her irritable and a willing victim of Brett's.

She also thought that the gigantic consequences of the act was the most illogical, even diabolical, happening nature could have thought up. A second of unison and you filled your body with a child. And then the further illogicality was that the goodness or the badness of the act was decided by a ceremony, during which a man said you are now married and gave you a piece of paper to that effect. She hadn't got to sleep for a long time.

But whatever it was that had changed her, she was undoubtedly different, and Angus naturally put it down to his love-making.

She said to him now, 'How much would you have to pay for a second-hand lorry?'

He screwed up his eyes at her. 'Seven hundred; anything less would be like what I've got, held up by paper and string. But . . . but what are you getting at?'

'Take the money that you're going to put down on this and put it on a lorry. You can pay it off by instalments, just as if you were buying this.'

He came and stood close to her, his bulging chest almost touching her. 'You'd give up this so's I could get a lorry?'

The look in his eyes embarrassed her and she turned her glance away as she said lightly, 'Perhaps I'm after something bigger, and the only way to get it is for you to get more business.'

He pulled her round squarely to him. 'It could mean staying in number twenty-four for God knows how long, you realise that, don't you?'

'Yes.'

'And you don't mind?'

The question was silly and he knew it, but when she answered truthfully, 'Not as much as I used to,' he nodded at her, and after a moment during which his gaze burrowed deep into hers, said, 'You'll do.' It was a compliment. Then stepping back from her, he ended, 'You know, if I give it up I'll lose fifty quid.'

Her reaction was immediate. 'Oh no! He'll give it back to you.'

'I can't see him doing it.'

'But I thought you knew him.'

'Oh, aye, I know him; but business is business.'

'I'll go with you; I'll help to explain.'

His head went back and he laughed. Then looking at her again he said, 'I think you would an' all.'

'Well,' she began walking down the narrow hall towards the front door, 'you can tell him that when, one day, we go after a bigger place we'll put the business in his hands.'

She found herself swung round, and the next minute her breath was taken away with his kisses, which covered her mouth, her eyes, her neck, and she became filled with panic when she thought where his frenzy of loving might lead: daylight would hold no obstacle, they were alone in this house. She managed to press herself from him and to say between gasps, and in an airy fashion, 'Come on, come on; there's fifty pounds at stake.'

He looked at her, at her flushed skin, which was like tinted cream, and he swallowed deeply; then with a rumbling laugh he pulled her arm tightly against his side, and he held it there as he locked the door. Then they walked down the path, but before they went through the gate he drew her to a stop and, leaning his face close to hers, he said, 'I'm so happy I could bust.'

The summons came on the Wednesday afternoon. It was served by a policeman.

In the usual way Angus wouldn't have been in the house on a Wednesday afternoon, but he had wanted to show Vanessa the lorry; after all, it was she who had really got things moving.

Reg Walker had given him back his deposit without much demur – a five-pound note had eased the situation here – and on the Saturday afternoon he and Fred Singleton had gone lorry hunting and had found one, but Angus hadn't been able to pick it up until an hour ago, when the owners' use for it had come to an end.

Vanessa and Emily had stood on the pavement and admired the new acquisition, which showed up to disadvantage Fred's lorry. They were both on their way to a job, but now they returned to the kitchen and the cups of tea Emily had poured out for them, also to continue the discussion of hiring another man for the old lorry. Angus was eager for this move, but Fred seemed reluctant. Angus was wondering about Fred. There was, he put it to himself, something up with him these days. He hadn't the interest in the business he once had, yet he had started it. It was his missis, Angus thought; she was a nagger. She didn't belong to these parts and had never settled. Doncaster was her home.

Angus was saying, in answer to Fred's statement that it was risky engaging another driver, 'You've got to take a risk, man; I've put me lot into that out there,' when the knock came on the front door.

Emily returned to the kitchen. She stared at Angus for a full minute before she said, 'It's for you. It's the polis.'

'The polis?' He looked puzzled, he had forgotten about Friday night. Then under his breath he muttered in horror, 'It must have been nicked, the lorry.'

Emily shook her head, then stood aside as he thrust himself into the passage. And now she looked at Vanessa, who had come to her side, and whispered, ''Tisn't the lorry.'

Vanessa knew what it was before Angus returned to the room. He walked past them and to the table, and there he flung down the sheet of paper, then put his fist on it and looked first at Emily then at Vanessa. He looked at her for quite a while before he turned his gaze to Fred, and it was to him he spoke. 'That bugger, Cornell, that I told you about; he's summonsing me.' He always tried to curtail his swearing in front of Vanessa, but his good intentions went by the board at this moment. 'The bastard, summonsing me for assault. I told you, Fred, he started all this. He's a good three inches taller than me and could give me a stone any day, and if one of his blows had contacted, as drunk as he was, I don't suppose I'd have stood much of a chance. He's got fists and feet on him as hard as a bull. I've felt them on the field many a time when we've been in the scrum, and he's summonsing me!'

'Aw, Angus, you don't want nowt like that at this

time.' Fred pushed his cap on the back of his head. 'Summonsing means money, a solicitor. And then there'll be a fine; as likely as not you'll get fined.'

'I'll not, you know.' Angus rounded on him. 'I'll not you know. I'll tell them exactly what happened. And you will an' all, won't you, Van?' He was glaring at her.

'Yes, yes, of course, Angus.' Her voice was low but firm.

'There; he'll not get his own way in this. By God, no!'

'What does the charge say?' It was the first time Emily had spoken, and he picked up the paper and after a moment read, 'Assault occasioning actual bodily harm.'

Emily said nothing for a while, but her colour faded. Then she sat down and muttered, as if to herself, 'That's bad . . . You'll have to get help.'

'I'll get help all right, don't you worry.' He looked at the summons again and said scornfully, 'Actual bodily harm!'

'Don't you think you should go and see that Mr Fowler?'

He stared at Vanessa; then said, 'Aye. Fowler . . .' His voice was high now. 'Aye, yes, you've got something there, Van. Funny, he thought something might come of it. He said if I should need him he'd speak up for me, but by damned I never dreamed I would. It just shows you, doesn't it? It was a little punch up, clean, nothing dirty.' He was speaking to Fred again. 'And that was that. Finished as far as I was concerned. And now this.' He swiped the paper aside; then looking at Vanessa, said, 'I've got to go through the town, I'll drop in and see him if he's there.'

'I'll come with you.'

'Oh, there's no need; not yet, anyway.'

'I'd like to come.'

'Aye, let her go along of you,' said Emily, and Angus shrugged his shoulders. It looked an indifferent, nonchalant movement, and it covered up the fact that he was glad she was coming. He turned to Fred. 'I shouldn't be more than fifteen minutes behind you, all right?'

'All right,' said Fred. 'You be as long as you like.'

'Time's money and it looks as if I'm going to need it, doesn't it?' He nodded from one to the other.

Andrew Fowler's office was a surprise to both of them. It stood in a new block of buildings. There was a secretary in the outer office, and she asked if they had an appointment.

'No,' said Angus, 'but Mr Fowler told me to look him up.'

The secretary spoke into the phone, and listened, and she'd hardly replaced the phone and said, 'Will you wait a moment?' when Andrew Fowler appeared at the connecting door. He looked pleased to see them. 'Hello,' he said; then, 'I'm going to give a guess. He didn't waste much time.'

'You're right there.' Angus smiled and nodded towards him, as he handed him the summons.

'Come in.' He stood aside and allowed them to walk into the inner office; and pushing a seat towards Vanessa, he said, 'Do sit down.' And he motioned to another for Angus to be seated. He did not go round the desk and sit in his chair but perched himself on the corner of the desk, and after reading the summons he looked from one to the other and said, 'Well, I'm not at all surprised. He's a vindictive beggar, Cornell, nasty piece of work. But assault occasioning actual bodily harm, that's laying it on. And he'll likely have a good solicitor. You'll have to be well prepared. Have you a solicitor?'

313

'No, and I don't feel like paying for one. I'll do my own defending. I can only speak the truth, and my wife here will tell exactly what happened. And . . . and then there's you.'

'Oh well, you can rely on me. I'll put them in the picture.' He laughed now, adding, 'And as much as I'd like to hear you defending your own case I think it would be wise to get a solicitor.'

'How much would that cost?'

'Oh, it all depends. Fifteen, twenty guineas. If you lose you'll have to pay the costs. And then the fine can be pretty stiff for what's stated here, I think.'

'How much?'

'Oh, I'm not sure, fifty I'd say.'

They both looked at Vanessa because she had groaned, and she, looking at Fowler, said with a weak smile, 'And this morning he bought a new lorry.'

'You did?' He looked at Angus with interest, then asked, 'You've got another man?'

Angus moved his tongue quickly around his upper lip and after a pause said, 'No, not yet; but I've got the promise of a fellow.' And he added, 'It looks as if I'm going to need half-a-dozen lorries, and the blokes to go with them, afore I'm finished.'

'Oh, I don't think it'll be as bad as that. A lot depends on who's on the Bench and how they're feeling.'

'And . . . and you don't mind speaking up for me?'

Andrew Fowler looked at the big fellow before him. He looked rough, he walked rough, but there was something about him that attracted one. It had certainly attracted the daughter of Jonathan Ratcliffe. He would like to know the real ins and outs of how it came about, and he would through time. In the meantime he liked the idea of giving the fellow a hand.

Andrew Fowler was honest enough, as he always was with himself, to see the philanthropic gesture to Cotton as a round-about way of getting his own back for past slights received from distant relatives. Who knew, but if this rough diamond rose he might come to be an embarrassment to the combined families of Ratcliffe and Braintree. As it was, he must be something of an embarrassment to the Ratcliffes, for had he not stormed the citadel of the mighty and snatched their convent-bred lily white chick from under their noses? Indeed, yes. And from the little he had seen of her the chick was adapting herself to her changed circumstances. She was out to push this rough man of hers. He would like to bet it was she who reminded him about coming here this morning; it was she who certainly had brought up the subject of the lorries again. They said she was seventeen. She looked older, nineteen at the least. Having a child likely did that; and, of course, being under the tuition of Mr Angus Cotton.

He chuckled. Andrew Fowler in his puckish way liked people. He liked these two, and no matter how it worked out he would enjoy giving them a lift. And he wouldn't lose anything by it, of that he was sure. Not if young Cotton got some lorries going, he wouldn't. He nodded inwardly and said, 'By the way, I'm going to look at a site yon side of Durham some time this week. Plastows have got the contract for excavating. He's not all that big and I know that he's often very glad of an extra lorry or two when any of his fellows are laid off, and this can happen, especially after a long run and they get a bit tired and want a break, a couple of weeks' holiday or something. Will I mention your name?'

'Aye, yes. Thank you very much.'

'How are you fixed now?'

'Oh, I'm set for the next month up at the quarry, Peterson's.'

'Well, look me up before that . . . Oh, I forgot; we're most certainly sure to meet before then, aren't we?' He slid off the edge of the table, saying, 'And don't worry too much about this. If I were you I'd go and have a talk with a solicitor. Millard's a good chap. Millard and Fogerty, you know, in the Market Square.'

'Thanks, I'll think about it.'

Angus waited until they reached the outer door, and there, turning to Andrew Fowler, he said, 'Thanks again for everything.'

'A pleasure.' Fowler nodded his head. 'And don't be afraid to pop in any time.'

'I won't. Good-bye.'

'Good-bye, Mrs Cotton.' Andrew Fowler inclined his head towards Vanessa, and she answered, 'Good-bye, Mr Fowler.' She wanted to thank him, but she refrained; Angus had done that.

In the lorry, Angus turned towards home, and presently he said, 'It isn't often you meet blokes like that, is it?'

'No. I think he's very nice; and – and he could be a great help to you.'

He glanced quickly towards her; then back to the wheel again before saying, 'Do you think so?'

'Yes, yes, I do indeed.'

Angus was quiet now. All of a sudden he was wondering why this stranger was going out of his way to help him. Or was he aiming to help himself to something that didn't belong to him? You could never trust blokes and she would catch anybody's eye; and that fellow had a discerning one. Yes, he could say that. He didn't look at her as he asked, 'Is he married?'

Vanessa bit on her bottom lip and with a great

effort she did not smile or laugh but answered, 'I don't know.'

'But you had met him before; he said you had.'

'Well, if I did I don't remember.' Then she added a little comfort. 'He's not the kind of man one would remember, is he?' She was learning quickly.

After a while he said, 'When we're down this far I'll drop in at the station yard and see if some spares have arrived; those bits I sent for out of the catalogue, you know. You don't mind waiting a minute?'

She smiled and said, 'No, of course not.'

In the station yard he got out of the cab, saying, 'I won't be a tick,' and she answered, 'Don't hurry. I want a magazine; I'll get it from the stall.'

'Well, come on then.' He held up his arms and gripped her waist and lifted her down. Whenever he touched her now he wanted to kiss her, and his hands stayed on her longer than was necessary. Her face had been smiling when he used to lift her into the garden barrow. Now, as on the very last time he had done this, he saw her expression change, and for the same reason.

She was looking over his shoulder, and he turned round and saw Jonathan Ratcliffe and his wife passing at a distance of not more than six yards, and in spite of his toughness his heart began to bounce and he was filled with apprehension, as if she'd be snatched away from him.

Vanessa's heart, too, was bouncing; she had an almost irresistible urge to run forward. She knew that her mother would have stopped if her father hadn't been there. It was he who had caught sight of her first, and the look he had sent across the distance told her that he didn't know her, nor did he want to.

She stood watching them until they reached the car,

then she turned away and was quite unable to check the flood of tears that rained down her face.

'Get up.' His voice was rough and he almost pushed her back into the cab. He revved up the engine as if he were at the start of a race, and he drove out of the yard ahead of Jonathan Ratcliffe's car. 'Bloody nowts!' He was muttering under his breath, swearing with every other word; but she remained silent until they reached the house. And when they entered the kitchen Emily asked, 'What's happened now?' She moved towards Vanessa, then looking quickly at Angus said, 'What is it?'

'I dropped in at the station, and she saw them . . . From up there. And she could have been a mongrel dog for all the notice they took of her.'

When Vanessa sat down at the table and dropped her head on to her arms it was Emily who went to her and said comfortingly, 'Never mind, lass. Never mind. Time heals everything.'

'My – my mother would have stopped. I – I think she would.' She raised her head and looked up at Emily. 'I'm sure she would.'

'Aye, I'm sure she would, lass. But it's him. Men are like that. But one of these days you'll come across your mother on her own and then you can have a crack. You'll see; the opportunity'll present itself, it always does.'

Vanessa now looked towards Angus. His face was hard and tight, and she said, 'I'm not really dying to see them, or anything like that. It's the truth. I would never go back even if I had the chance; but it was just, just coming on them like that.'

'Aye,' he said. Then turning abruptly, he added, 'I'm off.'

She got up hastily and followed him into the passage, and at the door she said quietly, 'After all, Angus, they are my people. You,' her voice dropped to a whisper, 'you – you would defend Emily to the last gasp. You know you would.'

'Aye,' he said again, 'but not if she let me down when I most needed her. That would have finished me. But it's all right.' He put out his hand and tapped her cheek. 'See you later.'

When she returned to the kitchen, Emily said brusquely, 'Take no notice of him. Men look at things differently. Of course you would be upset seein' them; you would have been unnatural if you hadn't. Now go an' wash your face, and I'll make a cup of tea. And then I'm goin' to do a bit of bakin'. I'll show you how; it's about time you learned. You can try your hand at a lemon pie and a fruit loaf; he's fond of both. Go on now.'

Vanessa went into the scullery, and as she sluiced her face under the tap she asked herself why she had to run into her parents at this time. She knew that there was always a possibility of meeting up with her mother, or Susan; her father she was less likely to meet as he was in the works all day. She had often pictured meeting her mother, and she always imagined them talking; there would be an interval filled with embarrassment and then they would come together, and talk, because her mother, although narrow, wasn't as hard grained as her father.

But that she should see both her mother and father on this particular day, and when she was with Angus, was most unfortunate. He had enough to think about with the summons. And that was another thing. They had more than likely heard of the fight; such kind of news travelled fast. In their estimation, she would have now sunk even further, if that were possible.

319

As she swilled the water around the shallow sink there returned to her a momentary longing for the material comforts of her home, the bathroom in particular, and on this thought came regret that she had turned down the bungalow. Oh, she was tired of it all. She had made a mess of her life, if anyone had.

As despondency flooded over her she gazed at herself in the small mirror on the wall to the side of the sink. Her face looked longer; she looked white and miserable. This was how she looked, and felt, before she took the pills. She stepped back from the mirror as if frightened of what she saw. There must be no more of that; she had caused enough trouble to so many people. Her parents might not want to have anything to do with her; nor anyone from her own class; and she was not unaware she was merely living under kindly toleration from the class she was in now, even from Emily and Rosie; but there was one person who did want her, one person all along who had stood by her, and who needed her. And not only sexually. In an odd sort of way she knew that to him she was the equivalent of a gold medal at the Olympic Games, or of a knighthood; in short, she was an honour. Men needed honour, recognition of having done something, acquired something, something that caused other men to look up to them or hate them as Angus did her father.

Angus and her father were opposed in every way. Yet oddly their aims were the same, both were ambitious for recognition.

She thought it strange that she had this knowledge of them while they hadn't it of themselves.

10

The case was due to be heard on Thursday, a day over three weeks since the summons had been issued.

The tension in the house had been mounting over the last few days, and as Rosie had remarked, on a laugh, last night, the case was causing nearly as much interest in the town as a Cup Final. The lasses in the factory were betting on it, as were the people roundabout the doors. Would Cornell, with his money and influence, win by a length? Or would Cotton, who was defending his wife from insults, romp home? It was anybody's guess.

Vanessa herself was very uneasy. Up till two o'clock on the Wednesday afternoon when she returned home – it was half-day closing – she had made her concern centre around the size of the fine that would be imposed on Angus; she wouldn't allow herself to think of an alternative. But once she entered the house the suppressed dread that Angus could be sent to prison burst into the open and she was forced to face it.

She had just got in the door when Emily, turning to her, said, 'Aw, there you are, lass. You've just missed him by about five minutes. He came in over the moon. He thought old Cargill and Howard were goin' to be on the Bench the morrow, but old Cargill's laid up, and he hears that Mrs Brett's takin' his place; so he'll be all right . . . What's the matter? You feelin' funny?'

'Just a bit. I . . . I felt a bit sick in the train.'

'It's an empty stomach; that's what's the matter with you. Get somethin' down you and you'll be all right.' She walked towards the oven. 'And you're worryin' about the morrow. But you can rest your mind easy; everythin' will go smoothly now. It's ten to one she'll say "Case Dismissed", like that.' She turned and snapped her fingers towards Vanessa before stooping down and bringing a dish from the bottom shelf. 'Mr Brett thought a lot of our Angus. It was a bad day for him and everybody else when he went . . . What is it, lass?' She looked towards Vanessa where she was hurrying into the scullery. Then going to the door she said, 'Well, it's better up, whatever it is.'

A few minutes later Vanessa, returning to the kitchen, said, 'Do you mind if I lie down for a minute, Emily? I couldn't eat anything yet.'

'Go on, lass, go on. Put your feet up. I'll bring you a cup of tea in. But try an' get over it afore teatime, for he plans takin' you out somewhere, the pictures, or some place in Newcastle, because, as he says, if we sit here the night we'll be jabberin' about nothin' else but the morrow. He should be home early, he says; there was only a few more loads and they'll be finished up at the quarry. They're not startin' on a new lot until Monday. Go on now.'

In the room Vanessa stood with her back to the door and pressed her hand tightly across her mouth, as if to prevent from escaping the groan that was straining up through her body. Irene Brett being kind to Angus!

The charge was assault occasioning actual bodily harm. They had never put it into words in the house but they all knew that men were sent to prison every day in the week on that charge.

And Irene Brett was to be Angus's judge! Irene knew that Brett was the father of her child. She had seen the knowledge in her eyes the morning Brett died; her look had been full of bleak hate, and it had found its target.

But Irene had said nothing. Why hadn't she come to the house and openly accused her of stealing her husband? Of causing his death? She had asked the question of herself at the time, but now she asked herself no longer for she knew the reason why Irene Brett had remained silent. It had been gall to a woman of her calibre that she should lose anything she considered hers, especially to a young, unformed girl, and one of no particular ability; she had kept silent because she couldn't bear the public ignominy of having been passed over.

But at ten o'clock tomorrow morning she would have her revenge. She'd pay her out through Angus, and it would be the maximum sentence she would give. She could almost see his face stretching in surprise that Mrs Brett should do this to him.

When Emily brought her in the cup of tea she was sitting in the chair by the fire, and Emily said, 'Now why don't you take your shoes off and put your feet up?'

'No; it's passing off a little; I'm all right now.'

'You don't look it. You never had much colour, but you're as white as a sheet. It's the morrow you're worrying about, I know by meself. Me stomach's been as sick as a dog's, but since he was in and told me about Mrs Brett I feel better. She does a lot of good work, does Mrs Brett; she gets things done. Some don't like her. But there it is; if you get things done people don't like you, do they? Now drink that up, and do as I say and put your feet up for a while.'

When she was alone again Vanessa joined her hands tightly between her knees and began to rock herself slightly; then, taking off her shoes, she got to her feet and began to walk from one side of the small room to the other . . . She had to do something. She stopped in her pacing. She would go and see her. NO. NO. That would mean going to Brampton Hill and she couldn't bear to go so near her old home. Would she be able to find her in one of the offices in the Town Hall? But wasn't there some rule about getting at the jury? She shook her head. But she wasn't a jury, she was a magistrate. Well, it might still hold good. And what would she say when she did see her? . . . What could she say? 'Will you please be lenient with Angus?' No, no; that wasn't the line to take with Irene Brett. She picked up the cup of tea from the low table, and although it was still hot she drank it almost at once; and as she put the cup down again she knew what she was going to do.

A few minutes later, when she again entered the kitchen with her coat on, Emily turned to her in surprise, saying, 'Where you off to? What's up?' But all she said was, 'You don't have any stamps, do you?' knowing full well that Emily never had any stamps.

'No. What would I do with stamps, lass?'

'I've run out and I want to write a letter. And Angus will be needing some; there's two letters he must get off tonight.'

'You don't look fit to go out; I'll go along for you.'

'No, no, Emily; the walk will do me good, give me something to do. And when I come back I'll have my dinner.'

'Please yourself. Please yourself.' There was the old

tart note in Emily's voice, but Vanessa was used to it now. As Angus said, it meant nothing.

She hurried down to the bottom of the street, walked along the main road to the pedestrian crossing, crossed over and walked a little further up the far pavement to the telephone kiosk. She knew the number; her mother had at one time frequently phoned next door. She stared down at the phone for a full minute before she picked it up. Then she inserted the coins and dialled Fellburn 538506. She knew it wasn't likely that either Colin or Paul would answer the phone; and if the house was running as it had done for some time past there would be no woman there in the afternoon – Irene had no au pair girl now but a daily who came twice a week in the mornings; so it would be Irene or silence.

When she heard Irene Brett's voice her lips moved but she couldn't speak.

'Hello. This is Fellburn 538506.'

'Mrs Brett?' She did not say Auntie Irene, nor yet Irene.

'Yes.' There was a pause. 'Who . . . who's speaking?'

'Vanessa . . . Cotton.' She had almost said Ratcliffe. There was no sound on the line now, and Vanessa said quickly, 'Are you there?'

'What do you want?'

'I just want to tell you something; and . . . and it isn't that Brett was the father of my baby because you already know that, don't you?'

The line seemed to be dead, but Vanessa knew that Irene Brett was still at the other end, and she swallowed and went on, 'What I want to tell you is, that if you take out your spite on me through Angus I'll stand up in Court and shout out the reason why you're doing it. If you send Angus to prison he'll come out again, but you'll never be able to come out from where this town will put you. You'll be fin –' There was no longer anyone on the other end of the line, the receiver had been banged down.

She leant against the dust-covered side of the kiosk and closed her eyes for a second. Would she do what she had said she would if Angus received a prison sentence? Would she stand up and cry, 'She's only doing this for spite because her husband gave me a baby'? She didn't know; she wouldn't know until the moment came. She had already made a name for herself in this town, but if she did that her mother and father, the whole family, and, she imagined, the family that Susan had married into would be bent low with embarrassment. And once sentence was passed, would it help Angus? Perhaps not; the only thing it would do would be to show him that she cared what happened to him. But again, would Angus thank her for publicly naming the father of her child? He had never pressed her to know who it was, but at times she felt his curiosity. How would he respond when he knew it was 'Mr Brett', the man he admired who had done this to her?

Well, whatever she would do tomorrow morning, the main thing was, she felt, she had convinced Irene Brett that she was quite capable of acting on her word.

She came out of the box and walked farther along the road, until she was opposite the little sub post office. And there she waited for an opportunity to cross . . .

As Vanessa had come out of the kiosk Angus had passed her in the lorry. It was impossible in the traffic to attract her attention, but he went round the island and came back up the other side of the road, and as he parked he saw her going into the post office.

He was waiting for her when she came out, and the first thing she said was, 'How long have you been here?'

'Oh, only a minute. I . . . I saw you as I was passing.' He did not mention seeing her coming out of the phone box, although he wondered who she was phoning; but he said quickly, 'Mam all right?'

'Yes, yes, of course. Why shouldn't she be? You were in at dinner time?'

'Oh, aye.' He stared at her. She looked paler than usual, her eyes larger.

'You all right?' he asked.

'I felt a bit sick when I came in. It was the train; it was packed, being Wednesday; I had to stand all the way. Are you finished for the day?'

'Yes,' he answered; 'but I've picked up another bit of business that'll keep Fred and me busy until the start of the quarry again. Come on, get in; I can't leave her parked here. And I'll have a cuppa before I put her away.'

Seated next to her, he said, 'Where to, modam?'

Taking his cue, she replied, 'Twenty-four Ryder's Row, Cotton.'

'Very good, modam.'

He had to drive to the next side turning, back into it, and come down the main road again before he could enter the street, and as he drove he thought, 'Why hasn't she said who she was phoning?'

When they entered the house Emily greeted them with, 'Oh, there you are. Going out in ones and coming in in twos. I suppose you want a cuppa.'

'That's the idea.' He nodded at her.

Then she said to him, 'I think you should see she goes and lies down; she's out of sorts.' She jerked her head towards Vanessa.

'Now, does she ever take notice of anything I say?' He was keeping things light.

Vanessa went into the room and took her coat off,

327

and a few minutes later he joined her. He had a cup of tea in his hand and, sitting down and crossing his legs, he looked at her and asked casually, 'Who were you phoning?'

He watched her mouth open and close again and her expression changed, her face becoming even paler; and he uncrossed his legs and said, 'Well, who were you? I saw you coming out of the box.'

She was so taken aback that she hadn't a lie on her lips. He got to his feet and moved slowly towards her, the cup of tea still in his hand, and after surveying her for a moment he asked thickly, 'What's the mystery?'

'There's no mystery.'

'All right then,' he inclined his head towards her patiently, 'who were you phoning? It's as simple as that. Give me a straight answer. Who were you phoning?'

When she didn't answer at all but made to turn from him he put the cup down noisily on the table, grabbing her arm at the same time. Then pulling her round to him, he looked deep into her face as he said, 'You weren't in the telephone box to rob it, were you? And you weren't in there to do wilful damage, were you? You were in there to phone . . . Who were you phoning?'

'A – a girl in the shop.'

'But the shop's closed this afternoon.' His voice was very low and ominously quiet.

'I know the shop's closed this afternoon. I – I phoned at her home.'

'What's her name?'

This was easy. 'Teresa Bumpstead.'

'And her number?'

Could she think of a number? Of all the thousands, the millions of numbers in all the directories in the country she couldn't think of one number. All she could remember was that all Newcastle numbers began with 53, and she stammered, 'Five, three . . .'

'Don't think too hard,' he said. Then, his voice rising slightly, he added, 'Are you going to tell me the truth?'

If she said, 'I was phoning Mrs Brett,' he would say, 'What the hell did you want to do that for? She's on my side.' And he would believe this until tomorrow, when he found she wasn't.

'You were phoning your house, weren't you?'

'Oh, no! No, Angus.' Her voice was high with relief. 'No, I wouldn't do that.' She watched his face relax for a moment, then tighten again as he said, 'Well then, it was some bloke . . . Fowler. You were phoning Fowler?'

'Oh, Angus!' She closed her eyes and put her hand to her cheek and smiled faintly. 'Why would I want to phone Mr Fowler?'

'Because he's breaking his neck to help me, and all the while I'm wondering why; and I tell meself I haven't far to look for the reason. Why would he want to help me if it wasn't for you being a sort of distant family connection? . . . And mind,' he stabbed his finger at her, 'I'm being kind when I think along those lines, because he's got an eye wide open, he has.'

'Don't be silly.' Her voice was harsh now; it was a woman's voice showing impatience with an unreasonable man.

'All right.' He turned and walked to the fireplace. 'If it wasn't Fowler, then tell me who it was. Look.' He swung round and glared at her fiercely. 'It's as easy as that. Just tell me who you were phoning, because I'll not let up on you until I know. I'm made like that. It'll niggle and niggle at me mind, getting bigger and bigger every minute. I've got a mind that makes mountains out of molehills where you're concerned. You know that already, don't you, and you're playing on it?'

'I'm not, Angus. That's unfair; I'm not. I don't play on people's emotions.'

Dropping down into the chair, he said, 'All right, I'll be reasonable. Let's start from the beginning, eh? You went to the phone; I saw you coming out. You must have gone to phone somebody. I've asked you a simple question and you can't give me a simple answer. Now this is how I look at it. If you've nothing to hide why can't you tell me truthfully who you were phoning?'

She stared down into his face; then said slowly, 'All right, Angus; I'll tell you who I was phoning . . . tomorrow dinner-time.'

He screwed up his eyes at her. 'After the case you mean? Is it to do with the case?'

'Yes and no. There's more to it than that.'

'But why did you . . .? Who did you get in touch with? Look. I'll be all right; you've got no need to worry.' He got to his feet and gripped her arms. 'If you're worrying about me, stop it. I've got a good solicitor. And there's our Mr Fowler.' He smiled a tight smile and made a deep obeisance with his head. 'And above all, I've got somebody on the right side of the Bench, Mrs Brett.'

She lowered her head slightly and she kept her eyes shadowed with her lashes as she said, 'I'll tell you tomorrow. Have patience with me, Angus. As I said, there's more in it than that, I mean the case. I – I promise you I'll tell you tomorrow.'

After staring at her bent head for a moment his grip on her arms tightened and he shook her once before grinding out below his breath, 'You're not going to walk out on me, are you? That's not what you're going to tell me?'

She was looking at him, half-smiling now, as she said quietly, 'No, Angus, that's not what I'm going to tell you.'

He drew in a deep, shivering breath, and after a moment he said, 'Reprieved. For a while at any rate. But one of these days you will, won't you, Van? You'll say to me: I've had enough, I'm going back . . . And you know what I'll do on that day . . . do you? Do you know what I'll do? I'll kill you. I mean it.' He nodded his head at her.

She gave a little huh of a laugh and unwittingly her smile held derision as she said, 'Well, I won't have to tell you, will I, because now I want to stay alive at least a little longer.'

He couldn't stand being laughed at, or taken lightly. He turned away and punched his fist into the palm of one hand, then went to the little table in the corner and sat down, and, picking up the letters that had come that morning, he read them once more. One was a request for his estimate on clearing a building site. It had been sent to him direct, and not to Fred – although Fred always passed any correspondence on to him – and he felt he had Andrew Fowler to thank for it. A lot might depend, he knew, not only on his estimate, but how he got it out and also on the accompanying letter.

He put his hand slowly up to the little bookcase and lifted down Fowler's 'King's English,' and opened it at a page on which the heading read: 'On sustained metaphor'. A page of Egyptian hieroglyphics would have posed no greater problem, and he did at this odd moment what he had been wanting to do for weeks, but had been too proud to voice his need. 'Will you take me through this?' he said. He lifted up the book to shoulder height but did not turn round, and when she did not answer he moved his head slowly until he had her in the corner of his eye. Then he said, 'It'll be a laugh for you. I've made so many bloomers you could fill a book. "Those are them" won't be in it. I've got some prize ones.'

She was standing by the side of the table now, and she looked into his face, saying softly, 'Don't, Angus.'

'Don't what?'

She did not add, 'You know what I mean,' and he pushed it no further.

Taking the book from his hand, she looked at it, saying softly, 'I'd love to help you, you know that. There's a lot I don't know, although English was my best subject. We,' she glanced down at him, 'we could learn together.'

He covered her hand on the book, pressing it hard, saying, 'You know, this is only another ruse to keep you, you know that, don't you? Everything I do is aimed at keeping you.' He was looking at her in a way he sometimes did, like a small boy who was asking to be needed, and loved. But he wasn't a small boy, he was a man, a rough, arrogant, bumptious man, who would, as he said, kill her if he thought she was going to leave him.

The issue seemed to have moved away from the telephone box to the region of raw emotions, but she could cope with this. And so she turned from him, saying, 'Go and put the lorry away. I haven't had any lunch yet; I'll get it, and then we'll go out.' She half turned her head. 'You were thinking of going out, weren't you?'

'Who told you that? Oh, me mam. She can't keep her mouth shut, that one.' He rose swiftly and stalked out of the room, and she heard him crying to Emily, 'You and your big mouth, Ma Cotton; you can't even let me spring a little surprise on me own.'

He was covering up the things that hurt and embarrassed him. During the past half hour he had been the questioning jealous husband, the young man pleading for education, two kinds of small boy, one loving, one rough, loud-mouthed, but threading all his attitudes was a man with a deep need.

There came, in the region of her heart, a restricted feeling that turned into an ache. The ache spread until her body was filled with it. If he went to prison, what would she do? She'd be lost. Yes, without him she'd be lost. She – she was in love with him. No; not just in love, she loved him. How had it come about that she should love Angus Cotton because he was . . .? She didn't tell herself all the things he was, but she went over all the things he wasn't. Was, or wasn't, it didn't matter; what did matter was that if he went to prison she wouldn't live until he came out again. She loved him.

They shouted to Angus as he and Vanessa went down the street the following morning: 'Good luck, lad.' It was as if they had been waiting behind their doors for him. One wit cracked, 'See you at the assizes, Angus,' and Angus turned a laughing face towards the man and shouted, 'And I wouldn't be surprised at that an' all, Jim.'

'Ten years' hard, you'll get, Angus, ten years, not a day less. You might as well have been in the train robbery.'

'Aye, Mrs Grant, you're right there; I might as well.'

When they were on the bus he turned to her and said, 'They were enjoying themselves, weren't they?' There was a kind of pain in the back of his eyes, and she answered softly, 'I don't think they meant to be unkind.'

'Huh!' He jerked his chin up. 'You defending "me ain folk"? Oh, I know them, I know them all like the

333

back of me hand. They'll all come round and help you when you're in trouble, but that doesn't stop them being happy that you are in trouble, somebody else is getting it, not them . . . Do you follow me?'

Yes, in a way she did follow him, and she was surprised at the depth of his knowledge concerning his . . . ain folk, as he called them.

He kept on talking. 'Human nature all over, that is. If you move away from the street you're a nowt, an upstart; if you stay in the street you're a stick-in-the-mud, you've got no gumption. You can never be right. I used to worry about it at one time.' He turned his face fully towards her. 'Can't imagine me worrying, can you?'

'Yes, Angus, yes, I can imagine you worrying.' She had a desire to take his hand; he was worrying now. He had been worrying since he got up. He had never stopped talking, which was proof that he was worrying.

'I used to worry because I couldn't get Mam into a better house. I used to worry because I hadn't got a decent job; then when I got promoted I used to worry in case I got demoted. Still do. And the more I worry the louder I yell.' His mouth was wide now and his smile cynical. 'I've been yelling since I got up, haven't I?'

She wanted to laugh, she wanted to cry. She touched his fingers and found her hand grasped painfully tight.

They got out at the market square and walked across the open space which, tomorrow, would be packed with stalls, and went through the iron gates that guarded the flower-decked space in front of the Town Hall where the Court was being held, and at the bottom of the steps he said, 'Are you sure you want to come in?'

'Yes, yes, I want to be there.'

'You've a stronger stomach than me mam. Funny isn't it, she just couldn't stand to come and hear it. You'd think

334

I was going to get the long drop. Oh, there they are,' he said under his breath, as he saw the solicitor standing in the distance talking to Andrew Fowler. And he added, 'I hope they look as happy when it's all over.'

The two men were laughing together as Angus and Vanessa came up to them, but they stopped immediately, and when Angus introduced Vanessa to the solicitor, he inclined his head deeply and said, 'How do you do, Mrs Cotton?'

She always felt it strange to be addressed as Mrs Cotton.

'Our – our opponents are already seated,' said Andrew Fowler to Angus, 'and our Mr Cornell's face is still showing signs of the fray.' He slanted his glance sideways at Angus. 'It's a good job old Cargill's indisposed and you have Mrs Brett to deal with.'

'Yes, indeed, indeed,' said the solicitor. 'Although when I saw her upstairs a few minutes ago she looked as if it was a murder charge she had on her hands. Likely suffering from indigestion. But usually she's fair, except for desertion or maintenance, and then, oh dear, does she jump on them. But as you're up for neither,' he glanced with a thin smile at Vanessa, 'I think we're fairly certain of having her on our side.'

His tone changing, he now spoke directly to Angus, saying, 'The main issue as I see it is: you were protecting your wife; he was making a nuisance of himself and he did it repeatedly . . . not once, but repeatedly. You had warned him, but he would take no heed. You know the line to take. You were protecting your wife from being annoyed. Mr Fowler, here, will vouch for all that; we have been all over it. Ah, here we go.' He answered the summons of a policeman standing before two double doors at the far end of the hall and he went forward.

Angus followed, walking at one side of Vanessa, while Andrew Fowler walked at the other. And so they entered the Court.

Half-an-hour later they re-entered the hall and they stood in a circle, and looked at each other; then Mr Millard said almost angrily, 'It's preposterous, ridiculous. She was utterly bitchy.' He looked from Andrew Fowler to Vanessa, and then to Angus again, and repeated, 'Utterly, absolutely bitchy. Old Cargill wouldn't have made it anything near as stiff as that even at his worst. It was the maximum.'

Angus said nothing. He felt stunned. He was remembering how Mrs Brett had looked at him as she said, 'You're lucky I am not passing a prison sentence on you. I am dealing with you leniently this time, but should you come before this Court again on a similar charge then there'll be no option of a fine, I can assure you of that. This town can do without your sort. Too long we have put up with big heads and bruisers: it has got to stop. Decent people can't have an evening out, or approach an old friend, but they are punched in the face. Their teeth are knocked out . . .'

It was as if she had got the wrong fellow. All she had said to him she should have said to Cornell. And he wasn't the only one who thought so; the whole Court seemed confused. Even Cornell was surprised. Pleased; oh aye, pleased, but nevertheless he was surprised . . . Mrs Brett! Angus couldn't understand it. He had spoken to her numbers of times since he was just a lad; and it was her husband who had pushed him on. He just couldn't understand it. It was as if she had hated his guts. One hundred pounds and costs! It was unbelievable. And besides that, she could have sent him along the line

336

for six months. She had said so. What was the matter with him anyway? Everything was hitting him. It was coming at him from all sides.

He looked along the hall now to where his solicitor and Cornell's were chatting amiably together, quietly and amiably together. Somehow he thought that shouldn't be. Yet they did it on the telly, try to cut each other's throats in the courtroom and pat each other on the back when they came out of it, like 'The Defenders'.

He wanted to get home out of this; he wanted to think. He felt he had been dealt a dirty deal somehow. He thought again: Mrs Brett! Mrs Brett! All right, she could have fined him, but to slam into him in front of everybody like that as if he was one of the local tear-aways, why? Why? He said abruptly to Vanessa, 'Come on, out of this.'

'Just a minute.' It was Andrew Fowler touching him on the arm. 'I know you're puzzled,' he said soothingly. 'So am I. So are they all. But it's over and done with . . . Listen, did you get a letter this morning from Fenwick?'

'Fenwick?' Angus had to think, and Vanessa put in quietly, 'Yes, yes, about estimates.'

'Oh aye, I've got a letter.'

'Well, it'll be O.K.,' said Andrew Fowler; 'I'll see to it. Make yourself a good margin. You might have to hire a couple more lorries and more men. Pop in tomorrow and we'll have a word.'

'Aye, all right. Thanks.' He spoke as if in a daze, and his 'Thanks' was desultory, and Vanessa, looking at Andrew Fowler, said firmly, 'Thank you, Mr Fowler.'

'It's a pleasure.'

He watched them going down the steps. The smile

had gone from his face now and he was nipping his lip. There was something fishy here. Why had Mrs Brett flayed him like that? Evidently he didn't know, he had looked flabbergasted. Cotton had counted on her being on the Bench – her husband had apparently been a kind benefactor to him when he worked at Affleck and Tate's. Had she taken that attitude because her neighbour's daughter had stepped over the rails? But that was nothing to her, surely. There was something here he would like to get to the bottom of. He liked to get to the bottom of things. Knowledge was power even if you didn't use it. He wondered how he could go about finding out. Well, something would happen that would give him a lead; it usually did.

Three days later not only had he a lead but the whole reason why Irene Brett had come down like a ton of bricks on Angus Cotton.

11

'It's a bloody shame!' everybody said. They called to
him across the main road; 'Just heard, Angus. It's a
bloody shame.' They said it in the street: 'A hundred
quid and costs! It's a bloody shame, Angus.'

Emily said it standing behind the kitchen table. 'She
didn't!' she said. 'Mrs Brett? No. One hundred pounds
and costs? Oh, no! lad.'

'She did. But that's not all, Mam. You should have
heard her. I mean, if she had gone for Cornell in the same
way I could have understood it, everybody could have
understood it, couldn't they, Van?' He turned towards
Vanessa, but all Vanessa did was nod her head. 'She flayed
me in front of everybody, talked to me as if I was a tough,
running scatty, knocking people on the head in the main
street, telling me what she would do if I came afore her
again. You know what I feel like doing? . . . Going along
there and asking her why, I do, honest to God, Mam.'

Vanessa went into the room, took off her coat and
stood waiting. In a short while he would get over this
shock to some extent, and then he would say, 'Ah now,
time's up. You're going to tell me who you phoned
yesterday.' So she wouldn't wait for that, she'd come
straight to the point.

When he entered the room she turned stiffly towards him and, looking him straight in the face, said, 'I can tell you, Angus, why she did it.'

'You?' He moved near to her. 'You mean you know why she got at me?'

'Yes . . . You – you wanted to know who I phoned yesterday. Well – well it was her.'

'Mrs Brett?' His eyes were screwed up tightly at the corners.

'Yes; I – I phoned her because I knew that when you came up before her this morning she would get at me through you; I was afraid she would give you a prison sentence. I threatened that if she did I would shout it out in the Court.'

'Shout what out? What are you talking about, girl? You all right?'

'YES! YES!' She had almost yelled. Then clamping her hand over her mouth, she bowed her head and said, 'She hates me because . . . because she knows who was the father of the baby.' Her head bent lower and her voice was hardly audible as she ended, 'It was Brett, her husband.'

From underneath her lowered lids she could see his body up to the waist, and it was perfectly still. Then his silence forced her to raise her head and the expression on his face turned her cold. It had in it the essence of incredulity, but something more, a surprising quality for him to show towards her, disgust. His lips moved well back from his upper teeth before he said, 'Mister Brett and you!'

Her head was moving down again and her voice was a whimper. 'It just happened. He – he was very sad, lonely, unhappy . . .'

'Christ!' The exclamation was like a crack of a whip.

'Aren't all old married men unhappy, lonely, sad? But that doesn't mean you've got to lie with them . . . You and Brett! He was as old as your father . . . Brett!'

As he continued to stare at her he remembered that he had always liked Mr Brett, that Mr Brett had been kind to him, but he also remembered, and with a sense of deep shock, that when he wondered who had given her a bairn he had imagined it to be a lad of her own age. He had imagined him carried away on the first real wave of emotion and being borne under with the pressure of it. He had imagined them both fumbling at the act without enjoying it; then the boy skulking away and keeping his tongue quiet while she carried the can. He had even admired her for not revealing who the young fellow was . . . But she had been under the hands of no young fellow, she had been with a man old enough to be her grandfather; aye, he could have been her grandfather.

He had the urge now to take her by the neck and choke her. He had been made a fool of. She had let everybody blame him while she could have put a stop to it, a real stop to it, by naming the fellow next door . . . But there hadn't been any fellow next door had there when the balloon went up? No, he had skedaddled, gone touring, supposedly getting orders for the firm; and when he came back and found what happened to her, what did he do? He hanged himself. It was a pity he hadn't done it earlier. How often had he had her?

There was a strange feeling in him now. He didn't want to go near her, or touch her. When she said, 'Angus, I'm sorry. Don't look like that. It – it was a sort of accident; it only happened . . .' he put in quickly, 'I don't want to hear.' He curled his lip at her. 'But you know something. I'll tell you something. I thought you had been let down by a young lad, and I could understand that and I could put up with it, but not when it was a bloke like Brett, with a son as old as me, and two others.'

He walked towards the door, then turned to her and said in a tone that was frightening because for him it was quiet, 'You're no better than the rest. You know something? I wouldn't marry May because I found she'd been with other blokes. Bit illogical you might say, when I've had my whack, but I'm made that way. I stomached what happened to you because, as I said, I thought it was a slip between two young 'uns, not a calculated get-together, as it must have been atween you and him, because a man of Brett's age wouldn't jump in feet first, he'd know he'd have to tread warily until he was sure of his ground. And he was sure, wasn't he?'

She was so stunned by his attitude that she could make no reply. All her mother and father had said, the treatment she had received from her friends, nothing she had gone through, affected her like Angus's reaction.

When he went out of the room he didn't bang the door behind him. Presently she heard the murmur of his voice coming from the scullery. He would be telling Emily.

He had no need to tell Emily, she already knew. She had picked enough up from standing at the kitchen door to put two and two together, and now she was looking at her son and saying bitterly, 'What are you going to do?'

'Nothing.' He looked out of the scullery window. 'Damn all. What's the good of raking up muck, you only get more smells, and at the present moment me nose is full of them. I couldn't stand any more.'

'I thought it must have been a young lad.'

'Aye.' He turned and looked at her. 'Aye, that's what I thought an' all; and I took the rap because of that. But

342

do you think for a moment if I'd guessed it had been Brett I would have? As sorry as I was for her, I would have seen her in hell first.'

'Mr Brett. MR. BRETT. He was a quiet, refined, gentlemanly . . .'

'Oh, Mam, for God's sake come off it. Gentlemanly. They do it an' all; even royalty has to be born. What's maddening me is that I've been made the scapegoat, and that bitch on the bench finished it the day. She's right about one thing though . . .' He jerked his head back towards the room. 'It's ten to one if she hadn't got on that phone yesterday and threatened what she might do I might quite easily be along the line at this minute.'

Emily shuddered. She knew that what he said was true; he could easily have been along the line. That lot! That lot! Look what they had done to her lad. Turned him into a lorry driver when he should have been in the drawing office. Then fining him a hundred pounds and blamin' him for the bairn, when all the time it was Mr Brett.

She was working herself up into a fury when Angus said, 'I'm going.'

'Where? Where you off to?'

'To get the lorries ready.'

'What time will you be back?'

'I don't know.' His voice was flat.

She followed him to the yard door and, her voice a low murmur in case someone was sitting in the lavatory beyond the wall, their ears cocked, she said, 'Don't go and get sozzled; that won't solve matters.'

He turned and looked at her once, then moved away down the back lane; and she returned to the scullery, and as she stood gripping her forearms with each hand her anger mounted into a white blaze, strangely not against Vanessa, but against her parents, and the Bretts, the whole family of Bretts, those two grown-up sons who must have been stone blind not to guess what their father was up to.

She was thinking along similar lines to Angus. This thing couldn't have happened like the snap of your fingers. There must have been some outward sign somewhere, to show that Brett – she did not now think of him as Mr Brett – had his sights on the young lass next door. And next door? Had they been stone blind an' all? God-Almighty Ratcliffe and his missus? And the things they said. Aye. She was recalling practically every word they had said to her regarding Angus, and the manner in which they had said it.

Her anger seemed to lend wings to her feet now and she was upstairs donning her hat and coat and downstairs again within a few minutes. Opening a cupboard, she grabbed up her handbag, looked in it to see if she had enough for the fare, then went out of the house, taking the well-known road towards Brampton Hill again.

12

Irene Brett was pouring tea in the drawing-room. It was seldom she had tea in this room; except when there were visitors, and they were few and far between. But today she was serving tea in the drawing-room because Paul was home. It was the first day of the Easter vac and tomorrow he would be off on another of his walking tours. She had little time to impress him, and her future lay very much in his hands; in fact, how long she could remain in this house depended on him.

If everything had gone to Colin, as it should have done, he being the eldest son, she would have known a sense of security, whereas now she felt she was dealing with a younger edition of her husband. She had urged Colin to contest the will, but for some reason or other he wouldn't. This was another thing that irked her; although the brothers were as different in character as chalk from cheese there was an affinity between them that she had no part of.

Her object now was to persuade Paul to sell some of the mouldering antiques in order that she might have the ground floor, at least, redecorated. When she had broached the subject at Christmas he had said neither yes nor no to the matter. He was like his father there, a ditherer . . . His father! When she thought of his father she knew she wouldn't live long enough to erase the hate of him that burned in her. She had always known she was capable of strong emotions, but she had never imagined that a man like Arthur, a weak, vacillating creature such as he could have aroused in her this unrelenting feeling of hate and resentment. And then there was that girl . . . Her thoughts sank into the depths and dragged up adjectives, and it was as much as she could do not to voice them. She had a picture of Vanessa sitting in Court staring at her, daring her to do what she most desired, send Angus Cotton down. She wished now she had defied her threat and done it. Oh, if only she had.

'Been a busy day for you?'

She brought her face round to her son, whom she couldn't look at without seeing his father, and she made herself say lightly, 'So-so, rather upsetting; some cases tend to be upsetting.'

'You take it all too seriously.'

'Perhaps.'

'You should have a holiday.'

'You know I can't have a holiday, Paul.'

He was silent, and the feeling of guilt that he always had now when he was with her mounted. He knew that within a few minutes she would bring up the subject again about selling the furniture. He supposed he would have to give in; although he would like to keep things intact as his father had done. But times were changing. Sooner or later the whole place would have to go, house, land, the lot. It was too big anyway for any one family these days. It had been too big for years. He wished he could feel more sympathy towards her but somehow he couldn't. He had never been able to understand the driving force that animated her thin body. There was too much of his father in him, he supposed. Poor Dad. When his thoughts were touched with pity he always addressed his father in his mind as Dad. He had wanted so little, and that's what he got, so little. He wished that tomorrow was here and he could get away. The house wasn't the same. Nothing was the same. Perhaps he had grown up suddenly, or perhaps it was the events that had happened in the last year. Whatever it was, life didn't appear bright and starry anymore.

When the ring came on the bell he rose and said, 'I'll take it'; and when he opened the front door there stood Emily Cotton. After a moment's pause he said, 'Emily! Oh, hello, Emily.'

'Your mother in?' No 'Master Paul' now.

'Mother? Yes, yes. You want to see her?'

'Yes, I want to see her.'

There was something wrong here; Emily was in fighting mood. He said, 'Come in a minute,' and when she'd walked past him and stood in the hall he closed the door and went quickly towards the drawing-room door, which he pushed behind him but not closed before he went to his mother and said softly, 'It's Emily, Emily Cotton, you know.'

He watched the cold blue of her eyes turn to a steely grey and her narrow jaws tighten.

'Will I bring her in?'

'No, I'll see her in the hall . . . Stay here.'

When she entered the hall she closed the drawing-room door behind her, then looked at the cheaply dressed, unshapely woman, and, aiming to take command of the situation, she said, 'Yes, Emily. What can I do for you?'

'Don't you come that tone with me, Mrs Brett; you know what you can do for me. By! you've got a nerve.

347

You know what you are?' Emily advanced two steps. 'You're a vindictive bitch, that's what you are.'

'How dare you! And stop shouting, woman. You forget yourself.'

'I'm tellin' you not to come that line with me. I'm not forgettin' meself; you're the one, Mrs Magistrate, who forgot yourself when you were up on that bench this mornin'. You forgot why you were put there. You were put there for justice, not to dish out personal spite. An' that's what you did, didn't you? If it hadn't been for Vanessa phoning you and threatenin' you yesterday that she would broadcast who was the father of her bairn if you sent my Angus along the line, you would have done just that, wouldn't you? You would have sent him up for six months, just to get back at her.'

'Be quiet, woman! And get out.' Irene was hissing at her now.

But Emily had no intention of being quiet or of leaving until she had had her say, and she said it even louder now.

'Be quiet, you say. When I'm ready an' not afore. I tell you again you're a bloody, vindictive bitch, and that's swearing to it. Your man took a young lass down, a schoolgirl, and then he took his life because he couldn't face it. An' you knew about it; you knew this all the time my lad was being blamed for givin' her this bairn, but you let it go on. Councillor Mrs Irene Brett, Magistrate, Chairman of this an' God knows what else, couldn't stand the racket of being shown up . . .'

'Get out! Do you hear me. GET OUT.'

'Aye, I'll get out, but I'm not goin' very far, just to your neighbours . . .'

'You wouldn't dare!'

348

'I wouldn't what?' Emily was bawling now. 'You tell me what I wouldn't dare?'

'I forbid you, woman.' They were standing close to each other now, Irene's words spitting between her teeth. 'Do you hear. I forbid you. This is between her and me . . . Vanessa.'

'Aw, but that's where you've made a mistake. It's not atween you and Vanessa, it's atween you and my lad. His name's been blackened all over this town, and beyond. He had dared to step over the white line and have an affair with one of his betters, that's what was said. A few years ago they would have had him flogged. Old Ratcliffe would have taken a horsewhip to him. Something similar was done to one of the grooms from Brampton Manor, an' that was in the thirties, not so very long ago. But times have changed, except on the bench, where there's upstarts like you . . . An' don't you call me woman . . .' She thrust her lower jaw outwards. 'I'm clearin' me lad's name. If it's the last thing I do I'll do that, an' people won't have to guess why he got it hot and hard from you this mornin'.'

'It will be you who'll be in Court next if you're not careful.' Irene's voice was trembling now, as was her whole body.

'All right, summons me, but you'll have to give me a summons for telling the truth. That's how you'll have to word it. Emily Cotton accused of telling the truth, the suppressed truth.'

Emily's eyes were brought for a moment from Irene Brett's bleached face to the open drawing-room door, where stood Paul, so changed that she thought for a moment she was looking at his father.

She turned now and walked towards the front door, and after she had opened it she jerked her head round to give one parting shot, but checked it as she saw Irene Brett and her son staring at each other. She had said enough, she was satisfied, in this quarter anyway. Mrs Magistrate had her son to deal with, and from the looks of him he was going to have her work cut out.

Her body was still quivering with indignation, she marched down the drive along the road, through the open gates and to the house in which, as she herself had said, she had spent a greater length of time over the past eighteen years than she had in her own home. She did not take the tradesman's path to the back door but made for the front door, and as she looked at the car standing on the drive she thought, 'Good. Madam Susan's here.' Then she pressed the bell with her thumb, holding it tight for some seconds.

The door was opened by a young woman who was wearing a small frilled apron over an ordinary house-dress, which in itself told Emily that there was company. 'Yes?' said the woman, looking her up and down.

'Your missus in?'

'What do you want?'

'You tell Mrs Ratcliffe that Emily's here and wants to see her. Just say that.' Then she put her hand out quickly, adding, 'You needn't close the door; I'm not goin' to pinch anything; I worked here when you were still in nappies. Go and tell her.'

The young woman's eyes were wide, but she made no further protest; she had heard of Emily Cotton. Emily followed her slowly and stood in the hall, and as she waited her eyes roamed around, and she noted, with some chagrin, that everything looked as usual. When the lounge door opened the maid came out alone and said to her, 'The mistress will see you in a minute.' Then she went on into the kitchen, and Emily waited.

She waited a full three minutes before her late mistress made her appearance.

Jane Ratcliffe closed the lounge door carefully behind her; then, coming slowly forward, she said unsmilingly, 'Good-afternoon, Emily.'

Emily did not return the greeting but said, 'Do you know why I'm here . . .?' She had almost said ma'am but checked herself in time.

'No, Emily, I don't know why you're here.'

'I've come for an apology.'

'For what?'

'You heard, for an apology.'

'Come – come into the morning-room, please.'

'No, I'm not goin' into any morning-room, missus; what I've got to say I'll say here, where there's ears cocked at the doors, an' they'll be my witnesses . . . Is he in?'

'If you're referring to the master, no, he's not, Emily.' Jane Ratcliffe's voice was trembling.

'That's a pity. That is a pity, because it's him I want to see more than you; but you can pass on what I've got to say. I suppose you know about my lad being up afore the Bench this mornin'. He was up there because he was defending your daughter – for the second time mind – against a man who was pestering her, and what did he get? He gets fined one hundred pounds an' costs. And, you know, he was lucky to just get fined. If it hadn't been for Van phonin' next door yesterday an' tellin' Madam Councillor, Mrs Irene Brett, that she would stand up in Court this mornin' and yell the truth at her if she dared send my Angus along the line, he would have been along the line at this minute.'

'Emily! Emily, please, come into the morning-room.'

'I'm not goin' into any mornin'-room; you can save

your breath. And I haven't finished yet. You know what Van was goin' to shout at Mrs Brett, do you?' She bent her body almost double. 'She was goin' to shout out the name of the man who gave her the bairn, an' the name was Mr Brett. Your esteemed neighbour . . . Mr Brett! That's who gave her the bairn. And his wife knew it, she knew it; an' she knew it was because of that he committed suicide . . . Aye,' her voice dropped a tone lower as she looked at Jane Ratcliffe supporting herself by the banister. 'I thought you would need some support. But you didn't think me or me lad needed any support, did you? You made him out to be the scum of the earth. He was accused of takin' Van down because he had been seen talkin' to her once or twice, and all the time 'nder your very noses a man old enough to be her grandfather was having his fun with her; an' you knew nowt about it. Of course, of course.' Her voice changed. 'You could trust people like Mr Brett; he was a gentleman. The same goes for Mr Brian Cornell, another gentleman. He can say what he likes and gets off with it, but because my lad had neither money nor position he didn't stand a chance.'

'Will you please go, Emily!' Jane Ratcliffe's voice had a far-away sound to it. She was standing stiffly upright now staring straight ahead, and Emily said, 'Aye, I'll go when I say this. My Angus is a bloody fool, that's what he is, for, knowin' that he was playing into your hands, he goes an' marries her. He marries her out of sympathy 'cos he finds her living in a filthy dump in Newcastle. Do you know Batterby Bay Road? No. I don't suppose you do. But your husband will. Oh, aye, there's not a man in this county who doesn't know of Batterby Bay Road. It's where the prostitutes hang out, an' that's where he found her. And he brought her from there an' married her, and he hadn't,' she paused, 'he hadn't given her the bairn . . .'

The lounge door was pulled sharply open at this stage and it checked Emily's spate, and she watched Susan Ratcliffe, or Braintree as she now was, going quickly towards her mother, saying, 'Come along, dear. Come along.'

As Susan put her arms round her mother she turned and looked at Emily and said, 'I think you'd better go. You've had your say, now get out.'

The young man standing in the doorway didn't speak, but he looked at Emily for a full minute and she at him before she said, 'Aye, I'll go. But I haven't finished me say yet; this town's goin' to hear the truth. Your lot's treated my lad as if he was a Geordie lout, an' there's not one of you fit to wipe his boots. Well, now we'll see what the town thinks and how the so-called gentleman from next door'll stand up against Angus Cotton.'

There were two reactions to Emily's outburst. The one in Bower Place was that Jonathan Ratcliffe refused to listen to his wife's pleas to move. Angus Cotton wasn't putting him on the run. All right, let the town know, let them talk, but he wasn't going to be frightened out of his home by that young slob.

He was still fighting Angus Cotton, more so now than ever, because Angus Cotton had got the better of him. He was in the right and the town would be laughing. Oh yes, behind their hands they would be laughing. Young Cotton had taken the blame of giving Ratcliffe's daughter a child just so that he could marry her and get his foot in.

Jonathan Ratcliffe was still convinced that Angus Cotton's motive in marrying Vanessa was to inveigle himself into her family's good books.

353

The other reaction took place in the kitchen in No. 24 between Emily and Angus. He had been utterly astounded when she told him where she had been. For a moment he could say nothing, then his wrath poured over her. She was a bloody, silly old cow, an interfering, stupid old swine. Why the hell couldn't she mind her own business! Hadn't there been enough talk and tittle-tattle without her going stirring things up? All right, all right, he knew he had been wrongly accused, nobody knew better, but that was his business.

'Thanks!' Emily screamed. 'Thanks! That's what I get. You're a bloody, ungrateful sod. Your name's been mud in this place for months now, aye, even round the doors. They said you had a nerve, and it was a dirty trick to take a young lass down like that an' her still at school, and a convent into the bargain. Virgin huntin' in the right place, they said. Taking advantage of his mother being up there, they said. Well then, I was determined they weren't goin' to say that no longer; they were going to know the truth an' this is what I get.'

'You haven't got half of it yet. For two pins I'd slap yer mouth for you.'

'Begod you would!' She thrust her hand back and grabbed up a large sauce bottle from the dresser; but at this moment Vanessa came out of the room. She stood in the doorway and, her voice louder than it had ever been raised in this house or anywhere before, she cried, 'Stop it! Stop it! I'm sick of you, do you hear, the both of you. I'm sick of your shouting and fighting. You're like wild animals, the pair of you. That's all you are, wild animals.'

Perhaps it was surprise that silenced them, for they both turned towards her and made no reply; they just looked at her. Her hair was tangled as if she had been running her hands through it; her clothes looked dishevelled as if she had been lying in them; her face was bloated with crying; she looked tired and weary, but above all she looked an angry woman. 'All right!' she said. 'I'm the cause of all this, but I'm going to end it, I'm leaving.' She was looking at Angus directly now, 'Do you hear me? I'm leaving?' When he still made no comment she went into the room and banged the door.

There was now exchanged between Emily and Angus a shame-faced look before he went slowly across the kitchen and into the room. With his back to the door he stood for a moment watching her pulling her dresses from the hanging wardrobe in the corner, and when she had put them in the case he approached her and said grimly, 'What d'you think you're doing?'

She glanced up at him with a look that was new, because it was defiant. She was looking at him as May might have looked at him when she was on the point of telling him to go to hell.

When he put his hand out and caught hers as she went to close the case, she jerked it away, and he said flatly, 'You're not leaving. Make up your mind to that; you're not leaving.'

'You can't stop me. If I don't go now I'll go once you leave the house; you can't keep watch over me all the time.' She was staring straight into his face, and he held her eyes with an unblinking stare as he said, 'You know what I said I'd do to you the other night if ever you left me. Well, you might have thought it was a joke, but it wasn't. If you walk out I'll drop everything till I find you, and I'll bring you back. Every time you go off I'll find you and I'll haul you back again. I mean it.'

She stepped back from him as she asked, 'Why? Why do you want to keep me here? Yesterday I thought I knew,

355

but not now, because you were disgusted when I told you the truth. You were, you were disgusted. Just because it was Brett who was the father you were disgusted. You had already accepted the situation because you thought I had been with a boy. Why, I could have been with a boy twenty times, fifty times and nothing could have happened and you wouldn't have known anything about it, but because this happened with Brett once, just once, your whole attitude towards me changed. It was as if you had suddenly heard that I'd had a baby; or, if you thought it was yours, then found out it was Brett's, you couldn't have reacted worse. I – I can't understand you.'

'You can't understand me! That's rich. But then I can't understand meself. I don't know why in hell I bother about you, but I do, so there's a pair of us who can't understand me. But you think it's odd I was disgusted when I heard it was Brett, an' I was disgusted, that's the right word; and it wasn't only because he was an old man, oldish anyway,' he flung his head upwards, 'but because, well, I liked him. I'd always liked him, and was fool enough to look up to him, thinking he represented something big, something fine, even great.' His voice dropped. 'I looked up to him the same as I looked up to you . . .'

It was his last words that took all the fight out of her. She turned from him and, going to the little table, sat before it and dropping her head on to her arms began to cry, painful, quiet crying.

He remained where he was, looking at her. The defiant woman was gone, and he saw a young girl again. Once, she said. She had only been with him once. He thought back and tried to remember when Brett had gone abroad. It must have been pretty near when it happened, for it was three months later when he came back, at the time when they were looking for somebody to pin it on. He must

356

have known that there was a chance she might fall and he had scurried away like a frightened rabbit, jumped at the opportunity to get away, because he now recalled that when Mr Cribber went into hospital, Mr Bindley was going to get the chance of going out abroad to fill in. He knew this because he often had a word with him at the Tech, where he did spare teaching at nights, but then Brett had gone instead.

She had been left high and dry by them all: Brett, her own family, and now, it must appear to her, that he was another one of them. Quite suddenly it didn't matter any longer who had been the father of her bairn; it was a thing that was over and done with. He went to the case and, lifting the lid, took out her dresses, one by one, and put them over his arm. Then going to her, he said, 'Hang these up.'

She raised her tear-streaked face and looked at him for a moment before, getting to her feet, and saying, quietly, 'No, no, Angus, it's not going to be like that. I don't care what you say, or what you do, I'm . . . I'm going. I'm not living in sufferance any longer.'

'Sufferance? What do you mean?'

'Just what I say. You married me because you were sorry for me. I – I thought you loved me; I imagined that you needed me; but now I know that was all girlish imagination. Another reason why you married me was so that you could cock your snoot at my folks. Oh, I know, I know.' She flapped her hand in front of her face. 'You'll deny it, but it's true. You were letting them see, father in particular, that you could marry anyone you liked, that you were as good as they were. So you married me, but you've never said one endearing word to me in all the months since then. Oh, yes,' her voice was scornful now, 'you can kiss me and hug me until I can hardly breathe; you can show me how strong you are, what a man you are; but you've never once said you've cared for me. I could have been that May woman you used to know.' The impetus went out of her voice and she ended, 'You don't really care for me, Angus, so why do you want to keep me? Just to hold me up and say, "Look what I've got; someone from Brampton Hill"?'

He was shaking his head slowly at her, bewilderment showing in every feature of his face, and, his voice humble now, he said low in his throat, 'You've got it all wrong, Van, you've got it all wrong. Admittedly I was shaken when I knew it was Brett, but the feeling's past, it's over. But about the other, how I feel about you, you've got it all wrong. You want fancy words. Well, I'm not up to it. It's almost impossible for me to express how I feel about you in words, but I thought I was showing it in a thousand and one other ways. If it means anything to you, I live in dread every day of you walking out, and that bit about what I would do if ever you left me, about bringing you back, and even polishing you off, it's just talk, wind, the big fellow bellowing . . . Look, if you go out of that door now, Van, I won't try to stop you. I'll know you're going because you can't stand the set-up or me any longer. And don't worry, I won't even ask you to come back, because who in their right senses would want to come back to this?' He flung one arm wide. 'Not even an ordinary lass from around the doors would have put up with what you've put up with. I know all this, and I've tried to tell you I know it, but I'm no hand at expressing meself that way. The only thing I can say now, and I've never said it afore, not in so many words is . . . I love you, that I've loved you since you were a nipper, and I'll go on loving you to the end of me days. That's not saying, if you leave me I won't take anybody else. I'm a man, I need somebody, but that isn't love. It's you I love, an' it's you I want. If you go, you go, but if you stay . . . well . . .'

All this time he had been holding her dresses over one arm, and now he went and put them on top of her case again, and when he turned round she was standing near him. But he did not touch her, not even when her hands went up to her face in distress and her fingers pressed so tightly across her mouth that her nose was pushed out of shape did he touch her, not until, her body leaning forward, she drooped her head against his shoulder did his arms go around her. And then his face, falling into her hair at the back of her neck, he muttered, 'Aw, Van. Van. God, don't you know how I feel about you?'

Her body began to shake again with her sobbing, and, his own voice thick and broken now, he said, 'It's a new start; we'll go on from here, no more looking back. I love you, love you, love you. Do you hear that? Always have and always will. It goes past lovin' what I feel for you. I need words now. I adore you, Van. Aye. I do. I adore you. Teach me words, Van. Teach me words so as I can tell you just how much I adore you . . . But there's one thing I don't need fancy words for, an' it's this.' He held her from him and looked deep into her tear-blinded eyes as he ended. 'I'm going to make you a promise and I'll carry it through by fair means or foul. I mean to put you back where you belong afore I'm finished. Brampton Hill, or even beyond. Now that's a solemn promise.'

When the shaking of her body increased with her sobbing he took it as a sign that she was pleased with the prospect. He was quite mistaken.

PART THREE

PART THREE

1

It was a week before Christmas, almost eighteen months from the day Angus had left Afflecks. Two things of import had happened to him and Vanessa since that day. First, and most important, was that Vanessa was going to have another baby, and it was due any time now. The second thing, and hardly of less importance, was that Angus Cotton was now a haulage contractor with his own name on ten lorries, and a respectable bank balance, together with a less respectable but equally important horde of five-pound notes in a cavity under the floor boards.

Angus's rise in the contracting world had been swift, even taking into account the many men who had made quick piles in this line of business. His success had really started when he thought he was finished altogether. It was on the day Fred Singleton asked him if he would buy his lorry because he was moving – the wife wanted to get back to her people in Doncaster.

Fred had thrown this bombshell on the very day Angus had secured a sub-contract to clear the rubble from a complete street of demolished houses. He had come by the contract through the help of Andrew Fowler, and it was to him he went to say that he couldn't go on with it;

one man and one lorry couldn't do the job and he hadn't any cash at the moment to buy Fred Singleton's lorry. It was at this point that Andrew Fowler said, 'Why don't you strike out on your own? Take a chance, borrow the money. Hire a couple of men and take a chance.'

Where, asked Angus, could he borrow the money without any security behind him?

'From me,' Andrew Fowler had answered; 'at five per cent. I won't be over-charging you or under-charging you. I'm willing to take a chance if you are, and, as you've seen, I can push a lot your way. If you take this chance I think you'll find it very much worth your while – and mine too.' He had nodded his head slowly. 'We can come to an agreement.'

Angus didn't know then whether Andrew Fowler was a bit of a sharp-shooter or not, and even now he didn't know; but what he did know at this present time was that if he kept going ahead during the next two or three years at the rate he had done these past months he would be set fair for the top. And tonight's little transaction would undoubtedly help it along.

'Move over, love,' he said. He dropped on to his knees on the hearth rug as he spoke; and as Vanessa rose to her feet he didn't immediately pull the mat back but, putting his arms around her waist, he pressed his face against the bulge of her stomach, and shouted, 'Hurry up, you in there. Hurry up. Do you hear me?'

Vanessa gave a contented laugh, saying, 'Angus don't. Look, you'll have me over.'

''Bout time too,' he said; ''bout time.' Then poking her stomach again gently he said in a lowered tone, 'Get a move on, d'you hear? Somebody else has got claims as well as you, you know.'

She turned away, biting on her lip, her head slightly

lowered. He was raw, uncouth in many ways, and she doubted if he would ever change. Definitely, the English lessons and selected reading had made no notable impression on him; but it didn't seem to matter, she loved him; she loved him as she hadn't imagined loving anybody. She had never imagined what it would be like to love like she loved him; it was a consuming feeling. Yet she wasn't happy.

She turned now and looked on his bent head as he put a knife down between the two floor boards and prised them upwards, then lifted a metal box on to the mat, from which he began counting out five-pound notes.

When he had counted to eight she said in some surprise, 'What are you going to give him?'

'A hundred.'

'A hundred pounds, Angus?'

'Aye.'

'But – but will he take all that from you?'

'Take me hand off for it an' all.' He grinned up at her with slanted glance.

He now replaced the box under the floor boards, and after straightening the mat and putting the chair back on it he counted the money again before putting it in an envelope.

When he looked at Vanessa she shook her head and said, 'I can never believe that he takes it.'

'You can believe it all right.' His head was bouncing up and down. 'That's how these blokes get rich, that's how all blokes get rich. You never find a rich honest business man. I mean, not one sticking to the books, everything down in black and white. Such men make a profit but they don't get stinkin' rich. And our kind friend, Mr Fowler, intends to get . . . stinkin' rich. And he should do with all the pies he's got his fingers in.'

'But he helped you at first without taking anything.'

'Aye, aye, you're right he did; but he had his eye on the future, and I soon picked things up. I know which side me bread is buttered.' He jerked his head at her.

'What if you hadn't given him any money on the side?'

'What do you think? I'd have been dropped. I'd have managed a one-man little business, just keeping afloat but nothing like where I am now, and where Stan is. It would appear we all took a chance and it paid off. Do you know how much Stan picked up last week? Forty-seven quid. Mind you, he had to work for it. And there's our Rosie going on about him coming home late. She doesn't say that when she goes and spends a small fortune on her clothes on a Saturday afternoon. She wants her ears scudded, that one.'

Vanessa said now, 'How long will you be? They're coming round tonight.'

'Oh, about an hour I should say. We'll just have a drink together and a natter . . . and a little exchange.'

'Why doesn't he transact the business in the office?'

'Not this kind of business, honey.' He leant towards her and tickled her chin. 'He's a very wise guy, is Mr Andrew Fowler. He's got a secretary there and secretaries have ears and noses. As he said himself, the walls have ears. No, he's cunning and cute, yet likeable. You know, I like him. You can't help liking him because, in a way, he's sort of honest about it. "Come for a walk along the river bank," he'll say, and there we go out of the office and along the river bank, and he'll say to me something like he did a month ago, like this. "Threadgill's are putting out a tender. They're opening up the land beyond Dark Town. It's just a sort of pilot scheme; your ten lorries could manage it. There's a fellow called Richardson there; he's got a lot of influence, but he's got a weakness for presents – a television, or a crate or two, or something like that." I said, "Wines?" and he said, "No. His taste runs to something a bit stronger, whisky."'

'But you got that contract, didn't you? I wrote – '

'Yes. Yes, I got the contract. Of course I did. That's what's been pulling it in these past few weeks.'

'And . . . and did you send him a . . . present?'

'Aye. Aye, I did. I didn't tell you about it at the time because I felt a bit chipped about doing it, sort of, well, half-ashamed like.'

She came and stood close to him and looked into his face, 'A television set?'

'No; nor whisky. You'd never believe in a month of Sundays what I sent him. Go on, have a guess.'

'A wrist watch?'

He shook his head.

'Gold cuff links?'

Again he shook his head.

'Was it something for himself?'

'Not exactly.'

'I give up.'

'A donkey.'

'A what!' Her face was spread wide with laughter. 'A donkey?'

'For his daughter; a very good donkey an' all. Now who would suspect anyone of doing a graft through a donkey? Sixty-two quid it cost me, that donkey. And it's not a donkey really, it's a pony, and a spanker.'

'Oh, Angus! Oh, Angus!' She leant against him sideways and they both began to laugh. 'And you know something else?' They were still laughing. 'I heard yesterday from Fowler that he's looking for a little go-cart, what they used to call a governess trap, you know. I haven't seen one in me life, and Fowler can't remember seeing one either, but that's what Mr Richardson's looking for, so Mr Angus Cotton is going to enquire if anybody's got a governess trap hanging about their back yard that they don't want.' They were holding on to each other shaking. When he released her she wiped her eyes, then held her hands on her high stomach as she asked, 'But what's the hundred pounds for?'

'I'm not sure meself yet.' He turned his head slowly towards her again. 'But if it means what I think it's going to mean that'll be the first of a few hundred I'll be dishing out . . . Now, now.' He put his hand up to her cheek. 'You don't have to worry; this is how business is done. Your big, ignorant slob of a man has learned a lot in the last few months, and he's got a lot to learn yet. But whatever he learns he's going to make it pay, because – because he's promised his wife something.' He took her chin firmly in the palm of his hand and squeezed it. 'I'll never rest until I fulfil that promise.'

'There's no need, Angus. Please, I've told you. I – I would rather you got the work in the ordinary way, I would, believe me, Angus, rather than run risks.'

'Risks? Oh! Oh! Now you're on the wrong track. There's no risk. I told you. Fowler walks me along the river bank; I buy a donkey for Mr Richardson's daughter. Why do I buy a donkey for Mr Richardson's daughter? Because Mr Richardson's daughter tells me that she is looking out for a donkey and I happen to see one going reasonable and I go and buy it. Does Mr Richardson pay me for it? Of course he does . . . That would be the way it would go if anybody said anything. There's no risk.' His face suddenly becoming straight, his jocular manner disappearing and his eyes hardening, he said, 'No risk, only the feeling you want to kick somebody up the backside every time they give you a hint a backhander is required if you want the job. When I see tenders put out it makes me laugh – grimly.'

There now came to them the sound of a door opening and Rosie's voice high and excited coming from the kitchen. The next minute both she and Emily were in the room, and Emily cried, 'What do you think? Rosie says Old Davis has died at the corner.'

'Aye?' Angus looked from one to the other. Then addressing Rosie, he said, 'What do you expect me to do? Send him a wreath? I've hardly seen him for years.'

'Don't be so daft, man.' Rosie pushed her hand out towards him. 'The house. He's been living there by himself since his wife died. The house; it'll be empty.'

'Oh, aye, aye.' He nodded at her. 'You've got something there, our Rosie. You don't miss much, do you?'

They both flapped their hands at each other; then Vanessa, coming forward, said, 'But there'll be a waiting list.'

'Not for these places,' said Rosie scornfully. 'They're all up for comin' down. Five years is the limit. Well don't stand there, our Angus; go and do somethin'. If we hadn't got that place last month I'd have been after it like a shot.'

'When did he die?' asked Angus, picking up his coat and going towards the door.

'About half-an-hour ago I should say. I saw Mrs Green coming out of the house. She's just washed him.'

'God! He's hardly cold.'

'Warm or cold, it doesn't matter to him now,' cried Emily. 'Go on, get yourself away. It'll be a godsend, that house especially, 'cos there's a bath in it.'

369

'Oh yes.' Angus turned quickly towards Vanessa. 'I forgot about the bath. There was quite a to-do in the street when he put it in. I'm off . . . Wait a minute.' He went back into the room towards the small table and, opening a drawer, took out three pounds, saying, 'I want more than this. Have you got any loose?'

Vanessa went to a chest of drawers to the right of the fire place and took her bag from the top, saying, 'How much do you want?'

'Oh, give me what you've got. A fiver should help get me into that bath. If not, it can be doubled.'

As he was passing Emily he gripped her wrinkled face tightly between his fists and, bending towards her, he quoted,

> 'Between the dark and the daylight,
> When the night is beginning to lower,
> Comes a pause in the day's occupation
> That is known as the Children's Hour.'

He ended on a deep note, thumbing towards Vanessa, 'Hurry that Children's Hour up, will you, 'cos I can't stand much more. If I have another night like last night I'll never live to see him. I was twisted up with cramp.'

Emily jerked her head from his grasp and pushed him through the kitchen, crying, 'Go on. Go on, you great big gowk.' But when they reached the front door the laughter went from his face and his bantering tone vanished as he said under his breath, 'See to her, won't you? Don't leave her?'

'Look,' said Emily, 'bairns have been born afore, and they'll be born again. This is just one of millions.'

'Aw, no, aw no.' He jerked his head at her. 'One in a

million, that's what you mean. One in a million. Now do as I tell you, stay with her, don't leave her for a minute. You won't go out, will you?'

'I'm not barmy, lad, or in me dotage. Go on, get on with your job an' I'll get on with mine; and she'll get on with hers. What's the matter with you? Gone soft all of a sudden? Go on an' get the contract. An' get that house. And anything else you can lay hands on.'

He nodded at her; then said slyly, 'Will do, Mrs Cotton. Will do.' Then he stepped across the narrow pavement and into his car, a ten-year-old Rover, which he had chosen, because it was the remains of a good thing. That was to be his policy, he told himself, all the way up: he'd rather have the remains of a good thing until he could get the good thing. No shoddy tin-pot new stuff, not for him or his.

Vanessa, Rosie, Emily and Stan waited in the kitchen for him coming back. He had said to Vanessa he would be an hour, but taking into account his visit to the rent agent they gave him another hour. That should have brought him back into the house at eight o'clock. At nine, he hadn't returned, and at half-past nine Vanessa's pains began; and Emily began to swear. He was a thoughtless, ignorant swine, that's what he was. In some pub likely, or fancy hotel, stuffing himself. There was the supper spoilt and them all starving. He thought of nobody but himself. He was a selfish swine, he always had been and always would be. Damn him.

At ten o'clock they began to get worried. At half-past ten Vanessa was sitting in her coat with her bag packed waiting to be taken to the hospital in Angus's car.

'If he comes in sodden,' said Emily, 'I'll brain him.

371

We won't see him till closing time, you'll see. The night of all nights.'

Rosie, pacing the kitchen, stopped at this point and looked at Stan and said, 'If you did this to me, Stan, you'd have your eyeballs served up to you the next day, and I'm tellin' you.'

Stan grinned sheepishly at her, and then said, 'Somethin's keepin' him. You know for a fact he's as worried as if he was going to have it himself.'

Nobody said there could have been an accident, only the thought was constant in Vanessa's mind. Over the last half-hour she had resorted to prayer. It was as if she was back in the convent listening to the nuns: 'Hail Mary, full of grace, the Lord is with thee . . . Blessed Michael, the Archangel, defend us in the day of battle; be our safe-guard against the wickedness and snares of the devil; rebuke him, we humbly pray . . . Angus, Angus, hurry up. Please come home. Hail Mary, full of grace, the Lord is with thee. Let him come now, please.'

Her last prayer seemed to receive a lightning answer, for there came the sound of a car drawing up outside. The next minute Angus was in the room. He wasn't drunk, as they all expected, but he wasn't rightly sober. He stood in the doorway and raised his hands for silence, crying, 'Now all of you, all of you don't say it. I'm telling you, don't say it.' He didn't seem to take in the fact that Vanessa was sitting in her coat. 'I've done it. A treble up . . . Mrs Cotton Junior, Mrs Cotton Senior, Mrs Rosie Barrett, Mr Stanley Barrett, you see before you a successful business man, a man who's going up and up. I've pulled off the Henson quarry deal, two years' work. I've got the whole contract. Twenty lorries I'll need. Twenty lorries and twenty men, Stan. And,' he moved slowly towards Vanessa, 'you're moving, Mrs Cotton Junior, to a house with a bathroom. But it's only temporary; this is only the beginning.' He wagged his finger down into her pale but smiling face. 'And now for the last news, the top of the treble.' He turned to his mother, where Emily was standing at the far end of the table, her fists thrust into her hips, her face grim. 'Mrs Cotton Senior, your son has had an honour bestowed on him. You always said it would happen. Give the lad a chance, you said and it'll happen. And it has.' He leant across the table towards her. 'I've been put forward as a member of the Round Table. Now what do you think of that?' He straightened up and looked from one to the other. There was both pride and scorn on his face. 'Me, Angus Cotton, asked to represent the contractors of this town in the Round Table, because you know,' he shook his head widely, 'only one man can be in there representing one profession. Profession mind; I said, profession.'

Whatever Emily felt at her son's success, at this moment what she said was, 'You big, gormless gowk, shut up. Shut your trap a minute if you can. What do you think's been happenin' while you've been swillin' beer? She's had her pains all night since you left, an' we've been waitin' for you. She wouldn't let Stan get a taxi. She's a fool; she wanted her husband to take her, an' she's been hangin' on. Now, pick up that case, that's if you're able to carry it, an' get goin'.'

Angus was deaf to Emily's bawling. He was looking down at Vanessa and she up at him, and he said softly, 'Aw, honey.'

His voice was cut off by Rosie saying airily, 'Well, you should have known what was happenin'. Didn't you have your pains?' On this, both she and Stan began to laugh heartily. Then their laughter was checked abruptly by Vanessa's body doubling forward.

'Look!' cried Emily. 'Get her into the car as quick as you can.'

'No . . . o. No . . . o.' Vanessa refused to move from the chair. She was gripping Angus's hands, her fingers digging into his flesh.

After a few minutes, when the pain didn't subside, Emily looked from one to the other and said, 'God, no!'

But it was God, yes.

When Angus tried to get Vanessa to her feet she slumped down his legs on to the mat, saying between gasps, 'Get . . . get the doctor.'

While Stan flew for Doctor Carr they all tried in various ways to get Vanessa to her feet and into the bedroom, and when Angus put his arms under to lift her up she cried out in agony, 'No! No!'

It was Rosie who said, 'Get an eiderdown and sheets to put under her.'

They managed to do this, and it was only fifteen minutes later when, on the mat in front of the fire, in the kitchen of the house where he himself had been born, Angus saw, to his horrified gaze, the head of his son coming into the world.

When Doctor Carr hurried into the room and took over, Angus went down the yard and was violently sick; and when he returned his mother was holding a screaming child in her arms. He did not look at it but went and knelt at Vanessa's side.

Vanessa looked at him. She was smiling. 'It's – it's a boy,' she said.

He nodded at her, unable to speak.

'It's been a day.'

374

He nodded again.

'You know something?' Her voice was faint. 'I want to laugh.'

'You can laugh the morrow.' His voice was shaking. 'What you want to do now is to go to sleep. Here's the doctor.' He moved aside and stood bewildered at what was going on around him. Rosie was gathering some pieces of linen from the floor and his mother was saying, 'Put them in soak and get me a dish of hot water. And here,' she turned to him, 'this belongs to you, so hold him until I find some place to put him. Make yourself useful for once.'

He took into his arms the thing he had created. It looked old and wrinkled, mummified, but it was his son, the beginnings of a man. He had been born on a mat in a condemned house. That shouldn't have happened; it was his fault. But he would remedy that. Oh aye, by God he would. His son would have education, the best money could buy, boarding school, public school, the lot. He'd have no memories of Ryder's Row, number twenty-four or number two. Angus Cotton's son would be a gentleman . . . He'd show them.

2

The Rover 2000 swerved expertly into the car park and to the corner opposite the side door of the club. Angus got out, and after adjusting his Aquascutum overcoat he went towards the building, not to the side door, but around to the main entrance of Ransome's Club.

Ransome's had first been established in 1864; it said so on a brass plate discreetly embedded in an alcove in the lobby. It was, supposedly, a non-political club, but it was rarely you found any well-known member of the Labour Party registered on its books. But there was one thing necessary to become a member of Ransome's . . . money.

The name of Mr Angus Frederick Cotton had been on the books for over six months now. He wasn't a frequent visitor, sometimes a fortnight would go by and he wouldn't look in, but whenever he did visit the club he came dressed in his best.

On the admission of Mr Angus Frederick Cotton to Ransome's it had lost one distinguished member. Mr Jonathan Ratcliffe had met Mr Cotton in the lobby, and Mr Ratcliffe's reactions had been apoplectic, and the town had something else to chuckle over.

The town was very interested in the situation that

376

existed between the house of Angus Cotton – still after five years at the corner of Ryder's Row – and the house of Mr Jonathan Ratcliffe of Bower Place, Brampton Hill. It was said over both pints of beer and sherry before dinner that there was nothing against people getting on, but they shouldn't forget themselves and play God Almighty. The definition over the sherry might be reduced merely to God, but it meant the same thing: Jonathan Ratcliffe had become too high-handed, too uppish for the forthright, outspoken, down-to-earth citizens of Fellburn.

Now young Angus Cotton: there was a lad who had got on but who hadn't forgotten himself. This was almost entirely the view of the beer drinkers. He knew where he was going right from the start did Cotton. Not only did he take on Jonathan Ratcliffe's girl when she was going to have a bairn – and not by him mind, and that was the telling point, and it hadn't come out till after. Oh aye, that was a great telling point, to take on somebody else's bairn; it showed what a man was made of. Well, not only had he done that, but he had gone into business as a one-lorry man, and whether he had begged, borrowed or stolen the money, nobody knew, but in next to no time he had got two lorries, then four, then six, and seemingly overnight he had a fleet because you couldn't walk yards in the town without seeing one of Cotton's lorries. But he hadn't forgotten himself, had Angus Cotton.

At least, not yet, said the sherry drinkers. They were watching him very closely. He still lived in the same street as his mother, and although his wife was turned out in the best, as were his two bairns, Ryder's Row wasn't an address for a member of Ransome's.

Yes, both quarters of the town were very interested in the doings of Angus Cotton. And he knew it, and thrived on it.

He left his hat and coat in the cloakroom, looked at himself in the mirror above the wash-basin, rubbed his hands lightly over his discreetly oiled hair, opened his mouth wide and brought his fingers down tightly against each cheek to make sure there was no stubble, then straightened his tie and adjusted his coat and walked quietly out and into the hallway. Here he looked about him for a moment before saying to a passing waiter, 'Mr Fowler about?'

'Yes, sir; he went into the Brown Room just a minute ago.'

'Thanks.'

The Brown Room had an ornate high ceiling. Its walls were covered with faded red wallpaper on which was hung portraits of past distinguished members of the club. There were deep leather armchairs and down cushioned settees. In an armchair in a far corner sat Andrew Fowler. And he raised his hand as Angus entered the room.

'Hello, there.' Angus took his seat opposite Fowler, then said, 'I'm sorry I couldn't make it yesterday; I had to go down to Lessington; they are taking it too easy in that quarter.'

Andrew Fowler smiled, nodded, then said, 'What are you having?'

'Oh, a brandy.' He would have preferred a beer, but beer wasn't drunk in this room; he had learned that early.

Andrew Fowler hailed a waiter who was bringing drinks to other occupants of the room. Having given his order, he settled back and said, still with a smile on his face, 'Served you right if you had missed it.'

'Missed what?'

'Oh.' Fowler jerked his head to the side. 'Just something I thought you should know about.'

'Well, let's have it,' said Angus. 'You're just bursting at the seams . . . Don't tell me they're going to pull the new Town Hall down in Newcastle and they want me to salvage it?'

They both laughed a little; then Fowler said, 'How would you like to live on Brampton Hill?'

'What!'

'You heard me. How would you like to live on Brampton Hill?'

Angus's face was straight, his eyes hard. 'It all depends which part. Brampton Hill's a long hill and there's all kinds of houses on it. I don't know whether I'd like to live there or not.' He lay back in his chair and stretched his neck out of his collar. 'It's not the place it was; a lot of the big houses are in flats now.' He surveyed Fowler. He was giving nothing away to him, not about Brampton Hill, he wasn't. There were things about Fowler he couldn't understand. Sometimes he thought he was playing him like a puppet. He didn't like the idea.

'The Larches is to be put up for sale.'

Angus felt a wave of heat cover him. It was as if he'd had an injection straight into an artery. His head seemed to be swelling and he knew his face was a deep red. The Larches. Brett's place. The house next to Jonathan Ratcliffe's. There was a tightness in his jaws that was painful. He drew in a long, steady breath. Was this it? Was this what he had been waiting for? Striving for? He had promised her he'd put her back where she belonged, even on the hill, but he'd never dreamed of anything on the scale of The Larches. The Larches up for sale. And all that land. God, yes. He screwed his buttocks farther back against the soft leather of the chair. This was it. This was what he had been waiting for. He'd put her in The Larches.

'What are they asking?' he said.

'I don't rightly know; the bills aren't out yet. And then most likely it'll be put up for auction. But it'll fetch money, big money, because of the land. Six acres, all with river frontage; that'll bring money.'

'Oh,' Angus moved his head deprecatingly, 'not as much as all that; it's controlled, isn't it? No building there.'

'Not for a while. But they're pulling off the controls everywhere. Anybody getting it could hang on for a few years and then they'd be in clover, no matter what they had to pay for it now.'

'Have you any idea what it will go for?'

Andrew Fowler pushed his head back into the chair and looked upwards for a moment before saying, 'Well, the house needs a lot doing to it, both inside and out, I understand. I would say anything up to fifteen thousand. That's playing up the supposition that you'll never be able to do anything with the land, only as a garden. But if there's a breeze of a whisper that it could be used for building land in a few years' time when we have a change of Government,' he pulled his nose at Angus, 'the price will soar; it could go as far as thirty.'

Angus gave a low whistle, then said, 'Who's got the business?'

'Pearson.'

'You know Pearson.'

'Yes, I know Pearson.'

'Could you do anything?'

'I might.'

Suddenly Angus tossed his head from one side to the other and gritted his teeth and muttered under his breath, 'For God's sake, don't stall, Andrew. I hate this cat and mouse business. Could you?'

Andrew Fowler's expression took on a slightly cold look now and he said, 'You get too agitated, Angus. That's your trouble. Play it cool; it pays off in the long run. I've got something else to tell you. It isn't only money you've got to worry about, Ratcliffe's after it. He's been at Pearson already; it could be sold privately before the sale.'

Angus didn't ask why Ratcliffe didn't go next door to the Bretts and do a deal straight-away; he guessed there had likely been no interchange between those two houses since the morning his mother had visited them both.

'Do you know what he's offering?'

'Sixteen thousand. But here's another thing. He's not doing it himself, he's working through a third party. Crafty, very crafty.'

Angus took a drink from his glass, then bent towards Fowler saying, 'I'll go seventeen.'

'Won't that be rocking your boat?'

'Aye, I suppose it will. But if it means twenty-seven and it almost sinks me, I mean to get that house . . . And another thing, tell Pearson I'll see him all right.'

'What would you suggest? It might be steep.'

'Five hundred?'

'Five hundred, it is.'

They both drew in deep breaths, and then Fowler said, 'There's another thing I'd like to talk over with you, Angus, while we're on the subject.'

'Aye, come on, let's have it; I thought we weren't finished.'

'Well, you know me.'

'Nobody better, Andrew.' Angus's lip was up at the corner.

Fowler ignored the implication and went on: 'As long as you buy the house and use it as a habitation, well

and good, but should you sell the land for building
. . . well, then I think there should be a little agreement
on that.'

Angus stared at his mentor for a moment before saying,
'Fair enough, fair enough. Do you want it in writing?'

'Yes, I think that would be wise, Angus.'

'What per cent?'

'Well, don't let's be greedy, say trade price.' He
smiled. 'Thirty three and a third.'

'Let's drink to it.'

Andrew Fowler raised his glass, and after they had
drunk he got to his feet and added, 'Now we can have
our dinner in peace. By the way, how's Vanessa and the
children?'

'Fine, grand.'

'What's she going to say when you tell her about this
latest venture?'

'I'm not going to tell her.'

'What! You're not . . .?'

'No. At least until it's all signed and sealed. How long
will it take?'

'Oh, don't gallop, Angus; I've got to put the wheels
in motion first. And then it can be a slow business:
solicitors, Land Registry, one thing and another, they
take time. Once we get going two months should see it
all cleared up.'

'Two months! As long as that?' He bit on his lip and
his step quickened unconsciously as he left the room,
and he thought, 'I'll not sleep for two months, I'll not
know a minute's peace until it's mine, MINE . . .'

And Angus's sleep was fitful for the next eight days,
during which time the price of The Larches rocketed
from seventeen thousand to twenty-three thousand, but
on the eighth day he wrote out a cheque for five per cent

of twenty-three thousand pounds to be paid to James Pearson Esq., Estate Agents, being the deposit required to purchase The Larches from the joint owners, Colin, Paul and Michael Brett.

Now Angus was bursting to tell Vanessa, but a wariness in him warned him to keep quiet until the whole thing was legally settled. He believed if he were to tell her now she'd put a spanner in the smooth-running works, she'd bring up the excuse it was too close to her people. But once the thing was settled and he'd saddled himself with a liability of twenty-three thousand pounds she couldn't do much else but accept the house with a good grace, and oh, to see her ensconced next to the folks who had thrown her off as if she were a dirty clout. Parents or no parents, she was bound to feel one up on them, if only for his sake, because he had done as he said, and in a short time at that, and put her back where she belonged.

And he had no doubt in his own mind where Vanessa belonged. She didn't belong in Ryder's Row, and if she lived to be a thousand she would never fit in there. She stuck out like a sore thumb; she was as great an embarrassment to those around her as he would be, God helping him, to Jonathan Ratcliffe.

Although he constantly told himself he wanted the house for Vanessa he knew that, with even more intensity, he wanted that house for Angus Cotton. Oh, to come out of that drive in the morning in a Bentley. Aye, the next car he would get would be a Bentley. And which Bentley would make way for which when they met in the road? He couldn't wait to find out. And another thing, he'd have his mother with him. Aye, that would be a feather in his cap, and in hers. She'd be going back to Brampton Hill, and not as a skivvy. No, she'd be going into the kitchen only to give her orders. He didn't conjure up what part

383

Vanessa was going to play in this arrangement, but told himself he'd employ a couple of maids and a gardener; he'd have The Larches the show-place of the town. And one more thing, his bairns, they were going to be educated . . . Private school for Andrew, and then public school. God, aye, he'd see to that. There'd be no Ryder's Row for his family. He'd let Ratcliffe see how Angus Cotton did things. Angus Cotton, the contractor, who, but for being blamed for giving his daughter a bairn, might be still Angus Cotton the foreman. When he came to think of it he had something to thank God-Almighty Ratcliffe for after all, and he would thank him one day . . . Aye, but spitting in his eye. And the first spit would be when he moved into The Larches. Hurry up, hurry up, the days, the weeks; he couldn't wait.

Feeling as he did he had to tell somebody, so he told Emily.

Emily had just finished soaking her feet in a tin dish before the fire and he sat on his hunkers on the edge of the mat and told her, and she was so thunderstruck by his news that she let him go on talking. The water got cold and her legs began to turn blue and shiny, and when he said, 'Well, say something, say something. Don't sit there looking like a stuffed duck with your feet in the water. Say something, woman,' she closed her eyes, heaved a deep sigh, then, taking up a towel where it had been warming on the fender, she put it on the hearth rug and lifted her feet on to it before she turned and looked at him and said, 'You're bloody-well stark, staring mad, lad.'

There was a short silence before he brought his body upwards in a bound, saying, 'Aw, for crying out loud, Mam! Have you heard what I've been saying to you? I've bought The Larches. Me, Angus Cotton, I've bought The

384

Larches in Brampton Hill, and all you can bloody well say is that I'm mad. Do you know what this means? We're all going to live on Brampton Hill.'

'Who? Me?' She dug her thumb into the hollow of her neck. 'Oh, no, lad. Now, you can count me out of your scheme. Me live on Brampton Hill? Now get this into that great, big, swollen head of yours, the only time you'll get me up Brampton Hill again is if they take the hearse up that way. But that's not even likely as it's the long way round to the cemetery.'

'Well, we can't go and live up there and leave you down here, woman.'

'Look. Look.' She stood up now and walked to the edge of the towel, which brought her close to him. 'You're not my keeper. You're married, you've got a wife and family. You see to them an' that'll take you all your time, but what I do is my business. This is my home and until they pull it down I'm stayin' here. And then I'll go into whatever they provide. But I'm not livin' with you and Van on Brampton Hill, or any other bloody hill. Now get that . . . And here's somethin' else I'll give you to think about. You said you haven't told her, you're keepin' it a secret; well, if I'm any judge, you're in for one great, bloody, shock. And it wouldn't surprise me if you haven't got a twenty-three-thousand-pound white elephant on your hands. What you still don't understand, lad, after five years is you've married somebody quite different to yoursel'.'

'Oh, for God's sake, Mam, don't talk bloody tripe. I know what I married, nobody better.'

'But you don't, lad, you don't. 'Cos if you think she's goin' to go on livin' next door to her folks just like that, then you don't. She's a highly sensitive lass. Some folk call it breeding. Anyway, she's different, an'

I can't see her lettin' you push her up there right on to their doorstep. She couldn't stand it. You know,' she stabbed her finger at him and smiled a tight smile, 'I know why you're doin' this. I know why you've bought Brett's place, an' I don't blame you. Oh, I don't blame you. And I'd be laughin' up me sleeve if you were takin' anybody else up there but his daughter. In fact, if your wife wasn't any connection of his I'd go up there on a Saturday night and have me knees up in the garden just to show him an' all.' Her voice dropped to a sad note as she ended, 'But you did marry his daughter, and if I know anythin' about your Van she's not going to like your little surprise, 'cos to say the least, it's sort of tactless like.'

'Tactless be-buggered. Look, Mam, don't give me the jitters. Twenty-three thousand I've spent. Do you realise, twenty-three thousand! I'm going up fast, but twenty-three thousand takes some finding. And that's not all. With the side lines I've had to keep going to get the damned place I'll be lucky if I get away with twenty-five thousand when I'm finished.'

Emily's voice was still quiet, but had a touch of laughter in it now and her smile was smirky as she said, 'It should be a nice experiment for you playing with thousands. Now who would have thought that the snotty-nosed, shock-headed, ugly mug, Angus Cotton, whose mam was the Ratcliffe's daily for years, can now talk in thousands, twenty-five thousands, when up to a few years ago twenty-five shillings spare would have been a Godsend to him. It's a credit to you, lad, and it's your mother that's saying it. Go on, lash out with your thousands, but don't think,' her voice rose sharply, 'that you're goin' to push me around, or that you're goin' to make your wife do somethin' that will be against every grain in her body.' She thrust out her hand and thumped him on the shoulder, her voice barking now as she finished, 'If you want my advice, you'll spend the next few weeks preparing yourself for a disappointment, sort of building yourself up, if you get what I mean, 'cos your big-head is goin' to have a puncture.'

'Aw, to hell with you!'

As he stalked out of the kitchen she bawled after him, 'An' to hell with you. And if you see me there, don't you open your mouth to me because I'm particular about the company I keep. I've no room for upstarts. You're goin' the same road as the man you're fightin'.'

When the door banged she quickly padded into the front room, and, standing to the side of the window, watched her son marching down the street. A big, well-dressed, prosperous-looking man, who had just been in this little box of a house talking about spending twenty-five thousand pounds as if they were shillings. Life was strange. Would he persuade Van to go and live in a house next to her parents? He persuaded her to do most things. It was always a mystery to her what Vanessa saw in her son; that she herself should know his worth was a different matter altogether. She knew him to be a good man, big-headed, bumptious, argumentative, all the qualities that went to make a rough northerner; he took after herself, and she knew what she was all right, nobody better, and him being the flesh of her flesh she could appreciate him; but how did it come that a girl like Vanessa could appreciate him? What did she see in him? She didn't talk much ever, never opened up, and she didn't seem to have any life of her own. She was his wife, the mother of his children; his secretary, aye, an' his teacher, she had been learning him for years to speak properly, grammer an' that. She had seen his

387

efforts on his desk but she hadn't remarked on them; she knew better. She didn't want to spoil a good thing. Yet he showed no evidence of improvement when he was talking to her. No, he was the same old ha'-penny dodger. But that lass; everything she did was for him, and what did she get out of it? Damn little that she could see. He could have got her into a decent house long afore this but he had put it off and put it off, partly, she had thought, because he didn't want to move away from herself. But now she saw the real reason for him staying put. He had been after big game all along, no modern bungalow or imitation Regency house for him; it had to be on Brampton Hill, and not only on Brampton Hill, it had to be one of the biggest houses; and not only one of the biggest, but the place that had the most land left. He was going too fast; he was rising too high; he'd blow himself up unless something, or somebody, put the brakes on him.

3

It was in the afternoon that she went down the street
to the end house. She knew Vanessa's routine. It being
after four o'clock Andrew and Annabella would be out
with Mary Ridley in the park, and Vanessa would be
preparing the evening meal.

She found her in the kitchen, a small, modern,
well-equipped kitchen, and she said, 'Oh, hello, lass.
Isn't it close? And it's going to pour afore the day's
out; I can tell by me feet.'

'Aren't they any better?' Vanessa looked down at
the swollen ankles bulging over the top of black-
laced shoes.

'No, lass; an' they won't be until I'm in me coffin.
And I bet you what you like, the swellin'll go down
immediately then. Enough to make you kick yourself.'

'Oh, Emily!' Vanessa was laughing. She always got
a laugh and felt happy when Emily was about. It
was a different kind of happiness from that which
she experienced with Angus; that happiness was a
taut, high-tensioned feeling. She said now, 'Rosie
popped in. She's just gone along to Stodart's; she'll
be back in a short while. She was coming down
to you.'

'Stodart's! For more shoes? She's always buyin' shoes. How many pairs is that she's got?'

'At the last count,' said Vanessa, breaking an egg into some flour, 'eighteen.'

'God above! Eighteen pairs of shoes. She would have to be a centipede to get her wear out of them.'

Vanessa was laughing again. 'She likes shoes.'

'She likes too many things, that one. The money's gone to her head; she's never done spendin'. Have they got owt in the bank? She won't tell me; she says it's none of my business.'

'Oh, I think they're all right, Emily. Stan's sensible where money is concerned.'

'It would take him to be. She'd have him on the rocks else . . . Van.'

'Yes, Emily?' Vanessa turned her head round, but still kept beating the egg and flour together.

'Can you stop a minute? I want a word with you, serious like.'

Serious? Vanessa laid down the fork and wiped her hands and turned about, and Emily, going into the living-room, said, 'Come an' sit down a minute; I want to get it over afore our Rosie comes in. This is atween you and me, understand?'

When they were seated Emily bent forward and repeated, 'Mind, lass; this is just atween you and me. I want your word on it.'

'Something's wrong, Emily . . . Angus?'

'Aye, Angus. Oh, it's all right. Don't look like that; it's not that kind of wrong.' She reached out and roughly pulled Vanessa's hand away from her mouth and, holding on to it, she said, 'Now listen, lass. Have you noticed any difference in him lately, the last week or so?'

Vanessa considered a minute, then said, 'Well, yes.

He's not sleeping. He seems excited about something; bursting out singing one minute, and gloomy the next. Yes. Yes, I've noticed it.'

'But you didn't say nothing?'

'No, Emily.'

'Well, I can tell you he is excited an' all, because he's keeping somethin' back from you. He's done somethin' an' he's not tellin' you until the matter is clinched. An' when it is it'll be too late to alter things; or so he thinks. You know, he's your husband, Van, but I don't think he really knows you. I feel I know you a damn sight better than him; but then, of course, I've known you longer, haven't I?' she smiled.

'What's it all about, Emily?' Vanessa's voice was quiet; her whole demeanour was quiet. She had grown into a rather reserved young woman. She was very seldom gay, unless she was with her children, and then she had to be alone with them before she could let herself go. She added now, 'Tell me. Tell me quickly, please, because Rosie might be back at any minute. And Angus himself will be in shortly.'

'Well, hold on to your seat there, lass. Here it comes . . . He's buying the Bretts' place, The Larches.'

Emily watched the colour drain completely from Vanessa's face. She thought for a moment she was going to collapse, and she said, 'Now steady on, lass. Steady on. Don't let go. This is not the time for lettin' go; you've got to put your thinkin' cap on.'

'The Larches? He's buying The Larches for us?' Vanessa's voice came as the smallest whisper.

'For you. He's goin' to give you the surprise of your life. He gave me the surprise of mine when he out with it. He was bustin' at the seams, like a bairn with a new toy. I've never stopped worryin' since. I told him he was mad . . . You don't want to go an' live in The Larches, do you?'

'Oh, Emily. Me! Live in The Larches? In Brett's house? O-Oh!' The last word came as a groan. 'I couldn't. I couldn't live there even . . . even if it wasn't next door to home.' She still thought of Bower Place as home. 'And just think what it would do to mother and father. They wouldn't stand for it; they would leave.'

'Aye, aye, I'd thought of that.'

'And . . . and they love that place. Oh. Oh, how could he, Emily? How could he?'

'He could because he's barmy; he thinks that because you came from there you want to go back there. It's no use tellin' him. But that's not the only reason he bought the place; the other is he's wantin' to get one back on your father. That's at the bottom of it; he wants to show him.'

'I'll never go there, Emily.'

'I know that, lass.'

'He'll just have to sell it again.'

'An' that'll knock the spunk out of him if anythin' will. And I'd hate to see it happen, 'cos he's mine, and I know how he'll feel. But as I see it there's nothing else for it. I thought I'd better tell you because if he sprung it on you and you hadn't time to think there might be a flare-up. And it's like this.' She smiled now. 'Him an' me, an' our lot, we can flare up and threaten to murder each other one minute, an' we'll be shakin' hands the next, but if you had a flare-up you wouldn't get over it easily. Would you now?'

Vanessa looked from the dyed-hair to the prematurely wrinkled face of her mother-in-law, and she thought: She's right. She's always right. But what was she going to do about this, this latest venture, which must appear to him as the summit of his aims? This is what he had been waiting for, working for, striving for, wearing himself out for, to give her this. Her refusal must be made in such a way that a flare-up, when it came, would not burn him out, burn them both out. Their marriage, as she saw it, was a precarious union, resting as it were on a knife's edge, and this in spite of love and two children.

At this moment they heard Rosie coming pitter-pattering up the stairs on her high heels and, after looking hard at each other, they went quickly out of the room, and Emily greeted her daughter with, 'You want your lugs scudded, buying more shoes.'

'Shoes are made for walking,' Rosie sang, as she pranced round the table in her latest acquisition. Then stopping suddenly, she looked at Vanessa and said, 'Oh, by the way. What's going with our Angus these days? Stan says he's like a dog with two tails.'

Vanessa and Emily refrained from exchanging glances; then Rosie exclaimed, 'You're not,' she shook her head before adding, 'again?'

'No, Rosie. I'm not again.' Vanessa smiled.

'Well; what is it?'

'Oh,' Vanessa turned towards the fireplace, 'I suppose it's because things are going well.'

'Oh, it isn't only that. Stan says they've been going well for a long time; and he wasn't like this. Stan says he's all keyed-up, just as if he was going to take off by parachute.'

'Very likely is,' said Emily now, going towards the door. 'You never know what he's goin' to do next. The only thing is, I hope he doesn't forget to pull the strings afore he hits the ground.'

On this enigmatic comment, enigmatic at least to Rosie, Emily left them.

*   *   *

393

Life seemed to follow the usual pattern until almost a week later. It was in the evening. Angus was late and Vanessa had just got the children to bed, promising them that their father would come and see them immediately he entered the house. But they were sound asleep by the time he did get in.

He looked tired tonight, and somewhat strained, and so she let him have his meal and cleared away before she said, 'I want to talk to you, Angus.'

'Talk?' He cast a sidelong glance at her. 'Well, fire ahead.'

She swallowed deeply and walked the length of the sitting-room and back to him before she said, 'I understand you are buying me a house?'

She watched his head turn from her and swing from side to side, and when his fist crashed on to the table she said, 'She had to tell me.'

'The big-mouthed-old-bitch!' He spaced each word. 'That's all she is, a great, big, loose-mouthed, old bitch.' His head stopped its swinging, his fists relaxed, and then slowly he turned and looked at her and asked in an entirely different voice, in which she detected a plea, 'Well, what do you think? Go on, tell me what you think?'

'I . . . I think it's wonderful that you could pay so much money for the place.'

'Is that all?' His shoulders stiffened. 'Aren't you excited? You know what place I've bought, don't you? Brett's. Now. Now.' He thrust his hand swiftly out towards her and jerked it back and forwards. 'Don't get me wrong. It isn't animosity; nothing like that; not against Brett; it's just that I wanted you to be back on the Hill, where you belong.'

'I – I understand, Angus.'

'Do you? Aw,' his head was swinging again, 'I don't think you do really.'

'Yes, yes, I do; and I think it's marvellous. There's only one thing.'

'Aye, one thing. Well, what is it?' His face looked grim now, for he expected her answer to be, 'I can't live there.' But it wasn't. What she said was, 'Would you do something more for me?'

'Anything.' His voice was full of relief. The tension went out of his body; he grabbed her hands, saying softly, 'Anything in the wide world. You know that. I don't have to tell you.'

'But this is something big, different; you – mightn't be able to understand why I'm asking it.'

'Well, I won't,' he smiled at her, 'not until you tell me.'

She dropped her eyes down to their joined hands, and then said softly, 'Would you have the house put in my name, not jointly, in – in my name?'

This request was the last thing in the world he imagined her making. It sounded utterly preposterous. He wanted to think he hadn't heard her aright, but he had. Put the house in her name? He wanted it for her but it was to be his property. He wanted to own The Larches, his name on the title deeds. That was one of the things he was living for, to see Angus Cotton written on the deeds of The Larches.

'Why? Tell me why?' he said flatly. 'Jointly, aye; but why do you want it in your name?'

She raised her lashes but didn't look at him; she looked beyond him as she said, 'It's – it's just a whim, I suppose.'

He stared at her. Just a whim, she said. If he didn't satisfy her whim what then? She'd think him mean. All his life she'd consider him mean, and it would raise a barrier between them. Another one to be broken down. He spent his life breaking down barriers. The one that stood between Brampton Hill and Ryder's Row was about to fall, but if he didn't comply with her wish in this, even when the barrier was down, wouldn't she in some way, like a woman, hold it against him? He was always saying that everything he did was for her, now he'd have to prove it by giving her the house.

She was at the window looking down into the street. She was standing very still. She could do that, stand still with no muscle moving. He stared at her long, straight back. Even the lines of her could churn up his stomach any time of the day, and that after nearly six years. Aw, to hell! Who was to know whose name was on the deeds? The house would be known as Angus Cotton's place, and Van wasn't the kind of woman to go loud-mouthing it round the town that it was in her name. She wasn't like his mother. Wait till he got his tongue around that one. She had knocked all the guts out of his plans. The excitement of driving Van up there when the thing was signed and sealed and saying, 'This is yours. I've bought it for you. Didn't I say I'd put you back where you belong?'

He said now, 'Well, if that's how you want it, that's how you'll have it. It'll be in your name.'

She turned round. 'Thanks, Angus,' she said. 'Thanks.'

That was all, just, 'Thanks, Angus.' No throwing her arms around his neck and hugging him and telling him that he was the most generous man on earth, that it was wonderful the things he had achieved in so short a time. Nothing like that. Just, 'Thanks, Angus.' Aye, well; that's how things went. Coolly. That was part of her makeup, coolness. If he ever could hate her it would be when she was cool.

'How long will it be before everything is settled?' She had her face averted as she asked the question, and he said, 'Oh, a few weeks. The solicitor will have to make a few more alterations now, but the papers haven't gone up to the Land Registry yet. It won't be too long. A month; five weeks perhaps.' His voice sounded flat as if he had lost interest in the whole project, and turning away, he added, 'I think I'll go down to the club.'

There was a pause before she answered, 'Yes. Yes, I would do that; it will relax you.'

'I don't need relaxing.' His voice was brittle as he turned and faced her again, and there was about his face an explosive look, and she combated it by saying quietly, 'All right, you don't need to relax. But you need a change. Go on; you'll feel better when you get back.'

He stared at her. There was something here he couldn't get to the bottom of. She should be a bit elated that she was having a twenty-three thousand pound house as a gift. She should be acting differently, not sending him out casually to a club, as if it was an ordinary night in an ordinary week – as if he was an ordinary bloke . . . Aye, as if he was just an ordinary bloke who hadn't one penny to rub against another. He had a feeling inside that things weren't right, the kind of feeling he had years ago when everything was going against him. He wanted to talk, to get to the bottom of it, but he couldn't do any probing with Van, not with the cool mood on her. But there was someone he could talk to, that loud-mouthed old bitch down there. He'd go down and blow her sky high.

He was in the street before he decided against visiting Emily; the mood he was in he'd want to bawl her down, and she didn't seem able these days to stand up to him as she used to. He cursed deep in his throat, got into his car and drove to the club. It was coming to something when he had to go to Ransome's to be appreciated.

When the house door banged Vanessa, sitting down suddenly on a chair, closed her eyes and thought, 'This is just the beginning. He'll want to kill me when he finds out.'

4

The day was dull and chilly. It had started with rain, which had slowed to a drizzle, and this in turn had developed into a wet mist. The streets were greasy. The town traffic bustled through the heavy greyness as if making for more pleasant scenes beyond.

Vanessa made her way down to the main street to Tiller's Garage and asked for a taxi, and when she was seated in it she held her large handbag upright on her knees and tightly between her hands. In her handbag were the deeds of The Larches. She'd had them in her possession since eleven o'clock when the solicitor had smilingly handed them to her and she had surprised both him and Angus by saying, 'I want to keep them with me for today.'

'Look; what's up with you? They're yours,' Angus had said. 'Let Mr Black hold them with all the other stuff.'

'Just for today,' she had repeated; and he had shaken his head and said, 'All right, all right, have it your own way.'

He had an appointment at half-past eleven but he was coming back about one for her and they were going up to . . . their house. It was a blind date, he said, because he had never seen inside The Larches. Fancy that, buying a place without looking it over. Had she ever heard of anyone doing that?

When she said to the taxi-driver, 'Brampton Hill, Bower Place, please,' she shivered. She was going home. For the first time in years she was going home. Deep down in her there was a suppressed longing to visit her old home, to see her mother and Susan, and . . . even her father. Knowing her father's temperament, she was well aware that if it lay with him she would never see the inside of her old home again, and that already, under the circumstances, he would be preparing to leave the house he had built, the house he loved; and this also he would have chalked up against her. She was aware that she was about to do something extraordinary, and something that would likely drive Angus mad, for the time being anyway. But as things stood, no word of hers would convince him that she would find it impossible to live next door to her people, and, in particular, in Brett's house. Angus wasn't insensitive, on the contrary, but he was totally blind in some instances to what was right and proper.

She was still shivering when the taxi drew up outside the gates of Bower Place. She had asked the driver not to go into the drive, and she paid him off for she did not know how long she would be.

She timed her visit. They would just be sitting down to lunch; they wouldn't be able to say he wasn't in.

It was strange to ring the doorbell. She could never remember ringing the doorbell. She wondered what kind of a maid they had at the moment.

When the door opened, Susan confronted her, a

plumper, older Susan, Susan with her mouth open and her eyes popping out of her head.

'Hello, Susan.'

Susan was unable to speak. She turned her head and cast a glance quickly back across the hall, then said on a high whisper, 'Vanessa.' She looked her up and down for a moment. Her younger sister was now a woman, a tall, beautiful woman, very well dressed. She knew a moment's keen envy of her. She didn't ask her to come in but stood staring at her, until Vanessa said, 'Are they in?'

'Yes. At – at lunch.'

'Will you tell them I'm here? I'd like to see them.'

'Vanessa,' Susan shook her head, 'he's in a dreadful state. You've . . . your . . .'

'I know, I know; me and mine. It's that I want to see him about. Things will be different from now on.' She smiled reassuringly down on her sister. She felt older, oh so much older than Susan at this moment. Susan looked dowdy, harassed, surprisingly commonplace. This fact made her slightly more at ease, but it didn't stop her body trembling.

'I – I'll put you . . . I mean, you'd better go into the morning-room. I'll – I'll break it to them.'

'All right, Susan.' She looked about the hall for a moment before crossing to the morning-room door. It was as if the years had rolled away and all in them was but a dream and she was back home once more. The morning-room was the same, except that there was not so much silver dotted about. She stood looking out of the window waiting. And she waited . . . and waited. And then her mother came in alone.

They looked at each other across the length of the room until Vanessa moved slowly forward, saying, 'Hello, Mother.'

401

Jane Ratcliffe nipped at her lower lip and gulped gently in her throat before saying, 'Hello, Vanessa.' The words came out on a hoarse whisper as if she had a cold.

'How are you, Mother?'

'Quite – quite well, thank you.' She did not ask her daughter to sit down; she just stared at her, because she was surprised at what she saw. She had caught a glimpse of her now and again in the town; once with her children; once a few years ago coming out of a store laden with shopping bags. But this woman before her was no relation to the girl she had known. She had never seen her before. This woman who had been associating with the common people for years was poised and dignified and looked sure of herself. She said stiffly now, 'Why have you come? Haven't you wrought enough havoc on us?'

It was some seconds before Vanessa answered: 'The reason for my visit is to try and rectify that in some small way. I would like to see Father.'

Jane Ratcliffe closed her eyes and said, 'That's impossible; he won't see you.'

'But I mean to see him. I must see him. I don't suppose it's news to you that Angus has bought The Larches.' She looked back into her mother's unblinking eyes, then went on, 'He has given it to me. It's in my name and I can do entirely what I like with it. I – I propose to sell it to father for what it cost Angus. He's always wanted the land, and I know he would have bought it only Angus went over his head. Well, that's why I'm here.'

Jane Ratcliffe blinked now. Then, after a moment, she exclaimed on a relieved note, 'That's very kind of you, Vanessa, very kind. I'll go and tell him.'

Again Vanessa waited, but not so long this time. And

402

when the door opened again her father entered, and her mother was behind him.

She hadn't seen her father since that morning in the station yard. He had looked no different then from how he had always looked, but now there was a difference. Although he was only in his middle fifties he looked an old man, a bitter, tight-faced old man. She forced herself to speak, to break the tension-filled silence in the room. 'Hello, Father,' she said.

He did not answer for a moment, and then his thin lips scarcely moving he said thickly, 'Feeling triumphant, aren't you? Having dragged yourself up from the gutter you come to show off, bearing a gift, I understand, from your husband. Well,' his bony lower jaw jutted outwards, bringing his lower lip overlapping his upper one, and he went on in a spate of scarcely controlled fury, 'you can take his gift back to him and tell him he's dealing with the same man that used to be his master. You can tell him that. I've never accepted gifts from menials and scum and I'm not starting now.'

She choked as the words rushed from her, her anger almost matching his now. 'He knows nothing about it. He didn't send me to you; he wouldn't because he loathes you. But I knew you couldn't stand us living next door. And what is more, I don't want to live next door to you. It was my own idea to offer you the house, because you've always coveted the land, but he knows nothing about it. As for being scum, don't you dare call him scum. He's worth more –'

His voice cracked at her like a whip, breaking off her words.

'I didn't ask you into this house. If I'd had my way you wouldn't have been allowed through the door. Now get out! You made your choice years ago when you went to live in the gutter, and I repeat gutter, with your upstart.' He moved two steps towards her, his head poked forward. 'You think because he's making money that he can buy himself into decent society. Well, wherever he goes he'll be like a pig in a parlour and an object of derision.'

'You would like to think so, wouldn't you?' She was glaring back at him. 'You hate him; you've always hated him, and you wish that all the things you're saying were true. But they're not. He's getting on, rising fast, and he is accepted. Because he's himself, he's accepted. You called him an upstart. I – I wonder if you know what people call you.'

'Vanessa!' It was her mother speaking. 'Would you please go now.'

'No. No, I won't until I've had my say.' She kept her eyes on her father as she answered, 'If there's anybody you should have hated it should have been Brett, but even knowing what he did you wouldn't have hated him, because you had felt guilty about him for so long. You had done him out of his job, his rightful job.'

'Vanessa! Do you hear me? Leave the house this minute.'

Vanessa now took three steps along the side of the breakfast table. It was a long way round to the door and she talked as she moved. 'Brett never stood up to you. He hadn't the spunk to stand up to you, not as my Angus' – she stressed the 'my' – 'stood up to you when he was just Emily's son . . . and scum, as you have so kindly called him. And there's something I've learned over the years, and it's being proved at this moment, for even if he were still scum he'd be twice the man that you are, and he'll be a name in this town when you're forgotten, like you forgot your own people, my grandfather Ratcliffe.'

'GET OUT!' Jonathan Ratcliffe's hand moved towards the sideboard and groped blindly for something to grip, to throw, to hurl, while his eyes remained fastened on his daughter; and Jane Ratcliffe, rushing in front of him, cried at Vanessa, 'Go, will you! Go!'

It was Susan who, coming into the room, grabbed her sister's arm and pulled her into the hall and to the front door, and almost pushed her through it as she cried, 'You were mad to come here. You know he'll never forgive you. You've only made things worse. And if you were actually aiming to get him to leave this house you've achieved it.'

It was because she knew every inch of the curved drive that she could walk down it with her hand covering her eyes. It was as she turned out of the drive into the main road that a car raced towards her and pulled up with a skidding of brakes, and Angus shot out and stood confronting her, his face livid with an anger that had bleached his rugged complexion white and which had the power to frighten her as her father's anger had not done.

'YOU! YOU!' The spittle sprayed from his lips, and when she bent her head and fell against him, muttering his name, his body remained rigid, and he growled, 'Don't you bloody-well "Oh Angus" me. I'm going in there and getting that deed, if it means I do life for it.'

She was gripping his coat as she sobbed, 'He . . . he hasn't got it. It's here.' She lifted her arm, from which hung the bag, and he snatched it from her and, tearing it open, looked at the long, thick envelope that was wedged inside. He brought the air into his body so quickly that it sent him coughing and spluttering, and he turned from her and leant against the car.

He hadn't been able to take it in when his mother had told him where she had gone. She'd said she'd better tell him in order to break his fall. To break his fall! He had worked for years to get even with that bastard of a Ratcliffe and to see Vanessa installed in her rightful sphere, and what does she do? She takes all his efforts, his early strivings, his sixteen to eighteen hours a day, running, scurrying, planning, aye, and cheating, cheating other men out of contracts with the help of Andrew Fowler, and hands it to the one man he'd like to hang.

His mother had dared to tell him that Vanessa had asked to have the house in her name precisely in order to be able to go to her father and sell it to him, and at the same price. Not only had she tricked him but she had got his mother on to her side an' all, because the old bitch had bawled at him that no man in his right senses would expect his wife to go and live next door to her people after the way they had treated her, and that his wife wasn't out for revenge, only him. And he had bawled back at her that Vanessa would live in that house if he had to tie her in it, and let anybody get in his way to try and stop him getting that deed back from Ratcliffe, and they wouldn't live to tell the tale. And that went for her an' all!

And here he was within a few yards of his new home and his wife crying as if he had knocked her teeth in. And that's what he'd like to do at this very minute. He gripped her by the arm and pushed her into the car. Then, taking his seat, he turned the car swiftly about, drove down to the next gate and into the drive of The Larches.

Vanessa had been sobbing so much that she didn't realise where she was until the car stopped and she looked out of the window. Then she blinked upwards and turned to him and whimpered, 'Oh, no! No, Angus.'

'Get out!' He reached down and pulled her on to the gravel. Then taking firm hold of her, he mounted the steps, put the key in the lock, turned it, and pushed her before him into the house.

They stood in the hall, Vanessa with her head down, he with his up looking about him. He was in Arthur Brett's house. No, no; he was in Angus Cotton's house; but what he saw didn't please him. The hall was big and dark; the panelling browning to black; the twisted rails of the stairs gave them an old-fashioned appearance. This was an old house; it would take thousands to modernise it. He left her and moved towards a door and looked into a room with an ornate and very high ceiling and windows at the far end looking out on a tangle of undergrowth. He passed her once more and looked in another room. It was smaller and the walls looked as if they hadn't been papered or the woodwork painted since the place had been built, and his knowing eye detected the bulge of dry rot in the two-foot high skirting board to the side of the fireplace.

Vanessa stood perfectly still all the while he looked round the ground floor, and when he stood before her again he said quietly, 'It'll be all right when it's done up.'

Now, she looked straight into his face. 'I'll never live here, Angus,' she said. 'You can't make me.'

'Then why did you let me go on and buy the bloody place?' He was bawling now in a restrained way.

'Because I knew I couldn't stop you. You had to buy it. You had to do something to get even with father.

Well, now you've got even with him. When I asked you to put it in my name I saw it was a way of getting the hatred out of your system and making up for what I had done to them, because I don't hoodwink myself about that point, Angus. What I did shook the foundations of their life. It might be narrow; they might be mean-spirited, they are mean-spirited; so what I did had a greater effect on them than it would have had it happened to parents more generous-minded. Their whole aim in life was social prestige, and I tore the foundations of it from under their feet. I . . . I might as well tell you now, I've wanted to go back for years; I've wanted to see them, not because I loved them, but, well, I can't really explain, ties, blood, kinship, what you will, but I've wanted to see them; I wanted to know if I was forgiven; and I've found out . . . They'll never forgive me. My father will live and die hating me. I knew he'd rather be crucified than be under the slightest obligation to either of us, and – and it saddens me to the very soul. I can't help it. That's how it is.'

The mighty wind was being taken out of his sails. A deflating calm was settling on him. He fought it by saying, 'We could pull it down and build.'

'No, no, Angus; it wouldn't make any difference. You see, I couldn't bear to live near them. And anyway, they wouldn't allow it, they'd move.'

'That's what I was hoping.' There was iron in his voice again. 'To put them on the move; to let them see that he isn't the only one that can crack a whip and see men jump.'

'And what would that achieve? He would move to a bigger and better place. He could raise the money; his name is good.'

'Meaning mine isn't?'

'You know I don't mean that.'

'Look, I don't mind telling you now that I've had to do some twisting and bribing to get this piece of land. The house doesn't matter; it's the land. Yet all the while I've seen you here in this house, where you belong.'

'I don't belong in this house, Angus. What is more, I've never liked this house. I belong,' she paused, 'I belong where you belong; but you don't belong here. Face it; you don't belong here.'

He turned from her, the colour rushing into his face, and she said softly now, 'I realised a long time ago that I never belonged here either. I was the odd one out. I couldn't help being born here no more than you could being born in Ryder's Row.'

She watched him walk away from her and open the doors that led on to the overgrown terrace, and slowly she followed him. Her heart beating rapidly she followed him down the steps and along the narrow path that led into the wood, and all the while she knew what he was thinking. Somewhere in here they used to meet, him and her. She had known all along; at least since she had learned he had bought the place, that this moment would come, but she prayed now he wouldn't make his way down to the river and the summerhouse.

He stopped under an oak tree, almost on the spot where Brett had kissed her good-bye on that last night before he died, and standing dumbly before him she returned his look, his questioning, probing look; then, her voice breaking, she said, 'Come away from here, Angus, please. Please. I'm asking you, begging you. Please.'

He turned and walked silently up into the house, through it and to the car. His jaw was stiff and his eyes hard.

When they reached the bottom of Brampton Hill she broke the silence by saying, 'Would . . . would you like to drive me out to the quarry, Angus?'

He cast a quick glance at her; then, his eyes on the road again, he growled, 'Why the quarry?'

'. . . I would like to show you something.'

'At the quarry?' His mouth was square.

'Yes, YES, ANGUS.' She shouted the last two words, and when again he glanced at her she was looking out through the windscreen and she said, quite loudly still, 'You don't seem to take anything in unless it's bawled at you.' Another time this would have made him smile, even laugh, but his expression didn't change; yet when they came to the roundabout he didn't go back into town but went straight ahead.

Fifteen minutes later he drew the car up in yellow mud beside a great hole; and when he alighted he didn't open the door for her to get out but stood by the bonnet waiting, silent and tense. She came now and stood beside him, her hands resting on the bonnet as she asked, 'How much would you have to pay for it, I mean the quarry itself and the bit of hill beyond?' She nodded into the distance.

'Pay for it? You mean buy it?' He screwed up his face at her.

'Yes.'

'In the name of God what for? Why should I buy a hole? There's nothing more I can get out of it, it's finished.'

She walked away from him on to flat ground, stepping on hard surfaces where she could find them, and made her way past stone outhouses that were the only remains of a country house that had once stood where the sandpit was now. She climbed a slope, not looking back to see if he was following, and at the top she stood and looked about her.

Angus stopped when he was a yard or so from her. He didn't want to go near her at the moment. If she had been May or someone like May he would have skelped her lugs long afore this, and likely given her a black eye into the bargain. Making a blasted fool of him. But she wasn't May, or someone like May. Funny, he should think of May now; she hadn't crossed his mind for years. He supposed he had thought of her, because she was the kind who wouldn't have thwarted him; his word would have been law to her. She wouldn't have wanted to have brought him down to pocket size.

Vanessa was pointing now. 'Look,' she said; 'down there. There's the river. It's like a scaly snake going round the town, isn't it? And over there.' She pointed to the right. 'You can see for miles and miles, open countryside.' She came towards him and put her hands on his thick, broad chest before she said, 'I'd like you to build our house here, Angus.'

He strained back from her, his face all creased up, his head moving slowly. Then with a jerk he was free from her hands, and he kicked the earth as he said, 'Here! You must be bloody well barmy, woman.'

'I'd – I'd like it built here, Angus.' She was smiling now. 'I can see it. I came out last week and measured.'

'You what!' His shout resounded down the valley.

'That's it, shout.' She nodded at him. 'You'll hear the echo of it from up here.'

He spoke a few tones lower now as he said, 'You came up here and measured . . .?'

She stared at him. She thought he was going to choke. She felt strangely calm now, at peace, and, more strangely still, in control of the situation . . . and him.

411

'Yes, I came up here and measured. I want it long and low, and spreading, with a paved terrace all about it. And that,' she swung round and pointed to the quarry, 'that'll be a lake with a boat on it. Two boats; and a diving board just there.' She pointed farther away to the side.

'Christ Almighty!' He had his head bowed now, holding his brow.

'How much land is there altogether, including . . . the hole?'

'You're not serious?'

'I was never more serious. That's a trite phrase.' She smiled tightly. 'What I should have said was, I'm doing something on my own for the first time in my life . . . besides having babies.' Her smile widened. 'How much land is there?' she repeated.

'About four acres.'

'Very nice.' She put her head on one side. 'There used to be heather on this part of the fell at one time, and not so very long ago because I can remember it. We'll have heather again, a heather garden, and shrubs, rhododendrons and azaleas. And the house on the rise here.' She spread an arm wide. 'And the gardens running down to the road on that side, and down to the lake on that.'

She was walking away from him now, down the slope towards the stone buildings. The door of the first one was half ajar and she went in and looked about her. The place had three rooms. One had been used as an office, the other two as a storage place for tools. She saw Emily living here, near Angus, yet still independent. She said so as soon as he came through the door.

He stood staring at her again. She looked different, more beautiful, more of a woman at this moment than she had ever been before; even after having the bairns.

412

She was stately, mature, classy; aye, that was the word, classy. He was still furious inside at her, at the position she had put him in; at the way she had brought his castle tumbling down as if she had barraged it with a twelve-pounder, and now she was asking for favours . . . No, she wasn't asking, she was demanding. She had her plans all made, and he knew that when he had time to simmer down and think he would realise that she was right about building above the hole. He knew that she had what he would never have, vision. And she had thought of his mother an' all. He would remember that, aye.

She had her back to him and she startled him now by saying, 'You don't have to buy me anymore, Angus.'

'WHAT!'

'You heard what I said. You still think you have to buy me; you've got to give me something to keep me with you. I've so many clothes I don't know where to put them, and jewellery that I never wear. You know, Angus, your imagination is limited, even to your own capabilities and attraction. Oh yes, you're always yelling about what you can do, but inside you're always fearful of not being able to accomplish it. It's true isn't it?' She waited, and when he didn't answer she went on, 'I've never really talked to you, shown you my real feelings, and you've been aware of this all the while, but I'd like you to know something now. It's just this, that whether I knew it or not I loved you when I married you, and now I can't love you any more . . . I mean,' she moved her head hastily, 'I can't love you any more than I do; I'll never be able to love you any more than I do at this moment. If you gave me everything in the world it wouldn't make any difference. As to yourself, I don't want you to change, no matter what you think. I know

that only with you, and through you, can I be happy
. . . There's been a sort of vacant spot in me for a long
time. You didn't fill it, and the children didn't fill it, so
I thought it was the miss of my people, and my venture
today was as much to see them and find out to make
things right in other ways. But now I know that we're
cut off for good and all, the void, in a strange way, is
filled, and . . . and I'm not unhappy about it now. One
thing I know is that I want to start a life of my own, on
my own plane, on our own plane, neither lower-class
nor middle-class, but our class. Your mother and Rosie
have ceased to stress how different I am from them by
every look and word, yet they still look upon me in the
same way as they did when I first came into their lives.
Beneath the surface we haven't mixed. But you and I
are different, Angus; we've rubbed off on each other.'
Her voice was trembling as she finished, 'I love you,
Angus; and – and not just out of gratitude, as you've
always thought.'

Her whole body trembled as he came towards her,
and when he held her face between his rough hands
she put hers up and cupped his. Slowly now he
dropped his head forward on to her shoulder and
muttered thickly, 'Thanks, Van. Thanks.' Then after
a moment he added, haltingly, 'I love you so much
I'd go crazy without you. You know that, don't you?'
Her heart beats were sending the blood flowing fast
through her veins and she was about to answer, 'You'll
never have to be without me, darling, never.' But that
was a reply she could have made to Arthur Brett
had she married him. It was a formal, acceptable,
reply. What she wanted was a reply to fit the plane
on which they were going to live from now on. If
Emily had ever been called upon to reply to such

a statement undoubtedly she would have said, 'You might go crazy without me, lad, but there's an even chance you'll go bloody well stark staring mad with me.' But she wasn't Emily, and she couldn't bring herself to swear to be amusing. Yet she wanted him to laugh as Emily could; she wanted to bring him back to normality; she wanted to set the pattern for the future, and so she ventured, in a good imitation of her mother-in-law's voice, 'Aye, I do, an' I'll Emily Cotton well see that you never get the chance to be without me, lad.'

The result was even more successful than she had anticipated. His head came up and he stared at her blankly for a moment; then he dropped it back on his shoulders and let out a roar of deep laughter, such laughter as she hadn't heard from him for a long time. It seemed to sweep away the obsession of his years of striving, and, as he picked her up, as if she were a child, and swung her around, she laughed loudly too.

When they were standing still again, he gathered her into his arms and he looked into her face before he said, with a self-conscious shyness that was new, 'Remember Mam's bit of poetry? Well, I'm always saying it in me mind to you:

> "I have you fast in my fortress,
> And will not let you depart,
> But put you down into the dungeon,
> In the round tower of my heart.
>
> And there will I keep you for ever,
> Yes, for ever and a day,
> Till the walls shall crumble to ruin,
> And moulder in dust away."'

'Oh, Angus. Angus.' For the first time in their joint lives her mouth dropped fiercely on to his.

Bower Place and Ryder's Row were merging.

THE END

COLOUR BLIND

AUTHOR'S NOTE

The characters in this book are entirely fictitious and have no relation to any living person.

Although the setting is Tyneside, and several actual place-names have been used, the fifteen streets, Casey's Wharf, and other parts of Holborn are imaginary.

Owing to the difficulty in comprehension by the uninitiated, the Tyneside dialect has not been adhered to.

In this story I make no effort to solve a problem. The solution, if there is one, for the living conflicts, the half-castes, would seem to lie in the far, far future.

CONTENTS

PART ONE

PART TWO

PART THREE

PART FOUR

PART ONE

CHAPTER ONE

ME DAUGHTER BRIDGET

'Glory be to God and his holy Mother. Well, well I never! And it to happen on me birthday an' all! . . . Did y'ever now.' Kathie McQueen threw her great head back and opened wide her full-lipped mouth and let the resounding waves of her laughter free. Her huge breasts and hanging stomach wobbled with it, and her feet, encased in the remnants of a pair of slippers, slapped at the bare floorboards alternately.

The boy, standing at the side of her chair, holding a letter in his hand, smiled up at her. He did not laugh with her, although his heart was racing and leaping inside his narrow chest. Having lived with the McQueens for four years he was used to their laughter, and perhaps it was the extravagance of it that subdued the laughter in himself, for his face rarely stretched beyond a smile. The McQueens frequently chipped him about this, saying, 'Go on, Tony, stretch your gob. Go on, give your face a day off, lad. Go on, forget about your leg; the inch you've lost on that you've got in your napper.' They meant it kindly. All the McQueens were kind to him, even Matt. But no matter how kind they were, or what they did for him, he could never laugh with them. For there was something he didn't understand about their laughter; at times it even brought a fear to him.

Into the sound of the laughter came a dull thumping on the back door, and the boy, raising his voice, shouted, 'There's someone at the door.'

'What?' Kathie brought her streaming eyes down to his. 'Someone at the door? Away then and open it.' And in the next breath she called, 'Come in, there.'

Before the boy had limped half-way to the door, it was opened, and a small girl with a coat over her head came into the kitchen.

'Me ma says can yer lend her yer gully, Mrs McQueen?' The black coat, forming a hood about her face, emphasised the pinched cheeks and hungry eyes, and the voice, too, sounded thin and hungry as it issued from the shadows of the coat. 'She won't keep it a minute. We've got some bread and me ma's got a ticket to get some groceries. But we've got the bread now . . . and . . .' Her voice trailed off.

'Yer ma got a ticket? God be praised! But I thought ye got yer gully out last week,' said Kathie, reaching across the table and picking up a long bread-knife.

'It had to go back with the fire-irons so as to get the bread.' The child's voice seemed to come from more remote depths of the coat.

'Ah well, times like these won't last much longer.' Kathie handed the child the bread-knife. 'Yer Da's bound to get set on now . . . cough, spit an' all. They'll be taking the blind and the deaf soon, they'll take owt during a war, God bless the Kaiser!'

Kathie's head was again thrown back, and the boy and girl stood regarding her solemnly, fascinated by the great pink and grey cavity of her mouth.

Her laughter seemed to remind her of the previous bout, and its cause, and she stopped suddenly, saying, 'It's good news we've got the day . . . what d'ye think? Me daughter Bridget's on her way home . . . Tell yer ma, Milly.'

'Brid coming home? Oh, I will, Mrs McQueen.'

'An' tell her she's married, at that . . . Me daughter Bridget's married, tell her, to a seafaring gentleman. Now what d'ye think of that? Go on now, tell her. And let me have that gully back!' she shouted to the departing child; 'they'll all be in in a minute, and I want it for the tea . . . Eeh, Tony lad' – she turned once more to the boy – 'read it again. No . . . give it me here.'

She took the letter from his hand and held it at arm's length, and, pulling her chin into the rolls of fat on her neck, she said slowly, ' "Dear Ma, I'll be home on Friday night. You will be surprised to know I am married. He goes to sea. My name is Mrs Paterson. Ma, there's something I should tell you, but I can't write it down. I'll have to come home. Love, Brid." '

The boy looked at her in admiration. He knew she couldn't read a word . . . she couldn't even write her own name. But her grotesque, fat body seemed to be the storage house for everything she heard; she had only to hear a thing once to remember it for ever.

'I know what she's afraid to tell me, Tony lad.' She leant towards him and whispered with a natural frankness, 'It's a baby she's goin' to have, ye know.' She joined her arms together and rocked them as if

429

a child lay on them. 'Ye know, like my Eva upstairs. Now there's no disgrace in having a child if ye're married and the priest's blessing on ye, is there, Tony? Now is there? But me Bridget was always the shy one.'

The boy regarded her in silence. Women with protruding stomachs were a common sight to him; he had only to walk down the back lane any time of the day to see one. In the summer he looked down on great cones of flesh hanging out from open blouses as the women sat on their front doorsteps suckling their babies. Eva upstairs had always appeared ugly to him, with her young fat and her red hair, but when her stomach had bulged she had been repulsive. And when her babies were born – for they were twins – they, too, were repulsive; and had grown more so, with their skinny bodies and rickety legs.

Yet here was Mrs McQueen classing Bridget, his beautiful Bridget, with Eva. If Bridget had a baby, it would be beautiful, like her, and its hair would be fair, and the grey of its eyes would dance at you. But it wouldn't laugh all the time, for Bridget was the only one of the six McQueens who didn't laugh all the time.

Tony blinked his eyes in startled surprise as Kathie McQueen's hand brought him a playful slap across the face. 'It's a solemn puss ye have on ye. But ye like me Bridget, don't ye?'

He nodded but made no answer. Liking was a poor word for the feeling he had for Bridget. She was the star that had filled his dark sky since the day his mother died and an aunt, his only living relative, had refused his claim on her. It was the McQueens who came forward, and without any preamble took him into their already full house. But only the fifteen-year-old Bridget brought him comfort. When they sat round the fire at night, huddled close to its often small embers, but always shouting and laughing, it was she who would sit next to him, with her arm about him. And when the lads called after him 'Hoppy on the Don!' it was she who would walk by his side, and at times fill him with curious pain when she affected to limp slightly, saying she had a pain in her hip. She championed him until he reached twelve, when he suddenly started to grow. But from then Matt had taken notice of Bridget's attentions to him. If she brought him some little tit-bit from her daily place, Matt would say, 'Stop making a blommin' fool of him. Why don't you give him a dummy?' At times there would be fierce rows, and he felt he was the cause. And the rows always took place in the wash-house, where Matt would push Bridget, and their voices, low and thick with rage, would filter into the house. One thing Tony noticed was that Matt didn't corner his sister when their father was about. And it was after one of these rows, which seemed to mount with the years, that Bridget suddenly went away. And for weeks afterwards Matt hadn't laughed.

And now Bridget was coming back, and she was married. This fact did not touch Tony's own feeling for her, but into his mind there crept a fear – a fear of Matt's reactions when this knowledge should be made known to him – and he thought, I won't look at his face when he reads the letter.

Cavan McQueen was the first to come in, his laugh in the back yard heralding his approach. The booming of his voice and the depth of his laughter were in striking contrast to the short, slight body. And his shortness was emphasised as he stood by his wife. He threw his bait tin with a clatter on to the table before bringing his hand with a resounding whack across Kathie's buttocks.

'We're set, lass. The war's only been on three days and the sods are begging us to do overtime.'

He was lifting his hand again to repeat the slap when she yelled, 'Stop it, ye little rat, ye!' Then her voice dropped to a thick caressing tone. 'Cavan lad . . . guess what. Ye'll never guess in a month of Sundays . . . read that.' She pulled the letter out from her blouse, then stood with her arms folded on the shelf of her stomach watching him. She saw the smile follow after the laughter, to leave his face wearing the blank, stiff look she hated.

When he made no comment she cried angrily, 'Ain't yer pleased? What would ye be wanting? The child's coming home an' she's married. Ye're wearing a look as if ye'd heard she'd been dropped with a bairn and no-one to father it. She's married, man, an' all respectable – they call her Mrs Paterson. And what's more, she got him herself. She hadn't to drag him to the altar rails like Eva had that miserable swine up there.' She flicked her eyes towards the ceiling.

Cavan rubbed his greasy hand over his moustache and said dully, 'Aye, there's that in it,' and handed the letter back to Kathie. Then, turning slowly, he went to the corner of the room, took off his coat, and proceeded to wash himself in a tin bath of hot water which was standing on a low shelf attached to the wall. He dried himself on a piece of sacking that had been hemmed into a square, and which still bore the sugar manufacturer's name across it. He took no heed of the upbraidings of Kathie as she pounced round the kitchen; he could stop her effectively whenever he wished, and she knew just how far she could go. His mind was trying to grasp the fact that his lass . . . his own lass . . . was married, and him not knowing. Of his four children, his heart laid claim only to one. In varying degrees he liked Eva, Matt and Terence, but Bridget he knew he loved.

He scrubbed himself more vigorously with the sacking to cover up the thought. Bridget had the knack of making people love her. All men seemed to love Bridget, even those that shouldn't . . . His thoughts swung to his son . . . That had been the trouble: Matt hadn't let Bridget live any life but that which he chose. If it hadn't been for Matt, Bridget would never have left home, to go all that way to London to work; and then to Liverpool.

Cavan stopped rubbing himself and stared down into the bath of dirty water. He was trying to see through his thoughts, but they were as opaque as the water. Yet this much he could see: if Bridget had not got married away, she would never have got married at home . . . not as long as Matt was alive.

Kathie's voice, raised in laughing greeting to their younger son, brought Cavan's mind from Matt, and he turned from the contemplation of the water and threw his greeting to the lad who was a replica of himself. 'How's it gone?'

'Oh, champion.'

'Was it hard?'

'Aye, a bit. But I'll get used to it. The stink of the chemicals made me sick at first, and you get covered all over with white dust. Most of them have overalls . . . can I have a pair of overalls, Ma?'

'Ye can have owt ye like, lad, if ye bring the money in.'

'Well, I'll be doing that. A pound a week, and me only sixteen!'

'Aye,' his father put in, with unusual seriousness, 'you'll be a millionaire shortly. But look out, and don't let on to anyone, for when the Government get wind you're having three meals a day they'll find some bloody way of bringing them down to one, or nowt.'

Terence took no notice of this, but said, 'Da, you said if we all got set on you were going to try for a house in the middle or top end.'

'Aye, I did.'

'Well you'd better look slippy then, for they're being snapped up; the men coming to work in the Barium are looking round. They want to live as near as they can.'

'Oh, there'll always be plenty of houses if ye've got the money to pay the rent. But we'll stick where we are till we see how long this war's goin' to last. It might only hang on a few weeks, and then where'll we be if we move, eh? Best forget moving for the time.'

But as Cavan sat down to his tea he was thinking as much about the possibility of moving as he was about Bridget's coming. They were both entwined in his mind; for hadn't he always promised Bridget that one day they'd move back into the middle of the

434

fifteen streets . . . or, with a bit of luck, perhaps the top end. It was a great pity they couldn't have moved before she came back, but he had learned too much from life to take a step like that without being sure the present flood of work would last. Here they had a roof over their heads. And it wasn't a workhouse roof, although he knew that the latter contingency had only been avoided by his wife's laughing tenacity and Matt's pilfering, and the pulling in of his own belt to let what food there was go to the others. But God was good, and had showered his special Providence over them, when all around, weeping women and grim-faced men had watched their last sticks of furniture being carried out by the bums before wending their heart-breaking way down the Jarrow Road to East Jarrow, through Tyne Dock and down Stanhope Road, to where Talbert Road showed the grim gates at the far end, which, once entered, a family was no longer a family but merely segregated individuals, with numbers on each of their garments. When this happened the McQueens had stood close together, defying Life's blows with their laughter. Bridget and the boy Tony hadn't laughed much, but the others made up for them.

It was said that only the scum of the earth lived in the fifteen streets, but Cavan would have considered himself one of the fortunate of the earth if he could have moved into the middle section, where the houses possessed four box-like rooms, and you went upstairs to bed; and where you were the proud possessor of your own back yard, and what was more – a netty. There you hadn't to stand waiting for your turn until your bladder nearly burst, or see

435

the bairns doing the wet dance while they waited, for he would allow none of them to foul the yard.

Here, in these two rooms that dared to flaunt the name of a downstairs house, the lavatory had to be shared with the family upstairs, although since Eva had come to live above them the situation had eased considerably. Before the previous tenant had taken the long trek to the iron gates there had been nineteen of them sharing the yard and its amenities.

When Cavan heard his quarter referred to as the 'stink-pot' or the 'buggy-boxes' his laughter would disappear, and he would yell at the offender, asking how he could expect anything else. During one of his angry spells he started a campaign against the bugs and enlisted a number of the neighbours. Paper was stripped off the walls, which were soaked with carbolic. This was quite effective if both upstairs and downstairs co-operated. But poverty dulls incentive, and the war against bugs needs to be wholesale, so many were soon back where they started. But not 42 Powell Street; for Cavan became almost a maniac with the carbolic, the smell of which permeated their clothes and food.

Cavan's thinking had reached a point where he was asking himself if it was the living conditions as much as Matt that drove Bridget away from home when Matt came in.

Matt seemed to spring into the kitchen – there was a spring in his every step. If he laughed when he walked, the combination became a beguilement, bringing the children after him and the eyes of the girls on him. His body, like his father's, was thin; but he had height with it, and a steely sinuation that spoke of arrogant maleness. His face was narrow and overhung by a thick mop of sandy hair, growing low on his brow. It was his eyes that were the most noticeable feature of his face; they were like large jet beads, and not even his laughter could lift the brooding veil from them.

Kathie's greeting to him was shriller than ever, and her laughter caused Tony to fix his eyes on his tin plate; it was the kind of laughter that frightened him, for somehow he didn't think it was meant to be laughter at all.

'I'll give yer a month of Sundays, Matt,' Kathie was yelling, 'to guess what's happened. Go on: Jesus in Heaven, ye'll never guess it.'

Matt look questioningly at his father; and Cavan returned his look, but said nothing.

'What is it?' Matt turned to his mother.

Still laughing, she said, 'Get the grease washed off yer, and come an' have yer tea – I've a steak as thick as a cuddy's lug for yer. Oh, ye'll never guess.' And her laughter and chattering filled the time until he came to the table.

'Let him have his tea,' said Cavan.

Kathie stopped her laughing and said soberly, 'Yes. Yes, I will.'

'I'm not having any tea till I know what's up.' Matt stood by his plate looking at his mother.

She looked at Cavan, and when he nodded his head she put her hand inside her blouse again and handed the letter to her son.

Tony did as he had promised himself: he didn't look at Matt while he read the letter. With great deliberation he wiped up the last of the gravy from his plate with a piece of bread, going round and round it until the tin shone with a silver gleam. Under his lowered lids he saw the letter flung on to the table. He saw Mr McQueen, too, wiping his plate clean with his bread.

Then Mrs McQueen's fist banging the table made him jump, and her voice nearly deafened him as she yelled, 'That's the last damn time the Cullens will get a loan of me gully. I've sworn it afore an' I'll swear it again! Here's me having to tear me own bread while those hungry hounds are lording it with me gully.'

Tony saw Matt's legs moving with unusual slowness towards the door. When he heard it close he lifted his head and watched Matt disappear down the back yard and into the September dusk. Mr and Mrs McQueen with one accord left the table and went into the other room; and Tony was left with Terence, who, taking advantage of the situation, cut a piece off Matt's congealing steak and motioned to Tony to do likewise. But Tony took no heed; he was tense with the feeling of nervous expectancy, longing for, yet dreading the time when Bridget would be in the kitchen again.

As Matt walked out of the fifteen streets into the main road he turned the lapels of his coat across his chest to hide his dirty shirt, for he had come out without his muffler. The air was soft and close, but he shivered, and a girl crossing the road called to him, 'Hallo there, Matt – you look as if ye'd seen the Kaiser. Have they called yer up?'

The sound of his laugh was sufficient answer for her, and she went on her way, laughing too.

Laughter was easy – when everything else failed you could always laugh. Then why hadn't he stayed in the house and laughed this off? No, he'd had to make a bloody fool of himself and come out! It was the shock. Bridget married! Well, he knew she'd marry sometime, didn't he? He knew that once she got away on her own some fellow would get her. He twisted the torn lining of his coat pocket round his fingers, tearing it still farther. He'd thought that in the months following her surprising departure he had worked the whole thing out; he'd imagined he had got her out of his system, for life, although emptier, became easier without her. The tearing, mad feeling of possessiveness faded, and he lost his hate of all mankind because she was not near to bestow her smile on it. He had been mad – he could see that now. But he could also see now that he would be mad again. What possessed him? Why was it he should feel like this about her? All his life he had suffered and enjoyed the torment of this feeling for her. He could remember himself as a tiny child holding her and knowing that she was his; still a baby himself, he had washed and dressed her; no-one was allowed to take her to school but himself; he had even stolen for her. He knew he would have let the others go hungry to death, and they would have done, or else to the workhouse, if Bridget's grey eyes hadn't told him that there was a gnawing in her stomach . . . And now she was married, and was coming home to flaunt her catch – the bitch! She was just doing it to torment him, By God, he'd kill her! No, no! . . . He wiped the moisture from his lips with the back of his hand. Whatever was the reason for her coming back, it wasn't to torment him. He would give her her due; she would never do that intentionally. Then why was she coming?

It was dark now, and he walked on through Tyne Dock, down Eldon Street and into Shields. If it had been light, he would have cut through the Deans into the park. He had been taking walks in the park often of late; to get away from the grime and muck of the fifteen streets, he had thought. Yet up to Bridget's going away he had never noticed their grimness. Vaguely he knew that to make his life bearable he needed something. Her personality, in such contrast to his, and her strange beauty had supplied that something. Now he was searching blindly to replace it. The park, in the minutest way, brought Bridget back to him. Was it its colour and cleanness? – for Bridget had always been clean. Or was it just some quiet place where his thoughts could move around her without the perplexing agony of her presence? He didn't know.

She would likely be home now, and they'd all be about her, laughing at the tops of their voices, and she would be smiling at them, that lovely wide smile. He turned abruptly and walked towards Jarrow again. After she had quietened them all, as she had the power to do, she would look around her and say, 'Where's Matt?' Yes, she would ask for him, for she knew as well as he did that some part of her belonged to him. And she could never rob him of it, husband or not.

When he passed the dock arches and reached the quiet stretch of road joining Tyne Dock to East Jarrow he started to run swiftly and lightly, with the loping grace of some forest animal. He kept on running, past the slacks where the water flapped at the bank to the side of his feet, past the Barium chemical works, where Terence had started that day, past Bogie Hill, and on to the fifteen streets.

He was panting when he reached the back yard, for it had been a long run, and as he paused behind the closed door of the yard, looking towards the gas-lit blind of the kitchen window, he was at once struck by the odd quiet that prevailed. He knew, as if he could see her, that Bridget had come. She was there, in the kitchen. Then why was there no laughing, no yelling? He looked to the upstairs window. It was alight, and he could see Eva moving back and forth with the unwieldy bulk of a child on her hip. Why wasn't she downstairs with the rest?

He turned the lapels of his coat back and straightened his shirt neck, and walked slowly up the yard. His hand hovered over the latch of the door; then he thrust it open, and with his usual spring entered the kitchen.

They were all there except Eva: his mother and father, Terence and Tony, and Bridget. They all stared at him, and the almost audible pleading in Bridget's eyes was also in those of the others. But he looked at none of them, not even at Bridget; for his eyes were riveted in stupefied amazement on the massive Negro standing behind Bridget's chair with his hand possessively covering her shoulder.

CHAPTER TWO

A SEAFARING GENTLEMAN

'Oh, it's ye, Mrs Cullen – did ye want to borrow something?'

Jane Cullen knew it was a danger signal when Kathie addressed her as Mrs. She stood within the door, hugging her shawl about her, and looked in envy at this neighbour whom no sorrow or tribulation could affect. She guessed Kathie was a bit upset about the black man, but nothing to speak of – if it had happened to one of her lassies she would have died with shame. She said gently, 'I was wonderin', Kathie, if ye'd lend me yer boots. I've got to go into Jarrow and it's pourin', and there's not a sole on mine. If he gets the job of night-watchman I'll get meself a pair.'

'Ye've been saying that for the last year, Mrs Cullen. If it isn't me gully, it's me boots!'

Jane looked at Kathie for a moment, then turned silently to the door.

'Here, take them.' The boots were thrust against Jane's arm, and as she took them with a low murmur of thanks Kathie remarked grandiosely, 'I'll soon be able to pass them on to yer altogether, for me daughter Bridget is buying me a new pair. She's able to buy anything she likes now she's married such a well-set-up gentleman. Did yer hear that she's setting up in the middle streets? Four rooms she'll have at that. They're down in Shields this very minute getting the furniture, and for the whole house, mind yer . . . there'll be no beg and scrape for me daughter Bridget.'

Jane nodded her head and smiled weakly. 'I'm glad for her, Kathie.'

For a second longer the two women stared at each other, then Jane sidled out, and Kathie, turning to the fire, stood grinding her strong teeth together until her jawbones ached. She'd let them see; no-one would pity her. She had laughed longer and louder these past few days than ever before, and she had made the others laugh too, saying, 'If ye laugh, they won't pity ye, and if they don't pity ye they'll envy ye.' Cavan, Terence and even Tony had done as she bid. But not Matt . . . Matt seemed to have been transfixed into silence from the moment he saw the Negro. And Eva – that big daft slobbery bitch. Kathie turned up her eyes and their venom was enough to penetrate the ceiling. Playing the respectable married woman! And getting all virtuous like – the silly sod, when her belly was full of Harry McGuire before she'd dragged him to the altar rails!

Eva had always envied Bridget; and rightly too, Kathie thought; but now she refused even to speak to her sister. And so Kathie had taken Bridget's marriage lines and held them under Eva's nose. But Eva, with an air that nearly drove her mother mad, had pointed out that a Registry Office marriage

444

was no marriage; so besides the awful disgrace of having a black man, Bridget was also living in sin, and she'd soon have Father O'Malley on her track. And, blast her, she was right, too . . . about the priest, anyway, for he had never been off the doorstep since he'd got wind of the affair.

He had managed to corner Bridget but not him . . . Kathie couldn't bring herself to call her son-in-law James. To his face she addressed him as 'Mr Paterson'; and time and again she wondered at the ordinariness of such a name for such an extraordinary man, and wondered too what in the name of God made her Bridget marry him. She couldn't get a word of explanation out of Bridget. When she asked her, Bridget just drooped her eyes and clasped her hands on her lap, and sat still and tense, until Kathie cried, 'Then why did ye come back?' And to this Bridget answered simply, 'I wanted to be near you all when he's away at sea . . . and the bairn coming.'

A bairn coming. Kathie held her head between her hands. A black bairn. For it would be a black bairn, she was sure; there was too much of him in comparison with Bridget's whiteness. The child would be black both inside and out, and her Bridget would have to push a black bairn around the streets. Mother of God! How could a daughter of hers stand up under the shame of it? She rocked her head with her hands. But Bridget didn't seem to be ashamed: there she was, away now in Shields, walking openly with him in the broad daylight! Hadn't she watched her go down the street with never a look to right or left, her head held high as if she had something to be proud of? What had come over her? Why had she

445

done it? Kathie beat the top of her head with her fist. Would the good God tell her why she had done it?

Something of the same question was passing through Bridget's mind as she faced the look of ill-concealed scorn in the eyes of the shop assistants. She had watched her husband put down the five pounds deposit and sign his name with a proud flourish on the form which was an open sesame to a choice of oil-cloths, of beds and bedroom suites, of half-sets of china and Nottingham lace curtains. Never had she dreamed that she would be able to set up house with thirty pounds' worth of furniture. She should be mad with the joy of it; but there was no spark of joy in her, only pain and pity, and gratitude and abhorrence – the pain and pity and gratitude were the feelings that the bulk of towering blackness evoked in her; the abhorrence was for herself and the thing she had done.

When they left the shop it was her husband who showed her out. Taking the door from the hand of the shopwalker he stood aside to allow her to pass. But the closing of the door did not shut out the tittering from the shop, and its sound brought an angry flush to Bridget's cheeks, and a higher tilt to her chin. They laughed at her because he treated her like a queen! If she had married one of them she would have been made aware of her inferiority for the remainder of her life, and if she had married one of her own class never would she have known the meaning of worship – not to speak of consideration; never would she have known what it was to be loved as this man loved her. Then why was she ashamed of him? Why did it take all the rallying of her forces to brave the streets with him at her side?

When they were together, closed in by four walls, with no eyes upon them, the shame would fade, and then a strange tenderness for him would fill her. Even at times a feeling she thought might be love for him would sweep over her. This often happened in the night when he woke her with his loving, for even with his passion, which lifted her into realms hitherto unknown, his love-making never lost the adoring quality that gave to it a gentleness. But she wished again and again that he would not show this gentleness to her in public, for it was this as much as anything that brought the guffaws and smiles of ridicule upon them. She wanted to tell him, but she could not bear to hurt him. She had soon found that she could hurt him with a look or a word; and she knew that she must never do this . . . she must never hurt him more than she had done by marrying him. She did not blame him for marrying her – if she had been in her right senses it would never have come about – Matt had always warned her . . . Matt . . . She shuddered. She had Matt to face yet. Oh God, give her strength for the day when Matt would speak to her, and drag from her the reason why she had done this thing.

Her husband's hand in her arm pulled her closer to him, and his thick bell-toned voice, speaking his short-cut English, fell on her head. 'You cold? . . . You shivering? . . . Me, I'm big selfish beast. I take you home right away, eh?' He bent down and looked into her face. 'Eh, honey? We go home, eh?'

She smiled at him. 'I'm not cold – someone was walking over my grave.'

'Someone on your grave? . . . Sh!' He pulled her still closer. 'You don't talk of graves; you make me have creeps too. No grave will get my Rose . . . By way, your mam don't like me calling you Rose, do she? But you Rose all through . . . Bridget, it is hard sound – like – like a swear, eh?' He laughed, his head thrown up and his massive shoulders shaking.

His laugh was infectious, but the passers-by did not join in as they would have done had he been alone . . . a black man and a white girl was something not to be condoned in any way. In the unmoving depths of his mind James Paterson knew this, but in the conflicting groping layers nearer the surface, where his thoughts jumped and clung to anything that would bring him a level nearer to the white man, he told himself that the looks of the women were jealousy of his Rose's beauty, and those of the men, envy of himself for his luck in possessing her.

He believed in luck . . . he believed he was born lucky. Had he ever starved like other black men? No. Hadn't he been to school? Couldn't he read and write? . . . By God, yes! And hadn't he always had any woman he wanted? Again, by God, yes! There were times when he had to push them off . . . white women liked black men; and they weren't all women of the bars, either; no, by God, they weren't. But one thing he never had until he took Rose; and that was a virgin. He knew then that Rose must belong to no man but him. It had been hard work getting her, and he'd nearly lost his boat. It would have been the first time he had missed a trip, either through drink or women, but he had been prepared to do it for Rose . . . The nagging thought came again . . . would she have married him had she not discovered there was a baby coming? . . . Yes; yes, she would. For his Rose loved him; and the colour of his skin meant nothing to her.

He pulled her even closer to him until he bore her weight on his arm. He wanted to lift her up and carry her through the streets; he wanted to show all men by some definite sign that she was his; he wanted to touch her and caress her. He said softly, 'We call at our own house – what you say?'

She consented readily, for anything was better than going home when Matt would be in, and have his eyes avoid hers and his silence beat at her.

As they turned into Dunstable Street James spoke a cheery 'good evening' to a small group of men standing at the corner. They answered him in low growls, turning their heads away and becoming engrossed in each other's conversation.

And Bridget felt a desire to stop and shout at them, 'He's as good as you – he's better than you. He wouldn't let his wife trail round the bars after him to get what was left of his pay; nor yet have his beer if the bairns went naked – you lot! What are you, anyway? . . . Scum . . . scum.'

She was shivering again when they entered the empty house; and James, all concern for her, said, 'I know you got chill, honey – come, we go to your home – there's big fire there.'

'No, it's all right; I want to stay here awhile.'

449

She smiled at him. 'We'll plan where we'll put the furniture.'

He responded to her, as pleased as a child: 'Oh, my, yes. Tomorrow when it all come – my!' He shook his head. 'We have our home – my Rose has a beautiful home . . . And me . . . between watches I sit on deck and think of you sittin' here thinkin' of me – eh?' He took her chin in his great black hand and tilted her face up to his. Her grey eyes were moist with the pity that was foremost in her mind at that moment, and he said, 'You not sad?'

She turned from him and went into the little bare kitchen, and he followed her in concern. 'You not like the house and the pretty furniture?'

The expressive, appealing gesture of his out-stretched arms wrenched the words out of her! 'Oh yes, yes – it's only that I'm happy.' She sniffed and blew her nose. 'I always cry when . . . when I'm happy.'

As his laughter resounded from the bare walls she knew that in a way she had spoken the truth, for she would be happy in this house with all her lovely furniture. She would have four rooms all to herself, and a back yard to herself, and she could bolt the door and be shut away from people. Apart from those looking down on the yard out of the windows opposite, no-one would see her if she did not wish it. And she would have the added comfort that her people were near if she wanted them. Oh yes, she would be happy. She was happy. She could believe it; for now they were alone together.

The soft light that had been the magnet that first drew him was in her eyes, and he pulled her away from the window to the dark corner near the fireplace.

'You love me, Rose?'

She nodded.

'Always?'

She nodded again.

'No other man, ever?'

She shook her head.

'Not when I'm away at sea, like some white women?'

'No, no, never that!' Her protest was vehement.

His enormous lips slowly traced the outline of her face. The moving black blur filled her with such conflicting emotions that she became faint under them. His unfinished words ran into one another, forming a lulling drawl. 'Rose love . . . my beautiful Rose. No other woman in world like you . . . You marry me 'cause you love me. You don't mind colour, and our baby . . . my baby, she be a girl; we call her Angela, eh? like angel . . . Rose Angela.' His fingers moved down the waist-band of her skirt and pressed gently on her stomach. 'I feel her heartbeat . . . she'll be like you, Rose . . . white and beautiful with long limbs and . . .'

The sound that checked his words was of someone breathing. The both remained still, pressed close against each other for a second longer, listening to the hiss of the indrawn breath. James turned slowly, but Bridget almost jumped into the centre of the kitchen at the sight of the priest standing in the front-room doorway.

If it had been an ordinary man, James would have demanded 'What the hell you up to, eh?' before, perhaps, whirling him through the air into the street. But a priest to him was not a man, so he said with laughing irony, 'Why, sir, you near scared me white.'

The priest looked from James to Bridget, and the expression in his eyes bore down her courage. Her head drooped and the old childhood fear of him overcame her.

'I told you to bring him along to the vestry.' Father O'Malley might have been speaking of an animal, and his words seemed to have been pressed thin in their effort to escape his tight lips.

'I . . . I didn't tell him, Father.'

James looked enquiringly from one to the other. Although he didn't like the tone the priest was using to his wife, nor the way he was looking at her, the smile still hovered about his face. Bible-punchers were funny; all bible-punchers were quaint men.

Father O'Malley again addressed Bridget. 'You have told him what must be done?'

She shook her head, her eyes still directed towards the floor. 'No, Father.'

The priest adjusted his thick glasses and brought the pin-points of his eyes to bear on James. 'You must be married; and you must take instruction.' He separated each word, and the effect was very much that of James's stilted English. 'I will marry you on Saturday morning at eight o'clock.'

'Marry? . . . Me? . . . We be married?' James looked in perplexity at Bridget's bowed head. The smile had left his face, and his body was stretched to its fullest height, making the small priest appear like a dwarf in comparison. 'What you mean, married? I got paper all signed – we married.'

'Not in the eyes of God. A Christian marriage cannot be performed in a Registry Office; and you must take instructions to become a . . .'

'But me am Christian.' A patient smile began to hover around James's lips; he felt he knew now why the priest was so concerned. 'Why, sir, I was baptised – yes, yes, I know all about Christ Jesus . . . Mr Edwards, he very good missionary – splendid fellow, he learned me Jesus Christ all through, and what those bloody Jews did for him. A good man, Jesus Christ . . . Yes, me Christian all right.' James's smile widened, spreading the corners of his mouth to meet the expanse of his broad nostrils. 'You no need worry 'bout me.'

'The missionary wasn't a Catholic – it isn't the same. This is your fault!' Father O'Malley hurled the accusation at Bridget.

'Here, here! You no speak to her like that.' James stepped to his wife's side and placed a protecting arm around her shoulders. 'You man of God all right, but you no speak like that, please. You mean me isn't Christian 'cause me not Catholic-Christian? Christ Jesus all kinds Christian. The Catholic Father he came and play chess with Mr Edwards, and laugh fit to bust over jokes. They both Christian men. Once Catholic Father say to me I am name same's Christ's brother, and I should be fisherman. Always that stay in my head. An' one day I leave my home for the water. Me was never fisherman, but me always on water . . . That Catholic Father was good man. He know me Christian all right.'

'Be quiet!' The sharpness of the command whipped the returning smile completely from James's face, and his scalp moved, shifting his mop of wire curls from side to side. The priest went on, looking now with open contempt at Bridget, 'This is no marriage and you know it. You have sinned enough already, and naturally as night follows day retribution will come upon you. Your only atonement can be to ensure the safe keeping of the soul of your child; and God knows it will need that to be in safe keeping. Be at the church at eight o'clock on Saturday morning; and I will take him for instruction whenever he is in port.'

'You what, by God!'

James made to follow the priest as he went through the front room, but Bridget clung on to him, crying, 'Please, James . . . James. Don't for my sake . . . James, we will see Father Bailey . . . he's different . . . he'll explain to you.'

James became still. His eyes were puzzled and sad as they looked down into hers. 'You no want us do this thing – to go be married again? If we do this, no dignity left. Mister Edwards always say "Keep dignity", and here I feel' – he pointed to his chest – 'dignity be gone if we do this. We married all right in here' – he pressed his hand on his heart – 'I know we'm married all right . . . Very much married. But him, he say we not married at all.'

Bridget's mind suddenly cried at her, Oh God, if only Father O'Malley was right, and it was no marriage! But it was a marriage all right. The night she had slept with James hadn't made it a marriage; but when a man with a greasy collar had mumbled some scarcely intelligible words over them and they had written their names in a book, that had made it a marriage. Why? but why? The cry against man's social order that had rung through unhappy unions down the ages found only one answer in her mind, You've made your bed and you'll have to lie on it.

She said to James, repeating the formula that had been drilled into her at school, 'The Catholic religion is the only one true religion.' Then she added, 'You've got to be married in the Catholic Church before – before it's all right with God.'

It was a bright Saturday morning and the streets were warm, and women, the respectable ones, were kneeling on the pavement washing their steps. Some were covering a large half-moon of the pavement with bath brick, taking care to get a smoothness in the distribution, regardless of the fact that within an hour, perhaps less, the feet of the children would have stamped it black; clean patches seemed to draw children like magnets. But this morning the women turned from the daily sign of their respectability to stare at Kathie McQueen and her man Cavan, all dressed up . . . and Kathie in her funeral coat too! One after the other, after answering Kathie's loud greeting, they knelt back on their heels and stared after her swaying figure encased in the tight black satin coat, and at Cavan, who from the back appeared like a boy walking with his mother, and silent, too, like some boys who are forced to walk with their mothers on some disagreeable errand, for he gave no greeting to the women, nor yet cast a glance at them.

'We are off for a jaunt with me daughter Bridget and her man.' Kathie threw this information to the last remaining women in the street, before they turned into the main road.

'And what better morning for it, eh?'

And the women answered back, 'None better.'

In the comparative quietness of the main road Cavan, still looking straight ahead, said, 'Ye're foolin' nobody but yersel'.'

And after a moment's silence Kathie replied, 'That's as may be; but I'll not have their pity . . . see?' She turned her head aggressively on him. 'They'll think as ye want them to think, in the long run . . . I've seen it afore . . . it's always the way.'

They walked on in silence again, and Kathie adjusted her large satin-covered hat that had once been black but was now a variety of shot greens, then hitched her coat into an easier position under her breasts, and hoped as she did so that the button wouldn't give way; and she cursed Father O'Malley at the same time. If he had to marry them again he could have waited a bit; and with Cavan in work she might have got herself a coat, for this one had seen its day. Eighteen years it had been on the go, and it second-hand when she got it. She'd had her nine-and-six worth out of it, and many a proud moment it had given her, for hadn't it come from a big house and been worn by a lady? You only had to smell it to know that. But she never thought she'd wear it to go and see her daughter married a second time to a nigger. The humiliation weighed her down and caused her greetings to the step-washers in Dunstable

Street to be even louder. And when she knocked at Bridget's door the satin of the coat was rippling and changing its greasy hue with her laughter.

The door was opened instantly, as if Bridget had been waiting for her knock, and Kathie was unable to keep up her laughter to cover her annoyance when Bridget, without a word, stepped into the street, and James, looking more massive and black than ever because of the stiffness of his body and the sombreness of his face, followed her. He, too, gave them no greeting; but locked the door; then, taking his place by Bridget's side, walked down the street, Kathie and Cavan following.

Kathie yelled at Cavan; she yelled to the step-cleaners again; she yelled to no-one in particular; and some of her words, even to herself, were unintelligible . . . To be turned back at the door like that; not to be asked in and given a drop of something to help things along a bit. God knew that at ordinary funerals and weddings you needed something; and this was no ordinary wedding; yet not a drop of anything. What were things coming to, anyway . . .

The church was empty when they arrived, and self-consciously they filed into the back seat after genuflecting towards the main altar; all except James, who did not bend even his head; nor did he follow the others' example and kneel down, but sat with his arms folded across his chest and his cheek-bones making tight the skin of his face with their pressure.

Presently an altar-boy, trying hard to cover his amusement, came with an order from the priest;

and they rose and filed down the aisle to the altar-rails. They had barely reached them when Father O'Malley appeared on the other side, his face as stiff as his vestments. With a peremptory finger he motioned James and Bridget to kneel down. And so the service began.

The priest's voice was not even audible. There was a hurried guttural mumbling of words, the flicking over of leaves of the prayer-book, the passing from one hand to the other of a penny, then the flinging of the words at James, 'Will you have this woman to be your lawful wedded wife?'

James flung the responses back in a voice that made the priest start in spite of his grim control; but so low was Bridget's 'I will' that the priest accepted it without having actually heard it.

It was over, and Cavan and Kathie followed the couple to the vestry. Cavan's face was the colour of chalk and Kathie's so red as to appear on the verge of apoplexy.

Once the register was signed it was as if Father O'Malley couldn't get rid of them quickly enough. Scrambling up the aisle ahead of them, he led the way to the church door, and without a word watched them file past him into the street, his eyes, like rapier-points, piercing each one of them in turn. James was the last to leave, and the door was allowed to swing behind him, almost catching his heels.

'Of all the rotten holy Joes in this world, he's one!' Kathie could contain herself no longer. 'I hope he finds himself dead in his bed one of these mornings, and God forgive me for sayin' such a thing; but that's me curse.'

'Shut up!' Cavan's voice was deep and angry. He was hurt to the very soul with the indignities his daughter had brought upon herself. 'We've reached rock-bottom when you curse the priest; we've had enough bad luck; hold your tongue!'

'I'll not hold me tongue; one of these days I'll tell him me opinion of him to his face, and chance Hell's flames for it, ye'll see.' Kathie talked at her husband all the way to the fifteen streets; but she did not laugh; nor did she address her daughter or son-in-law; she allowed them to walk well on in front until they reached their own street, where they stopped and waited for her. Then all she said was 'I'll see ye later.' Her laughter had failed her.

Bridget and James entered their house in silence, and as Bridget made to go upstairs James pulled her to him and stared at her fixedly; and Bridget was hurt by the look on the usually laughing face of her husband. Compassion for his bewilderment overcame her, and she laid her hand on his cheek. 'I'm sorry, James; it had to be done. Perhaps you'll understand later when you've had instructions.'

His face softened, and she was surprised at the relief she experienced with the sound of his voice; but for his answers at the altar-rails he had said no word to her since leaving the house; it was as if he were striving to keep the dignity he prized so much.

'Now you feel we married?'

She nodded dumbly.

'That's all right then.' He drew her into his arms

and held her gently for a while in silence. Then holding her away from him, he smiled at her, saying, 'Now we can be happy; for two more days we can be happy. You sorry I'm sailing Monday, Rose?'

'Yes.'

'Truly?'

'Yes – yes.'

'You don't want me to leave you?'

'No.'

'You know I don't want leave you. I don't want leave you ever.' He sat down and drew her on to his knee and, taking off her hat, ran his hands over her hair. 'Most beautiful hair in the world. My Angela have hair like this . . . Rose—' He buried his face between her breasts.

'Yes?'

'I want ask you something . . . If German get my ship and I not come back, you not let her forget me . . . you tell her about me?'

'Please, Jimmy, don't say that. Never fear, you'll be all right.'

She felt the strong conviction within herself that God would make her suffer all her life for her mistake, and that James would be immune from danger so that her punishment might be meted out to her. She repeated, 'Never fear.'

The broad sweep of his eyebrows lifted, showing more white to his eyes. 'Me? I don't fear nothing or nobody – not for me I don't. But for you, yes. I won't tell no lies 'bout what I fear: two men I fear for you, 'cause they both make you afraid. One is that goddam priest, and the other is . . .' He stopped; then went on slowly, '. . . your brother. He like me worse than the others. When I am here he can't touch you, for he knows I would break him like that.' He clenched his huge fist until the knuckles showed pink beneath the black skin. 'But when I'm gone, you very afraid of Matt.' The last was a statement.

'No – no I'm not – I won't be; he's all right.' She avoided his eyes and screwed nervously at the bottom of his waistcoat.

'No lie, Rose. Your brother mad because you marry black man – your brother like you very much. Me, I know. Your mother, da and others all right, but Matt . . . he black inside. Me, I know men. From twelve years I work with men – all kinds of men – down stokehold. Eight years I been in same ship, and the Chief he say to me, "New bunch this trip, Jimmie. What you make of them?" The Chief, he think lot of me. I would have been his donkey-man many times over but for this.' He tapped the skin of his hand. 'Chief ask my opinion of men, not 'cause he don't know men. He big Geordie fellow. But he like talk with me, and he know I know men . . . Oh! you no cry. Rose. Please you no cry.'

She leant against him and her sobs mounted; and he beseeched her, 'You no cry. Me, I am sorry, Rose; but I am full of fear for you – don't – don't. Why you cry so?'

She continued to sob and he swung her up into his arms; and as he rose to his feet with her she gasped out, 'Don't go, James; don't go away.'

'I got to go, honey, you know that.' He smiled down on her. 'But I mighty glad you don't want me go. And you no worry any more; I see that brother and I fix him 'fore I go. We go upstairs now, eh? And you put on pretty dress and new hat with feather, and we go out and make everybody look at my Rose, and fellas turn and say, "Him lucky fella . . . him marry twice same girl.'"

He smiled down on her; then opened the stair door with his foot and walked sideways up the stairs, hugging her closer to him.

CHAPTER THREE

MATT

James had been gone three days and Bridget was feeling strangely lonely. After the first flush of relief she began to miss him and his deep broken speech telling her how wonderful she was; she missed the feeling of strength and protection he gave her; she missed him at night, and this caused her to feel wicked. In the night she lay tossing and turning, fighting the feeling of wanting him; in the night she never thought of him as black, for the night made all colour one. It was in the daytime, going about the work of the house, that the barrier of his colour would loom up and terrify her. She knew that in marrying James she had committed a sort of outrage, and that this had lifted her in one sweep off the plane of her people; but it had not dropped her on to the plane of James's people; it left her in a no-man's-land where, as far as she could see, there was only herself.

As hour added to hour, she felt less inclined to leave her house, for she knew she was vulnerable to the hostile looks of the men and women of the fifteen streets, and for once she felt thankful and glad that the war was on, for in the excitement and sudden rush of prosperity they would, she thought, have less time to give to the scandal she had created; not that they would miss taking some action should the worst among them give tongue. So, for the time, she stayed within the precincts of her own four small rooms, and some part of her was rested with their sanctuary.

That she must soon face the people and even work among them she knew, for James's monthly half-pay note of two pounds fifteen shillings would scarcely keep her for four weeks and pay the rent, coals and light, which came to eight shillings a week. Then there were the instalments of five shillings per week to pay on the furniture. Although James had provided for this by leaving with her the remainder of his fortune, fifteen pounds, she had the desire not to touch a penny of what was to her a vast sum, but rather to add to it. She knew that he must have spent a great part of his earnings on women and drink, but the habit, started by the missionary, of saving a little of his earnings had stuck, and not a penny James had put into the Post Office in eighteen years had he withdrawn; until he met her. Thirty-five pounds he had saved, and the feeling of the growing wealth, Bridget felt, had in no small way added to the dignity he so greatly prized.

Only once during the past three days had Bridget visited her mother, for Matt was on night shift and she was afraid of encountering him without the shield of James. She sat now beneath the gas mantle that sported a pink porcelain shade, sewing at a minute flannel petticoat. Her expression was a mixture of tenderness and apprehension, and unconsciously her lips moved as she repeated the prayer that was never long out of her mind; and now it was almost audible; and as she murmured 'Please God, make it all right!' the knocker of the front door banged once, and after a moment's hesitation she rose slowly and laid the petticoat on the table; then stiffening her body she went through the front room and opened the door.

Her relief made her exclaim in an unnaturally high-pitched voice, 'Why, Tony! Come in . . . I'd been wondering when you were coming.'

Tony limped over the step and into the dark room, and Bridget, her hand on his shoulder, guided him to the kitchen. 'Come and sit down; have you had your tea?' She pulled a highly varnished wooden chair towards the glowing fire.

'Yes.' He sat down without taking his eyes from her face.

She sat opposite to him and for a while they smiled at each other. Then she said awkwardly, 'It's funny me having a house, isn't it?'

He nodded, and the broken peak of his cap jerked further down his brow. He pushed it up and continued to stare at her.

'Do you like it?' She made a small motion with her hand around the room.

Reluctantly he took his eyes from her face, and screwed round on his chair to take it all in. 'Eeh, it's fine, Bridget.' Stretching out his hand he shyly touched the fringe of the green chenille cloth covering the table. 'It's lovely!'

'Come on, I'll light the gas and show you the front room.'

She ran from him, and he followed more slowly,

465

his grey eyes wide with wonder, for she appeared to him now like the girl he saw when he first came to their house.

In the front room she pulled down the new cream paper blind, with its edging of imitation lace, and lit the gas. Tony looked from one piece to the other of the suite: four single chairs, two armchairs and a couch, each one defying comfort with its stiff back and red plush seat. He looked at the bouquets of flowers forming large diamonds on the linoleum; at the plant-stand before the window, holding a fuchsia which was actually in flower; then at the mantel border, an elaborate piece of black satin on which were pen-painted three large and unreal birds, and there was genuine admiration in his voice and in his eyes when he said, 'I've never seen anything like it, Bridget; it's beautiful.'

'Come on upstairs.' She was as eager as a child. 'Wait until you see the dressing-table.'

On the way upstairs he stopped and touched the corded stair-carpet with his hands; but his wonder was suddenly covered with embarrassment when he entered the bedroom. He had to walk close to the great iron and brass bedstead to get to the dressing-table, and as he did so he realised for the first time that Bridget was no longer the Bridget of the McQueens' laughter-filled kitchen; she was married . . . she was a married woman, and she was married to a nigger.

'Look,' Bridget was saying, 'it has three mirrors, and the two side ones swing back and forward – like this. Have you ever seen anything like it?' And when he made no answer, Bridget turned to him and looked down on his lowered eyes, and his embarrassment reached her.

They went down the stairs in silence, and now Tony knew that in some way Bridget was aware of what he was thinking, and there was an agitation in him to reassure her. Bridget mustn't be hurt – she mustn't think he was like the others. He said suddenly, 'I like Jimmy – I like him better than anyone I know.'

She smiled sadly, and his heart twisted inside him as he saw the wet mist cover her eyes.

He began to talk with unusual rapidity. 'I've got a job, Bridget . . . I'm starting at Crawley's grocer's shop the morrer – I'm going in the back first, weighing up spuds and flour. He's giving me five shillings a week, and I'll soon get a rise if I do all right, he says. I would have got more if I'd been able to go out with the orders, but it's me . . . Anyway, I'll soon be serving in the shop. I'm glad the war's on; I wouldn't have got it if the war hadn't been on.'

'Oh, I'm glad for you, Tony – oh, I am!' Bridget was mashing the tea. 'We'll have a cup of tea . . . you'd like a cup, wouldn't you?'

'Yes, Bridget. Yer ma's going to get me a pair of long trousers . . . new ones . . . as soon as I get a pay.'

'Oh, that'll be grand.'

'I'm dying to get into long trousers . . . Bridget, you know in six years and ten months I'll be twenty-one; and you'll be twenty-six. You'll only be five years older than me then.'

She turned to him, puzzled and wondering at the odd turn of his thoughts. 'But I'm five years older than you now – I'll always be five years older than you.'

'Yes, yes, I know' – he wrung his cap between his hands – 'but I'll be grown up then . . . I'll be able to do things . . . if people . . .' He took his gaze from her, and his dark lashes cast a long shadow on to his thin, pale face, giving to it an almost girlish delicacy.

Bridget, looking at his bent head, read his unfinished words wrongly. 'Nobody will ever say anything about you, Tony – your limp isn't really noticeable, and you're growing now. Why, you are nearly as tall as me. And, you know, you're nice-looking – yes you are.'

As he gave an impatient shake with his body, saying, 'Oh, it wasn't that,' Bridget exclaimed, 'Hush a minute!' and they both stood listening to the rattling of the backyard door-latch.

'Is it locked? Will I go and open it?' he asked.

'No; drink your tea.'

He drank it, standing near the table, his eyes watching her listening as she moved about the kitchen. When the front door-knocker banged he put down his cup and asked, 'Will I go home, Bridget?'

She answered him on her way to the door, 'Yes, Tony, you'd better; but come again – come often.'

Matt stood on the pavement, the distant light of the street lamp emphasising the piercing blackness of his eyes. He did not even glance at Tony sidling past him, but stepped into the room and closed the door.

With the first sight of him Bridget had returned to the kitchen, where she now stood, staring down into the fire, her hands gripping the brass rod. She waited for him to speak until she could wait no longer, and she turned to where he stood just within the kitchen door, surveying her.

'You needn't think you're coming round here to frighten me, our Matt, because you're not . . . James told you – I know he told you what would happen if you did anything.' Her voice trembled with the fear she denied, and she went on, throwing her words at him, 'You always wanted everything your own way – well, you can't run my life. I would never have left home if it hadn't been for you.' She had said all the things she had told herself she wouldn't say.

'Why did you do it?' Each word was thin and had a piercing quality that cut deep into her.

She shivered, but rapped out, 'That's my business.'

'You were drunk, weren't you?'

Her bust and shoulders lifted in an attempt at denial, but no words came. Their eyes fought each other's; then her head drooped and she flung round to the fire again.

'I warned you, didn't I, to keep off it . . . I always told you it made you a sloppy, dribbling sot. You can't carry it . . . I told you, you bloody young fool.' Every syllable dripped with his contempt of her.

'Well, you nor nobody else will have to pay for my mistake.' Her head was resting on the rod now, and her voice was flat and quiet.

'Won't we?' He took three rapid steps forward which brought him to the table. 'We're just the laughing-stock of the streets, that's all! Our street was raised yesterday, with Cissie Luck making that fat swine of hers stand aside to let her into her front door; he put his toe in her backside and she screamed up the street, "Now me next bairn'll be khaki."'

Bridget winced as if in physical pain; and Matt went on, 'And then Pat Skinner linked with his seedless piece when they were passing the corner, and the chaps nearly cracked their sides with laughing. They were yelling, "Give her the Paterson touch, lad" . . . Nobody paying for your mistake!' He spat past her into the fire. 'By God! We're all paying for it, every damned one of us. And let me tell you this – we've only just started. As for you, you can thank your lucky stars there's a war on. If there hadn't been, they would have hounded you out of the place; and they'll likely do it yet. Some of the men in the Barium were throwing their quips at Terry yesterday; they were saying why should black swines have the houses when they've got to travel across the water each day.'

He was standing behind her now and the gusts of his breath were on her neck: 'Do you know what me ma heard that Dorrie Clark say? Do you?'

Bridget remained silent and still.

'She was spouting in the shop that you should be sent down to Holborn, among the Arabs. And do you know what the others said – that the Arabs wouldn't allow a dirty nigger among them.'

Bridget swung round on him, almost knocking him over. 'Shut up you, shut up! Don't you dare call him a dirty nigger. He's better than you or any of them around these doors – he's too good for me. Yes he is, yes he is.' She was screaming now. 'He knows how to treat a woman, that's more than the men here do. If they bring in their wages they think they're gods, and the women have to wait on them hand and foot from the day they marry them; and even when they are giving them bairns and wearing them out they are pawing at whoever will let them. They've got room to talk – they have, the men around here! And the women too, for that matter – dirty-mouthed lot.'

'At least they have white bairns.' As always when he had succeeded in arousing her anger, his own subsided. He spoke quietly now, but his mild barbed words had more effect on her than had his rage.

Bridget put her hand up to her throat and tore at it; and moved her head from side to side as if trying to free herself from some fearsome grip. Matt saw the colour drain from her face; and when she staggered and groped for a chair, he stood watching her, fighting the torrent of feeling that was pouring back into his veins now that they were together again, and as she slid from the chair on to the floor he sprang to catch her, crying, 'Bridget! . . . here, Bridget! . . . what's up?'

For a few minutes she lay lifeless on the mat, while he gripped her bloodless face, still entreating, 'Bridget; here, come on – what's up with you?'

It was strange, but never before had he seen a woman in a faint; women of his knowledge didn't faint, even when carrying bairns. So he kept calling to her, and when at last she opened her eyes his voice was soft with his anxiety. 'Brid, what's up? Are you all right? Can I get you something? Have you anything in the house – a drop of anything?'

The shake of her head was almost imperceivable.

'Come on, get up.' He lifted her into a chair and supported her with his arm, and she pointed weakly to the tea-pot, saying, 'Give me a drink.'

The tea did nothing to revive her, and he stood

over her, his voice harsh again, yet threaded with his anxiety. 'You take the damn stuff when you shouldn't, yet when you need it you haven't got any. Will you be all right till I go and fetch you something?'

'I don't want anything.'

The weakness of her voice only strengthened his determination. 'You've got to have something to pull you round. I won't be a minute. Lie on the mat if you feel bad again.'

He was gone and she was left alone. The fear of him, too, was gone: it was ousted by the fear he had brought to the surface, the fear that she would have a black baby. Her mind was sick and her body shivering with the fear . . . and all because she had got drunk.

She had known Matt knew how she had come to marry James and would make her admit it. The twice he had seen her drunk was at New Year parties. The first time, when she was seventeen, she only took two glasses of whisky, but those were enough to make her throw her arms around Len Bryant and kiss him in front of everyone. She could never remember doing it, as she disliked Len Bryant because he was always trying to touch her, and she wouldn't believe Matt; but she believed her father when he told her.

It was the following New Year's Eve before she again touched whisky . . . her previous reaction to it having faded from her mind. She only knew that the smell of whisky held a fascination for her, and she liked the cutting taste, and in spite of – or perhaps because of – Matt's scowling eye she took a proffered glass. This time she lifted up her skirts and danced, and Frankie Flanagan, whose house the party was in, lifted her on to the table. . . and his wife punched him in the face; and she herself had been slapped sober in the wash-house by Matt.

It was after this she swore to herself never to touch whisky again, for she knew she couldn't carry it. But looking back now she saw that the chain of circumstances that led to her next being drunk could not have been foreseen by even the most wary of individuals; for who would have thought getting friendly with another house-parlourmaid in London would have been the main link? This girl's sister had recently married a man who was managing a public house in Liverpool, and they had written asking her to work for them. Soon Bridget herself received a letter from her friend, with a glowing account of the highly paid jobs to be had in Liverpool; and it was no time at all until she found herself in such a daily post; and getting half as much money again as she had been receiving in London, but paying out much more than the half for an attic room above a stable attached to the public house; and it was the simplest thing in the world to grant the request of the sisters to help in the rush-time on a Saturday night; also the simplest thing to get merry in the back room afterwards with a few of the regular seafaring clients – the honour of being called into the back room being an inducement to the men to empty their pockets again at the end of the next trip. There she met James . . . but she couldn't remember taking him to her room, she could only remember the horror of her awakening; and from then till now seemed but four hours instead of four months.

Her mind raked up again the humiliations that attended her marrying James; the scorn of her one-time friends; the order to get out by the supposedly outraged sister; the expressions on the faces of the many landladies; until she felt she could bear it no longer and that she must brave the shock that James would be to her people and go to them. She had imagined, too, that once inside the fifteen streets she would find a measure of peace and protection among her own kind; but when she thought this, the enormity of her crime in all its entirety had not been brought fully home to her . . . it needed the return to her own class to do this.

'Here, drink this.'

She had not been aware of Matt's return. The smell of the whisky from the glass held close to her face brought her to herself, and she turned her head away, saying, 'I don't want that.'

'Don't act the goat – here, get it down you!'

'I tell you I don't want it . . . Matt, I don't want it!' She gazed up at him pleadingly. 'I promised I wouldn't . . .' She broke off and shook her head. 'I'll be all right; this'll pass.'

Matt stood staring down at her, his lower lip pressed out. Who had she promised? That dirty black swine? She had promised him she wouldn't drink, had she! . . . after he had dropped her! Well, the nigger had got her through drink; then, by God, it would be through drink that he would lose her! He gripped the back of Bridget's head; then, putting the glass to her lips, forced the whisky between them.

CHAPTER FOUR

THE BIRTH

In such communities as that of the fifteen streets there is often found an outstanding personality, a personality that is respected for its self-sacrificing and good qualities, or one that is held in awe or fear for some power it is credited with possessing – mostly evil. Such a personality was Nellie Milligan. She was known as a fixer. Despairing women, realising that once again they had fallen, would immediately turn their thoughts to Nellie Milligan and wonder how the sovereign could be raised; but raise it they would, even to the extent of pawning every bit of bedding a pawnshop would accept, to enable them to pay for having the burden removed.

The days of the twelve or fifteen in a family were past; but to see up to half a dozen children with hungry eyes was more than enough for some of the women; so, ironically, many called God's blessing on Nellie Milligan, while here and there a woman, trailing out the remainder of her life only half alive, cursed the day she had seen her.

No-one knew Nellie's age . . . some of the old women said she was 'getting on' when they were young. She was known to possess various powers; she was a wart-charmer and she could also mix a concoction that would remove hair from the faces of women suffering 'the change' – that the new growth was stronger only called for a stronger potion; she was also known to possess powers which could overcome sterility; but these supposed powers she was chary of using. Apparently the most propitious time for using these powers was after she had fixed somebody; and when, some years ago, Maisie Searle, who had never shown the sign of one during the ten years of her marriage, found she was carrying, and that after going to see Nellie who had just fixed Mrs O'Leary of her ninth, Nellie's reputation was itself fixed, and both the priest and doctor were powerless against her.

Nellie never did anything straightforward . . . all her jobs were surrounded by mystery. Even when she told the cards, it would be behind drawn blinds and before a coke fire, winter or summer; and all her fixing jobs were attended, at least on the patient's part, by drinking bottles of evil-smelling liquids. Most of the women did not mind this, as after drinking the prescribed doses they had little or no recollection of what followed.

It was rarely a woman went to Nellie with a first child; although sometimes a bride, finding herself flung into the maelstrom of life and seeing herself fast becoming like the child-weary women about her, would become fear-stricken; and she would pay Nellie a visit on the quiet.

Of all her jobs it was really only the first 'uns that brought Nellie any satisfaction; and nearly always she was cheated out of these. If it wasn't a young outraged husband threatening to strangle her for attempting to deprive him of the visible evidence of his manhood, it would be the older women themselves threatening to split on her if she did it. They would remain blind and dumb should she help one of them; but with a first, almost to a woman they would be against her. But none of them knew about Bridget Paterson. Nellie herself hadn't thought about it until a week ago, when she had been telling Kathie McQueen her cards . . . and then with no intention of fixing it . . . that had been Kathie's idea. Never before had she been called upon to do a job like this, not when the bairn was just on being born; and she wasn't quite easy in her mind about it.

She made her way now up and down various back lanes on her way to Dunstable Street. She was thankful that it was snowing, for other than a few stray children playing there was no-one about . . . but even if she were seen, who would dream she was going to fix a nine-months one. She reached Bridget's back door, and like a thin black shadow on the white snow she sidled up the yard and tapped on the kitchen door.

The door was opened with the utmost caution, and Kathie peered at the black-shawled figure standing in the yard. She held a warning finger to her lips before pulling the old woman over the threshold into the scullery.

'Not a sound above a whisper out of ye, for God's sake, Nellie.'

Nellie let the shawl fall from her head, to disclose an almost bald scalp, and she stared at Kathie with small, bird-like eyes, while her toothless jaws champed together as if she were munching something tough.

'Have ye got everything?'

The old woman nodded.

'Oh my God, I hope ye know what ye're doin'.'

The small figure bridled, and her jaws stopped their munching. 'Ye want it done? And anyway, is she the first I've tackled?'

'No; I know.'

'Are ye sure she's for havin' it away? She's late in the day in thinkin' about it.'

'Of course I am . . . only she's too proud to say so. What do ye think she's been on the bottle these past months for? She's scared of the thing being black.'

'But I thought it wasn't due for two or three days yet?'

'So did I, but ye know what first ones are. I wouldn't have known she was even bad, but the boy Tony was here, and he came back and told me she had gone to bed. So I sent him straight to you.'

'Ye think it's near?'

'As near as makes no odds . . . have ye got the stuff?'

'Aye.'

'But how'm I gonna get her to take it, all in a hurry an' all, like this?'

'I've bought a bit of horse-flesh.'

'Horse-flesh! What in the name of God for?'

'To burn . . . there's nothing smells like burnt horse-flesh. Fry it in the frying pan till it burns and waff it up the stairs, then run up with the drink to her. She'll be so parched she'll gulp down anything. And by the way' – she knocked a drop off the end of her nose with the back of her hand – 'it's a drink we'll be needing ourselves, to get through . . . have you got owt?'

'I've got a wee drop of rum. But will the stuff knock her off?'

'Enough for me to do what I've got to do.'

'Ye won't use the crochet hook on her, Nellie? Ye won't hurt her?'

'I've told you before, there'll be no need . . . it isn't an abortion you want.'

'And ye won't do owt to it, Nellie, if it's white, will ye?'

'No; but haven't I told ye? I saw it in your cards as plain as the nose on your face . . . it's black it'll be, like night.'

'Aye.' Kathie rolled her head on her mountainous chins. 'Aye, ye did tell me, and I've never known a minute's rest since. And it won't look as if it had been . . . ?'

'Not a sign . . . it'll be stillborn.'

'But if she knows it's you up there—' Kathie wrung the corner of her apron. 'She hasn't been near me since she saw us together a week past.'

'She'll not know a thing once she takes the stuff; and if she does, she'll think it's a doctor fiddling about with her . . . Now come on and get me the pan.'

As Kathie watched Nellie bring a thick collop of horse-flesh from under her shawl she shuddered. 'God protect us! Where d'ye get it?'

479

'Never ye mind . . . it'll cost ye a shilling . . . And, Kathie' – the beady eyes closed still farther – 'it's a pound, mind, when the job's done!'

'If it's dead.'

'It'll be dead all right.'

'But mind, not if it's white, mind, Nellie . . . don't touch it if the colour's all right.'

As Nellie was about to place the pan on the fire she turned to Kathie, saying, 'Look, before I start: ye're sure she hasn't sent for the doctor, or the nurse or somebody? I've me name to think of, and it's late in the day.'

'How could she? I was round here within five minutes of the boy telling me. And she hardly knows what it's all about, anyway . . . it's her first, isn't it? No, she couldn't have sent for anybody; and she's never been one for making neighbours, thank God for that! She's kept herself to herself for months now.'

The horse-steak sizzled on the hot pan, and Nellie stood silently watching it. For a moment the terrible cold menace of the shrivelled old woman was borne home to Kathie, and she had the urge to fling her out of the door; but the dread of being a grannie to a black bairn was too strong. So she, too, stood silent and waiting, until the stench began to fill the kitchen, forcing her to go to the back door. As her hand went to the latch Nellie's fingers, like cold steel, gripped her arm, and without a word she was drawn back into the kitchen again, choking and spluttering. And Kathie's fear of Nellie increased when she saw that the choking fumes were having little or no effect upon the old woman.

'Here, take the pan up on the landing and waft it about while I get the stuff ready.'

Kathie, her eyes streaming and her apron held across her mouth, took the pan and groped blindly for the stair door. Never before in her life had she smelt anything like this, and she had smelt some smells. God, why had she got herself into this? She crept up the stairs, the pan held at arm's length, but before she reached the top Bridget's voice came to her.

'What's that smell, Ma? What are you doing? Oh, what's that smell?'

'A bit of steak . . . it dropped in the fire.' She coughed and spluttered. 'It'll be all right in a minute, I'm gonna open the window.'

Not being able to stand any more herself, she went hurriedly down the stairs again, and as she burst into the kitchen she let out a squeal like a trapped rabbit, for standing in front of Nellie, like some threatening giant, was Dr Davidson. The pan tipped in her hand and the charred steak fell on to the mat.

'So it's you, is it?' The doctor's eyes struck fire at Kathie. 'Giving her a hand, are you? . . . My God! Now listen to what I am saying.' His finger stabbed her in the chest. 'If anything goes wrong with that child up there, I'll see you both behind bars.'

For a moment Kathie was unable to utter a word, and her head rolled as if it would drop off her shoulders; then, sick with fright, she began to bluster. 'Behind bars, is it? And what, may I ask, am I goin' behind bars for . . . for burning a bit of meat?'

'Burning a bit of meat . . . !' The doctor turned his attention to Nellie again. She had not uttered a syllable, but her eyes, stretched to their small wideness, had never left his face.

'You . . . you fiend of hell! I've wanted to catch you red-handed for years. And now I've got you . . . with your' – he coughed – 'damned incantations.'

Still Nellie said no word; but her eyes slid to the table; his followed, and he said, 'I'll relieve you of that.'

His hand reached out to the unstoppered bottle, but, as quick as lightning strikes, Nellie was there before him. She grabbed up the medicine bottle; and whether by accident or design, Kathie, stooping in front of him to retrieve the steak, blocked his way; and Nellie, minus her shawl, escaped through the front room.

The doctor bestowed a look on Kathie that should have shrivelled her, but with relief filling her she faced him boldly. 'What's got into ye, Doctor, may I ask ye? What's got into ye?'

Doctor Davidson took a deep breath and almost choked. 'As long as something hasn't got into your daughter you'll be safe, Mrs McQueen . . . this time! But I'll see to it that your friend has killed her last child around these parts.'

He was forced to stop and cough into his handkerchief, and Kathie, regaining her confidence and belligerence, broke in, 'What do you know about it all? . . . You with your belly well fed. Nellie Milligan has saved many a poor soul from destruction around these doors. You and the priest between you are the ruination . . . the priests keep on tellin' yer, ye must do yer duty as a wife, and ye do it, from sixteen to sixty; and yer belly's full of bairns every year. And who's to feed and clothe them, and pay the doctor? . . . Aye, pay the doctor, eh? Nellie Milligan has been a godsend, I tell ye, to many a poor soul. Ye like bringing bairns into the world, because, given half the chance, ye cut them up so as ye can see their insides and try to find out where ye went wrong with the last one ye knocked off . . . Oh, I know all yer tricks.'

Dr Davidson stood surveying Kathie for a moment after she had finished. Then, between short coughs, he said, 'Well, if you've had your say, Mrs McQueen, I'll go upstairs; but for your information I'll tell you that your daughter wants this baby, black or white. Perhaps you didn't know that?'

He left Kathie, her mouth half open and her hands on her hips, staring after him.

So the girl had suspected her mother was up to something, and rightly, too, Dr Davidson thought as he mounted the stairs. Sending that strange, urgent little note to him, which told him nothing in the actual lines, but volumes between.

As he entered the bedroom, Bridget, in her night-dress, rose from the side of the bed, one arm hugging her waist. She showed evident relief at the sight of him, and said, 'I've got the pains, Doctor.'

'And what do you expect to have, eh?' He laughed as he placed his bag on the wash-stand.

'What's that dreadful smell, Doctor?'

'Oh, that . . . Your mother's been doing some fancy cooking and tipped a steak into the fire.'

'A steak? . . . But why should she?'

'Come; get into bed.'

As she slowly got back into bed he picked up a

bottle from the wash-stand and looked at it curiously. It was a bottle of disinfectant, and next to it were two neatly folded hand towels, while on a chair nearby stood a number of sheets and clothes; and before the fire in the small grate was a towel-rail with baby clothes arranged upon it. She certainly had everything ready. And disinfectant, too. He was surprised and pleased. The nearest they ever got to antiseptic in the fifteen streets was carbolic soap; and even the old hands rarely had everything ready and neat like this. Marrying that Negro had seemingly done her little harm. But hadn't he heard something about her taking to drink? Must have been idle rumour, for the house didn't look that of a drunk.

'You've got everything ready, I see,' he said, smiling down on her. 'And a very nice little place you've got here, too . . . haven't seen better.' He knew she was pleased, and he continued to talk to her as he examined her. 'You've sent for Nurse Snell?'

'No, Doctor.'

'Oh, but you should have done. And, you know, you should have come and seen me before . . . Who's going to look after you?'

'My mother.' Her tone did not reveal her fears, but she made no protest when he said, 'I think we'd better have the nurse, just for the first few days, eh?' He patted her shoulder, saying, 'It won't be long . . . it nearly got here before me. How long have you had the pains?'

'Since early this morning.'

'Oh, you're going to be lucky, it's coming quick . . . When is your husband due back?'

'Tonight or tomorrow.'

'Good . . . good. Here, pull on that . . .' He tied a piece of sheeting to the bed-rail and left her gripping it while he went downstairs again, where, without any preamble, he said to Kathie, 'You know where Nurse Snell lives? Go and tell her I would like her to come along here at once. If she isn't in, leave word to that effect. And don't give the wrong message.'

'Nurse Snell, is it?' cried Kathie. 'Look ye here, Doctor, if I want a nurse I'll get Dorrie Clark. In any case, I can do as good as either of them; and I don't charge seven and six or fifteen bob! I can see to me own daughter.'

'Yes, you very nearly did see to her! Now get yourself away this minute; if you're not gone on that errand before I reach the top of the stairs, I'll inform your daughter what the smell is she's so anxious about, and what her mother and Mrs Milligan were up to . . . Now what do you say?'

'Blast ye for an interfering swine! That's what I say.' Kathie snatched her shawl off the door. 'Don't think you'll frighten me . . . you! . . . nor a battalion like you. You and Father O'Malley would make a fine pair.'

God forbid, thought Dr Davidson, as the door banged behind Kathie.

When he again entered the bedroom it was to find Bridget crying. 'Oh, come now. Come now,' he laughed, 'you'll forget all about the pains once the little nipper's here.'

Bridget shook her head. She could not tell him it wasn't the pain that was making her cry, but the dread of its result. For days now the child had lain comparatively quiet within her, and she had soothed herself by thinking that if it was black it would be full of vigour and life, and be making itself felt. Then despair would seize her, and she would imagine the baby's stillness was because it was black and content and good-tempered like James. But whatever she imagined its quiet movements to mean, she did not imagine the baby to be dying. Not for a moment did she want the movements to stop altogether and signify her release . . . no, she wanted this child, as something that James might have for his own. But oh, Jesus, Jesus, she didn't want it to be black!

Soon the pains, gathering on themselves, formed a mountain that she must climb, and in the climbing there was no place for worry about colour. She was aware, as time went on, that the nurse was with the doctor, and when the child left her body all anxiety and worry flowed out with it. It was over. Whatever colour it was could not be altered; she should have realised that from the very beginning. She had been silly to worry.

When she heard the doctor chuckling, a deep rounded chuckle, she thought, he's laughing because it's quaint; all black babies are quaint.

The baby was twenty-four hours old when James got in. He came in like a wind, a hot driving wind. Kathie cast startled eyes on him when he flung open the kitchen door, then turned her back to him; but Cavan rose from his seat by the fire and there was understanding and sympathy in his look. James, his eyes holding a depth of emotion and anxiety, uttered one deep-belled word, 'Well?'

'It's what you was wantin'.'

Before Cavan finished speaking, James pulled open the stair-door. He took the stairs in three leaps, but pulled up for an instant on the landing. It might be what he wanted, but was it what Rose wanted?

Bridget's eyes were closed when he neared the bed; he did not know whether she was asleep or not. Although his attention was riveted on the blanket-wrapped bundle lying on the far side of her, he stopped before going round the bed, and stooping, gently laid his face against hers. Because she made no movement whatever, he knew she was awake, but he said nothing, and going round to the other side he reverently picked up the bundle.

Through half-closed, sleepy lids, two brown eyes looked up at him, so like his own that a leaping, choking happiness that was almost an agony tore through him; but it was nothing to the ecstasy when the wonder was borne in on him that his child was white, with skin the colour of thick cream, and hair that was straight; it was as black as his own, but it was straight. The lids widened and the child gazed at him in fixed concentration, as if, he thought, she knew him. And when her hand wavered from the folds of the blanket and plucked at his finger his joy mounted, passing out of him and flying in thanksgiving to the God he was aware of, and to others dimly sensed. He raised his eyes to the ceiling and struggled to find words adequate to this feeling, but only one word came to his mind. He had first heard it outside the bars around the Liverpool docks, when, rain or shine, abused and laughed at, the Salvation Army had beaten its drums and tinkled its triangles in praise of God. He threw back his head and his voice resounded through the house, startling all but the child as he cried, 'Alleluia! Alleluia! Alleluia!'

PART TWO

CHAPTER FIVE

A MUCH-RESPECTED MAN

The fog-horn, blasting from a tug, seemed to carry its force through the grey drifts of mist right into the forecastle without losing any of its strength. James, pulling the cord of his white sailor-bag tight, unconsciously screwed up his face in protest. There were few things he hated about the sea, but he hated the sound of the fog-horn; its melancholy note seemed to search out an answering chord within himself.

'You're not losing much time, Jimmy?' An old fireman, lying in his bunk, rolled on to his side and stared at the great black head level with his own.

'Not much time to lose.'

'Lucky for you we came to the Tyne to load this trip.'

'Yes, lucky for me.' James thumped his kit-bag on the floor to give him a better hold of the top, pulled his cap firmly down on his head, turned up the collar of his blue reefer jacket, then, thrusting the bag up the companionway, climbed on to the deck with the voice of the old man shouting after him, 'Don't forget me, Jimmy, when your wife's givin' out that new bread, mind.'

The deck was abustle, the hatches were off, and the men, working by the light of naked gas jets run by piping from the jetty to the holds, were grabbing at the tubs from the swinging cranes and tipping the coal into the hatches as if the devil was after them.

The voice of the chief engineer spoke from out of the mist, 'Just off, Jimmy?'

'Yes, Chief.'

'Dirty night.'

'Yes, 'tis, Chief.' Jimmy turned towards the wavering outline of the engineer. 'If old man changes his mind, you let me know, Chief?'

'I will, Jimmy; but you know as well as me that it's no good. I told you what he said; and we are off as soon as she's loaded; he's been at the gaffer to stir those dock tykes up.'

'She out of breath with running, she catch her barnacles on the bottom one of these days. Good night, Chief.'

'Good night, Jimmy. Make good use of your time, and remember me to the nipper.'

Jimmy's smile wasn't evident to the engineer, but he could feel it in the voice as it came to him. 'I will. Sure I will, Chief. She always talks of the engineer-man; she never forgotten you bought her that doll, Chief . . . and that near two years ago. Yes, I tell her 'bout you.'

The massive bulk of Jimmy was lost in the fog before he reached the gangway, but the chief continued to gaze in the direction he had taken. He felt uneasy in his mind about the man; he had done so for a long time now. At one time, Jimmy used to talk to him, especially about his white wife. At first, this association with a white woman had sickened him, but then he had asked himself why should it; Jimmy was a better man than some of the whites on the ship. Of course he was an exception, for most niggers made him sorry the old overseer's whip was out of fashion; but Jimmy was a good type, and there was no need to feel sorry for his wife. In any case, Jimmy was likely a damn sight too good for the type of woman who would marry a black man; any pity that was to be thrown about should go to him. Something had been wrong this long while, and it had to do with the wife, for he rarely spoke of her now; all his talk was about his child, his Rose Angela . . . highfalutin name, that. She was an unusually bonny child. A pity, though, there was evidence of the tar-brush in her. The Chief stood for a moment longer looking in the direction James had taken; then, shaking his head, he turned towards his cabin to take comfort in his bottle. What could you expect, anyway? The sins of the fathers left their mark . . . or was it the mother in this case? . . .

As James passed the dock-policeman's little stone office by the side of the main gates the policeman on duty peered at him. 'Oh, hullo there, Jimmy. Why couldn't you bring better weather with you? In for long?'

'All the weather they would give me, boss,' James laughed. 'No, it tip, fill and run trip . . . same as ever.'

'Good night, Jimmy.'

'Good night, boss.' He squeezed sideways through the small door in the gate and sprang across the road to the Jarrow tram and threw his bag on to the platform just as the tram moved off. He pushed the bag under the stairs and stood on the platform until the conductor said, 'Inside; there's a seat there.'

James took the seat – the corner one next to the door.

He gave a greeting to an old woman sitting opposite, who smiled at him, saying, 'You got back again then, Jimmy?' And he was about to answer her when the evident recoil of a young woman at his side froze his reply. He became still inside as he realised she was withdrawing her skirt from contact with him by tucking it under her hip. Slowly he turned and looked at her, but her eyes were staring straight ahead.

The old woman again spoke, her voice, loud and strident, filling the tram. 'Ye've just missed the Victory teas, Jimmy . . . they've had 'em in nearly all the fifteen streets. Eeh! they've had some do's . . . tables the length of the street, and the stuff to eat you wouldn't believe. And sports for the bairns; an' dancin'.' She rattled on, but James was not listening to her; he was conscious only of the inch of brown wooden lathe that separated his clothes from the girl's. It was many years since an incident like this had happened to him. He liked to think that the war had wiped all this feeling away, in England anyway, and he wanted to turn to the girl and say, 'I'm a steady, sober man, miss. I've worked to be respected, and I am respected. The people hereabouts know me and like me . . . you should have heard how dock pollis spoke to me, same as white man. And on my ship they call me Lucky Jim. I have a wife and a child, and money

494

in bank. I do nothing bad . . . I keep my dignity
. . . I'm much respected man.'

But he said nothing to the girl, he just sat staring,
like her, ahead, reassuring himself that he was a
. . . much-respected man, and a very lucky man.
Any man who had a daughter like his Rose Angela
was a lucky man, wasn't he? And Rose, wasn't he
lucky to have Rose? He refused to answer himself
this question, but instead asked, 'How she be this
time, I wonder? Will she be in temper or crying fit
to burst?'

The thought of his wife overshadowed for the time
the hurt he was feeling, and as the tram jogged along
he sat brooding, as always now when his thoughts
touched on Bridget. What was wrong with his Rose?
What had come over her? It started right back before
the child was born. His home-comings then found
her irritable, but he excused that because the child
was heavy on her. But after it was born she became
worse; and once, looking at her unusually puffed
face, he said seriously, 'Rose, you drinking!' Her
fury had silenced further accusation, and for a time
he believed his guess was wrong, until his reason told
him he had seen the results of drink on too many
women not to know that she was drinking, and
drinking heavily. But what he could not make out
was why she never took it when he was home. The
longest he had been home during the past four years
was a fortnight, and he remembered it as a period
of stress. He also remembered her passionate crying
when he was leaving, her begging him not to go – to
get a shore job. But he needed the sea, and, what was
more, the war was on, and the sea needed him.

But now the war was over, and, big as the wrench would be, he was going to look for a shore job. He had tried to tell the chief during this trip, yet somehow he had been unable to bring himself to it; but next trip would be his last, he had made up his mind. This docking for only twenty-four hours had decided him; he'd thought they'd be in for at least a week, as the old tub needed her bottom scraping.

At the corner of the fifteen streets he rose from his seat, and he looked once more at the girl. And this time she returned his look, and the hostility in her eyes hurt him. She would have a separate tram-car for coloured people, he thought, as they did in some countries. And he wondered, as he had often done before, why one adverse look could outweigh, even totally obliterate for a time, the acceptance of the majority.

The old woman, lumbering off the tram, called, 'You'll be glad of something inside you a night like this, comin' off the water an' all . . . Bridget'll have the old broth pan goin', I bet.'

'She don't know me coming; but all the same she have broth pan going. Good night.'

'Good night, Jimmy.'

He strode along the main road towards his own street, his mind heavy with the feeling of uncertainty now that he was nearing home. How would she look at him? If only that soft light of old would be in her eyes. She was sorry she had married him . . . he knew that . . . and yet she wanted him . . . he knew that too. Life could be heaven, and life could be hell; but it had been mostly hell lately. He shifted his bag from one shoulder

496

to the other, stiffening his back in the process.

He was nearing his door when the thick silence of the street was split by laughter, loud, high laughter that checked his step. It was Rose's laugh, but he had only once before heard her laugh in such a way – that night in the back room of the bar in Liverpool. He did not knock on the door, but stood listening, and he knew she was drunk again and that she wasn't alone. He became still; no anger filled him, only a questioning, and he began to reason with himself quietly, Now you find out . . . now you know what it all about . . . take things quietly . . . go round back: she not drinking alone. This thing happen before to other men . . . why you think it not happen to you? Into the stillness within him bored a pain, twisting the muscles of his chest. Not Rose . . . she not bad. He wiped the moisture from his face with his hand. You go find out. You don't be fool. You soft you know in some way . . . you been clarts where Rose concerned, she got you on a string, she know it. No . . . you no knock – it was as if something stayed his hand – you go clear this thing up. Gone on long enough it has. You don't know what matter with her half the time. You not coward 'bout other things, don't be coward 'bout this.

When he left the door, Rose's laugh followed him; it seemed to add weight to his legs, slowing his steps as he went round the bottom corner and up the back lane. Gently he tried the latch of the back door and found it locked, so, placing his hands on the top of the wall, he drew himself up and over, and, softly withdrawing the bolt, lifted his bag into the yard; then he re-bolted the door again.

497

Now, inside the yard and only a few feet from Rose and whoever was with her, the reasoning stillness was deserting him, and his muscles were knotting themselves. For a moment he hated Rose for being the cause of this undignified creeping up his own back yard.

When he reached the kitchen window her voice came to him, thick and fuddled, 'We'll have a tune – Sister Susie – eh?'

James bent down and put his head level with the bottom of the blind. He could see nothing, but the slow wail of a man's voice came to him:

> 'Pad-dy wrote a letter
> To his Irish Molly-oh,
> Saying if you don't receive
> Please write and let me know.'

Into the wailing broke a voice which brought James upright; it was saying, 'That's Tipperary, you fool! It's on the other side. Wind the damn thing up, and empty that glass.'

Before the last word died away James had thrust open the door and was in the kitchen. Bridget, her mouth open and moving in a vain effort to voice her surprise, was leaning back against the dresser, and the glass half full of whisky she held in her hand was spilling in a steady trickle to the floor. Matt, who had been in the act of pouring some beer from a tin can, placed the can on the table with an abruptness that caused the froth to shoot up in a spray and cover his waistcoat.

In one sweeping glance James took in every detail

of the kitchen: the untidy hearth with the ashes filling the pan, the dirty dishes on the table, Rose Angela's clothes lying in a heap by the side of the fireplace, and the order of drinking. There was one beer glass and one whisky glass, and Matt had the beer glass. A hot fury swept through James, opening his pores and bringing the sweat in large greasy beads on to his face! Here was the answer to all his bewilderment . . . Matt! Matt, who had always hated him for marrying his sister. Here was the explanation for the mirthless sneer in Matt's eyes.

Matt and he met seldom, but when they did the sneer was there, not only in his eyes but in the curl of his lip. Never had James encountered Matt in the house before, all their previous meetings having taken place in the McQueens' kitchen; but here was a man, James saw, who was very much at home, so much so that he himself was the intruder.

Matt, kicking his chair to one side, backed towards the little dresser, and his eyes, black with hate, never left James's face. James, throwing up his head, sniffed loudly in an unconscious primitive gesture, then, tearing off his coat, he cried, 'You not try get away; we settle this in yard. You pay for this, you dirty louse!'

'Jimmy, no! . . . look, I'll tell you.' Bridget thrust out a wavering arm to him, but it was knocked to one side as Matt's hand flung back to grab at a knife lying on the dresser top.

'Who's trying to get away?' As Matt brought the knife forward Bridget screamed, and James, with a lightning stroke, swung up the flat iron that was standing on the pan hob and whirled it across the

499

narrow space, just missing Matt's hand but striking the blade of the knife and sending it spinning into the air. Bridget screamed again; and she clasped her hands over her face as the knife scattered dishes to the floor. With a shove of his hand James thrust the table aside, and Matt and he were facing each other.

Matt's mouth was square, and his venom was ground from beneath his clenched teeth. 'You black swab! Why couldn't you stick to your own breed? You took her when she was drunk; well, you can have her now. She's so whisky-mad that you nor nobody else can stop her. So come on!'

James's fist almost covered Matt's face as it struck him, sending him crashing back against the dresser. His strength could have finished off any ordinary man with a single blow, but Matt was no ordinary man. He was possessed of a hate for the black man that gave him the tearing power of a lion. With a shake of his head he recovered from the blow and bore right into James, bringing both his fists and feet into play.

The gramophone and the little table on which it stood were whipped into the hearth, sending the pan off the hob in their flight. The soup spluttered into the fire and a shower of ash and steam filled the kitchen, and Bridget's screaming mingled with the hissing. She wrenched open the kitchen door and yelled, 'Help! . . . My God! Help, somebody . . . help!' She turned, still screaming, and saw Matt and James locked together as if in a passionate embrace: then she saw James free himself with a heave from Matt's entwined arms, and with one hand thrust him away and with the other deliver a blow under the chin that lifted him from the floor and sent him crashing on to the fender.

Bridget's world became very still; in the kitchen, in the yard, and all beyond there was no movement; the only sound was James's heavy breathing. She stared from the doorway in petrified horror at the still, limp figure of Matt, with the long gash in his cheek and the blood gushing from his temple. She lifted her eyes to James. His face seemed no longer black, but grey, and he was standing motionless, staring down at Matt. She moved slowly towards him and stood by his side. 'My God! What've you done? . . . Oh, Holy Mary!'

He said nothing; and she stooped and touched Matt's wrist, and, with her hand still holding her brother's, turned her face up to her husband and whispered a terrified whisper.

She dropped Matt's hand; and as she stood looking at James with a startled look as if she had never seen him before, the stair-door opened and a voice whimpered, 'Ma.' She did not look at her child, but spoke her thoughts as they came to her. 'They'll hang him . . . it was my fault, but they'll hang him . . . Oh my God, what have I done?'

James did not move or answer her, but he screwed his head slowly round and looked at his daughter. She was crying and biting her knuckles, and, as a tiny smile for him broke through her tears, a fear never before experienced swept over him . . . If Matt was dead, then he, too, would soon be dead, and never again would he see his Rose Angela, nor she him.

As a curl of fog came into the kitchen, seeming to

bear on its grey tendrils the enquiring cries from the back lane, James shook himself, first his head and then his shoulders . . . they'd hang him for sure . . . no black man could hope to get off after killing a white; he'd seen the result of that more than once. It would be no use telling them he hadn't meant to kill Matt, that he didn't kill him, it was the corner of the steel fender that had done it . . . it would be no use talking at all; there was one justice for the white and one for the black. He was no fool, he told himself; all his steady living would be forgotten in the face of the crime he would have to answer for. But he didn't want to die. He lifted his head, listening now to the yelling from the back lane:

'Are you all right, Bridget? What's up? Open the door there. Come on there, open up!'

If they once got hold of him there'd be no escape, he'd die all right. But he wasn't going to die, he'd get away. If he could reach the ship he'd be all right – yes, that was the way out. He must get to the ship and see the chief. He wouldn't be the first the chief had got across the water. The chief held his own ideas on justice. The thumping on the back door told him that the time he had to accomplish this was very limited. He grabbed up his coat from the floor, but stopped in the act of thrusting his arms into it; if he went now there would be no return, he would never see his Rose Angela again. He looked from her to Rose, and at this moment there was in him no feeling but bitterness for his wife. She had brought him to this, to running away, to hiding for the rest of his life, and to separating him from his daughter. Even if he lived he might never see his child again. Suddenly he knew that this would be unbearable. He could suffer anything but to be separated for ever from his child. Where he went, the child must go, for she was all his; Rose did not need her as he did. Intuitively he knew that Rose resented the knowledge that their child held more of him than her, despite its looks to the contrary.

Bridget, shocked into soberness, watched her husband stoop towards Rose Angela. She knew that his intention was to escape, and she thought he was about to embrace the child. Even when he swung her up and into the shelter of his coat she did not for one moment imagine he would attempt to take her with him. Only when, clutching Rose Angela to him, he ran through the front room did it dawn on her, and then she screamed louder than she had done before, 'No, James! . . . Jimmy! Jimmy! No! Don't . . . leave her be.'

When she reached the front door there was no sign of James and she stood on the road with the fog swirling round her, crying like a child herself. 'Jimmy, come back . . . bring her back . . . bring her back.'

Once clear of the streets and running along the main road, James's mind began to work, planning out a way to evade the pursuers he knew would soon be following him. In between his planning he soothed the child, saying, 'You no cry, you with your da; you all right.' He would make straight for the ship, for they wouldn't expect him to be mad enough to go back to her. But he couldn't get to her through the dock gates, so he would have to enter the docks by way of the river. This would be no easy task in the fog, but if there was a sculler lying at the slipway, he'd chance it. If there wasn't, he'd climb the sawmill wall and thread his way to the jetty where his ship lay. Of the two ways, he preferred taking the sculler and running the risk of being rammed, for if he went by the wall he might be spotted by someone inside the docks.

Rose Angela was crying again, her cries jerking out of her with his running, and as he spoke to her a voice shouted through the fog, 'Why, Jimmy, is that you? Is that you, Jimmy? What's up?'

Although he recognised the voice, he did not stop, not even when he heard the uneven hop of Tony's run following him. But coming to the slipway, he paused and listened. There was no sound other than his own harsh breathing and the quiet whimpering of the child, so he judged that Tony had gone back to the fifteen streets; and as he ran down the narrow path leading to the water he felt a regret that he had not given Tony some last word, for he knew that the lad's liking for him was sincere.

There was no sculler tied to the wall at either side of the narrow slipway. He splashed frantically through the rim of the tide, feeling for one, but his hand encountered only the iron ring in the wall, and he cursed. There was nothing for it now but to climb the sawmill wall. Running up the path to the road again, he went more carefully, keeping to the grass verge to deaden his steps. Rose Angela was quiet now, as if asleep, and as he left the lane and came into the main road again the pale blur of the gas lamp showed him the slight figure of

Tony. He knew it was him before he heard the voice asking again, 'Is that you, Jimmy?'

'Yes, it's me!'

'What on earth's up?'

Between deep gulps of air James answered, 'I row with Matt. He dead. I got to get away, Tony.'

'Matt dead? My God!'

'I no mean to do it, Tony.'

'But, Jimmy, why've you got the bairn with you?'

'I take her with me . . . she mine.'

'You can't do that, man.'

'Yes, she go with me . . . she all mine.'

'But, Jimmy, what about Bridget?'

'Sh!'

They both stood silent, listening. The sound of pounding feet and shouting came through the fog, and James started to run again, with Tony hopping unevenly by his side.

'I get over sawmill wall to my ship.'

'You're mad, man, you'll never be able to get over that wall with the bairn. They'll be on you before you can do it.'

'You hand her to me . . . yes, you do that.'

'Listen, man, can't you hear them?'

James could hear them, and the voices were almost paralysing his legs. His body was wet with sweat, yet he was cold with the fear that penetrated to the core of him. He had seen black men collared before by angry whites.

'Jimmy, for God's sake don't get caught! If you keep running, they'll get you – if not here, at the docks. Look, I can't keep up . . . Jimmy, look, it's your last chance.' Tony grabbed at his arm. 'Drop down here beside the slack bank and let them get by, then you can make your way to the sawmill wall keeping under cover of the bank.'

Whether it was Tony's reasoning or his own fear that made him follow the boy's advice James didn't know, but he dropped down the bank and lay on his side, pressed close to the wet seaweed-tangled grass, with Tony lying alongside him and the child lying as still as death between them. James pressed Rose Angela's face close to his own, but she made no sound, seeming to know that his life depended on her silence.

The men were passing them now, calling to each other as they ran:

'The dock pollis will nab him.'

'The trams and roads'll be watched.'

'They'll get him. The bairn will be the finish of him, anyway, the black swine!'

The black swine . . . James stared into the chilling darkness. It didn't take long for a black man to jump from a damn good sort to a black swine . . . you were given no benefit of the doubt if you were a black man.

'You see? You can't go on the road, Jimmy. There'll likely be more coming as it gets round the streets. You'll have to keep under cover of the bank and get into the sawmill yard from the gut side; and you'll have to plodge into the mud and water for a way.'

James made no answer. He knew that Tony was right, and that that was the only means of escape now. But he could only get that way on his own; it would be impossible to take the child. He pressed her closer to him, and Tony, guessing his thoughts, whispered urgently, 'Jimmy, man, you can't take her. And anyway, you could never keep her on the ship, can't you see? Get away while the going's good. Go on, man, for God's sake don't let them catch you! Matt's not worth swinging for . . . he's bad, right through. I've been wanting to tell you for some time what he was doin', but I couldn't.'

After a space, during which only the lapping of the water could be heard, James's strangled whisper came through the grass to Tony. 'No comin' back, Tony – if I go without her, she forget me.'

'No she won't, Jimmy . . . I won't let her. I promise you, man. I'll tell her what a fine fellow you are. I promise on my oath, Jimmy. And when she's older perhaps there'll be some way of her comin' to you . . . I won't let her forget you, Jimmy, I won't, only for God's sake get away.'

As fresh footsteps passed above them Tony felt the quivering of James's body. He put his arms about the child and drew her from James's clinging hands. 'She'll be all right, Jimmy, as God's my honour. I'll see to her.'

'I come back, Tony . . . some time I come back.'

'All right, Jimmy, only go on now . . . hurry, man.'

As James's hand moved over his child's head Tony knew he was crying, and as he felt the Negro's hand pressing for a moment on his cap he turned his face into the grass to stifle his own emotion.

It was Rose Angela's whimpering, 'Da! I want me da,' that brought Tony up the bank and on to the road.

Not wishing to encounter anyone from the fifteen streets, he walked on the pathless side of the road, and in this way he brought Rose Angela home without being stopped.

There was a crowd around Bridget's door, silent, weird, misshapen bulks, all so intent on watching the stretcher being carried from the house to the vehicle standing in the road that they took no notice of Tony and the child. The sight of the workhouse ambulance puzzled him . . . why were they taking Matt away? Would they bring the ambulance just to take him to his mother's to be laid out? He felt not the slightest touch of sorrow for Matt being dead. In fact, as he made his way to the back door, he knew a great surge of relief that Matt would no longer be Bridget's evil genie.

When he entered the yard Kathie's shouting came to him. 'He'll swing, what's left of him when Sam Luck and the lads get hold of him; they'll leave the print of their hobnails on his face, God speed them, the murderin' swine!'

Tony pushed the open door wide and entered the kitchen. It was crowded with the McQueens, and Eva was crying noisily. Only Bridget was seated, and Tony noticed that the last vestige of the girl was gone. Drunk or sober, he would never see the girl Bridget again. She was a woman with the stamp of sorrow on her. She became blotted from his gaze as the family surged round him. 'In the name of God where'd ye find her? Have they got the swine?'

'Have they got him?'

In Mr McQueen's moderate tone Tony seemed to detect an odd anxiety, and as he pushed his way through them all to Bridget he answered, 'No, he was well on the road to Newcastle the last I saw of him.'

'Have you told the pollis?' screamed Kathie.

'No.'

'Then somebody off and tell them. The Newcastle road, go and tell them!' Kathie threw her order from one to the other, but no-one obeyed her . . . they were looking at Tony as he faced Bridget, who was standing now, leaning heavily on the table with one hand. The child was still clinging to him, and he said to Bridget, 'I promised Jimmy I'd look after her.'

'You what? Christ! Listen to him!' cried Kathie.

'Shut up yer mouth!' said Cavan.

Tony stared steadily at Bridget. He, too, in the past hour, seemed to have left his youth behind and become a man, so much so that he voiced his first and only criticism of Bridget. 'You can't blame Jimmy for this . . . you asked for it.'

Bridget's head drooped, and for a space there was an uncomfortable, startled quiet in the kitchen. But it was soon shattered by a squeal from Kathie. 'Blame him be damned! If my Matt dies it'll be a rope's end for him. As it is, when they get him he'll get ten years for what he's done. Blame him, the . . . !'

'What?' Tony swung round on her. 'He isn't dead, then?'

It was Mr McQueen who answered. 'It's touch and go; he may not last the night. We've got to go down in an hour or so. Terry's gone in the van. It was Mr Steel on his motor bike that got them here so quick. He brought the pollis back an' all.' Cavan stopped and looked about him with a helpless air. 'I'd better go and tell them we've got the bairn.'

Matt wasn't dead, then, and there was the chance he would go on living. Although Tony knew that Matt's survival had lifted the dread of hanging from Jimmy, at least for the present, a sense of disappointment enveloped him, and he experienced a feeling of shock that was not unmixed with horror when he realised that Mr McQueen felt the same with regard to his son.

As Bridget took the child from his arms he wondered why, loving her as he did, he did not mind her being married to a black man, yet had always hated the fact that she spent a moment alone with her brother. If Matt didn't die and Jimmy couldn't come back, what would happen? There would only be him to stand between Bridget and Matt. And he would stand. He was eighteen and he was no longer a boy. Matt laughed at him because he was skinny and had a limp; they all either laughed at him or were sorry for him; well, he would show them. He struck Kathie speechless for a moment by saying, 'You want to get yourselves all away home and let Bridget and the bairn get some rest.'

Eva let out a laugh, then checked it abruptly and stood for a time looking somewhat shamefaced, until Cavan said, 'He's right; come on. Some of us must go down to the hospital, anyway.' Then she said, more to herself then anyone else, 'Well I never did. What next!'

Kathie took up Eva's words. 'What next! Aye, God Almighty, I wonder what next!' She stood behind Tony and her wavering forearm told of her desire to 'land him one'. But Cavan said authoritatively, 'Come on, the lot of you . . . I'll see you later, lass.'

He went out, followed by Eva and her docile husband, but Kathie stood for a moment longer glaring at the uneven line of Tony's shoulder. Cavan's voice calling, 'D'ye hear, you?' broke the concentration of her gaze, and she swung up her coat from the chair and flung it about her, saying, 'Some people are getting too big for their boots and they'd better watch out.' Her voice broke as she remembered her trouble, and she went on, 'As if I hadn't enough to put up with, me lad bein' battered to death an' all, without ye trying to be cock o' the midden.' She went out, shouting warningly, 'I'll see ye later, me lad!'

As the door banged Bridget sat down again, holding the child tightly to her. She looked vacant, as if her mind was emptied of thought, and when Tony said gently, 'Put her to bed Bridget, and go yourself, and I'll bring you up a cup of tea and clear up here,' she looked up at him, saying, 'If they catch him before the pollis they'll beat him up.'

He took her elbow and raised her to her feet. 'Don't you worry, they won't catch him.'

As he led her to the stairs, she said, 'I can't go to bed, Tony, I'll get her to sleep and come down. And Tony' – the tears flooded her swollen eyes again – 'will you stay with me until I know?'

'As long as you want me, Bridget.'

He watched her going up the stairs, lifting one foot slowly after the other as if they were weighted, and he knew a queer feeling of possession. So surprising was it that it caused him to flush, and he turned sharply and started to clear the kitchen.

The McQueens had made no effort to straighten the upturned articles of furniture; even the broken crockery had been kicked under the dresser to make room for their feet. The fireplace was still a shambles, and for a moment Tony looked around helplessly, not knowing where to start. Then abruptly he took off his coat and hung it behind the door. The act of doing this made him pause, and his hand rested for a moment on the nail . . . his coat hanging behind Bridget's door! It held a significance.

In his wideawake dreams of the night he imagined wild, wild things, such as something happening to make Bridget lean on him. Lean on him! That was laughable and fantastic. He knew this in the daytime, but in the night it was feasible. He had even pictured himself doing just what he had done this minute . . . hang his coat up . . . for when a man hung his coat up in a house . . .

What was he thinking, when there was poor Jimmy running for his life! If they caught him he'd be gaoled; if they didn't catch him he would come back some day, as he said. So wasn't Bridget still married? Slowly he dropped on to his knees and started to clear the fireplace.

CHAPTER SIX

ROSE ANGELA

All the children in the class knew that Miss Flynn didn't like Rose Angela Paterson; and when Miss Flynn got at Rosie, all their attention would be riveted on Rosie's face. The would screw round from their various positions to watch her, and they would wonder if her eyes could possibly become any larger, and how long she could stare at Miss Flynn without blinking. A day seldom passed without their being entertained in some way; but today Miss Flynn had been at Rosie twice . . . this morning because she hadn't danced the way they all did, and this afternoon because one of her long jet-black plaits had come undone.

As Rosie stared at her teacher she knew that she must remain silent, for it was no use trying to answer the question of how she lost her ribbon; if she said, 'Ribbons won't stay on my hair,' Miss Flynn would say she was insolent. She had long since learned that silence was the best defence, although she knew she would be punished for this too.

'Come out here!' Miss Flynn's voice was as thin as her body; the combination of her prominent boned face and thinly-covered scalp had justifiably earned her the name of 'Scrag-end' among the children.

Even the motion of Rose Angela's walk was enough to arouse a deep feeling of resentment in Miss Flynn. As she watched the child thread her way among the desks towards her she wanted to dash at her and shake that quiet, maddening poise out of her. She did not question herself as to her reason for hating this child; consciously she told herself that the child was the outcome of a sinful union; she was a half-caste, and looked it, with that thick olive skin and those great eyes. She didn't need to have thick lips and a pug nose for anyone to see that her father was a black man. That's what came of sinning. All men were sinful. She was glad, oh God, she was glad, that never once in her life had she done anything wrong or impure; she had never been out with a man and she never wanted to. She stared down on Rosie and wet her lips, one over the other, as she arched the cane back and forward between her two hands . . . she'd knock some of the sin out of her.

'Hold your hand out!'

Rose Angela held out her hand, trying not to think that when the cane lashed her palm her heart would leap. She kept her eyes on the piece of cabbage fixed firmly between Miss Flynn's front teeth, but when the cane descended for the third time she closed her eyes tightly.

'Now perhaps you'll keep your hair plaited. No-one wants to see the length of your hair. If I had my way I'd cut the lot off and relieve you of your vanity.'

If a pair of scissors had been at hand at that moment, Miss Flynn would not have been accountable for her actions. Of all the things she disliked about the child she disliked her hair most of all. She also resented the fact that this half-caste, with a runaway bully of a Negro for a father and a mother who was a daily servant, should be cleaner and better dressed than the other children. But of course there was that other man – that cripple. He was, she understood, the mother's fancy piece. That's where the money came from to dress the child like this . . . oh, the sins of some people!

'Get yourself to confession tonight and ask God to forgive you for your pride, for the proud can never enter into the Kingdom of Heaven,' she threw at Rose Angela's unsteadily retreating figure; and she added, 'Your road to Heaven, in any case, is going to be long and thorny . . . if you ever get there.'

After this outburst Miss Flynn felt curiously better, and for the rest of the afternoon peace reigned; but the children's minds, as porous as sponges, absorbed the feeling Miss Flynn had given out, and when school was over four of the girls who were usually Rose Angela's travelling companions to and from the fifteen streets dashed away and left her.

Walking alone out of the school yard, the sadness that this wholesale desertion always created settled on her. Although she knew that tomorrow they would be pally with her again, she could never understand why Florrie Tyler, her best friend, should leave her and go with the others, when they hadn't quarrelled in any way. This had happened before. She found she was either with them all or she was standing alone, facing something that she could feel but as yet could not fathom.

Turning the corner of the school wall, she came face to face with her schoolmates. They had formed a blockade across the pavement, faces strained to keep from laughing, eyes wide and hands joined.

Janie Wilson, who lived next door to the McQueens, was the spokesman. 'We ain't goin' to let you play with us any more, are we?'

The other three shook their heads vigorously.

'An' we don't want a loan of your schoolbag. An' you can keep your Saturday penny and stick it, can't she?'

Again there was vigorous nodding of heads. Then in silence they waited for some response.

The quietness with which it came left them at a loss, and aggravated them more than any shouting would have done. 'All right, it doesn't matter.'

Rose Angela watched them as they formed a ring and whispered together; then, with one accord, they broke from each other and ran some way along the road before turning and shouting, 'Rosie Paterson, you'll never go to Heaven. Even if you get up there they won't let you in, 'cause you ain't white.'

The startled expression on Rosie's face amply repaid them for her previous lack of response, and Janie Wilson's voice came above the others. 'Miss Flynn's got it in for yer . . . you ain't white and you can go to confession, but you'll not get to Heaven. I asked me ma, and she said yer da was a blackie, and you'd never get into our Heaven. You'll go down' – she pointed her thumb violently towards the pavement – 'and be pitched into the fire.'

For a long time now it had seemed to Rose Angela that she had been gathering to herself different kinds of fear. There was the fear of going home and finding her ma crying, sometimes with her head on her arms on the kitchen table, sometimes lying across the bed upstairs. At these times the fear would paralyse her limbs and she would want to be sick. The fear would disappear if, as sometimes happened, her mother put her arms blindly about her and there was no smell of whisky from her.

Then there was the fear that Uncle Tony might die . . . that he would fall under a tram, or that on a dark night he would slip into the water of the slacks, for if anything happened to Uncle Tony who would she have to talk to? or, what was more important, listen to? What would happen if a Sunday should pass and he didn't take her for a walk and sit or stand at the same spot on the slack bank, and tell her what a grand man her da was and that she must never be ashamed of him, for one day he was coming back? She knew why they stood at the same spot, for when she stood there a voice, deep and thick and melodious, echoed through her mind, murmuring words that were only intelligible by the feeling of warmth they created in her.

Then there was that other fear, the fear that caused her to wake up, trembling and sweating, in the night, and cry for her mother, but being aware as she cried that her mother could lift this fear from her did she so wish, that hers was the power to say to Uncle Matt, 'Don't come into this house any more!' In her Uncle Matt Rose Angela saw her idea of the devil; the jet-black eyes in the white face, with one end of the long scar on his cheek pulling down the corner of his eye while the other end pulled up one side of his mouth, were terrifying to her. When her Uncle Matt stood looking at her without blinking she wanted to scream. She had done so once, and her mother turned on Matt, saying, 'Get out!' But he didn't go, he just stood with his head bent, muttering, 'That's it . . . you turn on me too. The lasses go in their back doors when they see me comin'. And who's to blame, eh? I didn't start this.' Matt's voice sounded to Rose Angela as if he were crying, but his eyes remained dry and hard. Her mother had sat down and beaten her fists slowly on the corner of the table . . . that had been terrifying too.

So because of her Uncle Matt Rose Angela had a great desire to qualify for Heaven, for in the other place there'd be a man like him. And now here was Janie Wilson saying that she wouldn't go to Heaven.

She stood still, watching the girls hitching and skipping into the distance, and, try as she might, she could not stop her tears. As they rained down her cheeks she reassured herself: she would get to Heaven – she'd be good and she would go to Heaven. She wouldn't miss Mass and she'd go to Communion every week. Jesus, Mary and Joseph, say she would get to Heaven . . . Her tears threatened to choke her. Why was everyone so nasty? Miss Flynn and the girls and Uncle Matt, and even Granma. What had she done? . . . She made her way with bowed head along the road. She'd go into church, it'd be quiet there and she would get over her crying. She couldn't go home like this.

In the empty church she knelt out of habit in her class pew, and endeavoured to pray. But as her thoughts, dwelling on Janie Wilson, would form no set prayer, she made a mental note that she must confess the sin of 'wilful distractions at prayers' when she next went to confession. She knelt until her knees ached and her head swam; but her tears had stopped, so she rose, genuflected towards the main altar where Christ stayed, and left the church.

She was standing in the porch blowing her nose when the door opened behind her, and Father Bailey came through. Startled, she looked at him, wondering where he had sprung from, for the church was empty. She dropped her head as he said, 'Hallo there, Rosie.'

'Hullo, Father.'

'Have you been paying a visit to the Blessed Sacrament?'

'Yes, Father.' She began to breathe more evenly; he hadn't heard her crying or he'd surely be saying something.

'That's a good girl. Always keep a devotion for the Blessed Sacrament and you won't go far wrong in life.' He placed his hand on her hair and felt its silkiness. 'By, it's beautiful hair that you have, Rosie; it has the sheen of the starling on it.'

Forgetting her tears, she gazed up into his round, red face and her heart swelled. It wasn't wrong to have nice hair then. Here was the priest saying it was nice . . . she wasn't sinful, then, as Miss Flynn made out, because she kept her hair nice. But what was the good of having nice hair if you were destined for Hell? Suddenly Rose Angela knew that she couldn't bear the indecision – to go on all tonight and all the morrow, and perhaps for ever, knowing she mightn't be going to Heaven was unbearable. But here, standing right before her, was Father Bailey, and if anyone could tell if she were going to Heaven he could . . . he could even send her there if he liked, for he knew so much about it.

'Father, could I ask you something?'

The pleading in her eyes that always affected the priest brought him a step nearer to her, and he whispered jocularly, 'Anything you like, Rosie. But mind, I'll charge you tuppence for it.'

A smile appeared for a moment on her face, but was gone again as she asked tentatively, 'Father, will they let me into the white Heaven?'

'The white what?'

'The white Heaven, Father.'

'Are you getting mixed up? You don't mean Heaven, surely. Are you meaning the public on the Cornwallis Road, The White Heather? Now what would you be wanting to get in there for, might I ask?'

'I do mean Heaven, Father . . . God's Heaven.'

The priest straightened his stubby figure and tugged at the bottom of his waistcoat with both hands. 'Now what makes you ask such a question? Of course you'll go to Heaven, providing you're a good girl.'

'But they said . . .'

'Who said?' he asked sternly.

She hung her head again. 'The girls said, Father . . . because me da was black I won't get into the . . . proper Heaven.'

The priest remained silent, staring at the bowed head of this eight-year-old child who was already feeling the weight of 'man's inhumanity to man'. The tears in the church were the forerunner of many she would shed. God help her. Although he smiled at her there was an unsteadiness in his voice as he said, 'Look at me, Rosie, for I have something to tell you. You're a very ignorant child, you know.' He shook his head with a hopeless gesture. 'Has no-one ever told you that God is colour-blind?'

'Colour-blind . . . ? No, Father.' Her eyes were stretched to their widest.

'Haven't they now? Are you quite sure?'

'Yes, Father . . . is he?'

'He is so . . . as blind as a bat where colour is concerned . . . of course, mind, he can make out the flowers, but not people; he doesn't know a black from a white, nor a yellow from a red . . . God help him.' Father Bailey threw back his head and laughed; and with a mixture of appreciation of his wit and profound relief Rosie joined him.

'Ah! Rosie' – Father Bailey wiped his eyes – 'the good Lord appreciates a joke, even against himself. Now away home you go. Good night and God Bless you.'

'Good night, Father.' Rose Angela paused in her turning from him. 'And I'll get in, Father?'

He patted her head gently. 'You'll get in, Rosie. You of all people, I should say, will get in. And remember what I've told you about God being colour-blind, for it's the truth – one of the great truths.'

'I will, Father – I'll always remember.'

'That's it. Now let me see you smile – you don't

smile enough. Ah, that's better. Now off you go.'
With a push he helped her on her way, and she ran
the whole distance home, her feet just skimming the
pavement, so light was her body with relief.

Arriving at the corner of the fifteen streets, she
again met Janie Wilson, accompanied by a new crony
this time. Janie had acquired a large slice of bread,
and she almost choked herself in gulping a mouthful
when Rose Angela, with a hitherto unheard of assurance, said, 'You were wrong, Janie Wilson, I will
get in, Father Bailey said so . . . so there!' And with
a lift of her head she was about to walk on when a
violent push landed her against the wall.

'Who're you settin' your old buck up to?' Janie's
face was purple with indignation and the dry bread
wedged in her gullet. 'Take that, you cheeky bitch.
And that!'

Rose Angela took the smacks on the face, and
instead of the blows, as usual, frightening her, they
aroused a strange exhilarating feeling in her, the
feeling of wanting to strike back. She knew she
could never hope to stand up to Janie, so she used
her schoolbag. With a swing of the long strap she
brought the bag in contact with the side of Janie's
head. The manoeuvre was very effective, for Janie
screamed and kept on screaming. Rose Angela did
not stop to enquire why she screamed, but ran off,
thinking, I'm glad I hit her . . . I'm glad . . . I'm
glad.

It was a strange feeling; never could she remember
standing up to anyone before. She had always been
aware that the other children made use of her, and
imposed on her; somehow she knew that because her

colour was not exactly like theirs she qualified for all the dirty work of their play. She always allowed them to make her the finder in 'Deady-one', and when broken bottles and jars and other glassware had to be smashed still further to provide the imaginary contents of sweetshops it was she who had to sit before a stone, with another in her hand, breaking the glass, often with bleeding fingers. They liked her when they could use her; and she hadn't minded being used, for it made them happy, and she wanted people to be happy and laughing. But now she was going to stick up for herself: she was as good as them. The priest had said so hadn't he? Well . . . he said she would get into the same heaven as them, and that was the same thing, wasn't it? But her mind refused to dwell on this point; it didn't matter, anyway. If anyone hit her again she would hit them back, and if Miss Flynn got at her she would say . . . What she would say to Miss Flynn she never told herself, for as she reached her back-yard door she heard her grandmother's voice, shouting as usual. It slowed her running to a walk, and she entered the house unsmiling and serious.

Her mother and Uncle Tony and her grandmother all turned and looked towards her. Rose Angela's eyes came to rest on Tony. Why, she had forgotten it was Wednesday and his half day – fancy forgetting that!

'Go on, stare at him!' her grandmother rapped out at her. 'Go on, worship him. If ever there was a mean sod in this world it's your Uncle Tony. But go on, stare at him and put him to shame.'

Rose Angela looked swiftly from one to the other.

Her mother was ironing at the table and didn't raise her head; her Uncle Tony was staring at her grandmother, and, as always when he was angry, his nose was twitching.

Kathie was sitting entirely obliterating a wooden armchair, and each movement of her body was creating still more bulges of flesh. Her eyes, nestling in two full pouches, fastened themselves on her grandchild, and she went on, 'What would ye say if I told ye yer Uncle Tony had come into a house and a fortune?'

'It's no fortune, I'm telling you, it's forty pounds.'

Kathie, dismissing Tony's protests with a wave of her hand, went on addressing herself to Rose Angela. 'What's forty pounds but a fortune in these times? And a house, mind, a grand house with six rooms. And an estate around it.'

'Oh my God!' Tony held his head. 'A bit of a garden . . . look here . . .'

'An estate, I said, with trees and flowers and vegetables – taties and cabbages an' everything an' all.' She thrust her finger into Rose Angela's chest. 'He could sell the house, and get God knows how much for it . . . but will he? Be God, no! And will he let us go there to live in it? Eh?' Her eyes rolled sideways to Tony, and he, using her full title as he had done from a child, cried, 'Look, Mrs McQueen! I'm going to have no more of it . . . I've told you . . . and don't keep on.'

'There we are, five grown-ups stuck in two bug-ridden boxes, and never a sight of a big tree for miles, as ye well know yerself, child. And him that I brought up and treated as me own refusing to give us house-room. I could understand him not jumping at Terry's scheme to start a grocery business, but to refuse us house-room, packed as we are . . . !'

'Well, I'll soon alter that!' cut in Tony. 'I can make one less any day.'

'That's it, threaten to walk out on us.' She turned her attention from Rose Angela. 'The fix I'm in, with only Matt workin', and him on half time, and not knowing where the next bite's coming from. That's gratitude for you.'

Although Kathie still shouted, her eyes were wide, and showing in them was anxiety. Tony saw it, and blamed himself, but, oh God, if she'd only give over! She would try the patience of a saint. Why, oh why, he asked himself, had he not moved at the end of the war when they were all working, and she had money to squander but never to save. He was heart-sick of sharing the same room with Matt and Terry and of eating with them all, for now there was Eva and her growing brood to share the table.

When he received the letter three weeks ago asking him to go to Denver's, the solicitor in King Street, and there being told that his mother's only sister, she who refused to have him as a boy, had died, leaving him the money and the house, his first thoughts were, I don't want anything of hers, the upstart; she would have let me go into the workhouse! On reflection, however, he saw that this could be an answer to his unspoken prayers. Hadn't he longed for enough money to buy a special boot? Time and again he had saved the few pounds that would be necessary, only to hand them to Kathie 'just as a loan' to pay the rent, or the coals, or the tally man, or, more recently, to buy food. When asking for fresh loans, Kathie's conscience never seemed to trouble her about the dozens of unpaid ones, and Tony had come to think that all his life he would have to pay for her past kindness to him. But with regard to the unexpected legacy he was standing firm. When he had bought his boot, and perhaps a suit of clothes, and rigged Rosie out, then he'd see to Mrs McQueen, but he'd be damned if he was going to let her get her hands on the whole of the money. He knew what it would mean – a grand bust-up to show off to the neighbours, clothes for them all . . . so that when the money was gone there'd be plenty to pawn!

Kathie was still talking, addressing her remarks once again to Rose Angela . . . How wonderful it would be not to hear her voice ever again . . . Well, the choice was his . . . he had a house now, all his own, packed with good furniture and linen, and a little garden, the like he had not even dreamed of. He could go there and live, there was nothing to stop him. Of course it would be a long way to travel to the shop, right from High Jarrow to yon side of Harton village, but he would soon get used to that.

He stared at Bridget's hands moving the iron back and forward, back and forward, into the gatherings of Rose Angela's dress . . . What was he thinking about? Why was he playing games with himself? He could no more leave the vicinity of Bridget than he could walk without limping. There was only one way he could live in that house, and that dream was as impossible as . . . He was recalled sharply to Kathie again.

'Yer Uncle Tony thinks the world of ye. Then why

don't he let ye and yer ma rent his fine house; and then she can let us have this un.'

Bridget, putting her iron quietly down, looked at her mother. 'I've told you before, Ma, I'm not leaving this house.'

'No.' Kathie jumped up with surprising agility. 'Ye're as mean a swine as he is. Four rooms for ye and the bairn . . . ye could let us share this and we'd all have lived as happy as larks. But no. What ye keeping it for, may I ask? Hopin' for yer black man to come back? Well, God speed him to ye! And it's meself that'll escort him to clink, and make sure that he gets ten years for making my lad look like a beast . . . As for you' – Kathie turned her venom on Tony – 'standing there like a weakly bull gaping at a cow – whatever ye're keeping yer house for, remember . . . what God has joined together let no man put asunder . . . she's married till she knows the nigger's dead!' The door banged and she was gone.

After a moment of surprised silence Tony hopped for the door, crying, 'She's not getting off with that!'

But Bridget checked him, her voice quiet and even. 'It's no use, Tony, the less said the better.'

He turned to her, his face scarlet, and Bridget, picking a fresh iron from the heart of the fire, spoke to Rose Angela, 'Go upstairs and change your pinny and wash yourself up there . . . there's water in the jug in my room. And your tea'll be ready in a minute or so.'

Without a word Rose Angela went upstairs; and Bridget, testing the iron by holding it near her face, said, 'Don't worry, Tony; you know my mother doesn't mean half what she says . . . she never stops to think.'

He stood watching her across the table. He was as tall as her if he supported himself on the toe of his short leg, and now he wanted every centimetre of his height. He squared his shoulders to give him breadth. In the next few minutes she must see him as other men. He said slowly, 'She did mean it, she's not blind . . . I supposed nobody is blind enough not to notice how I feel about you, Bridget.'

There, it was out; and with the voicing of what seemed to him the feelings of a thousand lifetimes his courage grew. 'She was right. Your mother's no fool; she knows that the only one who'll get that house will be you and the bairn.'

'Tony!' Bridget stopped moving the iron. Her calmness was probed and her face now showed her concern. 'Don't be silly; you're no longer a boy!'

'I'm glad you've noticed that, anyway.'

She flicked her head impatiently. 'Well, act like a man and have some sense . . . Look, Tony; use that house, and use it now. It's a gift from God. Don't sell it.' She leant across the table towards him. 'Tony, there's Molly Cullen; she's a nice girl and she dotes on you. Now here's your chance. Be sensible, and get away from here. Molly's a cut above the rest; she'll live up to Harton, given the chance, and . . .'

He waved his hand at her. 'Bridget, save your breath, there'll be no Molly Cullen nor anybody else for me, and you know it.'

'And you know nothing can come of this' – her voice was harsh – 'so why do you keep on? If you think I'll go and live with you in your house . . .'

'Who asked you? There'll be plenty of time to refuse me when I ask you. I'm offering you the house, with no tags to it.'

As they stared at each other, the look in her eyes and the excited churning of his stomach told him that at least she regarded him as a man.

Bridget resumed her ironing again. 'Have you forgotten Jimmy?' she asked quietly.

'No.'

'And you still believe what you've told her for years?' She indicated the stairs with a nod.

There was a slight pause before he answered, 'I used to; but now I don't know . . . Bridget, look at me . . . If there wasn't Jimmy, would you have me?'

She remained silent, her eyes fixed on his.

'Answer me.'

'I don't know . . . I've never looked at it that way, because . . . Anyway, I'm so much older than you. Oh, it's all so mad. Don't let's start any of that talk. All I want is peace and quiet; I've had enough.' She turned abruptly away from him and the table.

'Listen here!' His voice compelled her to stop. 'You've got to look at it that way! Jimmy might come back the morrow, and he mightn't come back for years . . . or never; but one way or the other I've got to know how you feel. Do you want Jimmy to come back?'

The direct question startled her, and she stood gripping the rod and staring at the maker's name on the iron front of the fireplace: Greave & Gillespie, Jarrow-on-Tyne. Over the years the blackleaded words had formed a focus point for her thinking. Did she want James to come back? At times, yes. At times she longed for him, and had she known where he was she would have gone to him. But when these times passed she knew that the longing had been mainly of the body; most of the time her mind was filled with recrimination of herself for the trouble her folly had wrought. Father O'Malley foretold that retribution would fall on her for making such a marriage. It had fallen, and was still falling. Each day she paid. At first it was the stigma of the colour; but when James removed that with his flight he saddled her for life with Matt, with his twisted face and mind.

The first sight of Matt's face and the knowledge that his hold on her was greater than ever had made her resort again to the refuge of the bottle. But half a dozen glasses of whisky were not enough to shut out all her trials and to give her a brief feeling of gaiety; whereas before, two had done so. Rather, the effect of the whisky was to accentuate her troubles. But even though she knew its numbing effect was gone, she still retained the desire to drink. The habit was strong, and it needed an independent fight to conquer it. And only during the past few months had she known any real respite. She had never blamed Matt for making her drink, for it was her belief that no-one could make you do anything you didn't want to do. And because of this opinion, she had also pointed out to herself time and again that some part of her must have wanted James enough to have married him. The only question she had been unable to answer was: would she have done so if she hadn't been afraid of having a baby? . . . And likely as not in the workhouse, for she would never have come home.

And now Tony was asking did she want James back. If it would mean living quietly, as they had done during the first few months of their marriage, yes – even if it meant bearing the stigma of his colour again. But should he come back, her mother and Matt would see that his liberty was short; and knowing he was in jail would be worse than not knowing where he was . . . But she must not go on thinking of James, she must answer Tony. If she said she wanted James back, would Tony go away? She turned quickly and looked at him, as if to assure herself that he was still there, and in a revealing moment she knew that life without him would become unbearable. Up till now she had not known how much she relied on him, on his kindness and his patient devotion and steadfastness; and on the buffer he made of himself and placed between her and Matt. And in this moment, too, she realised that the feeling he bore her was no ordinary one; it had stood the iron test of witnessing her maudlin drunk. Her head drooped at the thought. Not once had he seen her drunk but many times, and yet here he was offering her his house, and all he was asking in return was to know she cared for him. If need of him meant caring, then she realised he was her life. For the first time she saw him, not as Tony, the boy, but as a man who loved her. She looked at his deep-set eyes, at his mop of light-brown hair, which seemed too weighty for the delicacy of his face, at the uneven slope of his shoulders that did not mar his bearing but lent to it an air of nonchalance, and she wished from the depths of her being that they had been of the same age. Then, in spite of Matt, she might never have left home; for at this moment she knew it would have been an easy thing to love Tony. But now it must not come about, it was too late. She had made her bed and she must lie on it alone; she must not drag him into the mire of her life. He must get away from the fifteen streets and all that they stood for. If he could not see Molly Cullen now as a mate, perhaps he would later, or find someone else; but under no circumstances must he remain invisibly tied to her. At least she would do this decent thing.

She watched the pain come into his eyes as she said harshly, 'Isn't it natural I should want him back? I married him, didn't I?'

She returned to the table and proceeded to force out the creases from her blouse with a partly cold iron, knowing that his eyes were on her.

'It's all right, Bridget, it makes no difference' – the quietness of his voice brought a smarting to her eyes – 'the offer still stands. If you don't take the house, it'll stay there. I'm not selling it – nor living in it.' He turned towards the door. 'Tell Rosie I'll be round for her after tea.'

She could not restrain her tears as she watched him limping down the yard. She was filled with relief, while at the same time despising herself. He wasn't going . . . he wouldn't go, no matter what she said. Oh, it was wrong, all wrong, but – oh God – she was thankful that he felt as he did. He was like an anchor to which she could tie herself to stop the drift towards drink and, she sometimes thought, towards madness.

Rose Angela came quietly into the kitchen. 'Has Uncle Tony gone?'

'He's coming back for you after tea . . . I won't be a minute, I'll just finish this. The kettle's boiling.'

Rose Angela stood looking at her mother. She saw that Bridget had been crying; but it hadn't been the kind of crying that was caused by the whisky bottle, so she was filled not with fear and revulsion but with a feeling of blinding love, which caused her to go to Bridget and shyly put her arms about her waist. As she hid her face under her mother's breast Bridget slowly placed the iron on the flat tin lid. The feeling from her child seeped into her, and, putting her arm about Rose Angela, she said gently, 'What is it, hinny?'

Rose Angela moved her face against her mother, and the action was so like that of James that Bridget took a deep breath to steady herself.

'It doesn't matter if we don't go and live in Uncle Tony's house . . . I love you . . . I love you, Ma.'

Bridget pressed the child to her. Her emotion, a mixture of remorse for having withheld her love from this child and the tenderness now flooding her, was almost unbearable. She was searching in her tear-flooded mind for appropriate words to express this tenderness when a commotion in the back yard caused her to push Rose Angela from her.

From between the curtains she could see Sarah Wilson striding up the yard, dragging her Janie with her. She knew that Sarah Wilson was no friend of hers, and now her raucous voice, louder than usual, was proclaiming that something was wrong. But what, and why was she coming here?

Bridget did not move towards the door but hastily dried her eyes and stood waiting until Sarah, peering into the kitchen between the gap in the curtains, called, 'You there, Mrs Paterson?'

Mrs Paterson! Something was wrong . . . only when you were in the black books did you receive your full title. Bridget opened the kitchen door, saying 'What is it? What's wrong?'

'What's wrong? Ah, ye might well ask. Here' – she pulled the straining Janie towards her – 'hev a look at this.' She tried to force Janie's hand, which was holding a bloodstained cloth, away from her face, but Janie cried, 'Aw, don't Ma . . . don't; it'll bleed again.'

'Take yer blasted hand away and let her see!'

'Don't shout like that, Mrs. Wilson!' Now Bridget was on her dignity. 'Come inside if it's got anything to do with me.'

'Don't shout!' cried Sarah, pushing Janie into the kitchen. 'Don't shout! Wouldn't you shout if yer bairn's eye was nearly put out?'

'But how . . . ?' began Bridget in perplexity.

'Aye, how? By that 'un there.' She pointed to Rose Angela, whose face was almost comical in its amazement.

'Rosie?'

'Aye – Ro-see.' There was definite mimicry in Sarah's tone. 'Let her see.' She tore her daughter's hand down, and Bridget saw an ugly cut about half an inch long to the side of Janie's cheek-bone.

She looked from Janie to Rose Angela. The child was staring in horror at Janie's face. 'Did you do that?'

Rose Angela shook her head slowly, and Janie cried, 'Yes you did. You did it with your schoolbag.'

'Aye, with her schoolbag,' added her mother. 'She can't fight with her hands, like other bairns.'

As Bridget stared in amazement at Rose Angela, whose meekness was sometimes a source of irritation to her, she was conscious of the back door opening, but she didn't turn round. The whole incident so bewildered her that she just stood staring at her daughter and listening to Sarah.

'She used the buckle side deliberately, didn't she?'

Janie nodded at her mother. 'And what's going to be done about it? That's what I want to know. Marked for life, my bairn'll be, all through that one's wickedness . . . through her not having proper control. Spoilt, that's what she is, decked up to the nines . . .'

'That's got nothing to do with you, Mrs Wilson.'

'Ain't it? Ain't it though? If she wasn't spoilt, this wouldn't have happened. Wild she is, and dangerous, like him that was her da was.'

'You never said a truer word.'

Bridget swung round to find Matt surveying them from the doorway.

'Aye, you've had some of it. Look at my bairn's face, Matt.' Janie's face was turned up for Matt's inspection, and from it Matt's eyes travelled to Rose Angela, and their expression needed no translation. The hate was plain for all to see, so much so that Sarah said, 'Aye, well, it's enough to make anyone turn on their own kith and kin what you've had, lad. But it should be knocked out of her before it gets any worse. That's all I say, Matt, it should be knocked out of her.'

Matt, with his eyes still riveted upon Rose Angela,

muttered, 'Aye, it should be knocked out of her.'

'If there's any chastising to do, I'll do it.' The sharpness of Bridget's tone brought Matt's gaze away from the shrinking child.

'Aye, you will, like hell,' he said. 'Soft as clarts you are with her, because she puts on her mealy-mouth to you – butter wouldn't melt in it, but I know her; I've watched her outside. This doesn't surprise me' – he pointed to Janie's face – 'I've seen it coming.' His voice gathering deep in his throat, he went on, 'For two pins I'd take the buckle-end of me belt . . .' His hand moved as he spoke to his trousers.

'Just you try it and you'll see who'll get the belt,' cried Bridget, blocking Rose Angela from Matt's sight by standing in front of her. 'And now clear out, the lot of you. And Mrs Wilson, if you take Janie to the doctor right away he'll put a stitch in it, and I'll pay – it'll heal all right if it's done now.'

'Aye, it'll heal . . . like this.' Matt slapped his distorted cheek with his palm.

'Get out, I've told you!' Bridget's eyes blazed at her brother.

Mrs Wilson went out, pushing Janie before her, crying, 'You haven't heard the last of it, by a long chalk.'

Matt, pausing at the door, spoke with chilling quietness, 'The buck nigger will never be dead as long as she's alive, and I hope she lives long enough to pay for this.' He again slapped his face. 'And she will pay, and with her physog too. I'll fix her one of these days so she won't mark anyone else.'

He was gone, and the kitchen was filled with dark premonition. It chilled Bridget, turning her faint and weak. She looked at Rose Angela. The child was leaning against the wall, and her face, pallid with stark terror, seemed more beautiful than ever before. She was too beautiful, Bridget thought – such looks brought nothing but trouble. And it was her face that enraged Matt – it always had – and given half a chance he would destroy it. My God! If he did anything to spoil the bairn's face! As if his intention was imminent, she pulled Rose Angela to her, and held her tightly, saying, 'It's all right, don't be frightened – your Uncle Matt won't do anything. Why did you hit Janie Wilson?'

She could feel the tenseness sinking out of Rose Angela's slight body while she waited for an answer. And when it came, it was in whispered gasps. 'Janie slapped my face, 'cause I told her I'd get to Heaven. She said I wouldn't 'cause . . . 'cause my da's a nigger. And I asked Father Bailey and he said I would . . . 'cause God's colour-blind, he said.'

Bridget's arms became stiff, and her eyes, staring at James's fretwork pipe-rack on the wall, were fixed in their pity.

'I didn't mean to hurt her . . . I just swung my bag at her . . . Ma! . . . Oh, Ma!'

'Sh! Sh! don't cry, hinny.'

'Ma, will Uncle Matt—' She was stiffening again.

'No, no.'

'But he said . . .'

'Sh . . . I'll not let him. Don't worry, don't cry.' As Bridget's arms tightened around the sobbing child she knew that only constant vigilance would save her from Matt's hands.

She had always known that there was something

odd about Matt. When she was a girl she had been able to ignore it for long spells during which he was 'just like any of them', but when unintentionally she aroused his anger by laughing or joking with one of the lads she would be brought into painful awareness of the oddity. Even when, her own rage aroused, she was fighting him, she would be wondering all the time why he should be like this. She knew no other brother who treated his sister as he did her – sisters generally came in for scorn and derision.

She had expected her marriage to alienate him from her; but it hadn't, and the result was his twisted face. Nor did this, contrary to what she had imagined, direct his bitterness towards her. Instead, he used the disfigurement to bind her to him, to draw on the affection he could get in no other way. That he hadn't vented his venom and bitterness on her wasn't, she knew, because he didn't feel bitter; she was only too well aware that every fibre of his being was corroded with bitterness. It was towards the child that it was directed, and it always would be. Bridget, looking ahead down the succession of coming years, realised that she would always have to watch Matt in order to protect the bairn, just as her da and Tony watched him to protect her.

PART THREE

CHAPTER SEVEN

THE WORKLESS

The cancer of unemployment was eating the country, and the Tyneside in particular. It was eating into initiative and hope, and doubling despair. A man, becoming unemployed, went on the dole; and he would sign on each day before vainly doing the round of the shipyards. And in the evening he would stand at the corner with his pals, who were in the same predicament as himself, and they would hide their feelings in jokes. If he lay in bed at night and wondered what was to become of him and the wife and bairns once the dole was finished, he gave little sign of it during the day.

It is said that man can get used to any condition if he is in it long enough, and it would seem there was truth in this, for, as the years went on and the dole bred the Means Test, most of the men on the Tyne had forgotten how it felt to carry a bait tin – in fact they doubted whether there had ever been a time in their lives when they had worked. The younger men didn't have to wonder about this; those born just prior to or during the 1914 war never knew what it was to be employed. Even those apprenticed to the few small firms still in existence were stood off immediately they reached the age of nineteen.

It was strange, too, how stark poverty changed the flavour of the jokes from sex to food.

'Well, I'm off for me dinner.'

'What's it the day, lad?'

'Chicken.'

'Chicken agin?'

'Aye . . . I'm so bloody full of chicken I've got the urge to gan an' sit on a clutch of eggs.'

And so it went on. Here and there a man suddenly ended the struggle, and the effect on his mates, oddly enough, was such as to stiffen their fibre. 'It's no use taking things like that,' would be their attitude; 'things can't get any worse; the bloody Government will have to do something if they don't want trouble. Hang on a bit longer.'

There were protests, mass meetings, matches, but no perceptible change. In many houses the furniture was sold bit by bit, until only the table and mattresses remained. The sight of the bairns standing around the table to their meagre food hurt a man, but when the wife sat on the boards to feed the youngest, blazing anger would fill him; and so there would be more shouting at meetings, more protests. But even anger cannot be sustained on an empty stomach, and it would fade, except in the case of the few, in whom injustice burned as a fuel. These carried the fight in London – even to 10 Downing Street itself; but their sincere cries were lost in the noise of the rabble they gathered to themselves on the march.

The slump had long been with the McQueens – Cavan's last full week's work was in 1922, and his last work of all in 1926. Terence, too, had early joined the band of unemployed. Only Matt found work, odd days here and there. The McQueens seemed to think that Matt would always have work, however small . . . for life owed him this. But latterly, even Matt had failed to achieve even a day a week; and now Tony was the only one to go out at a regular hour.

Although most shops sported a sign 'No more credit given' and the windows showed more and more empty cartons, Mr Crawley's two shops still managed to keep their heads above water. Tony for some years now had been managing the second business, a small one-windowed shop in a side-street, and the fact that he was in the glorified position of manager and had never been out of work, added to which he was receiving the great sum of ten shillings per week rent for his house, surrounded him with an atmosphere of unwilling respect and thinly veiled resentment. If he had not been the asset that kept the wolf from the door, Kathie's spleen and Matt's venom, together with Terence's jealousy, would have been openly hurled at him. Only Cavan was grateful to him. It infuriated Kathie to know that for years now Tony had stayed in her house because, by doing so, he was helping Bridget . . . He'd had the nerve to tell her he'd cut down the extra five shillings he had been giving her each week if she sponged on Bridget. Sometimes Kathie thought she hated Tony worse than she had the nigger . . . for, give the devil his due, the nigger had been good for a few bob or so every trip, with no conditions attached.

And another infuriating thing was that her daughter Bridget, her that had been the apple of her eye, her who she had brought up like a lady, had withdrawn herself from them all during the years. Only Cavan seemed welcome in her house . . . and, of course, her fancy man. It was the desire of Kathie's heart to hurl this latter accusation at Bridget, but fear of the consequences kept her tongue in her cheek. If Tony should go, God knew how she would manage. As it was, with such a lodger, she appeared to be in comfortable circumstances compared with those of her neighbours, and to shine in any way helped to make life bearable. It was good to be able to say to Jane Cullen, next door, 'It's a stone of flour I'm after bakin', and two dozen fresh herrin's I've got in the oven this minute. Oh, it's a tea they'll have the night,' for it gave her a queer sense of satisfaction to see Jane unconsciously moving her tongue over her blue lips whenever food was mentioned. On baking days she would open her back door and window wide to allow the smell to waft into the Cullens' hungry house.

The Cullens were meek, and Kathie despised them. Most of all did she despise Mollie, who had grown hollow-eyed and grey-faced waiting for Tony to take up with her. At this moment Kathie was thinking of the Cullens as she banged her oven door on a shelf of baking potatoes . . . 'Gutless lot!' There were the scrap-ends of bacon Tony had brought home at dinner-time to be fried; she'd kick up such a stink of food that the smell would knock them all out.

Phew, it was hot! As she wiped the sweat from her neck with the oven rag Eva's youngest boy called through the open door, 'Grannie, Rosie's home. She's got her case an' all.'

'What?' Kathie swung round on the boy. 'When?'

'Just now.'

'My God, she's lost her job again.' Kathie turned abruptly to Cavan, who was sitting on the edge of the bed and peering over the top of a pair of wire rimmed spectacles at the boy.

He closed the book he was reading and asked quietly, 'Are you sure?'

'Aye, I am – she give me a ha'penny.'

Taking off the spectacles, Cavan placed them in an old black case, and put them in his waistcoat pocket.

As he slowly took his coat from the back of the door Kathie said, 'Three weeks she's been in that job . . . my God!' and as he went out of the door she called after him, 'Mind, if she gives you owt, you stump up.'

Cavan threw an angry glance back at her, but said nothing. He turned into the back lane, dusting the front of his greasy coat as he went. What was it this time? It couldn't be the same thing again . . . surely to God not. What was the lass going to do? If only she could get married or something. But there would be small chance round here – the fellows would be willing enough, God knew, but their mothers and sisters wouldn't be. It wasn't only the bit of colour in her that turned the women upon her, but something else – what, he didn't know – he couldn't lay a finger on it – it wouldn't go into words. Was it the proud way she walked that maddened them? or the quietness of her? or her voice, so like her father's, him that must be dead these many years? or was it her face? Aye, it was likely her face, for it did something to men, particularly married ones.

How many times had she been given a week's money in advance and sent packing? He had lost count. And it was bad that she should be out of work at this time, too, with Bridget off an' all. He doubted whether he'd come in for anything at all the night. She was always liberal with her bit pocket-money – rarely did she see him without slipping a sixpence into his hand. And he always made the same protest, 'No . . . no, lass, ye've got little enough'; but she would smile and say, 'Get yourself a bit baccy, Granda.' Aye, she was good; both her and Bridget – his pipe would have cracked many times during the past years had it not been for them. It was strange, he thought, that he felt no humiliation in taking from either of them, yet if Kathie threw him tuppence his stomach bridled.

Funny what life did to you; funny how people changed. Time and things that happened made you change. And many things had happened to him during the past ten years. But more so during the past two; for who would have thought the desire to work would go completely from him, that it would be sent packing by this other strange desire that filled him?

He walked slowly, taking the long way round to Dunstable Street . . . He was sixty-two, and it was only during these last two years of abject poverty that he had become aware of living. It happened in an odd way, so odd that he trembled when he thought that but for a fight about St Patrick's nationality, and being laughed into spending his last threepence on buying a hundred books that he didn't want, he would never have known this new world.

He remembered the night that Kathie bullied him into making a barrow out of a soap box and a couple of old bicycle wheels so that he should go to the tip and pick cinders. The barrow would hold twice as much as a sack, and he had been given the ultimatum of picking more cinders or going without food, for she couldn't buy both coal and food. His protest that the tip ripped the soles from his boots brought the retort from Kathie that he wrap old sacking about his feet and leave his boots at home. He had done this, but, like a great number of other men, not until it was dark.

Part of the tip burned continuously, and this saved many of the men from their death, for in the chill, often mist-ridden dawns they would huddle together as near the blazing parts as was safe. It was during one such dawn that the row began. A big Irishman was expounding, half in fun and whole in earnest, on the merits of being Irish, when a quiet voice from among a little group of men said, 'If it's such a grand country, why don't you go back there?'

'By me patron saint! Are ye meanin' to be insultin'?' the Irishman had demanded.

'Not necessarily,' went on the voice, 'but it's odd that you lot who are so bigoted about your country couldn't pick an Irishman for your saint.'

'What! In the name of God what is St Patrick but the most Irish of the Irish?'

'English . . . St Patrick was English.'

That did it. The men had all their work cut out

to keep the Irishman from throwing the man into the blazing tip. When the row subsided, Cavan, taking up his barrow, urged the young fellow to leave and come along with him.

Half-way home Cavan burst out laughing. 'It was funny the way you got him on the raw, joking about St Patrick being English.'

'I wasn't joking – he is.'

'You're funning.'

'No, not a bit of it – he was English, all right.'

'How do you know?'

'Oh, I read it.'

'Well, you can't believe all you read. Was it in the paper?'

'No, of course not.'

They went on pushing their barrows; and Cavan looked through the drizzle of rain at this young fellow, tousle-haired, dirty and thin, as they all were, whose calm assurance was making even him have his doubts as to St Patrick's nationality. But he felt he must warn the lad of making it an open statement, particularly around these quarters.

'I shouldn't repeat it too often, lad.'

'Why not?'

'Oh well, you know.'

'Aye, I know . . . for the same reason that folk don't like to remember that Christ was a Jew. They like to think he was an Englishman, or God, which amounts to the same thing with some of the bloody church-going lot.'

Cavan was aghast. 'But why, man, he was God!'

'All right, if you think so. He may be to you, but he isn't to me; nor is he to two-thirds of the world.

I think he was the greatest man who has yet lived, but I don't think he was God.'

Cavan stopped pushing his barrow.

'You serious, lad?'

'Yes, why shouldn't I be?'

The positive tone silenced further questioning. Cavan had never heard anyone talk like this.

It wasn't until Cavan was leaving him to continue his journey alone to Jarrow that the young fellow said, 'Do you read much?'

Cavan rubbed his sleeve across his face. 'Not in my line, lad. Although, mind' – he gave a superior nod – 'I've got some books – stacks of them – nigh on fifty. There was nearly a hundred, but the wife stuffed some up the wash-house flue.'

The young fellow put the handles of his barrow down on to the road. 'What kind of books?'

'Oh, all kinds; some in foreign tongues; but some of the English ones are as bad – I can't make head or tail of them. Some are about science and some are about the Middle Ages. Some've got one pound marked on 'em. Fools and their money, I say. They all belonged to an old wife who died, by the name of Peggy Flaherty. The bums sold up the house to meet the back rent, and I went along 'cause I'd now't better to do, an' when they put the books up, just for a lark I said threepence . . . and be hanged, I got them. Laugh – the place was razed. And there was me and all the bairns in the neighbourhood carrying the books home in a long procession, and Kathie raised Cain and made me dump them in the wash-house. Still they've come in handy.'

'Can I see them?'

'Why, aye, lad.'

And that had been the beginning. Ted Grant saw the books and convinced Cavan of their value, not in money but in knowledge. He was absurdly grateful for the dozen that Cavan gave him, and he persuaded Cavan to take the rest into the house, which he did, and stacked them under the bed; and so impressed was he by Ted's praise of them that he threatened to annihilate Kathie if she stuffed any more of them up the flue.

Ted was a married man, with three children all under six. He was also an embittered man, because, having won a scholarship to the High School, his parents were forced by circumstances to take him away at fifteen. He was further embittered through having been so weak as to marry while on the dole, for he became dependent on his wife. He was still dependent on her, for she went out to work, leaving him to see to the house and the children. His trek to the tip was made mostly from choice, for it helped him to keep his self-respect – he was doing work of a sort, and among men.

Cavan's conversion to reading seemed to happen overnight. From Ted Grant, who was young enough to be his son, he learned, sitting half the night listening to him, being guided by him, step by step, until now he could read his own books with understanding. And there was rarely a day passed but he did not quote his tutor's words to the joking yet admiring men at the corner, 'They can starve your bellies, but only you can starve your mind.' So although there was little or no prospect of work for Cavan in the next few years, after which he would be really too old to bother, there were times now when the thought of sudden prosperity, returning life to its normal routine of the war years, was actually frightening to him. He wanted nothing to interfere with the orderliness of his days and nights – his sitting on the tip, except in very severe weather, from ten at night till five or six in the morning, his sleeping for six hours, and the rest of the day being taken up with his reading and keeping his eye on Matt. The only part of his present life which he resented was this trailing of his son – this casual shadowing of Matt whenever he thought he was making his way to Bridget, and his sitting in Bridget's kitchen in his endeavour to outstay Matt – wasting precious hours of his reading time in shielding Bridget from . . . From what was he trying to shield Bridget? Cavan had never put it into words; but the feeling that he was preventing something happening never left him; and it was being strengthened as he watched his son's face becoming even more twisted, and his step losing its spring and beginning to slither, and his fingers plucking the front of his coat. This last habit was a recent addition to his queerness. Cavan noticed it first when Matt, Bridget and he were in the kitchen, and Rosie unexpectedly came in. Matt, his black, gimlet eyes fixed on the girl, who never looked at him if she could help it, began to pluck his coat like a woman plucking a hen.

Cavan began to dread the times when Rosie would be at home. It was one thing keeping his eye on Matt where Bridget was concerned, but he felt utterly inadequate to stand between Rosie, the girl, or the woman as she now was, and Matt. He had formed one point of the protective triangle in which she had stood as a child, the other points being Bridget and Tony; but as soon as she went into service the triangle became useless. And now here she was home again. He turned into Dunstable Street's back lane and into the house, and found Bridget alone in the kitchen.

'Well, lass?'

He took off his cap and hung it on the knob of the chair.

'She's back again.'

'Aye, I heard.'

'Somebody's been quick.' Bridget's tone was sharp.

'It was Johnnie.'

'It isn't her fault.'

'I never said it was, lass.'

Bridget doubled her fists and beat her knuckles together, betraying her worry. She stood gazing unseeingly out of the kitchen window, and as Cavan looked at her straight back he felt a stirring of pride that he, a little shrimp of a man, was father to such a fine, upstanding figure as Bridget. Here she was, on forty, with no grey hairs and a body as straight as a die. The only part of her showing the stamp of her trials was her face, which had a stiffness about it that at times he likened to enamel. He cleared his throat and spat into the fire.

'It's no use taking on, lass.'

'But this is the third place she's had in two months.' She swung round and faced him. 'Why in God's name can't they leave her alone?'

Cavan rasped his hand across his chin, and gazed down on his boots so covered with patches that there was no sign of the originals left.

'And she hasn't given her a reference.'

Cavan's head jerked up. 'That's bad . . . what'll she do?' Bridget turned to the window again, saying, 'God knows . . . where can she get without a reference?'

In the silence of the kitchen Cavan sat pulling his lower lip in and out between his finger and thumb; and when Bridget turned from the window and thumped the kettle on to the fire he said, 'Don't worry, lass, something'll turn up – she'll drop into a good place one of these days.'

'Where?' asked Bridget harshly. 'Oh, I could kill them all!' She ground the kettle into the cinders . . .

Upstairs, Rose Angela, too, asked herself where she could go now – no decent mistress would take her without a reference. She sat on the side of the bed and looked at the reflection of her face in the little mirror of the dressing-table, and not for the first time she told herself how she hated that face – it had brought her nothing but misery. The brown of the eyes, in the depth of which lay the pain and mystery of her father's race, were deepened still further by the sweep of the long, black lashes, which shadowed the skin until it reached the cheek-bones, changing its colour from a creamy tint to that of deep olive.

It was this face which laid her open to men like Mr Spalding – oh, Mr Spalding and his hands – she shuddered and closed her eyes – waking her up in the night, moving over her in the dark. She had wanted to scream, but she knew it would bring his wife, so

553

she had pleaded, 'Leave me alone . . . please leave me alone.' But she did scream; even with his hand over her mouth she screamed. But apparently not even the scream convinced Mrs Spalding that her husband was at fault – Rose Angela had enticed him, and would have to leave. But such was Mrs Spalding's mentality that she said nothing the next morning, and allowed Rose Angela to continue with her usual routine of doing the washing; but when this was finished she handed her three days' wages and told her to go. Rose Angela did not even protest that she was entitled to a week's wages in lieu of notice; she packed her things and went, tired, and slightly dazed, and burning under the humiliation of yet once again losing her place and having to go home.

What was she to do? She saw her head shaking in the mirror. Should she try to get into some shop? But there were so many trying, and one stood little chance because of the married women, who pleaded a family to support. She could perhaps go into the working-man's café . . . No! She stood up and began to unpack her case, stacking her uniform neatly in the drawers of the dressing-table, her morning pink prints and big white aprons, her black afternoon dress and little frilled caps. No! She would first try to get a place somewhere.

She began to move about the room, straightening things out of habit. Always on her return from the big houses her home seemed smaller and the fifteen streets more grim. She paused in her moving and looked down into the street. The children as usual were filling the pavement, more so immediately below the window. When they were chased from other doors they invariably settled outside twenty-eight, for Bridget never shooed them off. Rose Angela watched them with the yearning that had never left her. How often had she stood as she was doing now and watched their play. The longing to join them was past, but the hurt of being ostracised by them still remained.

This being cast out was not due entirely to the tint of her skin, but because, since the day she marked Janie Wilson, she had become suspect . . . there were two people now in the fifteen streets scarred, and by a Paterson; and mothers warned their children, 'Keep clear of that Rosie Paterson, mind,' and the children, ever anxious to create bogies, fed their inherent cruelty on this ready-made one. The spark of courage Rose Angela had felt after hitting Janie Wilson had been crushed, and had never risen again. More and more she began to sit by the fire, sometimes thinking and wondering why her thoughts hurt her, sometimes listening to Bridget reading stories. But very seldom did she hear a story right through, for when her Uncle Matt came in Bridget would send her upstairs. There had been a period of stark fear, she remembered, after she hit Janie, when she was afraid even to go to school, and would walk with her head bowed and her arms ready to shield her face. Her fear, she knew, was not unwarranted, for her mother would often be at the school gate to meet her, and if this were impossible she would tell her to go along to her place and wait there. The years did little to lessen the fear.

Directly below her a group of children were taking turns at kicking the bottom of a broken bottle into chalked squares. They were doing this while standing on one foot and with their hands behind them. Rose Angela looked at the smallest among them, a child of five, Janie Wilson's child, and thought how like her mother she was. A boy was manipulating a piece of tin, through the centre of which were drawn two pieces of string. As he pulled the string the tin whirled, making a sawing noise, and he dashed among the girls, working it against their faces. There were screams and yells, and they scattered and ran, all except Janie's child, who stood fixed and screaming. Rosie was about to knock on the window when a big girl pounced on the boy, crying, in a very good imitation of her elders, 'Get out of it! Do you want her to be marked for life, like her mother?'

Rosie turned sharply from the window. Marked for life! The mark of the buckle had shrunk until now it wasn't a quarter of an inch in length. It had not spoiled Janie's looks, for she had none to spoil. Rosie had long suspected that this lay at the core of Janie sustaining the hate over the years. Oh, what did it all mean . . . She sat down on her bed again. What did living amount to? Fear and hate, fear and hate, that's what her living amounted to. It always had and it looked as if it always would. She could count on one hand those who had never caused her to be afraid – her mother and Uncle Tony, her grandfather, Father Bailey and Mrs Kent. If only Mrs Kent hadn't died – she would still have been with her, and happy. Mrs Kent had made her feel as if she was different; and not because she was a half-caste, either. She would come to the kitchen at nights and talk about her husband, who had been killed in the war. But more often she would talk about Rose Angela herself. Frequently during the two years they were together she had said, 'Don't you worry, my dear, you won't always be doing this. You'll see . . . you'll marry, and marry well, and I'll live to see it.' But she was dead, and Rose Angela often thought that if those two comparatively happy years could have gone on she would have been content to let Mrs Kent's prophecy of a happy marriage go forever unfulfilled.

Her mother's voice came to her from the foot of the stairs, 'Rosie, there's a cup of tea . . . your granda's here.'

'I'll be there in a minute, Ma.' She straightened the coils of her shining black hair and smoothed down her grey print dress; then she went downstairs.

'Hallo, Granda.'

'Hallo, lass – how are you?'

'Oh, all right, Granda.' She smiled at him, and took a cup of tea from her mother's hand, then sat down near him; and Cavan, returning her smile, thought, You can't blame the chaps, really. God in Heav'n, but she's bonny! While he was thinking this he felt that the description was not quite right, but how could anyone find words to fit the effect she had on a man? He could well see her driving a fellow crackers, and doing so unconsciously, because he knew she was unaware of her power. Her movements were so natural and unaffected, yet in them was the sensuousness that tore at a man's control . . . God help and protect her! Where would she end?

'How's your reading going, Granda?' There was a faint twinkle in her eye.

'Oh, fine, lass.'

'And the professor?'

'Oh, Ted's still goin' strong.'

'Has he unravelled any more mysteries?'

'My God, yes.' He hitched his chair nearer. 'Do you know something, Rosie?' He stopped and pinched his lip and nodded to himself before going on. 'I'd like to be letting on to Father O'Malley about this – aye, well, I might an' all some day – Well, do you know there's not a bit of truth in this Adam and Garden of Eden business – never has been.'

Rose lifted her eyebrows.

'Yes, it surprised me, but there's been books written about it . . . do you know it's the belief – and that of men of great learning – that we come from . . .'

'Monkeys!' put in Bridget, endeavouring to forget her anxieties by joining in her father's pet pastime.

'Not a bit of it. Life in the first place was nothing but slime. Now can you take that in? Slime. And another thing; do you know why a snake's the length it is, eh?'

'No, Granda.'

'Well, because it wanted to be that long.'

Both Bridget and Rose Angela remained silent during his impressive pauses, knowing that it gave him great pleasure to expound the knowledge gathered from his books and Ted Grant.

'And do you know why a bull has horns?'

'No. Granda.' Rose Angela shook her head.

'Because it thought them up.'

Here Bridget and Rose Angela laughed.

'Ah, you can laugh, but it's a fact. It's all in a book by a fellow called Lemarck . . . the bulls and cows and such had only their heads to fight with, and they wanted something hard there so much that it affected their glands and things, so horns started to grow out of the tops of their heads.'

'They weren't made by God, then?' The twinkle was evident in Rose Angela's eyes now. 'Where does he come in, then, Granda?'

'Ah, ye've asked me something there. Where does he, lass? It makes a fellow think. It made me think a bit, I can tell you, 'cause, as Ted says, he could've made the slime in the first place; but that does away with this business of making the world in seven days. But then again Ted says it was only them Romans who chopped time up into days. A day could've been the word that meant a million years, for all we know. And then, as Ted says again, who's to know how long he took over making it? That's if he did. He's never told anybody, for Ted says half them prophet fellows, if they were about the day, would be shut up as loonies. People believed them in bygone times 'cause they was always frightened of what they couldn't understand. Aye, and that's another point. Have you ever thought of how our lives are ruled by what other people say? They say God wants you to do this or that, but how does anybody know what God wants of them, other than what the good part of their hearts tells them, eh?'

'Don't you believe in God then, Granda?'

'I don't know, lass; I just don't know.' He stroked the bare part of his scalp with two fingers. Then, looking from one to the other, he laughed. 'Be damned, it's funny, but I just don't know.'

Bridget, getting up to refill the cups said, 'Then I wouldn't let on to Father O'Malley about it.'

And while they were all laughing together Rose Angela thought, This is nice, just the three of us here. If only there could be more times like this. She listened to her Granda with only half her mind – she was thinking how strange it was that he should have become so altered by the reading of a few books, and him an old man. Perhaps when she was old she would get to love books, too; but now she only wanted to look at things, and listen. If only she could go to far-away places, where there was colour – lots of colour – earth colours and water colours and sky colours. And if only she could sit and listen to music. Oh, if only she had a wireless, a wireless all her own, so she could listen to music – any kind of music, for any music was better than none.

'Do you believe in God, Rosie? Do you believe Jesus Christ was God?'

'Of course, Granda.'

'That's right, then, that's right. Stick to your belief. But I wonder, would you still believe if I was to lend you some of my books? Now there's one by that fellow called Darwin – a right stink that fellow kicked up at one time . . .'

Cavan's voice went on, getting more excited, and Bridget rose and cleared the cups away, and Rose Angela, her eyes intent on her grandfather, followed her own thinking. She would always believe in God – life would be unbearable without this belief. How often, when a child, had Father Bailey's words 'God is colour-blind' soothed and comforted her. And how often now did she turn to that saying for comfort. Should she lose her belief in God, then she would be lost indeed, for she had come to know that He alone in all the world was . . . colour-blind. Even her mother, whom she loved with a deep, unshakable love . . . she wasn't colour-blind. Rose Angela knew that when Bridget stared at her without seeing her she was seeing her husband. She looked at Bridget now, and not for the first time realised just how lonely her mother's life was. She had been alone for years. Even loving Uncle Tony hadn't filled her life.

Rose Angela could look back to the day when she first discovered that her mother loved Uncle Tony. It was a Sunday, and Uncle Tony came to take her for the usual walk. As they were leaving Bridget said, 'Don't tell her that any more.' And she had watched her mother and Uncle Tony stare at each other; and when they were outside Tony looked happy, and suddenly he laughed. But from that day he never again told her that her father would come back. Was her father dead? Sometimes she thought he was. At other times she was strongly convinced he wasn't. Now and again she experienced an odd feeling that he was speaking to her, in a sort of pleading way, as if he were asking her not to forget him. There was no fear of her ever forgetting him – he was too much a part of her, too deeply buried in her being, to ever throw him off, even if she desired to. And never once had that been the case. Even as a child, realising he was black, she did not want him to be other than he was; for it was the man himself she loved, not in the way she loved her mother, but in a protective way. The term seemed silly to apply to the great black man she could still remember with astonishing clearness . . . but would she know him now if she saw him?

She was recalled to what her grandfather was saying by him tapping her knee. 'And did you know there is a fly that flutters about in a horse's stomach and drives him mad? Did you know that?'

'No, Granda.'

'Well, there is. And can you explain this? When the horse sees that fly buzzing around him, trying to find a sore patch to lay his eggs on, he nearly goes mad and no-one can hold him. Off he dashes, hell for leather. Now how does the horse recognise that fly? And how does he know what it will do to him? 'Cause if he'd already had a dose of him, he'd be dead . . . Now can you explain that?'

'No, Granda.'

'No, nor nobody else . . . And here's another thing that'll surprise you . . .' What the other thing was Cavan didn't explain, for the kitchen door opened and Matt entered. And the harmony of the kitchen was immediately shattered. Cavan spat into the grate and said, 'I'm sorry, lass, I've marked yer hob.'

'That's all right.' Bridget took up a paper, and, folding it, began to swat flies vigorously.

Rose Angela, after one startled look at Matt as the door opened, remained still. It was difficult to sit still with Matt's eyes on her, but lately she had told herself she must run no more – she must show him by her stillness that he could scare her no longer. If only she could make a pretence of not being afraid it would be something, for inside of her, always and forever, she knew she would fear Matt and what he might do. Her voice sounded a little cracked as she said, 'You were telling me about the horse, Granda.'

'Aye, aye, I was.' Cavan, now slowly and laboriously, went on talking, while Bridget banged the paper against the walls, on the table and against the window pane.

No-one spoke to Matt, nor he to them. He had moved into the kitchen and was standing leaning against the cupboard door, picking his teeth with a broken match-stick. The years had brought a stoop to his thin figure, and his face had grown two different kinds of skin – the puckered side was faintly blue, with the scars showing silver, like a winding river seen from a great height, while on the other side the skin was of a deadly whiteness and unrelieved by a trace of colour. His hair was sparse over his pointed head, and his eyes seemed to have narrowed to slits, from which jets of red light darted. For a time his gaze followed Bridget and her banging; then it again became focused on Rose Angela. The match-stick worked up and down the crevices of his teeth as his eyes swept their menacing light over her. They came to rest at length on her face, and forced her eyes to meet his. And when, despite her efforts, he saw the fear in their brown depths, his lip curled and he said, 'Been at your whoring again, eh? And got the . . . ?'

Before he could finish speaking the newspaper struck him across the mouth. 'I've warned you, haven't I?' Bridget's face was livid.

Matt made no answer, but stood looking at his sister. The red light from his pupils seemed to have diffused itself into his skin, for the top part of his face was pink-hued. Dead flies from the swatter were sticking to the stubble of his chin; and their squashed bodies, adding to the terribleness of his face, together with his accusation, were too much for Rose Angela. Pressing her hands over her mouth she fled upstairs.

Cavan, too, felt a great sickness rising in him as he looked at his son, and not for the first time he wished with all his heart that the nigger had done the job properly, for he knew that Bridget's blow had been in the nature of a caress to him – Matt did not mind what Bridget did as long as she noticed him. Why should this be? Cavan asked himself. Why should he have bred a man with this unnatural feeling? He could find no answer within himself, nor would his books be able to provide him with the reason, as they did for so many things; and it wasn't a question he could ask of anyone, so he would never know the answer.

CHAPTER EIGHT

THE JOB

The night had been exceptionally close, and Rose Angela lay waiting for the light to break. She had slept hardly at all. The heat of the past few days had made the houses like ovens, and the nights were not long enough to allow them to cool before another day dawned and their bricks were re-baked. As she lay listening to a baby crying in a house across the street she knew that she should be everlastingly grateful for having a room to herself, when all around her four to a room was privacy. Yet she could feel nothing but a great anxiety – what was to become of her? For three weeks now she had walked the streets of the towns on both sides of the river, but when there were girls with good references what chance had she? To every place she went she had to admit that her last mistress wouldn't be likely to give her a reference. When asked why, she could only say, 'We had words.' She would offer the name of her previous mistress, but with the women practically lining up for jobs why should a mistress bother herself about this person, who dared to 'have words', and who was undoubtedly a half-caste – it would be inviting trouble. Rose Angela could read the thoughts of prospective mistresses as their calculating eyes surveyed her. Now, after weeks of tramping, her mind and body were tired and a despair was settling on her. It would have to be that café – he said he would always set her on – the manager with his big red hands, and his fat body which seemed to have been poured into his greasy suit. And there wouldn't be him alone, but the riff-raff of the waterside, with whom, in comparison, the men of the fifteen streets were gentlemen. But she must have work of some kind, things were getting desperate. Her mother had only been able to secure two half-days a week for some time now, and so she was afraid the necessity might arise when her Uncle Tony would stop the extra he now gave to her grandma to give to them. And this would mean more bickering, more rows, with her grandma yelling for all the world to hear. Oh, what would it be like to really live in one of the houses in which she had worked, where you couldn't hear what the people in the next house were saying? . . . Or in Uncle Tony's house, that little red house all by itself ? Why had he never gone to live there? Was it because of her mother? If only he had taken them away from the fifteen streets years ago when he had first come by it. In that quiet, sheltered house she would have been free from her Uncle Matt's eyes, and the fear of him would have died. Why had her mother stayed on here? Was she waiting for her father to come back? He would never come back now after all this time. Anyway, what would she do about Uncle Tony if he did come back?

She turned restlessly over and lay on her stomach, and one long black plait hung down by the bed-side and brushed the floor. The light through the blind began to change, and she lay waiting to hear the sound of the barrows as the men passed the street corner. This was usually her time-signal, a signal without pain now, for the men would be dry and warm. But in the winter the creaking of the barrow wheels filled her with pity and despair . . . there they were now, the wheels on the bricks. She could hear a man singing . . . 'Oft in the Stilly Night' . . . the song of reflection,

The eyes that shone,
Now dimmed and gone,
The cheerful heart's now broken.

Oh, why must they sing? And that song with the heart-breaking words. She thrust her fingers into her ears, shutting out the unquenchable spirit of man, but almost instantly she released them as the unusual sound of the front door-knocker being banged came to her. Who on earth could it be at this hour of the morning?

She was on the landing pulling a coat round her when Bridget, opening her door, said, 'Wait, I'll go.' She had forgotten it might be her Uncle Matt. So she stood aside and let her mother go down-stairs; but when Cavan's voice came to her from the kitchen she ran downstairs and asked, 'What's wrong, Granda?'

'Wrong? Nothing, lass.' He wiped the dust and

sweat from his face with a piece of rag. 'I've just been telling your mother if you're lucky you'll be getting a job this mornin'.'

'A job?'

'Aye, lass. You know Ted's wife was in a good place in Shields? Well, she's ricked her foot.' He tried to cover his excitement and to appear sympathetic. 'Bad job altogether. Poor Ted's proper cut up about it, and he doesn't know what's going to be done now.'

He wiped his face again and sat down, while Bridget and Rose Angela watched him, waiting for him to go on.

'It'll likely be weeks before she can go back there again, for it takes a young 'un to climb over them sleepers and such like to get to the house; and then there's the stairs; and with him a bit cranky – he has the house cleaned every day.'

'What you talking about, Da?' asked Bridget impatiently. 'I thought you said it was a good place.'

'It is.'

'Well, what's this about getting over sleepers? . . . And who's the mistress?'

'Where is it, Granda?' asked Rose Angela. 'I don't mind how much work there is.'

'Off Holborn, hinny.' Cavan rubbed the back of his hand sheepishly under his nose.

'Holborn!' Both Bridget and Rose Angela spoke the name together.

'Off, I said. Look, give me a chance to tell you. Do you know Cassy's Wharf? No, you don't. Well, it's by a cut off the Mill Dam bank afore you get to Holborn proper. It's never been used for years as a wharf, but long ago – God knows how long – somebody built a house there. By all accounts the builder must have been as cranky as the chap who lives there now – great windows it has. Anyway, there was once a field all round the house. That was God knows how long ago, too, but it was gradually surrounded by sidings. Then the field became the graveyard for all the old bogies and wagons. But the house still stands there, and this painter fellow has it done out white twice a year, and everything's to be cleaned every day. And he hardly ever sees it, 'cause he's always up top painting. Ted says Bessie used to get tired going up trying to get him to come to a meal. When he's the mood on him, he'll paint night and day, then sleep for days and get up roaring for something to eat and go for her if it isn't ready.'

'But, Granda' – Rose Angela's voice was quiet – 'there isn't a woman there? He's not married?'

'No, lass, that's what I was going to tell you. You see' – he looked apologetically from her to Bridget and back to her again – 'you see, you won't need to fear him – Ted's Bessie says he dislikes women. He never paints owt but men and boats, and they've both got to be on their last legs afore he'll do either.'

'Is he mental?' asked Bridget.

'No, he's just cranky. But cranky or not, he makes money; and he must spend it, 'cause he gave Bessie a free hand. And she makes quite a bit, so Ted says, out of the housekeeping. So, lass, if you get a place like that . . .'

'If she gets a place like that, we won't depend

on anything out of the housekeeping,' said Bridget, stiffly.

'Well, I was only saying, lass,' said Cavan, getting up; 'I was trying to do me best.'

'Look, Granda,' Rose Angela said soothingly, 'sit down a minute and I'll make you a cup of tea. And go on, tell me more about it. When did this happen to Mrs Grant, and what's the man's name?'

'Just last night, hinny. She tripped over a sleeper, and a bloke found her and went for the painter chap; and he put her in a taxi-cab and sent her home. Ted says all you've got to say is you've come in Mrs Grant's place until she's better. But mind, hinny' – he nodded cautiously at her – 'you'll have to give it up when she's better. Ted was clear about that.'

'Oh yes, Granda, I understand – that's only fair. But what's the man's name?'

'Stanhope. It's easy to remember . . . like Stanhope Road in Shields. Mr Michael Stanhope. And there's another bloke; but he's away most of the time. He's in Austria now, in a place called Teeroll or some-such. He's another painter. Although he's madder by a week than this one, Bessie says, you can have a laugh with him, where you can't with the Stanhope bloke. I think Bessie's just a bit scared of him.'

'Are you sure he's not mental?' asked Bridget again.

'Not as far as I can make out, lass.'

'I'll soon find out when I get there, Ma.' Hope had almost made Rose Angela gay. 'And I don't care if he is a bit mental, I'll look after him.'

'You'll have nothing to do with the place if he's not all there; you'll go and get yourself—' Bridget was

570

about to say 'murdered', but she feared the word, so she substituted 'in trouble'.

'There's always been trouble down there,' she went on. 'Look at that Saturday a few years back, when the Arabs rioted around the shipping office and stabbed them three policemen.'

'You couldn't only blame the Arabs for that,' Cavan put in sharply; 'it were our blokes agitating them not to sign the P.C.5 form that did that, together with those bloody Arab boarding-house masters who bleed them dry. Look what them masters did a while back . . . sent the Arabs in droves up to the workhouse. Blackmail it was, just to compel the town to give them outdoor relief, so as the poor skinny scabs could tip up their dibs to them again. It was the white agitators and the black masters who caused that shipping trouble, I'm telling you . . . Anyway' – he turned towards Rose Angela – 'you won't be near them. As I've told you, Cassy's Wharf cuts away from Holborn.'

'What time did Mrs Grant start, Granda?'

'Eight, hinny.'

'All right, I'll be there at eight.' She touched his stubbly cheek. 'Thanks, Granda. You know, it's a good job for me that you read.'

'How do you make that out, hinny?'

'Well, if you hadn't got interested in books you wouldn't have had Ted Grant for a friend, and he would likely have given someone else the chance to fill his wife's place.'

The deduction pleased Cavan, and he laughed. 'Aye, there's that in it.' And when Rose Angela handed him his cup of tea he raised the cup to her, saying, 'Here's to Bessie's slow recovery. Not that I'm wishing her any harm, mind you, but—' He chuckled and winked at her. 'Good luck, lass.'

Rose Angela took the seven o'clock workmen's tram into Shields. The appellation was a mere courtesy title – now only a sprinkling of miners and odd workmen occupied it. She alighted by the slaughterhouse, where the piteous bellowings of the beasts were already to be heard. She had left the tram earlier than was necessary in order that she might ask the way of some 'white person', for beyond the Mill Dam lay Holborn, and Arabs. And strange though it appeared, her dislike of Arabs exceeded that held by most white people. When on one or two occasions an Arab had spoken to her, his very approach had seemed an insult. Yet it was this feeling of revulsion which gave her the insight into how the Negro was viewed by a white, and helped her to understand a little the white man's deep dislike of the Negro who was penetrating his preserves. But her understanding did not make her situation easier to bear, even though the touch of colour in herself, at least outwardly, was slight.

She reached the top of the Mill Dam bank without meeting any women, so she stopped an old man and enquired of him the whereabouts of Cassy's Wharf.

'Cassy's Wharf? Aye, I know where that is, but it's a job to get at. Why d'ya want to get there?'

'I'm after a job.'

'Funny place for a job – a lot of queer characters around this quarter, you know, lass – although it isn't as bad as it used to be in my young days, except for the bloody Arabs. They're swarming like flies here. But now let me see, which is your best way.' He ruminated for a moment. 'Aye, look. Go down that street there – it's the only street you need touch if you follow where I tell you. At the end of it you'll see a narrow cut between two warehouses. Go down there, it'll bring you to the river bank; then turn right and keep straight on . . . well, you won't be able to keep straight on, for you'll have to dodge between trucks and things, but keep as near the river as you can and you can't miss the wharf. They tell me there's still a house along there. Is that where you're going?'

Rose Angela said it was, and, after thanking him warmly, followed his directions. All the doors in the street were closed; the blinds of the windows were still drawn, and the bright morning sun intensified the blackness of the passageways separating every other house. The place seemed entirely dead; the only live thing was herself, and the only noise the heels of her shoes on the pavement. She came to the cut between the warehouses, and this was as dark as the passageways, for the towering buildings seemed to meet above the narrow slit. She couldn't see the end of the cut, only where it curved in the dim distance. But as she rounded the curve she saw coming towards her a man with lowered head. He was walking slowly and was merged in the duskiness of the passage. It was well he wasn't fat, she thought, for the breadth of the cut was hardly wide enough to allow two people to pass. It was with an inward shrinking she realised that the approaching man was an Arab. She could see him peering at her across the narrowing distance. He stopped, and, standing with his back to the wall, waited for her to pass. She did not look at him or alter her pace, but as she passed him her coat brushed him and her heart thumped in agitation. He did not speak, but she knew his eyes were fixed on her, and as she walked on she was conscious of his gaze on her back. She wrinkled her nose in distaste – that sweet-scented smell peculiar to most Arabs hung in the air. When as a child sitting in a tram she had first smelt this heavy aroma she had wondered if her father too had that kind of smell, only to dismiss it as impossible.

Immediately beyond the passage she came to the river, and turned right; but as the old man said, she was unable to keep straight on for long – the banks seemed a graveyard for old trucks, some wheel-less, some on their sides. An old railway carriage, also without wheels, and sunk in coarse sea grass, attracted her attention, and she glanced through a window, only to hurry quickly on again, for two men fully dressed were lying in huddled positions on its floor.

Climbing over piles of stacked rails, walking in and out of the maze of wagons, she felt she was entering a sort of waking nightmare, and this feeling leapt into certainty when she saw the house. The jumble of debris stopped suddenly, and there ahead of her was a clear space of about thirty feet, with a narrow red-brick house at the end of it, the windows and door shining startlingly white. She stopped, and for no accountable reason a surge of happiness welled in her. She knew she had never seen this house before, yet it was familiar. It was as if she had known it, and through knowing it had been happy. She entered the clearing and began to walk slowly towards the house . . . Would he be up? It wasn't yet eight. She had better find the back door.

As she turned round the side of the house the river, too, turned, seeming to follow the line of the bright golden beach pathway; and when she came to the back she stopped again in pleased surprise. There lay the wharf not eight yards from the house, with the sun thick and warm on the fawn-coloured planks of the landing and lining the black water-marked piles of the jetty with silver streaks. A vivid splash of blue moving gently on the sparkling water drew her to the jetty edge, and she looked down almost tenderly on a little boat with a white furled mast lying down at its centre . . . how lovely! If only the man himself turned out to be all right and she could work here.

'Well, and what do you want?' The deep grunt of the voice, and the unexpectedness with which it came, nearly caused her to topple into the water. She gripped the jetty post, and, turning, looked towards the house. Her first jumbled impression was that the whole back of the house was made of three huge panes of glass, the widest being the top one, out of which was thrust the wildest looking head she had ever seen. She opened her mouth to explain her presence, but his next words halted her, and she experienced a faint tingling of pleasure at them.

'I don't want a model – I have more than I can cope with.'

She looked at his eyes sweeping over her, but felt not the slightest embarrassment. She could not name the expression they held; she only knew they were

575

without that look she had come to fear in the eyes of man.

'I don't do women, anyway.'

'I am not a model, Mr Stanhope – I came to take Mrs Grant's place until she's better . . . that's if I'll be suitable.'

He blinked down on her as if recalling who Mrs Grant was.

'Oh yes, the blasted woman hurt her foot. Well, come in.'

Breathing quickly, she moved towards the door, set back in a little porch, and entered the house. If only he would take to her! Oh, Holy Mother, let me get this place.

She stood waiting for him in the most beautiful kitchen she had ever seen. The woodwork, she noticed, wasn't white, but of the palest blue. There were cupboards all along one side of the room and the little fireplace was blue-tiled, and never made for cooking, she thought. She turned to the window. The wharf and a large stretch of the river was framed in it like a picture. She had never imagined the Tyne looking like this . . . and the sight of a boat moving swiftly, with the grace of a dancer, across the middle of the pane intensified her prayer; Dear, dear God, let me get this place.

'What's the matter with your legs?' The bellow, coming from somewhere inside the house, startled her.

Was he shouting at her? Who else, if he lived here alone? She moved towards the half-open door and stepped into the hall, which for all its whiteness appeared dark after the sun-filled kitchen. Before her was the side of the staircase, and she looked up, but could see no-one, so she asked softly, 'Were you calling for me, sir?'

'Yes. Are you deaf?'

Quickly she mounted the stairs, her steps making no sound on the thick dark-blue carpet, but when she came to the landing it was empty. She looked at the four closed doors, then at the second flight of stairs, and went hurriedly up these; and there he was, standing in the doorway of a room, seeming to fill it not with height so much as with breadth. He was not much taller than she, but his solidness made him appear like a giant to her. Her eyes went to his hair, which looked like a tangled matting of coarse rope. She couldn't tell what colour it was, for the light behind him made it a mixture of red and brown, while the piece hanging over his brow appeared black.

'There's nothing the matter with your legs, is there?' He looked at them with close scrutiny, but his gaze did not offend her.

She shook her head slightly; and he turned into the room, saying, 'All the women I had before Bessie had legs – bad legs, swollen legs, stiff legs. They had a job to get here, and when they did the stairs were too much for them. Are stairs too much for you?' His voice was staccato and his eyes held an angry look, as if he was indulging in a row.

'No, I'm used to stairs.'

She was now in the room, and the scene bewildered her. From floor to ceiling the walls were covered with paintings. The sun, pouring through the great window, merged them into one rainbow

577

whole, but apart from the window-seat there was not another fixture or article of furniture in the room – not even an easel stood on the bare floor. He walked to the window and turned there, his back to the light; and she stood in the centre of the room, facing him. The sun was dazzling her eyes and he became indistinct, only the vivid blue of his eyes remaining clear.

'How long is Bessie likely to be? Can you cook?'

'I don't really know – yes, yes, I can do . . .'

'Don't say it!' He held out a hand, short-fingered and square, in protest. 'Plain cooking! Floating cabbage and fries!'

She smiled, in no way offended. 'They tell me I'm a good cook.'

'What wage do you want?'

She was nonplussed at the question – to be asked what wage she wanted! She'd be sleeping out, so dared she ask for . . . twenty-five shillings? No, she'd better make it a pound. But then he might come down.

'Could I ask a pound?'

'A pound!' His face was wrinkled in the light.

Now she had done it. She began, 'Well, I . . .' when he cut in, 'Bessie got thirty-five shillings; you'll have the same if you suit.'

Thirty-five shillings! She could only swallow and say, 'Yes, sir.'

'What's your name?'

'Rose Angela Paterson – I'm called Rosie.'

'Well, all right.' Half turning, he blinked into the sun, and stifled a yawn. 'I'm hungry and I want a meal. But listen' – he swung round on her again, his manner more aggressive than before – 'I don't want my breakfast at nine, and dinner at one, and tea at six. If you don't think you'll like that arrangement, say so now. And I knock down when I want a meal – I don't have bells, I don't like them. And when I say I don't want to be disturbed I mean it. When I want you I knock, you understand?'

Still she said nothing, knowing he wasn't finished.

'And I want the rooms dusted every day, not with a duster but with a wash-leather. Why do I want unused rooms done every day? Because I hate dirt and muddle. Get rid of the idea that any old thing or condition does for an artist. Another thing – I don't mind being robbed, but I don't want it overdone.' He paused, waiting for some response; and when none came he went on, 'Why don't you bridle and say that you're an honest woman and don't touch anything that doesn't belong to you?'

She regarded him steadily, and said, 'Because I know it's done.'

'Oh, you do?' He nodded his great head at her. 'Well, you're honest about it, anyway, that's more than most of them are. Where were you last?'

Dear Lord, here it came!

'At Mrs Spalding's in Paddington Road. But that was three weeks ago – I haven't been well.' Would he ask for her card? If he did she would tell him the truth and chance it.

But he didn't ask for the card.

He said, 'We'll try it a week and see how it goes. And now I want a meal – a big meal, a dinner. And strong coffee. You'll find plenty of stuff downstairs. I'll have it in the drawing-room.'

'Yes, sir.'

She turned quickly away, only to be pulled up by his next words, 'And take that frightened look off your face, there's nothing to be afraid of here.'

She wanted to say, 'I'm not afraid of you,' but after a pause she went on her way without saying anything. Her body was feeling inflated and light with relief. She had got the place, and he was nice. Her mind questioned how anyone so abrupt and who said such unorthodox things could be nice, but he was, and she knew she would like working for him in this lovely, quaint house.

She ran down the last flight of stairs to the kitchen. He wanted a dinner. What would she make him? Something tasty and quick. She tore off her coat and opened one door after another. The cupboards in the kitchen were well stocked, and in the larder was a half chicken and a piece of cooked fresh salmon – a salad, yes – but something hot before – soup. Lentils, an onion and a little curry powder. After searching at frantic speed she found all that she required.

The soup was simmering and the fruit pie baking, and she was standing at the table by the window arranging the salad when her hands became still and her eyes widened . . . her master, for she thought of him as that already, was walking, practically naked, towards the end of the wharf, his body looking even broader without clothes. His hair was still on end, and as she watched him she had a great desire to laugh. When he dived he became lost to her view, and she resumed her hurried preparations. But when the squat lumbering line of a tug ploughing up the centre of the river caught her eye, she stopped again, for in line with it she saw the shining lift of an arm cutting the water with regular precision. A figure leaning over the side of the tug waved, and a hand from the water answered the salute, and a faint call that could have been a greeting came to her. The atmosphere was homely, and she felt a warmth growing inside her . . . he must swim often, the tugmen knew him. And he'd be hungry . . . If only he liked the dinner . . .

Half an hour later she was standing dropping little squares of bread into boiling fat, to serve with his soup, when she heard his footsteps in the hall. Oh, if only he didn't bang or call for a minute, and then everything would be ready.

There was neither bang nor call, and when she took the soup in to him her knees were trembling so much that she felt her body was about to fold up, the consequences of which would be disastrous.

He was lying fully dressed on a divan; his eyes were closed, and as she said quietly, 'Your dinner, sir,' he opened one eye and looked at her.

'Dinner?'

For one moment she thought that his order had been a joke, for his tone was full of surprise, so that when he got up at once and went to the table her sigh of relief was almost audible. But if she expected any word of praise for her quickness or the quality of the meal she was disappointed.

She left him with his coffee and prepared herself a cup of tea, for she could eat nothing – excitement being her food at this moment.

She had barely finished the tea when his voice came to her, not from the drawing-room but from the upstairs window. Was he calling her? She sprang up, but stopped on her way to the open door, for there, in the middle of the wharf, looking upwards, were two men, one tall and thin and the other a dwarf, whose head was sunk deep into his shoulders and whose features were so strong and shapely as to give the impression of a sculptor's cast.

'I told you I didn't want you till three o'clock!'

'Yes, guv'nor.' It was the tall man who spoke.

'Well, what the hell're you nosing round for?'

'Just takin' a walk, guv'nor.'

'Walk be damned! Then walk some place else – this is my back yard, or front yard. It's private, and you know it.'

'We were just thinkin', guv'nor . . . we were just wondering—' The man broke off. He was still looking up, and the stretched sinews of his neck cast their own deep shadows. The silence continued until the man raised his hand and grabbed at the coin flashing through the sunlight. He touched his brow with his finger, saying, 'Thanks, guv'nor – we'll be here at three.'

There was no response from the upper window, and Rose Angela watched the men shambling off, ludicrous in their different heights, and pitiable in their crumpled threadbare clothes. Why hadn't they come and asked for a bite or something? She guessed these were the two men who had been lying in the railway carriage.

As she returned to her cup of tea her master's voice again startled her.

'Pete! You, Pete!'

The dwarf reappeared from the side of the house.

He did not speak but stared up at the window.

'Seen anything of that fellow yet?'

'I asked him. He won't come.' The dwarf's voice was guttural and the words strangely clipped.

'Why not?'

'He says he don't want to be painted.'

'Did you tell him I'd give him two shillings an hour?'

'Yes.'

'Where does he live?'

There was a slight pause before the dwarf answered, 'I dunno.'

'You're a liar – you do.'

The dwarf remained silent, gazing upwards.

'Murphy!'

As if being produced from a gigantic hat, the tall man sprang round the corner. 'Yes, guv'nor?'

'Where does that fellow live?'

Murphy dropped his gaze from the top window to the dwarf's face, then he lifted it again. 'I dunno, guv'nor.'

'You're a liar, too.'

'Yes, guv'nor.'

'Look, I'll give you a pound if you get him here.'

'A quid!' Again Murphy dropped his eyes to the dwarf, but whatever he saw there wasn't reassuring. 'I'll try, guv'nor, but I ain't promising owt.'

'I'll make it two.'

They both stared upwards in silence, then turned slowly away; and once again it was quiet on the wharf.

Offering them two pounds just to get a man to come and sit for him! He must be made of money.

Rose Angela went into the drawing-room to clear the table, and as she looked about the room she thought again, He must be made of money.

In her various places she had come to recognise good furniture from shoddy imitations, and although her knowledge of antiques was limited she knew that every piece in this room had been specially picked, for here, with the air of age and elegance, was comfort. The main tone of the room was brown, a deep patina brown, relieved in the upholstery by a shade of green that was almost blue. The window of this room, which ran the whole length of the house, looked out on to a white trellis, constructed to shut off the jumble of debris beyond. She would have liked to linger and examine the room further, but the desire was checked when she remembered what still had to be done with the wash-leather.

By mid-day she had finished the ground floor and the four rooms on the first floor. One of these had taken very little doing, as it was another studio belonging to the 'other one', whom her grandfather had referred to as being 'madder by the week' than her master. In contrast, the bedroom adjoining this studio was, to Rose Angela's mind, more like an overcrowded sitting-room, and unlike her master's, which was practically bare, without even a carpet on the floor, a large orange rug being the only covering on the bare polished boards.

She did not venture to the top of the house, and as the afternoon wore on she began to await anxiously the summons for another meal. It was close on three o'clock when it came . . . a dull thumping from above. With fast-beating heart she mounted the stairs and knocked on the studio door, and entered, only to find it empty. Staring along its length, she saw a crumpled rug lying on the boards by the window. Had he been sleeping on the floor?

Her conjecturing was interrupted by his voice coming through a partly-opened door to the right of her. 'Rosie!'

It was as familiar-sounding as if he had used her name every day for years. There was none of the harshness of the morning in his tone.

'Yes, sir.' She went into the room and saw him standing at a table, stretching some canvas over a frame. He did not lift his eyes from his work, nor speak further, until he had taken some tacks from his mouth and hammered them home.

'I'll have a pot of tea. Make it strong. Nothing to eat; but you can make me a meal about six. You needn't stay to clear – do that in the morning.'

'Is there anything particular you would like, sir?'

He walked to an easel, with a full-length empty canvas set on its pegs, and moved it to the side of a dais which ran the breadth of the room.

'No – as long as it's nothing hashed up, it'll do . . . I like fresh food.'

'Yes, sir. About the ordering, sir – do I do that?'

'Yes, yes, of course. Bessie always did. But mind' – he swung round and faced her, and his tone took on the edge that she associated with him as natural – 'sixteen pounds a month's my limit – not a penny more.'

'Sixteen pounds a month for food!' Her expression carried further the surprise of her voice.

'Yes, for food.' His eyes narrowed and their blueness became intensified. 'What do you think? It's not enough?'

Sixteen pounds a month to keep one man and a daily maid in food. Was he a fool? No, she dismissed the idea. Had Bessie been charging him all that? If so, it was absolute robbery. It was understandable her wanting to make a bit extra, with the family to feed, but four pounds a week for food! . . . Yet Bessie would be coming back, she must be careful what she said.

His narrowed, concentrated gaze remained fixed on her, and she met it. 'It will be more than enough, sir.'

'I'm glad of that.'

He turned to his easel again and she went out. Was there a touch of sarcasm in his voice? One couldn't blame him if there was – as he had said that morning, he knew he was being robbed. But four pounds a week!

She had just reached the bottom of the stairs when his voice came again. 'Rosie! Tell those two men to wait for a quarter of an hour or so. I'll shout when I want them.'

'Yes, sir.'

As she reached the kitchen there was a tap on the open door, and there stood Murphy and Pete . . . she thought of them immediately by their names. On closer inspection they looked more disreputable than they had looked on the wharf.

'You can come in and sit down. Mr Stanhope will knock when he wants you.'

'Thank you, miss. You're new, aren't you? What's

happened to the other one?' It was Murphy who did the talking.

'She's hurt her foot.'

She made the tea, conscious of the men's eyes gravely watching her movements, and as she went out of the room with the tray she said, 'I'll make you a cup when I come back.'

But when she returned to the kitchen Murphy spoke again, hesitantly and sadly. 'I'd better tell you, miss – he doesn't like it, the guv'nor don't. He don't like us getting anything.'

'Has he said so?'

'Aye; at least he told Mrs Grant we weren't to come begging here or he'd stop us sitting.'

'Has he ever said anything to you himself?'

'No.'

Would a man who knew he was being robbed by his servants begrudge a bite and a cup of tea to these half-starved men? If Bessie wouldn't give them anything, it would be for reasons of her own.

'He hasn't said anything to me, so until he does you can have what's over – he doesn't like things hashed up.' And with a feeling of one in authority Rose Angela went to the pantry, and Murphy's long furrowed face gazed down on Pete with an almost angelic smile. But Pete did not return the smile. His eyes were riveted on the door, waiting for Rose Angela's return; and when she motioned them to the table his gaze did not flicker from her.

As hungry men will sometimes do, they began to eat the food in small bites, with a seeming finickiness – it was the habit of making a little go a long way; and they were only half-way through their plates of food when a hail from above brought them to their feet.

'Look, miss, we are much obliged. Could we put it in a bit paper and take it with us?'

'Yes, go on, I'll see to it.'

Murphy went into the hall rubbing his mouth vigorously, but Pete, standing in front of Rose Angela, asked abruptly, 'What's your name?'

'Rosie.'

'Your other name – full name?'

'Rose Angela Paterson – why?'

The dwarf did not answer, but hurried after Murphy; and about a minute later, when passing through the hall, Rose Angela was amazed to see them still standing halfway up the stairs. They both looked silently down on her and she up at them.

'What the hell you doing down there, Murphy?'

At the bellow from the upper landing they turned and sprang up the remaining stairs, and Rose Angela went on her way to the drawing-room, wondering if she had been wise, after all, to break Bessie's rule. For what were they up to, she wondered, looking at her like that and whispering on the stairs?

CHAPTER NINE

THE AWAKENING

It was eighteen days since Rose Angela came to Wharf House, and she knew now that one of the main things she wanted from life was the opportunity to manage a house; not just to work in one, but to control it – to be able to say, as she was doing now, 'I'll order this today,' or 'I'll make that for dinner the morrow.' Never could she remember being so happy; yet the eighteen days had not been without their worry.

She disliked fighting or arguing of any kind, and, on such occasions, had always found herself strangely backward with her tongue; yet the way she had stood up to the grocer had been gratifying, even if the meeting with Mrs Grant had still to be faced.

The barefacedness of the twisting that Mrs Grant and the grocer's man worked incensed her – four pounds' worth of groceries, fowl, meat and fish were certainly bought, but only half the amount was delivered to the house. The rest was divided between the two of them. She had wanted to change to another shop, but was afraid of doing so in case this particular shop had been the master's choice; but she was firm in her ordering, and with ham at sixpence a pound and streaky at threepence, and eggs a penny each, while cooking ones were twenty-four a shilling, not to overlook the fact that one pound of steak with a rabbit thrown in was little more than a shilling, a great deal of food could be bought for two pounds. She knew her refusal to co-operate with the man would make it awkward when she met Mrs Grant, but she could feel no regret. In any case, Mrs Grant would likely return to her own system, for it was doubtful whether the master would notice any difference, since so far she had given only one order of her own and perhaps she would not give another, for only yesterday Cavan had regretfully told her that Mrs Grant's ankle was considerably better.

Slowly she crumpled the pastry in the bowl as she looked out of the window towards the wharf. The sun had gone in and the river was lead-coloured and choppy, but it was still beautiful. Soon she would no longer be able to look at it, in either sunshine or shadow. As she was staring at the water the blue boat ran alongside the wharf, and for the moment Mrs Grant and her impending return were put aside. The scones would be done – perhaps he'd like one with his coffee; it would have been cold on the water.

As he entered the kitchen she trembled a little, as always when in his presence; yet she wasn't afraid of him.

'There are some scones just out of the oven, sir. Would you like one with your coffee?' She turned her head towards him, her hands still rubbing the pastry.

'Yes . . . yes, I would – nice smell.'

He sniffed the air, and she said, 'I won't be a minute, sir, I'll bring it up.'

She was clapping the flour from her hands over the bowl when he said, 'I'll have it here.'

He pulled a chair to the table and sat down, and so great was her surprise that she stood with her palms pressed together and stared at him.

'You don't mind?'

'Oh no, sir – no.'

'Cold on the water.'

'Yes, sir.'

In spite of his abruptness, she knew he was trying to be pleasant, and a little whirl of happiness went through her.

'How old are you, Rosie?' The question was brusquely put, as were all his enquiries.

She turned, and for a flash of time looked directly into the blue eyes surveying her before answering. 'Twenty, sir.'

'You look older.'

'Yes, I know I do, sir.'

He pulled off his top boots and placed them by the side of the hearth, asking as he did so, 'What have you done all your life? This kind of work?'

'Yes.'

'What have you wanted to do?'

'Just this, sir – look after a house.'

'My God! Nothing more?' He twisted round and looked up at her incredulously.

'It isn't everyone who's lucky enough to do even that these days.'

Her voice was serious, and he answered more curtly still, 'Yes, I know all about that; but you . . . haven't you wanted something different – to be a dancer or get on the films? or be a mannequin, or an artist's model? . . . you'd make a good model, you know – not that I want to do you.' He raised his hand as if pressing her away. 'No, no; but there are plenty who would.'

She waited until she returned from the scullery with the coffee before saying, 'I can't see myself getting such work around the Tyne, sir.' And she smiled ruefully as she placed his coffee on the table.

'The Tyne! You don't want to stick around here all your days, do you? Get up to London and you'll be snapped up.'

'You think so, sir?' Her voice held no belief, but her smile broadened and she gazed for a moment on his bent head as he stirred his coffee briskly. London, and mannequins and artists' models! Who would want such things if they could work in a house like this, with the river flowing by and him up there painting away and thumping occasionally on the floor, and the peace that prevailed even when he was bellowing down the stairs. And now him sitting here talking to her! She experienced a feeling of satisfaction as she watched him bite into one of her scones – his mouth was full-lipped, and wide, like the rest of him; his hair still bore its numerous partings, and even without the sun's misleading light was of different colours. She often tried to guess how old he was, for on different days he looked a different age. Today he looked youngish, about thirty.

Tomorrow, painting like mad, his hair standing up on end, he would look anything up to forty-five. She couldn't tell what his age was.

A knock on the kitchen door checked something further he was about to say, and Rose Angela, opening it, found Murphy there.

'Can I see the guv'nor, miss?'

'What do you want?' Stanhope called.

Murphy sidled into the kitchen, cap in hand and his long body swaying.

'Well? What you after?'

'I've got him, guv'nor.'

'The fellow?' Stanhope rose to his feet, his excitement evident.

'He'll come the morrow.'

'Why not today?'

'Well . . . ye see . . . he's been bad.'

'Bad! – Pah! You're just stalling to push me up a bit, like you've done all along . . . I'm not rising, Murphy.'

'No, guv'nor, honest to God! Just when he said he would come, he took bad – week afore last he was took bad.'

'Well, I'm giving you nothing on account this time . . . I want to see the fellow first.'

'Yes, guv'nor.' There was disappointment in Murphy's voice.

Stanhope sat down again and looked at Murphy, at the long, shambling length of him – By God, he had got him on to that canvas – every undernourished pore. And the little fellow too. It should shake them up, there . . . but he wouldn't send it until this other fellow was done . . . Now he should make a picture, especially if he could get him to look as he had done that day when he first saw him gazing across the river. He'd get him all right; he'd work on him night and day.

His attention was drawn to Murphy's working mouth and the saliva at the corners of it. 'I suppose you could squeeze a cup of coffee into that fat carcass of yours, eh? Well, you'd better get round Rosie – she makes quite good coffee . . . or perhaps you know that?' His eyes were crinkled at the corners and he threw a quick glance towards Rose Angela, and as a tinge of colour mounted her cheeks he laughed and scraped his chair back from the table, but his rising was checked by the abrupt opening of the door. He turned, with Rose Angela and Murphy, and stared at the young woman surveying them. The door in her hand, she looked from one to the other before coming into the kitchen; then she advanced with such a proprietary air that even Stanhope for the moment seemed in a subordinate position.

Rose Angela, strangely enough, had never met Bessie Grant, but the faintness in the pit of her stomach told her who this plump, fair woman was. She wasn't much older than herself, but she had all the assurance in the world.

'Good morning, sir.'

'Oh, hallo, Bessie. You're better then, I see.'

'Yes . . . yes, I'm better.' The look she threw towards Murphy said plainly 'and not before time'.

Stanhope rose and walked towards the hall saying, 'Come upstairs a minute, Bessie, will you?' His voice had lost the harsh note usual to it – it was now soft, and even pleasant. Perhaps he was glad to have her back, Rose Angela thought, with an accompanying pang.

Bessie, in the act of unbuttoning her coat, stopped. She looked at Rose Angela, and Rose Angela managed to smile at her and say, 'I'm glad you're better, Mrs Grant.'

To this pleasantry Bessie made no rejoinder, but with the same air of being in command she followed Stanhope.

Rose Angela turned to the window. She was finished, then. She hadn't thought it would be like this, like a bolt from the blue – she had imagined there would be a little warning, such as her granda saying, 'Bessie's better. I think she intends starting next week, lass.' But this suddenness, and coming at a time when everything was so wonderful . . . him sitting there drinking his coffee at the kitchen table, much the same as her Uncle Tony or her granda would have done . . . and poor Murphy and Pete – there'd be no more bits and pieces for them . . . and herself – there would be the round again – the humiliations, the despair. He said she could get a job as a model any day in London. Should she try? She knew it was a stupid question to ask herself, for she had not the courage to leave the small security of her home, and Bridget, Tony and her granda, for a life she thought would be just as hostile towards her as this one was, together with added dangers.

'I'm sorry, miss.'

She turned towards Murphy. 'Well, I was only temporary, you know, Murphy.'

'You'll be goin' right away, then, this mornin'?'

'Yes.'

'We'll miss yer, miss.'

'I'll miss you, too, Murphy, and Pete . . . I'll miss everything.' She turned blindly towards the window again. It would have been better if she'd never got the job . . . oh, a thousand times better.

'Look, miss' – Murphy came up behind her – 'could ye pop this way the morrer? Round about eightish.' He was whispering now. 'Pete and me – we've got something for ye – a surprise, like. If ye could come just to the carriage, round about eight, miss – could you?'

'Oh, I don't think so, Murphy . . . it's very kind of you . . . but—' She turned to him and her refusal was checked by the look of utter disappointment on his face. 'All right,' she added listlessly, 'I'll come.'

It would be a chance to see the house again, even if only from the outside, and she'd have to be out early going the rounds, anyway.

As Murphy, turning to go, muttered, 'I'm dead sorry you're going, miss,' she remembered the drink she had been about to get him, and she said, 'I forgot your coffee, Murphy. Just a minute; I'll get it.' But as she went into the scullery the sound of a door closing overhead reached them, and Murphy whispered, 'Never bother, miss. Thanks all the same, but I'd best be off.'

'No – wait.' If it was the last drink Murphy was to have here, he should have it, in spite of Bessie.

Suddenly Rose Angela found she heartily disliked Bessie. She had disliked her before she met her, because of her blatant robbery and her meanness towards these half-starved men.

She listened to the quick, soft padding on the stairs, and as she handed the cup to Murphy her eyes turned towards the kitchen door, awaiting Bessie's entry. But it didn't come. Instead, the front door banged with such violence that the window panes rattled, and Murphy almost dropped the cup.

Rose Angela and he stared at each other; then Murphy, putting down his cup, went quickly out of the house. He was back again in a minute, his body jangling with excitement and his enlarged Adam's apple jerking inside the loose skin of his neck.

'She's gone, miss . . . in a tear too – like the divil was after her. What d'ye make of it?'

What could she make of it? She shook her head and watched Murphy gulping the coffee, his face crinkled and happy – she dared not think of what she could make of it.

Murphy, wiping his mouth with the back of his hand, beamed on her. 'It looks as if ye might be set, miss.'

He left her, and from the window she watched his shank-like legs running across the wharf . . . Her being set would mean a lot to Murphy and Pete, but what would it mean to her?

She worked on in a daze, awaiting a summons upstairs, but none came. His dinner was ordered for two o'clock, and when she took it into the drawing-room he was there waiting. But he did not speak until she was leaving the room; then, quite briefly, he said,

'Bessie isn't coming back. Would you like to stay on?'

After a moment of silence, during which he turned his head and looked at her, she said quietly, 'Yes, sir, thank you.'

That was all; but as usual after any nervous strain she wanted to be sick, and she stood in the closed scullery, retching and asking herself what had happened. What could have happened? Surely Bessie hadn't come to give her notice in. She dismissed the idea – when Bessie came through that door it was into 'her kitchen'. Every particle of her declared it. Whatever had happened, she would likely have to wait until Ted told her granda before she knew.

At half-past six she closed the kitchen door – her kitchen door now – and went home. She had never felt so gay in her life before, nor so free. She had a job that she could see stretching on for ever; she could look ahead and say, 'I'll save up and buy things . . . I'll save up for Christmas and buy things for me ma and granda, and Uncle Tony. And perhaps some day I'll be able to buy a fur . . . Oh to have a fur!' She'd always wanted a fur – a long one . . . As she hurried over the sleepers and around the wagons she kept her mind from the man who had made this possible. Later tonight she would think of him and the events of the day, but now to get home and tell Bridget, and talk of the things she'd buy in the future.

Coming out on to the piece of clear ground before she entered the passage, she saw the Arab. He was standing as usual leaning against the broken wall surmounting the river bank, and as usual on her approach he took a step or two from the wall and awaited her coming. She had ceased being actively afraid of him; and now she wondered curiously if he was dumb, for since their first meeting in the passage she had encountered him both morning and evening, rain or shine, and always in the same place – against the broken wall. And never had he spoken, but tonight, adding to the events of the day, he said, 'Good evening.'

Her present happiness held down her fear of him, and she answered, 'Good evening,' but quickened her step as she did so.

'Excuse me . . . please don't be afraid. Can I walk with you?'

His hand came out to check her flight, but she swerved aside, saying, 'No – no thank you.'

'It's all right.'

The words reached her as she entered the passage. He was making no attempt to follow her, and she breathed more easily. She could even smile to herself about it. It was like something one read in a book – 'Good evening – may I walk with you?' Not . . . 'Goin' my road?' or 'Who's tyekin' ye hyem?' His precise English was surprising, for the Arabs one heard talking in the trams jabbered, and he looked so different from any of the others in his tight blue suit, except perhaps a bit taller. All Arabs looked the same to her, of medium height and extreme thinness.

But if, at any time, he should attempt to walk with her, what would she do? There was plenty of time to meet that when he tried it. Anyway, all she'd have to do would be to tell Mr Stanhope. Yes, she'd tell Mr Stanhope, for he didn't like the Arabs, and one bellow from him would scare a dozen Arabs. She laughed to herself – it was like a child saying, 'I'll tell me ma, mind!', or 'I'll tell me da, mind' – only she had never said the latter.

The journey to Jarrow seemed interminable, and when she alighted at the fifteen streets the sight of Matt standing with a group of men at her Grannie's street corner did not, as usual, stiffen her with apprehension. She would be afraid of nothing or no-one today . . . she was happy . . . she had a permanent job, and what a job! The sound of someone spitting followed her. She knew it was Matt, and that it was meant for her, but what did it matter? She walked on, her head high, her step free and swinging, and her face alight, but the moment she entered the kitchen the light was quenched, for there, sitting facing her, was Bessie Grant. On the other side of the hearth sat her Uncle Tony, it being Wednesday, and her mother sat by the table. They were all three quiet, but it was a quietness that any moment could have snapped with extreme tension.

Bridget rose and said, 'I suppose you know why Mrs Grant's here?'

'Oh, she knows, all right.' Bessie uncrossed and recrossed her thick legs.

'Wait a minute.' Bridget put out a gently suppressing hand towards Bessie. 'One story's good till another one's told. We'll take one thing at a time. Rosie – did you tell Mr Stanhope about the – the grocer? . . . You know . . . about Mr Pillin?'

'No, not a word. He knows nothing about it. I only cut down one week, and he hasn't seen the bill.'

'Hasn't seen the bill!' repeated Bessie, with utter scorn.

'He hasn't,' said Rose Angela heatedly, 'for it's in my bag. I've kept it here all the time.'

'Sh!' said Bridget, silencing them both. 'Then how was it, Rosie, that Mr Stanhope could tell Mrs Grant that she had been . . . well . . . getting a bit too much stuff?'

'Not through me. I tell you I've never said a word to him, and he couldn't have heard what I said to Mr Pillin because he was out. He was up the river at the time.'

'Then,' said Bessie, emphasising each word with a nod of her head, 'it's merely a damned excuse, as I said it was.'

'You'd better be careful what you're saying, Mrs Grant.' Tony rose to his feet. 'You can be made to pay for such statements.'

'Made to pay!' Bessie rounded on him. 'What with, eh? When she's even taken the bread out of me bairns' mouths because she's low enough to supply Mr bloody Stanhope with something that I wouldn't! I might have known – but that's what you get for helping people.'

At this moment Bessie was cursing her husband for persuading her, as she liked to think, to let her job to old McQueen's girl, who had been up against it. She was forgetting that at the time she thought it was a good idea, for had she asked any of her friends to take over, they would have known a little

601

too much of her business – and Mr Pillin's, and she didn't want that. But she had considered McQueen's grand-daughter would be so grateful she'd keep her mouth shut. Yet what had happened? Yes, what had happened? It was as plain as a pikestaff – she knew now why this young bitch couldn't keep a job with a mistress. It had been easy going for her with no mistress at Wharf House. The Stanhope bloke was supposed not to like women, but he was a man, and that type of bitch would soon let him know how much of a man he was.

She looked at Rose Angela, and said with insinuating quietness, 'I wouldn't do what you're doing, not for thirty-five bob a week, I wouldn't. But perhaps you've come to some arrangement, eh? You can call the piper now. The lot of you here'll be decked out soon, and be moving, for he's rotten with money.'

Bridget, with set, white face, moved towards the door. 'You'd better be going, Mrs Grant.'

'Aye. I'll go . . . but mark you, don't think she's heard the last of this. Oh no, I'm not taking this lying down – I'll see me day with her, if it's the last thing I do.' She nodded, emphasising her threat as she passed Bridget.

The door closed, and Bridget turned towards Rose Angela, saying quietly, 'Now let's hear what you've got to say.'

'You don't believe her – do you?' Rose Angela stood supporting herself against the table edge.

'I don't know what to believe.'

'Ma!'

'Well, why has he kept you on when she's been with him over a year, if he knew nothing about her doing him? She's known to be a good, clean worker.'

'He didn't know from me.'

After a moment, during which Bridget's eyes bored into her daughter's, she turned to the fire, and took up her attitude of staring at the grate, her hands moving slowly back and forth along the rod. Her voice sounded muffled as she murmured, 'Mrs Grant said she found him in the kitchen with you this morning – you were having coffee together, and laughing; and all the time she was there he never came into the kitchen half a dozen times – he always used the front door.'

Through the righteous anger that was rising in her against Bessie Grant and her mother, and anyone who should think this of her, streaked a feeling of pleasurable surprise that he should have altered even slightly his habits since she had come to live in the house. But the pleasure vanished as quickly as it was born, for here was her mother half-believing Bessie Grant's implications. If Bridget believed this, what could be expected of others?

'I'd rather you left there,' said Bridget softly, 'rather than get yourself a bad name.'

Leave the house, and the river . . . and . . . and him . . . leave such a job, all because of Bessie Grant's spite. 'I'll not leave the job . . . I'll not leave there until he sacks me. As for what people believe – who's going to stop them if I leave tomorrow, when you believe what she said.'

Bridget turned in surprise at Rose Angela's tone. 'I don't want to believe it; but can't you see yourself it looks fishy? Why has he kept you on?'

'I don't know . . . I only know I've found a job I like, and I'm going to stick to it. And you can all think and say what you like.'

So finishing the most forcible words of her life, Rose Angela swung round and went upstairs, leaving Tony and Bridget staring after her.

Nothing could have confirmed her guilt so much in Bridget's eyes as this bold stand . . . her shy, timid Rosie to speak out like that! She could have come to such courage, Bridget reasoned, through one thing only – she was no longer a girl, she had been with that man. Bessie Grant had been right. The Rosie upstairs now was a different Rosie from the one who had returned so often from other places. A great sadness settled on Bridget . . . it wouldn't even be her own case over again, for such a man as the artist was, with money an' all, he wouldn't marry her. And if there was a bairn . . . Bridget was unaware of wringing her hands together until she felt Tony's hands gently unloosing her fingers. Impatiently she pulled them away from him. Here she was blaming her girl for what, all things considered, it was a wonder she hadn't done years ago, for even as a child she must have been aware of what was going on in the house between Tony and herself. Bridget dropped into a chair and bowed her head, saying dully, 'I'm to blame for this.'

Tony looked down on the beloved head and his face fell into lines of sadness. 'You mean, because of us, Bridget!' She did not answer the appeal in his voice, nor raise her eyes to his, and he went on, 'She could have been brought up a thousand times worse. You have nothing to blame yourself for – any blame

there is rests on me; I badgered you into it. But I'd
do it again and again if need be . . . Bridget, look at
me.'

When she did not raise her head he took her face
gently between his hands and lifted it to his. 'Don't
worry, love' – he smiled down on her the gentle,
comforting smile that had warmed her heart for
years – 'she's your girl – she'll be all right. Do you
know' – his smile broadened – 'looking at her just
now I had the feeling she's coming into her own,
somehow – she's been awakened.'

His artless words had other than the desired effect
– Bridget groaned. 'Aye, she's been awakened all
right!' she said.

CHAPTER TEN

THE RETURN

There was a wind blowing from the river, a cold, damp wind. It seemed to fill the cut with a solidness that had to be forced apart. Rose Angela pressed against it, head bent, and her coat hugged tightly to her. She was so cold that she felt she would never be warm again. All night she had been cold – the only warmth that was in her life had been wrenched out last night, not by Bessie Grant's accusations but by her mother believing it so rapidly. How could she? was the question she kept asking herself. Hadn't she left place after place to avoid that very thing? Her name now, she knew, would be so much dirt in the fifteen streets, not because she was suspect of being 'thick' with her boss so much as of having done Bessie Grant out of her job by it. What if the rumour should reach her master's ears? She shivered, imagining the violence of his reaction. Thank God the fifteen streets were miles away. To her knowledge he had never been there, nor was he ever likely to go.

Why was life like this? No little joy or happiness lasted; only the fears and hurts lasted, and the feeling of inferiority. And now the old tormenting questioning was upon her again: why, being a half-caste, were you credited with inheriting the lowest traits of both parents? The injustice had been hard to bear before, but now, since her mother, of all people, was holding her suspect, life looked black and hopeless. She could, of course, prove to her mother that she was wrong by giving up the job; but that would be madness – it was the best place she'd had since Mrs Kent's, and she knew, anyway, that now the job was hers she would never leave it until he sacked her.

After passing through the cut she again saw the Arab standing, sheltering from the wind, close against the wall. He made no move towards her, but said, with a strangely pleasant smile, 'Good morning; the wind is cold.'

Here was a coloured man in a foreign land who likely felt very much as she did. It should be natural to feel in sympathy with him, but all she felt was revulsion, yet so courteous was his greeting that she could not but answer him civilly, 'Yes, it is cold.'

'Can I speak with you a moment?'

'No, I'm late.'

'I won't keep you a minute. Don't be afraid – I mean you no harm.' He moved from the wall. 'Won't you let me talk to you?'

'No!' she shouted back at him, her walk on the verge of becoming a run.

Talk to an Arab! She had only to be seen doing that and . . . Once your name was coupled with an Arab you were . . . taboo. The word was associated in her mind with two girls she knew of who had 'taken up with' Arabs. One had married an Arab and gone to live in Holborn, the other wasn't married but just lived there – they were both taboo. Having heard the word connected with the disgrace of going with an Arab from her childhood, she now put no other construction on it; and she had plenty of fears in her life, she told herself, without a taboo being realised. To be accused of having a 'fancy man' was bad enough, but it was an entirely separate and pure thing compared with having your name coupled with that of an Arab. For a moment she thought of her mother, and, knowing the temper of the fifteen streets, she wondered at her ever being allowed to stay there with a black man. And she had been married.

Pete was outside the railway carriage, protecting a fire built in a hollow scooped out of the earth – he was kneeling, his back to the wind, holding the sides of his coat about it. He glanced up at her, but gave her no greeting, nor did the sombre expression on his face alter. Yet she knew he was very much aware of her, and had been before he glanced up. If, like Murphy, he was pleased she was being kept on he certainly didn't show it. He was a strange man, she thought, for only once had he spoken to her – the time he asked what her name was.

She wished that Murphy was about, for she felt that if she told him about the Arab he would walk with her to the Mill Dam each night, especially as the nights were cutting in. She remembered now he had asked her to be here at eight o'clock; yet he wasn't here. But when she reached the wharf she saw him talking to the guv'nor. They both turned at her approach and she shuddered at the dripping nakedness of 'the master' – he had just come out of the river and was pressing the water out of his hair with both hands. And once again she had the impression of immense strength. Her eyes barely touched him, yet in their flicking she was more acutely aware of Bessie Grant's accusation than she had been before.

His tone was unusually gay as he called to her, 'Breakfast, Rosie; and plenty of it.'

She surmised he was excited about this man coming, who must be even worse than Murphy and Pete to arouse his interest like this. Murphy had been strangely reticent about the new model when she questioned him shortly after her coming here, so she had not brought up the subject since. Doubtless she, too, would have been interested in the man's coming, but for last night – and her mother's reaction.

At nine o'clock the breakfast was over and the dishes washed, and the master was upstairs waiting for the man. She had orders not to leave the kitchen until he came. At quarter past nine he had not arrived, and Stanhope came into the kitchen, his good humour decidedly strained.

'Nine o'clock sharp he was to have been here. No sign of him, eh?' His laughter of yesterday was as if it had never been.

'No, sir.'

'I'll break that blasted Murphy's neck – he did this to me once before. It's my own damn fault – I shouldn't have given him a penny until I had the fellow here.'

Rose Angela made no comment, and he looked at her, his eyes narrowed and scrutinising. 'What's the matter? You all right?'

'Yes, sir.'

'Not bad or anything?'

'Oh no, sir.'

'Did you . . . have you come across Mrs Grant?'

Rose Angela replaced three plates on the delf rack before answering, 'She came to my home last night.'

'Ah!' The sound was expressive. 'Well, don't let her worry you – her notice was coming to her anyway. I was only waiting. If it hadn't been you it would have been someone else.'

She could find nothing to say, and as he left the kitchen muttering to himself about Murphy she thought that even the knowledge that Mrs Grant would have been dismissed in any case wasn't going to be much consolation to her now, for her mother wouldn't believe it.

Stanhope couldn't have reached the top of the stairs when a tap came on the back door. With hardly any interest, and with not the slightest emotion that could be indicative of a premonition, Rose Angela opened it.

The man confronting her was tall; he could at one time have been described as massive. He was still big, but it was merely the framework of bone. He was hatless and his frizzy black hair was greying to a whiteness about the temples. His neck, chin and the lower part of his cheeks were badly disfigured with deep pock marks; and one ear was distorted out of all semblance to an ear, and was twice its normal size. Rose Angela saw all these things at a glance – they were part of the dreadful and pathetic whole – yet her ready sympathy and pity was not touched by them, for she was filled with an incredible emotion. It had not come into her

611

being at this moment at the sight of the man; it seemed to have been born when her body was born and to have lain waiting, to be touched into life on looking into this Negro's eyes. For the eyes resembled those she saw when she herself looked into a mirror.

She was conscious that her mouth was agape, and she felt dazed and stupid as if she had received a blow. She drew slowly aside and allowed him to step into the kitchen, and in his moving his eyes never left hers and hers became fixed in their amazement. She closed the door and stood with her back pressed to it and her hands gripping the sides of her apron. She was aware of the Negro's mouth working and his lips forming words that gave no sound. She saw his eyes glaze and a tremor pass down his body; then, outside herself, she heard the quick padding on the stairs again, and part of her mind shouted at her, 'Be careful!' But she still stood where she was, even when Stanhope entered the kitchen. He, however, did not notice her, for he was looking at the Negro, and when he spoke his voice was quiet, almost tender.

'There you are, then. So you got here.' Stanhope's eyes were devouring the Negro, moving over him with an ecstatic look such as a dealer would bestow on a rare gem.

'Yes, sah.'

The sound of the voice lifted Rose Angela immediately to the slack bank; the darkness was again around her, and she was smelling the rough smell of the jacket, a mixture of tar and mothballs and brine, and the voice that had lived in her mind only by the feeling of warmth its memory aroused was in her ears, speaking now, 'My Rose Angela – she mine.' She had never been able to remember one word from that night, but the simple 'Yes, sah' was the unlocking of the door, closed all these years, on the dim yet cherished memory. This was her da . . . the eyes had told her, and the voice wiped all doubt away.

'Come this way.' Stanhope held an arm out as if to guide the Negro, and added, 'Have you had anything to eat?'

'Yes, sah, thank you.'

He did not look at Rose Angela again, but went into the hall, guided by Stanhope's hand, and Rose Angela leant against the door, repeating stupidly to herself, 'After all these years . . . after all these years. It can't be. And to come here!' She could think of nothing clearly, her thoughts were racing and tumbling about. Only one impression stood out in the jumble of her mind – she was shocked at the sight of this man. If he was her da, and she had no doubt about it, he could not look more unlike what she had imagined. Only his eyes remained true to her picture of him, the picture her Uncle Tony had kept bright for years by saying, 'Your eyes are the same as your da's.' Her Uncle Tony . . . oh, her mother and Uncle Tony! What would her Uncle Tony do if her mother went back to her father? But would she go back? This wasn't the man she had married, not with all those pock marks and that ear. But the eyes must be the same as those her mother knew – gentle, with the gentleness lying deep in their warm brown . . . He mightn't look the same, but he was the same. Somehow she knew this. She looked up to the ceiling – up there was that great battered man who was her da. A faintness overcoming her, she groped her way to a chair and sat down. Mr Stanhope was painting him. What would he say if he knew? Would he look into his eyes and notice the resemblance? No, she doubted it. He would see the Negro as a whole . . . she shuddered . . . or what was left of the whole. The master was only interested in one thing, she thought – getting on to his canvas the last dregs of life. Yet Murphy had seen . . . or was it Pete? Yes, Pete's eyes saw everything. But he must have had something to go on. What? She would likely know later. Was this Murphy's surprise? He had asked her to come back this morning. What must she do now? Her thoughts raced again. What would happen when her Uncle Matt got to know? There'd be murder, for her Uncle Matt would surely overpower this great shadow of a man.

She sat on, her hands stretched out before her on the table and joined as if in prayer, until she was startled by two simultaneous sounds – the hall clock striking ten and a thudding from above. As she mounted the stairs she had to hold on to the banisters for support, and after she had tapped on the studio door she was thankful for the pause before Stanhope's voice called, 'Here!'

She went in, telling herself not to look towards the dais, but immediately her eyes were drawn to it. There he was sitting on the platform, his legs slightly apart and his hands lying palm upwards, one on each thigh. His back was supported by a cunningly contrived rotten hulk of a boat, kept in place by packing-cases; and the double effect of decay was such as almost to make her cry out.

Stanhope was standing before a full-length canvas, and as he softly called her to him his hand, moving the charcoal in swift, broken lines, did not stop, nor did his eyes stray from their darting back and forth to the platform.

'Make some coffee, Rosie, and bring some brandy up. And about twelve o'clock make a meal – something good. I'll have it up here. Bring enough for two.'

His voice stopped and she moved away without emitting the usual, 'Yes, sir.' As she reached the door she knew the Negro's eyes were following her, yet he was apparently gazing straight ahead. It was like the picture of the nun she had in her bedroom – wherever you moved the eyes followed you.

In the kitchen the old feeling of sickness threatened to overcome her, and it took all her will-power to conquer it. When she took the coffee up, Stanhope stopped work, and, pouring a generous amount of brandy into the cup, handed it to the Negro, saying, 'Drink this and have a break. How're you feeling?'

'All right, sah.'

The sound of the voice sent a pain through Rose Angela, and she knew a sudden longing to be alone and to cry. She stumbled uncertainly downstairs, and in the kitchen she had to upbraid herself, saying, 'It's no use going on like this . . . pull yourself together – he wants a dinner for twelve o'clock, and when he says twelve he means twelve; you know that.' But the upbraiding did little good and she commenced the preparations like a sleepwalker.

Once, going to the corner of the house where the dustbin was, she saw Murphy and Pete. They were standing looking speculatively towards the house from the edge of the clearing. She withdrew sharply from their gaze, for she wanted to talk to no-one yet about this thing . . . not until she had first talked to him. How long would the master keep him? As long as he could sit or stand, she supposed.

She made three journeys in all when she took the dinner up, but never once did she allow herself to look towards the Negro; yet when he rose and slowly stretched himself she was conscious of his every movement. Nor did she look at the master, for part of her was daring to question his gay mood – did this man's presence call for gaiety and bantering jokes?

As the afternoon wore on she wondered when she would get a chance to speak to him – she shied from using the word da, even to herself. Would she manage it when he came downstairs?

But she did not speak to him when he came downstairs, for Stanhope was with him, shepherding him as if indeed he was a precious jewel. He even walked out to the wharf with him, solicitous to the last moment, saying, 'Now are you sure it hasn't been too long? We'll cut it down tomorrow if it has.'

His gentleness and consideration sounded strange, this manner being utterly unlike that which he showed to Murphy and Pete. The Negro seemed to have adopted the tone Stanhope had set, for his voice sounded quite gay as he replied, 'No, sah. No hard work 'bout that – jus' settin'.'

'Well, I'm glad you think so. You'll be here the same time tomorrow?'

'Yes sah, same time.'

Through the window Rose Angela watched him walking away until he disappeared round the corner of the house. Stanhope, too, watched him until he disappeared from sight; then he came slowly into the kitchen, rubbing the palms of his hands together as if savouring his day's work.

'Well, what do you think of him? Marvellous specimen, isn't he?'

She turned towards her master – that's all he was to him, a marvellous specimen. For a second she felt a strong feeling of resentment against this man who saw misery only as something to paint; then it was replaced by a feeling of dread which his next words evoked.

'Poor devil, he's not long for the top . . . he'll be lucky if he sees the winter out.'

She put her hand up to her lips and closed her eyes, and his voice, for a moment, receded from her.

'What is it, Rosie? Are you ill? Come and sit down.' He placed a chair for her and she walked unsteadily towards it. His hand hovered uncertainly over her shoulder as if about to touch her. 'What's upset you today? Are you still thinking about Bessie?'

She gave a slight nod, and he went on, 'You're a silly girl. Look here, go and lie down on the couch in the drawing-room for a while, and go home as soon as you are feeling fit again.'

'I'm all right, sir.'

She rose to her feet, and he said harshly, 'You're not all right, but you'll do as you like, I suppose.

You want to get this into your head – your life will be one long hell if you take notice of what the other fellow says – in this case the other woman.'

'Yes, sir.'

'Oh, for God's sake, don't agree with everything I say. And don't keep saying "Yes, sir".'

She marvelled at her own audacity when she asked quietly, 'What do you expect me to do – contradict you?'

His lips twisted into a smile that brought a boyishness to his face and his eyes twinkled at her. 'That would stagger me, wouldn't it?'

As he laughed she thought how she would have enjoyed this little exchange yesterday, or more probably the day before, but now she could think of nothing but what he had recently said. When she gave no reply to his bantering he went out abruptly, saying, 'Do what I tell you and get off home.'

He's not long for the top . . . he's not long for the top . . . the phrase kept repeating itself. Her da was not long for the top. She had scarcely met him, yet already she knew he was marked for death by the words that had always created pity in her – old so-and-so's not long for the top. Now pity for this great, battered, grotesque man began to rise in her; it obliterated the disfigured face – all she could see were the eyes, looking at her with love and pleading in their depth, and all she wanted now was to meet him and confirm the certainty of the kinship.

At six o'clock, as usual, she gave a last look round, adjusted the cloth cover on the supper tray and went out, closing the kitchen door behind her. She tried not to hurry, and her step was unusually slow as she entered the chaotic jumble of wagons. She felt he would be waiting for her somewhere along here . . . but where? She must not miss him.

He was sitting on the step of the railway carriage; and at the sight of her he rose, and she went towards him, still walking slowly. When within a few feet of him, she stopped, and they took their quiet fill of each other.

'You know me, Rose Angela?' The appeal in his voice brought a pain to her heart.

'Yes.' She wanted to say 'Da', but she felt shy of the word.

'Long time, Rose Angela.'

'Yes.'

'You remember me, way back?' His voice was deep, yet had a hollow ring.

She nodded.

'All the years I want to see you . . . I think of you. But you more beautiful than I think.'

His voice cracked and the wet mist was in his eyes again, and she could bear no more. Her arms went out, and with a sound that was forced out of the suppressed depth of him he flung out his own, and they held each other. Their tears mingling, they stood pressed face to face, and as her lips touched his pock-marked cheek he let escape a cry as he had done on the day of her birth, but this time there were no words to it. After a time, during which neither of them spoke, she began to feel the shaking of his limbs as if the bones beneath his skin were jangling, and she said anxiously, 'Sit down.'

Like a child he obeyed her and sat down on the step again. 'You're cold,' she said, bending over him. 'Go inside.'

'No, I'm all right. Inside not very clean, but they not help it. Them good fellows . . . good fellows,' he repeated. He put up his hand to her. 'Sit down here, close by me, and you talk. All years I wait to hear you talk, Rose Angela.' His voice slurred over her name, making it sound like a caress.

She sat below him on the block of wood that formed the step, but she could not talk. Her feelings could not be interpreted into speech, but she bowed her head and pressed it against his knee and held his hands tightly with her own; and slowly the feeling was born in her that although she looked like and loved her mother, she was not of her, she never had been . . . she was of this man. Were he ten times as black, it would be the same.

He's not long for the top. As Stanhope's words came to her she sat up and looked into James's face. 'You're not well, you haven't been well – what's wrong?' she asked gently.

'Oh, that.' He shook his head and gave a laugh that was punctured by a little clicking sound in his throat that couldn't be called a cough. 'I was sick for time . . . but now me get like fighting cock.'

'What were you sick with?' she asked with concern.

He pointed silently to the pock marks on his face; then said, ''Fore this I was big fine fellow, go round with fair and boxed twice a day – twenty rounds I could take. But you wait' – he held her face lovingly between his hands – 'you wait. Now nothing stop me getting fit again.' So convincing was his tone that she believed him . . . She would look after him and get him well; she would spend on him the ten shillings a week she had intended saving to buy Christmas presents and clothes; she would feed him and feed him.

She asked suddenly, 'How did Pete and Murphy know who I was?'

He said again, 'Them very good fellows – them best fellows.'

'But how did they know?'

He turned his head away and looked across the river. 'I been in lower part of town three months, but I been sick. I want to go to fifteen streets, but no know how land lie. Pete, he scout for me; he talk to men around docks.' James paused, then looked at his daughter again. 'Matt still bad . . . still hate me . . . I no want to go to gaol before I see you little time.'

'Oh, Da!' the word escaped her.

'Long time I wait to hear that.' He stroked her cheek and went on, 'You no worry, I not go.' He touched the corner of her eyes with a gentle trembling finger. 'Pete, he say he knew you by your eyes – they like mine. When he think you my girl he ask your name, then Murphy, he make sure and follow you home. Me, I near mad 'cause I not come right away – I laid up with little cold.'

Not one word had he said about Bridget, and as Rose Angela gazed up into the eyes so like her own she knew why, and a hot flush covered her body. Murphy, in his scouting, would have heard more than just how her Uncle Matt felt – he would have heard, too, of the relationship that existed between

Tony and her mother. That relationship would now have to end – her mother must be told. Her da couldn't return to the fifteen streets as long as Matt was there, but her mother could come to him here – he must want to see her so much. She forced herself to mention Bridget's name. Gently she said, 'My mother will get a shock, but she'll be glad.'

James looked away again to the river: 'No tell your mother, Rose Angela. She might come down here, and Matt, he guess. No tell anyone I here.'

For a moment she believed the reason he gave, and unwittingly said, 'But Uncle Tony . . . I could tell Uncle Tony; he would be safe.'

By the stillness of him she knew she had made a mistake, and she murmured, 'I'm sorry.'

He turned quickly towards her, reassurance in his tone. 'You no worry; I have all I want now I have you. We not be parted again, eh?'

The question had a timorous sound; and he inhaled deeply and slowly when, shaking her head, she said, 'Never again.'

After a silence, during which they each seemed to be savouring the other, James went on, 'Tony always good boy . . . him quite a man now.'

There was no bitterness in his tone, so she could say, 'He's always been very good to me.'

'Yes . . . that's what he promise: Me, I look after your Rose Angela, he said. Me, I tell her what a fine fellow you are . . .' His smile took on a piteous twist.

'He did – every Sunday for years he took me to the slack bank and talked about you.'

'He did?' There was some amazement in James's voice.

'Yes, for years; until I think he thought I was too big.' She did not even admit to herself that the Sunday walks had stopped from the time she happened upon her mother and Tony in the front room in each other's arms.

Again a silence fell between them; until James said sorrowfully, 'Me, I never thought I'd come back to you like this; always I dream I have pots of money, and always I see myself decking you out . . . I think I make so much money I even square Matt.'

As Rose Angela listened, her throat tight with tears, she knew that in a thousand lifetimes James could never have made enough money to placate Matt's hate – that was something beyond the bounds of bargaining or reasoning.

'You know I try and take you with me that night?'

He watched her nod.

'Yes, and I always mad I not do it. I could have got you away all right – not even old man know I was on board, and you were good child, quiet and making no trouble. You would have been all right in chief's cabin till ship got clear; then old man if he did find you not do nothing. Things been different perhaps if you with me.'

He shook his head musingly towards the river, and Rose Angela asked, 'What became of the chief?'

James straightened up on the step. 'Him die on next trip, when boilers bust. Sometime I tell you 'bout it . . . not now. Now we just talk of us, eh? Rose Angela' – he bent above her – 'will you take your hat off?' The request was humble, as if asking her to confer on him a great favour, but as Rose Angela's hands went readily to her head he stopped

623

her with a warning movement of his hand, 'Sh! we got company; I hear somebody.'

Rose Angela had heard nothing, but, bending forward, she glanced between the wagons, and then saw the Arab.

'It's an Arab,' she said uneasily; 'he's always about here. He stands by the wall at the bottom of the passage nearly every day.'

James was in no way perturbed; in fact his expression showed pleasure. 'Oh, then, that be Hassan. He all right. Like me, he like river. Every day he come to river. He quite good sort, not like some.'

'Do you know him?'

'Yes – I work for him 'fore I was sick. He got eating-house . . . he quite rich man. But him not like some . . . him like the river and talk 'bout places and other peoples.'

She turned her head and watched the Arab coming into view, and she saw the blank look of astonishment appear on his face when he saw her and James together. James raised his hand to his forehead in salute, and after a moment, during which he stood stock still, the Arab, too, raised his hand; then came forward.

'You courtin' river again?' said James.

The Arab nodded and smiled, but his eyes rested on Rose Angela; and James, standing up, said with deep pride, 'This my daughter . . . you never believe I had white daughter that time I tell you, did you?'

The Arab continued to smile, and shook his head slowly. Rose Angela did not return his smile, but as she looked at him she thought, Now he will speak to me; if I meet him in Shields he will speak to me, and people will see us, and that will be the end of any name I have left. But this thought did not fill her with the usual fear and apprehension, and she wondered at it. Instead, she felt a new strength flowing through her veins, bringing with it courage. She looked at James. She had a da, and she was going to look after him and keep him safe. She had a feeling of belonging, of moving out of the inbetween world in which she had lived her life into another, more steady, planet. In this moment she experienced a sense of exhilaration in which she feared nothing or nobody . . . no – she made her mind gather the words together and present them to her – not even her Uncle Matt!

PART FOUR

CHAPTER ELEVEN

THE BOOKS

'Go ye down now and put yer spoke in and she'll do it.' Kathie leant across the table towards Cavan, who was sitting, his hands clenched on the arms of the chair, gazing stonily at her. 'She's got to do it. And why not for, I ask you? To let her brother sleep in her house a few nights. If it was her fancy man there wouldn't be two ways about it.'

Still Cavan said nothing, and Kathie went on, 'Christmas soon upon us an' all, an' ye know, none better, how we are fixed for coppers. It's worse I'm off since they put Terry on that job, with his tram fares and him eating like a ravenous loon, and wantin' pocket-money an' all . . . and now this to happen – to bring Matt up for a means test! God in Heaven, don't ye see it's less than nothing he'll get when they know Terry's bringing a penny in, an' us havin' a lodger an' all? But if he says he's sleeping out, for there's no place to sleep five of us in these two rooms, then he'll likely stand a chance of getting his full seventeen shillings. Don't you see?'

'Aye, I see.' Cavan's voice rasped like a jangle of steel filings. 'And he's not sleeping there! He can get a bed anywhere around for five bob or so a week.' As he glared at his wife he wondered if she was being purposely blind to Matt's feelings for Bridget – or was she just a fool?

'Five bob or so a week! Will ye listen to him! Five bob or so – the Virgin stand by me side and guide me. We have so much, sure we have, that we can throw five bobs about! Listen to me, Cavan McQueen. My Matt's goin' into nobody's house while his sister sports two rooms with not a soul lying in them.'

Cavan stood up. 'If she had ten empty rooms, he's not going there.'

'An' who the hell are you to say he's not goin' there?'

'I'm the same bloke who used to give you a hammerin'. It's a long time since you had one, but you're asking for it now.'

'Go on, ye little bantam, ye try it on.' Kathie stepped back from the table and rolled up the sleeves of her blouse.

'Oh, away to hell!' Cavan waved her off with a deprecatory move of his hand. 'Don't tempt me . . . only listen to this! We've heard the last of Matt goin' to Bridget's – do you hear that?'

Kathie was almost black in the face with the torrent of mixed emotions filling her great bulk – her thoughts moved from Matt and the means test to a more personal trouble – more than anything at this moment she desired that Cavan should hit her; his refusal to do so was like an insult. She watched him move towards the door, and so great was her feeling that her usual flow of invective was checked, and she stammered and stuttered, 'You . . . you . . .

sod! I'll get even with you. Ye won't lift a finger to help yer own kith and kin, but I'll get even with ye – by God, I'll get even with ye before many hours have passed over yer head.'

The door banged and she was left yelling at the walls. 'I'll see me day with ye. Like me fine daughter Bridget ye are, getting too big for yer boots – with her loose piece of a girl giving her twenty-five shillings a week. And I know where that-'un'll end, too. And she's another mean sod, for not a penny has she given me since she started. But you' – she flung herself to the window and yelled fruitlessly – 'yer Rosie gives you a backhander, don't she!' The sound of her voice echoed around the walls, and the words seemed to fall about her and hurt her. She turned into the room and beat the table in her rage. He hadn't lifted a finger to her, and she had gone at him like that! Years ago, when the bairns were young, he often landed her one, and then he was sorry and she cooked him a good feed after; but now . . . now, nothing. Her head swung from side to side. Bridget and Matt were entirely forgotten, only her own failure confronted her. She could no longer rouse her man; nothing she did could touch him. How long was it since he last slapped her a wallop across the backside? Years; not since he had started that reading business. She no longer meant anything to him – she was just a fat hulk that he even turned from in bed at night. He wasn't always like that – by God, no! At one time she could say yes or nay, but not since he took to that reading. Her head stopped swinging . . . It was them books that had made him different . . . he wanted nothing but them books.

Pity for herself turned to rage again. She looked towards the shelf that held eight books, all brown paper-backed and stacked according to their size. Cavan had made the shelf and hung it above the bed. As she stared, her fingers cupping one great breast began to twitch, and the fire dropping in the grate sent a glow into the darkening kitchen and showed up her mouth and eyes, stretching in their portraying of her thoughts. Who said she couldn't touch him? Didn't she say she'd get even with him? And what better way? She'd let him see she wasn't dead yet. Scorn her, would he? Sit there, hour after hour, reading and never a word out of him, never a laugh, never a joke? Well, she'd finish all that.

With three steps and a sweep of her hand the books were scattered over the bed and on the floor, and as she stooped to pick one up the enormity of her intention stilled her hand for the moment. Then with a growl which seemed to emerge from some dark depth, even beyond that of her enormous body, she gripped the pages and wrenched them out; and she threw them on the fire. But the dull glow of the cinders seemed to hesitate before sending even a small flame to lick their edges, and Kathie, taking a poker, scattered the pages, the more readily to catch the flame; and when they were alight she threw on the mutilated book cover. One book after the other followed until the fire was banked high with smouldering cardboard and blackened paper. And when there was no more to tear she thought of the box under the bed – she'd make a clean job of it. Scorn her, would he? She'd make him sorry he had ever imagined he could live without her.

Once his books were burnt he'd be finished, for he'd never have the face to go into Shields to the library; even if he had the nerve he'd never go because he wasn't decently put on. And whichever way he went – Jarrow or Shields – it meant walking miles there and back; and he hadn't the boots, anyway. No, she had him right enough. Like some unwieldy animal she went down on her knees and dragged the tin box from under the bed.

Still kneeling, she went on working in a frenzy, pulling and tearing at the books and telling herself that no-one would slight her and get off with it; least of all that little rat who had chased her for months before she'd look at him. He'd thought nothing about reading in those days, nor did it matter a damn that she could neither read nor write.

That it was forty-five years ago Cavan had pursued her did not enter into her reasoning; nor had her illiteracy troubled her in the least until recently, when she imagined that part of Cavan's indifference was bred by scorn of her ignorance. She knew that the days of love-making were long past, and she herself was past wanting them renewed, but there had been little acts of endearment between them which, with the years, had taken the place of passion – such as him bringing her a wallop across the backside after being supplied with a good feed, or his feet searching and twining around hers in the night. But during the past two years even these had ceased.

Deaf to all sound but that of her rage, she did not notice the opening of the door; and so astonished was Eva's Johnnie at the sacrilege being perpetrated that he could not speak. For a time he remained still, watching his grannie; then silently closing the door, he ran off to tell his granda, whom he had just left standing at the corner of the street.

'Granda! Granda' – he flung himself against Cavan's legs – 'me grannie's gone off her chump – she's throwing your books on the fire!'

Cavan had not run for years, but now his running had an arrow's swiftness to it that far outstripped Johnnie's youthful legs; nor did his speed slacken until he reached the kitchen door. Still in his stride, he flung it open and was brought up sharply by the sight of the fire piled high with his treasures. Kathie turned and confronted him, pieces of charred paper clinging to her hair and face, which, with her frantic exertion and the heat, was looking like a great red balloon. For perhaps a moment Cavan stared at her, his mouth and eyes stretched wide; then rushing forward, he plunged his hands into the smouldering mass, and flinging handful after handful on to the floor, began to stamp on it, seemingly unaware that they were no longer his books, but small pieces of paper, most of them charred.

Standing amid the smoke and the paper, Kathie taunted him as he thrust his hands again and again into the now flaming jumble; and when, as if at a given signal, he stopped his vain efforts, her voice faded away in her throat, and she stood slumped, watching him looking helplessly down at the debris. He lifted his head and stared at her through the smoke, and she saw how useless had been her effort. Not even this would make him lift his hand again to her, for in his eyes was only sorrow and pain.

Her flesh seemed to shrink from her bones as she watched the tears gathering in his eyes – never had she known her man to cry. She watched him stumble to a chair and sit down, and spread his burned hands out before him on the table; and when he dropped his head between them and began to sob, she, too, groped for a chair and sat down; and the knowledge that Cavan was not made hers again by the loss of his books but gone from her for ever made her great body tremble. Entirely forgotten now was the cause of the row, and she began searching her mind for a reason, asking herself what had led her to do such a thing. A surge of emotion she was unable to understand and had no power to control rushed upon her. Like a penance, it filled her with sorrow and regret; feelings that were both new to her, so new that they made her fearful – of what, she didn't know. She only knew that she was sorry and she must cry . . . she, who had laughed so much in her life, must cry as if for the first time. Slowly and painfully her sobs mingled with Cavan's; and the sound and the sight scared Johnnie, who was standing staring through the window; and since his mother wasn't in he ran to tell his Aunt Bridget.

Bridget was standing in her favourite position, hand gripping the brass rod and her eyes resting on the words 'Grieve Gillespie, Jarrow-on-Tyne' on the stove. How many times during the years had she faced a problem standing thus, and mostly about the man behind her now? She stood listening to his voice, soft and whining, and she thought for the countless time, Oh, if he were only dead! and for the countless time she was shocked and grieved at her thoughts.

'Just for a little while . . . I won't be in your way.'

'Matt' – her voice, too, was soft – 'I've told you. You can't stay here . . . Look, don't let's have any more rows over it – I've told you what I'll do – I'll give you a few shillings towards you getting a room for a week or two.'

'But why should I, when you've got two rooms doing nothing? And what'll folks say? They'll think it funny, I'll tell you, when me own sister won't take me in for a night or two.'

Bridget sighed. 'It's immaterial to me what people say.'

'Is it?' There was a challenge in his tone.

Bridget did not reply, and he went on, 'If your great managing director was to ask, he wouldn't be refused – he never has yet.'

'You know that's a lie!' She swung round on him. 'He's never stayed here at nights.'

'No, he gets what he wants before that.'

She raised her hand and dropped it helplessly. 'Matt – you're not staying here, and that's final.'

Bridget's rage was always more bearable to Matt than her indifference or her reasonableness. Now she was trying to be reasonable, to put him off with soft words, and it maddened him. Why was she trying to put him off? He knew why – because of that dirty half-caste. It was strange that although he hated Tony, the feeling was as nothing compared with that which even the thought of Rose Angela

636

could rouse in him. Rose Angela still stood as a symbol of the thing that had taken his Bridget away from him; every part of her reminded him of the man whom he held responsible for his distorted face and the frustrations of his life.

Years ago he would have taken what he deemed his just revenge on Rose Angela's face, but for the knowledge that in doing so he would be cutting himself off for ever from Bridget. The hate of Rose Angela the child had been bearable because he knew that Bridget bore her no real love, but from the time he sensed the change in Bridget's affections his hate, when Rose Angela was present, often made it almost impossible for him to restrain his urge to destroy.

He would not admit to himself that the reason Bridget was refusing him was because she didn't want him in the house – he could not face the fact that his Bridget did not want him. She was, in his mind, the only one who did want him. And were it not for that 'un she would take him in like a shot; it was because of her he was being refused.

'I know why you won't have me here.' He addressed Bridget's back as she took a table cloth from the dresser drawer preparatory to laying the table. She did not answer him, and he went on, 'It's because of that 'un, isn't it?'

Still Bridget made no rejoinder.

'Well, it looks as if that reason will soon be moved.'

Bridget swung the cloth over the table.

'She's changed her fancy man. The funny thing is, the other bloke must be in the dark, as she's still working for him.'

'What badness are you concocting now?' Bridget's mouth was grim as she jerked round and faced him.

'I'm concocting nothing – it's the truth. She's picked up with one of her own kind.'

The muscles of Bridget's face sagged, and her voice shook as she said, 'Matt, be careful – I can only stand so much.'

'You'll have to stand this sooner or later; if not from me from somebody else.'

'Go on.'

'She's thick with an Arab.'

Bridget remained still.

'You don't believe me? Well, get on to Jack Rundall. He was with me the first time I saw them. She was standing talking to an Arab in the open near the ferry, as brazen as brass she was, and he eating her with his eyes.'

Matt was quiet now, both inside and out, for he had roused Bridget not to anger but to fear. Her face was stiff with it.

'No!' Her whisper was scarcely audible, but Matt heard it and said, 'It's true. And then there was last night, I watched her. The same Arab was waiting for her near the river, at the end of the cut that leads into Holborn. I saw them under the lamp. She gives him her hand and they start talking, then off they go, right into Holborn . . . into a café affair; and you don't have to be told what those places are.' His voice had assumed an almost sympathetic tone.

Bridget whispered again to herself, 'No, oh no, Rosie.'

Last night she was late – it was nearly nine o'clock when she came in. She had been late other nights, too, because, she said, there were some people staying with Mr Stanhope and she had to cook a late dinner. It sounded so feasible, and she had tried not to think there might be another reason for the lateness . . . and all the time she was going with an Arab. Oh God! Bridget folded her arms about her waist and began to rock herself . . . Not that, not an Arab. Yet could she be blamed? What example had she to follow? What had she thought all these years about her mother marrying a black man, not to speak of what she knew of Tony? . . . But an Arab! James had been handsome in his way, but the Arabs were like weeds. And then, what about her master?

Bridget had just said she cared nothing for people's gossip. For herself, she could bear it; but when it touched her daughter, it tore at her. Because of Bessie Grant, people had for months looked askance at Rose Angela, but now she would be stamped 'a real loose piece'; and she wasn't bad, somehow she wasn't bad. Lately when Bridget covertly watched her daughter's face she was forced to say to herself, 'If she's bad, then there's no good in heaven or earth.' No, she wouldn't believe it – Rose Angela would never go with an Arab, she had always been afraid of them. This was another of Matt's tricks. He was evil – she stopped her rocking – but strangely enough he wasn't a liar. This fact forced itself on her mind and she muttered to herself, 'Oh my god, there must be something in it, somehow.' And Matt said Jack Rundall had seen her and all. If that was so, then most of the fifteen streets knew about it by now. Suppose they did to Rose Angela what they did to Rene

Batten a few years ago . . . pelt her out of the streets. Oh Holy Mary, don't let this happen to my lass!

As Bridget sent up this fervent prayer Johnnie's voice came screaming up the yard, 'Aunt Bridget! Aunt Bridget!' And Bridget turned sharply as he burst into the kitchen, crying, 'Stop that yelling, you!'

'But Aunt Bridget' – he stood panting, the saliva running over his loose lower lip – 'there's hell on at me grannie's; she's burnt all the books an' me granda kept putting his hands in the fire and he's crying.'

'What! What you talking about?'

'They've been fightin'. Me ma's not in . . . oh, come on Aunt Bridget!' he pleaded. 'I tell you me granda's cryin'.'

Momentarily Bridget's personal worries were thrust on one side; but she looked suspiciously at her nephew, and, remembering his tendency to practical jokes, said, 'You're not having me on, Johnnie, are you, for I can't stand your games the day.'

'No, no, Aunt Bridget, strike me dead. They were rowin' and me granda went out and me grannie threw his books on the fire, and now she's cryin' an' all.'

Her ma crying! Bridget ran up the stairs for her coat, and when she returned to the kitchen Matt said, 'It'll be a damn good job if she has burnt the lot of them; he's been dotty since he got them books.'

If what Johnnie said was true, Bridget realised it would be nothing less than a catastrophe for her father, and as she hurried through the streets, Matt shuffling at her side, her own trouble was obliterated for the moment. If her da's books were gone, life

640

would be finished for him. There were thousands of other books, she knew, but the motley assortment with their fund of varied topics were his books, even though sometimes she had been a little scornful in her own mind regarding his attitude towards them, thinking that he showed signs of senility in his treating them like children.

As they neared the back-yard door Matt exclaimed, 'By God, she must have done it . . . smell that?'

The yard was full of the smell of burning and Bridget's uneasiness grew; and when she entered the kitchen she was appalled at the sight of her parents sitting one each side of the table in utter dejection amidst the chaos of the room, but more so was she shocked by the look of her father. His already small body seemed to have shrunk and he now looked a tiny old man; and her heart was wrung when, lifting his brimming eyes to her, he said with the simplicity of a child, 'She burned me books, Bridget; she's burned all me books, lass.' It was as if he had said, 'She has burned all I hold dear in life; I am finished; there is nothing more to live for.'

That his dejection should then cause a slight irritation to assail her surprised Bridget. She knew her mother had done wrong in taking her spite out on him by burning his books, but need he take it like this? It wasn't as if he'd been a great reader all his life, and she doubted whether he understood one quarter of what he read. He remembered interesting facts and outstanding episodes, and delighted to relate his knowledge, also to pass on that which he gleaned from Ted Grant. But then again

Bridget recalled that he had been happier during the past few years than she had ever known him to be, and her irritation vanished – he'd be happy no more.

She looked at her mother, pitiable with age and slobbery fat. She hadn't laughed so much lately. Strangely, in contrast with Cavan, she had seemed less happy these past two years. Was this why she had destroyed the books, because they had brought him happiness? But she was old, and she shouldn't feel like this. Yet, as Bridget continued to stare at her mother, the thought came to her that age brought no respite – there still remained the worries, the fears and hurts . . . the tearing of one human being to shreds by another. Life was ruled by emotion, and when emotion was frustrated this was the result – people died while they still breathed. And although, of the two, Bridget liked her father best, her sympathy at this moment went to her mother.

Rose Angela had been at Wharf House four months now. At times she could not believe this; it seemed like four years, or even fourteen, for the events before she came here were dim and dream-like in her mind, and no day up till today had been long enough for her. She wanted the hours to spread themselves so that she could savour the two great things that had come into her life – her father's return and their nightly meetings; and this other great thing, which she would not admit openly to herself but which made her days joyous and coloured her dreams at night with what might be if miracles could happen. But this latter had been thrust into the background and now only the thought of her father filled her mind. For last night she had left the house as usual at six o'clock and made her way to the spot where she always met James, near the railway carriage. But he was not there.

It was their custom, if it was dry, to walk along the river bank, but if a gale was blowing they shared the shelter of the railway carriage with Murphy and Pete. The railway carriage had been turned into winter quarters, the windows being covered at night with pieces of sacking nailed on to frames to hide the light of the fire in the home-made stove, and more recently, the light of a little lamp supplied by Rose Angela. Into the company sometimes came the Arab, Ali Hassan; and the contrasts of the men gave Rose Angela food for thought as she sat, silent mostly, listening to their individual tales – the Arab, the Negro, the dwarf who was half-Russian, and Murphy, born of an English mother and father unknown and brought up in the workhouse. And she often marvelled that never once in all the talks she had sat through was a swear word used in her presence. The courtesy with which they each treated her often brought a lump to her throat. It was as if she were someone of note – even a queen, she sometimes thought, could not receive more respect than she did. And the many sore places in her heart were soothed.

But last night her father was not waiting for her, nor was there any sign of Pete or Murphy, and she was filled with panic.

Hassan, waiting at the entrance to the cut, quiet and patient as always, seemed to her, at that moment, like a comforting angel, and she ran to him, crying, 'Oh, Hassan, where's me da?'

And he replied soothingly, 'Don't worry; he's a little sick and can't get out, but I'll take you to him.'

When she asked where Murphy and Pete were he said he understood they had gone that morning across the river, where, they'd heard, lay the chance of some odd work.

Rose Angela did not know where her father lodged. On this he had been firm. When she had asked him to tell her in case an emergency such as the present one arose, he had laughed and said, 'Me, I be ill no more now.' Nor did she know exactly what was wrong with him, for he would not talk about himself.

Hassan had called into his eating-house and collected some food, and as he led her along narrow streets and through short, black alleyways where she could see nothing but felt that in the thick depths figures were standing, she began to understand why her father had refused to bring her here; and on reaching the house, his firmness on the matter was made absolutely clear to her. The house was one of a number which led out of a yard, and the yard was approached by a passage from the street. The ground floor was in darkness and silence, but on the first landing pale shafts of light came from beneath numerous doors, and voices in strange tongues came to her. They passed another landing and mounted yet another flight of stairs, and the air, after the freshness of the river, almost stifled her. The prevailing smell was of dirt, dirt such as she had never yet encountered even in the worst part of the fifteen streets. Even before she followed Hassan into the room she was sick at heart for her father, but when she saw him in the rusty iron bed, his back supported against the bare rails, pity and love overwhelmed her. He grasped her outstretched hand, but he did not speak, for he was holding a rag over his mouth.

The beating of her heart stopped for a moment as she saw the red streaks on the cloth – consumption! Oh God! Yet he had no cough, just that little tickling sound in his throat. She imagined all consumptives coughed and spat, like that man who travelled on the Jarrow tram and spat into a bottle. She could never make up her mind which was the worst, spitting on to the floor or into a bottle. But her father to have consumption . . . and spitting blood with it! As his eyes looked into hers with unbearable love and tenderness she knew what she must do – she must come and live here and look after him.

During the past four months she had grown to love him with a love so deep it amounted to worship; and each day she was made more poignantly aware of what she had missed by being brought up without him, and of the unnatural load of fear that had been bred in her because of his absence. But now, the knowledge that he was near was building up in her a courage that had already ousted much of her fear. Yet there were always new fears waiting to be born. She had imagined he was getting better, for he looked better and talked as if whatever was wrong with him was now cured; but this – she knew what consumption meant, especially bleeding from the mouth.

They mustn't be separated again . . . for the time that was left to him she must be with him, even in this house.

She drew his head to her, and as he leant against her she felt him sigh, and a fresh surge of strength, like the strength that had once been his, flowed into her, and she knew she would need this strength if she was to stick to her decision. First, her mother must be told. To face Bridget and say 'I am leaving home, I am going to sleep in' would be the final confirmation in her mother's mind that she had 'gone wrong'; but far rather let her think she was living with Mr Stanhope than she was living in Holborn.

The simplest course for her, she knew, would be to tell her mother the truth, but there the simpleness would end, for she felt she knew her mother enough to know that even were there no Uncle Matt to be considered the return of this gaunt Negro into her life would fill her with nothing but pain and embarrassment, to say the least. It would also deprive her of what happiness she had with Tony . . . Rose Angela felt a separate pang of sorrow for Tony; he had been so good; he had lived his life just to serve her mother and her. No, things must remain as they were. Her father was wise – he knew the situation was only bearable as it was now. She could not tell whether he harboured any bitterness towards Bridget, for he never spoke of her, but she guessed there were a number of reasons why he did not want her mother to know of his whereabouts.

After a while, when she told James what she intended doing he became agitated, saying, 'No, Rose

Angela, me better tomorrow. She not do this, Hassan, eh?'

Although Hassan said no and that it would be unwise to do so, his eyes were telling her that above all things he wanted her here, not in this house, but in Holborn.

Rose Angela was well aware of Hassan's feelings towards her, but so well had she come to know him that she no longer feared him, or resented the fact that he should love her; and at times she thought it a waste and a pity that he should care for her as he did, for never could she return a spark of such feeling. Even if this other great love had not come into her life, she would have never considered Hassan.

To soothe James she had complied with his wishes of last night and had gone home, but she had been borne down with anxiety. This morning she'd had to wait until word was brought to her regarding his condition for she could not have found her way to the house alone. Murphy came in the middle of the morning, and his words 'I'm afraid, miss, he'll soon kick the bucket' had decided her. She told Murphy that as soon as she was finished work she would go home and get her things, and she asked if he would meet her at the cut and take her to the house. She also asked him if Hassan had sent for a doctor, and Murphy said he had.

There were still two more hours before she could leave. She longed intolerably to get away, yet she shivered at the thought of facing her mother.

She was brought from her thinking by her master entering the kitchen. He had not 'thumped' for his afternoon tea – at least she didn't think he had. 'You didn't knock, sir?' she asked.

'No – I thought I'd have it down here – it's warmer. Not in your way?'

'No, sir, of course not.'

She began immediately to get his tea, thinking that if only she hadn't so much on her mind she could enjoy this moment. Twice before during the past few days he had taken his tea with her and talked to her, and she had lain awake at night thinking over the things he had said. She looked at him now, sitting in the basket chair by the little blue stove, and it came to her that he seemed lonely; and another phrase was added to that feeling which she thought could not be enlarged.

He startled her by turning his head suddenly and holding her gaze. 'You look pale today, Rosie. Are you over-working?'

'Oh no, sir.'

'You don't still take notice about that wash-leather business I barked at you when you first came, do you? I always used that technique on the types they sent me from the agency. You see, I was a lone man and I found they always wanted to run me as well as the house; that wash-leather was a very good way of putting them off.'

She smiled and said, 'You mustn't have been fierce enough, sir; it had no effect on me.'

'I'm glad of that.'

She turned from his eyes and began to set the tray; and he looked into the fire again, and a quietness that was weighed with peace filled the kitchen; and Rose

Angela forgot for the moment what lay before her this evening.

'Rosie, would you mind coming in on Christmas Day?'

'Not at all, sir. I expect to.'

'If Mr Collins is here I won't ask you, for then we'll go out somewhere.'

'It won't matter in the least, sir. I'll come in.'

'Rosie' – he was still looking into the fire – 'what do you want most? Is there something that you've longed for and never been able to have? Tell me – I want to give you a Christmas present.'

She stopped in the act of pouring his tea out. What did she want most? That her father should be better. He couldn't give her this; but the other great desire he could fulfil, and him only. Her face began to burn and although his eyes were not on her she turned away in case he should look up and see what madness she had come to. It was one thing to surrender her soul to him in the deep privacy of her being, but it would, she thought, destroy itself through exposure.

'I've . . . I've never wanted very much, sir; I have all I want – a job, a very good job,' she added.

'Oh, Rosie, for God's sake don't be so humble.' He was aggressive again, his jaw thrust out and his eyes glinting. 'You shouldn't be humble; there's nothing about you to create humility. Why, you could—' He paused. 'Look; tell me truthfully; is there anything you've ever dreamed about?'

What words he used! She pushed the little trolley up to the fire, and now she was near him, looking down into his face, into those startlingly blue eyes. What could she say? Could she say a wireless? But that would be so expensive. A fur? Oh no . . . some little thing – a brooch.

'Perhaps a brooch, sir.'

'A brooch!' His tone ridiculed the word. 'You're a disappointment, Rosie.'

'Yes, sir.'

'Sit down and have some tea with me.'

She hesitated for a moment, and he yelled, 'Go on, sit down, woman! There, you've got me bellowing again . . . you shouldn't cross me.'

As she sat down on the opposite side of the hearth to him she caught the glimmer of a twinkle in his eye, and her own was forced to respond, and they laughed together.

'You must think me a funny old man.'

'I don't think you old, sir.'

'Well, I am; I'm nearly twice your age. I'm close on forty.'

'You don't look it, sir.'

'Nice and polite of you. Why are you not married, Rosie?'

The abruptness of the question caused her to stammer, 'Well . . . well . . .'

'I suppose you're waiting until you have enough money.'

'No, I am not waiting.' To herself her voice sounded cold and unemotional, giving no indication of the inner turmoil. She was conscious of drawing herself up, as if to defend her pride, as she went on, 'I've never been asked.'

He continued to look at her for a time before saying softly, 'There are more damn fools in the world than I thought.' Then he returned to his previous question. 'Now, tell me the truth, what would you like for Christmas? . . . Besides a brooch, that is. By the way, I hate brooches, and I can't stand women who plaster themselves with jewellery.' He looked so aggressive as he said this that she was forced to smile again, thinking it was well she knew him.

'There's nothing really, sir.'

'Well, I'm not buying you a brooch. I'll give you the money and you can get what you like.'

'That's very kind of you, sir.' She turned to the table to hide her pleasure at this, for above all things at the present time she needed money.

'You know, Rosie, you are the most formal individual I have ever come across. Tell me, are you afraid of me?'

'Oh no, sir.' Her assurance was so sincere that there was no doubt that it was true; but he went on, 'Then if you're not afraid of me you are of someone or something.'

Rose Angela looked down at her plate and broke her cake into small pieces. 'I have been afraid of many things in my life, but lately they have all gone, or nearly so.'

She said no more, and he did not press the question, but continued with his tea in silence until she rose and went to the oven; and he asked, 'What have you in there? It's a lovely smell.'

She called back to him from the scullery, 'It's your Christmas cake, sir'; and he repeated laughingly, 'It's your Christmas cake, sir.'

When she returned to the kitchen he was standing by the table, and as she readjusted her apron and straightened her cap he nodded towards her head and said, 'It still isn't straight.' There was a quirk to his lips.

She flushed and said, 'It's my hair, nothing will stay on it.' And she again attempted to straighten the cap.

'That's another thing I detest – caps. Take it off and never wear it again.'

She paused, her hands raised to her head, and at his next words her feelings almost suffocated her.

'You are very beautiful, Rosie.'

As her hands brought the cap from her head she forced her eyes from his in case she should betray herself, and the wisdom of this was given to her as he went on, his tone brusque again, 'Don't worry . . . I am merely paying you a compliment.'

He went out in his quick, bustling way, and she sat down by the table, the cap still held in her hands. 'You are very beautiful, Rosie . . . I am merely paying you a compliment.' Was that the artist speaking or was it the man? She sat quiet until the chimes of the clock from the hall told her that soon it would be time to go, and there were other things that she must think of; and she wondered why everything should have come into her life at once . . . her love for this man, and the coming of her father . . .

Rose Angela's nervous system was like a highly tensed wire. The fears of her childhood and teens had played on it with such regularity that it responded with a feeling of acute sickness and anxiety when anything of a worrying nature affected her. Now, as she faced Bridget, she felt so sick that it was as much as she could do to stand. She had told Bridget that Mr Stanhope had people staying and that she was going to sleep in for a little while. She had managed to face her mother's blank stare as she said this, but under Bridget's silence her new-found courage was failing her. She knew that her mother did not believe a word she said, yet she forced herself to go on bluffing. 'It'll only be for a little while. I'll still let you have something each week . . . perhaps it won't be so much for the time being, as . . . as I'm living in.' It would have been difficult enough to lie if Bridget had believed her tale, but under the circumstances she was finding it almost impossible.

'Are you going to live with your master or the Arab?' Bridget's voice was without tone or colour. It seemed like the voice one would expect to hear from the dead, could the dead speak.

Rose Angela mouthed 'The Arab?' without any sound coming from her lips, and Bridget said, 'Yes, the Arab . . . you are going to live in Holborn, aren't you, where you've spent a good many of your evenings these past weeks?'

Rose Angela could only stare at her mother. It was Hassan she was meaning . . . someone had seen her with Hassan. But who? It had always been dark when she saw him, except that once by the ferry, and then there had been no-one about . . . Oh, this was worse than anything she had ever imagined. Her mother mustn't go on thinking this. Oh no, she couldn't let her think this. She must tell her about James, no matter what it entailed: Matt's vengeance and Tony's unhappiness; she must tell her. She could have allowed her to go on thinking she was Mr

Stanhope's mistress, but not this. To have married an Arab would have been bad enough, but to casually live with one . . . no, she would be foolish to allow anyone to think this, most of all her mother.

Relief flooded her with the knowledge that she was about to straighten things out, and she put out her hand to Bridget, saying, 'It's true I'm going into Holborn, but just to – well, lodge there.'

Bridget did not take the proffered hand, and as Rose Angela, knowing that she was about to give her mother a shock, said gently 'Sit down a minute, Ma', there came to her the sound of stormy voices from the back yard, and one at least brought the sickness over her again.

Within a second Matt and Tony were in the kitchen, and Matt, not pausing from his battle of words, directed the onslaught of his bitterness against the thorn that was forever in his flesh. 'That's the cause of all the trouble – there!' He thrust out his arm and pointed his finger at Rose Angela.

'Don't be so daft, man; she wasn't here when your ma and da were rowing.' Tony, too, was angry and his nose was twitching rapidly.

'She didn't need to be, but it was through her. She's at the bottom of everything. If me ma goes off her head I swear to God I'll kill her.'

'It'll take a lot to knock your ma off her head,' said Tony, scathingly.

'What is she, then, but nearly daft, running round the streets begging folks to give her books for me da?'

'That's remorse for the thing she did to him, and it'll do her good to feel like that, but it'll take more

654

than that to knock her off her head . . . It's your old man you should be worrying about, not her. She's burned more than his books the day.'

Matt was not in the least concerned about his father, but his dauntless, laughing, loud-mouthed mother had always held his respect, and during the last few hours she had shocked him by going soft and begging the silent Cavan to forgive her, promising to get him all the books he could ever read. To Matt, her final humiliation was her actual begging for books, and it was all because Bridget wouldn't put him up for a night. And why wouldn't she? Because of that Arab whore.

'If she has,' he answered Tony, 'who's to blame but that dirty Arab supplier? Whites don't suit her now, she must get herself an Arab.'

Before Tony could bring out a startled exclamation and the sound of Bridget's groan escaped her lips, Rose Angela's voice rang through the kitchen louder than it had ever been raised in that room before. 'How dare you say such a thing! You're a liar! Do you hear, a liar!' There was no sign of fear in her as, for the first time in her life, she faced up to Matt. 'You and your filthy mind! You're like a sewer.' She turned from him and confronted Tony. 'Uncle Tony, do you believe I'm going to live with an Arab?'

'No, lass. I'd never believe that, never.'

'Then why,' put in Bridget beseechingly, 'are you going to live in Holborn, lass? Tell us that.'

The three stared at her, hanging on her reply.

Rose Angela looked from one to the other, and as her lips opened her eyes came to rest on Matt.

655

She had only to say 'because James is there' and she would be clear; yet in doing so she would be handing him over to this maniac. She couldn't do it. She knew from the look in her mother's face that she believed the worst of her, and now even her Uncle Tony's expression was showing bewilderment and doubt at the mention of her going to live in Holborn. She looked at her mother again; then dropped her lids to shut out Bridget's tortured gaze and turned away, saying flatly, 'No matter what I said, you wouldn't believe me. Think what you like, I'm going to get my things.'

Matt hadn't spoken since she had called him a liar. To say the least, her bold front had startled him, and it was strange that he, who in the first place had accused her of going with an Arab, was now the only one to believe her when she denied it, even in spite of having with his own eyes seen her talking to one. He was astute enough to know that it had taken a very powerful emotion to arouse that outburst against himself, for he knew that he could instil the fear of God, as he put it, into her. He stood, his eyes fixed on the staircase door, awaiting her return and asking himself the question 'Why should she be going to live in Holborn, if not with somebody? And if it wasn't the Arab, then who was it?'

The gas began to flicker, and Bridget, moving heavily towards the mantelpiece to get some coppers from the toby jug for the meter, shoved him aside, and in putting out his hand to steady himself he touched the fretwork pipe-rack on the wall, the hated relic of the damned nigger! His whole instinct was to whip his hand away as if it had come in contact with molten steel, but his hand remained still as something clicked in his brain, and his widening eyes seemed to draw from the pipe-rack the answer to his probing. Slowly his fingers began to move into the holes, until they hung like talons from the rack. God Almighty! Could it be? Who else?

The gas went up with a plop and Bridget came back into the kitchen, and Matt turned from the pipe-rack and looked from her to Tony. Who else. Who else? They didn't know, they suspected nothing. Nobody knew, only that half-black rat up there. Hadn't she nearly given the game away to clear herself, just a minute ago? She had pulled up only just in time. No, nobody knew but her . . . and now him. God Almighty!

Slowly he began to rub the scar on his face. How long was it? Sixteen years . . . sixteen years! His fingers nipped the flesh about the scar at the corner of his mouth. Sixteen years he'd carried this, sixteen years of nights he'd lain tossing and turning. He looked back to the days when he had laughed with the lasses. He had wanted nothing from them but to laugh with them, not even to touch them. There was only one woman he had wanted to touch. Yet from when they laughed no more with him a desire to extract something from them had arisen, adding to the torment of his days and the agony of his nights; and now he who caused all this was back. He must be . . . that was the only answer to that lily-livered rat up there having the spunk to face him. Perhaps all these years she had been on the look-out for the nigger – she'd had it ground into her enough as a bairn by that blasted fool Tony that her da would come back. He'd heard him at it time and again before he got thick with Bridget. A pain like a knife twisting in his bowels went through him, and his fingers moved up the scar, nipping the silver flesh into momentary redness . . . Well, if his surmise was right, Master Tony would soon have the tin hat put on him; he knew his Bridget well enough to follow her reactions to the nigger's return.

He turned his eyes to the staircase door. She would get brave, would she? By God, she'd need to be brave before he'd finished with her. Stand up to him, would she? He'd see about that. He'd plaster her name with the Arab's so thick about the fifteen streets that she wouldn't dare put her nose inside them, much less come home again to live. If her own mother and Tony could believe she was thick with an Arab, how much more gullible would be the neighbours. And what about the painter bloke? Aye, what about him!

And if she was willing to forgo what was left of her good name to cover up for the nigger, it would be the crowning thumb-screw on her if he nabbed him – and by God, nab him he would, or die in the attempt.

CHAPTER TWELVE

THE END OF THE WAITING

Rose Angela would have laughed to scorn anyone who would have told her a fortnight ago that there were many worse places to live in than the fifteen streets, and that there would come a time when she would miss them, miss the privacy of a house, of going upstairs to bed, of walking from one tiny room to the other, and miss the streets themselves, and the greetings and conversation thrown carelessly across their narrow widths; for in Holborn the tongues were many and varied, and she never could make out whether the neighbours in the rooms around were rowing or merely talking.

She saw very little of her neighbours, or of Holborn itself, for she went out in the dark of the morning and returned in the dark of the evening, yet the atmosphere pressed down on her and was as strange as that of a foreign country. But her days were too full to allow the change to penetrate farther than the fringe of her mind. What did penetrate and cast a shadow over her days was the rift between Bridget and herself. She wondered if anyone before had experienced so much happiness and unhappiness at the same time; there was James's love and this other love, but they were unable to ease the separation from her mother. She did not much care now what the people of the fifteen streets or of the town thought about her, but she still cared very much what Bridget thought. But for this, she felt there could be no-one happier; her da was so much better – it seemed as though her presence had given him a temporary lease of life; and then this impending thing; for she did not hide the fact from herself that something was impending and that she was waiting for it, waiting with her heart racing so fast at times that she thought such emotion could not be borne and that something within her was bound to give way.

What would happen when at last her master spoke? She knew what would happen – she would become his mistress and so qualify for the name the fifteen streets had already given her. If this thought brought with it a sadness, she told herself she'd rather be his mistress than any other man's wife. Two weeks ago she would not have allowed herself to dream of becoming his mistress, for to her mind he had given no indication that he thought of her other than as a very good servant; but from the night he told her she was beautiful there had been a decided change in his manner towards her. For the three days following he almost ignored her, never looking at her, and when he spoke his voice was harsh and more clipped than usual; nor did he stay in the kitchen either for his morning coffee or for his tea, but used it merely as a passage from the hall to the wharf. Although the weather was at its worst, he spent most of his time on the river, and after one severe day he developed a cold. It was the cold that broke down his defence. He remained indoors the following day, and Rose Angela, without being summoned, took up a hot drink to the studio. He was painting on a small canvas, and on her entry he took the canvas off the easel and laid it face upwards on the table in the corner of the room, saying, 'I didn't knock.'

'I know, sir, but I thought you needed this.'

For the first time in days he looked at her. 'What are you thinking, Rosie?'

'That you should be in bed, sir.'

'That all?'

'You have a nasty cold.'

'I know I have – and I'm annoyed. I've never had a cold for years, and you're to blame.'

She didn't ask the inane question 'But why me?'; she just looked at him, her skin growing pink and the brown of her eyes deepening, and he turned from her, saying, 'You are either so full of humility, Rosie, that you are not quite woman, or you are so full of the wisdom of the serpent that you are laughing at me.'

She did not at the moment try to unravel his references; only one thing was clear to her and that was she was not laughing at him – whatever feeling he had for her could not arouse her laughter. He said no more, and she went downstairs.

Although, since then, his manner towards her had been gentle, he did not resume his habit of sitting in the kitchen; and she knew he was fighting her, and at times this knowledge filled her with glory and she waited, doing nothing to precipitate the moment yet longing for it to come about.

He was out now, in Newcastle she thought, for he had said he might not be back before she left. Only twice before had she seen him 'dressed', as she put it, and today she thought he looked very grand; and she knew a qualm of fear – his heavy tweeds and large trilby seemed to remove him from her – he looked too grand. Could anyone like him think of her in the way she was imagining? Yet she thought of his words as he left the house. 'Don't wait for me, Rosie, I may not be back before six,' and it seemed to her that he wanted them to convey the opposite meaning – it was as if he were saying 'Wait for me'. It would have been nice to have waited, on the pretext of giving him a hot meal, but she knew how much her da longed for her return, and she never kept him waiting a minute longer than she could help.

It was now half-past five and she went around the house doing the final touches of the day, building up the drawing-room fire, taking the counterpane off the bed and turning back the bed clothes; and as she left his room she glanced towards the flight of stairs leading to the studio. How empty the house was without him up there . . . even if she never heard him for hours his presence would seep down to her. The feeling to be nearer to the things that were part of him now enveloped her and she went slowly up the stairs and into the first studio. She did not switch on the light but passed through into the other, the room where he spent most of his life. She pressed one of the switches on a board near the door and the light appeared high up in the far corner of the ceiling. This was part of the system of lighting by which he worked at night. A reflector directed the light on to an easel, on which stood the small canvas he had been working on for days. She had not seen this picture, for his breadth always obscured it, and once she remembered him taking it down when she was in the room. Now she moved towards it and saw it was hidden behind a covered frame clipped to the top of the easel and leaving only a narrow strip of the canvas visible. Gently she lifted up the frame and stood staring at the picture . . .

Had she known this was what she would see? Was that why she was drawn up here? Did she really look like that, her mouth half smiling and her eyes sad? But were her eyes as sad as that? And her hair . . . did the coiled plaits appear like a silver and black halo where the light touched them? Surely she didn't look like this. No, this wasn't meant to be the picture of the self that she saw in the mirror, it was rather the picture of what she knew herself to be inside. The little things she laughed at were there in her lips, but the fears of her life were in her eyes. She unhooked the frame from the easel and the light fell full on the picture. And now she was confronted with another aspect . . . she looked superior, or, to use the fifteen streets' term, 'stuck up'. But she wasn't stuck up

– no-one could be less stuck up – for what had she to be stuck up about? Nevertheless, there it was on the canvas. Was this how he saw her? She moved back and sat down and stared at the portrait, her hands gripped tightly in her lap. No matter how he saw her, he had painted her, and hadn't he said, 'I never paint women?'

'Well, what do you think of it?'

She swung round on the stool, her hands clutching the front of her dress. He was standing in the door-way, still in his outdoor clothes, and the sight of him made her dumb. She was afraid of having been found here, for this was his sanctum sanctorum, and it was an unwritten law that it would always be held as such.

As he walked towards her she turned to the canvas again; and when he stood behind her and she felt his coat against her shoulders a painful stillness filled her.

'Do you like it?' His voice was unsteady.

Still she could utter no word. His hand came down on her shoulder and moved slowly to her chin, and as her head was tilted back the stillness vanished; the waiting was over, and wave after wave of trembling happiness washed through her as she looked up at his great tousled head.

Now his other hand was on her face, cupping it. 'You know, Rosie, don't you?'

She closed her eyes against the light in his and felt herself swung round and to her feet.

'You know I love you. For God's sake say something! Stop me making a fool of myself. I know I'm a damned fool, but I can't help it. God knows I've tried.' He pressed her clasped hands into his chest. 'Tell me I'm not a fool . . . tell me, Rosie.'

Still she could release no words; it was as if her happiness had locked all expression of itself within her; but she leant towards him and all that her being held was in her eyes, and he kissed her, kissed her with a fierceness that met and satisfied the deep demand that lay hidden beneath her calm exterior. She stood crushed in his arms, pressed into him, almost crying from sheer happiness.

'Rosie; Rosie; Rosie—' With each murmur of her name he rocked her gently. 'How I've longed to do that. For months and months I've longed just to do that . . . even from the very first day. Do you know you've driven me nearly mad?' He held her from him. 'I'd sworn never to paint another woman, and you see what I had to do?'

Dimly she registered the fact that he had at one time painted women; and a woman was likely the reason why he had stopped. But what did anything of his past matter? He was hers now . . . hers . . . hers.

She was in his arms again and he was murmuring into her hair, ' "What's your name?" I asked you that first day. Do you remember? "Rose Angela Paterson", you said. Rose Angela. There has never been anyone more like their name, half flower, half angel.'

She lifted her head and laughed at his flowery exaggeration, such a gay, happy, free laugh that she could not believe it came from her; and with a naturalness as if she had spoken it instead of merely thinking it every day she said his name . . . 'Michael.'

'Say that again.'

'Michael.' Her lips shyly framing the word seemed to hold it while she drew fresh joy from the utterance. As she was borne away on his emotion, part of her questioned the reality of what was happening. But reality or dream, it did not matter as long as she remained in this state.

'Come' – he took her by the hand and led her to the door – 'I've something to show you . . . something that you asked for.'

But at the door he stopped; and there was laughter in his eyes. 'What do you want most, Rosie? Tell me. But this time I want the truth, mind.'

And when she gave him the answer she had wanted to give him that night in the kitchen he swung her off her feet and up into his arms and carried her down the stairs.

She made no protest, but lay against him; and as he sat her down in the drawing-room, saying like a boy with his first love, 'I'll never let you walk up or down those stairs again – it will be an excuse to hold you,' she dared to say teasingly, 'Even when you bellow for me?'

His face became serious. 'To think I ever bellowed at you!'

Diffidently she put up her hand and touched his cheek. 'I used to long for you to bellow so that I could come up to you.'

He was on his knees, his arms about her again. 'You love me, Rosie?'

'Yes . . . oh yes. I've always loved you, right from that first day when you looked down on me from the window and said, "I don't want a model."'

666

'And all the time you put me off, by looking either frightened or aloof . . . You'll never look afraid again; from now on I'll make your life such as no fear will touch it.'

She moved her hands through his hair. 'It all seems too good to be true.'

'Nothing will be too good for you . . . I'll take you travelling – I'll show you the world. Not that I think much of the world at the present moment, but you must see places. We'll go through France to Germany, and through the Black Forest . . . you'll like that.'

She answered slowly, 'Yes, perhaps . . . but I don't know. I can think of no better life than to stay here in this house with you.'

'Rosie, your humility is painful, but I love you for it. Where's that damn box?'

He patted his pockets and dragged the greatcoat that he had flung on to the carpet towards him. 'There' – he thrust the small parcel into her hands – 'that's what you asked for.'

She undid the wrapping, and she flashed him a look of gratitude before opening the black box lying in the palm of her hand. It would be the brooch. It was the brooch, but such a one as she had never seen before. In an oval of finely wrought silver lay a rose worked in stones glinting with red and purple lights. She had no knowledge of precious stones, but she knew that in this exquisite setting lay something of great value, something that she was afraid to accept.

'Well, what do you think? You asked for it, you know; though what you want a brooch for God alone knows. You shouldn't wear jewellery – you have all the jewels you need.' He moved his fingers round the circles of her eyes.

'It's beautiful; but it's too much.'

'Too much!' he scoffed. 'Rosie you are the only beautiful woman I have met . . . in fact the only woman, beautiful or otherwise, who didn't think she was worth the earth. You must put a greater value on yourself.' He pressed her face tightly between his hands. 'After you've lived with me for a while you will – I'll make you know your own value . . . Oh, my love!' He laid his head on her breast; and his voice took on a touch of sadness. 'You don't know what you've done for me. I never thought I'd allow a woman into my life again. Years ago I received a nasty knock and it turned me against all your kind, but from the moment I first saw you, you changed that. And then to find you possessed a sense of fair play – you seemed too good to be true.'

He lifted his head, and she looked down into his eyes, the blue now dark and soft, and her mind was awhirl with the wonder of him and his love for her that was making him tremble. At last. At last life was coming right. You only had to wait and be patient and happiness came to you. Oh, Holy Mary! She felt she wanted to go down on her knees and pray. But the thought of praying brought a self-consciousness with it; if he didn't mention marriage – and she was sensible enough to know that there was very little likelihood of him doing so – and she went to him, as she knew she would, what about praying then? It didn't matter . . . nothing mattered but him. What was marriage and religion, anyway? Look at the

lives the married people led in the fifteen streets . . .
good Catholics, too! She would let nothing come
between them. She would take this love whichever
way it was offered and stand the consequences. But
the consequences could only be good. And as she
listened to his voice she felt the certainty of this.

'That day you told our enterprising Mr Pillin
what you thought of him, you didn't know I was
in the boat alongside the wharf, did you?' She shook
her head. 'I had started up the river, but found there
was some gear missing, and when I came back you
were in the thick of it. You did something for me
that day, Rosie: you more than saved me nearly
two pounds a week; you gave me back my faith
in human nature – the female side, anyway. It was
surprising to know that a woman could be honest –
a beautiful woman – and just for the sake of honesty,
with no ulterior motive behind her action. Oh, Rosie,
Rosie, I love you for so many things.' He gazed at
her tenderly. 'What are you going to do about it?'

The onus was on her, and it brought the colour
flooding to her face. She shook her head and
swallowed, and he asked gently, 'Would you . . .
would you come and live with me, Rosie?'

Her eyes fell away from his and she said simply,
'Yes.'

'Rosie! Oh, Rosie, my dear!'

He held her gently, and a silence fell on them that
was not entirely devoid of embarrassment.

He rose from her side, saying, 'We'll have a drink,
then dinner, eh?' But he hadn't reached the cabinet
before she was on her feet, protesting, 'Not tonight!
I'd forgotten the time . . . I must go home.'

'What! Now?' He turned in surprise. 'But you can't, Rosie.' He came towards her, his heavy brows gathering into a furrow. 'You don't mean to go yet.'

'I'll have to. Look, it's quarter to seven. He . . . they'll be worrying.'

'Surely not for an hour or so? Stay and have something to eat with me, and then I'll take you home. I've always wanted to take you home . . . next to keeping you here.' He stood close to her, not touching her, but his eyes tracing each feature of her face.

'Oh, I'd love to stay . . . you know I would.' She took his hand and held it to her cheek.

'Then why don't you?' He covered the hand that held his with his own.

'Because they're expecting me.'

He remembered it was Friday and she had been paid, and he surmised it was for this they would be waiting.

'All right, then, but I'm taking you home.'

At this her mind whirled into a panic, and saying she must get her things she turned from him . . . He thought she was going to the fifteen streets. What would he have to say to her living in Holborn? And what further would he say when he knew the Negro was her father? He would have to be told, but not tonight. Anyway, she must hurry. What on earth would her da be thinking? He'd be lying worrying. But how was she going to put Michael off?

'It's raining, and you've still got that cold . . . don't come out again.' Even to herself, her effort sounded feeble.

'Don't go out; but let you go alone, and over that road too?' He was his bustling self again. 'I don't know what I've been thinking of all along to allow you to go alone in the dark through that jumble of debris. God knows what might have happened to you.'

She was forced to smile at his solicitude. For months now she had walked through the debris and she doubted if he had even thought of it.

But his next words brought a tenseness to her body. 'I would have seen you to the tram, in any case, tonight, for I had to warn off one of those damned Arabs as I came in. I found him standing at the edge of the clearing, apparently surveying the house. Have you had any trouble with them coming here when I've been out?'

'No.'

As he was shrugging himself into his coat again he said, 'I'll break the first one's neck I find with his foot on my ground – I can't stand the oily blighters.'

Poor Hassan. At one time she had felt that way too. She still did towards most of the Arabs, but towards Hassan she felt nothing but sympathy. But she guessed this feeling would be hard to explain to this love of hers, who in many ways was a law unto himself. She would explain her acquaintance with Hassan after she told him about her da – it really shouldn't come as any great surprise to him to know that her father was a Negro, for he must see she had coloured blood in her veins. It was always a matter of amazement to her that the likeness in the eyes had escaped him. Yet her da had sat for him every day for a week, and he hadn't noticed.

As he insisted on buttoning a mackintosh of his over her coat she probed his feelings on the matter

671

of her colour by asking shyly, 'Michael, do you mind about me being . . . coloured?'

'Coloured? Oh, my dear, I wouldn't mind if your father was an orang-outang as long as you were you.' He drew her to him. 'Never mention that again. I adore you . . . I always shall. Right from the day I first saw you I knew what would happen to me. Coloured! Where you are concerned I'm colour-blind.'

She laughed. 'Oh, how funny. You're like God, then.'

'God?' His eyebrows shot up into his hair. 'Me?'

'Well, I think you must be the only one besides him in all the world who is colour-blind. Our priest told me when I was a child that God was colour-blind; I've never found anybody else who is. Oh, and I love you for it. Oh, Michael, Michael!'

She kissed him with a fervour that prolonged the departure and made him plead again, 'Stay a little while . . . just a little while.'

'I can't. Tomorrow night I will, I promise.'

Yes, she would stay later tomorrow night. She would tell her da and he would understand.

As soon as they were outside she began to talk, as a warning to Hassan, whom she knew would be waiting. Stanhope held her by the arm, her elbow pressed into his side and her fingers laced tightly through his own; and going up the dark bank towards the market-place he pulled her into the deep shadow of a wall and kissed her, a silent, wordless kiss. But as they walked across the steel-glistening empty market-place to the tram it took all her gentle persuasion to counter his voluble insistence that he should accompany her home, and she did not feel safe until she stood on the platform of the tram as it jogged out of the market-place, watching him receding into the distance, the blueness of his eyes seeming to pierce the darkness until he was lost from her sight.

The tram stopped four times before she alighted; then she stood, uncertain for a moment what to do. She must give him time to get well out of the way before she ventured back to the Mill Dam again.

When she did come to the bank she kept to the shadow of the wall until she entered Holborn and, although she now breathed more freely, her steps became slower, for she had never before traversed these streets alone in the dark.

She had hardly covered the first deserted street when she heard quick padding footsteps behind her and a well-known voice call softly, 'Rose Angela.' She stopped in relief and laughed into the darkness, 'Oh, Hassan! I am glad to see you!'

Hassan made no reply, but walked quietly by her side; and because of his silence she knew that he was aware of what was between her and Stanhope. He would have seen them; perhaps he had followed them. Thinking of the dark bank leading to the ferry, she blushed and decided to bring the matter into the open. It would be the best way.

'Mr Stanhope set me to the tram tonight, he doesn't know that I'm living down here.' It was difficult to go on, for Hassan's displeasure was as visible as the wet darkness, and as cold. 'You wouldn't believe it, but he doesn't know James is my da. After painting him, too! It's odd, isn't it?'

Still Hassan made no comment, and they walked in awkward quietness until they reached the house, but in the darkness of the hall he spoke softly and rapidly, holding her gently by the arms as he did so. 'Rose Angela. You know I have a great love for you. No, don't say anything yet . . . I am not as others. I want one woman and one only, and that woman is you. I have money – much money. I can take you and your father away from here and send you both to Switzerland, where the healing air will prolong his life. But above all things I want to make you my wife . . . I want to marry you. The painter will never marry you – he comes of a class that scorns any colour but their own.'

She said nothing. The darkness hid his face from her, but she was filled with pity for him.

'Think it over. I don't want to hurry you, Rose Angela, but . . .' He did not finish, and they stood in silence again. He was waiting for her to speak; and as they stood it was brought to both of them that their silence was part of an unusual quietness that pervaded the whole house. Usually at this time of night the house was alive with clatter and noise. Only when danger threatened the inhabitants or something unusual was afoot would there be this silence.

Hassan drew closer to Rose Angela and whispered, 'Something is wrong. Go up and stay in the room, I'll be up later. Don't come downstairs again, not until I've found out what the trouble is.'

He gave her a gentle push towards the stairs, and she ran quickly from him, and each door she passed showed no light, nor gave forth any sound.

Only from the bottom of her own door did a light shine. She paused, and the ecstatic happiness of the evening became submerged under the weight of a dread. Reluctantly her hand went to the knob, and she turned it slowly and went in.

For the past hour James had lain watching the door. Soon she would be here, and his day would begin. His days for the past two weeks had started at half-past six in the evening, when his Rose Angela came through the door, and ended at half-past seven in the morning when she left him. All day long he lay quiet, reserving his strength for her. He had little to say to Murphy or Pete, or even to the generous Hassan, while they sat with him giving him the news of the river. Only when they commented on the change Rose Angela had wrought in this room did he allow himself to be roused. Yes sir, by Jove . . . she wonderful.

He looked now to the corner where her shakedown was curtained off with a piece of gay chintz, and at the window to the side of him where the same material shut out the sight, if not the sound, of the torrential rain; even the rusty bedrail was removed from his gaze by her neat draping. His hands, long and bony, with the nails startlingly pink, moved lovingly to the glass jar of yellow chrysanthemums on the bamboo table by the bedside . . . she thought of everything. Flowers for him! And the food she brought him, food that now he couldn't eat. Two years ago he could have eaten it; how he could have eaten it. If he'd had food then there might have been a chance for him. Or if he had waited a little longer and hadn't sailed in that hell ship, with short commons and rotten boilers that sweated the flesh off a man. But hadn't he waited too long, years too long, always hoping that he would strike the money and come back and shower gifts on his Rose Angela?

It was strange how the thought of his once beloved Rose had been thrust into the background by the love for his child. Had he always known that Bridget wouldn't wait for him? He supposed so. Yet it came as a shock when he knew it was Tony she had chosen . . . Tony, the boy who had taken Rose Angela from his arms that night long ago; Tony, who had always liked him. He did not blame Tony. Women were the devil – they had always been the devil, all except his Rose Angela. Yet she played the devil with men, too, tenfold more than her mother had been capable of doing. Hassan . . . Hassan was mad about her. But he was glad she no want Hassan. He was good fella and kind, but he was not for his Rose Angela. He did not want her to marry any coloured man. No sir. She was mostly white and he wanted a white man for her. If she married coloured man all her life she'd be in trouble, inside of her and outside, whereas if she marry white man she be protected by his colour alone. The painter man he like his Rose Angela, there were many signs of that. He bellow a lot, but not at her; he look at her when she not looking, and his voice soft and kind when he speak to her. But would he marry her? Liking and marrying were two different things. And him a swell . . . And his Rose Angela. How did she feel about the painter man? She no say nothing, not even last night when he noticed strange light in her eyes when she came in, and he say to her, 'You happy?' and she replied, 'I'm happy to be back with you.'

'Who bring you?'

'Murphy, and he's practically drowned, but he wouldn't stay – it's blowing a gale.'

Murphy had not brought that light to her eyes, but as yet she did not wish to tell him who had, so he had turned the conversation.

'It blowing great guns all day – river'll be in a temper. I no like wind much. You like wind, Rose Angela?'

'No, I don't.' She touched his brow with her lips. 'That's another thing I've got from you, you know.' She looked lovingly into his face. 'You look heaps better today.'

'Me? I'm fine.' And to prove it he had hitched himself up and talked to her as she emptied the basket and set about preparing the evening meal. 'Me? I never like wind, 'cause I don't understand him, how him come about. Harvest – it no mystery; you put seed into earth. You can see the earth and see the seed, but you no can see wind. Only things that it touches you can see. Me, I see it touch one part of tree, other part still as death; and I see it wave one blade of grass – just one. Clever fellow on boat, he say it was worm or insect at bottom. Wasn't worm or insect on the tree. No, I no like wind. I hate fog and I no like wind, yet I love the water. And water and wind are cousins, they say. Strange. Me, I can never understand it. You like fog, Rose Angela?'

'No, I can't stand it either – it makes me afraid. I always expect something strange to loom up out of it.'

677

He nodded understandingly. 'Me same.'

The tie of kinship seemed to be stronger because she had inherited his fears, and he became silent, content just to watch her.

Later she told him she had seen a little house they could rent, not actually out of Holborn, but away from this quarter, and it pained him to witness her disappointment when he said, 'I no move from here, Rose Angela; Matt not get down this part. If I no sick I not mind, but . . .' He left the sentence unfinished, then went on, 'I be able to get up next week, and you go back home.' He hung on her reply, and it was like new life pouring into his veins when she said, 'You are my home.'

Was it any wonder he lived only when she was near him? But would he live enough days to make up for the years they had been separated? With the hope that is the heritage of the consumptive he thought he would and longer . . .

He was lying now, still and unmoving, his great eyes watching the door, but at half-past six she did not come. Nor yet at seven o'clock, and the fear of the wind became lost under the weight of apprehension filling his wasted body. And when half an hour later the noise and clamour of voices that always filled the house became gradually still and into their place came a scuffling of feet on the stairs as if someone was being dragged up them, he hitched himself up in the bed and waited, the sweat pouring down his body; and he fell back almost in a faint when the door was pushed open and a man was thrust into the room by Murphy and Pete.

Across the bedrails James and Matt surveyed each

678

other, and both for the moment forgot all else but the terrible change that time had brought to each face.

Then the years fell away, and the hate that had reached its destroying climax in Bridget's kitchen sixteen years before filled the room. Matt's body jerked spasmodically with it; he made sounds in his throat but did not speak; only his eyes, riveted on James, spoke for him.

Murphy and Pete released their hold on him but remained threateningly close, and Murphy said to James, over the bed-rail, 'We had to bring him up – the Greek tipped us off he was watching the house. We couldn't nab him in the street, we had to wait until he got into the yard.'

Matt growled again, and Murphy, raising his forearm, warned, 'Mind yersel'.' Then he repeated, 'We had to bring him up; he knew you were here, Jimmy. He would have come up on his own or got the polis.'

James made no comment, but lay returning Matt's stare, and Murphy asked, 'What's to be done with him?'

The ominous question brought Matt's gaze from James and he glanced from Murphy to Pete, then swiftly around the room.

'Aye, have a good look,' said Murphy. 'The only way out is the way you come in.'

As Matt's eyes darted to the door the sound of running footsteps, intensified by the quiet of the house, came to him; and the other three men also turned their eyes to the door and waited. When it opened, Matt looked at Rose Angela standing there with her hands over her mouth, and a flash of his old power wiped out for the moment his own fear. Where was her bravery now? His eyes held hers as she came into the room and backed towards the bed, and when, without looking at James, she groped for his hand, Matt growled, 'Thought you were smart, didn't you? Well, you weren't smart enough, were you?'

'Shut yer gob, else I'll shut it for yer!' Murphy lifted his hand threateningly, and James interposed in a surprisingly calm voice, 'Let him talk, Murphy. There lots he wants off his chest.'

The sight of Rose Angela's fear seemed to restore Matt's courage, and he cried, 'There's one thing I'm gonna say, you needn't think I was fool enough to come down here without lettin' on to anyone, so you can tell these two tykes of yours they better be careful what they're up to.'

'Why you come, anyway?' James asked.

'You know bloody well why I came . . . to get you!'

'You too late.'

'I don't know so much about that.' Matt's eyes darted to Rose Angela. 'I'll never be too late as long as that-'un's about.' Matt's sense of power mounted as he saw James's calm vanish and the hand holding his daughter's visibly shake. 'One of you'll pay for this.' Matt jerked his chin to indicate his scarred face.

James said, 'You no blame anyone but me . . . you asked for what you got, you try to ruin . . . my wife.' The word wife had a stilted sound, as if stiff for want of use.

'Your wife! A bit of a lass you took down when she was drunk. Your wife! I wonder, if she could see you now, what she'd think of her great, swaggering nigger. You made a mess of me, but, by God, it's

680

a flea-bite to what you look like! That's why you didn't send for her on the quiet, eh? Didn't want her to see what a fool she'd been.'

The jerking of James's fingers within her palm told Rose Angela that Matt's surmise was one of the reasons why her father hadn't wanted to see Bridget; and when Matt went on, 'She knew she'd been a fool all right, long before you went, and you weren't gone five minutes before she had another bed-warmer,' she cried out, 'Don't believe him; he's lying! It was years after, years and years.'

She looked pleadingly down on James, and he, calm once more, reassured her. 'You no worry; that no matter . . . makes no difference.' He lay back and, staring at Matt over the bed-rails, said quietly and pointedly, 'When Bridget took other man I not know, but you did. Must have been very devil for you that!'

The words, like a knife-thrust, turned Matt's face to the colour of dirty silver. 'You black swine!'

He drew his body up as if to spring, and Murphy cried, 'I wouldn't if I was you.' And as he said this Murphy stepped a little to the front of Matt to prevent any movement he might make towards the bed, leaving exposed to Matt's right the little kitchen table, on which stood a lamp, an old-fashioned affair with a painted iron stalk and an oil container in the shape of a round flower surmounted by a tall lamp-glass.

In this tense, passion-filled atmosphere, Matt's mind was attuned to take advantage of any opening, and in the lamp he saw the weapon to his hand. Like a cat he sprang sideways, and in an instant he was at the far side of the table with the lamp in his hand. For a second, surprise made the others still. They stared at him, unbelieving, as if he were some demon capable of conjuring up separate selves. It was Murphy who made the first move, and Matt yelled, 'You stir from there and I'll hurl this on to the bed!' Slowly his eyes ranged from one to the other, and he said softly, 'Now who calls the tune?'

As Murphy made to move again Rose Angela cried, 'Don't Murphy, don't . . . he's mad . . . he'll do it.'

'Yes, I'll do it . . . you know your Uncle Matt, don't you?' He spat across the table at the term 'uncle'. 'But before I do it I'll do something else . . . come here, you!'

'You no move.' James was sitting upright, his voice hoarse with fear. 'I go.'

'I don't want you yet, I want her. I'll deal with you later. You come here. If you don't, you know what I'll do with this lamp.'

Wild-eyed and staring, as if her eyes were already fixed in death, Rose Angela loosened James's fingers from her coat, and pressed him back into the bed; and skirting Murphy and Pete, slowly walked towards the table.

'Not that side . . . this side.'

Like a marionette she obeyed him, until she was standing less than an arm's length from him, with the table at her back. Now she knew the summit of all fears . . . the total fears of her childhood and her teens were one minor tremor compared to the emotion now paralysing her. She felt that all her years had been a waiting for this moment. In the ecstasy of Stanhope's kiss she hadn't told herself, like most girls would, that all her life she had been awaiting such a moment . . . that this was what her thoughts and dreams had promised her, but now, standing fascinated under Matt's diabolical stare, she knew that this was the moment she had been awaiting, this moment in which he would destroy her face. Every atom of feeling in her was transformed into fear; it was shaking her limbs as if with ague.

'You're sick with fright, aren't you? Go on spew – you always spew when I frighten you.'

Without taking his eyes from her face Matt spoke to Murphy. 'Stop that dirty nigger from getting out of that bed, and you two listen to me. I'm gonna do something, and if any of you as much as move a finger when I'm at it I'll hurl the lamp into her half-breed face, d'you hear me?'

The desire to destroy both James and Rose Angela was burning its way through Matt like an acid. Inside his tortured mind he sensed that, whichever way things went, this was the end for him, but end or no end he was going to do things in his own way. For the first time in his life the desire for Bridget was lost under a greater desire – he would crash the lamp into her face if it was the last thing he did! But first there was something else he would do. For how many years had he wanted to feel the contact of his fist between those eyes? He could not remember a time when this urge had not swayed him. As he glared into Rose Angela's blanched face he realised that his hate of the daughter exceeded a thousand-fold that of the father.

His body began to sway and his hand with it, and the lamp sent the shadows of Murphy and Pete across the ceiling like crouching demons leaping through space. The room for the moment became strangely silent, with all the figures motionless and stiff. Then Matt, shouting another warning to Murphy, flung the silence into pandemonium.

As his fist crashed between Rose Angela's eyes Murphy sprang. He hurled himself on Matt, or more correctly where Matt had been, for Murphy's hand slid off Matt's twisting shoulders as if they were greased and he measured his length with a thud on the floor.

Pete did not move, but his unblinking eyes never left Matt; not even when James's swaying body rocked towards Matt did he remonstrate. Not until Matt threw the lamp did he spring. Then, like an enraged monkey he hurled himself sideways across the table, knocking Rose Angela flying as she stood swaying and moaning, her hands covering her face. Still with the antics of a monkey, he caught the lamp, and fell to the floor with it, balancing it upright like some circus clown.

Murphy, rising to his knees, clawed wildly at Matt's legs as he rushed towards the door, but he did not succeed in checking him . . . It was James, looking more weird and grotesque than ever, his long, wasted legs sticking like props from beneath his shirt, who blocked Matt's way. Once more he and Matt confronted each other, and James's anger was even greater now than it had been on that faraway night, but his strength was as a child's. As his feeble hands were raised to strike, Matt's foot shot out, aiming at his stomach, but catching him on the thigh and sending him sprawling against the wall.

The way clear now, Matt flung himself out on to the landing and went down the stairs, rocketing against the walls as he went, and through his brain rocketed only one regret – the lamp had missed her! All through that blasted dwarf! As he neared the hall he knew by the thundering on the stairs above that they were after him, and in the yard, where no vestige of light showed, not even a glimmer from the street lamp, for that had been put out, he knew himself to be running for his life, and that every man's hand was against him. By a stroke of luck he found the alleyway, but in the street, shadows that seemed darker than the night loomed at the end by which he had entered, so he turned in the other direction.

He was running as he had been wont to do years ago, with long loping strides, springing from one foot to the other. He became conscious as he ran of a strange and new feeling of freedom; his body seemed light and young once more . . . he would beat them yet . . . When had he last felt like this? The night he had run home to see Bridget and saw the black swine for the first time . . . Bridget, Bridget, why did you do it? It was as if the years were being flung off with each flying step until he was back to that very night, walking the black streets and crying like a child as he walked, 'Bridget, Bridget, why did you do it?'

He was now in a maze of buildings, warehouses mostly, and this told him he was near the river. If only he could find an alleyway. He paused in his running and listened. Yes, blast them, he could hear their feet pounding the cobbles . . . Where was there a damned alleyway? He groped along one wall and laughed in relief as the wind, rushing up the alley, brought him the tang of the river. Once on the bank, he could make his way to the Mill Dam; he would slope them yet. His legs became infused with revitalised life; he was young again, really young. He had done something he had wanted to do for years – he had bashed that one's face. And now he was going to tell his Bridget that the nigger was alive, but was less than useless. He wouldn't trouble her, but it would put paid to Mister Tony, and his Bridget would be alone again, and would turn to him. Oh, Bridget, Bridget! His running cut through the wind like the keel of a ship through the water, and his head filled with the wind. It swelled and swelled, making his body so light that he was no longer on the ground. The wind became a whirlwind; until finally the roaring of it culminated in a bang and his head burst into stillness.

He came to a sudden stop on the very edge of the wall that hemmed in the river, and below him he could hear the lap-lap of the water against the wall. He put out his hand and felt the walls of the warehouses that closed him in on both sides. He put out his foot and there was nothing. This last action conveyed only one thing to the hollowness of his mind – he must not jump down there because he couldn't swim. He lifted his hand to his brow and his fingers groped at the emptiness under them. What had he been thinking when he was running? Had he been running? Yes, he had been running . . . but what had he been thinking? He must try to remember what he had been thinking. The sound

686

of the pounding feet came to him again, and they carried another single thought into the hollowness . . . he must hide. But there was only the river, with the sheer wall down to it.

It was impulse that made him lower himself over the wall. Alongside the warehouses the shelf of the wall was scarcely more than a hand wide, but the finishing stones had been left in parapet form and to these he clung, and edged himself a foot or so out of the line of the alleyway. His legs were in the water up to his thighs, and when his toes, scraping against the wall, found a niche where a brick had been washed out, he thrust his feet in, and this lifted the weight from his hands; and he hung there, listening to the footsteps, their coming and their going, and he began to laugh softly.

CHAPTER THIRTEEN

THE FEET OF THE BELOVED

It was ten o'clock when Rose Angela stumbled over the last sleepers towards the clearing, and the white-painted door and windows of the house shone at her like welcoming beacons. Never had she loved the house as she did at this moment; nor needed its comforting warmth and colour so much; and once inside, with Michael's arms about her, all her mental and physical pain would be eased.

She pressed her hand to her brow, where the pain was most acute. How would he take the sight of her face? She must tell him everything . , . everything but how she came by the blow. She would say that she fell – she must not tell him Matt did it, for not even to him must she say that she had seen Matt last night, for as yet she did not know what had happened to him. Hour after hour she had sat waiting by the side of James for Murphy or Pete to come back with some word, but they hadn't come. Nor yet had any of the neighbouring men looked in, or the women, and this augured bad, so she must not say she had seen Matt.

The terror of last night would remain with her, she thought, until she died, and after, and the terror had not ceased when Matt had flown, for the scarlet blood pouring from James's mouth had been equally terrifying. But this morning he seemed better, yet she knew that last night's events had precipitated his end, and she had been loath to leave him even for the short time it would take to tell Michael the reason for her absence. Oh to be with Michael just for a few minutes, to rest against him and have his sympathy flow over her. She broke into a run, and when she rounded the narrow shingled path to the back door she could not restrain herself from calling his name aloud, 'Michael! Michael!' If he was up in the studio he would hear her and come bounding down the stairs, to stand horrified for the moment at the sight of her face – yes, she knew her face would shock him.

She turned the handle of the door and, finding it locked, called again, 'Michael!'

He mustn't be up yet, and it was after ten. Likely he had been working most of the night. Automatically her hand went to the beam that supported the roof of the porch, but her fingers, groping behind it, did not come in contact with the key. When she had tried the other side, and been met with the same emptiness, she turned and looked at the blue boat bobbing forlornly against the side of the wharf. She was nonplussed. If he was not down in the morning the key would still be behind the beam, where she left it at night. Again her fingers traced the key's hiding place; then panic seized her. If he had gone out, he would have left the key. Perhaps he had been taken ill and couldn't get downstairs . . . perhaps he was dead.

'Michael!' She battered with her fist upon the door. 'Michael!'

When she heard his steps in the kitchen only the tight painfulness of her face prevented her from laughing with relief, and he had barely opened the door before her hands went out to him. But they found no answering grip. His arms did not pull her to him, exclaiming in horror at the sight of her face, nor did he demand in his impetuous way where she had been until this hour. After staring fixedly at her face for a moment, he merely turned from her and put the width of the table between them.

As she stared at him in astonishment her whole body began to shake, and her voice, too, trembled as she asked softly, 'What's the matter?'

He did not answer her immediately, but continued to look at her with eyes so coldly blue that she appealed to him as a child might, saying, 'But what have I done?'

She watched him pass one lip over the other, and his voice was so quiet when it came as to be scarcely recognisable at his.

'Are you living in Holborn, Rosie?'

The racing of her heart warned her of what was to come, and she answered with difficulty. 'Yes, but I was going to tell you . . . I . . .'

A small deprecatory movement of his hand checked her hesitant words.

'With an Arab?'

'No. No!' She screamed the words at him; and again he checked her, asking sharply, 'Last night you never went to the fifteen streets, you got off that tram and went back to Holborn, didn't you?'

She was unable to answer him – her eyes were fixed on his face like a fear-paralysed rabbit.

'That Arab I chased was waiting for you, wasn't he?'

Still no words would come, and he went on, 'I see he has thrashed you for your duplicity. He has that to his credit, anyway.'

'Michael' – she gasped his name fearfully – 'I'm not living with him. It's true he was waiting for me. He's . . . he's a friend. He takes me into Holborn. I'm living with my father . . . the Negro, the one that you painted.'

She watched his eyebrows rise, then draw into a thick furrow. 'Your father, eh? My God!' He shook his head as if at his own gullibility. 'Rosie, I wouldn't have believed you capable of such barefaced lying.'

She leant across the table towards him and cried beseechingly, 'Believe me, oh, believe me, I'm not lying. I know it looks bad, but I'm not lying.'

'Be quiet!'

At his low-growled command she straightened herself and tried to draw on what little pride and strength she had left to face up to this man, who was now neither master nor lover. But it was no use. Under his contemptuous glance she not only bowed her head but her body also, and she leaned her hands on the table for support as he went on, 'May I ask where your mother comes in, in this scheme of things? Why isn't she with your father?'

'I can explain—' She made to raise her head.

'Wait. If I remember rightly, you told me your mother was a widow, and that your father died when you were a child.'

Yes, he remembered rightly, and she could remember his question 'Is your father out of work?' and her answer, to save explanations and more humiliation, 'He's dead. He died when I was a child.'

She spoke with difficulty from under her breath, 'That was a lie, but it's the only one I've told you.'

'Rosie!' His tone as he uttered her name was quiet but heavy with scorn. 'Don't make matters worse. Look at those.' He placed two letters on the centre of the table. 'Do you recognise the writing?'

She shook her head.

'They are anonymous letters about you.'

'About me?' Her head came up with a jerk, and her mouth hung agape in amazement.

'Why do you appear so surprised? Everyone isn't blind, you know; I happen to be an exception. One of those letters, I know, is from Bessie, who tells me it's about time I found out I was being fooled. Apparently she had her own ideas of why I kept you on. The other is from someone, I should imagine, who knows you very well. One sentence interests me very much. It says you can assume a cloak of timidity and fear so as to hoodwink people. I once said to you that I wasn't sure whether you were so full of humility as not to be a woman or so full of the wisdom of the serpent that you were being amused by me, and, my God, how you must have been amused! What was your game, anyway? Did you think you could get off with it?'

'Please M—' She could not now speak his name. 'Please don't say any more ... you're wrong. Those letters are full of lies.'

'Yes?' He picked up one of the letters. 'This writer points out that you have always been a great source of worry to your mother, and that she tried to stop you from going into Holborn. But you wouldn't listen to her. Is that a lie?'

'Yes . . . no . . . She did try to stop me, but . . .'

'Why didn't you tell her then about . . . your father?'

'Because he didn't want me to . . . he was ill, as you know and changed.'

'How was it I didn't notice any tender relationship between you during his visits here? Throwing my mind back, I never once remember you even looking at the man. Why, in the name of God, must you bring him into all this?'

'Because I've told you . . . he's my father.'

Stanhope scrutinised her for a moment, then said softly, 'And the Arab is just a friend? He waits for you each night and takes you home?'

Knowing her answer would bring down his contempt on her head, she hesitated before saying, 'Yes.'

'What do you take me for? If it had been a white man I would have had my doubts, but an Arab! And to term him a friend. You know as well as I do that no man, black or white, could be merely a friend to you, and an Arab least of all.'

Oh God! It was like the scene of her frequent dismissals over again, only intensified a thousandfold. She had often wondered what her master would be like were he in a real rage. Then, she had thought, his bellow would reach such volume as to scare even the bravest. She had never imagined that his rage would produce no bellows, that his voice would be low-toned and even. Nor had she imagined that his eyes could express such disgust and a disdain that would make her feel unclean, unmerited as it was.

The terrible coldness of his manner was having a numbing effect on her already failing senses, and as his voice went on she had to grip the edge of the table for support.

'And your face . . . the Arab didn't do that?'

'No, he didn't.'

In spite of her faintness her words carried conviction. But when he asked, 'Who did then?' and she answered, 'I fell on the stairs,' he made a sound like a laugh.

'Do you take me for a fool altogether? In my young days I used to box, but had I never given or received a blow between the eyes I would know that it was a fist that had hit you.'

Rose Angela knew that there were levels of pain she had not yet probed. What she was suffering now would be nothing compared to the agony that would be produced by the emptiness of a life separated from this man's . . . She must tell him about Matt.

'It was a fist. My uncle did it – the one that wrote that letter. He's always hated me and lied about me.'

'Oh, your uncle, now! Is he lying when he says you have been turned out of situation after situation because of your double-dealings with men, and that you've never kept a job more than a few weeks?'

Rose Angela stared at Stanhope without seeing him. What was the use? Living or dead, Matt's work went on. She could do no more; yet through all the turmoil of her feeling ran a thread of bewilderment at what appeared to her a determination on Stanhope's part not to believe anything she said, for only last night hadn't he told her it was her honesty that had altered his opinion of women?

Then, as she stood swaying on her feet, his voice, losing its levelness and sinking into his throat with bitterness, brought her sharply back from the oblivion that was upon her; and she knew part of the reason for his unrelenting attitude towards her, for, as much as he hated her at this moment, he hated and loathed himself even more.

'Last night I asked you to live with me, but after you had gone I knew that wouldn't be enough . . . I must marry you and make sure of you. Make sure of you . . . that's funny, isn't it? And when this morning I received these two letters it was history repeating itself, for all this has happened to me before. When I was about to be married, twelve years ago, I received such a letter as that.' He flicked Matt's letter with his nail. 'The girl was as beautiful as you, and as practised a liar.' He paused for a while, and ran the side of his finger across his lips as if wiping something distasteful from them. 'I felt a young fool, then, but now I feel an old one. And that I find harder to stomach!'

Now she knew the uselessness of trying to convince him. The giddiness swam over her again, and his voice came to her as if from the end of a long corridor, saying, 'There's a week's wages in lieu of notice. And you may keep the brooch. It is of some value, as doubtless you expected when you asked for such a simple gift.'

When the mist cleared from her eyes she found that she was alone. She hadn't heard him go. His movements, like his voice, were now quiet and final.

She leant over the table, her body trembling. Her hand went to her throat, and, groping at the brooch fastening her blouse, she undid it and placed it on the table near the money he had laid there. Then unsteadily she left the kitchen.

Outside, she stood watching the sun's watery rays reflected on the river. It was over – just like that . . .

She walked on, almost blindly, over the rails and sleepers and she wondered vaguely why she was shedding no tears, for inside she was crying as she had never cried before: in many ways at one and the same time, like a child that had been misjudged, and like a girl who had been spurned, and like a woman who had drunk bitterly of humiliation. The child was crying, 'It's always the same. Oh, I wish I was dead! Oh, I wish I was dead!' And the girl was crying, 'He believed everything in that letter, about the men an' all.' But the woman's cry overshadowed the others, for she was crying, 'It's my colour. If I'd been all white he would have let me convince him, in spite of that other girl. Last night he said colour didn't matter, but I know, I know. It will always matter, and balance the scales; it's still like when I was a child.'

She drew to a halt and stared at the river. The fitful gleam of the sun had vanished, leaving the water a broken mass of steely grey. There was a way out – it was deep by the broken wall, and once in she would never get out. There was only her da to really mourn her; and then not for long, for he would soon go . . . Mourning. All her life had been one long mourning; mourning because she was what she was. She was tired, so tired, and her face was like a sheet of hot pain. She had been born to misery, so why had she imagined that anything might come right for her? And of all things, Stanhope's love! She had been like a child, firmly believing that a fairy-tale could become reality.

She started to run over the sleepers, tripping and stumbling like someone drunk. She passed the railway carriage and was deaf to Murphy's voice calling after her. And she had actually mounted the broken wall before she was pulled to a halt.

'Here, here! Steady on. What is it, lass? What you running like that for? . . . Look, stop it!' Murphy put his arms tightly about her, restraining her until she suddenly became still. 'That's better. What is it? What's happened to you?'

She leant against him, her head resting on his greasy muffler, and he held her gently until she murmured, 'It's him.'

'Him? Who?' asked Murphy.

'The guv'nor.' She used Murphy's own term for Stanhope. 'He won't believe me. He won't believe I'm not living with Hassan.' She was speaking slowly, with the dull simplicity of a child, and Murphy stared at her perturbed as he repeated, 'Living with Hassan? God Almighty! What put that into his head?'

'Matt. Matt sent him a letter; and Bessie too.'

'Why, blast the pair of them for lying skunks! Look, lass, come inside the cabin a minute and get yourself warmed; you're all in.'

She allowed him to lead her back and into the railway carriage, where he sat her on the backless chair before the fire and began clumsily to chafe her stiff hands, talking all the while and trying to break through the strange light in her eyes. And he looked apprehensively at Pete when she broke in on him, saying dully, 'He was going to ask me to marry him, and I would have been Mrs Stanhope then, Murphy.'

Murphy pursed his lips and jerked his head approvingly. 'Aye, fit to marry anyone, you are, Rosie . . . you'll marry him all right, won't she, Pete?'

Pete nodded, sparing his words as usual.

'Not now,' she said, 'because it's all happened before.'

'There, there then. Are you warmed? . . . I'll brew some tea. There ain't any milk, but it'll be hot. Been through a bit too much, you have. Lean back against the wall . . . he'll marry you all right, don't you worry.'

'No . . . he wouldn't believe about Matt . . . about him always being bad.' Murphy's hand became still for a second as he measured the tea into the black can, and his eyes darted towards Pete's; then he turned the thread of her thoughts by saying, 'Not that Pete and me want you to marry and be skedad-dled off to some place else, do we, Pete?'

Pete shook his head.

'Best friend we've ever had, you've been. Not many like you about. No wonder yer da dotes on you. It'll be a bad day for all of us when we lose you, I can tell you that.'

Bad day for all of them when they lost her . . . best friend they'd ever had. She felt a momentary glow of comfort . . . there were kind people in the world –

these men were kind. And they believed in her, they who had known her so short a time. Not like her mother, who knew her even before birth, and him who last night had told her he adored her from the moment he set eyes on her and would continue to do so every moment of his life.

The crying and inward sobbing began to mount. It was Pete's unused voice that caused her pent-up tears to break, betraying himself by look and word as he said briefly, 'Nobody's good enough for you . . . the Stanhope bloke nor nobody else.'

This was a long speech for Pete, and as Rose Angela looked at the dwarf his love penetrated the mist of her mind, and all the pain within her gathered itself into her throat, and as it found release she covered her face with her hands and sobbed, great tearing sobs that convulsed her body.

The men stood helplessly by, gazing at her bent head. When the sobs, gathering on themselves, threatened to choke her, their hands hovered towards her but did not touch her. It was as if they both realised that this safety valve must not be checked. Twice the crying died down, only to burst out afresh, and it was only when her body sagged almost double that Pete intervened by motioning to Murphy to give her the tea.

Clumsily Murphy straightened her hat, saying, 'Come, Rosie, lass, and have your drop of tea.' He took the mug from Pete's hand and held it to her lips. 'There now, drink that, and we'll get you a drop of water, for your face and hands are in a mess.' His voice was placating, he was humouring her as if she were still the strange distraught child he had pulled from the wall.

But after she had sipped the tea she spoke to him, and her voice was as he knew it. 'I'm sorry, Murphy.'

Murphy's face showed his relief. 'There, there, it's all over now.'

She sat in silence, the two men watching her. Was it all over? Wasn't there more to come?

'Where is Matt?' She asked the question as she stared down into the mug of black tea.

After a pause Murphy muttered, 'We don't know.'

She cupped the mug in her cold hands and the steam rising from the tea wafted about her face. 'What happened last night?' Her voice betrayed her premonition.

There was another pause before Murphy said, 'We chased him and he went down the drop alley.'

'The drop alley?' She looked quickly up at Murphy. 'But there's no way out of there but the river.'

Pete's eyes were fastened on the floor, and Murphy turned his head aside as he replied, 'I know. Me and the fellows waited to see if he'd come back, and Hassan and Pete went along to the sculler steps to nab him if he came up that way. But he didn't come . . .' He paused, and then went on hopefully, 'He could have swum along the river and come up somewhere, though, and is hiding out, trying to scare us.'

Rose Angela looked through the carriage window to where the river was moving swiftly in black and grey patches. 'He couldn't swim,' she said flatly.

Neither Murphy nor Pete made any comment or movement, and she went on fearfully, 'There'll be an enquiry if they find him, and if there are any marks on his body . . .'

'Honest to God, we didn't touch him, Rosie,' Murphy put in. 'We never got near enough to him, or I don't know what we might have done at the time . . . but we never laid a hand on him, did we, Pete?'

Pete gave the usual reply with his head.

'If there are enquiries, you'll have to be careful.' She was talking quietly now, as if it were an ordinary, everyday topic. For the moment all the turmoil seemed to have been swept away on the flow of her tears, and being thus quiet she asked herself questions, and the answers brought no pain. She asked herself did she hope Matt was dead; and the answer came: Yes, oh yes! She asked herself why she had pleaded so much with Stanhope. Had she stormed at him, as most women would have done under the circumstances, would she have convinced him? Her head shook slowly from side to side. No. Anyway, she could never have stormed at him.

All her life she had been humble because openly and in covered ways she had been given to understand that her mixed blood was like a poster advertising some inferior form of human being, and she had never used the argument, 'Is it our fault we are what we are? Must we go around searching for others like ourselves to form a world apart? The blame lies with them that bred us.' To have taken this view would have meant criticism of her mother and her da. Yet in this moment she dared to wonder what life would have been like had each stuck to his own kind, for it was borne in on her that Stanhope's unrelentlessness, whether he realised it or not, was due not so much to the fact that he had been duped before but that this time it had been done by a half-caste . . . The thought laid hold of her. Last night when he said that colour did not matter it was because he wanted her – men would say anything to get what they wanted. Life had taught her that lesson thoroughly. Last night he and God were colour-blind; now there was, as before, only God.

She surprised Murphy by rising abruptly and saying, 'I'll go now. Don't come . . . I'll be all right,' and adding calmly, 'If you are questioned you'd better say you were in with us till ten o'clock. And Hassan too . . . we must all say the same thing, mustn't we?'

They did not answer her, and she turned from them and went out of the railway carriage, and together they moved towards the door and watched her walking away with a step that had in it some quality that reminded them strongly of James. And as she walked, Rose Angela herself had the strange feeling inside her, in some depths where no white mind could reach, that most of her father walked with her.

Murphy watched her until she disappeared from view, then he turned to Pete. 'What do you make of it?'

Pete shook his head.

'She was ready for the high jump then, all right. Think she'll be all right now?'

Pete nodded.

'Can't understand the guv'nor taking notice of them letters, can you? He don't take no notice of what nobody says as a rule. What do you think we best do?'

Pete brought his eyes from where in imagination they were following Rose Angela, and said briefly, 'Tell him about Hassan?'

'Aye, that would be the best thing.'

Murphy pulled the door of the railway carriage to, then they set off walking slowly over the sleepers – slowly, as if they did not relish coming to the end of their short journey. Murphy did not speak again until they reached the wharf, when he said, 'What if he's mad?'

Pete's answer was to indicate the door with a motion of his head, which said plainly, 'Knock and find out.'

Murphy knocked four times on the door, but received no answer. It took courage to go round the house and ring the front door-bell; but even this brought no response, and only when they came to the back door again and knocked once more was the studio window thrust up with a bang; and Murphy and Pete stepped back and looked up at Stanhope. No word was spoken for quite some seconds, for Stanhope's expression froze Murphy's tongue. He was used to hearing the guv'nor going off the deep end and to see his face become furious with sudden temper, but the man up there was not in any way connected with the guv'nor he knew. His face was white, almost livid, and he did not yell at them, as usual, with, 'Well, what the devil do you want?' but stood waiting for them to speak.

In keeping with the unusual that seemed to be the order of the morning, it was Pete who spoke.

'Can we have a word with you?' he said.

Murphy looked swiftly from Stanhope to Pete and back to Stanhope again, who asked curtly, 'What about?'

'Well' – it was Murphy starting now – 'it's like this, guv'nor. Y'see . . .' His Adam's apple jerked swiftly and he swallowed and brought out, 'It's about Rose Angela.'

'What about her?' The words seemed to take their time in reaching them; they were weighed with something that chilled Murphy and curbed his ready tongue.

'Well, there's been a mistake made, guv'nor' – he dared not say 'You have made a mistake,' and went lamely on – 'about Hassan. The Arab fellow, y'know.'

'Yes?' This word came sharp now, like a rapier.

'Well, she said you . . . Well . . . you've got the idea—' Murphy hesitated. 'It's a bit of a mix-up, guv'nor.'

'And she sent you along here to explain it away?'

'No, no. But we thought you should know . . .'

'She's living in Holborn, isn't she?'

'Aye, she is.'

'Who with?' Again the words were heavy.

Once more Murphy brought his gaze down to Pete's. Here was a complication they hadn't given themselves time to foresee. If they said Jimmy, one thing would lead to another and before they knew where they were they would be talking of Matt; then of last night; and the less who knew about that affair the better.

But Murphy was not required to answer this particular question, for Stanhope threw another at him. 'Who gave her the black eyes?'

'What's that?'

Murphy's mouth was agape as he stared up at him. It was as if he hadn't heard, or having heard, the question did not make sense to him.

This pose of stupidity seemed too much for Stanhope. In a moment he became the guv'nor they recognised, only more vehement than they had ever seen him before.

'Get the hell out of it, the pair of you! Get!'

It was as if he would topple out of the window on to them with the force of his passion.

'But look here, guv'nor . . .'

'I'll give you a minute to get going. If you aren't gone by the time I come down I'll throw the pair of you in the river!' His voice rose to a yell, and before he had crashed the window down they were off the wharf, for they were too experienced to attempt to reason with anyone in the state he was in.

'What do you think we'd better do?' asked Murphy as they returned to the railway carriage.

'Wait and tell him the morrer.'

'But what will we tell him then?'

'The lot.'

'The lot?' Murphy stopped in his stride. 'Oh, I think we'd better see Jimmy afore doin' that.'

'Aye,' Pete assented with a nod.

'Will we go now?'

Again Pete nodded.

'But how about taking a look round first in case he's . . .' Murphy did not add 'come up'. And once more Pete's head inclined agreement, and without further words they walked along the river bank, their eyes turned towards the water.

CHAPTER FOURTEEN

COLOUR

The quietness was still with Rose Angela as she mounted the stairs to James, but it was now a frozen quietness, and she knew that when it melted there would be pain to bear greater than ever she had known before.

James's eyes, burning in their great sockets, fastened on her from the moment she opened the door, and his voice came as a hollow, cracked whisper from the bed, saying, 'You not long.'

'No.' She went straight to him and took his hand. 'How do you feel now?'

'Oh, a lot better . . . heap better.' He stared up into her face, his eyes searching hers. 'What wrong now? Something more wrong now? They find him?'

'No.'

'Well, what wrong? You been crying mightily.'

'Don't talk any more. Now lie quiet.' She put his arms inside the clothes, then turned from him and took off her hat and coat.

'Your face pain?'

'Yes.'

'Rose Angela . . .'

'Yes, dear, what is it?' She turned at the entreaty and bent over him.

He stared at her in silence for some time before answering, 'I feel in here' – his hand was moving under the bed-clothes with its old gesture of patting his chest – 'things not right with you . . . Painter . . . Mr Stanhope, he all right . . . him not mad at you staying off?'

She had to prevent her eyelids from closing to shut out the pain, for now the quietness was melting, and it was a moment before she answered, 'Yes, he's all right.'

'And you hear nothing about . . . the other one?' James could not bring himself to pronounce the name.

'No.'

'Sure?'

'Yes. Now don't talk, dear; I'm going to make you a drink.'

'I got to talk. It won't make no difference, one way or other. Sit down by me.'

She was lifting a chair to the bedside when a tap came on the door, and to her 'Come in' Hassan entered, and she saw immediately that he was disturbed.

'You've heard something?' she asked hesitantly.

He shook his head, but said nothing, only continued to stare at her, and James called feebly, 'Hassan! Here!'

Hassan went to the bed and James motioned him to sit down. 'What happen?'

'Nothing.'

'No sign of him?'

'No.'

'Perhaps him get back home somehow.'

'No; they're looking for him.'

'You been up?'

'I sent up.'

There was silence in the room for a time until Rose Angela came to the bed with a drink for James and she said to Hassan, 'Could you stay for a short while? I've got to get some oil and things.'

He nodded, but still he did not speak to her, only stared up into her face.

She put on her hat and coat again, and saying, 'I won't be more than a minute or two,' she left the room.

She had hardly closed the door when James hitched himself up on his pillows and said urgently, 'Something wrong with her – something more wrong. She come in and she been cryin' sore. You know what 'tis, Hassan?'

Hassan looked away, and James urged, 'If you know, you tell me – I not long for top and I want her be happy.'

'Jimmy' – Hassan leant forward and took James's hand – 'I want to marry Rose Angela. You know that, don't you, without me telling you?'

James stared fixedly at the Arab without answering, and Hassan went on, 'I can make her happy. I know I can.'

James shook his head.

'I tell you I can. What have you against it? You married a white woman.'

Again James shook his head, and his voice rose above its whispering quality, and for a moment there was the echo of the deep timbre note in it again. 'It very wrong thing for black man marrying white woman. It bad enough for man, for him sore inside all his days, but for white woman it hell. And bigger hell for children. What you think the real reason I no let my wife know I'm here? It because I know she happy with white man. That's as should be – colour to colour. But me . . . I not blaming you, Hassan, for wanting my Rose Angela, for only when fellow near death can he be wise. When life leaps inside him no man wise.'

'But Rose Angela's different . . . she's not all white.'

'She is' – James was sitting up now in agitation – 'she's white. I tell you she is white.'

'All right, all right, Jimmy,' Hassan said soothingly. 'Outside she may look more white than black, but inside she's all you – and that's a good thing.'

He smiled into James's troubled eyes, and James leant back and said between gasps, 'You say kind things, Hassan. I always like you, but I near death and I must speak truth. I no want my Rose Angela marry you. Anyway, the . . .' James looked down on his hands, almost transparent in their thinness, and went on lamely, 'I think she loves painter fellow.'

'Yes, and he's turned her out.'

Hassan had risen to his feet, his voice harsh and angry, and James's eyes darted up his thin frame to his face. 'What you say?'

'That fellow Matt wrote and told him she was living with me, and without any evidence he believed it. That's the kind of white god he is. And he turned her out, and she nearly threw herself . . .'

Hassan pulled up too late, and James said fearfully, 'Go on.'

'It's all right. She was a bit overdone – I'm sorry I said anything. She's all right now.'

James bent over and gripped Hassan's arm. 'She try throw herself in river?'

'She's all right now. Don't you worry.'

'My God! You say don't worry. Go after her. Don't leave her, and bring her back.'

'But she wants me to stay.'

'Go now – go.'

Hassan turned from the bed; then swung round again. 'If I ask her and she will marry me, what then?'

James closed his eyes. 'I said my say, Hassan.'

When Hassan had gone, James lay back weak and exhausted, and for some time he did not move. Only his fingers clutched and gathered up the white Marcella bedspread. After a while he moved his head to one side on his bank of pillows so that the knob of the bed should not obstruct his vision, and now he could see the three statues standing on a shelf to the side of Rose Angela's shake-down. There was a statue of St Joseph and one of the Virgin, and another of Jesus. Years ago he had bought them at the door of the church because the man there, who said he was a brother of St Vincent de Paul, also said that many blessings went with these statues. He remembered Rose Angela, from when she was a tiny child, claiming them as hers, and they were among the few possessions she had brought here. Now, in his mind, he began to talk to the statues, as he had often done of late, but this time with added urgency. 'You not let this come about, you not let the painter fellow believe this. You can't do this. You not let her marry Hassan, or kill herself in river.' He hitched himself a little farther to one side and appealed across the distance, 'I not want to die till she fixed up right. You can understand that. Don't let me die till she fixed up right.'

He waited in his thinking, and a narrow shaft of sunlight, the only shaft in the day that ever found its way into the room, fell across the face of the figure of Christ, and for the moment obliterated it in light; and James became still inside in wonderment.

He lay quiet and at peace now, watching the streak of sunlight narrow before it disappeared altogether. When it had gone he shook his head at himself. 'Me, I imagine things. All my life I imagine things.'

He lay staring at the statues until the drowsiness which was becoming more frequent of late took hold of him, and as he dozed off he wondered whimsically if, when he went into the long sleep, he would meet the people the statues represented.

He did not know what he would find in the coming long sleep. Perhaps he would see God, perhaps not. Perhaps God died when the brain could function no more. Perhaps he had done his work then. But if, on the other hand, he did meet him, what then? What had he to show for his life? Drowsily he shook his head again. Only a kindness here and there . . . and loving. Yes, he had loved. Love had been the driving force, the force that had brought him to this way of dying. Then perhaps it had to be . . . perhaps he had followed the pattern cut out for him. But it did not matter either way. He allowed himself to slip farther down the bed. All that mattered was that his Rose Angela should know happiness, happiness such as he knew existed but which had escaped him. If his daughter could have this happiness, then the pattern of his life had been a good pattern; and working it out was like paying in advance for another life – Rose Angela's life.

Hassan guessed that Rose Angela had gone to a little group of shops off Commercial Road, and he made for there. But as he turned the corner of the street he actually ran into her, and in her surprise at seeing him she clutched at his arm, exclaiming, 'He's not . . . ?'

'No, no – he's all right. He asked me to come and help you with the basket.'

She looked at him in disbelief. 'What's wrong, Hassan? There was something the matter when you came in.'

She started to walk rapidly towards the house, and he took the oil-can from her hand and said without looking at her, 'There are two men I'd like to kill, and one's that painter.'

She stiffened, and he went on, 'I must talk to you, Rose Angela. Will you come to the café for a minute?'

She shook her head. 'I must get home.'

'Just for a minute.'

With the appeal of his voice she turned her head towards him and said kindly, 'You know I can't leave him for long.'

They were crossing the yard now, and it was empty of people, as was the dark hallway, and inside

715

he brought her to a halt. 'Listen just one minute, Rose Angela. Tell me, are you afraid of me?'

'No, oh no, Hassan!' Her answer was so spontaneous that it brought a smile to his face.

'Thank you, Rose Angela. Do you . . . do you like me?'

'Yes, I like you. No-one could help liking you, Hassan.'

'You are not afraid of me and you like me.' He took the basket from her hand and laid it, together with the oil-can, at the foot of the stairs. Then he gathered both her cold hands in his. 'Will you believe me when I say I can make you love me?'

She stared into his eyes and saw there the released fire of his feelings.

'Will you believe me?'

'Oh, Hassan!'

She bowed her head, and he pulled her to him. 'I love you so much, Rose Angela, that I would give my life for you. You cannot believe it at this moment, but there would be no pain with my love as there would have been with his.'

She made a movement to withdraw her hands, and he gripped them closer. 'Listen. All your life you will be colour-conscious. I know, for I have watched you. You feel inferior. Inside you feel inferior . . . you, who could be a queen. And could he take that inferior feeling away? No. And however he might have overlooked it, his fine friends would not, and he has plenty of fine friends. But with me you will never feel inferior. Instead of knowing you are looked down on, you will be looked up to – adored, worshipped; and you will want for nothing . . . Oh,

Rose Angela, look at me. Tell me, Rose Angela.'

She did not raise her head, for his words were finding resting-places in her mind. He was right. Always inside she felt inferior, but never so much as she did at this moment; and as he said, with him it would go. She could believe this, for he did not feel racially superior to her. With him she could stop fighting; once joined to him she could allow the stamp of her colour to rise to the surface and she could accept what she was, and with acceptance would come release.

For a moment the face of Stanhope came before her eyes, as it had been last night, saying, 'What are you going to do about it?' He hadn't thought her good enough to marry, then; only this morning in the midst of rejecting her he could say he had been going to marry her. It was easy, then, when there was no possibility of its taking place. Into the pain and despair that seemed to be finding passage through each vein of her body was mingled a feeling of bitterness against him, and against her mother. Bridget was also in her mind at this moment, for was she not another, the only other one that mattered, who had so readily believed the worst of her? And if she were to marry Hassan she would not have to suffer the shock of breaking it to her, for that had already been endured. And yet another worry that Hassan could relieve her of was money, for she had only a few pounds she had saved up to provide extras at Christmas. All her wages had been spent on James and the room. If she was to support him she must find work; for the short time left she must find work – or else. She raised her eyes to Hassan. He

717

had said, 'You will want for nothing.' Well, she had never wanted very much from life, and the little she had got, which amounted to food and a few clothes, was acquired only through long hours of labour at the beck and call of others. And these had always been punctuated by the fight against men. So what had she to lose if she married Hassan?

Hassan sensed the change in her, and he pressed his point. 'Tell me, Rose Angela.' And although he was urging her answer, when it came he was rendered dumb with surprise.

'Give me time, and I'll try.' And as she said it there swept over her a wave of sound, full of her father's voice, crying, 'You not do this.'

It was done, but as Hassan leaned forward to place his lips on hers she recoiled, saying, 'No, no, not yet.'

'All right, I can wait.'

There was pain in his eyes, and she turned from him and picked up the basket and the oil-can, and went heavily up the stairs.

CHAPTER FIFTEEN

PAYMENT

After Stanhope had rushed down the stairs to carry out his threat to Murphy and Pete, and found he was not called upon to do so, he again locked the back door; then he stood and glared around the kitchen. He looked at the delf rack. The dishes she had washed yesterday were all arrayed neatly and gleaming, and his anger was such that he had to place the utmost restraint on himself not to raise his arm and sweep the lot on to the floor.

He flung out of the kitchen and into the drawing-room. The cold deadliness of his feeling was passing and he was wanting to storm. He caught a glimpse of himself in the mirror, and was brought to a halt. He looked as he felt, wild with temper.

He sat on the couch and, resting his elbows on his knees, he gripped his hair with both hands as if he would pull it out by the roots. God, why had he let himself in for this? The first time was bad enough, but nothing compared with this. She had got into his blood and maddened him, and in spite of her lies, this raving ache would go on and on . . . The lies, the bare-faced lies! He might have questioned the truth of that man's letter if she hadn't actually admitted she was living in Holborn. To think he had put her on the tram and she had doubled back into Holborn!

Anyway, it served him right, at his age, falling for a bit of a girl! . . . But she wasn't a bit of a girl; she was mature, with the knowledge of life in her eyes; and by God, she must have it, too, living in Holborn! And he had been such a fool as to fall for her simplicity. Living with her father in Holborn!

He lifted his head and let out a staccato laugh. That black he had painted! Why on earth had she to pick on him? Had there been the slightest resemblance between them he would have noticed it . . . wouldn't he? It was a pity the painting had gone . . . His thinking brought him upright, and before the thought ended he was up the stairs and into the studio. He pushed aside a number of files that stood against the wall, until he came to one with the word 'Hulk' written across it. This he lifted on to the table and flicked over the loose sheets it contained, most of them being rough sketches of a boat rotting in the mud. And when he came to the sketches of the Negro he became still, devouring each line of the drawings. This one was a quick sketch, done when he first saw the man. It was made up of only a few lightning strokes, because, finding he was being sketched, the Negro moved off. Then this one, a side view, showing that enormous ear. And this, just his mouth. Was there any resemblance between that mouth and hers? . . . None! But he had done one full-faced. He flung over more drawings, depicting hands and feet. Then he came upon it: the ear, the pock marks, and the emaciation, all there.

But out of this, James's eyes, almost alive, stared up at him, and for a moment the man became submerged in the artist, and he thought, with a sense of awe, of his own achievement: I got those eyes. Then, still looking down into the charcoal eyes of the Negro, he began to place odd pieces of paper over the face. In all positions he placed them, until only the eyes were left, and as he stared an uneasiness grew in him; and he protested, speaking aloud, 'It isn't so. I would have known; I would have detected it.'

He looked around the room, at the various paintings hanging there, as if they would confirm him in his belief . . . 'I would have known.' Yet the eyes looking up at him were the eyes of Rose Angela.

My God! Supposing she was speaking the truth! But the Arab . . . he was waiting for her all right. And her face. Who had really done that to her?

He was still staring down into the eyes when a faint tap, tap came to him. There was someone at the back door again, blast them! Murphy come back, perhaps. No . . . Then Her? He gave himself no answer, for it would not be her; she would not come here again – his reception having blasted her as far as another continent from him.

Well, who the hell was it, then? He marched to the window, and, flinging it up, looked down on to the wharf and into the upturned face of a woman.

'Mr Stanhope?'

He found himself answering quietly, 'Yes.'

'I'm Mrs Paterson. I've come to see my daughter.'

For a long moment he stared at her. Then he said, still quietly, 'Wait a moment, I'll be down.'

He would not allow himself any pondering as he went hastily down the stairs. But when he unlocked the back door he was made to wonder what this woman's visit could portend.

Bridget and he appraised each other for some seconds, and it was she who spoke first. 'Can I see my daughter, please?'

His reply was to step aside and say, 'Will you come in?'

Silently Bridget passed him and walked into the kitchen, into the blue kitchen that Rose Angela had described so vividly. She stood stiffly waiting, and he pulled a chair from the table and said, 'Please sit down.'

She sat down, and looked towards the door that led to the hall, as if expecting Rose Angela to make an appearance.

Stanhope looked at this woman, the mother of Rose Angela, the woman who had married a coloured man. She was a fine-looking woman with a stately bearing, but there was a stiffness about her that wasn't a veneer of the moment. It seemed to emanate from within her.

She looked up at him and asked, 'Is Rosie in?'

'No.' He turned from her and looked out of the window towards the river. 'I'm afraid, Mrs Paterson, she is not here.'

'Not here? You mean she's gone?'

He nodded.

'When?'

'This morning.'

'This morning,' she repeated. 'Mr Stanhope' – she

was on her feet now, looking at his back – 'do you know where she's gone?'

'No.'

He heard her swallow in the silence that followed his answer. Then she burst out:

'Mr Stanhope, you know something, you know where she's gone. Has she gone into . . . Holborn? Is she living there altogether?'

He did not answer her, and she went on, 'Has she been working here all along?' And he said, 'Yes, up to yesterday.'

'And is she not coming back?'

'No.'

Slowly Bridget sat down again. 'If I'd only come yesterday.' She was talking softly as if to herself. 'I knew something was wrong. Mr Stanhope' – she entreated the forbidding solidness of his back – 'you know more than I do, for God's sake tell me!'

He remained for a moment longer staring at the river. Then turning slowly, he pulled a letter from his pocket and handed it to her. 'Read that.'

Wondering, she took the letter from him, and he watched her closely as she began to read it. He saw the colour of her face change; and before she had read very far she turned to the back of the letter in search of the signature. Then she said in an awed whisper, 'My brother wrote this.'

She read a little farther, then again she stopped, and the glisten of tears was in her eyes. 'Oh, it's lies, all lies. She was the best lass in the world, she never caused me a moment's trouble. Not until . . . these last few weeks. But this about having to leave

723

her places, it's a pack of lies. She left because she wouldn't . . . well, the men wouldn't leave her alone, and her mistresses . . . It wasn't her fault. Matt, my brother, has always hated her.'

She read on to the end of the letter, then folded it slowly and handed it back to him. 'There's not a line of truth in it, except . . .' She bit her lip and pulled at the fingers of her thin black gloves. 'He . . . Matt, my brother . . . he said he saw her with an Arab. And then she said she was going to lodge in Holborn. But somehow, knowing her, the more I thought of it the less I could believe it, in spite of what I did.' For an instant her eyes flicked away from his. Then she murmured in perplexity, 'But if she's left here and is . . . in Holborn . . .'

Stanhope pushed his hand through his hair. 'I don't know, I don't know what to think. An hour ago I would have said she was with the Arab all right. Now I'm not sure. And if I'm wrong . . .' The enormity of his thought brought his movements to a stop, and he stood, his hand in his hair, staring at the table, as if lying there for him to see was some disastrous result of his doubting.

'Mrs Paterson' – he dropped into a chair opposite to her – 'I think I'd better tell you . . . You see, I loved Rosie. I was no better than any of her other bosses, but not up till last night did I tell her . . .'

'Not till last night? Then she wasn't . . .?' Bridget caught herself up.

He shook his head at her. 'No, she wasn't living with me.'

'I'm sorry I . . .'

'Don't be. Last night I was quite willing that that's

724

how things should be; but then, on reflection, I knew I must marry her. I went with her to the tram and saw her get on it – as I thought, to go home. Prior to this I had chased an Arab away from outside. Then this morning I received this letter. And not only this one, but another from Mrs Grant. Then Rosie came. You can imagine how I was feeling.' He looked away from Bridget towards the window again. 'But I can see now that the distress she was in was genuine. And her face, her beautiful face, was scarcely recognisable.'

Slowly Bridget rose up from the chair. 'What about her face?'

'It was disfigured.'

'Disfigured? With a knife?'

'No, no, not with a knife; the blow had been done with a fist, right between her eyes. She said her uncle did it, but I didn't believe her; I thought the Arab had done it.'

'Oh, my God! What's it all about?' Bridget clutched at the front of her coat. 'Matt always said he'd spoil her face. I went in fear for years that he'd do it. And yesterday morning he went out, and hasn't been seen since. My other brother's been looking for him half the night; and this morning we had to tell the polis. Oh, Mr Stanhope, I'm afraid of our Matt and what he'll do to her. Was she alone last night when he caught her?'

'I don't know.'

'Have you any idea at all where I'll likely find her?'

'Apart from knowing she's in Holborn, I can't say. She said she was . . .' He stopped and stared at Bridget. 'Mrs Paterson, is your husband alive?'

Bridget stared back at him, and murmured, 'I don't know.'

'It's some years since you saw him?'

'I saw him last when Rosie was four years old. He had a fight with my brother and he thought he'd killed him, and he ran away. I haven't seen him since.'

'Sit down, I won't be a minute.' Stanhope left the kitchen, and in a matter of seconds was back with a single sheet of paper in his hand. He put this face downwards on the table and, leaning towards Bridget, said gently, 'Mrs Paterson, this may come as a shock to you . . . or it may mean nothing. Do you recognise this man?' He turned over the drawing for her to see. He watched her eyes widen and her lips slowly drop apart; then he saw her body fold up as if it had been released from a spring, and she slumped face forward over the table before he could reach her.

Lifting her limp head he urged, 'Come on, Mrs Paterson,' but she made no response. He hurried into the drawing-room, and when he returned with some brandy she was raising herself up. And her face was blanched.

'Drink this.'

He put the brandy to her lips, and she sipped it and shuddered, then said, 'I'm all right.'

'Take another drink.'

She shook her head. The drawing was still on the table, and she looked down on it again, but did not speak. Nor did Stanhope, for he was seeing Rose Angela's face as she said, 'I'm living with my father . . . the Negro . . . the one you painted.'

Every word she spoke had been true, then, and he had kicked her out. He closed his eyes.

Bridget's voice, low and trembling, was saying, 'This is my husband. He's changed . . . but it's him. Where is he?'

'If that is your husband, then, Mrs Paterson, he's in Holborn. And he's been living there for some time. And Rosie is living with him. That is the explanation of it all. The only thing I can't see now is why she had to keep it secret.'

Bridget took her handkerchief and wiped the moisture from her face. Her conscience was suggesting one reason why James had remained hidden. She stared at the drawing again. The eyes were as she remembered them, but that ear and the pox about his chin and the hollowness of his cheeks all spoke of hardship. Remorse and pity rose in her! Oh, Jimmie, Jimmie! And Rosie knew. All the time she knew and stayed with you, and put up with everything rather than let on in case Matt found out. Yes, that would be one of the reasons why she had kept quiet . . . in case Matt found out. Oh, Rosie, lass!

Stanhope touched the outline of the drawing with his finger. 'He was a very sick man when I drew that . . . You should know he was dying with consumption.'

'Consumption?'

'I'm afraid so. And after I'd finished painting him he seemed to disappear. Murphy and Pete, two friends of his, never mentioned him again, and I took it for granted he was dead.'

Bridget gripped the edge of the table and brought herself to her feet. 'Now I know!' She turned startled eyes on Stanhope. 'Matt knew about him' – she nodded to the drawing – 'about Jimmie being here. He's been queer for the last week or so; he's been queer for some time. But lately he's been saying strange things; I thought he was going mad. Only yesterday morning he said' – she paused as if to recall each word – 'he said, soon he'd be able to tell me something and I'd be really free; he said there wouldn't only be one funeral. You see, me father's ill. He had an accident and burnt his hands; then he got soaked sitting on the . . . being out one night, and he took pneumonia and we thought he was going to die. But my mother's pulling him through.'

She paused again, and Stanhope could see her mind probing, and for the moment, he knew, she was no longer with him but back in a number of yester-days, piecing together what well might be a tragedy.

Since coming downstairs this morning his life had been changed completely. Yesterday he was lord of all he surveyed – the house, the wharf – and last night, Rose Angela. In spite of the torment of his growing passion for her his days had been full and smooth; he had his work and material, for it swarmed about him. But now, after a few hours, he was being drawn rapidly into the maelstrom of lives, each converging to a climax that had its begin-ning when this woman married a Negro. That she foresaw tragedy he could see by her expression – the terror in her face conveyed itself to him – and he thought, I likely could have prevented anything further happening if I hadn't been such a blasted fool and had listened to Rosie.

'If they meet, Matt'll kill him,' Bridget spoke

again. 'He always said he would. I must find Rosie. When I find her I'll find him.'

'Likely they have met already. When your brother hit her he must have cornered her somewhere, for it's not likely he'd try it on in the street.'

'But he hasn't come home! You don't know Matt; he'll keep at a thing until it's done.'

'But where are you going to start to look for her? You know the people in that quarter – they can be like oysters if they choose . . . Wait! What am I thinking of? Murphy, the man who lives in the railway carriage, he'll take us. I'll get my coat.'

When he returned, Bridget said, 'But it's putting you to a lot of trouble.' And he answered soberly, 'Trouble, Mrs Paterson? If I can't gain Rosie's forgiveness, then I'm only at the beginning of my trouble.'

They stood for a second longer looking at each other and understanding each other, as if this was but one of many meetings during which their hopes and fears had been laid bare.

He opened the door for her and she went out before him, and as they hurried over the sleepers he took her elbow to help her, and this action thrust her painfully back into the past – Jimmie had done things like this . . . Tony didn't. His loving showed itself in other ways; like the men of the fifteen streets, he practically ignored women in public, at least when it meant doing any service that would qualify him for the name of 'Sloppy' and bring derision on him and the recipient of his affection. But, she remembered, Jimmie had not minded. He, like this man, had done these little things naturally. Her heart

729

began to ache with an intolerable ache. Poor Jimmie! She should never have married him; she should have had the courage to have the bairn. But he had wanted her so. And she was young and silly, and ignorant.

And now he was dying; and he'd been living in the town and hadn't troubled her; and Rosie had stood all that scandal about living with an Arab rather than give him away. Would Rosie ever forgive her? What must she have felt when everybody turned against her! Oh, Rosie, lass, Rosie!

Stanhope's tongue, clicking with impatience, brought her thoughts from Rosie. He was looking through the railway-carriage window.

'They're gone!' He turned a disappointed face to her. 'The thing is now, where to look for them, for they may have gone across the water. Yet there's the chance they may still be knocking around the market place or the ferry.'

So, for an hour or more Stanhope and Bridget walked about the market and the ferry and beyond them, but saw no signs of Murphy and Pete. Then Stanhope suggested that Bridget, who was looking very tired, should return home and that as soon as he found Murphy he would send her word.

But Bridget was reluctant to comply with his suggestion, even when he pressed the point that they would likely go on for hours without success. At last, when he intimated that he stood more chance of finding something out if alone, she agreed; and, as he had put her daughter on the tram for home last night, now he did her, reassuring her once more that as soon as he had any news he would send for her.

Alone again, he hurried down the Mill Dam bank;

but stopped before turning into Holborn. It would be a good idea to leave a note at the railway carriage telling Murphy, should he return, to wait there for him. Forgotten now completely was the fact that a short while ago he had threatened to throw him in the river.

He was going through the narrow cut, when, to his surprise and relief, he saw Murphy entering it from the river end. Murphy had, however, seen him first, and was already making a hasty retreat when Stanhope shouted. 'Hi there! Murphy!'

Murphy did not stop, so Stanhope broke into a run, calling, 'Just a minute! What's the matter with you, man?' And when he came abreast of him he demanded, 'Are you deaf? Couldn't you hear me?'

Murphy looked at him out of the corner of his eye and cautiously answered the latter part of the question, 'Aye, guv'nor.'

Then, remembering the reason for this caution, Stanhope said, 'I'm sorry about that; I was a bit mad. But something's happened since then, and I want your help, Murphy.'

'Aye, guv'nor.' Again Murphy looked sideways at him.

'I want you to take me to Rosie.'

'What?' Now Murphy was fronting him. 'Take you to Rosie! Oh, well, guv'nor.' He rubbed his chin with the palm of his hand. 'Well, it's like this. I can't do it . . . not right away I can't. I'll have to have a talk with . . . Well, you see . . .'

He stopped, and Stanhope said, 'It's all right; I know who Rosie's father is. Her mother has just been to see me.'

'To see you,' repeated Murphy. 'But God, guv'nor, she don't know nowt about Jimmie being here!'

'She does now.'

'How?'

'By the drawing I did of him.'

'But he don't want her to know.'

'She knows, anyway, and it's right that she should. And she's worried about Rosie. I'm worried about Rosie, too, Murphy.'

Murphy had never before detected such a tone in Stanhope's voice, and he moved from one foot to the other, saying, 'Well, guv'nor . . . I dunno . . . I suppose it'll be all right.'

'It will be, I assure you.'

'I wish Pete was here.'

'Where is he?'

'Gone along the river looking for a sign of . . .' He stopped; it wasn't likely the guv'nor knew anything about Matt. 'Seeing if there's anything doing,' he ended.

'Take me now, Murphy,' Stanhope urged. 'If you don't, I'll find them anyway. It will take me longer, but I'll find them.'

'Aye, there's that in it.' Murphy again looked sideways at him, and his next words would never have been spoken had he given thought to them. But as he stared at this big, blustering man, they seemed to be drawn to his lips. 'You're a bloody funny bloke,' he said, and his mouth fell agape at his own temerity.

After a moment they laughed together, then turned and went through the cut and into Holborn.

Hassan came thoughtfully down the stairs. His first

love offering had just been refused. When previously he had left Rose Angela he returned to his café and had there packed a basket of delicacies for James, and for her he had selected, from a small hoard of such things, a ring, a very valuable ring. Although he had given a lot of money for it, he knew he had paid only about a third of its real value. Rose Angela, however, had merely glanced at it and shook her head, and instead of allowing him to place the ring on her finger she had placed her fingers on her lips to ensure his silence so as not to disturb James's sleep. And when he left the ring on the table she picked it up and followed him on to the landing and whispered, 'No, Hassan, I can't take it. Not yet, anyway.' And he simply said, 'All right,' and told himself that he must go carefully, and that time was young. Give her a few weeks to recover and she would turn to him; she would be his . . . he would make her his; only let her not see that painter and she would forget.

It was at this point that he reached the foot of the stairs, and, as if his thought of the painter had conjured Stanhope up, he saw him. Through the open doorway he saw him and Murphy enter the yard, and as fire will sweep over oil, so a flame of hate swept over him.

He stood guarding the foot of the stairs; and when Murphy, coming first through the doorway, said, 'Watcher, there,' he made no reply. He did not even look at Murphy, but kept his eyes riveted on the breadth of the man protruding behind him.

Stanhope, coming abreast of Murphy, faced Hassan, and he recognised in this thin tall Arab the man he had chased from the house last night. Also, even before Hassan spoke, he knew him to be the Arab whose name was coupled with that of Rosie, and immediately guessed that if rumour was wrong it was not this man's fault.

'What do you want?' Hassan pointedly addressed Stanhope.

And Stanhope tried to override his own dislike, for, after all, this was a man, and if his feeling for Rosie was to be compared with his own, then, whatever his race, he was to be pitied. So, with unusual calmness for him, he replied, 'Don't you think that's my business?'

'No, I do not.'

The English was precise and clipped, not the pidgin kind, and this too impressed Stanhope that he was not dealing with the ordinary run of Arab who manned the cargo ships running back and forth from the Tyne. So again he curbed the hot retort on his tongue and said, 'Well, whether you do or not is beside the point. Now, if you'll move . . .'

'I'll see you in your own particular hell first!'

'Why, Hassan, man' – Murphy was gaping open-mouthed – 'what's come over you? Look, the guv'nor just wants to see Rosie and . . .'

Hassan turned on Murphy and repeated, 'Just wants to see Rosie! You fool!'

Murphy stood dumb with amazement. Never before had Hassan taken this line with him. To him Hassan was a warm man, and a very decent bloke, better than many whites, for he always had a civil word and would sit and crack with you. But now he was speaking to him as if he was a dog.

And no coloured man, however decent he might be, was going to speak to him like a dog! After all was said and done, what was he but an Arab, even if he had money. No, by God, he'd soon let him see who he was speaking to!

'What the hell's up with you! The guv'nor's come to see Rosie, and he's goner see her!'

Murphy's tone now brought Hassan's gaze back to him, and his anger for a moment was touched with sorrow: Murphy was no longer Murphy, he was a white man, taking another white man's part against colour. And Jimmie, in his wilful ignorance, thought Rose Angela could entirely escape this!

Hassan's voice was quieter now as he addressed Murphy, but bitterness lay deep in it. 'A few hours ago you saved Rose Angela from jumping in the river, because of this man's treatment of her. Now you bring him to her. Well, it's too late, she's going to marry me.'

'What' – the loose goose-flesh skin of Murphy's neck rippled – 'marry you!' He turned and looked at Stanhope; but Stanhope was showing no surprise at this preposterous statement, for inside he was sick with this new knowledge, that because of him Rosie had tried to drown herself.

'Marry you!' gulped Murphy. 'Why, man, you must be mad.' He knew that Hassan was fond of Rosie, but so was he, and so was Pete. Aye, by lad, Pete was very struck on Rosie. But would any of them think they could marry her? Yet here was Hassan saying he was going to. Why, it was enough to make the guv'nor bash his face in. He looked again at Stanhope, who was looking at Hassan . . . not as he should do, in one of his mad tears, but quietly, and what was more puzzling he was speaking quietly too. Funnily quiet, Murphy thought.

'I am here to see Rosie, and I am going to see her! As for what she does, that is for her to decide.'

'You're so sure of yourself, aren't you? You think you only have to see her again and tell her you know now she wasn't living with an Arab and everything will be all right!' Hassan's lip curled back, miming the scorn against himself the last words implied.

And Murphy thought, I shouldn't have told him. I want me head look'n.

'Will you get out of my way?'

Hassan's reply was to remain staring down at Stanhope from the vantage point of the bottom stair. There were now spectators on the scene, some on the stairs above and some in the doorway. Stanhope was not aware of them; he was only aware that his tolerance had reached its limit. With a lightning stroke for one so heavily built his hands shot up, and the Arab and he changed places. In almost the wink of an eye he had swung Hassan bodily from the step. But like lightning, too, Hassan's hand moved behind to his hip pocket in a movement that spoke plainer than words to the onlookers, for whereas before no-one had uttered a word, now there were cries of, 'Don't be a fool, man!' 'You know who'll get the worst of it, don't you?' and 'None of that, now; do you want to bring the polis on the house?'

Hassan's fingers still gripped the handle of his knife as Stanhope turned from him and walked up the stairs, followed by Murphy. And now the people in the hall and those on the stairs came and closed round Hassan, urging him, for his own sake, to be sensible and reminding him of the too swift justice that followed when a coloured man attacked a white.

As Murphy tapped gently on the door, Stanhope stood taut, waiting. His mind was in a turmoil; all he wanted to do in this moment was to savour the thought that he was about to see her again, but the scene just past and the significance of the Arab's statement that she was going to marry him, combined with the thought that but for Murphy she might have succeeded in drowning herself, all added to his confusion. And when the door was softly opened and Rose Angela stood there, a warning finger on her lips, all he could do was to stare at her.

As her hand dropped to her side, Murphy whispered, 'What did I tell you, eh, Rosie? Here's the guv'nor; he wants to see you.'

When neither she nor Stanhope spoke, Murphy went on, 'Is Jimmy asleep? Well, that will do him good.' The silence being too much for him, he moved from one foot to the other, then sidled past her into the room.

Stanhope said, 'I must talk to you, Rosie.'

With a backward glance towards the bed, Rose Angela stepped out on to the landing and pulled the door to behind her. And now they were within a foot of each other. He looked into her face, discoloured and bruised from cheek-bone to cheek-bone, her eyes swollen level and their expression without life; and his love at this moment became purified and selfless. All he wanted was to ensure that never again would she know fear or want;

and so deep was the sadness in her eyes that he felt that not in a lifetime could he erase it. That he had put most of it there he knew, and the responsibility lay like a weight on his tongue, making him inarticulate. 'Rosie . . . what can I say?'

She did not help him, she only looked at him, into his eyes.

'Oh, Rosie, if you had only told me at the beginning. Can you forgive me?'

He took her hand, and it lay passively in his. 'Can you?' His voice was deep with his feeling.

Slowly she inclined her head, and he sighed. 'Oh, Rosie, I'll never forgive myself . . . never.' He looked about the landing. The other two doors were closed, but he felt that behind them were straining ears, and he whispered, 'Come back with me, I must talk to you.'

She shook her head.

'But we must talk.'

He looked at the door behind her, and for the first time she spoke. 'My father is very sick.'

'Can I see him?'

'I would rather you didn't.'

The listlessness of her voice perturbed him, and he said, 'There's bound to be some way in which I can help.'

Again she shook her head, and it seemed to him she was growing more lifeless each moment.

'Rosie' – he meant the demand in his voice to stir her – 'go back to last night; try to forget what has happened in between. I will make you forget. I'm to blame, at least for this morning . . . Will you?'

Still looking into his eyes, she answered him, 'A

short while ago I promised Hassan . . .' But what she had promised Hassan she could not go on to explain. Instead she shook her head pitifully and Stanhope's brows gathered into a furrow and his jaw stiffened. 'You can't do it! You didn't mean it. You did it on the rebound, you know you did. And perhaps, naturally, to hurt me.'

'No. I did it because' – she looked away from him as if she was seeing the reason for her action beyond the walls of the house – 'because I'm tired of fighting.'

'Tired of fighting?' He echoed her words in perplexity.

She nodded, her gaze penetrating the future. 'With him there'll be no need to fight; I won't be ashamed any more of being what I am.'

'Rosie, you're mad! You don't know what you are saying. You, ashamed of what you are! You're tired and ill. You're not thinking rationally because of all you've been through.'

She turned and looked at him again. 'It's strange, but my mind is clearer now than ever before in my life. I've always been fighting inside myself because I felt inferior. I've always felt inferior and tried to hide it; and only Hassan could see it, for he, too, knows what it is like to be looked down on. But now there won't be any need to hide it.'

'Stop it!' Stanhope's voice had a touch of the old arrogance in it. 'You cannot compare yourself with him.'

'You don't like Arabs, do you?'

'No, I don't!'

'Yet I'm coloured too.'

739

'Rosie' – he swallowed hard and inhaled deeply in an endeavour to retain a hold on his calmness – 'why all this talk of colour? What's come over you? Last night you didn't take this line.'

'No, I didn't; I was still hiding from myself. But now I know it was because of my colour that you believed the worst of me.'

'My God, Rosie, you can't believe that! It never entered into it. Can't you see it was because, as I said, when I was to be married before, I found out about this girl, and the circumstances were pretty much the same? Rosie, Rosie, for God's sake get that out of your head!'

'But I kept telling you the truth, and you wouldn't listen to me.'

'Yes, I know, I know. But I was mad with jealousy because I loved you so much. Look' – he pulled her to him – 'you're not going to do this. You wouldn't only be wrecking your own life, but a number of lives. There's your mother – she's worried to death.'

Her face was close under his and she whispered, 'My mother?'

'She's been to see me. She knows about your father, and she's worried because your uncle hasn't returned home. And she's afraid he'll do you both further harm.'

'My mother's been to see you, and she knows?'
'Yes.'

He felt a sigh of relief pass over her, and the despair for a moment left her eyes.

'She's coming here?'
'Yes, as soon as I can get word to her.'

She looked towards the door of the room in which

740

James was lying. 'I must warn him.'

'Rosie, let me speak to him.'

She hesitated a moment, then said dully, 'All right.'

'And Rosie' – he pulled her closer – 'listen to me. I love you and I'm willing to spend my life trying to convince you of it, but I'd rather see you dead than married to that Arab. You love me, don't you? . . . Look at me. You can't look at me and say you don't. Look at me.'

But she did not look at him. Her eyes, wide and staring from her head, were looking at something beyond him. And he flung round from her, expecting to be confronted by the Arab. But he faced a man whom he had never seen before, and who was staring with a diabolical stare, not at him, but at Rosie. And before he had time to think, the man had sprung past him and at Rose Angela, and they were borne to the floor together.

Matt had lain all through the night and most of the day concealed between the wall of a warehouse and a rubbish dump. He had slept fitfully through the night, and each time he had woken he had groped at his head. Once he woke up laughing and punching at the air. When daylight came he kept awake, but did not move from where he was. He could not tell himself why he was staying here, but instinct was telling him that he must hide. There was a pile of shavings among the rubbish, and after a while he burrowed into this and lay trying to find something to hold on to in the hollowness of his head. He could not remember his name, nor where he had come from; he only knew he had been running . . . running,

running. But when he thought of himself running he felt disappointed, and groped at the feeling, but the reason for this, too, evaded him.

Although a drizzle of rain was falling, he did not feel cold, only hungry. But he was loath to move, until the fading light of the afternoon urged him to get up. And he had to struggle out of the shavings, for his limbs felt heavy. He gazed about him, but did not know where he was. The river meant nothing to him, and he turned from it and walked with dragging step to where an opening showed in the wall beyond the refuse heap. It was an alleyway, and at the farther end he could see people passing in the street; and, strangely, he did not fear them now, but had an urge to be near them. Yet, once in the street, he walked close to the wall, keeping his head down. He turned the corner and crossed a road as if he knew where he was going, and he had walked quite some distance before he stopped. He was beside a short passage leading into a yard. Some way beyond, on the pavement, two men stood talking to an Arab. He turned his back on them, and as though he had done it before he lifted his eyes to the tin plate nailed above the arch and read 'River Court, 1, 2, 3 and 4'. Then he went along the passage and into the yard, and looked from one to the other of the four doors leading from it.

In the centre of the yard a woman was emptying slops down the drain, and as she banged the bucket to dislodge some filth she turned and glanced at him, and he hung his head. She took no further notice of him, but went to a tap near the wall, rinsed the bucket, threw the water on to the yard, then went through an open doorway.

Matt looked around the yard, selected a door, and went towards it. As he reached it his hand went to his head again, and his fingers moved over his scalp. Two children coming through the doorway looked up at him, then continued on their way; and he walked into the hallway and up the stairs without meeting anyone. But when he reached the second landing he heard voices, and he stood still, listening. First a man's voice, then a woman's. The woman's did not come often, but he waited for it. It was soft, scarcely above a whisper, and his mind clung to it, and he knew that he knew it. It began to form a substance in the hollowness, yet he could not pin it down, for when he groped at it it evaded him, moving away swiftly, almost becoming lost in the void again, until the whisper was renewed. Then he could feel it, the something that would bring him back. But when, for a seemingly long time, the woman's whisper did not reach him, he began to mount the stairs, pausing on each tread to listen. He was half-way up when he saw the feet through the banisters. They were close together, the woman's and the man's. He mounted still farther, until now he could see the back of the man's head. Then he was at the top of the stairs, and the woman moved her head and he saw her face, and he knew.

Now he knew what he had been trying to remember: his life that had been wrecked, his days bare and his nights empty, and all because of her. And he had come back to level things off. Once he had done this he would be happy, and the remainder of the void within him would be filled again. The woman saw him and became petrified, so petrified that she could make no sound, and at the sight of her fear he experienced a feeling of pure glee. And when the man who was shielding her with his body turned, the way was clear, and he sprang.

His hands clawed at her flesh, and he felt her body under his as they went down together. He heard the rattle of pails and tins as they were scattered about them. Then he was no longer on the landing but swinging into the air. And as he fell the second time he clung to the thing that had lifted him and bore it with him. He was fighting now like a mad-man, with his teeth, his fists and his feet, until fresh hands tore at him and fresh faces milled around him . . . white faces, dark faces; and hands, thousands of hands; and voices, crying and scream-ing. Then as suddenly as the void had begun to fill, so it emptied again. He still fought and struggled, but now only to get away, because he had become afraid of something, not of the pain from the blows, but from something welling inside him. Above the noise and stamping of feet he heard a high scream; then the struggle ceased abruptly.

He was on his knees, and the front of his coat and shirt were ripped away, and on his bare chest there were spatters of blood. Someone was holding his arms, and someone else had hold of his hair and was pulling his head back. The strain on his neck was excruciating, and from this angle all he could see was an Arab standing some distance from him. His eyes strained from the face down the man's side to the knife clutched in the brown hand.

Then the grip on his hair eased, to fall away altogether. And now his eyes were looking at the floor and the dirty boards spattered with blood, and he felt a rising gurgle of laughter moving up through his stomach. But before it reached his lips it changed. He saw it changing. It was in the centre of the great empty void that was him. He saw it disintegrate, then form again. And it formed into a sorrow that he knew was his life. And the weight of it became so great inside of him that he felt he must tear it out. But he had no means of doing this, and he knew it. Then into the stillness came a terrifying sound. It was the thing that had frightened him, the thing that he feared. It was the sound of his own weeping.

Stanhope looked from the sobbing man to his arm. The long gap in his greatcoat, coat and shirt looked like a series of jagged red lips. He was feeling no pain; from the moment when a red hot needle seemed to rip his skin the arm became numb. His main feeling was one of amazement. Even in the heat of the fight he had felt this amazement, when he realised that the Arab was trying to knife him. When he first saw the knife gleaming in the Arab's hand he wanted to protest against its use on Matt, but the milling of six bodies, for by then Murphy and two other men had joined the fray, made it impossible. When the knife slit the front of his coat he thought it was an accident, but not when he felt the prick of it between his shoulder-blades. He had untangled himself from the arms that were trying to hold Matt down and turned, filled with fury, yet still amazed, to where he thought the Arab was, for in the dimness of the landing it was fast becoming difficult to distinguish one figure from another. Almost at the same moment as he heard Rose Angela scream he felt the knife go down his arm, and he was thrown against the wall by the force behind the blow.

And now there was quiet on the landing; even the people crowding the stairs were quiet; and Stanhope thought he must be light-headed when, in a matter of seconds, the stairs were emptied of people as if a hand had wiped them away. Doors on the landing, which had been open and filled with shouting women, were now closed. He saw the two men who had been very prominent in the mêlée glide like vapour down the stairs. And now there remained only Murphy, who was holding the kneeling Matt by the arms, Rose Angela, who was pressed tight in the corner of the walls, the Arab and himself.

He looked at the Arab, whose face appeared a dull grey, its expression a mixture of hate and bitterness, and he thought, The dirty greaser! He tried to do me in. And he'll try to pass it off on to the madman there. A flame of intense anger swept over him, and he knew that if he himself had a knife handy at this moment he would ram it home into the Arab's chest. His anger impelled him from the wall, and, shouting a gabble of words, he lunged at Hassan. But before he could reach him, Murphy was between them. He struck at Murphy with his good arm until, without any warning, his strength left him and he had to lean on Murphy for support. The sweat ran into his eyes, blinding him for the moment. Then again he was looking at the Arab. But the Arab was now staring at Rose Angela, and she at him.

For a seemingly long time he watched them stare at each other, until he pulled himself from Murphy's hands and stumbled towards them.

Hassan, turning his eyes from Rose Angela to Stanhope, seemed to be on the point of saying something; but, instead, he allowed his curling lip to convey the contempt he was feeling. Then, unhurriedly, he walked across the landing and into the black well of the staircase.

There seemed to be nothing left now but the sound of the crying. It was like the crying of a lost child, with snuffles and breaking sobs. And again, from the support of Murphy's arm, Stanhope gazed down in stupefaction at the man sitting on the floor, his clothes torn from his body and his face and chest spattered with blood. He could not reconcile this whimpering heap with the maniac he had been fighting, and to his disgust he felt a faintness overcoming him, and he retched.

James lay with his eyes closed. His heart was beating rapidly, but not so rapidly as it had done two hours ago. Then he had thought that each beat would sever the slender line with which he was holding on to life. His heart was pounding now because of what was to come, for at any moment the door would open and Bridget would be in the room.

He had thought he did not want to see her, but now he knew he had been lying to himself by way of comfort. What she had done with her life since he left her did not hurt him any more, nor was he worrying about what effect his changed appearance would have on her; not for much longer would he suffer from vanity or pride or whatever it was that had made him hate the idea that she should see him looking anything but . . . the big fine Negro man.

The murmur of whispering voices floated to him; Rose Angela's and the painter's. He was a man after his own heart, that painter, stubborn and generous. The doctor had been stubborn man too; he say the painter must go to hospital, and the painter, he say he not go. The painter was worried in case Hassan come back, but Hassan no come back, and that good thing. Yet he was sorry, very sorry, for he liked Hassan, and he wished things had worked out different, for he no want Hassan or any man to hide like he had to hide. But now Hassan think that painter put polis on him, and he lie low for time. Yet painter generous, for he had the chance when polis ask him who stab him, and he say he not see man who did it. And when polis ask could it be Matt, painter still say he not know.

James had always felt that life was full of strange contradictions. Things had puzzled him, and when he groped into the deep depths of himself in search of answers, he had only become more puzzled. Yet he would have stood by the theory that once you love, you always love, and once you hate, a groove is seared in the mind, a groove that can be filled with nothing but itself. He would have rejected the idea that he could allow pity to fill the groove, yet the groove of his hate for Matt had been filled with pity when he watched him for the last time through the open door and saw him propped against the banisters, crying, ceaselessly crying. There was something improper in a man crying like that, but instead of arousing his scorn, pity for this man who had directed his life into tragic channels rose in him; for, to all intents and purposes, Matt was a dead man. He was gone now; they had taken him away. And the doctor was gone. And Murphy was gone too . . . to fetch Bridget.

Life was strange. A man wanted something, and he got it; and he thought it make him happy; and he thought all things that came of it must be good things because it made him happy. He had wanted Bridget, and he had got her. And he was happy for a time. But it was not good. For sixteen years he paid for that bit happiness. And others paid too . . . Rose Angela, she paid; she paid too much. And Bridget, she paid; just how much he did not know. But she paid all right. And now Hassan, he pay. And Matt; yes indeed, he pay; he was bound to pay in some way. Everything in life must be paid for, but some things were charged too big a price. He had wanted the painter for his Rose Angela, but this, too, would have to be paid for, and by her.

The hoodwinking of himself, the pretence, the day-dreaming, all fell away, and in a moment of illuminating truth he knew that because of his folly his daughter must pay and go on paying, for, as Hassan said, inside Rose Angela was black, and the tragedy of his race lay buried in the blackness. In what way she would be called upon to pay he did not exactly know: perhaps with babies who would be black outside as well as in.

She had a saying that the priest had told her. It went: God is colour-blind. He had always had his doubts about this saying; he thought it would be better if God could see colour, for then he would see the black man as the white sees him, and seeing him so, and being God, he would certainly have given the black man some power wherewith he could command of the white and of all races their respect; for surely it was an indignity for a man to desire the flesh of his flesh to be a different colour from that of his own. God should not allow a man or a woman to be born to despise the seed of their body like that; he should not ask such a price for a life.

He raised his tired lids and looked at Rose Angela. She was bending over the painter as he sat in the old armchair by the fire. The strained look was gone from her face, but the sadness still remained. He watched the painter's hand go up to her cheek. Then she saw him rise and come towards him. He looked up at this man into whose keeping Rose Angela was going, and he knew a measure of contentment . . . if anyone could, he would make the payment easier.

He put out his hand, and the painter grasped it, and they gazed deep at each other – the need for words was past.

As the sound of a car came to them from the street below, Rose Angela bent over him, and softly and tenderly and with love she kissed him. Then with the painter she left the room, smiling at him before closing the door. And, his heart pounding again, he lay watching the door, waiting for it to open into his past.

THE END